THE CAPTAIN OF
THE 'POLE-STAR'

Sir Arthur Conan Doyle in 1904

Arthur Conan Doyle

THE CAPTAIN OF
THE 'POLE-STAR'

Weird and Imaginative Fiction

Edited, with an Introduction by
Christopher Roden and Barbara Roden

and with a Preface by
Michael Dirda

Ash-Tree Press
Ashcroft, British Columbia
2004

First published 2004
by Ash-Tree Press
P.O. Box 1360
Ashcroft, British Columbia
Canada V0K 1A0
www.ash-tree.bc.ca/ashtreecurrent.html

ISBN: 1-55310-068-9

Typesetting and design by Ash-Tree Press
Printed and bound in Canada by Morriss Printing Ltd.
Victoria, British Columbia

CONTENTS

THE CAPTAIN OF THE 'POLE-STAR'

IS DEDICATED

TO THE MEMORY OF

RICHARD LANCELYN GREEN

Preface

SOME AUTHORS, NO MATTER HOW BRILLIANT and varied their oeuvre, find that posterity remembers them only for one or two books. Who, aside from scholars of Victorian fiction, now reads anything by Thackeray other than *Vanity Fair*? The world-wide popularity of Sherlock Holmes early on annoyed Arthur Conan Doyle, and with some cause: the detective stories, wonderful as they are, tended to overshadow everything else he ever wrote, with the partial exception of *The Lost World*. Visit a used bookstore today and you will find a shelf of Sherlockiana. But if you wish to enjoy 'The Horror of the Heights' or 'The Great Keinplatz Experiment' or 'Lot No. 249', you may have to do a bit of searching. All three are superb stories, and yet it would be far easier to find 'The Three Gables'—the worst tale in the generally lacklustre *Case-Book of Sherlock Holmes*.

Conan Doyle's non-Sherlockian work suffers neglect because of the widespread misconception that he only rose above the conventions of his time when he wrote about the dynamic duo of Baker Street. His other works are thus regarded as period pieces, of interest mainly to professional Doyleans. Many readers imagine that historical novels like *The White Company* or *Micah Clarke* must be fustian, pseudo-antiquarian homages to Walter Scott—and nobody bothers with Scott any more, let alone his imitators. To modern ears, tales of prize-fighting, pirates, or late Victorian medical life merely sound dated and unappealing. What's more, some of Conan Doyle's best stories bear dull names like 'The Bully of Brocas Court' or 'J. Habakuk Jephson's Statement'— they lack the almost mythic quality of titles such as 'The Musgrave Ritual' or 'The Final Problem'.

Yet, as the contents of this much anticipated collection reveal again and again, Conan Doyle is just as compelling a storyteller when writing about a subterranean monster, killer mummy, or arctic ghost as when imagining a spectral hound let loose from the bowels of hell. Some of the tales here, like 'The Case of Lady Sannox', possess a tightly plotted O. Henry feel; the trapdoor slams shut in the final paragraph. Others recall leisurely Somerset Maugham-style reminiscences, tinged with a club-land atmosphere of brandy and leather armchairs and some elderly duffer announcing, 'Oh, yes, that reminds me of rather a rum thing that happened to me when I was young. Out East, don't you know.' Today an attentive modern reader may occasionally guess a plot twist, if only because some of Conan Doyle's tricks have been picked up and used by others: one recognizes almost immediately what will happen during the Keinplatz experiment because it's a common theme for farcical writing (see F. Anstey's classic *Vice-Versa*, P. G. Wodehouse's *Laughing Gas*, movies like *Freaky Friday*). But even here we happily read on, eager to see how Conan Doyle works out a screwball comedy that flirts with possible incest while also suggesting a heartless system for attaining immortality (compare H. G. Wells's treatment in 'The Story of the Late Mr Elvesham').

Like Guy de Maupassant, whom he admired, Conan Doyle knows how to tell a lean, fast-moving story, and to prefer variety to repetition. So he turns out a brilliant 'conte cruel' ('The Brazilian Cat'), a semi-humorous ghost story ('The Brown Hand'), a psychic adventure ('The Leather Funnel'), a tale like 'The Ring of Thoth' with elements of both the legend of the Wandering Jew and Haggard's *She*, and the macabre yet touching Grand Guignol of 'The Sealed Room'. He is a master of the first-person narrative voice, and, like the Wedding Guest in 'The Ancient Mariner', one cannot choose but hear. Just listen to the first sentence of the classically spooky 'Lot No. 249': 'Of the dealings of Edward Bellingham with William Monkhouse Lee, and of the cause of the great terror of Abercrombie Smith, it may be that no absolute and final judgment will ever be delivered.' It could almost be the opening to an H. P. Lovecraft shocker.

Good as these stories are in general, four or five are real masterpieces, with Conan Doyle providing far more than careful plotting, a mesmerizing narrator, or an example of the biter bit. 'The Captain of the "Pole-Star"' leaves one with thoughts that lie too deep for tears; it is as richly haunting a story of love and mystery as *Wuthering Heights* (a linkage examined in a fine essay by Barbara Roden*). 'J. Habakuk Jephson's Statement' is a worthy pendant to Melville's celebrated 'Benito Cereno'—two nautical mysteries built around racial hatred and an almost wilful social blindness. 'The Horror of the Heights' and 'The Terror of Blue John Gap' both deal with what one might call 'monsters of the id', the first evoking sublimity and awe (as well as panic), the other provoking terror, then pity. Such works as these touch on the archetypal, the numinous, and they linger long in the memory.

Barbara and Christopher Roden have aimed to include virtually everything that a reader might want in a collection of Conan Doyle's 'weird tales'. So you will find here his scarce 'The Haunted Grange of Goresthorpe'—his earliest known work of fiction—and his vampiric novella 'The Parasite'. They shrewdly underscore the continuity of their author's oeuvre by also including 'The Speckled Band'—the most nightmarish of the shorter adventures of Sherlock

---

* Barbara Roden, 'Fiery Passions and Icy Realms: "The Captain of the *Pole-Star*" and *Wuthering Heights*' in *ACD 3* (1992), reprinted in Barbara Roden, *I Am Inclined To Think . . .* (Ashcroft: Calabash Press, 2004).

Holmes—and the chilling account of the origins of 'the hound of the Baskervilles'.

Certainly *The Captain of the 'Pole-Star': Weird and Imaginative Fiction by Arthur Conan Doyle* is a volume that any devotee of the uncanny will want to own. Here are pages that sometimes call to mind the accomplishments of Rudyard Kipling, M. R. James, Lord Dunsany, and John Collier. Clearly, if he'd never given immortal life to Mr Sherlock Holmes and Dr John Watson, Sir Arthur Conan Doyle would be better honoured today as a superb writer in many genres, not least that of the strange and unsettling story.

MICHAEL DIRDA

INTRODUCTION

Introduction

EW OF THE VERY LARGE NUMBER of Victorian and Edwardian popular
storytellers are widely read today. In part this is because their work has
become inaccessible to modern readers, as it has disappeared from
publishers' lists; in part it is because their work simply has not withstood the
test of time. One notable exception is Arthur Conan Doyle, whose Sherlock
Holmes stories are still widely read—and widely copied by practitioners of
varying talents. Although the worldwide interest in Sherlock Holmes, fuelled
by the many dramatic and cinematic interpretations, seems at times to diminish
in intensity, it is fairly safe to forecast that the foggy, gaslit London streets of
the Holmes stories—that world where, as Vincent Starrett wrote, 'it is always
1895'—will be as popular with readers fifty years hence as they are today.

Conan Doyle would have disliked the thought of being remembered
primarily for Sherlock Holmes: he always considered his historical novels—*The
White Company, Sir Nigel, Micah Clarke, The Refugees,* etc.—to be his best,
and most important fictional writing; but it is an inescapable fact that Conan
Doyle's reputation as a storyteller was born with Sherlock Holmes, and that it
was Holmes who made Conan Doyle one of the wealthiest authors of his day.
Holmes, irrespective of whether or not he bore the influence of others—Edgar
Allan Poe, Émile Gaboriau, Robert Louis Stevenson, and Wilkie Collins among
them—was unique, as was, for the time, the manner of his presentation to the
public. Although Conan Doyle had dabbled with his detective creation in two
short novels prior to 1891—*A Study in Scarlet* (*Beeton's Christmas Annual,*
1887) and *The Sign of the Four* (*Lippincott's Magazine,* 1890)—it was the change
to the short-story format which established Holmes as a character the British
public would embrace with open arms: a change brought about by the advent
of many new monthly magazines, and one in particular—*The Strand Magazine.*
Conan Doyle commented in his autobiography *Memories and Adventures*:

> Considering these various journals with their disconnected stories it had
> struck me that a single character running through a series, if it only engaged
> the attention of the reader, would bind that reader to that particular
> magazine. On the other hand, it had long seemed to me that the ordinary
> serial might be an impediment rather than a help to a magazine, since,
> sooner or later, one missed one number and afterwards it had lost all interest.
> Clearly the ideal compromise was a character which carried through, and

yet instalments which were each complete in themselves, so that the purchaser was always sure that he could relish the whole contents of the magazine. I believe that I was the first to realize this and *The Strand Magazine* the first to put it into practice.

The Strand Magazine's first issue appeared in March 1891, and Conan Doyle's literary agent, A. P. Watt, had submitted one of the author's lesser-known pieces, 'The Voice of Science', presumably after initial publication announcements were made. The story duly appeared without a by-line, although Conan Doyle was credited in the magazine's index. And so began a relationship with *The Strand Magazine*, publisher George Newnes, and editor H. Greenhough Smith which would last until Conan Doyle's death in 1930 and beyond. Unquestionably, when he was at his most productive, and best, as a storyteller—between 1891 and 1906—Arthur Conan Doyle played a leading role in *The Strand*'s success, and, at the same time, established his own reputation, and his own fortune. George Newnes was obviously very happy with the situation: according to Conan Doyle's record of Stock Exchange business, 1892–8, he received a gift from Newnes of 500 preference shares in Newnes Ltd.[1]

ARTHUR IGNATIUS CONAN DOYLE (1859–1930) was a born storyteller, partly, one must assume, through 'art in the blood', as Sherlock Holmes would have said. He had a natural talent inherited from the artistic Doyle family—his grandfather, John Doyle ('H.B.'), was a fine political cartoonist and satirist; his uncle, Richard Doyle, a fine illustrator and diarist (famous for his covers for *Punch*); and his father, Charles Altamont, was also an artist, even if a lesser one. He also spent hours listening to tales of his forebears while sat at his mother's knee, and was an avid and rapid reader—so rapid, he tells us in *Memories and Adventures*, that a small library with which the family dealt gave his mother notice that books would not be changed more than twice a day. His tastes were wide-ranging, matching his early life experiences, and his willingness to explore new subjects, new authors, and new theories is shown to full advantage in the stories he was to produce as his writing career progressed.

Conan Doyle's life is so well charted that to delve too deeply into biography would be to repeat unnecessarily what others have written. However, an outline is essential for a fuller appreciation of some of the influences on Conan Doyle. He was born in Edinburgh, baptized into the Roman Catholic church, and educated by the Jesuits at Hodder and Stonyhurst in Lancashire, from where he returned home only occasionally, his mother's wish being that he should be isolated from difficult and deteriorating family circumstances as much as possible. At Stonyhurst he was often in trouble, and often disagreed with his masters,

---

1. Quoted in 'Account Books'. Christie's Auction Catalogue *The Conan Doyle Collection* (London: Christie's, 2004), p.53.

but he seems to have been an adequate student before matriculating from the University of London in June 1875 (he was placed eighty-first in the Honours Division).[2]

During his time at Stonyhurst, Conan Doyle began to question conventional religious beliefs, eventually rejecting Catholicism. It seems that the Jesuits were prepared to help him through his crisis of faith, possibly to assist with the situation they knew to exist back home in Edinburgh. In any event, it is well established that Conan Doyle ceased receiving the Sacrament at Stonyhurst, even though he continued to fulfil his duties as an altar boy.[3] But Stonyhurst was to provide Conan Doyle with an outlet for his storytelling skills and an introduction to drama: he would, in spare moments, read and tell stories to his fellow students, and the Stonyhurst archive retains copies of playbills which show that Conan Doyle performed minor parts in the Christmas plays of 1872, *The Omnibus* and *The Box of Mischief.*

After leaving Stonyhurst, Conan Doyle had one more year with the Jesuits, this time in Feldkirch, in Austria's Vorarlberg province. Here he played music (the Bombardon), and wrote short articles and verse for *The Feldkirchian Gazette.*[4]

In 1876 Conan Doyle enrolled as a student of medicine at Edinburgh University, from where he graduated MB, CM (Edin.) in 1881. It was while at University that he became a surgeon's clerk to Dr Joseph Bell, whom Conan Doyle later identified as the model for Sherlock Holmes. Bell was not alone in providing models for his fiction, however, and ACD also identified another of his Professors—Professor Rutherford, 'with his Assyrian beard, his prodigious voice, his enormous chest, and his singular manner'—as the model for Professor Challenger, who would debut in *The Lost World* in 1912.

Money, inevitably, was always short. In 1880, to supplement the family's income, Conan Doyle enrolled as ship's surgeon in the steamship *Hope*, a Peterhead whaler bound for the waters of the Arctic. The experiences of this adventure were later translated into one of ACD's finest ghost stories, indeed one of the finest of all Victorian ghost stories, 'The Captain of the "Pole-Star"'. A further term as ship's surgeon was served in 1881–2, when, following his graduation from Edinburgh University, Conan Doyle served on the steamer *Mayumba*, headed for West Africa. These further adventures seem to have served

---

2. Conan Doyle's Matriculation Certificate is illustrated in the Christie's Auction Catalogue, p.53.

3. Personal conversations with the late Fr. Frederick Turner, SJ, archivist at Stonyhurst College. See also Owen Dudley Edwards, *The Quest for Sherlock Holmes* (Edinburgh: Mainstream, 1983), ch.4.

4. Two issues, October and November 1875, handwritten entirely in Conan Doyle's hand, survive. Formerly part of the Conan Doyle Biographical Archive, these were among items offered at auction in May 2004. See the Christie's Auction Catalogue, p.17.

in the development of a further story in the present volume, 'The Fiend of the Cooperage'.

Modest literary success had already come Conan Doyle's way: his first published story, 'The Mystery of Sasassa Valley', was published in *Chambers's Journal* in September 1879. Other collections of Conan Doyle's weird stories have chosen to include 'The Mystery of Sasassa Valley', but the story is wholly rationalized, and is little more than an unsatisfactory fantasy. For that reason, we have chosen not to include it in the present volume. Sometime prior to this first success, however, and possibly as early as 1877, Conan Doyle had submitted a manuscript to *Blackwood's Magazine*. 'The Haunted Grange of Goresthorpe' may have been read by an editor, but little more. *Blackwood's* seems promptly to have consigned the manuscript to the filing cabinets, and there it lay until the *Blackwood's* archive was presented to the National Library of Scotland in 1942. Inevitably, it was some time later before this manuscript was re-discovered, and it was not until 2000 that the story finally saw publication.[5]

But the time had come for Conan Doyle to pursue his career and, following a disastrous partnership in Plymouth with the wily, conniving George Turnavine Budd, ACD found himself in Southsea, where he erected his plaque at 1 Bush Villas, and waited for patients. The semi-autobiographical *The Stark Munro Letters* (1895) provides an often hilarious account of this stage of Conan Doyle's life—a life which was about to change dramatically, and for the better.

In 1885, Conan Doyle was called upon to treat young John Hawkins, a patient suffering a sudden and violent illness arising from cerebral meningitis. His patient, unfortunately, died, and Conan Doyle was fortunate to escape criminal charges (by the good fortune of his having called in a colleague for a second opinion, suspicion was removed). John Hawkins was the brother of Louise Hawkins of Minsterworth in Gloucestershire, and Conan Doyle and Louise ('Touie') were now drawn closer together, and they married later that year. Louise was what ACD described as 'a very gentle and amiable girl', but there can be little doubt that Louise was extremely influential, too. 'In many ways,' wrote Conan Doyle in *Memories and Adventures*, 'my marriage marked a turning point in my life. A bachelor, especially one who had been a wanderer like myself, drifts easily into Bohemian habits, and I was no exception. . . . Up to now the main interest of my life lay in my medical career. But with the more regular life and the greater sense of responsibility, coupled with the natural development of brain-power, the literary side of me began slowly to spread until it was destined to push the other entirely aside.'

They say that behind every successful man there is a good woman, and there is no doubt that Louise Conan Doyle was a very good woman. She brought stability to Conan Doyle's life and provided him with two fine children, Mary Louise (born 1889) and Alleyne Kingsley (born 1892). While other

---

5. Arthur Conan Doyle, *The Haunted Grange of Goresthorpe*, Christopher Roden, gen. ed. (Ashcroft, B.C.: The Arthur Conan Doyle Society, 2000).

commentators have noted that Conan Doyle's Southsea medical practice was not a successful one, this is not true, as a letter to his sister Lottie confirms: 'In January 1884 I saw 82 patients—In January 1885 I saw 165.' In 1885 he reported '1,350 entries in my ledger'; in 1886, 1,850 entries. '. . . The practice is fairly brisk. . . .'[6]

Needless to say, the practice was not so brisk that Conan Doyle had to forego the time he could allow for writing, and from the time of his marriage to Louise he was to launch into his most productive years as a novelist and short story writer. But Conan Doyle could be a restless man. . . .

By 1891, he had given up his Southsea practice, had travelled to Vienna to attend lectures on the eye, presented by Dr Koch, and had returned to London disappointed. The family took rooms in Montague Place, and ACD set up an ophthalmology practice at 2 Upper Wimpole Street. No patients came, but Sherlock Holmes was born: it was during these few weeks that 'A Scandal in Bohemia' was written. A virulent attack of influenza decided the future for Conan Doyle: 'It was then, as I surveyed my own life, that I saw how foolish I was to waste my literary earnings in keeping up an oculist's room in Wimpole Street, and I determined with a wild rush of joy to cut the painter and to trust for ever to my power of writing. I remember in my delight taking the handkerchief which lay upon the coverlet in my enfeebled hand, and tossing it up to the ceiling in my exultation. I should at last be my own master. . . . It was one of the great moments of exultation of my life. The date was in August 1891.'

The Conan Doyles moved to a new home at 12 Tennison Road, South Norwood, and the increasingly successful author pursued his career with vigour. Contemporary photographs show a pleasant home, and a pleasantly happy husband, wife, and children. Life was certainly improving, but, as so often happens, fate was set to deal its unwelcome hand. Louise was diagnosed with tuberculosis; there was every sign of rapid consumption.

The South Norwood home was sold and Conan Doyle and Louise headed for Davos in the High Alps, where there seemed to be the best chance of killing the vicious microbe. ACD's sister Lottie was with them, and with her as a companion for Louise, Conan Doyle was able to head to America in late 1894 for a lecture tour.

On the advice of fellow author Grant Allen, Conan Doyle decided to build a new house, Undershaw, at Hindhead in Surrey, a location and climate suitable, it was felt, for Louise's condition, and a place where she might continue to improve. That Louise survived until July 1906 is a testament to the care and nursing she was given. However, though Louise's illness undoubtedly cast a shadow over Conan Doyle's life, and inevitably brought about a change in the marital relationship, a new woman had attracted Conan Doyle's attention. Jean

---

6. Quoted from 'Letters to Lottie Doyle'. Christie's Auction Catalogue, p.114.

Leckie, who was to become Conan Doyle's second wife a year after Louise's death, bewitched him. He was obsessed with her.

Conan Doyle always stressed that Louise came first; that he would have done nothing to hurt her feelings in any way; that his relationship with Jean Leckie, prior to their marriage, was strictly platonic. Conan Doyle's mother certainly knew, and approved, of the relationship with Jean Leckie. His sister Connie and her husband Willie Hornung seem to have been less approving: following an incident at a cricket match at Lord's, when Conan Doyle was seen in public, openly flirting with Jean Leckie, the relationship between Connie, Willie, and Arthur became quite frosty. Conan Doyle held himself to be doing nothing wrong, however. In a letter to his brother Innes, dated 17 June 1889, he wrote: 'You must not feel however [that any] harm will arise from it [the affair with Jean] or that any pain will ever be given to Touie. She is as dear to me as ever, but, as I said, there is a large side of my life which was unoccupied but is no longer so. It will all fit in very well, and nobody be the worse and two of us be very much the better. I shall see to it very carefully that no harm comes to anyone. I say all this lest you, at a distance, might fear that we were drifting towards trouble.'[7]

Did Louise suspect, or know, that her successor was in the wings? Almost certainly. Although Conan Doyle wrote to his mother in March 1901

> I am most careful at home and I am sure that at no time have I been anything but most considerate and attentive. But the position is difficult, is it not? Dear J is a model of good sense and propriety in the whole thing. There never was anyone with a sweeter and more unselfish nature.[8]

Conan Doyle's daughter Mary seems to have been quite adamant that her mother knew exactly what was going on, and stated privately that Louise actually mentioned the name of Jean Leckie as her (Mary's) future stepmother. In a letter, Mary wrote:

> Some two months before the end she [Louise] called me in for a talk. She told me that some wives sought to hold their husbands to their memory after they had gone—that she considered this very wrong, as the only consideration should be the loved-one's happiness. To this end she wanted me not to be shocked or surprised if my father married again, but to know that it was with her understanding and blessing.[9]

Whatever conclusions we may draw from our scant knowledge of events is, in reality, a matter of personal judgment. It appears that few family papers relating to Conan Doyle's first marriage now exist, and it is believed that many personal letters between Conan Doyle and Jean Leckie were destroyed, either

---

7. Quoted from 'Letters to Innes Doyle', Christie's Auction Catalogue, p.116.

8. Pierre Nordon, *Conan Doyle* (London: John Murray, 1966), p.179.

9. Quoted in Georgina Doyle, *Out of the Shadows: The Untold Story of Arthur Conan Doyle's First Family* (Ashcroft, B.C.: Calabash Press, 2004), pp.138–9.

by Jean herself, or by her family after her death.

Louise's failing health caused Conan Doyle to re-focus somewhat: he became involved in the Boer War on the medical staff for the Langman Field Hospital at Bloemfontein, and turned his writing skills to a History of the War and propaganda in support of the British involvement in South Africa. Such efforts earned him his knighthood in 1902, and afforded Louise the title Lady Conan Doyle for the final years of her life.

On board ship, returning from the Boer War, Conan Doyle met the novelist and journalist Bertram Fletcher Robinson, and the two struck up a friendship, which was later to result in a meeting from which the idea for *The Hound of the Baskervilles* emerged. Sherlock Holmes, about whom Conan Doyle had last written in 1893, had returned, albeit briefly for the moment; Conan Doyle was continuing to do what he did well—tell extremely good stories for the magazines—and he would continue to do so until Louise's death in July 1906.

During the black depression which followed Louise's death, Conan Doyle again became a campaigner: this time on behalf of George Edalji, the Parsee who had been convicted of cattle-maiming at Great Wyrley in Staffordshire in 1903. His campaign was eventually successful, and Edalji was freed in time to attend the wedding of Arthur Conan Doyle and Jean Leckie on 18 September 1907.

Of Jean Leckie's influence on Conan Doyle's writing after 1907, there is little positive comment to make. Other commentators are firm in their view that Sherlock Holmes was never quite the same in *His Last Bow* and *The Case-Book*, and many point to *The Valley of Fear* as being inferior to the other Holmes novels. The present editors do not concur with the latter judgment.

Jean Leckie, however, very definitely exercised a powerful influence over Conan Doyle, and it is difficult not to attribute his eventual total involvement in Spiritualism, and virtual abandonment of his writing of fiction from the early 1920s onwards, to that influence. Apart from the Professor Challenger series—and even Challenger was laughably involved in Spiritualism for his appearance in *The Land of Mist*—Conan Doyle wrote few very memorable pieces following his second marriage. Did Jean Leckie bring about a character change in Conan Doyle? Certainly he was, by the time of his second marriage, a wealthy man by contemporary standards, so perhaps the need to work hard at his writing was not as pressing a matter as it had been in earlier years; but there is also the question of how his first family was treated after he married Jean Leckie. Seemingly, under Jean Leckie's influence, both Mary and Kingsley were deliberately distanced, almost as if she wished to have no reminder of Louise in her life; and Conan Doyle seems to have been willing to oblige her. Accounts, such as the one now available in *Out of the Shadows*, may alter our perception of Conan Doyle somewhat. He remained a great man, even if a changed one; but his total and absolute commitment to Spritualism, his acceptance of Jean Leckie as a writing medium, his willingness to accept and believe in fairies and fairy photographs, and his strange reports of séances where the control Pheneas expounded all kinds of fantasies, remain as difficult, if not more difficult, than ever to explain.

Conan Doyle pursued much in his life: medical doctor, writer, war doctor, war correspondent, photographer, traveller, balloonist, skier, unsuccessful parliamentary candidate, psychic investigator, Spiritualist; he was an advocate for many causes, including Divorce Law reform, the Channel tunnel, protective body armour for soldiers in warfare; he was an indefatigable writer of letters to the press on all manner of topics—if an opinion could be held on a certain subject, Conan Doyle held one, it seems; he was knighted by Queen Victoria and held the position of Deputy Lieutenant of the County of Surrey. He was successful at a great many things (but not, by any means, everything that he attempted), most notably in writing short stories. His fiction was inventive, and we now move on to consider the background behind the remarkable collection of weird and imaginative fiction which forms the content of this volume.

* * * * *

ARTHUR CONAN DOYLE'S interest in the supernatural tale is not difficult to trace. We need look no further than one of his favourite authors, Sir Walter Scott, who was perhaps the first writer to place supernatural tales within the framework of his novels. In *Through the Magic Door* (1907), his reminiscences on books and reading, Conan Doyle recalled: '[T]he olive green line of Scott's novels . . . were the first books I ever owned—long, long before I could appreciate or even understand them. But at last I realized what a treasure they were. In my boyhood I read them by the surreptitious candle-ends in the dead of night, when the sense of crime added a new zest to the story.' Scott's 'Wandering Willie's Tale' from the 1824 novel *Redgauntlet*, generally acknowledged as the first of what we now recognise as the modern ghost story, was held in very high esteem by Conan Doyle. 'The great masters of our literature,' he wrote, 'Fielding, Scott, Dickens, Thackeray, Reade, have left no single short story of outstanding merit behind them, with the possible exception of "Wandering Willie's Tale".' Poe and de Maupassant, too, were held in high regard, but he was also inspired by other practitioners of the supernatural genre: Dickens, Le Fanu, Ambrose Bierce, Nathaniel Hawthorne and his son Julian, Arthur Quiller-Couch, and Bulwer Lytton, whose 'The Haunted and the Haunters' Conan Doyle called 'the very best ghost story that I know'.

It was hardly surprising, given his reading in the genre, that the aspiring writer should turn his hand to a ghost story; or that the result, 'The Haunted Grange of Goresthorpe', probably written around 1877 when the author was eighteen, is a typical Victorian ghost story with elements of the Gothic. Conventional in both form and narration, 'The Haunted Grange of Goresthorpe' does show flashes of promise; but it is a long way from the finely crafted, unconventional supernatural tales which its author would go on to produce. This early effort, originally submitted to *Blackwood's Magazine*, remained unpublished in Conan Doyle's lifetime. Indeed, it remained unknown for many years, as it had been consigned to the *Blackwood's* archives, and only came to light some years after those archives had been donated to the National Library of Scotland in 1942. The story was finally published by The Arthur Conan Doyle Society in 2000.

Conan Doyle first achieved publication in 1879, when 'The Mystery of Sasassa Valley' appeared in *Chambers's Journal*. Though this tale begins with strong hints of the supernatural, the supposed 'haunting' is wholly rationalized at the story's end. There is also a rationalized ending to his next published story, 'The American's Tale', although the horror written into this story qualifies it for inclusion in this collection. Published in the Christmas number of *London Society*, the story seems originally to have been titled 'The American's Story', and Conan Doyle's account book records that he was paid £1. 10*s*. 0*d*. for his efforts.[10]

One of Conan Doyle's very finest supernatural stories—indeed, one of the finest of all Victorian ghost stories—'The Captain of the "Pole-Star"', was published in *Temple Bar* in January 1883. When we consider that this story was the work of a twenty-two year old developing author, it is difficult not to marvel at the story's maturity and the manner in which it succeeds in freeing itself from many of the restraints typically associated with the Victorian ghost story. The background for the story is not hard to find: Conan Doyle's voyage to the Arctic between 17 June and 11 August 1880. It was a journey which was to influence him greatly, and one which left a warm impression of lonely days at sea. Writing on 31 July 1880, he noted: 'I shall never again see the great Greenland floes, never again see the land where I have smoked so many pensive pipes. . . Who says thou art cold and inhospitable, my poor icefields? I have known you in calm and in storm and I say you are genial and kindly.'[11]

Although it is impossible not to draw some parallels with Mary Shelley's *Frankenstein; or, The Modern Prometheus* (1818), Barbara Roden has commented on the striking similarities to another great work of fiction, Emily Brontë's *Wuthering Heights* (1847),[12] and it is entirely possible that Conan Doyle could have read, remembered, and been influenced by the latter. *Through the Magic Door* finds him noting: 'Whence came the intense glowing imagination of the Brontës—so unlike the Miss-Austen-like calm of their predecessors?'

In 'The Captain of the "Pole-Star"' Conan Doyle is comfortable and assured

---

10. Quoted from 'The American's Story' and 'Account Books'. Christie's Auction Catalogue, pp.28–9, 53.

11. Quoted from 'The Log of the Hope'. Christie's Auction Catalogue, pp.20–3.

12. Barbara Roden, 'Fiery Passions and Icy Realms: "The Captain of the *Pole-Star*" and *Wuthering Heights*' in *ACD: The Journal of The Arthur Conan Doyle Society*, Vol. 3 (1992); reprinted in Barbara Roden, *'I am inclined to think . . .': Musings on Sherlock Holmes and Arthur Conan Doyle* (Ashcroft, B.C.: Calabash Press, 2004), pp.52–7.

with the supernatural elements of his story, and it is interesting to see the way in which he anticipated several of the 'rules' of the ghost story laid down by the great Montague Rhodes James in his fiction and, more to the point, in his introduction to the 1924 Oxford World's Classics collection *Ghosts and Marvels*. There James stated that the way to go about constructing an effective ghost story is to let us 'be introduced to the actors in a placid way; let us see them going about their ordinary business, undisturbed by forebodings, pleased with their surroundings; and into this calm environment let the ominous thing put out its head, unobtrusively at first, and then more insistently, until it holds the stage. It is not amiss sometimes to leave a loophole for a natural explanation; but, I would say, let the loophole be so narrow as not to be quite practicable.' James disliked the convention of setting ghost stories in the long-distant past: 'On the whole,' he wrote, 'I think that a setting so modern that the ordinary reader can judge of its naturalness for himself is preferable to anything antique. For some degree of actuality is the charm of the best ghost stories; not a very insistent actuality, but one strong enough to allow the reader to identify himself with the patient.' All of this is anticipated in 'The Captain of the "Pole-Star"', even to the loophole, so narrow as to not be quite practicable, which allows the reader to believe that there was a natural explanation for everything which happened. In this story, Conan Doyle shows an affinity for the genre which holds out the promise of great things.

'The Winning Shot', published in *Bow Bells* in July 1883, makes use of the then fashionable interest in hypnotism/mesmerism for its chilling finale. Also from 1883, and further evidence of the attention Conan Doyle was paying to 'occult' sciences at the time, is 'The Silver Hatchet'. Here ACD makes use of alchemical devices to resolve a particularly nasty little horror, but the writing, disappointingly, shows little of the promise of 'The Captain of the "Pole-Star"'. Although Conan Doyle was tempted to use it in a collection of stories he attempted unsuccessfully to compile, it comes as no surprise that he paid it little further attention in later collections of his stories.

The Johnny-come-lately Argentine D'Odd of 'Selecting a Ghost' (alternatively titled 'The Ghosts of Goresthorpe Grange' and 'The Secret of Goresthorpe Grange' (not to be confused with 'The Haunted Grange of Goresthorpe')), spoofs Conan Doyle's own family: the apostrophised surname acknowledges ancestral variations such as D'Ouilly, D'Oyly, and D'Oel, while attempts to purchase suitable heraldic emblems prefigure ACD's own attempts to give prominence to the Doyle arms in the stained glass windows of his new house at Hindhead (and also the somewhat infantile attempts of Conan Doyle's son, Adrian, to adorn books by means of a dubious bookplate with a dubious Conan Doyle crest). The vulgarity of Argentine has, of course, little to do with reality; but one suspects that much laughter would have echoed around a gathering of Conan Doyles had the opportunity arisen for ACD to read this story in the presence of his genealogy-obsessed mother.

'J. Habakuk Jephson's Statement' (*Cornhill Magazine*, January 1884), Conan Doyle's 'solution' to the mystery of the *Mary Celeste*, caused a small sensation when it was published anonymously: one reviewer attributed the story to Stevenson; the Advocate General in Gibraltar announced that it was 'a fabrication from beginning to end'; and the *Boston Herald* took it as total truth. Conan Doyle appears to have received the princely sum of twenty-nine guineas for his efforts.[13] In later years, his editor at *The Strand Magazine*, H. Greenhough Smith, seems to have raised the possibility of a further piece concerning the *Mary Celeste*, or had occasion to discuss the story. In an undated response, Conan Doyle wrote: 'I did the Marie Celeste in Cornhill of 1885—republished in "The Captain of the Polestar". No one knows the story now.'[14]

'The Blood-Stone Tragedy', which appeared anonymously in *Cassell's Saturday Journal* for 16 February 1884, was not recognized as being by Conan Doyle until the mid-1980s, when a small amount of archival material from the publisher Cassell was auctioned in London. Amongst the material was a letter from Conan Doyle requesting permission to republish 'John Barrington Cowles' and 'The Bloodstone', 'both of which appeared in the "Saturday Journal".' Conan Doyle mentions that he is republishing a volume of his stories, and this ties in with John Dickson Carr's statement that ACD was working on compiling a collection of eighteen stories to be titled *Light and Shade*.[15] Volume one of Conan Doyle's Southsea notebook confirms that the material was sent off to a publisher on 27 November 1885,[16] but nothing seems to have come of the proposal, Green & Gibson noting that ACD was told that 'he would need to make his name known with a novel'.[17] By the time that a publisher was ready to accept Conan Doyle's proposal for a collection in 1890, the eighteen stories mentioned by Carr had been pruned to ten ('The Blood-Stone Tragedy' was not among them), the resulting collection being *The Captain of the Polestar and Other Tales*.

In itself, 'The Blood-Stone Tragedy' is an unremarkable piece. What is remarkable, however, is what it tells us about the speed with which Conan Doyle adapted current events for his fiction, and also the speed with which he was able to write a piece and place it before a publisher. The story is a fictionalised version of events concerning Dr William Price and his attempt to revive Druidism by the cremation of an infant. The newspapers were carrying the developing story through to the end of January 1884, and the writing and acceptance process must have been one of the most rapid on record, with the story seeing

13. Richard Lancelyn Green and John Michael Gibson, *A Bibliography of A. Conan Doyle* (Oxford: Soho Bibliographies, 1984), p.30.

14. Undated letter, Conan Doyle to H. Greenhough Smith, held in The Arthur Conan Doyle Collection, Toronto Reference Library.

15. John Dickson Carr, *The Life of Sir Arthur Conan Doyle* (London: John Murray, 1949), p.60.

16. Quoted from 'The Southsea Notebooks'. Christie's Auction Catalogue, p.38.

17. *A Bibliography of A. Conan Doyle*, p.27.

publication on 16 February. 'The Blood-Stone Tragedy' was first published in book form by The Arthur Conan Doyle Society in 1995.

A letter from Conan Doyle to the editor of *Belgravia* shows that 'John Barrington Cowles' was submitted to that magazine on 27 February 1884.[18] It must have been rejected by return, for it was then offered to *Cassell's Saturday Journal*, and was published there, on successive Saturdays, 12 and 19 April. Quite why *Belgravia* rejected the story is difficult to understand—perhaps the sinister effect of the mind on the body, and the wiles of the beautiful and young Kate Northcott, were considered a little too modern in outlook for readers of *Belgravia*. Despite its early rejection, 'John Barrington Cowles' remains one of Conan Doyle's most successful and better known stories of the supernatural, and we have suggested elsewhere[19] that it may have served to influence Arthur Machen when, ten years later in 1894, he came to write one of his earliest and best supernatural tales, 'The Great God Pan'. If Machen did borrow ideas from 'Cowles', then Conan Doyle can lay claim to having influenced one of the most effective supernatural works of recent years: Peter Straub's *Ghost Story* (1979), which drew scenes and characters from several masters of the genre. *Ghost Story*'s central character is a mysterious and beautiful woman who is, Straub admits, definitely based on Machen's *femme fatale* in 'The Great God Pan'.[20]

In 'The Great Keinplatz Experiment' the horror is that of a scientific experiment gone wrong—and the subsequent realization that one has changed places with a social and intellectual inferior. The story is a joyous piece, likely inspired by the recently published *Vice-Versa* (1882) by F. Anstey, and it was first submitted to the editor of *Belgravia* some time earlier than 5 January 1884[21] (we know this because of the existence of a letter of this date, in which Conan Doyle wrote 'You have a M.S. of mine entitled "The Great Kein-platz experiment". Should it not suit you I should be very much obliged if you would send it back to me.'[22] In February 1885 he was again querying its fate: 'I enclose stamps for its return should it be unsuitable to your pages.'[23] The story was finally published in the July 1885 issue of *Belgravia*, and it appears that ACD was in for an unpleasant shock. On 11 July we find him writing to

18. Letter, 27 February 1884, Conan Doyle to the *Belgravia*. Part of 'Arthur Conan Doyle's letters to the editor of *Belgravia* and Chatto and Windus' (accession number MA4500), Pierpont Morgan Library, New York.

19. Barbara Roden and Christopher Roden, 'From Arctic Wastes to Ancient Egypt: The Supernatural Fiction of Arthur Conan Doyle'. Unpublished paper presented to 'Footprints of the Hound', Toronto, 20 October 2001.

20. Stanley Wiater, ed., *Dark Dreamers: Conversations with the Masters of Horror* (New York: Avon Books, 1990), p.94.

21. Pierpont Morgan Library, New York.

22. Pierpont Morgan Library, New York.

23. Pierpont Morgan Library, New York.

Belgravia: 'I append a receipt for £3..17..6. I am bound to say that it is somewhat less than a third of what I have been in the habit during the past six years of receiving for stories of the same length.'[24] Admittedly, £1 per 1,600 words is hardly generous, but one wonders why Conan Doyle had no idea, in advance of publication, of the payment he would be receiving for a particular story. Perhaps, in his desire to gain a foothold with *Belgravia*, he had omitted to ask, and it seems that any acceptance letter he may have received omitted to note the magazine's payment rates.

'Cyprian Overbeck Wells', also known as 'A Literary Mosaic', is a wonderful little pastiche concerning the ghosts of the authors who are the subject of the exercise. It originally appeared in the Christmas 1886 issue of *Boy's Own Paper*.

The past few years had been busy ones for Conan Doyle. His Southsea practice was becoming established, and his marriage to Louise was off on a firm footing. By the end of 1886 he had also laid the groundwork for a major development, though he did not necessarily realize it at the time: in the March and April of that year he had been busy writing a longish story concerning a new detective. The story was *A Study in Scarlet*, and the detective, of course, Sherlock Holmes. Things would never be quite the same again.

As far as his weird and macabre fiction was concerned, a new problem would present itself in 1889. Many of Conan Doyle's early stories had been sold outright to the magazines in which they appeared (indeed, *A Study in Scarlet* was no exception to this, and ACD bemoaned the fact, for very many years afterwards, that he never received a penny for the story, over and above the £25 he had received from Ward, Lock for its copyright). Because of this situation, James Hogg, editor of *London Society*, brought together all of the stories which he held, and published them in a volume entitled *Mysteries and Adventures*. Conan Doyle was furious—Longmans was on the verge of publishing his own collection, *The Captain of the Polestar*, and Hogg's volume was seen as direct competition. Conan Doyle told the *Birmingham Weekly Mercury*: ' "Mysteries and Adventures" is a pirated edition of tales written years ago in London Society—some of them when I was little more than a boy. It is rough on me having these youthful effusions brought out in this catchpenny fashion, but I have no legal redress. The less reviewed or read they are the better.'[25] Conan Doyle regained certain rights when the volume was reissued by George Newnes, but meanwhile his favoured volume, *The Captain of the Polestar*, appeared from Longmans, Green & Co. in March 1890. In addition to stories we have already considered, one further weird tale was included in this volume: 'The Ring of Thoth', which had just been published in the January 1890 issue of *Cornhill Magazine*. If we need look for influences, we may recall that Conan Doyle had visited Paris and seen the Egyptian mummies in the

---

24. Pierpont Morgan Library, New York.
25. *A Bibliography of A. Conan Doyle*, p.27.

Louvre. Undoubtedly this inspired him to create his tale of undying love carrying through the ages. But, despite the name that Conan Doyle was making for himself, the story originally appeared anonymously. 'The Ring of Thoth' ranks as one of the earliest supernatural tales to take ancient Egypt as a setting—the true heyday of the Egyptological ghost story would not take place for another thirty years or so, when the discovery of Tutankhamen's tomb rekindled a craze for all things Egyptian. It is also worth noting that in 'The Ring of Thoth' Conan Doyle establishes what has since become one of the conventions of the mummy genre: that of an undying love which lasts through the ages, and which sees a reincarnated or immortal being searching in the present day for his partner from days gone by.

'A Pastoral Horror' had a long gestation period: it took six years for it to be published from the time Conan Doyle first submitted it to *Belgravia* on 11 March 1884. At that time it was titled 'The Man with the Mattock', but there is no known documentation to explain the eventual, better, title, nor do we know why it was rejected by *Belgravia*—again, quite possibly, the story's content, this time dealing with a series of murders carried out by a psychotic priest, may have been considered just a little too much for readers of *Belgravia*. The story is set in the Austrian village of Feldkirch, and doubtless draws heavily on Conan Doyle's time there as a Jesuit student for its descriptive passages. 'A Pastoral Horror' eventually appeared in *The People* in December 1890.

For our next selection we move ahead to 1892. Sherlock Holmes was established: in addition to *A Study in Scarlet,* he had made a further appearance in the *Lippincott's*-commissioned novel *The Sign of the Four*, and had been making regular monthly appearances in *The Strand Magazine* since July 1891. Conan Doyle never treated Holmes as a vehicle for the supernatural, or, as he did with Professor Challenger, a mouthpiece for his own Spiritualist beliefs. 'No ghosts need apply', he had Holmes say in 'The Sussex Vampire' as late as 1924; but he did allow Holmes the occasional foray into the strange and the macabre, and this is splendidly illustrated by the Gothic trappings surrounding the events of 'The Speckled Band', the eighth Holmes tale to appear (February 1892).

Although Conan Doyle was virtually a permanent feature of *The Strand* from 1891 onwards, the need to publish stories, other than those of Sherlock Holmes, meant that other magazines would benefit from his work, too. *The Idler*, which began publication in 1892, was a case in point; and, with a friendship struck with both Robert Barr and Jerome K. Jerome, the magazine's first editors, contributions from Conan Doyle began to appear in that magazine on a regular basis. 'De Profundis' (March 1892) is a somewhat gruesome tale that Conan Doyle seems to have ignored for some years following its first publication: it was not collected until 1911's *The Last Galley*, even though the collection *Round the Red Lamp* appeared in the intervening years.

The major story from 1892, however, remains a bona fide classic of the

supernatural genre, and is one of the most memorable of all mummy tales—
'Lot No. 249'. This is a much stronger and horrific effort than Conan Doyle's
first foray into Egyptology, and one can almost feel the mummy breathing
down the protagonist's neck as he tries to reach the safety of his friend's house:
truly the stuff of nightmare.

Also from 1892 comes 'The Los Amigos Fiasco' (originally, it seems, titled
'Fiasco of Los Anjelos'),[26] which concerns an execution gone wrong. Conan
Doyle's account book notes that he received £17. 10s. 0d. for this story, which
appeared in the *Idler* in December 1892.

'The Case of Lady Sannox' (*Idler*, November 1893) was one of the stories
written for the *Idler* which Jerome K. Jerome hoped would be as successful for
that magazine as Holmes was proving for *The Strand*. The intention was for a
series entitled 'In a Doctor's Waiting Room'. In the event, Conan Doyle proved
too strong for the public's taste (or, at least, the *Idler*'s readership's taste), and
Jerome only published three of the stories over which he held rights. 'The Case
of Lady Sannox' is a black, dark tale of mutilation, carried out at the insistence
of an aggrieved husband. It is one of Conan Doyle's most brutal and horrific
stories, and one wonders quite what was running through Conan Doyle's mind
at that particular time: January 1893 had seen publication of the Sherlock
Holmes story 'The Cardboard Box', in which severed ears were sent through
the mail in a box filled with preserving salt; November 1893 brought the horror
and mutilation of Lady Sannox; and this was to be followed in the July 1894
Strand by the mutilation and psychological horror of 'The Lord of Château
Noir'. Was there one specific thing? Was there something definite that caused
Conan Doyle to put 'The Cardboard Box' aside for twenty-four years, removing
it from its rightful place in *The Memoirs of Sherlock Holmes* until 1917, when he
allowed the story to be collected in *His Last Bow*? Was there something more
than his simply feeling that the material was not truly suitable for younger
readers? Was the mystery behind the suppression of 'The Cardboard Box' related
to the implied adultery in the story? Perhaps so: it is difficult to believe that
Conan Doyle felt that a pair of severed ears could be more horrific or offensive
than the mutilated lip of Lady Sannox, a story he never suppressed, and one
which was gathered into his *Round the Red Lamp* collection a short year after
its original appearance. Conan Doyle's account book shows that he probably
used 'Douglas Stone' as the working title for this story, as his entries for 1892
show receipt of £36. 0s. 0d. from the *Idler* for this work.[27]

'The Parasite', first published in four parts in *Lloyd's Weekly Newspaper*
during November/December 1894, is another of Conan Doyle's classic
supernatural tales: one that re-uses the theme of mesmerism which he utilised
first in 'John Barrington Cowles', but which develops the device of mind control

---

26. Quoted from 'Account Books'. Christie's Auction Catalogue, p.53.
27. Quoted from 'Account Books'. Christie's Auction Catalogue, p.53.

more dramatically, and to far greater effect. Green and Gibson note[28] that Conan Doyle's interest in the subject of mesmerism dates back to the time when he was in medical practice at Southsea, and they refer to a specific meeting of the Portsmouth Literary and Scientific Society on 1 April 1890. This meeting may well have rekindled his interest, but it seems more likely, given the late 1883/early 1884 composition date of 'John Barrington Cowles', that Conan Doyle was interested in, and reading about, the subject much earlier than this. 'The Parasite' presents us with a textual problem: when Constable published the first English book edition in December 1894, they chose to adopt the spelling 'Penelosa' for the name of one of the book's main characters. The original newspaper serialization spells the name 'Penclosa', and this seems to have been adopted for all subsequent editions. Certainly commentators over the years have made much Freudian-style comment about the name 'Penclosa', which makes little sense if the Constable version is to be believed. For the publication of the story in this volume, we have preferred the original style. One wonders whether Constable may have had access to Conan Doyle's hand-written version of the story: his written 'e' and 'c' could, at times, be difficult to distinguish, as could his 'a' and 'o' (which we will not, at this time, allow to develop into a Sherlockian dissertation on the Long Island Cove/Cave Mystery of 'The Red Circle'!).

Following publication of 'The Parasite' Conan Doyle turned away from the purely supernatural story, concentrating instead on his historical and adventure novels—*Rodney Stone* (1896), *Uncle Bernac* (1897), *The Tragedy of the Korosko* (1898)—his Brigadier Gerard stories, other tales of adventure and medical life, even a semi-autobiographical novel, *The Stark Munro Letters* (1895). *The Strand Magazine*'s readers, it seems, were always demanding more Conan Doyle and, with the exception of 'The Striped Chest' (July 1897), 'The Fiend of the Cooperage' (October 1897), and 'The New Catacomb' (1898), which appeared in *Pearson's Magazine*, the *Manchester Weekly Times*, and *The Sunlight Year Book* respectively, it was the *Strand*'s readers who generally got to appreciate a new Conan Doyle story before anyone else did.

With Sherlock Holmes well and truly despatched over the Reichenbach Falls, or seemingly so, Conan Doyle began a new series. 'I am quite open to reason about the title,' he wrote to Greenhough Smith, 'but "Round the Fire Stories" seemed to me to be good.'[29] Three of that series of twelve stories concern us here: 'The Sealed Room' (September 1898), 'The Brazilian Cat' (December 1898), and 'The Brown Hand' (May 1899).

'The Sealed Room' is a dark little tale which deals with a family tragedy— might there just be some self-recrimination here over Conan Doyle's father

---

28. *A Bibliography of A. Conan Doyle*, pp.85–6.

29. Undated letter, Conan Doyle to H. Greenhough Smith, held in The Arthur Conan Doyle Collection, Toronto Reference Library.

being confined in asylums for the final years of his life? 'The Brazilian Cat' is a further psychological horror story, which adds physical horrors, too, with the villain deliberately setting out to ensure that his victim will suffer the torture of being held in a confined space with a vicious panther, and planning that matters should be resolved by the cat's killing his victim.

'The Brown Hand' is much lighter, and is based on the conventional idea of a person searching for a missing body part after death, so that they might go whole to their grave. It is a far cry from the brooding darkness of 'The Captain of the "Pole-Star"' and 'John Barrington Cowles', but is effective nonetheless.

Also falling within this period, but not a 'Round the Fire' story, is 'The Retirement of Signor Lambert', published in *Pearson's Magazine* in December 1898. This is a re-working of the dramatic theme Conan Doyle utilised in 'The Case of Lady Sannox', but the effect, while horrific in itself, lacks the accomplishment and execution of the earlier story. Commentators have noted that, as the years went by, Conan Doyle re-used some of the plot devices of his earlier tales, most notably in the later Sherlock Holmes adventures, and this seems to be an early example of a re-worked plot.

'Playing With Fire' (*Strand*, March 1900) tells the story of a séance gone wrong, and was, we feel sure, intended to serve as a warning to those who were prepared to dabble with things beyond their understanding.

In 1901 came the moment that all *Strand* readers had anxiously awaited: the news that Sherlock Holmes was to be resurrected. All Conan Doyle was initially prepared to say, however, was that this was a story from Holmes's earlier days. There are those who would have us believe that *The Hound of the Baskervilles* is a novel of the supernatural. It is not: the story is wholly rationalized. There are those who would have us believe that it is the best detective novel ever written. It is not: Holmes, the detective, is absent from the action for a good deal of the time. *The Hound of the Baskervilles* succeeds because of its atmosphere and its setting, and because something which is inanimate, yet lives and breathes, is allowed centre stage: the Moor. All of the mysteries of the case, the problems of the Baskerville family and its 'curse', are explained at the end of the story. The one thing that is not explained away is the Legend of the Hound, as read by Dr Mortimer in the novel's second chapter. From the document Dr Mortimer presents we learn of the origins of the story of the hound which has supposedly haunted the Baskerville family; and while the original hound might well have been of flesh and blood, it is slightly harder to explain away subsequent events as detailed in the Legend, written at least one hundred and twenty years after Sir Hugo perished: 'If I have set it down it is because that which is clearly known hath less terror than that which is but hinted at and guessed. Nor can it be denied that many of the family have been unhappy in their deaths, which have been sudden, bloody, and mysterious.' Are the Baskervilles a spectacularly unlucky family? Or is there truly something supernatural behind the legend which Holmes dismisses so airily? We have chosen to give the Legend the benefit of the doubt, and hope our readers will share that view.

'The Leather Funnel' (*Strand*, June 1903) is a story which Conan Doyle seems to have held in particularly high regard. In an undated letter [1902] to Greenhough Smith, Conan Doyle wrote: 'Here is a mighty grim story for your Xmas number if you want it.'[30] Greenhough Smith obviously wavered at this— the story was, indeed, rather gruesome for Christmas reading—and Smith may well have expressed that view; but Conan Doyle had also offered the story to S. S. McClure for American publication, as he was later to tell Greenough Smith: 'S. S. McClure read it and wanted me to put in the detail of the torture. I think myself I have got the happy mean—the horror without the coarseness— but of course the thing must be gruesome, that is what it is for.'[31]

In a later letter to Greenhough Smith, Conan Doyle noted: 'The Leather Funnel appears in November in America. I still think it is par excellence a Xmas story.'[32] Whether Conan Doyle and Greenhough Smith argued the matter there is no way of knowing. What we do know is that the story was accepted, but Greenhough Smith moved its publication as far away from Christmas as he could manage, the story finally seeing print in *The Strand* in June 1903. While Conan Doyle would certainly have been pleased to see its eventual publication in England, he was less than pleased with its appearance. A further letter to Greenhough Smith finds him writing: 'Let me do a small grumble on my own account. That "Leather Funnel" was literature, or as near literature as I can ever produce. It is not right to print such a story two words to the line on each side of an unnecessary illustration. It's bad economy to spoil a £200 story by the intrusion of a 3 guinea engraving.'[33] It's unlikely that Greenhough Smith would have been too worried. Conan Doyle was back to writing Sherlock Holmes stories, and the first of the new series, 'The Adventure of the Empty House', was just four months away from its debut in the October issue of the magazine.

The period following the death of Conan Doyle's first wife, Louise, in 1906 saw the beginning of the decline in the volume of Conan Doyle's short story output, which is borne out by the fact that there are only eight stories selected for this volume from the period 1906–30. Conan Doyle's interests and activities were moving elsewhere—to public issues, to Spiritualism, and to a new wife and family. There remained highlights, however, not least Professor

30. Undated letter, Conan Doyle to H. Greenhough Smith, held in The Arthur Conan Doyle Collection, Toronto Reference Library.

31. Undated letter, Conan Doyle to H. Greenhough Smith, held at the Alderman Library, University of Virginia Library, Special Collections and Manuscripts.

32. Undated letter, Conan Doyle to H. Greenhough Smith, held in The Arthur Conan Doyle Collection, Toronto Reference Library.

33. Undated letter, Conan Doyle to H. Greenhough Smith, held in The Arthur Conan Doyle Collection, Toronto Reference Library.

Challenger and *The Lost World*. Challenger was a particular favourite of Conan Doyle's, and the development of that character is a story to which a whole book could be devoted—indeed, will be devoted in the near future. The genre stories that remain from that period, however, are still very good indeed.

One wonders just how much supernatural fiction, if any, Conan Doyle was reading at this time. It is easier to believe that he was paying more attention to Spiritualist tracts and other matters, but, given his apparent interest in supernatural fiction, it is rather strange that no comment or assessment of M. R. James's seminal collection *Ghost Stories of an Antiquary*, published in 1904, has been traced back to Conan Doyle. Where the writer of the ghost story was concerned, James had changed things forever, and, for several years, his admirers and imitators would produce 'antiquarian' ghost stories, often revolving around the somewhat cloistered university existence of James's protagonists. It is a practice that continues, successfully, to this day, and James is unquestionably the most imitated practitioner of the form. (There are probably those who would claim the crown for H. P. Lovecraft, but Lovecraft's approach to supernatural fiction—that it should involve a cosmic vision—was far removed from that of James. And it should be added that, although Lovecraftian imitation is seemingly boundless, the quality of much of it leaves a great deal to be desired.)

So, although a new standard was being set by James, it seems to have had little or no effect on Conan Doyle. Perhaps it was the case that, in everyday life, they moved in very different circles—although Conan Doyle's son Kingsley was a student at Eton at this time, and it is just possible that Conan Doyle and James may have become acquainted in some way. (Whatever the case, James was a *huge* admirer of Sherlock Holmes.) However, wholly disregarding the new standard set by James, Conan Doyle made his next offering 'The Silver Mirror' (*Strand*, August 1908).

Arthur may well have had the opportunity to visit Holyrood Palace during his Edinburgh years, and there was, after all, a minor family connection—his father Charles had been involved in the design of the fountain there. He would certainly have recalled the story of Rizzio's murder, and used it to splendid effect in his story. Disappointingly, E. F. Bleiler brackets this story with a number of items he considers 'are not significant';[34] but the fact remains that 'The Silver Mirror' is a compact piece, well narrated, and a rather pleasing approach to one of history's horrors.

Another location which would certainly have been familiar to Conan Doyle (from his time as Dr Richardson's assistant in Sheffield) was Derbyshire's Peak District (or 'The Peak country', as Dr Watson terms it in his narration of 1904's 'The Adventure of the Priory School'). It was here, in the Blue John caverns, that ACD set his next story of the supernatural, 'The Terror of Blue John Gap'

---

34. E. F. Bleiler, Introduction to *Arthur Conan Doyle's Supernatural Fiction* (New York: Dover, 1979), p.xiii.

(*Strand*, August 1910), though it has to be said that this is more of a weird, than a supernatural, tale, involving a prehistoric cave-bear.

The idea of a monstrous prehistoric creature surviving into the twentieth century was one which was on Conan Doyle's mind in 1910, when he was beginning to conceive the idea which would later become his novel *The Lost World* (1912), in which an assortment of prehistoric creatures is discovered on an isolated plateau in South America. ACD had become interested in paleontology, and in 1909 he met with the British explorer P. H. Fawcett, who had recently returned from South America, and asked for information about the area. Also in 1909, ACD had noticed fossil imprints in a quarry near his home in Crowborough, and informed the British Museum, which sent an expert to examine them. An article about Conan Doyle, published in 1913 in *The Bookman*,[35] mentions that on the floor of the author's billiard room stood 'two huge fossil feet of the prehistoric Iguanodon, and on the table above them is the flint head of an arrow that has survived the Stone Age . . . [It] was the discovery of these relics on the downs that stretch for miles before his own door that set Sir Arthur's imagination at work on the period to which they belong and resulted in the creation of the astonishing Professor Challenger . . .' It is not too much of a stretch to say that 'The Terror of Blue John Gap' was also a result of this interest of the author's, and may have been a trial run for the novel; although Conan Doyle realized that setting such a story in England had its limitations. In a speech on 'Literature' which he delivered at the Royal Society Club in London on 3 May 1910, ACD said, with tongue firmly in cheek, that writers of romance had a grievance against explorers, who, through their 'ill-directed energy', were continually filling the blank spaces of the world. The question, said Conan Doyle, was 'where the romance writer was to turn when he wanted to draw any vague and not too clearly defined region. Romance writers [are] a class of people who very much disliked being hampered by facts.'[36]

But where did the idea of a huge bear-like creature originate? That is certainly more difficult to discern, and it is tempting to offer a solution by suggesting that the creature in the Blue John cavern owes something to the Sasquatch or Bigfoot of North America, or to the Yeti, said to live in the Himalayas, and reported in the west as early as 1832. Certainly both creatures have long histories in their own countries, and it may be noted that Theodore Roosevelt records a detailed incident, said to be a true account of a Sasquatch attack in the mid-1850s, in his 1893 book *The Wilderness Hunter*. Interestingly, Conan Doyle and Roosevelt met in 1910, shortly before 'The Terror of Blue John Gap' was published.

What, our readers may well ask, is a story of pirates doing in a collection of supernatural and weird fiction? It's a valid question, and we hope that a reading

---

35. A. St John Adcock, 'Doyle's Crowborough Home' in *Bookman* 36, 1913.
36. *The Times*, 4 May 1910, p.10.

of the story will provide a valid answer. Captain John Sharkey of the *Happy Delivery* had previously featured in three stories published in *Pearson's Magazine* in 1897. Piracy was a subject in which Conan Doyle was obviously prepared to invest a little of his time—two of his research notebooks were specifically dedicated to notes on pirates and buccaneer lore.[37] Sharkey was unquestionably one of Conan Doyle's nastier and more colourful creations, and 'The Blighting of Sharkey', included here, is memorable for its specific horror. No more will be said; the reader will shiver for him- or her-self. Consistent with his desire to feed *The Strand* with much, if not all, of his new material, Conan Doyle offered this story to Greenhough Smith, but it appears not to have been well received. A reported letter to Greenhough Smith regrets objections to the story, 'for I feel it was of my best', and offers to modify the language if this would suffice, and also proposes to develop two sketches.[38] As events transpired, the story would be published by *Pearson's*, and that was only fitting, since they had carried the earlier Sharkey stories in their pages.

'Through the Veil', a story original to Conan Doyle's collection *The Last Galley* (1911), is a modest but pleasing offering which deals sensitively with the question of reincarnation. Less sensitive, and quite happy to deal a surprise at the reader's expense, is 'How It Happened' (*Strand*, September 1913). It's easy to believe that Conan Doyle had his own motoring experiences in mind when he wrote this story: John Dickson Carr notes an incident in 1904 when, returning from a drive with his brother Innes, ACD's Wolseley motor car bumped against one of the gate-posts of his Hindhead home, Undershaw. Then it shot down the drive towards the house, slurring gravel under its hard-rubber tyres. It lurched, swerved, climbed straight up the steep bank at one side of the drive, and turned over backwards on top of its two occupants. The full weight of the car—more than a ton—settled down across ACD's back and shoulders just below the neck. Conan Doyle managed to sustain the weight until help arrived to free him; all of which goes to prove that real life can be just as dramatic as fiction.

While 'The Horror of the Heights' could, justifiably, be regarded as early science fiction, it is the unknown—whatever lurked in the upper atmosphere, unknown to early aeronauts—that is the horror in this story. As with his mummy stories, and the forgotten civilization of *The Lost World*, Conan Doyle shows himself to be an innovative fictioneer in this story, which was published in *The Strand* in November 1913. In this case, in part answering his own question 'where was the romance writer to turn when he wanted to draw any vague and not too clearly defined region', Conan Doyle chose the spaces above the earth, a virtually unknown and unexplored area in the early days of flight. A very detailed study of this story has recently appeared, accompanying a facsimile

---

37. Quoted from 'Notebooks'. Christie's Auction Catalogue, p.47.
38. Quoted from '[Letters to] H. Greenhough Smith'. Christie's Auction Catalouge, p.140.

reproduction of Conan Doyle's original manuscript.[39] Conan Doyle was to receive comment on this story many years later from a first-hand source. In *Our American Adventure* he noted:

> I had an interesting talk while in Chicago with Major Schroeder, who broke the height record in 1920 in his aeroplane. He reached 37,000 feet. At that point something went wrong with his oxygen tube and he fell down in the car among the carbon monoxide which came from the exhaust.
>
> The poisonous stuff would soon have killed him, but the machine, left to itself, fell seven miles in less than three minutes. The improved air revived Schroeder and he was able to regain command when only 1,800 feet above earth.
>
> Fancy falling like a stone for seven miles! I am not sure if it is a nightmare or a dream of bliss. He had read my story 'The Horror of the Heights', and admitted to me that he always at great altitudes had a subconscious fear that he might meet some new form of life. 'Look out for those big angle worms!' they had called to him as he left the ground.
>
> After all, the deepest sea sustains life—why not the highest air? As a matter of fact, the only strange thing he ever saw was a flight of snow-white birds, like robins, flying at 12,000 feet altitude. Also drifting spider webs with spiders still on them.
>
> The great problem is to prevent your eyes freezing, which is done by double glasses with a sort of thermos arrangement. No one, he thinks, will ever get much higher, because the tenuous air will not give a grip to the machine. Altogether I was very interested in our talk.[40]

It would be a further eight years before Conan Doyle's final notable contribution to the genre appeared, in *The Strand Magazine* for November 1921. A few months earlier he had advised Greenhough Smith: 'I have a real good short boxing story on hand. "The Bully of Brocas Court". Should finish it this week.'[41]

'The Bully of Brocas Court' is almost unique among early ghost stories, in that the ghost is actually seen to cause physical harm to humans. This is a twist to the usual style of ghost story, in which ghosts generally do little more than frighten people—albeit, on occasion, with fatal consequences—and it enables Conan Doyle to fool his reader for a while. E. F. Bleiler called this 'one of Doyle's best stories'.[42] It is certainly one of his more unusual.

Our final selection, 'The Lift' (*Strand*, June 1922), is a piece of

---

39. *The Horror of the Heights: A Facsimile of the Author's Holograph Manuscript with Commentary*, Phillip Bergem, ed., John Bergquist, gen. ed. (Ashcroft, B.C.: Calabash Press in conjunction with The Sherlock Holmes Collections, Department of Special Collections, University of Minnesota Libraries; The Arthur Conan Doyle Society; and The Norwegian Explorers, 2004).

40. Arthur Conan Doyle, *Our American Adventure* (London: Hodder and Stoughton, 1923), pp.140–1.

41. Undated letter, Conan Doyle to H. Greenhough Smith, held in The Arthur Conan Doyle Collection, Toronto Reference Library.

42. E. F. Bleiler, Introduction to *Arthur Conan Doyle's Supernatural Fiction*.

psychological horror set in the modern surroundings of a seaside tower. It is unlikely that this story will be well known to genre readers, but we feel that it is a highly suitable piece, which supplies a fitting, tingling end to the collection.

In closing, mention must be made of other works of Conan Doyle's which have a supernatural flavour. In the main these are novels. *The Mystery of Cloomber* (1888) was never one of the author's own favourite works, and was the only novel excluded from the Crowborough Edition (1930). The influences of Wilkie Collins's *The Moonstone* and various ideas from Stevenson are apparent. *The Doings of Raffles Haw* (1892) was written for Harmsworth's penny paper *Answers*, and ACD began writing the novel shortly after his arrival in Vienna in 1891. He received 'my present scale' of £5 per 1,000 words for his efforts.[43] The novel deals with alchemy and was considered 'not a very notable achievement' by Conan Doyle.[44] *The Maracot Deep* (1929), originally titled 'The Fabricius Deep', illustrates ACD's interest in the Atlantean legend, and, while highlighting a cosmic battle between good and evil, really falls into the category of science fiction/fantasy. Finally, there is *The Land of Mist* (1925), the novel in which Conan Doyle allowed his Spiritualist beliefs and propaganda to intrude into his fiction. This novel should, in all fairness, be grouped with the semi-autobiographical *The Stark Munro Letters* (1895), as it does provide us with some evidence of Conan Doyle's activities as a Spiritualist. A modern reader, however, is unlikely to find it an absorbing read, and it is a sad epitaph for the splendid Professor Challenger that Conan Doyle demeaned his character in this manner.

E. F. BLEILER commented that 'Arthur Conan Doyle was not the towering figure in supernatural fiction that he was in the detective story or the historical novel . . . his was not a new vision; his was merely respectable accomplishment.'[45] Bleiler compared Conan Doyle's output to that of Bram Stoker, M. R. James, Algernon Blackwood, Arthur Machen, and Ambrose Bierce, and it is true that, where 'vision' is concerned, the comparison may not be a good one. But we should not overlook the fact that Conan Doyle's supernatural, weird, and imaginative fiction broke new ground—particularly in stories such as 'J. Habakuk Jephson's Statement', 'Lot No. 249', 'The Parasite', 'The Terror of Blue John Gap', and 'The Horror of the Heights'. It should also be acknowledged that where many authors in the supernatural field are content to write variations on the same theme for much of their career, Conan Doyle explored a wide range of supernatural themes and settings.

That Conan Doyle was interested in the supernatural story is demonstrated by the fact that the first story he is known to have written and submitted for

---

43. *A Bibliography of A. Conan Doyle*, p.43.

44. Arthur Conan Doyle, *Memories and Adventures* (London: John Murray, 1924), p.94.

45. E. F. Bleiler, Introduction to *Arthur Conan Doyle's Supernatural Fiction*, p.xiii.

publication, 'The Haunted Grange of Goresthorpe', was a ghost story. It was an interest which he was to maintain throughout his writing career: a career which spanned more than five decades, and saw him turn his hand to almost every form of fiction.

It is impossible not to share the enthusiasm that H. Greenhough Smith, editor of *The Strand Magazine*, felt when Conan Doyle's submissions first crossed his desk. As he wrote shortly after Conan Doyle's death:

> . . . good story-writers were scarce, and here to an editor, jaded with wading through reams of impossible stuff, comes a gift from heaven, a godsend in the shape of a story that brought a gleam of happiness into the despairing life of this weary editor. Here was a new and gifted story-writer; there was no mistaking the ingenuity of plot, the limpid clearness of style, the perfect art of telling a story.

Later he was to add:

> Now I take it that the mark of a good style—as it is of the medium of every art—is its capacity to achieve the purpose for which it was intended. Conan Doyle was one of the great story-tellers of the world, and his purpose was to tell a story; and this his style, simple, clear, and easy-flowing, never drawing off the reader's notice by any frills or gewgaws of its own, achieves to absolute perfection.

Who would argue with that? Conan Doyle's supernatural fiction was a very small but important part of this huge oeuvre, and many of his ghostly tales show him writing at the height of his ability. What is perhaps most overlooked today is the fact that Arthur Conan Doyle was one of the most accomplished and entertaining storytellers of his day, an author who was consistently able to satisfy his huge readership, virtually without respite, for a period of forty years. Above all, this is Conan Doyle's remarkable achievement as a fictioneer, and the reason why his work is still so highly regarded.

CHRISTOPHER RODEN
BARBARA RODEN
ASHCROFT, B.C.
May 2004

THE CAPTAIN OF
THE 'POLE-STAR'

A Note Concerning the Texts

THERE IS NO DEFINITIVE TEXT of Arthur Conan Doyle's stories. For example, Sherlock Holmes scholars have been arguing for years about various textual differences in the stories which, for them, are particularly significant. The fact is that Conan Doyle's stories have passed through so many hands and eyes, with each person adding fresh punctuation, and correcting what, in his/her opinion, are errors, and reading what they feel it is that Conan Doyle actually wrote—be it 'Long Island Cave' or 'Long Island Cove'—that many changes have undoubtedly been made to Conan Doyle's originals.

We have not, for example, been able to track down the original manuscript of 'The Parasite', and we have no way, therefore, of knowing whether Conan Doyle intended his character to be named 'Miss Penclosa' (as in most editions), or 'Miss Penelosa' (as in the first book edition).

The Crowborough Edition (1930) of Conan Doyle's works set out with good intentions: it was to be *the* definitive edition—Conan Doyle would revise the texts to his liking, and various new materials would be added. Regrettably, other commitments, and ill health, prevented the project from being seen through to a satisfactory conclusion; and the Crowborough Edition was destined to be re-workings of previous printings.

For *The Captain of the 'Pole-Star'* we have, generally, preferred the texts of the John Murray editions of Conan Doyle's stories, where those exist. In other cases, we have relied upon the texts which Richard Lancelyn Green and John Michael Gibson presented in their compilation of Conan Doyle's Uncollected Stories, correcting obvious errors as we encountered them. Overall, however, we have attempted to provide what we consider to be the most satisfactory presentation of the stories. Inevitably, errors of our own will have been introduced. We trust that we have kept such infelicities to a minimum.

The Haunted Grange
of Goresthorpe

A True Ghost Story

LOOKING BACK NOW AT THE EVENTS OF MY LIFE that one dreadful night looms out like some great landmark. Even now, after the lapse of so many years, I cannot think of it without a shudder. All minor incidents and events I mentally classify as occurring before or after the time when I saw a Ghost.

Yes, saw a ghost. Don't be incredulous, reader, don't sneer at the phrase; though I can't blame you for I was incredulous enough myself once. However hear the facts of my story before you pass a judgment.

The old Grange used to stand on my estate of Goresthorpe in Norfolk. It has been pulled down now, but it stood there when Tom Hulton came to visit me in 184–. It was a tumbledown old pile at the meeting of the Morsely and Alton roads where the new turn-pike stands now. The garden round had long been choked up by a rank growth of weeds, while pools of stagnant water and the accumulated garbage of the whole village poisoned the air around. It was a dreary place by day and an eerie one by night, for strange stories were told of the Grange, sounds were said to have come from those weather-beaten walls, such as mortal lips never uttered, and the elders of the village still spoke of one, Job Garston by name, who thirty years before had had the temerity to sleep inside, and who had been led out in the morning, a whitehaired broken man.

I used, I remember, to ascribe all this to the influence of the weird gaunt old building upon their untutored minds, and moralized upon the effects of a liberal education in removing such mental weaknesses. I alone knew however that the Grange had certainly, as far as foul crime was concerned, as orthodox a title to be haunted as any building on record. The last tenant as I discovered from my family papers was a certain Godfrey Marsden, a villain of the first water. He lived there about the middle of last century and was a byeword of ferocity and brutality throughout the whole countryside. Finally he consummated his many crimes by horribly hacking his two young children to

3

death and strangling their mother. In the confusion of the Pretender's march into England, justice was laxly administered, and Marsden succeeded in escaping to the Continent where all trace of him was lost. There was a rumour indeed among his creditors, the only ones who regretted him, that remorse had led him to commit suicide, and that his body had been washed up on the French Coast, but those who knew him best laughed at the idea of anything so intangible having an effect upon so hardened a ruffian. Since his day the Grange had been untenanted and had been suffered to fall into the state of disrepair in which it then was.

Tom Hulton was an old college chum of mine, and right glad I was to see his honest face beneath my roof. He brightened the whole house, Tom did, for a more good humoured hearty reckless fellow never breathed. His only fault was that he had acquired a strange speculative way of thinking from his German education, and this led to continual arguments between us, for I had been trained as a medical student and looked at things therefore from an eminently practical point of view. That evening, I remember, the first after his arrival, we glided from one argument into another but all with the greatest good humour and invariably without coming to any conclusion.

I forget how the question of ghosts arose; at any rate there we were, Tom Hulton and I, at midnight in the depths of a debate about spirits and spiritualism. Tom, when he argued was wont to produce a certain large briar root pipe of his, and by this time he was surrounded by a dense wreath of smoke, from the midst of which his voice issued like the oracle of Delphi, while his stalwart figure loomed through the haze.

'I tell you, Jack,' he was saying, 'that mankind may be divided into two classes, the men who profess not to believe in Ghosts and are mortally afraid of them, and the men who admit at least the possibility of their existence and would go out of their way to see one. Now I don't scruple to acknowledge that I am one of the latter school. Of course, Jack, I know that you are one of these "*credo-quod-tango*" medicals, who walk in the narrow path of certain fact, and quite right too in such a profession as yours; but I have always had a strange leaning towards the unseen and supernatural, especially in this matter of the existence of ghosts. Don't think though that I am such a fool as to believe in the orthodox spectre with his curse, and his chain warranted to rattle, and his shady retreat down some back stairs, or in the cellar; no, nothing of that sort.'

'Well, Tom, let's hear your idea of a creditable ghost.'

'It's not such an easy matter, you see, to explain it to another, even though I can define it in my own mind well enough. You and I both hold, Jack, that when a man dies he has done with all the cares and troubles of this world, and is for the future, be it one of joy or sorrow, a pure and ethereal spirit. Well now, what I feel is that it is possible for a man to be hurried out of this world with a soul as impregnated with some one all-absorbing passion, that it clings to him even after he has passed the portals of the grave. Now,' continued Tom, impressively waving his pipe from side to side through the cloud that surrounded him, 'love or patriotism or some other pure and elevating passion, might well be entertained by one who is but a spirit, but it is different, I fancy, with such grosser feelings as hatred or revenge. These one could imagine, even after death, clogging the poor soul so that it must still inhabit that coarse clay which is most fitted to the coarse passions which absorb it; and thus I would account for the unexplained and unexplainable things which have happened even in our own time, and for the deeply rooted belief in Ghosts which exists, smother it as we may, in every breast, and which has existed in every age.'

'You may be right, Tom,' said I, 'but as you say "*quod tango credo*" and as I never saw any of your "impregnated spirits" I must beg leave to doubt their existence.'

'It's very easy to laugh at the matter,' answered Tom, 'but there are few facts in this world which have not been laughed at, sometime or another. Tell me this, Jack, did you ever try to see a ghost? Did you ever go upon a ghost hunt, my boy?'

'Well I can't say I ever did,' said I, 'did you?'

'I'm on one just now, Jack,' said he, and then sat puffing at his pipe for some time. 'Look here,' he continued, 'I've heard you talk of some old manor or Grange you have down here, which is said to be haunted. Now I want you to lend me the key of that, and I'll take up my quarters there tomorrow night. How long is it since anyone slept in it, Jack?'

'For heaven's sake, don't think of doing such a foolhardy thing,' I exclaimed. 'Why only one man has slept in Goresthorpe Grange during a hundred years, and he went mad to my certain knowledge!'

'Ha! that sounds promising, very promising,' cried Tom in high delight. 'Now just observe the thick headedness of the British public, yourself included, Jack. You won't believe in ghosts, and you won't go and look where a ghost is said to be found. Now suppose there was said to be white crows or some other natural curiosity in Yorkshire, and someone assured you that there was not, because he had been all through Wales without seeing one, you would naturally consider the man an idiot. Well, doesn't the same apply to you if you refuse to go to the Grange and settle the question for yourself once for all?'

'If you go tomorrow, I shall certainly go too,' I returned, 'if only to prevent your coming home with some cock and bull story about an impregnated spirit, so good night, Tom,' and with that we separated.

I confess that in the morning I began to feel that I had been slightly imprudent in aiding and abetting Tom in his ridiculous expedition. 'It's that confounded Irish whisky,' thought I. 'I always put my foot into it after the third glass, however perhaps Tom has thought better of it too by this time.' In that expectation however I was woefully disappointed, for Tom swore he had been awake all night planning and preparing everything for the evening.

'We're bound to take pistols you know, old boy; those are always taken;

then there are our pipes and a couple of ounces of bird's-eye, and our rugs, and a bottle of whisky, nothing else, I think. By Jove, I do believe we'll unearth a ghost tonight!'

'Heaven forbid!' I mentally ejaculated but as there was no way out of it I pretended to be as enthusiastic in the business as Tom himself.

All day Tom was in a state of the wildest excitement, and as evening fell we both walked over to the old Grange of Goresthorpe. There it stood cold, bleak and desolate as ever with the wind howling past it. Great strips of ivy which had lost their hold upon the walls swayed and tossed in the wind like the plumes of a hearse. How comfortable the lights in the village seemed to my eyes as we turned the key in the rusty lock, and having lit a candle began to walk down the stoneflagged dusty hall!

'Here we are!' said Tom, throwing a door open and disclosing a large dingy room.

'Not there for Goodness' sake,' said I, 'let's find a small room where we can light a fire and be sure at a glance that we are the only people in it.'

'All right, old fellow,' answered Tom laughing. 'I did a little exploring today on my own hook and know the place pretty well. I've got just the article to suit you at the other end of the house.'

He took up the candle again as he spoke and having shut the door he led me from one passage to another through the rambling old building. We came at last to a long corridor running the whole length of one wing of the house, which certainly had a very ghostly appearance. One wall was entirely solid, while the other had openings for windows let in at every three or four paces, so that when the moon shone in the dark passage was flecked every here and there with patches of white light. Near the end of it was a door which led into a small room, cleaner and more modern looking than the rest of the house, and with a large fireplace opposite the entrance. It was hung with dark red curtains, and when we had got our fire ablaze it certainly looked more comfortable than I had ever dared to expect. Tom seemed unutterably disgusted and discontented by the result; 'Call this a haunted house,' he said, 'why we might as well sit up in a hotel and expect to see a ghost! This isn't by any means the sort of thing I have been looking forward to.' It was not until the briar had been twice replenished that he began to recover his usual equanimity of temper.

Perhaps it was our curious surroundings which flavoured the bird's-eye and mellowed the whisky, and our own suppressed excitement which gave zest to the conversation. Certainly a pleasanter evening neither of us ever spent.

Outside the wind was howling and screaming, tossing the trailing ivy in the air. The moon shone out fitfully from between the dark clouds which drifted across the sky, and the measured patter of the rain was heard upon the slates above us.

'The roof may leak, but it can't get at us,' said Tom, 'for there's a little bedroom above our heads with a very good floor too. Shouldn't be surprised if it's the very room where those youngsters were cut up by that model father of theirs. Well it's nearly twelve o'clock, and if we are going to see anything at all, we ought to see it before very long. By Jove, what a chill wind comes through that door! I remember feeling like this when I was waiting outside before going in for my oral exam at college. You look excited too, old boy.'

'Hush, Tom, didn't you hear a noise in the corridor?'

'Hang the noise,' said Tom, 'pass me over a fusee old boy.'

'I'll swear I heard a heavy door slamming,' I insisted. 'I'll tell you what, Tom, I feel as if your ambition was going to be realized tonight and I'm not ashamed to say that I'm heartily sorry I came with you on such a foolhardy errand.'

'Dash it all,' said Tom, 'it's no use funking it now—By Jove, what's that?'

It was a gentle pit pat pit pat in the room and close to Tom's elbow. We both sprang to our feet, and then Tom burst into a roar of laughter. 'Why, Jack,' he said, 'you're making a regular old woman of me; it's only the rain that has got in after all and is dropping on that bit of loose paper on the wall yonder. What fools we were to be frightened! Why here's the very place it dropped——'

'Good God!' I cried, 'what is the matter with you, Tom?' His face had changed to a livid hue, his eyes were fixed and staring, and his lips parted in horror and astonishment.

'Look!' he almost screamed, 'look!' and he held up the piece of paper which had been hanging from the mildewed wall. Great heaven! it was all freckled and spotted with gouts of still liquid blood. Even as we stood gazing at it, another drop fell upon the floor with a dull splash. Both our pale faces were turned upwards tracing the course of this horrible shower. We could discern a small crack in the cornice, and through this as through a wound in human flesh the blood seemed to well. Another drop fell, and yet another, as we stood gazing spellbound.

'Come away, Tom, come away!' I cried at last, unable to bear it longer. 'Come! God's curse is on the place.' I seized him by the shoulder as I spoke and turned towards the door.

'By God, I won't,' cried Tom fiercely, shaking off my grasp, 'come up with me, Jack, and get to the bottom of the matter. There may be some villainy here. Hang it, man, don't be cowed by a drop or two of blood! Don't try to stop me! I shall go'; and he pushed past me and dashed into the corridor.

What a moment that was! If I should live to be a hundred I could never shake off my vivid remembrance of it. Outside the wind was still howling past the windows, while an occasional flash of lightning illuminated the old Grange. Within there was no sound save the creaking of the door as it was thrown back and the gentle pit pat of that ghastly shower from above. Then Tom tottered back into the room and grasped me by the arm. 'Let us stick together, Jack,' he said in an awestruck whisper. '*There's something coming up the corridor!*'

A horrible fascination led us to the door, and we peered together down the long and dark passage. One side was, as I have said, pierced by numerous openings through which the moonlight streamed throwing little patches of light upon the dark floor. Far down the passage we could see that something was obscuring first one of these bright spots, then the next, then another. It vanished in the gloom, then it reappeared where the next window cast its light, then it vanished again. It was coming rapidly towards us. Now it was only four windows from us, now three, now two, one, and then the figure of a man emerged into the glare of light which burst from our open door. He was running rapidly and vanished into the gloom on the other side of us. His dress was old fashioned and dishevelled, what seemed to be long dark ribbons hung down among his hair, on each side of his swarthy face. But that face itself—when shall I ever forget it? As he ran he kept it half turned back, as if expecting some pursuer, and his countenance expressed such a degree of hopeless despair, and of dreadful fear, that, frightened as I was, my heart bled for him. As we followed the direction of his horror stricken gaze we saw that he had indeed a pursuer. As before we could trace the dark shadow flitting over the white flecks of moonlight, as before it emerged into the circle of light thrown by our candles and fire. It was a beautiful and stately lady, a woman perhaps eight-and-twenty years of age, with the low dress and gorgeous train of last century. Beneath her lovely chin we both remarked upon one side of the neck four small dark spots, and on the other side one larger one. She swept by us, looking neither to the right nor left, but with her stony gaze bent upon the spot where the fugitive had vanished. Then she too was lost in the darkness. A minute later as we stood there, still gazing, a horrible shriek, a scream of awful agony, rang out high above the wind and the thunder, and then all was still inside the house.

I don't know how long we both stood there, spellbound, holding on to each other's arms. It must have been some time for the fresh candle was flickering in the socket when Tom, with a shudder, walked rapidly down the passage, still grasping my hand. Without a word we passed out through the mouldering hall door, out into the storm and the rain, over the garden wall, through the silent village and up the avenue. It was not until we were in my comfortable little smoking-room, and Tom from sheer force of habit had lit a cigar, that he seemed to recover his equanimity at all.

'Well, Jack,' were the first words he said, 'what do you think of ghosts now?' His next remark was 'Confound it, I've lost the best briar root pipe I ever had, for I'll be hanged before I go back there to fetch it.'

'We have seen a horrible sight,' said I. 'What a face he had, Tom! And those ghastly ribbons hanging from his hair, what were those, Tom?'

'Ribbons! Why, Jack, don't you know seaweed when you see it? And I've seen those dark marks that were on the woman's neck before now, and so have you in your medical studies I have little doubt.'

'Yes,' said I, 'those were the marks of four fingers and a thumb. It was the strangled woman, Tom. God preserve us from ever seeing such a sight again!'

'Amen,' said Tom, and those were the last words we interchanged that night.

In the morning Tom, his mission ended, went down to London, and soon afterwards set sail for the coffee estates of his father in Ceylon. Since then I have lost sight of him. I do not know whether he is alive or dead, but of one thing I am very sure, that if alive he never thinks without a shudder of our terrible night in the haunted Grange of Goresthorpe.

The American's Tale

IT AIR STRANGE, IT AIR,' he was saying as I opened the door of the room where our social little semi-literary society met; 'but I could tell you queerer things than that 'ere—almighty queer things. You can't learn everything out of books, sirs, nohow. You see it ain't the men as can string English together and as has had good eddications as finds themselves in the queer places I've been in. They're mostly rough men, sirs, as can scarce speak aright, far less tell with pen and ink the things they've seen; but if they could they'd make some of your European's har riz with astonishment. They would, sirs, you bet!'

His name was Jefferson Adams, I believe; I know his initials were J. A., for you may see them yet deeply whittled on the right-hand upper panel of our smoking-room door. He left us this legacy, and also some artistic patterns done in tobacco juice upon our Turkey carpet; but beyond these reminiscences our American storyteller has vanished from our ken. He gleamed across our ordinary quiet conviviality like some brilliant meteor, and then was lost in the outer darkness. That night, however, our Nevada friend was in full swing; and I quietly lit my pipe and dropped into the nearest chair, anxious not to interrupt his story.

'Mind you,' he continued, 'I hain't got no grudge against your men of science. I likes and respects a chap as can match every beast and plant, from a huckleberry to a grizzly with a jaw-breakin' name; but if you wants real interestin' facts, something a bit juicy, you go to your whalers and your frontiersmen, and your scouts and Hudson Bay men, chaps who mostly can scarce sign their names.'

There was a pause here, as Mr Jefferson Adams produced a long cheroot and lit it. We preserved a strict silence in the room, for we had already learned that on the slightest interruption our Yankee drew himself into his shell again. He glanced round with a self-satisfied smile as he remarked our expectant looks, and continued through a halo of smoke:

'Now which of you gentlemen has ever been in Arizona? None, I'll warrant. And of all English or Americans as can put pen to paper, how many has been in Arizona? Precious few, I calc'late. I've been there, sirs, lived there for years; and when I think of what I've seen there, why, I can scarce get myself to believe it now.

'Ah, there's a country! I was one of Walker's filibusters, as they chose to call us; and after we'd busted up, and the chief was shot, some on us made tracks and located down there. A reg'lar English and American colony, we was, with our wives and children, and all complete. I reckon there's some of the old folk there yet, and that they hain't forgotten what I'm agoing to tell you. No, I warrant they hain't, never on this side of the grave, sirs.

'I was talking about the country, though; and I guess I could astonish you considerable if I spoke of nothing else. To think of such a land being built for a few "Greasers" and half-breeds! It's a misusing of the gifts of Providence, that's what I calls it. Grass as hung over a chap's head as he rode through it, and trees so thick that you couldn't catch a glimpse of blue sky for leagues and leagues, and orchids like umbrellas! Maybe some of you has seen a plant as they calls the "fly-catcher", in some parts of the States?'

'*Dianoea muscipula*,' murmured Dawson, our scientific man *par excellence*.

'Ah, "Die near a municipal", that's him! You'll see a fly stand on that 'ere plant, and then you'll see the two sides of a leaf snap up together and catch it between them, and grind it up and mash it to bits, for all the world like some great sea squid with its beak; and hours after, if you open the leaf, you'll see the body lying half-digested, and in bits. Well, I've seen those flytraps in Arizona with leaves eight and ten feet long, and thorns or teeth a foot or more; why, they could—But darn it, I'm going too fast!

'It's about the death of Joe Hawkins I was going to tell you; 'bout as queer a thing, I reckon, as ever you heard tell on. There wasn't nobody in Arizona as didn't know of Joe Hawkins—"Alabama" Joe, as he was called there. A reg'lar out and outer, he was, 'bout the darndest skunk as ever man clapt eyes on. He was a good chap enough, mind ye, as long as you stroked him the right way; but rile him anyhow, and he were worse nor a wild-cat. I've seen him empty his six-shooter into a crowd as chanced to jostle him agoing into Simpson's bar when there was a dance on; and he bowied Tom Hooper 'cause he spilt his liquor over his weskit by mistake. No, he didn't stick at murder, Joe didn't; and he weren't a man to be trusted further nor you could see him.

'Now at the time I tell on, when Joe Hawkins was swaggerin' about the town and layin' down the law with his shootin'-irons, there was an Englishman there of the name of Scott—Tom Scott, if I rec'lects aright. This chap Scott was a thorough Britisher (beggin' the present company's pardon), and yet he didn't freeze much to the British set there, or they didn't freeze much to him. He was a quiet simple man, Scott was—rather too quiet for a rough set like that; sneakin' they called him, but he weren't that. He kept hisself mostly apart, an' didn't interfere with nobody so long as he were left alone. Some said as how he'd been kinder ill-treated at home—been a Chartist, or something of that sort, and had to up sticks and run; but he never spoke of it hisself, an' never complained. Bad luck or good, that chap kept a stiff lip on him.

'This chap Scott was a sort o' butt among the men about Arizona, for he was so quiet an' simple-like. There was no party either to take up his grievances; for, as I've been saying, the Britishers hardly counted him one of them, and many a rough joke they played on him. He never cut up rough, but was polite to all hisself. I think the boys got to think he hadn't much grit in him till he showed 'em their mistake.

'It was in Simpson's bar as the row got up, an' that led to the queer thing I was going to tell you of. Alabama Joe and one or two other rowdies were dead on the Britishers in those days, and they spoke their opinions pretty free, though I warned them as there'd be an almighty muss. That partic'lar night Joe was nigh half drunk, an' he swaggered about the town with his six-shooter, lookin' out for a quarrel. Then he turned into the bar where he know'd he'd find some o' the English as ready for one as he was hisself. Sure enough, there was half a dozen lounging about, an' Tom Scott standin' alone before the stove. Joe sat down by the table, and put his revolver and bowie down in front of him. "Them's my arguments, Jeff," he says to me, "if any white-livered Britisher dares give me the lie." I tried to stop him, sirs; but he weren't a man as you could easily turn, an' he began to speak in a way as no chap could stand. Why, even a "Greaser" would flare up if you said as much of Greaserland! There was a commotion at the bar, an' every man laid his hands on his wepins; but afore they could draw we heard a quiet voice from the stove: "Say your prayers, Joe Hawkins; for, by Heaven, you're a dead man!" Joe turned round and looked like grabbin' at his iron; but it weren't no manner of use. Tom Scott was standing up, covering him with his Derringer; a smile on his white face, but the very devil shining in his eye. "It ain't that the old country has used me over-well," he says, "but no man shall speak agin it afore me, and live." For a second or two I could see his finger tighten round the trigger, an' then he gave a laugh, an' threw the pistol on the floor. "No," he says, "I can't shoot a half-drunk man. Take your dirty life, Joe, an' use it better nor you have done. You've been nearer the grave this night than will be agin until your time comes. You'd best make tracks now, I guess. Nay, never look black at me, man; I'm not afeard at your shootin'-iron. A bully's nigh always a coward." And he swung contemptuously round, and relit his half-smoked pipe from the stove; while Alabama slunk out o' the bar, with the laughs of the Britishers ringing in his ears. I saw his face as he passed me, and on it I saw murder, sirs—murder, as plain as ever I seed anything in my life.

'I stayed in the bar after the row, and watched Tom Scott as he shook hands with the men about. It seemed kinder queer to me to see him smilin' and cheerful-like; for I knew Joe's bloodthirsty mind, and that the Englishman had small chance of ever seeing the morning. He lived in an out-of-the-way sort of place, you see, clean off the trail, and had to pass through the Flytrap Gulch to get to it. This here gulch was a marshy gloomy place, lonely enough during the day even; for it were always a creepy sort o' thing to see the great eight- and ten-foot leaves snapping up if aught touched them; but at night there were never a soul near. Some parts of the marsh, too, were soft and deep, and a body thrown in would be gone by the morning. I could see Alabama Joe crouchin' under the leaves of the great Flytrap in the darkest part of the gulch, with a scowl on his face and a revolver in his hand; I could see it, sirs, as plain as with my two eyes.

''Bout midnight Simpson shuts up his bar, so out we had to go. Tom Scott started off for his three-mile walk at a slashing pace. I just dropped him a hint as he passed me, for I kinder liked the chap. "Keep your Derringer loose in your belt, sir," I says, "for you might chance to need it." He looked round at me with his quiet smile, and then I lost sight of him in the gloom. I never thought to see him again. He'd hardly gone afore Simpson comes up to me and says, "There'll be a nice job in the Flytrap Gulch tonight, Jeff; the boys say that Hawkins started half an hour ago to wait for Scott and shoot him on sight. I calc'late the coroner'll be wanted tomorrow."

'What passed in the gulch that night? It were a question as were asked pretty free next morning. A half-breed was in Ferguson's store after daybreak, and he said as he'd chanced to be near the gulch 'bout one in the morning. It warn't easy to get at his story, he seemed so uncommon scared; but he told us, at last, as he'd heard the fearfulest screams in the stillness of the night. There weren't no shots, he said, but scream after scream, kinder muffled, like a man with a serapé over his head, an' in mortal pain. Abner Brandon and me, and a few more, was in the store at the time; so we mounted and rode out to Scott's house, passing through the gulch on the way. There weren't nothing partic'lar to be seen there—no blood nor marks of a fight, nor nothing; and when we gets up to Scott's house, out he comes to meet us as fresh as a lark. "Hullo, Jeff!" says he, "no need for the pistols after all. Come in an' have a cocktail, boys." "Did ye see or hear nothing as you came home last night?" says I. "No," says he; "all was quiet enough. An owl kinder moaning in the Flytrap Gulch— that was all. Come, jump off and have a glass." "Thank ye," said Abner. So off we gets, and Tom Scott rode into the settlement with us when we went back.

'An allfired commotion was on in Main-street as we rode into it. The 'Merican party seemed to have gone clean crazed. Alabama Joe was gone, not a darned particle of him left. Since he went out to the gulch nary eye had seen him. As we got off our horses there was a considerable crowd in front of Simpson's, and some ugly looks at Tom Scott, I can tell you. There was a clickin' of pistols, and I saw as Scott had his hand in his bosom too. There weren't a single English face about. "Stand aside, Jeff Adams," says Zebb Humphrey, as great a scoundrel as ever lived, "you hain't got no hand in this game. Say, boys, are we, free Americans, to be murdered by any darned Britisher?" It was the quickest thing as ever I seed. There was a rush an' a crack; Zebb was down, with Scott's ball in his thigh, and Scott hisself was on the ground with a dozen men holding him. It weren't no use struggling, so he lay quiet. They seemed a bit uncertain what to do with him at first, but then one of

Alabama's special chums put them up to it. "Joe's gone," he said; "nothing ain't surer nor that, an' there lies the man as killed him. Some on you knows as Joe went on business to the gulch last night; he never came back. That 'ere Britisher passed through after he'd gone; they'd had a row, screams is heard 'mong the great flytraps. I say agin he has played poor Joe some o' his sneakin' tricks, an' thrown him into the swamp. It ain't no wonder as the body is gone. But air we to stan'by and see English murderin' our own chums? I guess not. Let Judge Lynch try him, that's what I say." "Lynch him!" shouted a hundred angry voices—for all the rag-tag an' bobtail o' the settlement was round us by this time. "Here, boys, fetch a rope, and swing him up. Up with him over Simpson's door!" "See here though," says another, coming forrards; "let's hang him by the great flytrap in the gulch. Let Joe see as he's revenged, if so be as he's buried 'bout theer." There was a shout for this, an' away they went, with Scott tied on his mustang in the middle, and a mounted guard, with cocked revolvers, round him; for we knew as there was a score or so Britishers about, as didn't seem to recognise Judge Lynch, and was dead on a free fight.

'I went out with them, my heart bleedin' for Scott, though he didn't seem a cent put out, he didn't. He were game to the backbone. Seems kinder queer, sirs, hangin' a man to a flytrap; but our'n were a reg'lar tree, and the leaves like a brace of boats with a hinge between 'em and thorns at the bottom.

'We passed down the gulch to the place where the great one grows, and there we seed it with the leaves, some open, some shut. But we seed something worse nor that. Standin' round the tree was some thirty men, Britishers all, an' armed to the teeth. They was waitin' for us evidently, an' had a businesslike look about 'em, as if they'd come for something and meant to have it. There was the raw material there for about as warm a scrimmidge as ever I seed. As we rode up, a great red-bearded Scotchman—Cameron were his name—stood out afore the rest, his revolver cocked in his hand. "See here, boys," he says, "you've got no call to hurt a hair of that man's head. You hain't proved as Joe is dead yet; and if you had, you hain't proved as Scott killed him. Anyhow, it were in self-defence; for you all know as he was lying in wait for Scott, to shoot him on sight; so I say agin, you hain't got no call to hurt that man; and what's more, I've got thirty six-barrelled arguments against your doin' it." "It's an interestin' pint, and worth arguin' out," said the man as was Alabama Joe's special chum. There was a clickin' of pistols, and a loosenin' of knives, and the two parties began to draw up to one another, an' it looked like a rise in the mortality of Arizona. Scott was standing behind with a pistol at his ear if he stirred, lookin' quiet and composed as having no money on the table, when sudden he gives a start an' a shout as rang in our ears like a trumpet. "Joe!" he cried, "Joe! Look at him! In the flytrap!" We all turned an' looked where he was pointin'. Jerusalem! I think we won't get that picter out of our minds agin. One of the great leaves of the flytrap, that had been shut and touchin' the ground as it lay, was slowly rolling back upon its hinges. There, lying like a child in its cradle, was Alabama Joe in the hollow of the leaf. The great thorns had been slowly driven through his heart as it shut upon him. We could see as he'd tried to cut his way out, for there was a slit in the thick fleshy leaf, an' his bowie was in his hand; but it had smothered him first. He'd lain down on it likely to keep the damp off while he were awaitin' for Scott, and it had closed on him as you've seen your little hothouse ones do on a fly; an' there he were as we found him, torn and crushed into pulp by the great jagged teeth of the man-eatin' plant. There, sirs, I think you'll own as that's a curious story.'

'And what became of Scott?' asked Jack Sinclair.

'Why, we carried him back on our shoulders, we did, to Simpson's bar, and he stood us liquors round. Made a speech too—a darned fine speech— from the counter. Somethin' about the British lion an' the 'Merican eagle walkin' arm in arm for ever an' a day. And now, sirs, that yarn was long, and my cheroot's out, so I reckon I'll make tracks afore it's later'; and with a 'Good night!' he left the room.

'A most extraordinary narrative!' said Dawson. 'Who would have thought a *Dianoea* had such power!'

'Deuced rum yarn!' said young Sinclair.

'Evidently a matter-of-fact truthful man,' said the doctor.

'Or the most original liar that ever lived,' said I.

I wonder which he was.

The Captain of the 'Pole-Star'

[Being an extract from the singular journal
of John M'Alister Ray, student of medicine.]

SEPTEMBER *11th*—Lat. 81° 40′ N.; long. 2° E. Still lying-to amid enormous ice-fields. The one which stretches away to the north of us, and to which our ice-anchor is attached, cannot be smaller than an English county. To the right and left unbroken sheets extend to the horizon. This morning the mate reported that there were signs of pack ice to the southward. Should this form of sufficient thickness to bar our return, we shall be in a position of danger, as the food, I hear, is already running somewhat short. It is late in the season, and the nights are beginning to reappear. This morning I saw a star twinkling just over the fore-yard, the first since the beginning of May. There is considerable discontent among the crew, many of whom are anxious to get back home to be in time for the herring season, when labour always commands a high price upon the Scotch coast. As yet their displeasure is only signified by sullen countenances and black looks, but I heard from the second mate this afternoon that they contemplated sending a deputation to the captain to explain their grievance. I much doubt how he will receive it, as he is a man of fierce temper, and very sensitive about anything approaching to an infringement of his rights. I shall venture after dinner to say a few words to him upon the subject. I have always found that he will tolerate from me what he would resent from any other member of the crew. Amsterdam Island, at the north-west corner of Spitzbergen, is visible upon our starboard quarter—a rugged line of volcanic rocks, intersected by white seams, which represent glaciers. It is curious to think that, at the present moment there is probably no human being nearer to us than the Danish settlements in the south of Greenland—a good nine hundred miles as the crow flies. A captain takes a great responsibility upon himself when he risks his vessel under such circumstances. No whaler has ever remained in these latitudes till so advanced a period of the year.

9 P.M.—I have spoken to Captain Craigie, and though the result has been hardly satisfactory, I am bound to say that he listened to what I had to say very quietly and even deferentially. When I had finished he put on that air of iron

determination which I have frequently observed upon his face, and paced rapidly backwards and forwards across the narrow cabin for some minutes. At first I feared that I had seriously offended him, but he dispelled the idea by sitting down again, and putting his hand upon my arm with a gesture which almost amounted to a caress. There was a depth of tenderness too in his wild dark eyes which surprised me considerably. 'Look here, Doctor,' he said, 'I'm sorry I ever took you—I am indeed—and I would give fifty pounds this minute to see you standing safe upon the Dundee quay. It's hit or miss with me this time. There are fish to the north of us. How dare you shake your head, sir, when I tell you I saw them blowing from the mast-head?'—this in a sudden burst of fury, though I was not conscious of having shown any signs of doubt. 'Two-and-twenty fish in as many minutes as I am a living man, and not one under ten foot.* Now, Doctor, do you think I can leave the country when there is only one infernal strip of ice between me and my fortune? If it came on to blow from the north tomorrow we could fill the ship and be away before the frost could catch us. If it came on to blow from the south—well, I suppose the men are paid for risking their lives, and as for myself it matters but little to me, for I have more to bind me to the other world than to this one. I confess that I am sorry for *you*, though. I wish I had old Angus Tait who was with me last voyage, for he was a man that would never be missed, and you—you said once that you were engaged, did you not?'

'Yes,' I answered, snapping the spring of the locket which hung from my watch-chain, and holding up the little vignette of Flora.

'Curse you!' he yelled, springing out of his seat, with his very beard bristling with passion. 'What is your happiness to me? What have I to do with her that you must dangle her photograph before my eyes?' I almost thought that he was about to strike me in the frenzy of his rage, but with another imprecation he dashed open the door of the cabin and rushed out upon deck, leaving me considerably astonished at his extraordinary violence. It is the first time that he has ever shown me anything but courtesy and kindness. I can hear him pacing excitedly up and down overhead as I write these lines.

I should like to give a sketch of the character of this man, but it seems presumptuous to attempt such a thing upon paper, when the idea in my own mind is at best a vague and uncertain one. Several times I have thought that I grasped the clue which might explain it, but only to be disappointed by his presenting himself in some new light which would upset all my conclusions. It may be that no human eye but my own shall ever rest upon these lines, yet as a psychological study I shall attempt to leave some record of Captain Nicholas Craigie.

A man's outer case generally gives some indication of the soul within. The captain is tall and well-formed, with dark, handsome face, and a curious way of

---

* A whale is measured among whalers not by the length of its body, but by the length of its whalebone.

twitching his limbs, which may arise from nervousness, or be simply an outcome of his excessive energy. His jaw and whole cast of countenance is manly and resolute, but the eyes are the distinctive feature of his face. They are of the very darkest hazel, bright and eager, with a singular mixture of recklessness in their expression, and of something else which I have sometimes thought was more allied with horror than any other emotion. Generally the former predominated, but on occasions, and more particularly when he was thoughtfully inclined, the look of fear would spread and deepen until it imparted a new character to his whole countenance. It is at these times that he is most subject to tempestuous fits of anger, and he seems to be aware of it, for I have known him lock himself up so that no one might approach him until his dark hour was passed. He sleeps badly, and I have heard him shouting during the night, but his cabin is some little distance from mine, and I could never distinguish the words which he said.

This is one phase of his character, and the most disagreeable one. It is only through my close association with him, thrown together as we are day after day, that I have observed it. Otherwise he is an agreeable companion, well-read and entertaining, and as gallant a seaman as ever trod a deck. I shall not easily forget the way in which he handled the ship when we were caught by a gale among the loose ice at the beginning of April. I have never seen him so cheerful, and even hilarious, as he was that night, as he paced backwards and forwards upon the bridge amid the flashing of the lightning and the howling of the wind. He has told me several times that the thought of death was a pleasant one to him, which is a sad thing for a young man to say; he cannot be much more than thirty, though his hair and moustache are already slightly grizzled. Some great sorrow must have overtaken him and blighted his whole life. Perhaps I should be the same if I lost my Flora—God knows! I think if it were not for her that I should care very little whether the wind blew from the north or the south tomorrow. There, I hear him come down the companion, and he has locked himself up in his room, which shows that he is still in an unamiable mood. And so to bed, as old Pepys would say, for the candle is burning down (we have to use them now since the nights are closing in), and the steward has turned in, so there are no hopes of another one.

September 12th—Calm, clear day, and still lying in the same position. What wind there is comes from the south-east but it is very slight. Captain is in a better humour, and apologised to me at breakfast for his rudeness. He still looks somewhat distrait, however, and retains that wild look in his eyes which in a Highlander would mean that he was 'fey'—at least so our chief engineer remarked to me, and he has some reputation among the Celtic portion of our crew as a seer and expounder of omens.

It is strange that superstition should have obtained such mastery over this hard-headed and practical race. I could not have believed to what an extent it is carried had I not observed it for myself. We have had a perfect epidemic of it this voyage, until I have felt inclined to serve out rations of sedatives and nerve-tonics with the Saturday allowance of grog. The first symptom of it was that shortly after leaving Shetland the men at the wheel used to complain that they heard plaintive cries and screams in the wake of the ship, as if something were following it and were unable to overtake it. This fiction has been kept up during the whole voyage, and on dark nights at the beginning of the seal-fishing it was only with great difficulty that men could be induced to do their spell. No doubt what they heard was either the creaking of the rudder-chains, or the cry of some passing sea-bird. I have been fetched out of bed several times to listen to it, but I need hardly say that I was never able to distinguish anything unnatural. The men, however, are so absurdly positive upon the subject that it is hopeless to argue with them. I mentioned the matter to the captain once, but to my surprise he took it very gravely, and indeed appeared to be considerably disturbed by what I told him. I should have thought that he at least would have been above such vulgar delusions.

All this disquisition upon superstition leads me up to the fact that Mr Manson, our second mate, saw a ghost last night—or, at least, says that he did, which of course is the same thing. It is quite refreshing to have some new topic of conversation after the eternal routine of bears and whales which has served us for so many months. Manson swears the ship is haunted; and that he would not stay in her a day if he had any other place to go to. Indeed the fellow is honestly frightened, and I had to give him some chloral and bromide of potassium this morning to steady him down. He seemed quite indignant when I suggested that he had been having an extra glass the night before, and I was obliged to pacify him by keeping as grave a countenance as possible during his story, which he certainly narrated in a very straightforward and matter-of-fact way.

'I was on the bridge,' he said, 'about four bells in the middle watch, just when the night was at its darkest. There was a bit of a moon, but the clouds were blowing across it so that you couldn't see far from the ship. John M'Leod, the harpooner, came aft from the fo'c'sle-head and reported a strange noise on the starboard bow. I went forrard and we both heard it, sometimes like a bairn crying and sometimes like a wench in pain. I've been seventeen years to the country and I never heard seal, old or young, make a sound like that. As we were standing there on the fo'c'sle-head the moon came out from behind a cloud, and we both saw a sort of white figure moving across the ice-field in the same direction that we had heard the cries. We lost sight of it for a while, but it came back on the port bow, and we could just make it out like a shadow on the ice. I sent a hand aft for the rifles, and M'Leod and I went down on to the pack, thinking that maybe it might be a bear. When we got on the ice I lost sight of M'Leod, but I pushed on in the direction where I could still hear the cries. I followed them for a mile or maybe more, and then running round a hummock I came right on to the top of it standing and waiting for me seemingly. I don't know what it was. It wasn't a bear, anyway. It was tall and white and straight, and if it wasn't a man nor a woman, I'll stake my davy it was something worse. I made for the ship as hard as I could run, and precious glad I was to find myself aboard. I signed articles to do my duty by the ship, and on the ship I'll stay, but you don't catch me on the ice again after sundown.'

That is his story, given as far as I can in his own words. I fancy what he saw must, in spite of his denial, have been a young bear erect upon its hind legs, an attitude which they often assume when alarmed. In the uncertain light this would bear a resemblance to a human figure, especially to a man whose nerves were already somewhat shaken. Whatever it may have been, the occurrence is unfortunate, for it has produced a most unpleasant effect upon the crew. Their looks are more sullen than before, and their discontent more open. The double grievance of being debarred from the herring fishing and of being detained in what they choose to call a haunted vessel, may lead them to do something rash. Even the harpooners, who are the oldest and steadiest among them, are joining in the general agitation.

Apart from this absurd outbreak of superstition, things are looking rather more cheerful. The pack which was forming to the south of us has partly cleared away, and the water is so warm as to lead me to believe that we are lying in one of those branches of the gulf-stream which run up between Greenland and Spitzbergen. There are numerous small Medusae and sea-lemons about the ship, with abundance of shrimps, so that there is every possibility of 'fish' being sighted. Indeed one was seen blowing about dinner-time, but in such a position that it was impossible for the boats to follow it.

September 13th—Had an interesting conversation with the chief mate, Mr Milne, upon the bridge. It seems that our captain is as great an enigma to the seamen, and even to the owners of the vessel, as he has been to me. Mr Milne tells me that when the ship is paid off, upon returning from a voyage, Captain Craigie disappears, and is not seen again until the approach of another season, when he walks quietly into the office of the company, and asks whether his services will be required. He has no friend in Dundee, nor does anyone pretend to be acquainted with his early history. His position depends entirely upon his skill as a seaman, and the name for courage and coolness which he had earned in the capacity of mate, before being entrusted with a separate command. The unanimous opinion seems to be that he is not a Scotchman, and that his name is an assumed one. Mr Milne thinks that he has devoted himself to whaling simply for the reason that it is the most dangerous occupation which he could select, and that he courts death in every possible manner. He mentioned several instances of this, one of which is rather curious, if true. It seems that on one occasion he did not put in an appearance at the office, and a substitute had to be selected in his place. That was at the time of the last Russian and Turkish War. When he turned up again next spring he had a puckered wound in the side of his neck which he used to endeavour to conceal with his cravat. Whether the mate's inference that he had been engaged in the war is true or not I cannot say. It was certainly a strange coincidence.

The wind is veering round in an easterly direction, but is still very slight. I think the ice is lying closer than it did yesterday. As far as the eye can reach on every side there is one wide expanse of spotless white, only broken by an occasional rift or the dark shadow of a hummock. To the south there is the narrow lane of blue water which is our sole means of escape, and which is closing up every day. The captain is taking a heavy responsibility upon himself. I hear that the tank of potatoes has been finished, and even the biscuits are running short, but he preserves the same impassable countenance, and spends the greater part of the day at the crow's nest, sweeping the horizon with his glass. His manner is very variable, and he seems to avoid my society, but there has been no repetition of the violence which he showed the other night.

7.30 P.M.—My deliberate opinion is that we are commanded by a madman. Nothing else can account for the extraordinary vagaries of Captain Craigie. It is fortunate that I have kept this journal of our voyage, as it will serve to justify us in case we have to put him under any sort of restraint, a step which I should only consent to as a last resource. Curiously enough it was he himself who suggested lunacy and not mere eccentricity as the secret of his strange conduct. He was standing upon the bridge about an hour ago, peering as usual through his glass, while I was walking up and down the quarter-deck. The majority of the men were below at their tea, for the watches have not been regularly kept of late. Tired of walking, I leaned against the bulwarks, and admired the mellow glow cast by the sinking sun upon the great ice-fields which surround us. I was suddenly aroused from the reverie into which I had fallen by a hoarse voice at my elbow, and starting round I found that the captain had descended and was standing by my side. He was staring out over the ice with an expression in which horror, surprise, and something approaching to joy were contending for the mastery. In spite of the cold, great drops of perspiration were coursing down his forehead, and he was evidently fearfully excited. His limbs twitched like those of a man upon the verge of an epileptic fit, and the lines about his mouth were drawn and hard.

'Look!' he gasped, seizing me by the wrist, but still keeping his eyes upon the distant ice, and moving his head slowly in a horizontal direction, as if following some object which was moving across the field of vision. 'Look! There, man, there! Between the hummocks! Now coming out from behind the far one! You see her—you *must* see her! There still! Flying from me, by God, flying from me—and gone!'

He uttered the last two words in a whisper of concentrated agony which shall never fade from my remembrance. Clinging to the ratlines he endeavoured to climb up upon the top of the bulwarks as if in the hope of obtaining a last glance at the departing object. His strength was not equal to the attempt, however, and he staggered back against the saloon skylights, where he leaned panting and exhausted. His face was so livid that I expected him to become unconscious, so lost no time in leading him down the companion, and stretching him upon one of the sofas in the cabin. I then poured him out some brandy, which I held to his lips, and which had a wonderful effect upon him, bringing the blood back into his white face and steadying his poor shaking limbs. He raised himself up upon his elbow, and looking round to see that we were alone he beckoned to me to come and sit beside him.

'You saw it, didn't you?' he asked, still in the same subdued awesome tone so foreign to the nature of the man.

'No, I saw nothing.'

His head sank back again upon the cushions. 'No, he wouldn't without the glass,' he murmured. 'He couldn't. It was the glass that showed her to me, and then the eyes of love—the eyes of love. I say, Doc, don't let the steward in! He'll think I'm mad. Just bolt the door, will you!'

I rose and did what he had commanded.

He lay quiet for a while, lost in thought apparently, and then raised himself up upon his elbow again, and asked for some more brandy.

'You don't think I am, do you, Doc?' he asked, as I was putting the bottle back into the after-locker. 'Tell me now, as man to man, do you think that I am mad?'

'I think you have something on your mind,' I answered, 'which is exciting you and doing you a good deal of harm.'

'Right there, lad!' he cried, his eyes sparkling from the effects of the brandy. 'Plenty on my mind—plenty! But I can work out the latitude and the longitude, and I can handle my sextant and manage my logarithms. You couldn't prove me mad in a court of law, could you, now?' It was curious to hear the man lying back and coolly arguing out the question of his own sanity.

'Perhaps not,' I said; 'but still I think you would be wise to get home as soon as you can, and settle down to a quiet life for a while.'

'Get home, eh?' he muttered, with a sneer upon his face. 'One word for me and two for yourself, lad. Settle down with Flora—pretty little Flora. Are bad dreams signs of madness?'

'Sometimes,' I answered.

'What else? What would be the first symptoms?'

'Pains in the head, noises in the ears, flashes before the eyes, delusions——'

'Ah! what about them?' he interrupted. 'What would you call a delusion?'

'Seeing a thing which is not there is a delusion.'

'But she *was* there!' he groaned to himself. 'She *was* there!' and rising, he unbolted the door and walked with slow and uncertain steps to his own cabin, where I have no doubt that he will remain until tomorrow morning. His system seems to have received a terrible shock, whatever it may have been that he imagined himself to have seen. The man becomes a greater mystery every day, though I fear that the solution which he has himself suggested is the correct one, and that his reason is affected. I do not think that a guilty conscience has anything to do with his behaviour. The idea is a popular one among the officers, and, I believe, the crew; but I have seen nothing to support it. He has not the air of a guilty man, but of one who has had terrible usage at the hands of fortune, and who should be regarded as a martyr rather than a criminal.

The wind is veering round to the south tonight. God help us if it blocks that narrow pass which is our only road to safety! Situated as we are on the edge of the main Arctic pack, or the 'barrier' as it is called by the whalers, any wind from the north has the effect of shredding out the ice around us and allowing our escape, while a wind from the south blows up all the loose ice behind us, and hems us in between two packs. God help us, I say again!

September 14th—Sunday, and a day of rest. My fears have been confirmed, and the thin strip of blue water has disappeared from the southward. Nothing but the great motionless ice-fields around us, with their weird hummocks and fantastic pinnacles. There is a deathly silence over their wide expanse which is horrible.

No lapping of the waves now, no cries of seagulls or straining of sails, but one deep universal silence in which the murmurs of the seamen, and the creak of their boots upon the white shining deck, seem discordant and out of place. Our only visitor was an Arctic fox, a rare animal upon the pack, though common enough upon the land. He did not come near the ship, however, but after surveying us from a distance fled rapidly across the ice. This was curious conduct, as they generally know nothing of man, and being of an inquisitive nature, become so familiar that they are easily captured. Incredible as it may seem, even this little incident produced a bad effect upon the crew. 'Yon puir beastie kens mair, ay, an' sees mair nor you nor me!' was the comment of one of the leading harpooners, and the others nodded their acquiescence. It is vain to attempt to argue against such puerile superstition. They have made up their minds that there is a curse upon the ship, and nothing will ever persuade them to the contrary.

The captain remained in seclusion all day except for about half an hour in the afternoon, when he came out upon the quarter-deck. I observed that he kept his eye fixed upon the spot where the vision of yesterday had appeared, and was quite prepared for another outburst, but none such came. He did not seem to see me, although I was standing close beside him. Divine service was read as usual by the chief engineer. It is a curious thing that in whaling vessels the Church of England Prayer-book is always employed, although there is never a member of that Church among either officers or crew. Our men are all Roman Catholics or Presbyterians, the former predominating. Since a ritual is used which is foreign to both, neither can complain that the other is preferred to them, and they listen with all attention and devotion, so that the system has something to recommend it.

A glorious sunset, which made the great fields of ice look like a lake of blood. I have never seen a finer and at the same time more weird effect. Wind is veering round. If it will blow twenty-four hours from the north all will yet be well.

September 15th—Today is Flora's birthday. Dear lass! it is well that she cannot see her boy, as she used to call me, shut up among the ice-fields with a crazy captain and a few weeks' provisions. No doubt she scans the shipping list in the *Scotsman* every morning to see if we are reported from Shetland. I have to set an example to the men and look cheery and unconcerned; but God knows, my heart is very heavy at times.

The thermometer is at nineteen Fahrenheit today. There is but little wind, and what there is comes from an unfavourable quarter. Captain is in an excellent humour; I think he imagines he has seen some other omen or vision, poor fellow, during the night, for he came into my room early in the morning, and stooping down over my bunk, whispered, 'It wasn't a delusion, Doc; it's all right!' After breakfast he asked me to find out how much food was left, which the second mate and I proceeded to do. It is even less than we had expected. Forward they have half a tank full of biscuits, three barrels of salt meat, and a very limited supply of coffee beans and sugar. In the after-hold and lockers there are a good many luxuries, such as tinned salmon, soups, haricot mutton, etc., but they will go a very short way among a crew of fifty men. There are two barrels of flour in the store-room, and an unlimited supply of tobacco. Altogether there is about enough to keep the men on half rations for eighteen or twenty days—certainly not more. When we reported the state of things to the captain, he ordered all hands to be piped, and addressed them from the quarter-deck. I never saw him to better advantage. With his tall, well-knit figure, and dark animated face, he seemed a man born to command, and he discussed the situation in a cool sailor-like way which showed that while appreciating the danger he had an eye for every loophole of escape.

'My lads,' he said, 'no doubt you think I brought you into this fix, if it is a fix, and maybe some of you feel bitter against me on account of it. But you must remember that for many a season no ship that comes to the country has brought in as much oil-money as the old *Pole-Star*, and every one of you has had his share of it. You can leave your wives behind you in comfort, while other poor fellows come back to find their lassies on the parish. If you have to thank me for the one you have to thank me for the other, and we may call it quits. We've tried a bold venture before this and succeeded, so now that we've tried one and failed we've no cause to cry out about it. If the worst comes to the worse, we can make the land across the ice, and lay in a stock of seals which will keep us alive until the spring. It won't come to that, though, for you'll see the Scotch coast again before three weeks are out. At present every man must go on half rations, share and share alike, and no favour to any. Keep up your hearts and you'll pull through this as you've pulled through many a danger before.' These few simple words of his had a wonderful effect upon the crew. His former unpopularity was forgotten, and the old harpooner whom I have already mentioned for his superstition, led off three cheers, which were heartily joined in by all hands.

September 16th—The wind has veered round to the north during the night, and the ice shows some symptoms of opening out. The men are in a good humour in spite of the short allowance upon which they have been placed. Steam is kept up in the engine-room, that there may be no delay should an opportunity for escape present itself. The captain is in exuberant spirits, though he still retains that wild 'fey' expression which I have already remarked upon. This burst of cheerfulness puzzles me more than his former gloom. I cannot understand it. I think I mentioned in an early part of this journal that one of his oddities is that he never permits any person to enter his cabin, but insists upon making his own bed, such as it is, and performing every other office for himself. To my surprise he handed me the key today and requested me to go down there and take the time by his chronometer while he measured the altitude of the sun at noon. It is a bare little room, containing a washing-stand and a few books, but little else in the way of luxury, except some pictures upon the walls. The majority of these are small cheap oleographs, but there was one water-colour sketch of the head of a young lady which arrested my attention. It was evidently a portrait, and not one of those fancy types of female beauty which sailors particularly affect. No artist could have evolved from his own mind such a curious mixture of character and weakness. The languid, dreamy eyes, with their drooping lashes, and the broad, low brow, unruffled by thought or care, were in strong contrast with the clean-cut, prominent jaw, and the resolute set of the lower lip. Underneath it in one of the corners was written, 'M.B., æt. 19.' That anyone in the short space of nineteen years of existence could develop such strength of will as was stamped upon her face seemed to me at the time to be well-nigh incredible. She must have been an extraordinary woman. Her features have thrown such a glamour over me that, though I had but a fleeting glance at them, I could, were I a draughtsman, reproduce them line for line upon this page of the journal. I wonder what part she has played in our captain's life. He has hung her picture at the end of his berth, so that his eyes continually rest upon it. Were he a less reserved man I should make some remark upon the subject. Of the other things in his cabin there was nothing worthy of mention—uniform coats, a camp-stool, small looking-glass, tobacco-box, and numerous pipes, including an oriental hookah—which, by the by, gives some colour to Mr Milne's story about his participation in the war, though the connection may seem rather a distant one.

11.20 P.M.—Captain just gone to bed after a long and interesting conversation on general topics. When he chooses he can be a most fascinating companion, being remarkably well-read, and having the power of expressing his opinion forcibly without appearing to be dogmatic. I hate to have my intellectual toes trod upon. He spoke about the nature of the soul, and sketched out the views of Aristotle and Plato upon the subject in a masterly manner. He seems to have a leaning for metempsychosis and the doctrines of Pythagoras. In discussing them we touched upon modern spiritualism, and I made some joking allusion to the impostures of Slade, upon which, to my surprise, he warned me most impressively against confusing the innocent with the guilty, and argued that it would be as logical to brand Christianity as an error because Judas, who professed that religion, was a villain. He shortly afterwards bade me good night and retired to his room.

The wind is freshening up, and blows steadily from the north. The nights are as dark now as they are in England. I hope tomorrow may set us free from our frozen fetters.

September 17th—The Bogie again. Thank Heaven that I have strong nerves! The superstition of these poor fellows, and the circumstantial accounts which they give, with the utmost earnestness and self-conviction, would horrify any man not accustomed to their ways. There are many versions of the matter, but the sum-total of them all is that something uncanny has been flitting round the ship all night, and that Sandie M'Donald of Peterhead and 'lang' Peter Williamson of Shetland saw it, as also did Mr Milne on the bridge—so, having three witnesses, they can make a better case of it than the second mate did. I spoke to Milne after breakfast, and told him that he should be above such nonsense, and that as an officer he ought to set the men a better example. He shook his weather-beaten head ominously, but answered with characteristic caution, 'Mebbe aye, mebbe na, Doctor,' he said, 'I didna ca' it a ghaist. I canna' say I preen my faith in sea-bogles an' the like, though there's a mony as claims to ha' seen a' that and waur. I'm no easy feared, but maybe your ain bluid would run a bit cauld, mun, if instead o' speerin' aboot it in daylicht ye were wi' me last night, an' seed an awfu' like shape, white an' gruesome, whiles here, whiles there, an' it greetin' and ca'ing in the darkness like a bit lambie that hae lost its mither. Ye would na' be sae ready to put it a' doon to auld wives' clavers then, I'm thinkin'.' I saw it was hopeless to reason with him, so contented myself with begging him as a personal favour to call me up the next time the spectre appeared—a request to which he acceded with many ejaculations expressive of his hopes that such an opportunity might never arise.

As I had hoped, the white desert behind us has become broken by many thin streaks of water which intersect it in all directions. Our latitude today was 80° 52' N., which shows that there is a strong southerly drift upon the pack. Should the wind continue favourable it will break up as rapidly as it formed. At present we can do nothing but smoke and wait and hope for the best. I am rapidly becoming a fatalist. When dealing with such uncertain factors as wind and ice a man can be nothing else. Perhaps it was the wind and sand of the Arabian deserts which gave the minds of the original followers of Mahomet their tendency to bow to kismet.

These spectral alarms have a very bad effect upon the captain. I feared that it might excite his sensitive mind, and endeavoured to conceal the absurd story from him, but unfortunately he overheard one of the men making an allusion to it, and insisted upon being informed about it. As I had expected, it brought out all his latent lunacy in an exaggerated form. I can hardly believe that this is the same man who discoursed philosophy last night with the most critical acumen and coolest judgment. He is pacing backwards and forwards upon the quarter-deck like a caged tiger, stopping now and again to throw out his hands with a yearning gesture, and stare impatiently out over the ice. He keeps up a continual mutter to himself, and once he called out, 'But a little time, love—but a little time!' Poor fellow, it is sad to see a gallant seaman and accomplished gentleman reduced to such a pass, and to think that imagination and delusion can cow a mind to which real danger was but the salt of life. Was ever a man in such a position as I, between a demented captain and a ghost-seeing mate? I sometimes think I am the only really sane man aboard the vessel—except perhaps the second engineer, who is a kind of ruminant, and would care nothing for all the fiends in the Red Sea so long as they would leave him alone and not disarrange his tools.

The ice is still opening rapidly, and there is every probability of our being able to make a start tomorrow morning. They will think I am inventing when I tell them at home all the strange things that have befallen me.

12 P.M.—I have been a good deal startled, though I feel steadier now, thanks to a stiff glass of brandy. I am hardly myself yet, however, as this handwriting will testify. The fact is, that I have gone through a very strange experience, and am beginning to doubt whether I was justified in branding everyone on board as madmen because they professed to have seen things which did not seem reasonable to my understanding. Pshaw! I am a fool to let such a trifle unnerve me; and yet, coming as it does after all these alarms, it has an additional significance, for I cannot doubt either Mr Manson's story or that of the mate, now that I have experienced that which I used formerly to scoff at.

After all it was nothing very alarming—a mere sound, and that was all. I cannot expect that anyone reading this, if anyone ever should read it, will sympathise with my feelings, or realize the effect which it produced upon me at the time. Supper was over, and I had gone on deck to have a quiet pipe before turning in. The night was very dark—so dark that, standing under the quarter-boat, I was unable to see the officer upon the bridge. I think I have already mentioned the extraordinary silence which prevails in these frozen seas. In other parts of the world, be they ever so barren, there is some slight vibration of the air—some faint hum, be it from the distant haunts of men, or from the leaves of the trees, or the wings of the birds, or even the faint rustle of the grass that covers the ground. One may not actively perceive the sound, and yet if it were withdrawn it would be missed. It is only here in these Arctic seas that stark, unfathomable stillness obtrudes itself upon you all in its gruesome reality. You find your tympanum straining to catch some little murmur, and dwelling eagerly upon every accidental sound within the vessel. In this state I was leaning against the bulwarks when there arose from the ice almost directly underneath me a cry, sharp and shrill, upon the silent air of the night, beginning, as it seemed to me, at a note such as prima donna never reached, and mounting from that ever higher and higher until it culminated in a long wail of agony, which might have been the last cry of a lost soul. The ghastly scream is still ringing in my ears. Grief, unutterable grief, seemed to be expressed in it, and a great longing, and yet through it all there was an occasional wild note of exultation. It shrilled out from close beside me, and yet as I glared into the darkness I could discern nothing. I waited some little time, but without hearing any repetition of the sound, so I came below, more shaken than I have ever been in my life before. As I came down the companion I met Mr Milne coming up to relieve the watch. 'Weel, Doctor,' he said, 'maybe that's auld wives' clavers tae? Did ye no hear it skirling? Maybe that's a supersteetion? What d'ye think o't noo?' I was obliged to apologise to the honest fellow, and acknowledge that I was as puzzled by it as he was. Perhaps tomorrow things may look different. At present I dare hardly write all that I think. Reading it again in days to come, when I have shaken off all these associations, I should despise myself for having been so weak.

September 18th—Passed a restless and uneasy night, still haunted by that strange sound. The captain does not look as if he had had much repose either, for his face is haggard and his eyes bloodshot. I have not told him of my adventure of last night, nor shall I. He is already restless and excited, standing up, sitting down, and apparently utterly unable to keep still.

A fine lead appeared in the pack this morning, as I had expected, and we were able to cast off our ice-anchor, and steam about twelve miles in a west-sou'-westerly direction. We were then brought to a halt by a great floe as massive as any which we have left behind us. It bars our progress completely, so we can do nothing but anchor again and wait until it breaks up, which it will probably do within twenty-four hours, if the wind holds. Several bladder-nosed seals were seen swimming in the water, and one was shot, an immense creature more than eleven feet long. They are fierce, pugnacious animals, and are said to be more than a match for a bear. Fortunately they are slow and clumsy in their movements, so that there is little danger in attacking them upon the ice.

The captain evidently does not think we have seen the last of our troubles, though why he should take a gloomy view of the situation is more than I can fathom, since everyone else on board considers that we have had a miraculous escape, and are sure now to reach the open sea.

'I suppose you think it's all right now, Doctor?' he said, as we sat together after dinner.

'I hope so,' I answered.

'We mustn't be too sure—and yet no doubt you are right. We'll all be in the arms of our own true loves before long, lad, won't we? But we mustn't be too sure—we mustn't be too sure.'

He sat silent a little, swinging his leg thoughtfully backwards and forwards. 'Look here,' he continued; 'it's a dangerous place this, even at its best—a treacherous, dangerous place. I have known men cut off very suddenly in a land like this. A slip would do it sometimes—a single slip, and down you go through a crack, and only a bubble on the green water to show where it was that you sank. It's a queer thing,' he continued with a nervous laugh, 'but all the years I've been in this country I never once thought of making a will—not that I have anything to leave in particular, but still when a man is exposed to danger he should have everything arranged and ready—don't you think so?'

'Certainly,' I answered, wondering what on earth he was driving at.

'He feels better for knowing it's all settled,' he went on. 'Now if anything should ever befall me, I hope that you will look after things for me. There is very little in the cabin, but such as it is I should like it to be sold, and the money divided in the same proportion as the oil-money among the crew. The chronometer I wish you to keep yourself as some slight remembrance of our voyage. Of course all this is a mere precaution, but I thought I would take the opportunity of speaking to you about it. I suppose I might rely upon you if there were any necessity?'

'Most assuredly,' I answered, 'and since you are taking this step, I may as well——'

'You! you!' he interrupted. '*You're* all right. What the devil is the matter with *you*? There, I didn't mean to be peppery, but I don't like to hear a young fellow, that has hardly began life, speculating about death. Go up on deck and get some fresh air into your lungs instead of talking nonsense in the cabin, and encouraging me to do the same.'

The more I think of this conversation of ours the less do I like it. Why should the man be settling his affairs at the very time when we seem to be emerging from all danger? There must be some method in his madness. Can it be that he contemplates suicide? I remember that upon one occasion he spoke in a deeply reverent manner of the heinousness of the crime of self-destruction. I shall keep my eye upon him, however, and though I cannot obtrude upon the privacy of his cabin, I shall at least make a point of remaining on deck as long as he stays up.

Mr Milne pooh-poohs my fears, and says it is only the 'skipper's little way'. He himself takes a very rosy view of the situation. According to him we shall be out of the ice by the day after tomorrow, pass Jan Meyen two days after that, and sight Shetland in little more than a week. I hope he may not be too sanguine. His opinion may be fairly balanced against the gloomy precautions of the captain, for he is an old and experienced seaman, and weighs his words well before uttering them.

*　*　*　*　*

The long-impending catastrophe has come at last. I hardly know what to write about it. The captain is gone. He may come back to us again alive, but I fear me—I fear me. It is now seven o'clock of the morning of the 19th of September. I have spent the whole night traversing the great ice-floe in front of us with a party of seamen in the hope of coming upon some trace of him, but in vain. I shall try to give some account of the circumstances which attended upon his disappearance. Should anyone ever chance to read the words which I put down, I trust they will remember that I do not write from conjecture or from hearsay, but that I, a sane and educated man, am describing accurately what actually occurred before my very eyes. My inferences are my own, but I shall be answerable for the facts.

The captain remained in excellent spirits after the conversation which I have recorded. He appeared to be nervous and impatient, however, frequently changing his position, and moving his limbs in an aimless choreic way which is characteristic of him at times. In a quarter of an hour he went upon deck seven times, only to descend after a few hurried paces. I followed him each time, for there was something about his face which confirmed my resolution of not letting him out of my sight. He seemed to observe the effect which his movements had produced, for he endeavoured by an overdone hilarity, laughing boisterously at the very smallest of jokes, to quiet my apprehensions.

After supper he went on to the poop once more, and I with him. The night was dark and very still, save for the melancholy soughing of the wind among the spars. A thick cloud was coming up from the north-west, and the ragged tentacles which it threw out in front of it were drifting across the face of the moon, which only shone now and again through a rift in the wrack. The captain paced rapidly backwards and forwards, and then seeing me still dogging him, he came across and hinted that he thought I should be better below—which, I need hardly say, had the effect of strengthening my resolution to remain on deck.

I think he forgot about my presence after this, for he stood silently leaning over the taffrail and peering out across the great desert of snow, part of which lay in shadow, while part glittered mistily in the moonlight. Several times I could see by his movements that he was referring to his watch, and once he muttered a short sentence, of which I could only catch the one word 'ready'. I confess to having felt an eerie feeling creeping over me as I watched the loom of his tall figure through the darkness, and noted how completely he fulfilled the idea of a man who is keeping a tryst. A tryst with whom? Some vague perception began to dawn upon me as I pieced one fact with another, but I was utterly unprepared for the sequel.

By the sudden intensity of his attitude I felt that he saw something. I crept up behind him. He was staring with an eager questioning gaze at what seemed to be a wreath of mist, blown swiftly in a line with the ship. It was a dim nebulous body, devoid of shape, sometimes more, sometimes less apparent, as the light fell on it. The moon was dimmed in its brilliancy at the moment by a canopy of thinnest cloud, like the coating of an anemone.

'Coming, lass, coming,' cried the skipper, in a voice of unfathomable tenderness and compassion, like one who soothes a beloved one by some favour long looked for, and as pleasant to bestow as to receive.

What followed happened in an instant. I had no power to interfere. He gave one spring to the top of the bulwarks, and another which took him on to the ice, almost to the feet of the pale misty figure. He held out his hands as if to clasp it, and so ran into the darkness with outstretched arms and loving words. I still stood rigid and motionless, straining my eyes after his retreating form, until his voice died away in the distance. I never thought to see him again, but at that moment the moon shone out brilliantly through a chink in the cloudy heaven, and illuminated the great field of ice. Then I saw his dark figure already a very long way off, running with prodigious speed across the frozen plain. That was the last glimpse which we caught of him—perhaps the last we ever shall. A party was organized to follow him, and I accompanied them, but the men's hearts were not in the work, and nothing was found. Another will be formed within a few hours. I can hardly believe I have not been dreaming, or suffering from some hideous nightmare, as I write these things down.

7.30 P.M.—Just returned dead beat and utterly tired out from a second unsuccessful search for the captain. The floe is of enormous extent, for though we have traversed at least twenty miles of its surface, there has been no sign of its coming to an end. The frost has been so severe of late that the overlying snow is frozen as hard as granite, otherwise we might have had the footsteps to guide us. The crew are anxious that we should cast off and steam round the floe and so to the southward, for the ice has opened up during the night, and the sea is visible upon the horizon. They argue that Captain Craigie is certainly dead, and that we are all risking our lives to no purpose by remaining when we have an opportunity of escape. Mr Milne and I have had the greatest difficulty in persuading them to wait until tomorrow night, and have been compelled to promise that we will not under any circumstances delay our departure longer than that. We propose therefore to take a few hours' sleep, and then to start upon a final search.

September 20th, evening.—I crossed the ice this morning with a party of men exploring the southern part of the floe, while Mr Milne went off in a northerly direction. We pushed on for ten or twelve miles without seeing a trace of any living thing except a single bird, which fluttered a great way over our heads, and which by its flight I should judge to have been a falcon. The southern extremity of the ice-field tapered away into a long narrow spit which projected out into the sea. When we came to the base of this promontory, the men halted, but I begged them to continue to the extreme end of it, that we might have the satisfaction of knowing that no possible chance had been neglected.

We had hardly gone a hundred yards before M'Donald of Peterhead cried out that he saw something in front of us, and began to run. We all got a glimpse of it and ran too. At first it was only a vague darkness against the white ice, but as we raced along together it took the shape of a man, and eventually of the man of whom we were in search. He was lying face downwards upon a frozen bank. Many little crystals of ice and feathers of snow had drifted on to him as he lay, and sparkled upon his dark seaman's jacket. As we came up some wandering puff of wind caught these tiny flakes in its vortex, and they whirled up into the air, partially descended again, and then, caught once more in the current, sped rapidly away in the direction of the sea. To my eyes it seemed but a snow-drift, but many of my companions averred that it started up in the shape of a woman, stooped over the corpse and kissed it, and then hurried away across the floe. I have learned never to ridicule any man's opinion, however strange it may seem. Sure it is that Captain Nicholas Craigie had met with no painful end, for there was a bright smile upon his blue pinched features, and his hands were still outstretched as though grasping at the strange visitor which had summoned him away into the dim world that lies beyond the grave.

We buried him the same afternoon with the ship's ensign around him, and a thirty-two pound shot at his feet. I read the burial service, while the rough sailors wept like children, for there were many who owed much to his kind heart, and who showed now the affection which his strange ways had repelled during his lifetime. He went off the grating with a dull, sullen splash, and as I looked into the green water I saw him go down, down, down until he was but a little flickering patch of white hanging upon the outskirts of eternal darkness. Then even that faded away, and he was gone. There he shall lie, with his secret and his sorrows and his mystery all still buried in his breast, until that great day when the sea shall give up its dead, and Nicholas Craigie come out from among the ice with the smile upon his face, and his stiffened arms outstretched in greeting. I pray that his lot may be a happier one in that life than it has been in this.

I shall not continue my journal. Our road to home lies plain and clear before us, and the great ice-field will soon be but a remembrance of the past. It will be some time before I get over the shock produced by recent events. When I began this record of our voyage I little thought of how I should be compelled to finish it. I am writing these final words in the lonely cabin, still starting at times and fancying I hear the quick nervous step of the dead man upon the deck above me. I entered his cabin tonight, as was my duty, to make a list of his effects in order that they might be entered in the official log. All was as it had been upon my previous visit, save that the picture which I have described as having hung at the end of his bed had been cut out of its frame, as with a knife, and was gone. With this last link in a strange chain of evidence I close my diary of the voyage of the *Pole-Star*.

[Note by Dr John M'Alister Ray, senior.—I have read over the strange events connected with the death of the captain of the *Pole-Star*, as narrated in the journal of my son. That everything occurred exactly as he describes it I have the fullest confidence, and, indeed the most positive certainty, for I know him to be a strong-nerved and unimaginative man, with the strictest regard for veracity. Still, the story is, on the face of it, so vague and so improbable, that I was long opposed to its publication. Within the last few days, however, I have had independent testimony upon the subject which throws a new light upon it. I had run down to Edinburgh to attend a meeting of the British Medical Association, when I chanced to come across Dr P——, an old college chum of mine, now practising at Saltash, in Devonshire. Upon my telling him of this experience of my son's, he declared to me that he was familiar with the man, and proceeded, to my no small surprise, to give me a description of him, which tallied remarkably well with that given in the journal, except that he depicted him as a younger man. According to his account, he had been engaged to a young lady of singular beauty residing upon the Cornish coast. During his absence at sea his betrothed had died under circumstances of peculiar horror.]

The Winning Shot

Caution—The public are hereby cautioned against a man calling himself Octavius Gaster. He is to be recognised by his great height, his flaxen hair, and deep scar upon his left cheek, extending from the eye to the angle of the mouth. His predilection for bright colours—green neckties, and the like—may help to identify him. A slightly foreign accent is to be detected in his speech. This man is beyond the reach of the law, but is more dangerous than a mad dog. Shun him as you would shun the pestilence that walketh at noonday. Any communications as to his whereabouts will be thankfully acknowledged by A.C.U., Lincoln's Inn, London.

THIS IS A COPY OF AN ADVERTISEMENT which may have been noticed by many readers in the columns of the London morning papers during the early part of the present year. It has, I believe, excited considerable curiosity in certain quarters, and many guesses have been hazarded as to the identity of Octavius Gaster and the nature of the charge brought against him. When I state that the 'caution' has been inserted by my elder brother, Arthur Cooper Underwood, barrister-at-law, upon my representations, it will be acknowledged that I am the most fitting person to enter upon an authentic explanation.

Hitherto the horror and vagueness of my suspicion, combined with my grief at the loss of my poor darling on the very eve of our wedding, have prevented me from revealing the events of last August to anyone save my brother.

Now, however, looking back, I can fit in many little facts almost unnoticed at the time, which form a chain of evidence that, though worthless in a court of law, may yet have some effect upon the mind of the public.

I shall therefore relate, without exaggeration or prejudice, all that occurred from the day upon which this man, Octavius Gaster, entered Toynby Hall up to the great rifle competition. I know that many people will always ridicule the supernatural, or what our poor intellects choose to regard as supernatural, and that the fact of my being a woman will be thought to weaken my evidence. I can only plead that I have never been weak-minded or impressionable, and that other people formed the same opinions of Octavius Gaster that I did.

Now to the story.

It was at Colonel Pillar's place at Roborough, in the pleasant county of Devon, that we spent our autumn holidays. For some months I had been engaged to his eldest son Charley, and it was hoped that the marriage might take place before the termination of the Long Vacation.

Charley was considered 'safe' for his degree, and in any case was rich enough to be practically independent, while I was by no means penniless.

The old Colonel was delighted at the prospect of the match, and so was my mother; so that look what way we would, there seemed to be no cloud above our horizon.

It was no wonder, then, that that August was a happy one. Even the most miserable of mankind would have laid his woes aside under the genial influence of the merry household at Toynby Hall.

There was Lieutenant Daseby, 'Jack', as he was invariably called, fresh home from Japan in Her Majesty's ship *Shark*, who was on the same interesting footing with Fanny Pillar, Charley's sister, as Charley was with me, so that we were able to lend each other a certain moral support.

Then there was Harry, Charley's younger brother, and Trevor, his bosom friend at Cambridge.

Finally there was my mother, dearest of old ladies, beaming at us through her gold-rimmed spectacles, anxiously smoothing every little difficulty in the way of the two young couples, and never weary of detailing to them *her* own doubts and fears and perplexities when that gay young blood, Mr Nicholas Underwood, came a-wooing into the provinces, and forswore Crockford's and Tattersall's for the sake of the country parson's daughter.

I must not, however, forget the gallant old warrior who was our host; with his time-honoured jokes, and his gout, and his harmless affectation of ferocity.

'I don't know what's come over the governor lately,' Charley used to say. 'He has never cursed the Liberal Administration since you've been here, Lottie; and my belief is that unless he has a good blow-off, that Irish question will get into his system and finish him.'

Perhaps in the privacy of his own apartment the veteran used to make up for his self-abnegation during the day.

He seemed to have taken a special fancy to me, which he showed in a hundred little attentions.

'You're a good lass,' he remarked one evening, in a very port-winey whisper. 'Charley's a lucky dog, egad! and has more discrimination than I thought. Mark my words, Miss Underwood, you'll find that young gentleman isn't such a fool as he looks!'

With which equivocal compliment the Colonel solemnly covered his face with his handkerchief, and went off into the land of dreams.

How well I remember the day that was the commencement of all our miseries!

Dinner was over, and we were in the drawing-room, with the windows open to admit the balmy southern breeze.

My mother was sitting in the corner, engaged on a piece of fancy-work, and occasionally purring forth some truism which the dear old soul believed to be an entirely original remark, and founded exclusively upon her own individual experiences.

Fanny and the young lieutenant were billing and cooing upon the sofa, while Charley paced restlessly about the room.

I was sitting by the window, gazing out dreamily at the great wilderness of Dartmoor, which stretched away to the horizon, ruddy and glowing in the light of the sinking sun, save where some rugged tor stood out in bold relief against the scarlet background.

'I say,' remarked Charley, coming over to join me at the window, 'it seems a positive shame to waste an evening like this.'

'Confound the evening!' said Jack Daseby. 'You're always victimising yourself to the weather. Fan and I ar'n't going to move off this sofa—are we, Fan?'

That young lady announced her intention of remaining by nestling among the cushions, and glancing defiantly at her brother.

'Spooning is a demoralising thing—isn't it, Lottie?' said Charley, appealing laughingly to me.

'Shockingly so,' I answered.

'Why, I can remember Daseby here when he was as active a young fellow as any in Devon; and just look at him now! Fanny, Fanny, you've got a lot to answer for!'

'Never mind him, my dear,' said my mother, from the corner. 'Still, my experience has always shown me that moderation is an excellent thing for young people. Poor dear Nicholas used to think so too. He would never go to bed of a night until he had jumped the length of the hearthrug. I often told him it was dangerous; but he *would* do it, until one night he fell on the fender and snapped the muscle of his leg, which made him limp till the day of his death, for Doctor Pearson mistook it for a fracture of the bone, and put him in splints, which had the effect of stiffening his knee. They did say that the doctor was almost out of his mind at the time from anxiety, brought on by his younger daughter swallowing a halfpenny, and that that was what caused him to make the mistake.'

My mother had a curious way of drifting along in her conversation, and occasionally rushing off at a tangent, which made it rather difficult to remember her original proposition. On this occasion Charley had, however, stowed it away in his mind as likely to admit of immediate application.

'An excellent thing, as you say, Mrs Underwood,' he remarked; 'and we have not been out today. Look here, Lottie, we have an hour of daylight yet. Suppose we go down and have a try for a trout, if your mamma does not object.'

'Put something round your throat, dear,' said my mother, feeling that she had been outmanoeuvred.

'All right, dear,' I answered; 'I'll just run up and put on my hat.'

'And we'll have a walk back in the gloaming,' said Charley, as I made for the door.

When I came down, I found my lover waiting impatiently with his fishing basket in the hall.

We crossed the lawn together, and passed the open drawing-room windows, where three mischievous faces were looking at us.

'Spooning is a terribly demoralising thing,' remarked Jack, reflectively staring up at the clouds.

'Shocking,' said Fan; and all three laughed until they woke the sleeping Colonel, and we could hear them endeavouring to explain the joke to that ill-used veteran, who apparently obstinately refused to appreciate it.

We passed down the winding lane together, and through the little wooden gate, which opens on to the Tavistock road.

Charley paused for a moment after we had emerged and seemed irresolute which way to turn.

Had we but known it, our fate depended upon that trivial question.

'Shall we go down to the river, dear,' he said, 'or shall we try one of the brooks upon the moor?'

'Whichever you like?' I answered.

'Well, I vote that we cross the moor. We'll have a longer walk back that way,' he added, looking down lovingly at the little white-shawled figure beside him.

The brook in question runs through a most desolate part of the country. By the path it is several miles from Toynby Hall; but we were both young and active, and struck out across the moor, regardless of rocks and furze-bushes.

Not a living creature did we meet upon our solitary walk, save a few scraggy Devonshire sheep, who looked at us wistfully, and followed us for some distance, as if curious as to what could possibly have induced us to trespass upon their domains.

It was almost dark before we reached the little stream, which comes gurgling down through a precipitous glen, and meanders away to help to form the Plymouth 'leat'.

Above us towered two great columns of rock, between which the water trickled to form a deep, still pool at the bottom. This pool had always been a favourite spot of Charley's, and was a pretty cheerful place by day; but now, with the rising moon reflected upon its glassy waters, and throwing dark shadows from the overhanging rocks, it seemed anything rather than the haunt of a pleasure-seeker.

'I don't think, darling, that I'll fish, after all,' said Charley, as we sat down together on a mossy bank. 'It's a dismal sort of place, isn't it?'

'Very,' said I, shuddering.

'We'll just have a rest, and then we will walk back by the pathway. You're shivering. You're not cold, are you?'

'No,' said I, trying to keep up my courage; 'I'm not cold, but I'm rather frightened, though it's very silly of me.'

'By jove!' said my lover, 'I can't wonder at it, for I feel a bit depressed myself. The noise that water makes is like the gurgling in the throat of a dying man.'

'Don't, Charley; you frighten me!'

'Come, dear, we mustn't get the blues,' he said, with a laugh, trying to reassure me. 'Let's run away from this charnel-house place, and—Look!—see!—good gracious! what is that?'

Charley had staggered back, and was gazing upwards with a pallid face.

I followed the direction of his eyes, and could scarcely suppress a scream.

I have already mentioned that the pool by which we were standing lay at the foot of a rough mound of rocks. On the top of this mound, about sixty feet above our heads, a tall dark figure was standing, peering down, apparently, into the rugged hollow in which we were.

The moon was just topping the ridge behind, and the gaunt, angular outlines of the stranger stood out hard and clear against its silvery radiance.

There was something ghastly in the sudden and silent appearance of this solitary wanderer, especially when coupled with the weird nature of the scene.

I clung to my lover in speechless terror, and glared up at the dark figure above us.

'Hullo, you sir!' cried Charley, passing from fear into anger, as Englishmen generally do. 'Who are you, and what the devil are you doing?'

'Oh! I thought it, I thought it!' said the man who was overlooking us, and disappeared from the top of the hill.

We heard him scrambling about among the loose stones, and in another moment he emerged upon the banks of the brook and stood facing us.

Weird as his appearance had been when we first caught sight of him, the impression was intensified rather than removed by a closer acquaintance.

The moon shining full upon him revealed a long, thin face of ghastly pallor, the effect being increased by its contrast with the flaring green necktie which he wore.

A scar upon his cheek had healed badly and caused a nasty pucker at the side of his mouth, which gave his whole countenance a most distorted expression, more particularly when he smiled.

The knapsack on his back and stout staff in his hand announced him to be a tourist, while the easy grace with which he raised his hat on perceiving the presence of a lady showed that he could lay claim to the *savoir-faire* of a man of the world.

There was something in his angular proportions and the bloodless face which, taken in conjunction with the black cloak which fluttered from his shoulders, irresistibly reminded me of a blood-sucking species of bat which Jack Daseby had brought from Japan upon his previous voyage, and which was the bugbear of the servants' hall at Toynby.

'Excuse my intrusion,' he said, with a slightly foreign lisp, which imparted a peculiar beauty to his voice. 'I should have had to sleep on the moor had I not had the good fortune to fall in with you.

'Confound it, man!' said Charley; 'why couldn't you shout out, or give some warning? You quite frightened Miss Underwood when you suddenly appeared up there.'

The stranger once more raised his hat as he apologised to me for having given me such a start.

'I am a gentleman from Sweden,' he continued, in that peculiar intonation of his, 'and am viewing this beautiful land of yours. Allow me to introduce myself as Doctor Octavius Gaster. Perhaps you could tell me where I may sleep, and how I can get from this place, which is truly of great size?'

'You're very lucky in falling in with us,' said Charley. 'It is no easy matter to find your way upon the moor.'

'That can I well believe,' remarked our new acquaintance.

'Strangers have been found dead on it before now,' continued Charley. 'They lose themselves, and then wander in a circle until they fall from fatigue.'

'Ha, ha!' laughed the Swede; 'it is not I, who have drifted in an open boat from Cape Blanco to Canary, that will starve upon an English moor. But how may I turn to seek an inn?'

'Look here!' said Charley, whose interest was excited by the stranger's allusion, and who was at all times the most openhearted of men. 'There's not an inn for many a mile round; and I daresay you have had a long day's walk already. Come home with us, and my father, the Colonel, will be delighted to see you and find you a spare bed.'

'For this great kindness how can I thank you?' returned the traveller. 'Truly, when I return to Sweden, I shall have strange stories to tell of the English and the hospitality!'

'Nonsense!' said Charley. 'Come, we will start at once, for Miss Underwood is cold. Wrap the shawl well round your neck, Lottie, and we will be home in no time.'

We stumbled along in silence, keeping as far as we could to the rugged pathway, sometimes losing it as a cloud drifted over the face of the moon, and then regaining it further on with the return of the light.

The stranger seemed buried in thought, but once or twice I had the impression that he was looking hard at me through the darkness as we strode along together.

'So,' said Charley at last, breaking the silence, 'you drifted about in an open boat, did you?'

'Ah, yes,' answered the stranger; 'many strange sights have I seen, and many perils undergone, but none worse than that. It is, however, too sad a subject for a lady's ears. She has been frightened once tonight.'

'Oh, you needn't be afraid of frightening me now,' said I, as I leaned on Charley's arm.

'Indeed there is but little to tell, and yet is it sorrowful.

'A friend of mine, Karl Osgood of Upsala, and myself started on a trading venture. Few white men had been among the wandering Moors at Cape Blanco, but nevertheless we went, and for some months lived well, selling this and that, and gathering much ivory and gold.

''Tis a strange country, where is neither wood nor stone, so that the huts are made from the weeds of the sea.

'At last, just as what we thought was a sufficiency, the Moors conspired to kill us, and came down against us in the night.

'Short was our warning, but we fled to the beach, launched a canoe and put out to sea, leaving everything behind.

'The Moors chased us, but lost us in the darkness; and when day dawned the land was out of sight.

'There was no country where we could hope for food nearer than Canary, and for that we made.

'I reached it alive, though very weak and mad; but poor Karl died the day before we sighted the islands.

'I gave him warning!

'I cannot blame myself in the matter.

'I said, "Karl, the strength that you might gain by eating them would be more than made up for by the blood that you would lose!"

'He laughed at my words, caught the knife from my belt, cut them off and ate them; and he died.'

'Ate what?' asked Charley.

'His ears!' said the stranger.

We both looked round at him in horror.

There was no suspicion of a smile or joke upon his ghastly face.

'He was what you call headstrong,' he continued, 'but he should have known better than to do a thing like that. Had he but used his will he would have lived as I did.'

'And you think a man's will can prevent him from feeling hungry?' said Charley.

'What can it not do?' returned Octavius Gaster, and relapsed into a silence which was not broken until our arrival in Toynby Hall.

Considerable alarm had been caused by our non-appearance, and Jack Daseby was just setting off with Charley's friend Trevor in search of us. They were delighted, therefore, when we marched in upon them, and considerably astonished at the appearance of our companion.

'Where the deuce did you pick up that second-hand corpse?' asked Jack, drawing Charley aside into the smoking-room.

'Shut up, man; he'll hear you,' growled Charley. 'He's Swedish doctor on a tour, and a deuced good fellow. He went in an open boat from What's-its-name to another place. I've offered him a bed for the night.'

'Well, all I can say is,' remarked Jack, 'that his face will never be his fortune.'

'Ha, ha! Very good! very good!' laughed the subject of the remark, walking calmly into the room, to the complete discomfiture of the sailor. 'No, it will never, as you say, in this country be my fortune'—and he grinned until the hideous gash across the angle of his mouth made him look more like the reflection in a broken mirror than anything else.

'Come upstairs and have a wash; I can lend you a pair of slippers,' said Charley; and hurried the visitor out of the room to put an end to a somewhat embarrassing situation.

Colonel Pillar was the soul of hospitality, and welcomed Doctor Gaster as effusively as if he had been an old friend of the family.

'Egad, sir,' he said, 'the place is your own; and as long as you care to stop you are very welcome. We're pretty quiet down here, and a visitor is an acquisition.'

My mother was a little more distant. 'A very well informed young man, Lottie,' she remarked to me; 'but I wish he would wink his eyes more. I don't like to see people who never wink their eyes. Still, my dear, my life has taught me one great lesson, and that is that a man's looks are of very little importance compared with his actions.'

With which brand new and eminently original remark, my mother kissed me and left me to my meditations.

Whatever Doctor Octavius Gaster might be physically, he was certainly a social success.

By next day he had so completely installed himself as a member of the household that the Colonel would not hear of his departure.

He astonished everybody by the extent and variety of his knowledge. He could tell the veteran considerably more about the Crimea than he knew himself; he gave the sailor information about the coast of Japan; and even tackled my athletic lover upon the subject of rowing, discoursing about levers of the first order, and fixed points and fulcra, until the unhappy Cantab was fain to drop the subject.

Yet all this was done so modestly and even deferentially, that no one could possibly feel offended at being beaten upon their own ground. There was a quiet power about everything he said and did which was very striking.

I remember one example of this, which impressed us all at the time.

Trevor had a remarkably savage bulldog, which, however fond of its master, fiercely resented any liberties from the rest of us. This animal was, it may be imagined, rather unpopular, but as it was the pride of the student's heart it was agreed not to banish it entirely, but to lock it up in the stable and give it a wide berth.

From the first, it seemed to have taken a decided aversion to our visitor, and showed every fang in its head whenever he approached it.

On the second day of his visit we were passing the stable in a body, when the growls of the creature inside arrested Doctor Gaster's attention.

'Ha!' he said. 'There is that dog of yours, Mr Trevor, is it not?'

'Yes; that's Towzer,' assented Trevor.

'He is a bulldog, I think? What they call the national animal of England on the Continent?'

'Pure-bred,' said the student, proudly.

'They are ugly animals—very ugly! Would you come into the stable and unchain him, that I may see him to advantage. It is a pity to keep an animal so powerful and full of life in captivity.'

'He's rather a nipper,' said Trevor, with a mischievous expression in his eye; 'but I suppose you are not afraid of a dog.'

'Afraid?—no. Why should I be afraid?'

The mischievous look on Trevor's face increased as he opened the stable door. I heard Charley mutter something to him about its being past a joke, but the other's answer was drowned by the hollow growling from inside.

The rest of us retreated to a respectable distance, while Octavius Gaster stood in the open doorway with a look of mild curiosity upon his pallid face.

'And those,' he said, 'that I see so bright and red in the darkness—are those his eyes?'

'Those are they,' said the student, as he stooped down and unbuckled the strap.

'Come here!' said Octavius Gaster.

The growling of the dog suddenly subsided into a long whimper, and instead of making the furious rush that we expected, he rustled among the straw as if trying to huddle into a corner.

'What the deuce is the matter with him?' exclaimed his perplexed owner.

'Come here!' repeated Gaster, in sharp metallic accents, with an indescribable air of command in them. 'Come here!'

To our astonishment, the dog trotted out and stood at his side, but looking as unlike the usually pugnacious Towzer as is possible to conceive. His ears were drooping, his tail limp, and he altogether presented the very picture of canine humiliation.

'A very fine dog, but singularly quiet,' remarked the Swede, as he stroked him down.

'Now, sir, go back!'

The brute turned and slunk back into its corner. We heard the rattling of its chain as it was being fastened, and next moment Trevor came out of the stable-door with blood dripping from his finger.

'Confound the beast!' he said. 'I don't know what can have come over him. I've had him three years, and he never bit me before.'

I fancy—I cannot say it for certain—but I fancy that there was a spasmodic twitching of the cicatrix upon our visitor's face, which betokened an inclination to laugh.

Looking back, I think that it was from that moment that I began to have a strange indefinable fear and dislike of the man.

Week followed week, and the day fixed for my marriage began to draw near.

Octavius Gaster was still a guest at Toynby Hall, and, indeed, had so ingratiated himself with the proprietor that any hint at departure was laughed to scorn by that worthy soldier.

'Here you've come, sir, and here you'll stay; you shall, by Jove!'

Whereat Octavius would smile and shrug his shoulders and mutter something about the attractions of Devon, which would put the Colonel in a good humour for the whole day afterwards.

My darling and I were too much engrossed with each other to pay very much attention to the traveller's occupations. We used to come upon him sometimes in our rambles through the woods, sitting reading in the most lonely situations.

He always placed the book in his pocket when he saw us approaching. I remember on one occasion, however, that we stumbled upon him so suddenly that the volume was still lying open before him.

'Ah, Gaster,' said Charley, 'studying, as usual! What an old bookworm you are! What's the book? Ah, a foreign language; Swedish, I suppose?'

'No, it is not Swedish,' said Gaster; 'it is Arabic.'

'You don't mean to say you know Arabic?'

'Oh, very well—very well indeed!'

'And what's it about?' I asked, turning over the leaves of the musty old volume.

'Nothing that would interest one so young and fair as yourself, Miss Underwood,' he answered, looking at me in a way which had become habitual to him of late. 'It treats of the days when mind was stronger than what you call matter; when great spirits lived that were able to exist without these coarse bodies of ours, and could mould all things to their so-powerful wills.'

'Oh, I see; a kind of ghost story,' said Charley. 'Well, adieu; we won't keep you from your studies.'

We left him sitting in the little glen still absorbed in his mystical treatise. It must have been imagination which induced me, on turning suddenly round half an hour later, to think that I saw his familiar figure glide rapidly behind a tree.

I mentioned it to Charley at the time, but he laughed my idea to scorn.

* * * * *

I alluded just now to a peculiar manner which this man Gaster had of looking at me. His eyes seemed to lose their usual steely expression when he did so, and soften into something which might be almost called caressing. They seemed to influence me strangely, for I could always tell, without looking at him, when his gaze was fixed upon me.

Sometimes I fancied that this idea was simply due to a disordered nervous system or morbid imagination; but my mother dispelled that delusion from my mind.

'Do you know,' she said, coming into my bedroom one night, and carefully shutting the door behind her, 'if the idea was not so utterly preposterous, Lottie, I should say that that Doctor was madly in love with you?'

'Nonsense, 'ma!' said I, nearly dropping my candle in my consternation at the thought.

'I really think so, Lottie,' continued my mother. 'He's got a way of looking which is very like that of your poor dear father, Nicholas, before we were married. Something of this sort, you know.'

And the old lady cast an utterly heart-broken glance at the bed-post.

'Now, go to bed,' said I, 'and don't have such funny ideas. Why, poor Doctor Gaster knows that I am engaged as well as you do.'

'Time will show,' said the old lady, as she left the room; and I went to bed with the words still ringing in my ears.

Certainly, it is a strange thing that on that very night a thrill which I had come to know well ran through me, and awakened me from my slumbers.

I stole softly to the window, and peered out through the bars of the Venetian blinds, and there was the gaunt, vampire-like figure of our Swedish visitor standing upon the gravel-walk, and apparently gazing up at my window.

It may have been that he detected the movement of the blind, for, lighting a cigarette, he began pacing up and down the avenue.

I noticed that at breakfast next morning he went out of his way to explain the fact that he had been restless during the night, and had steadied his nerves by a short stroll and a smoke.

After all, when I came to consider it calmly, the aversion which I had against the man and my distrust of him were founded on very scanty grounds. A man might have a strange face, and be fond of curious literature, and even look approvingly at an engaged young lady, without being a very dangerous member of society.

I say this to show that even up to that point I was perfectly unbiased and free from prejudice in my opinion of Octavius Gaster.

'I say!' remarked Lieutenant Daseby, one morning; 'what do you think of having a picnic today?'

'Capital!' ejaculated everybody.

'You see, they are talking of commissioning the old *Shark* soon, and Trevor here will have to go back to the mill. We may as well compress as much fun as we can into the time.'

'What is it that you call nicpic?' asked Doctor Gaster.

'It's another of our English institutions for you to study,' said Charley. 'It's our version of *fête champêtre*.'

'Ah, I see! That will be very jolly!' acquiesced the Swede.

'There are half a dozen places we might go to,' continued the Lieutenant. 'There's the Lover's Leap, or Black Tor, or Beer Ferris Abbey.'

'That's the best,' said Charley. 'Nothing like ruins for a picnic.'

'Well the Abbey be it. How far is it?'

'Six miles,' said Trevor.

'Seven by the road,' remarked the Colonel, with military exactness. 'Mrs Underwood and I shall stay at home, and the rest of you can fit into the waggonette. You'll all have to chaperon each other.'

I need hardly say that this motion was carried also without a division.

'Well,' said Charley, 'I'll order the trap to be round in half an hour, so you'd better all make the best of your time. We'll want salmon, and salad, and hard-boiled eggs, and liquor, and any number of things. I'll look after the liquor department. What will you do, Lottie?'

'I'll take charge of the china,' I said.

'I'll bring the fish,' said Daseby.

'And I the vegetables,' added Fan.

'What will you do, Gaster?' asked Charley.

'Truly,' said the Swede, in his strange, musical accents, 'but little is left for me to do. I can, however, wait upon the ladies, and I can make what you call a salad.'

'You'll be more popular in the latter capacity than in the former,' said I, laughingly.

'Ah, you say so,' he said, turning sharp round upon me, and flushing up to his flaxen hair. 'Yes. Ha! ha! Very good!'

And with a discordant laugh, he strode out of the room.

'I say, Lottie,' remonstrated my lover, 'you've hurt the fellow's feelings.'

'I'm sure I didn't mean to,' I answered. 'If you like I'll go after him and tell him so.'

'Oh, leave him alone,' said Daseby. 'A man with a mug like that has no right to be so touchy. He'll come round right enough.'

It was true that I had not had the slightest intention of offending Gaster, still I felt pained at having annoyed him.

After I had stowed away the knives and plates into the hamper, I found that the others were still busy at their various departments. The moment seemed a favourable one for apologising for my thoughtless remark, so without saying anything to anyone, I slipped away and ran down the corridor in the direction of our visitor's room.

I suppose I must have tripped along very lightly, or it may have been the rich thick matting of Toynby Hall—certain it is that Mr Gaster seemed unconscious of my approach.

His door was open, and as I came up to it and caught sight of him inside, there was something so strange in his appearance that I paused, literally petrified for the moment with astonishment.

He had in his hand a small slip from a newspaper which he was reading, and which seemed to afford him considerable amusement. There was something horrible too in this mirth of his, for though he writhed his body about as if with laughter, no sound was emitted from his lips.

His face, which was half-turned towards me, wore an expression upon it which I had never seen on it before; I can only describe it as one of savage exultation.

Just as I was recovering myself sufficiently to step forward and knock at the door, he suddenly, with a last convulsive spasm of merriment, dashed down the piece of paper upon the table and hurried out by the other door of his room, which led through the billiard-room to the hall.

I heard his steps dying away in the distance, and peeped once more into his room.

What could be the joke that had moved this stern man to mirth? Surely some masterpiece of humour.

Was there ever a woman whose principles were strong enough to overcome her curiosity?

Looking cautiously round to make sure that the passage was empty, I slipped into the room and examined the paper which he had been reading.

It was a cutting from an English journal, and had evidently been long carried about and frequently perused, for it was almost illegible in places. There was, however, as far as I could see, very little to provoke laughter in its contents. It ran, as well as I can remember, in this way:

> Sudden Death in the Docks—The master of the bark-rigged steamer *Olga*, from Tromsberg, was found lying dead in his cabin on Wednesday afternoon. Deceased was, it seems, of a violent disposition, and had had frequent altercations with the surgeon of the vessel. On this particular day he had been more than usually offensive, declaring that the surgeon was a necromancer and worshipper of the devil. The latter retired on deck to avoid further persecution. Shortly afterwards the steward had occasion to enter the cabin, and found the captain lying across the table quite dead. Death is attributed to heart disease, accelerated by excessive passion. An inquest will be held today.

And this was the paragraph which this strange man had regarded as the height of humour!

I hurried downstairs, astonishment, not un-mixed with repugnance, predominating in my mind. So just was I, however, that the dark inference which has so often occurred to me since never for one moment crossed my mind. I looked upon him as a curious and rather repulsive enigma—nothing more.

When I met him at the picnic, all remembrance of my unfortunate speech seemed to have vanished from his mind. He made himself as agreeable as usual, and his salad was pronounced a *chef-d'oeuvre*, while his quaint little Swedish songs and his tales of all climes and countries alternately thrilled and amused us. It was after luncheon, however, that the conversation turned upon a subject which seemed to have special charms for his daring mind.

I forget who it was that broached the question of the supernatural. I think it was Trevor, by some story of a hoax which he had perpetrated at Cambridge. The story seemed to have a strange effect upon Octavius Gaster, who tossed his long arms about in impassioned invective as he ridiculed those who dared to doubt about the existence of the unseen.

'Tell me,' he said, standing up in his excitement, 'which among you has ever known what you call an instinct to fail. The wild bird has an instinct which tells it of the solitary rock upon the so boundless sea on which it may lay its egg, and is it disappointed? The swallow turns to the south when the winter is coming, and has its instinct ever led it astray? And shall this instinct which tells us of the unknown spirits around us, and which pervades every untaught child and every race so savage, be wrong? I say, never!'

'Go it, Gaster!' cried Charley.

'Take your wind and have another spell,' said the sailor.

'No, never,' repeated the Swede, disregarding our amusement. 'We can see that matter exists apart from mind; then why should not mind exist apart from matter?'

'Give it up,' said Daseby.

'Have we not proofs of it?' continued Gaster, his grey eyes gleaming with excitement. 'Who that has read Steinberg's book upon spirits, or that by the eminent American, Madame Crowe, can doubt it? Did not Gustav von Spee meet his brother Leopold in the streets of Strasbourg, the same brother having been drowned three months before in the Pacific? Did not Home, the spiritualist, in open daylight, float above the housetops of Paris? Who has not heard the voices of the dead around him? I myself——'

'Well, what of yourself?' asked half a dozen of us, in a breath.

'Bah! it matters nothing,' he said, passing his hand over his forehead, and evidently controlling himself with difficulty. 'Truly, our talk is too sad for such an occasion.' And, in spite of all our efforts, we were unable to extract from Gaster any relation of his own experiences of the supernatural.

It was a merry day. Our approaching dissolution seemed to cause each one to contribute his utmost to the general amusement. It was settled that after the coming rifle match Jack was to return to his ship and Trevor to his university. As to Charley and myself, we were to settle down into a staid respectable couple.

The match was one of our principal topics of conversation. Shooting had always been a hobby of Charley's, and he was the captain of the Roborough company of Devon volunteers, which boasted some of the crack shots of the county. The match was to be against a picked team of regulars from Plymouth, and as they were no despicable opponents, the issue was considered doubtful. Charley had evidently set his heart on winning, and descanted long and loudly on the chances.

'The range is only a mile from Toynby Hall,' he said, 'and we'll all drive over, and you shall see the fun. You'll bring me luck, Lottie,' he whispered, 'I know you will.'

Oh, my poor lost darling, to think of the luck that I brought you!

There was one dark cloud to mar the brightness of that happy day.

I could not hide from myself any longer the fact that my mother's suspicions were correct, and that Octavius Gaster loved me.

Throughout the whole of the excursion his attentions had been most assiduous, and his eyes hardly ever wandered away from me. There was a manner, too, in all that he said which spoke louder than words.

I was on thorns lest Charley should perceive it, for I knew his fiery temper; but the thought of such treachery never entered the honest heart of my lover.

He did once look up with mild surprise when the Swede insisted on relieving me of a fern which I was carrying; but the expression faded away into a smile at what he regarded as Gaster's effusive good-nature. My own feeling in the matter was pity for the unfortunate foreigner, and sorrow that I should have been the means of rendering him unhappy.

I thought of the torture it must be for a wild, fierce spirit like his to have a passion gnawing at his heart which honour and pride would alike prevent him from ever expressing in words. Alas! I had not counted upon the utter recklessness and want of principle of the man; but it was not long before I was undeceived.

There was a little arbour at the bottom of the garden, overgrown with honeysuckle and ivy, which had long been a favourite haunt of Charley and myself. It was doubly dear to us from the fact that it was here, on the occasion of my former visit, that words of love had first passed between us.

After dinner on the day following the picnic I sauntered down to this little summer-house, as was my custom. Here I used to wait until Charley, having finished his cigar with the other gentlemen, would come down and join me.

On that particular evening he seemed to be longer away than usual. I waited impatiently for his coming, going to the door every now and then to see if there were any signs of his approach.

I had just sat down again after one of those fruitless excursions, when I heard the tread of a male foot upon the gravel, and a figure emerged from among the bushes.

I sprang up with a glad smile, which changed to an expression of bewilderment, and even fear, when I saw the gaunt, pallid face of Octavius Gaster peering in at me.

There was certainly something about his actions which would have inspired distrust in the mind of anyone in my position. Instead of greeting me, he looked up and down the garden, as if to make sure that we were entirely alone. He then stealthily entered the arbour, and seated himself upon a chair, in such a position that he was between me and the doorway.

'Do not be afraid,' he said, as he noticed my scared expression. 'There is nothing to fear. I do but come that I may have talk with you.'

'Have you seen Mr Pillar?' I asked, trying hard to seem at my ease.

'Ha! Have I seen your Charley?' he answered, with a sneer upon the last words. 'Are you then so anxious that he come? Can no one speak to thee but Charley, little one?'

'Mr Gaster,' I said, 'you are forgetting yourself.'

'It is Charley, Charley, ever Charley!' continued the Swede, disregarding my interruption. 'Yes, I have seen Charley. I have told him that you wait upon the bank of the river, and he has gone thither upon the wings of love.'

'Why have you told him this lie?' I asked, still trying not to lose my self-control.

'That I might see you; that I might speak to you. Do you, then, love him so? Cannot the thought of glory, and riches, and power, above all that the mind can conceive, win you from this first maiden fancy of yours? Fly with me, Charlotte, and all this, and more, shall be yours! Come!'

And he stretched his long arms out in passionate entreaty.

Even at that moment the thought flashed through my mind of how like they were to the tentacles of some poisonous insect.

'You insult me, sir!' I cried, rising to my feet. 'You shall pay heavily for this treatment of an unprotected girl!'

'Ah, you say it,' he cried, 'but you mean it not. In your heart so tender there is pity left for the most miserable of men. Nay, you shall not pass me—you shall hear me first!'

'Let me go, sir!'

'Nay; you shall not go until you tell me if nothing that I can do may win your love.'

'How dare you speak so?' I almost screamed, losing all my fear in my indignation. 'You, who are the guest of my future husband! Let me tell you, once and for all, that I had no feeling towards you before save one of repugnance and contempt, which you have now converted into positive hatred!'

'And is it so?' he gasped, tottering backwards towards the doorway, and putting his hand up to his throat as if he found a difficulty in uttering the words. 'And has my love won hatred in return? Ha!' he continued, advancing his face within a foot of mine as I cowered away from his glassy eyes. 'I know it now. It is this—it is this!' and he struck the horrible cicatrix on his face with his clenched hand. 'Maids love not such faces as this! I am not smooth, and brown, and curly like this Charley—this brainless school-boy; this human brute who cares but for his sport and his——'

'Let me pass!' I cried, rushing at the door.

'No; you shall not go—you shall not!' he hissed, pushing me backwards.

I struggled furiously to escape from his grasp. His long arms seemed to clasp me like bars of steel. I felt my strength going, and was making one last despairing effort to shake myself loose, when some irresistible power from behind tore my persecutor away from me and hurled him backwards on to the gravel walk.

Looking up, I saw Charley's towering figure and square shoulders in the doorway.

'My poor darling!' he said, catching me in his arms. 'Sit here—here in the angle. There is no danger now. I shall be with you in a minute.'

'Don't Charley, don't!' I murmured, as he turned to leave me.

But he was deaf to my entreaties, and strode out of the arbour.

I could not see either him or his opponent from the position in which he had placed me, but I heard every word that was spoken.

'You villain!' said a voice that I could hardly recognise as my lover's. 'So this is why you put me on a wrong scent?'

'That is why,' answered the foreigner, in a tone of easy indifference.

'And this is how you repay our hospitality, you infernal scoundrel!'

'Yes; we amuse ourselves in your so beautiful summer-house.'

'We! You are still on my ground and my guest, and I would wish to keep my hands from you; but, by heavens——'

Charley was speaking very low and in gasps now.

'Why do you swear? What is it, then?' asked the languid voice of Octavius Gaster.

'If you dare to couple Miss Underwood's name with this business, and insinuate that——'

'Insinuate? I insinuate nothing. What I say I say plain for all the world to hear. I say that this so chaste maiden did herself ask——'

I heard the sound of a heavy blow, and a great rattling of the gravel.

I was too weak to rise from where I lay, and could only clasp my hands together and utter a faint scream.

'You cur!' said Charley. 'Say as much again, and I'll stop your mouth for all eternity!'

There was a silence, and then I heard Gaster speaking in a husky, strange voice.

'You have struck me!' he said; 'you have drawn my blood!'

'Yes; I'll strike you again if you show your cursed face within these grounds. Don't look at me so! You don't suppose your hankey-pankey tricks can frighten me?'

An indefinable dread came over me as my lover spoke. I staggered to my feet and looked out at them, leaning against the door-way for support.

Charley was standing erect and defiant, with his young head in the air, like one who glories in the cause for which he battles.

Octavius Gaster was opposite him, surveying him with pinched lips and a baleful look in his cruel eyes. The blood was running freely from a deep gash on his lip, and spotting the front of his green necktie and white waistcoat. He perceived me the instant I emerged from the arbour.

'Ha, ha!' he cried, with a demoniacal burst of laughter. 'She comes! The bride! She comes! Room for the bride! Oh, happy pair, happy pair!'

And with another fiendish burst of merriment he turned and disappeared over the crumbling wall of the garden with such rapidity that he was gone before we had realised what it was that he was about to do.

'Oh, Charley,' I said, as my lover came back to my side, 'you've hurt him!'

'Hurt him! I should hope I have! Come, darling, you are frightened and tired. He did not injure you, did he?'

'No; but I feel rather faint and sick.'

'Come, we'll walk slowly to the house together. The rascal! It was cunningly and deliberately planned, too. He told me he had seen you down by the river, and I was going down when I met young Stokes, the keeper's son, coming back from fishing, and he told me that there was nobody there. Somehow, when Stokes said that, a thousand little things flashed into my mind at once, and I became in a moment so convinced of Gaster's villainy that I ran as hard as I could to the arbour.'

'Charley,' I said, clinging to my lover's arm, 'I fear he will injure you in some way. Did you see the look in his eyes before he leaped the wall?'

'Pshaw!' said Charley. 'All these foreigners have a way of scowling and glaring when they are angry, but it never comes to much.'

'Still, I am afraid of him,' said I, mournfully, as we went up the steps together, 'and I wish you had not struck him.'

'So do I,' Charley answered; 'for he was our guest, you know, in spite of his rascality. However, it's done now and it can't be helped, as the cook says in *Pickwick*, and really it was more than flesh and blood could stand.'

I must run rapidly over the events of the next few days. For me, at least, it was a period of absolute happiness. With Gaster's departure a cloud seemed to be lifted off my soul, and a depression which had weighed upon the whole household completely disappeared.

Once more I was the light-hearted girl that I had been before the foreigner's arrival. Even the Colonel forgot to mourn over his absence, owing to the all-absorbing interest in the coming competition in which his son was engaged.

It was our main subject of conversation and bets were freely offered by the gentlemen on the success of the Roborough team, though no one was unprincipled enough to seem to support their antagonists by taking them.

Jack Daseby ran down to Plymouth, and 'made a book on the event' with some officers of the Marines, which he did in such an extraordinary way that we reckoned that in case of Roborough winning, he would lose seventeen shillings; while, should the other contingency occur, he would be involved in hopeless liabilities.

Charley and I had tacitly agreed not to mention the name of Gaster, nor to allude in any way to what had passed.

On the morning after our scene in the garden, Charley had sent a servant up to the Swede's room with instructions to pack up any things he might find there, and leave them at the nearest inn.

It was found, however, that all Gaster's effects had been already removed, though how and when was a perfect mystery to the servants.

I know of few more attractive spots than the shooting-range at Roborough. The glen in which it is situated is about half a mile long and perfectly level, so that the targets were able to range from two to seven hundred yards, the further ones simply showing as square white dots against the green of the rising hills behind.

The glen itself is part of the great moor and its sides, sloping gradually up, lose themselves in the vast rugged expanse. Its symmetrical character suggested to the imaginative mind that some giant of old had made an excavation in the moor with a titanic cheese-scoop, but that a single trial had convinced him of the utter worthlessness of the soil.

He might even be imagined to have dropped the despised sample at the mouth of the cutting which he had made, for there was a considerable elevation there, from which the riflemen were to fire, and thither we bent our steps on that eventful afternoon.

Our opponents had arrived there before us, bringing with them a considerable number of naval and military officers, while a long line of nondescript vehicles showed that many of the good citizens of Plymouth had seized the opportunity of giving their wives and families an outing on the moor.

An enclosure for ladies and distinguished guests had been erected on the top of the hill, which, with the marquee and refreshment tents, made the scene a lively one.

The country people had turned out in force, and were excitedly staking their half-crowns upon their local champions, which were as enthusiastically taken up by the admirers of the regulars.

Through all this scene of bustle and confusion we were safely conveyed by Charley, aided by Jack and Trevor, who finally deposited us in a sort of rudimentary grandstand, from which we could look round at our ease on all that was going on.

We were soon, however, so absorbed in the glorious view, that we became utterly unconscious of the betting and pushing and chaff of the crowd in front of us.

Away to the south we could see the blue smoke of Plymouth curling up into the calm summer air, while beyond that was the great sea, stretching away to the horizon, dark and vast, save where some petulant wave dashed it with a streak of foam, as if rebelling against the great peacefulness of nature.

From the Eddystone to the Start the long rugged line of the Devonshire coast lay like a map before us.

I was still lost in admiration when Charley's voice broke half reproachfully on my ear.

'Why, Lottie,' he said, 'you don't seem to take a bit of interest in it!'

'Oh, yes I do, dear,' I answered. 'But the scenery is so pretty, and the sea is always a weakness of mine. Come and sit here, and tell me all about the match and how we are to know whether you are winning or losing.'

'I've just been explaining it,' answered Charley. 'But I'll go over it again.'

'Do, like a darling,' said I; and settled myself down to mark, learn, and inwardly digest.

'Well,' said Charley, 'there are ten men on each side. We shoot alternately; first, one of our fellows, then one of them, and so on—you understand?'

'Yes, I understand that.'

'First we fire at the two hundred yards range—those are the targets nearest of all. We fire five shots each at those. Then we fire five shots at the ones at five hundred yards—those middle ones; and then we finish up by firing at the seven hundred yards range—you see the target far over there on the side of the hill. Whoever makes the most points wins. Do you grasp it now?'

'Oh, yes; that's very simple,' I said.

'Do you know what a bull's eye is?' asked my lover.

'Some sort of sweetmeat, isn't it?' I hazarded.

Charley seemed amazed at the extent of my ignorance. 'That's the bull's-eye,' he said; 'that dark spot in the centre of the target. If you hit that, it counts five. There is another ring, which you can't see, drawn round that, and if you get inside of it, it is called a "centre", and counts four. Outside that, again, is called an "outer", and only gives you three. You can tell where the shot has hit, for the marker puts out a coloured disc, and covers the place.'

'Oh, I understand it all now,' said I, enthusiastically. 'I'll tell you what I'll do Charley; I'll mark the score on a bit of paper every shot that is fired, and then I'll always know how Roborough is getting on!'

'You can't do better,' he laughed as he strode off to get his men together, for a warning bell signified that the contest was about to begin.

There was a great waving of flags and shouting before the ground could be got clear, and then I saw a little cluster of red-coats lying upon the greensward, while a similar group, in grey, took up their position to the left of them.

'Pang!' went a rifle-shot, and the blue smoke came curling up from the grass.

Fanny shrieked, while I gave a cry of delight, for I saw the white disc go up, which proclaimed a 'bull', and the shot had been fired by one of the Roborough men. My elation was, however, promptly checked by the answering shot which put down five to the credit of the regulars. The next was also a 'bull', which was speedily cancelled by another. At the end of the competition at the short range each side had scored forty-nine out of a possible fifty, and the question of supremacy was as undecided as ever.

'It's getting exciting,' said Charley, lounging over to the stand. 'We begin shooting at the five hundred yards in a few minutes.'

'Oh, Charley,' cried Fanny in high excitement, 'don't you go and miss, whatever you do!'

'I won't if I can help it,' responded Charley, cheerfully.

'You made a "bull" every time just now,' I said.

'Yes, but it's not so easy when you've got your sights up. However, we'll do our best, and we can't do more. They've got some terribly good long-range men among them. Come over here, Lottie, for a moment.'

'What is it, Charley?' I asked, as he led me away from the others. I could see by the look in his face that something was troubling him.

'It's that fellow,' growled my lover. 'What the deuce does he want to come here for? I hoped we had seen the last of him!'

'What fellow?' I gasped, with a vague apprehension at my heart.

'Why, that infernal Swedish fellow, Gaster!'

I followed the direction of Charley's glance, and there, sure enough, standing on a little knoll close to the place where the riflemen were lying, was the tall, angular figure of the foreigner.

He seemed utterly unconscious of the sensation which his singular appearance and hideous countenance excited among the burly farmers around him; but was craning his long neck about, this way and that, as if in search of somebody.

As we watched him, his eye suddenly rested upon us, and it seemed to me that, even at that distance, I could see a spasm of hatred and triumph pass over his livid features.

A strange foreboding came over me, and I seized my lover's hand in both my own.

'Oh, Charley,' I cried, 'don't—don't go back to the shooting! Say you are ill—make some excuse, and come away!'

'Nonsense, lass!' said he, laughing heartily at my terror. 'Why, what in the world are you afraid of?'

'Of him!' I answered.

'Don't be so silly, dear. One would think he was a demi-god to hear the way in which you talk of him. But there! that's the bell, and I must be off.'

'Well, promise, at least, that you will not go near him?' I cried, following Charley.

'All right—all right!' said he.

And I had to be content with that small concession.

The contest at the five hundred yards range was a close and exciting one. Roborough led by a couple of points for some time, until a series of 'bulls' by one of the crack marksmen of their opponents turned the tables upon them.

At the end of it was found that the volunteers were three points to the bad—a result which was hailed by cheers from the Plymouth contingent and by long faces and black looks among the dwellers on the moor.

During the whole of this competition Octavius Gaster had remained perfectly still and motionless upon the top of the knoll on which he had originally taken up his position.

It seemed to me that he knew little of what was going on, for his face was turned away from the marksmen, and he appeared to be gazing into the distance.

Once I caught sight of his profile, and thought that his lips were moving rapidly as if in prayer, or it may have been the shimmer of the hot air of the almost Indian summer which deceived me. It was, however, my impression at the time.

And now came the competition at the longest range of all, which was to decide the match.

The Roborough men settled down steadily to their task of making up the lost ground; while the regulars seemed determined not to throw away a chance by over-confidence.

As shot after shot was fired, the excitement of the spectators became so great that they crowded round the marksmen, cheering enthusiastically at every 'bull'.

We ourselves were so far affected by the general contagion that we left our harbour of refuge, and submitted meekly to the pushing and rough ways of the mob, in order to obtain a nearer view of the champions and their doings.

The military stood at seventeen when the volunteers were at sixteen, and great was the despondency of the rustics.

Things looked brighter, however, when the two sides tied at twenty-four, and brighter still when the steady shooting of the local team raised their score to thirty-two against thirty of their opponents.

There were still, however, the three points which had been lost at the last range to be made up for.

Slowly the score rose, and desperate were the efforts of both parties to pull off the victory.

Finally, a thrill ran through the crowd when it was known that the last redcoat had fired, while one volunteer was still left, and that the soldiers were leading by four points.

Even *our* unsportsman-like minds were worked into a state of all-absorbing excitement by the nature of the crisis which now presented itself.

If the last representative of our little town could but hit the bull's-eye the match was won.

The silver cup, the glory, the money of our adherents, all depended upon that single shot.

The reader will imagine that my interest was by no means lessened when, by dint of craning my neck and standing on tiptoe, I caught sight of my Charley coolly shoving a cartridge into his rifle, and realised that it was upon his skill that the honour of Roborough depended.

It was this, I think, which lent me strength to push my way so vigorously through the crowd that I found myself almost in the first row and commanding an excellent view of the proceedings.

There were two gigantic farmers on each side of me, and while we were waiting for the decisive shot to be fired, I could not help listening to the conversation, which they carried on in broad Devon, over my head.

'Mun's a rare ugly 'un,' said one.

'He is that,' cordially assented the other.

'See to mun's een?'

'Eh, Jock; see to mun's moo', rayther!—Blessed if he bean't foamin' like Farmer Watson's dog—t'bull pup whot died mad o' the hydropathics.'

I turned round to see the favoured object of these flattering comments, and my eyes fell upon Doctor Octavius Gaster, whose presence I had entirely forgotten in my excitement.

His face was turned towards me; but he evidently did not see me, for his eyes were bent with unswerving persistence upon a point midway apparently between the distant targets and himself.

I have never seen anything to compare with the extraordinary concentration of that stare, which had the effect of making his eyeballs appear gorged and prominent, while the pupils were contracted to the finest possible point.

Perspiration was running freely down his long, cadaverous face, and, as the farmer had remarked, there were some traces of foam at the corners of his mouth. The jaw was locked, as if with some fierce effort of the will which demanded all the energy of his soul.

To my dying day that hideous countenance shall never fade from my remembrance nor cease to haunt me in my dreams. I shuddered, and turned away my head in the vain hope that perhaps the honest farmer might be right, and mental disease be the cause of all the vagaries of this extraordinary man.

A great stillness fell upon the whole crowd as Charley, having loaded his rifle, snapped up the breech cheerily, and proceeded to lie down in his appointed place.

'That's right, Mr Charles, sir—that's right,' I heard old McIntosh, the volunteer sergeant, whisper as I passed. 'A cool head and a steady hand, that's what does the trick, sir!'

My lover smiled round at the grey-headed soldier as he lay down upon the grass, and then proceeded to look along the sight of his rifle amid a silence in which the faint rustling of the breeze among the blades of grass was distinctly audible.

For more than a minute he hung upon his aim. His finger seemed to press the trigger, and every eye was fixed upon the distant target, when suddenly, instead of firing, the rifleman staggered up to his knees, leaving his weapon upon the ground.

To the surprise of everyone, his face was deadly pale, and perspiration was standing on his brow.

'I say, McIntosh,' he said, in a strange, gasping voice, 'is there anybody standing between the target and me?'

'Between, sir? No, not a soul, sir,' answered the astonished sergeant.

'There, man, there!' cried Charley, with fierce energy, seizing him by the arm, and pointing in the direction of the target. 'Don't you see him there, standing right in the line of fire?'

'There's no one there!' shouted half a dozen voices.

'No one there? Well, it must have been my imagination,' said Charley, passing his hand slowly over his forehead. 'Yet I could have sworn—Here, give me the rifle!'

He lay down again, and having settled himself into position, raised his weapon slowly to his eye. He had hardly looked along the barrel before he sprang up again with a loud cry.

'There!' he cried; 'I tell you I see it! A man dressed in volunteer uniform, and very like myself—the image of myself. Is this a conspiracy?' he continued, turning fiercely on the crowd. 'Do you tell me none of you see a man resembling myself walking from that target, and not two hundred yards from me as I speak?'

I should have flown to Charley's side had I not known how he hated feminine interference, and anything approaching to a scene. I could only listen silently to his strange wild words.

'I protest against this!' said an officer coming forward. 'This gentleman must really either take his shot, or we shall remove our men off the field and claim the victory.'

'But I'll shoot *him*!' gasped poor Charley.

'Humbug!' 'Rubbish!' 'Shoot him, then!' growled half a score of masculine voices.

'The fact is,' lisped one of the military men in front of me to another, 'the young fellow's nerves ar'n't quite equal to the occasion, and he feels it, and is trying to back out.'

The imbecile young lieutenant little knew at this point how a feminine hand was longing to stretch forth and deal him a sounding box on the ears.

'It's Martell's three-star brandy, that's what it is,' whispered the other. 'The "devils", don't you know. I've had 'em myself, and know a case when I see it.'

This remark was too recondite for my understanding, or the speaker would have run the same risk as his predecessor.

'Well, are you going to shoot or not?' cried several voices.

'Yes, I'll shoot,' groaned Charley—'I'll shoot *him* through! It's murder—sheer *murder*!'

I shall never forget the haggard look which he cast round at the crowd. 'I'm aiming *through* him, McIntosh,' he murmured, as he lay down on the grass and raised the gun for the third time to his shoulder.

There was one moment of suspense, a spurt of flame, the crack of a rifle, and a cheer which echoed across the moor, and might have been heard in the distant village.

'Well done, lad—well done!' shouted a hundred honest Devonshire voices, as the little white disc came out from behind the marker's shield and obliterated the dark 'bull' for the moment, proclaiming that the match was won.

'Well done, lad! It's Maister Pillar, of Toynby Hall. Here, let's gie mun a lift, carry mun home, for the honour o' Roborough. Come on, lads! There mun is on the grass. Wake up, Sergeant McIntosh. What be the matter with thee? Eh? What?'

A deadly stillness came over the crowd, and then a low incredulous murmur, changing to one of pity, with whispers of 'leave her alone, poor lass—leave her to hersel'!'—and then there was silence again, save for the moaning of a woman, and her short, quick cries of despair.

For, reader, my Charley, my beautiful, brave Charley, was lying cold and dead upon the ground, with the rifle still clenched in his stiffening fingers.

I heard kind words of sympathy. I heard Lieutenant Daseby's voice, broken with grief, begging me to control my sorrow, and felt his hand, as he gently raised me from my poor boy's body. This I can remember, and nothing more, until my recovery from my illness, when I found myself in the sick-room at Toynby Hall, and learned that three restless, delirious weeks had passed since that terrible day.

Stay!—do I remember nothing else?

Sometimes I think I do. Sometimes I think I can recall a lucid interval in the midst of my wanderings. I seem to have a dim recollection of seeing my good nurse go out of the room—of seeing a gaunt, bloodless face peering in through the half-open window, and of hearing a voice which said, 'I have dealt with thy so beautiful lover, and I have yet to deal with thee.' The words come back to me with a familiar ring, as if they had sounded in my ears before, and yet it may have been but a dream.

'And this is all!' you say. 'It is for this that a hysterical woman hunts down a harmless *savant* in the advertisement columns of the newspapers! On this shallow evidence she hints at crimes of the most monstrous description!'

Well, I cannot expect that these things should strike you as they struck me. I can but say that if I were upon a bridge with Octavius Gaster standing at one end, and the most merciless tiger that ever prowled in an Indian jungle at the other, I should fly to the wild beast for protection.

For me, my life is broken and blasted. I care not how soon it may end, but if my words shall keep this man out of one honest household, I have not written in vain.

Within a fortnight after writing this narrative, my poor daughter disappeared. All search has failed to find her. A porter at the railway station has deposed to having seen a young lady resembling her description get into a first-class carriage with a tall, thin gentleman. It is, however, too ridiculous to suppose that she can have eloped after her recent grief, and without my having had any suspicions. The detectives are, however, working out the clue.—EMILY UNDERWOOD.

The Silver Hatchet

ON THE 3RD OF DECEMBER, 1861, Dr Otto von Hopstein, Regius Professor of Comparative Anatomy of the University of Buda-Pesth, and Curator of the Academical Museum, was foully and brutally murdered within a stone-throw of the entrance to the college quadrangle.

Besides the eminent position of the victim and his popularity amongst both students and towns-folk, there were other circumstances which excited public interest very strongly, and drew general attention throughout Austria and Hungary to this murder. The *Pesther Abendblatt* of the following day had an article upon it, which may still be consulted by the curious, and from which I translate a few passages giving a succinct account of the circumstances under which the crime was committed, and the peculiar features in the case which puzzled the Hungarian police.

'It appears,' said that very excellent paper, 'that Professor von Hopstein left the University about half-past four in the afternoon, in order to meet the train which is due from Vienna at three minutes after five. He was accompanied by his old and dear friend, Herr Wilhelm Schlessinger, sub-Curator of the Museum and Privat-docent of Chemistry. The object of these two gentlemen in meeting this particular train was to receive the legacy bequeathed by Graf von Schulling to the University of Buda-Pesth. It is well known that this unfortunate nobleman, whose tragic fate is still fresh in the recollection of the public, left his unique collection of mediaeval weapons, as well as several priceless black-letter editions, to enrich the already celebrated museum of his Alma Mater. The worthy Professor was too much of an enthusiast in such matters to intrust the reception or care of this valuable legacy to any subordinate, and, with the assistance of Herr Schlessinger, he succeeded in removing the whole collection from the train, and stowing it away in a light cart which had been sent by the University authorities. Most of the books and more fragile articles were packed in cases of pine-wood, but many of the weapons were simply done round with straw, so that considerable labour was involved in moving them all. The Professor was so nervous, however, lest any of them should be injured, that he refused to allow any of the railway employées (*Eisenbahn-diener*) to assist. Every article was carried across the platform by Herr Schlessinger, and handed to Professor von Hopstein in the cart, who packed it away. When everything was in, the two gentlemen, still faithful to their charge, drove back to the University, the Professor being in excellent spirits, and not a little proud of the physical exertion which he had shown himself capable of. He made some joking allusion to it to Reinmaul, the janitor, who, with his friend Schiffer, a Bohemian Jew, met the cart on its return and unloaded the contents. Leaving his curiosities safe in the store-room, and locking the door, the Professor handed the key to his sub-curator, and, bidding every one good evening, departed in the direction of his lodgings. Schlessinger took a last look to reassure himself that all was right, and also went off, leaving Reinmaul and his friend Schiffer smoking in the janitor's lodge.

'At eleven o'clock, about an hour and a half after Von Hopstein's departure, a soldier of the 14th regiment of Jäger, passing the front of the University on his way to barracks, came upon the lifeless body of the Professor lying a little way from the side of the road. He had fallen upon his face, with both hands stretched out. His head was literally split in two halves by a tremendous blow, which, it is conjectured, must have been struck from behind, there remaining a peaceful smile upon the old man's face, as if he had been still dwelling upon his new archaeological acquisition when death had overtaken him. There is no other mark of violence upon the body, except a bruise over the left patella, caused probably by the fall. The most mysterious part of the affair is that the Professor's purse, containing forty-three gulden, and his valuable watch, have been untouched. Robbery cannot, therefore, have been the incentive to the deed, unless the assassins were disturbed before they could complete their work.

'This idea is negatived by the fact that the body must have lain at least an hour before anyone discovered it! The whole affair is wrapped in mystery. Dr Langemann, the eminent medico-jurist, has pronounced that the wound is such as might have been inflicted by a heavy sword-bayonet wielded by a powerful arm. The police are extremely reticent upon the subject, and it is suspected that they are in possession of a clue which may lead to important results.'

Thus far the *Pesther Abendblatt*. The researches of the police failed, however, to throw the least glimmer of light upon the matter. There was absolutely no trace of the murderer, nor could any amount of ingenuity invent any reason which could have induced any one to commit the dreadful deed. The deceased Professor was a man so wrapped in his own studies and pursuits that he lived apart from the world, and had certainly never raised the slightest animosity in any human breast. It must have been some fiend, some savage, who loved blood for its own sake, who struck that merciless blow.

Though the officials were unable to come to any conclusions upon the matter, popular suspicion was not long in pitching upon a scapegoat. In the first published accounts of the murder the name of one Schiffer had been mentioned as having remained with the janitor after the Professor's departure. This man was a Jew, and Jews have never been popular in Hungary. A cry was at once raised for Schiffer's arrest; but as there was not the slightest grain of evidence against him, the authorities very properly refused to consent to so arbitrary a proceeding. Reinmaul, who was an old and most respected citizen, declared solemnly that Schiffer was with him until the startled cry of the soldier had caused them both to run out to the scene of the tragedy. No one ever dreamed of implicating Reinmaul in such a matter; but still it was rumoured that his ancient and well-known friendship for Schiffer might have induced him to tell a falsehood in order to screen him. Popular feeling ran very high upon the subject, and there seemed a danger of Schiffer's being mobbed in the street, when an incident occurred which threw a very different light upon the matter.

On the morning of the 12th of December, just nine days after the mysterious murder of the Professor, Schiffer, the Bohemian Jew, was found lying in the north-western corner of the Grand Platz stone dead, and so mutilated that he was hardly recognizable. His head was cloven open in very much the same way as that of Von Hopstein, and his body exhibited numerous deep gashes, as if the murderer had been so carried away and transported with fury that he had continued to hack the lifeless body. Snow had fallen heavily the day before, and was lying at least a foot deep all over the square; some had fallen during the night, too, as was evidenced by a thin layer lying like a winding-sheet over the murdered man. It was hoped at first that this circumstance might assist in giving a clue by enabling the footsteps of the assassin to be traced; but the crime had been committed, unfortunately, in a place much frequented during the day, and there were innumerable tracks in every direction. Besides, the newly-fallen snow had blurred the footsteps to such an extent that it would have been impossible to draw trustworthy evidence from them.

In this case there was exactly the same impenetrable mystery and absence of motive which had characterized the murder of Professor von Hopstein. In the dead man's pocket there was found a note-book containing a considerable sum in gold and several very valuable bills, but no attempt had been made to rifle him. Supposing that any one to whom he had lent money (and this was the first idea which occurred to the police) had taken this means of evading his debt, it was hardly conceivable that he would have left such a valuable spoil untouched. Schiffer lodged with a widow named Gruga, at 49 Marie Theresa Strasse, and the evidence of his landlady and her children showed that he had remained shut up in his room the whole of the preceding day in a state of deep dejection, caused by the suspicion which the populace had fastened upon him. She had heard him go out about eleven o'clock at night for his last and fatal walk, and as he had a latch-key she had gone to bed without waiting for him. His object in choosing such a late hour for a ramble obviously was that he did not consider himself safe if recognized in the streets.

The occurrence of this second murder so shortly after the first threw not only the town of Buda-Pesth, but the whole of Hungary, into a terrible state of excitement, and even of terror. Vague dangers seemed to hang over the head of every man. The only parallel to this intense feeling was to be found in our own country at the time of the Williams murders described by De Quincey. There were so many resemblances between the cases of Von Hopstein and of Schiffer that no one could doubt that there existed a connection between the two. The absence of object and of robbery, the utter want of any clue to the assassin, and, lastly, the ghastly nature of the wounds, evidently inflicted by the same or a similar weapon, all pointed in one direction. Things were in this state when the incidents which I am now about to relate occurred, and in order to make them intelligible I must lead up to them from a fresh point of departure.

Otto von Schlegel was a younger son of the old Silesian family of that name. His father had originally destined him for the army, but at the advice of his teachers, who saw the surprising talent of the youth, had sent him to the University of Buda-Pesth to be educated in medicine. Here young Schlegel carried everything before him, and promised to be one of the most brilliant graduates turned out for many a year. Though a hard reader, he was no bookworm, but an active, powerful young fellow, full of animal spirits and vivacity, and extremely popular among his fellow-students.

The New Year examinations were at hand, and Schlegel was working hard— so hard that even the strange murders in the town, and the general excitement in men's minds, failed to turn his thoughts from his studies. Upon Christmas Eve, when every house was illuminated, and the roar of drinking songs came from the Bierkeller in the Student-quartier, he refused the many invitations to roystering suppers which were showered upon him, and went off with his books under his arm to the rooms of Leopold Strauss, to work with him into the small hours of the morning.

Strauss and Schlegel were bosom friends. They were both Silesians, and had known each other from boyhood. Their affection had become proverbial in the University. Strauss was almost as distinguished a student as Schlegel, and there had been many a tough struggle for academic honours between the two fellow-countrymen, which had only served to strengthen their friendship by a bond of mutual respect. Schlegel admired the dogged pluck and never-failing good temper of his old playmate; while the latter considered Schlegel, with his many talents and brilliant versatility, the most accomplished of mortals.

The friends were still working together, the one reading from a volume on anatomy, the other holding a skull and marking off the various parts mentioned in the text, when the deep-toned bell of St Gregory's church struck the hour of midnight.

'Hark to that!' said Schlegel, snapping up the book and stretching out his long legs towards the cheery fire. 'Why, it's Christmas morning, old friend! May it not be the last that we spend together!'

'May we have passed all these confounded examinations before another one comes!' answered Strauss. 'But see here, Otto, one bottle of wine will not be amiss. I have laid one up on purpose;' and with a smile on his honest, South German face, he pulled out a long-necked bottle of Rhenish from amongst a pile of books and bones in the corner.

'It is a night to be comfortable indoors,' said Otto von Schlegel, looking out at the snowy landscape, 'for 'tis bleak and bitter enough outside. Good health, Leopold!'

'*Lebe hoch!*' replied his companion. 'It is a comfort indeed to forget sphenoid bones and ethmoid bones, if it be but for a moment. And what is the news of the corps, Otto? Has Graube fought the Swabian?'

'They fight tomorrow,' said Von Schlegel. 'I fear that our man will lose his beauty, for he is short in the arm. Yet activity and skill may do much for him. They say his hanging guard is perfection.'

'And what else is the news amongst the students?' asked Strauss.

'They talk, I believe, of nothing but the murders. But I have worked hard of late, as you know, and hear little of the gossip.'

'Have you had time,' inquired Strauss, 'to look over the books and the weapons which our dear old Professor was so concerned about the very day he met his death? They say they are well worth a visit.'

'I saw them today,' said Schlegel, lighting his pipe. 'Reinmaul, the janitor, showed me over the store-room, and I helped to label many of them from the original catalogue of Graf Schulling's museum. As far as we can see, there is but one article missing of all the collection.'

'One missing!' exclaimed Strauss. 'That would grieve old Von Hopstein's ghost. Is it anything of value?'

'It is described as an antique hatchet, with a head of steel and a handle of chased silver. We have applied to the railway company, and no doubt it will be found.'

'I trust so,' echoed Strauss; and the conversation drifted off into other channels. The fire was burning low and the bottle of Rhenish was empty before the two friends rose from their chairs, and Von Schlegel prepared to depart.

'Ugh! It's a bitter night!' he said, standing on the doorstep and folding his cloak round him. 'Why, Leopold, you have your cap on. You are not going out, are you?'

'Yes, I am coming with you,' said Strauss, shutting the door behind him. 'I feel heavy,' he continued, taking his friend's arm, and walking down the street with him. 'I think a walk as far as your lodgings, in the crisp, frosty air, is just the thing to set me right.'

The two students went down Stephen Strasse together and across Julien Platz, talking on a variety of topics. As they passed the corner of the Grand Platz, however, where Schiffer had been found dead, the conversation turned naturally upon the murder.

'That's where they found him,' remarked Von Schlegel, pointing to the fatal spot.

'Perhaps the murderer is near us now,' said Strauss. 'Let us hasten on.'

They both turned to go, when Von Schlegel gave a sudden cry of pain and stooped down.

'Something has cut through my boot!' he cried; and feeling about with his hand in the snow, he pulled out a small, glistening battle-axe, made, apparently entirely of metal. It had been lying with the blade turned slightly upwards, so as to cut the foot of the student when be trod upon it.

'The weapon of the murderer!' he ejaculated.

'The silver hatchet from the museum!' cried Strauss in the same breath.

There could be no doubt that it was both the one and the other. There could not be two such curious weapons, and the character of the wounds was just such as would be inflicted by a similar instrument. The murderer had evidently thrown it aside after committing the dreadful deed, and it had lain concealed in the snow some twenty metres from the spot ever since. It was extraordinary that of all the people who had passed and repassed none had discovered it; but the snow was deep, and it was a little off the beaten track.

'What are we to do with it?' said Von Schlegel, holding it in his hand. He shuddered as he noticed by the light of the moon that the head of it was all dabbled with dark brown stains.

'Take it to the Commissary of Police,' suggested Strauss.

'He'll be in bed now. Still, I think you are right. But it is nearly four o'clock. I will wait until morning, and take it round before breakfast. Meanwhile, I must carry it with me to my lodgings.'

'That is the best plan,' said his friend; and the two walked on together talking of the remarkable find which they had made. When they came to Schlegel's door, Strauss said goodbye, refusing an invitation to go in, and walked briskly down the street in the direction of his own lodgings.

Schlegel was stooping down putting the key into the lock, when a strange change came over him. He trembled violently, and dropped the key from his quivering fingers. His right hand closed convulsively round the handle of the silver hatchet, and his eye followed the retreating figure of his friend with a vindictive glare. In spite of the coldness of the night the perspiration streamed down his face. For a moment he seemed to struggle with himself, holding his hand up to his throat as if he were suffocating. Then, with crouching body and rapid, noiseless steps, he crept after his late companion.

Strauss was plodding sturdily along through the snow, humming snatches of a student song, and little dreaming of the dark figure which pursued him. At the Grand Platz it was forty yards behind him; at the Julien Platz it was but twenty; in Stephen Strasse it was ten, and gaining on him with panther-like rapidity. Already it was almost within arm's length of the unsuspecting man, and the hatchet glittered coldly in the moonlight, when some slight noise must have reached Strauss's ears, for he faced suddenly round upon his pursuer. He started and uttered an exclamation as his eye met the white, set face, with flashing eyes and clenched teeth, which seemed to be suspended in the air behind him.

'What, Otto!' he exclaimed, recognizing his friend. 'Art thou ill? You look pale. Come with me to my—— Ah! hold, you madman, hold! Drop that axe! Drop it, I say, or by heaven I'll choke you!'

Von Schlegel had thrown himself upon him with a wild cry and uplifted weapon; but the student was stout-hearted and resolute. He rushed inside the sweep of the hatchet and caught his assailant round the waist, narrowly escaping a blow which would have cloven his head. The two staggered for a moment in a deadly wrestle, Schlegel endeavouring to shorten his weapon; but Strauss with a desperate wrench managed to bring him to the ground, and they rolled together in the snow, Strauss clinging to the other's right arm and shouting frantically for assistance. It was as well that he did so, for Schlegel would certainly have succeeded in freeing his arm had it not been for the arrival of two stalwart gendarmes, attracted by the uproar. Even then the three of them found it difficult to overcome the maniacal strength of Schlegel, and they were utterly unable to wrench the silver hatchet from his grasp. One of the gendarmes, however, had a coil of rope round his waist, with which he rapidly secured the student's arms to his sides. In this way, half pushed, half dragged, he was conveyed, in spite of furious cries and frenzied struggles, to the central police station.

Strauss assisted in coercing his former friend, and accompanied the police to the station; protesting loudly at the same time against any unnecessary violence, and giving it as his opinion that a lunatic asylum would be a more fitting place for the prisoner. The events of the last half-hour had been so sudden and inexplicable that he felt quite dazed himself. What did it all mean? It was certain that his old friend from boyhood had attempted to murder him, and had nearly succeeded. Was Von Schlegel then the murderer of Professor von Hopstein and of the Bohemian Jew? Strauss felt that it was impossible, for the Jew was not even known to him, and the Professor had been his especial favourite. He followed mechanically to the police station, lost in grief and amazement.

Inspector Baumgarten, one of the most energetic and best known of the police officials, was on duty in the absence of the Commissary. He was a wiry, little, active man, quiet and retiring in his habits, but possessed of great sagacity and a vigilance which never relaxed. Now, though he had had a six hours' vigil, he sat as erect as ever, with his pen behind his ear, at his official desk, while his friend, Sub-inspector Winkel, snored in a chair at the side of the stove. Even the inspector's usually immovable features betrayed surprise, however, when the door was flung open and Von Schlegel was dragged in with pale face and disordered clothes, the silver hatchet still grasped firmly in his hand. Still more surprised was he when Strauss and the gendarmes gave their account, which was duly entered in the official register.

'Young man, young man,' said Inspector Baumgarten, laying down his pen and fixing his eyes sternly upon the prisoner, 'this is pretty work for Christmas morning; why have you done this thing?'

'God knows!' cried Von Schlegel, covering his face with his hands and dropping the hatchet. A change had come over him, his fury and excitement were gone, and he seemed utterly prostrated with grief.

'You have rendered yourself liable to a strong suspicion of having committed the other murders which have disgraced our city.'

'No, no, indeed!' said Von Schlegel, earnestly. 'God forbid!'

'At least you are guilty of attempting the life of Herr Leopold Strauss.'

'The dearest friend I have in the world,' groaned the student. 'Oh, how could I! How could I!'

'His being your friend makes your crime ten times more heinous,' said the inspector, severely. 'Remove him for the remainder of the night to the—— But steady! Who comes here?'

The door was pushed open, and a man came into the room, so haggard and care-worn that he looked more like a ghost than a human being. He tottered as he walked, and had to clutch at the backs of the chairs as he approached the inspector's desk. It was hard to recognize in this miserable-looking object the once cheerful and rubicund sub-curator of the museum and privat-docent of chemistry, Herr Wilhelm Schlessinger. The practised eye of Baumgarten, however, was not to be baffled by any change.

'Good morning, mein Herr,' he said. 'You are up early. No doubt the reason is that you have heard that one of your students, Von Schlegel, is arrested for attempting the life of Leopold Strauss?'

'No; I have come for myself,' said Schlessinger, speaking huskily, and putting his hand up to his throat. 'I have come to ease my soul of the weight of a great sin, though, God knows, an unmeditated one. It was I who—— But merciful heavens!—there it is—the horrid thing! Oh, that I had never seen it!'

He shrank back in a paroxysm of terror, glaring at the silver hatchet where it lay upon the floor, and pointing at it with his emaciated hand.

'There it lies!' he yelled. 'Look at it. It has come to condemn me. See that brown rust on it! Do you know what that is? That is the blood of my dearest, best friend, Professor von Hopstein. I saw it gush over the very handle as I drove the blade through his brain. *Mein Gott*, I see it now!'

'Sub-inspector Winkel,' said Baumgarten, endeavouring to preserve his official austerity, 'you will arrest this man, charged on his own confession with the murder of the late Professor. I also deliver into your hands Von Schlegel here, charged with a murderous assault upon Herr Strauss. You will also keep this hatchet'—here he picked it from the floor—'which has apparently been used for both crimes.'

Wilhelm Schlessinger had been leaning against the table, with a face of ashy paleness. As the Inspector ceased speaking, he looked up excitedly.

'What did you say?' he cried. 'Von Schlegel attack Strauss! The two dearest friends in the college! I slay my old master! It is magic, I say; it is a charm! There is a spell upon us! It is—ah, I have it! It is that hatchet—that thrice accursed hatchet!' and he pointed convulsively at the weapon which Inspector Baumgarten still held in his hand.

The inspector smiled contemptuously.

'Restrain yourself, mein Herr,' he said. 'You do but make your case worse by such wild excuses for the wicked deed you confess to. Magic and charms are not known in the legal vocabulary, as my friend Winkel will assure you.'

'I know not,' remarked his sub-inspector, shrugging his broad shoulders. 'There are many strange things in the world. Who knows but that——'

'What!' roared Inspector Baumgarten, furiously. 'You would undertake to contradict me! You would set up your opinion! You would be the champion of these accursed murderers! Fool, miserable fool, your hour has come!' and rushing at the astounded Winkel, he dealt a blow at him with the silver hatchet which would certainly have justified his last assertion had it not been that, in his fury, he overlooked the lowness of the rafters above his head. The blade of the hatchet struck one of these, and remained there quivering, while the handle was splintered into a thousand pieces.

'What have I done?' gasped Baumgarten, falling back into his chair. 'What have I done?'

'You have proved Herr Schlessinger's words to be correct,' said Von Schlegel, stepping forward, for the astonished policemen had let go their grasp of him. 'That is what you have done. Against reason, science, and everything else though it be, there is a charm at work. There must be! Strauss, old boy, you know I would not, in my right senses, hurt one hair of your head. And you Schlessinger, we both know you loved the old man who is dead. And you, Inspector Baumgarten, you would not willingly have struck your friend, the sub-inspector?'

'Not for the whole world,' groaned the inspector, covering his face with his hands.

'Then is it not clear? But now, thank heaven, the accursed thing is broken, and can never do harm again. But see, what is that?'

Right in the centre of the room was lying a thin brown cylinder of parchment. One glance at the fragments of the handle of the weapon showed that it had been hollow. This roll of paper had apparently been hidden away inside the metal case thus formed, having been introduced through a small hole, which had been afterwards soldered up. Von Schlegel opened the document. The writing upon it was almost illegible from age; but as far as they could make out it stood thus, in mediaeval German:

> Diese Waffe benutzte Max von Erlichingen um Joanna Bodeck zu ermorden, deshalb beschuldige Ich, Johann Bodeck, mittelst der macht welche mir als mitglied des Concils des rothen Kreuzes verliehan wurde, dieselbe mit dieser unthat. Mag sie anderen denselben schmerz verursachen

den sie mir verursacht hat. Mag Jede hand die sie ergreift mit dem blut
eines freundes geröthet sein.

> Immer übel—niemals gut,
> Geröthet mit des freundes blut.

Which may be roughly translated:

This weapon was used by Max von Erlichingen for the murder of Joanna
Bodeck. Therefore do I, Johann Bodeck, accurse it by the power which
has been bequeathed to me as one of the Council of the Rosy Cross. May
it deal to others the grief which it has dealt to me! May every hand that
grasps it be reddened in the blood of a friend!

> Ever evil, never good,
> Reddened with a loved one's blood.

There was a dead silence in the room when Von Schlegel had finished
spelling out this strange document. As he put it down Strauss laid his hand
affectionately upon his arm.

'No such proof is needed by me, old friend,' he said. 'At the very moment
that you struck at me I forgave you in my heart. I well know that if the poor
Professor were in the room he would say as much to Herr Wilhelm Schlessinger.'

'Gentlemen,' remarked the inspector, standing up and resuming his official
tones, 'this affair, strange as it is, must be treated according to rule and precedent.
Sub-inspector Winkel, as your superior officer, I command you to arrest me
upon a charge of murderously assaulting you. You will commit me to prison
for the night, together with Herr von Schlegel and Herr Wilhelm Schlessinger.
We shall take our trial at the coming sitting of the judges. In the meantime take
care of that piece of evidence'—pointing to the piece of parchment—'and,
while I am away, devote your time and energy to utilizing the clue you have
obtained in discovering who it was who slew Herr Schiffer, the Bohemian Jew.'

The one missing link in the chain of evidence was soon supplied. On the
28th of December the wife of Reinmaul the janitor, coming into the bedroom
after a short absence, found her husband hanging lifeless from a hook in the
wall. He had tied a long bolster-case round his neck and stood upon a chair in
order to commit the fatal deed. On the table was a note in which he confessed
to the murder of Schiffer the Jew, adding that the deceased had been his oldest
friend, and that he had slain him without premeditation in obedience to some
uncontrollable impulse. Remorse and grief, he said, had driven him to self-
destruction; and he wound up his confession by commending his soul to the
mercy of heaven.

The trial which ensued was one of the strangest which ever occurred in the
whole history of jurisprudence. It was in vain that the prosecuting counsel
urged the improbability of the explanation offered by the prisoners, and
deprecated the introduction of such an element as magic into a nineteenth
century law-court. The chain of facts was too strong, and the prisoners were

unanimously acquitted. 'This silver hatchet,' remarked the judge in his summing up, 'has hung untouched upon the wall in the mansion of the Graf von Schulling for nearly two hundred years. The shocking manner in which he met his death at the hands of his favourite house steward is still fresh in your recollection. It has come out in evidence that, a few days before the murder, the steward had overhauled the old weapons and cleaned them. In doing this he must have touched the handle of this hatchet. Immediately afterward he slew his master, whom he had served faithfully for twenty years. The weapon then came, in conformity with the Count's will, to Buda-Pesth, where, at the station, Herr Wilhelm Schlessinger grasped it, and, within two hours, used it against the person of the deceased Professor. The next man whom we find touching it is the janitor Reinmaul, who helped to remove the weapons from the cart to the store-room. At the first opportunity he buried it in the body of his friend Schiffer. We then have the attempted murder of Strauss by Schlegel, and of Winkel by Inspector Baumgarten, all immediately following the taking of the hatchet into the hand. Lastly, comes the providential discovery of the extraordinary document which has been read to you by the clerk of the court. I invite your most careful consideration, gentlemen of the jury, to this chain of facts, knowing that you will find a verdict according to your consciences without fear and without favour.'

Perhaps the most interesting piece of evidence to the English reader, though it found few supporters among the Hungarian audience, was that of Dr Langemann, the eminent medico-jurist, who has written text-books upon metallurgy and toxicology. He said: 'I am not so sure, gentlemen, that there is need to fall back upon necromancy or the black art for an explanation of what has occurred. What I say is merely a hypothesis, without proof of any sort, but in a case so extraordinary every suggestion may be of value. The Rosicrucians, to whom allusion is made in this paper, were the most profound chemists of the early Middle Ages, and included the principal alchemists whose names have descended to us. Much as chemistry has advanced, there are some points in which the ancients were ahead of us, and in none more so than in the manufacture of poisons of subtle and deadly action. This man Bodeck, as one of the elders of the Rosicrucians, possessed, no doubt, the recipe of many such mixtures, some of which, like the *aqua tofana* of the Medicis, would poison by penetrating through the pores of the skin. It is conceivable that the handle of this silver hatchet has been anointed by some preparation which is a diffusible poison, having the effect upon the human body of bringing on sudden and acute attacks of homicidal mania. In such attacks it is well known that the madman's rage is turned against those whom he loved best when sane. I have, as I remarked before, no proof to support me in my theory, and simply put it forward for what it is worth.'

With this extract from the speech of the learned and ingenious professor, we may close the account of this famous trial.

The broken pieces of the silver hatchet were thrown into a deep pond, a clever poodle being employed to carry them in his mouth, as no one would touch them for fear some of the infection might still hang about them. The piece of parchment was preserved in the museum of the University. As to Strauss and Schlegel, Winkel and Baumgarten, they continued the best of friends and are so still for all I know to the contrary.

Schlessinger became surgeon of a cavalry regiment, and was shot at the battle of Sadowa five years later, while rescuing the wounded under a heavy fire. By his last injunctions his little patrimony was to be sold to erect a marble obelisk over the grave of Professor von Hopstein.

Selecting A Ghost

The Ghosts of Goresthorpe Grange

I AM SURE THAT NATURE never intended me to be a self-made man. There are times when I can hardly bring myself to realise that twenty years of my life were spent behind the counter of a grocer's shop in the East End of London, and that it was through such an avenue that I reached a wealthy independence and the possession of Goresthorpe Grange. My habits are conservative, and my tastes refined and aristocratic. I have a soul which spurns the vulgar herd. Our family, the D'Odds, date back to a prehistoric era, as is to be inferred from the fact that their advent into British history is not commented on by any trustworthy historian. Some instinct tells me that the blood of a Crusader runs in my veins. Even now, after the lapse of so many years, such exclamations as 'By'r Lady!' rise naturally to my lips, and I feel that, should circumstances require it, I am capable of rising in my stirrups and dealing an infidel a blow—say with a mace—which would considerably astonish him.

Goresthorpe Grange is a feudal mansion—or so it was termed in the advertisement which originally brought it under my notice. Its right to this adjective had a most remarkable effect upon its price, and the advantages gained may possibly be more sentimental than real. Still, it is soothing to me to know that I have slits in my staircase through which I can discharge arrows; and there is a sense of power in the fact of possessing a complicated apparatus by means of which I am enabled to pour molten lead upon the head of the casual visitor. These things chime in with my peculiar humour, and I do not grudge to pay for them. I am proud of my battlements and of the circular uncovered sewer which girds me round. I am proud of my portcullis and donjon and keep. There is but one thing wanting to round off the mediaevalism of my abode, and to render it symmetrically and completely antique. Goresthorpe Grange is not provided with a ghost.

Any man with old-fashioned tastes and ideas as to how such establishments should be conducted, would have been disappointed at the omission. In my case it was particularly unfortunate. From my childhood I had been an earnest student of the supernatural, and a firm believer in it. I have revelled in ghostly literature until there is hardly a tale bearing upon the subject which I have not perused. I learned the German language for the sole purpose of mastering a book upon demonology. When an infant I had secreted myself in dark rooms in the hope of seeing some of those bogies with which my nurse used to threaten me; and the same feeling is as strong in me now as then. It was a proud moment when I felt that a ghost was one of the luxuries which money might command.

It is true that there was no mention of an apparition in the advertisement. On reviewing the mildewed walls, however, and the shadowy corridors, I had taken it for granted that there was such a thing on the premises. As the presence of a kennel presupposes that of a dog, so I imagined that it was impossible that such desirable quarters should be untenanted by one or more restless shades. Good heavens, what can the noble family from whom I purchased it have been doing during these hundreds of years! Was there no member of it spirited enough to make away with his sweetheart, or take some other steps calculated to establish a hereditary spectre? Even now I can hardly write with patience upon the subject.

For a long time I hoped against hope. Never did rat squeak behind the wainscot, or rain drip upon the attic floor, without a wild thrill shooting through me as I thought that at last I had come upon traces of some unquiet soul. I felt no touch of fear upon these occasions. If it occurred in the night-time, I would send Mrs D'Odd—who is a strong-minded woman—to investigate the matter, while I covered up my head with the bedclothes and indulged in an ecstasy of expectation. Alas, the result was always the same! The suspicious sound would be traced to some cause so absurdly natural and commonplace that the most fervid imagination could not clothe it with any of the glamour of romance.

I might have reconciled myself to this state of things, had it not been for Jorrocks of Havistock Farm. Jorrocks is a coarse, burly, matter-of-fact fellow, whom I only happened to know through the accidental circumstance of his fields adjoining my demesne. Yet this man, though utterly devoid of all appreciation of archaeological unities, is in possession of a well-authenticated and undeniable spectre. Its existence only dates back, I believe, to the reign of the Second George, when a young lady cut her throat upon hearing of the death of her lover at the battle of Dettingen. Still, even that gives the house an air of respectability, especially when coupled with blood stains upon the floor. Jorrocks is densely unconscious of his good fortune; and his language when he reverts to the apparition is painful to listen to. He little dreams how I covet every one of those moans and nocturnal wails which he describes with unnecessary objurgation. Things are indeed coming to a pretty pass when democratic spectres are allowed to desert the landed proprietors and annul every social distinction by taking refuge in the houses of the great unrecognised.

I have a large amount of perseverance. Nothing else could have raised me into my rightful sphere, considering the uncongenial atmosphere in which I spent the earlier part of my life. I felt now that a ghost must be secured, but how to set about securing one was more than either Mrs D'Odd or myself was able to determine. My reading taught me that such phenomena are usually the outcome of crime. What crime was to be done, then, and who was to do it? A wild idea entered my mind that Watkins, the house-steward, might be prevailed upon—for a consideration—to immolate himself or someone else in the interests of the establishment. I put the matter to him in a half-jesting manner; but it did not seem to strike him in a favourable light. The other servants sympathised with him in his opinion—at least, I cannot account in any other way for their having left the house in a body the same afternoon.

'My dear,' Mrs D'Odd remarked to me one day after dinner, as I sat moodily sipping a cup of sack—I love the good old names—'my dear, that odious ghost of Jorrocks' has been gibbering again.'

'Let it gibber!' I answered, recklessly.

Mrs D'Odd struck a few chords on her virginal and looked thoughtfully into the fire.

'I'll tell you what it is, Argentine,' she said at last, using the pet name which we usually substituted for Silas, 'we must have a ghost sent down from London.'

'How can you be so idiotic, Matilda?' I remarked, severely. 'Who could get us such a thing?'

'My cousin, Jack Brocket, could,' she answered, confidently.

Now, this cousin of Matilda's was rather a sore subject between us. He was a rakish, clever young fellow, who had tried his hand at many things, but wanted perseverance to succeed at any. He was, at that time, in chambers in London, professing to be a general agent, and really living, to a great extent, upon his wits. Matilda managed so that most of our business should pass through his hands, which certainly saved me a great deal of trouble; but I found that Jack's commission was generally considerably larger than all the other items of the bill put together. It was this fact which made me feel inclined to rebel against any further negotiations with the young gentleman.

'O yes, he could,' insisted Mrs D., seeing the look of disapprobation upon my face. 'You remember how well he managed that business about the crest?'

'It was only a resuscitation of the old family coat-of-arms, my dear,' I protested.

Matilda smiled in an irritating manner. 'There was a resuscitation of the family portraits, too, dear,' she remarked. 'You must allow that Jack selected them very judiciously.'

I thought of the long line of faces which adorned the walls of my banqueting-hall, from the burly Norman robber, through every gradation of casque, plume, and ruff, to the sombre Chesterfieldian individual who appears to have staggered against a pillar in his agony at the return of a maiden MS which he grips convulsively in his right hand. I was fain to confess that in that instance he had done his work well, and that it was only fair to give him an order—with the usual commission—for a family spectre, should such a thing be attainable.

It is one of my maxims to act promptly when once my mind is made up. Noon of the next day found me ascending the spiral stone staircase which leads to Mr Brocket's chambers, and admiring the succession of arrows and fingers upon the whitewashed wall, all indicating the direction of that gentleman's sanctum. As it happened, artificial aids of the sort were entirely unnecessary, as an animated flap-dance overhead could proceed from no other quarter, though it was replaced by a deathly silence as I groped my way up the stair. The door was opened by a youth evidently astounded at the appearance of a client, and I was ushered into the presence of my young friend, who was writing furiously in a large ledger—upside down, as I afterwards discovered.

After the first greetings, I plunged into business at once.

'Look here, Jack,' I said, 'I want you to get me a spirit, if you can.'

'Spirits you mean!' shouted my wife's cousin, plunging his hand into the waste-paper basket and producing a bottle with the celerity of a conjuring trick. 'Let's have a drink!'

I held up my hand as a mute appeal against such a proceeding so early in the day; but on lowering it again I found that I had almost involuntarily closed my fingers round the tumbler which my adviser had pressed upon me. I drank the contents hastily off, lest anyone should come in upon us and set me down as a toper. After all there was something very amusing about the young fellow's eccentricities.

'Not spirits,' I explained, smilingly; 'an apparition—a ghost. If such a thing is to be had, I should be very willing to negotiate.'

'A ghost for Goresthorpe Grange?' inquired Mr Brocket, with as much coolness as if I had asked for a drawing-room suite.

'Quite so,' I answered.

'Easiest thing in the world,' said my companion, filling up my glass again in spite of my remonstrance. 'Let us see!' Here he took down a large red note-book, with all the letters of the alphabet in a fringe down the edge. 'A ghost you said, didn't you? That's G. G—gems—gimlets—gas-pipes—gauntlets—guns—galleys. Ah, here we are. Ghosts. Volume nine, section six, page forty-one. Excuse me!' And Jack ran up a ladder and began rummaging among a pile of ledgers on a high shelf. I felt half inclined to empty my glass into the spittoon when his back was turned; but on second thoughts I disposed of it in a legitimate way.

'Here it is!' cried my London agent, jumping off the ladder with a crash, and depositing an enormous volume of manuscript upon the table. 'I have all these things tabulated, so that I may lay my hands upon them in a moment. It's all right—it's quite weak' (here he filled our glasses again). 'What were we looking up, again?'

'Ghosts,' I suggested.

'Of course; page 41. Here we are. "J. H. Fowler & Son, Dunkel Street, suppliers of mediums to the nobility and gentry; charms sold—love philtres—mummies—horoscopes cast." Nothing in your line there, I suppose.'

I shook my head despondently.

'"Frederick Tabb,"' continued my wife's cousin, '"sole channel of communication between the living and the dead. Proprietor of the spirits of Byron, Kirke White, Grimaldi, Tom Cribb, and Inigo Jones." That's about the figure!'

'Nothing romantic enough there,' I objected. 'Good heavens! Fancy a ghost with a black eye and a handkerchief tied round its waist, or turning summersaults, and saying, "How are you tomorrow?"' The very idea made me so warm that I emptied my glass and filled it again.

'Here is another,' said my companion, '"Christopher McCarthy; bi-weekly séances—attended by all the eminent spirits of ancient and modern times. Nativities charms—abracadabras, messages from the dead." He might be able to help us. However, I shall have a hunt round myself tomorrow, and see some of these fellows. I know their haunts, and it's odd if I can't pick up something cheap. So there's an end of business,' he concluded, hurling the ledger into the corner, 'and now we'll have something to drink.'

We had several things to drink—so many that my inventive faculties were dulled next morning, and I had some little difficulty in explaining to Mrs D'Odd why it was that I hung my boots and spectacles upon a peg along with my other garments before retiring to rest. The new hopes excited by the confident manner in which my agent had undertaken the commission, caused me to rise superior to alcoholic reaction, and I paced about the rambling corridors and old-fashioned rooms, picturing to myself the appearance of my expected acquisition, and deciding what part of the building would harmonise best with its presence. After much consideration, I pitched upon the banqueting-hall as being, on the whole, most suitable for its reception. It was a long low room, hung round with valuable tapestry and interesting relics of the old family to whom it had belonged. Coats of mail and implements of war glimmered fitfully as the light of the fire played over them, and the wind crept under the door, moving the hangings to and fro with a ghastly rustling. At one end there was the raised dais, on which in ancient times the host and his guests used to spread their table, while a descent of a couple of steps led to the lower part of the hall, where the vassals and retainers held wassail. The floor was uncovered by any sort of carpet, but a layer of rushes had been scattered over it by my direction. In the whole room there was nothing to remind one of the nineteenth century; except, indeed, my own solid silver plate, stamped with the resuscitated family arms, which was laid out upon an oak table in the centre. This, I determined, should be the haunted room, supposing my wife's cousin to succeed in his negotiation with the spirit-mongers. There was nothing for it now but to wait patiently until I heard some news of the result of his inquiries.

A letter came in the course of a few days, which, if it was short, was at least encouraging. It was scribbled in pencil on the back of a playbill, and sealed apparently with a tobacco-stopper. 'Am on the track,' it said. 'Nothing of the sort to be had from any professional spiritualist, but picked up a fellow in a pub yesterday who says he can manage it for you. Will send him down unless you wire to the contrary. Abrahams is his name, and he has done one or two of these jobs before.' The letter wound up with some incoherent allusions to a cheque, and was signed by my affectionate cousin, John Brocket.

I need hardly say that I did not wire, but awaited the arrival of Mr Abrahams with all impatience. In spite of my belief in the supernatural, I could scarcely credit the fact that any mortal could have such a command over the spirit-world as to deal in them and barter them against mere earthly gold. Still, I had Jack's word for it that such a trade existed; and here was a gentleman with a Judaical name ready to demonstrate it by proof positive. How vulgar and commonplace Jorrocks' eighteenth century ghost would appear should I succeed in securing a real mediaeval apparition! I almost thought that one had been sent down in advance, for, as I walked round the moat that night before retiring to rest, I came upon a dark figure engaged in surveying the machinery of my portcullis and drawbridge. His start of surprise, however, and the manner in which he hurried off into the darkness, speedily convinced me of his earthly origin, and I put him down as some admirer of one of my female retainers mourning over the muddy Hellespont which divided him from his love. Whoever he may have been, he disappeared and did not return, though I loitered about for some time in the hope of catching a glimpse of him and exercising my feudal rights upon his person.

Jack Brocket was as good as his word. The shades of another evening were beginning to darken round Goresthorpe Grange, when a peal at the outer bell, and the sound of a fly pulling up, announced the arrival of Mr Abrahams. I hurried down to meet him, half expecting to see a choice assortment of ghosts crowding in at his rear. Instead, however, of being the sallow-faced, melancholy-eyed man that I had pictured to myself, the ghost-dealer was a sturdy little podgy fellow, with a pair of wonderfully keen sparkling eyes and a mouth which was constantly stretched in a good-humoured, if somewhat artificial, grin. His sole stock-in-trade seemed to consist of a small leather bag jealously locked and strapped, which emitted a metallic chink upon being placed on the stone flags in the hall.

'And 'ow are you, sir?' he asked, wringing my hand with the utmost effusion. 'And the missus, 'ow is she? And all the others—'ow's all their 'ealth?'

I intimated that we were all as well as could reasonably be expected, but Mr Abrahams happened to catch a glimpse of Mrs D'Odd in the distance, and at once plunged at her with another string of inquiries as to her health, delivered so volubly and with such an intense earnestness, that I half expected to see him terminate his cross-examination by feeling her pulse and demanding a sight of her tongue. All this time his little eyes rolled round and round, shifting perpetually from the floor to the ceiling, and from the ceiling to the walls, taking in apparently every article of furniture in a single comprehensive glance.

Having satisfied himself that neither of us was in a pathological condition, Mr Abrahams suffered me to lead him upstairs, where a repast had been laid out for him to which he did ample justice. The mysterious little bag he carried along with him, and deposited it under his chair during the meal. It was not until the table had been cleared and we were left together that he broached the matter on which he had come down.

'I hunderstand,' he remarked, puffing at a trichinopoly, 'that you want my 'elp in fitting up this 'ere 'ouse with a happarition.'

I acknowledged the correctness of his surmise, while mentally wondering at those restless eyes of his, which still danced about the room as if he were making an inventory of the contents.

'And you won't find a better man for the job, though I says it as shouldn't,' continued my companion. 'Wot did I say to the young gent wot spoke to me in the bar of The Lame Dog? "Can you do it?" says 'e. "Try me," says I, "me and my bag. Just try me." I couldn't say fairer than that.'

My respect for Jack Brocket's business capacities began to go up very considerably. He certainly seemed to have managed the matter wonderfully well. 'You don't mean to say that you carry ghosts about in bags?' I remarked, with diffidence.

Mr Abrahams smiled a smile of superior knowledge. 'You wait,' he said; 'give me the right place and the right hour, with a little of the essence of Lucoptolycus'—here he produced a small bottle from his waistcoat pocket—'and you won't find no ghost that I ain't up to. You'll see them yourself, and pick your own, and I can't say fairer than that.'

As all Mr Abrahams' protestations of fairness were accompanied by a cunning leer and a wink from one or other of his wicked little eyes, the impression of candour was somewhat weakened.

'When are you going to do it?' I asked, reverentially.

'Ten minutes to one in the morning,' said Mr Abrahams, with decision. 'Some says midnight, but I says ten to one, when there ain't such a crowd, and you can pick your own ghost. And now,' he continued, rising to his feet, 'suppose you trot me round the premises, and let me see where you wants it; for there's some places as attracts 'em, and some as they won't 'ear of—not if there was no other place in the world.'

Mr Abrahams inspected our corridors and chambers with a most critical and observant eye, fingering the old tapestry with the air of a connoisseur, and remarking in an undertone that it would 'match uncommon nice'. It was not until he reached the banqueting-hall, however, which I had myself picked out, that his admiration reached the pitch of enthusiasm. ''Ere's the place!' he shouted, dancing, bag in hand, round the table on which my plate was lying, and looking not unlike some quaint little goblin himself. ''Ere's the place; we won't get nothin' to beat this! A fine room—noble solid, none, of your electro-plate trash! That's the way as things ought to be done, sir. Plenty of room for 'em to glide 'ere. Send up some brandy and the box of weeds; I'll sit 'ere by the fire and do the preliminaries, which is more trouble than you'd think; for them ghosts carries on hawful at times, before they finds out who they've got to deal with. If you was in the room they'd tear you to pieces as like as not. You leave me alone to tackle them, and at 'alf-past twelve come in, and I lay they'll be quiet enough by then.'

Mr Abrahams' request struck me as a reasonable one, so I left him with his feet upon the mantelpiece, and his chair in front of the fire, fortifying himself with stimulants against his refractory visitors. From the room beneath, in which I sat with Mrs D'Odd, I could hear that, after sitting for some time, he rose up and paced about the hall with quick impatient steps. We then heard him try the lock of the door, and afterward drag some heavy article of furniture in the direction of the window, on which, apparently, he mounted, for I heard the creaking of the rusty hinges as the diamond-paned casement folded backwards, and I knew it to be situated several feet above the little man's reach. Mrs D'Odd says that she could distinguish his voice speaking in low and rapid whispers after this, but that may have been her imagination. I confess that I began to feel more impressed than I had deemed it possible to be. There was something awesome in the thought of the solitary mortal standing by the open window and summoning in from the gloom outside the spirits of the nether world. It was with a trepidation which I could hardly disguise from Matilda that I observed that the clock was pointing to half-past twelve, and that the time had come for me to share the vigil of my visitor.

He was sitting in his old position when I entered, and there were no signs of the mysterious movements which I had overheard, though his chubby face was flushed as with recent exertion.

'Are you succeeding all right?' I asked as I came in, putting on as careless an air as possible, but glancing involuntarily round the room to see if we were alone.

'Only your help is needed to complete the matter,' said Mr Abrahams, in a solemn voice. 'You shall sit by me and partake of the essence of Lucoptolycus, which removes the scales from our earthly eyes. Whatever you may chance to see, speak not and make no movement, lest you break the spell.' His manner was subdued, and his usual cockney vulgarity had entirely disappeared. I took the chair which he indicated, and awaited the result.

My companion cleared the rushes from the floor in our neighbourhood, and, going down upon his hands and knees, described a half-circle with chalk, which enclosed the fireplace and ourselves. Round the edge of this half-circle he drew several hieroglyphics, not unlike the signs of the zodiac. He then stood up and uttered a long invocation, delivered so rapidly that it sounded like a single gigantic word in some uncouth guttural language. Having finished this prayer, if prayer it was, he pulled out the small bottle which he had produced before, and poured a couple of teaspoonfuls of clear transparent fluid into a phial, which he handed to me with an intimation that I should drink it.

The liquid had a faintly sweet odour, not unlike the aroma of certain sorts of apples. I hesitated a moment before applying it to my lips, but an impatient gesture from my companion overcame my scruples, and I tossed it off. The taste was not unpleasant; and, as it gave rise to no immediate effects, I leaned back in my chair and composed myself for what was to come. Mr Abrahams seated himself beside me, and I felt that he was watching my face from time to time, while repeating some more of the invocations in which he had indulged before.

A sense of delicious warmth and languor began gradually to steal over me, partly, perhaps, from the heat of the fire, and partly from some unexplained cause. An uncontrollable impulse to sleep weighed down my eyelids, while at the same time my brain worked actively, and a hundred beautiful and pleasing ideas flitted through it. So utterly lethargic did I feel that, though I was aware that my companion put his hand over the region of my heart, as if to feel how it were beating, I did not attempt to prevent him, nor did I even ask him for the reason of his action. Everything in the room appeared to be reeling slowly round in a drowsy dance, of which I was the centre. The great elk's head at the far end wagged solemnly backwards and forwards, while the massive salvers on the tables performed cotillions with the claret-cooler and the epergne. My head fell upon my breast from sheer heaviness, and I should have become unconscious had I not been recalled to myself by the opening of the door at the other end of the hall.

This door led on to the raised dais, which, as I have mentioned, the heads of the house used to reserve for their own use. As it swung slowly back upon its hinges, I sat up in my chair, clutching at the arms, and staring with a horrified glare at the dark passage outside. Something was coming down it—something unformed and intangible, but still a *something*. Dim and shadowy, I saw it flit across the threshold, while a blast of ice-cold air swept down the room, which seemed to blow through me, chilling my very heart. I was aware of the mysterious presence, and then I heard it speak in a voice like the sighing of an east wind among pine-trees on the banks of a desolate sea.

It said: 'I am the invisible nonentity. I have affinities and am subtle. I am electric, magnetic, and spiritualistic. I am the great ethereal sigh-heaver. I kill dogs. Mortal, wilt thou choose me?'

I was about to speak, but the words seemed to be choked in my throat; and, before I could get them out, the shadow flitted across the hall and vanished in the darkness at the other side, while a long-drawn melancholy sigh quivered through the apartment.

I turned my eyes towards the door once more, and beheld, to my astonishment, a very small old woman, who hobbled along the corridor and into the hall. She passed backwards and forwards several times, and then, crouching down at the very edge of the circle upon the floor, she disclosed a face the horrible malignity of which shall never be banished from my recollection. Every foul passion appeared to have left its mark upon that hideous countenance.

'Ha! ha!' she screamed, holding out her wizened hands like the talons of an unclean bird. 'You see what I am. I am the fiendish old woman. I wear snuff-coloured silks. My curse descends on people. Sir Walter was partial to me. Shall I be thine, mortal?'

I endeavoured to shake my head in horror; on which she aimed a blow at me with her crutch, and vanished with an eldritch scream.

By this time my eyes turned naturally towards the open door, and I was hardly surprised to see a man walk in of tall and noble stature. His face was deadly pale, but was surmounted by a fringe of dark hair which fell in ringlets down his back. A short pointed beard covered his chin. He was dressed in loose-fitting clothes, made apparently of yellow satin, and a large white ruff surrounded his neck. He paced across the room with slow and majestic strides. Then turning, he addressed me in a sweet, exquisitely modulated voice.

'I am the cavalier,' he remarked. 'I pierce and am pierced. Here is my rapier. I clink steel. This is a blood stain over my heart. I can emit hollow groans. I am patronized by many old Conservative families. I am the original manor-house apparition. I work alone, or in company with shrieking damsels.'

He bent his head courteously, as though awaiting my reply, but the same choking sensation prevented me from speaking; and, with a deep bow, he disappeared.

He had hardly gone before a feeling of intense horror stole over me, and I was aware of the presence of a ghastly creature in the room, of dim outlines and uncertain proportions. One moment it seemed to pervade the entire apartment, while at another it would become invisible, but always leaving behind it a distinct consciousness of its presence. Its voice, when it spoke, was quavering and gusty. It said: 'I am the leaver of footsteps and the spiller of gouts of blood. I tramp upon corridors. Charles Dickens has alluded to me. I make strange and disagreeable noises. I snatch letters and place invisible hands on people's wrists. I am cheerful. I burst into peals of hideous laughter. Shall I do one now?' I raised my hand in a deprecating way, but too late to prevent one discordant outbreak which echoed through the room. Before I could lower it the apparition was gone.

I turned my head towards the door in time to see a man come hastily and stealthily into the chamber. He was a sunburnt powerfully built fellow, with earrings in his ears and a Barcelona handkerchief tied loosely round his neck. His head was bent upon his chest, and his whole aspect was that of one afflicted by intolerable remorse. He paced rapidly backwards and forwards like a caged tiger, and I observed that a drawn knife glittered in one of his hands, while he grasped what appeared to be a piece of parchment in the other. His voice, when he spoke, was deep and sonorous. He said, 'I am a murderer. I am a ruffian. I crouch when I walk. I step noiselessly. I know something of the Spanish Main. I can do the lost treasure business. I have charts. Am able-bodied and a good walker. Capable of haunting a large park.' He looked towards me beseechingly, but before I could make a sign I was paralyzed by the horrible sight which appeared at the door.

It was a very tall man, if, indeed, it might be called a man, for the gaunt bones were protruding through the corroding flesh, and the features were of a leaden hue. A winding-sheet was wrapped round the figure, and formed a hood over the head, from under the shadow of which two fiendish eyes, deep set in their grisly sockets, blazed and sparkled like red-hot coals. The lower jaw had fallen upon the breast, disclosing a withered, shrivelled tongue and two lines of black and jagged fangs. I shuddered and drew back as this fearful apparition advanced to the edge of the circle.

'I am the American blood-curdler,' it said, in a voice which seemed to come in a hollow murmur from the earth beneath it. 'None other is genuine. I am the embodiment of Edgar Allan Poe. I am circumstantial and horrible. I am a low-caste spirit-subduing spectre. Observe my blood and my bones. I am grisly and nauseous. No depending on artificial aid. Work with grave-clothes, a coffin-lid, and a galvanic battery. Turn hair white in a night.' The creature stretched out its fleshless arms to me as if in entreaty, but I shook my head; and it vanished, leaving a low, sickening, repulsive odour behind it. I sank back in my chair, so overcome by terror and disgust that I would have very willingly resigned myself to dispensing with a ghost altogether, could I have been sure that this was the last of the hideous procession.

A faint sound of trailing garments warned me that it was not so. I looked up, and beheld a white figure emerging from the corridor into the light. As it stepped across the threshold I saw that it was that of a young and beautiful woman dressed in the fashion of a bygone day. Her hands were clasped in front of her, and her pale proud face bore traces of passion and of suffering. She crossed the hall with a gentle sound, like the rustling of autumn leaves, and then, turning her lovely and unutterably sad eyes upon me, she said, 'I am the plaintive and sentimental, the beautiful and ill-used. I have been forsaken and betrayed. I shriek in the night-time and glide down passages. My antecedents are highly respectable and generally aristocratic. My tastes are aesthetic. Old oak furniture like this would do, with a few more coats of mail and plenty of tapestry. Will you not take me?'

Her voice died away in a beautiful cadence as she concluded, and she held out her hands as if in supplication. I am always sensitive to female influences. Besides, what would Jorrocks's ghost be to this? Could anything be in better taste? Would I not be exposing myself to the chance of injuring my nervous system by interviews with such creatures as my last visitor, unless I decided at once? She gave me a seraphic smile, as if she knew what was passing in my mind. That smile settled the matter. 'She will do!' I cried; 'I choose this one'; and as, in my enthusiasm, I took a step towards her I passed over the magic circle which had girdled me round.

'Argentine, we have been robbed!'

I had an indistinct consciousness of these words being spoken, or rather screamed, in my ear a great number of times without my being able to grasp their meaning. A violent throbbing in my head seemed to adapt itself to their rhythm, and I closed my eyes to the lullaby of 'Robbed, robbed, robbed.' A vigorous shake caused me to open them again, however, and the sight of Mrs D'Odd in the scantiest of costumes and most furious of tempers was sufficiently impressive to recall all my scattered thoughts, and make me realise that I was lying on my back on the floor, with my head among the ashes which had fallen from last night's fire, and a small glass phial in my hand.

I staggered to my feet, but felt so weak and giddy that I was compelled to fall back into a chair. As my brain became clearer, stimulated by the exclamations of Matilda, I began gradually to recollect the events of the night. There was the door through which my supernatural visitors had filed. There was the circle of chalk with the hieroglyphics round the edge. There was the cigar-box and brandy-bottle which had been honoured by the attentions of Mr Abrahams. But the seer himself—where was he? and what was this open window with a rope running out of it? And where, O where, was the pride of Goresthorpe Grange, the glorious plate which was to have been the delectation of generations of D'Odds? And why was Mrs D. standing in the grey light of dawn, wringing her hands and repeating her monotonous refrain? It was only very gradually that my misty brain took these things in, and grasped the connection between them.

Reader, I have never seen Mr Abrahams since; I have never seen the plate stamped with the resuscitated family crest; hardest of all, I have never caught a glimpse of the melancholy spectre with the trailing garments, nor do I expect that I ever shall. In fact my night's experiences have cured me of my mania for the supernatural, and quite reconciled me to inhabiting the humdrum nineteenth century edifice on the outskirts of London which Mrs D. has long had in her mind's eye.

As to the explanation of all that occurred—that is a matter which is open to several surmises. That Mr Abrahams, the ghost-hunter, was identical with Jemmy Wilson, *alias* the Nottingham crackster, is considered more than probable at Scotland Yard, and certainly the description of that remarkable burglar tallied very well with the appearance of my visitor. The small bag which I have described was picked up in a neighbouring field next day, and found to contain a choice assortment of jemmies and centre bits. Footmarks deeply imprinted in the mud on either side of the moat showed that an accomplice from below had received the sack of precious metals which had been let down through the open window. No doubt the pair of scoundrels, while looking round for a job, had overheard Jack Brocket's indiscreet inquiries, and promptly availed themselves of the tempting opening.

And now as to my less-substantial visitors, and the curious grotesque vision which I had enjoyed—am I to lay it down to any real power over occult matters possessed by my Nottingham friend? For a long time I was doubtful upon the point, and eventually endeavoured to solve it by consulting a well-known analyst and medical man, sending him the few drops of the so-called essence of Lucoptolycus which remained in my phial. I append the letter which I received from him, only too happy to have the opportunity of winding up my little narrative by the weighty words of a man of learning:

ARUNDEL STREET.

DEAR SIR: Your very singular case has interested me extremely. The bottle which you sent contained a strong solution of chloral, and the quantity which you describe yourself as having swallowed must have amounted to at least eighty grains of the pure hydrate. This would of course have reduced you to a partial state of insensibility, gradually going on to complete coma. In this semi-unconscious state of chloralism it is not unusual for circumstantial and *bizarre* visions to present themselves—more especially to individuals unaccustomed to the use of the drug. You tell me in your note that your mind was saturated with ghostly literature, and that you had long taken a morbid interest in classifying and recalling the various forms in which apparitions have been said to appear. You must also remember that you were expecting to see something of that very nature, and that your nervous system was worked up to an unnatural state of tension. Under the circumstances, I think that, far from the sequel being an astonishing one, it would have been very surprising indeed to any one versed in narcotics had you not experienced some such effects.—I remain, dear sir, sincerely yours,

T. E. STUBE, M.D.

Argentine D'Odd, Esq.
The Elms, Brixton.

J. Habakuk Jephson's Statement

IN THE MONTH OF DECEMBER IN THE YEAR 1873, the British ship *Dei Gratia* steered into Gibraltar, having in tow the derelict brigantine *Marie Celeste*, which had been picked up in latitude 38° 40′, longitude 17° 15′ W. There were several circumstances in connection with the condition and appearance of this abandoned vessel which excited considerable comment at the time, and aroused a curiosity which has never been satisfied. What these circumstances were was summed up in an able article which appeared in the *Gibraltar Gazette*. The curious can find it in the issue for January 4, 1874, unless my memory deceives me. For the benefit of those, however, who may be unable to refer to the paper in question, I shall subjoin a few extracts which touch upon the leading features of the case.

'We have ourselves,' says the anonymous writer in the *Gazette*, 'been over the derelict *Marie Celeste*, and have closely questioned the officers of the *Dei Gratia* on every point which might throw light on the affair. They are of opinion that she had been abandoned several days, or perhaps weeks, before being picked up. The official log, which was found in the cabin, states that the vessel sailed from Boston to Lisbon, starting upon October 16. It is, however, most imperfectly kept, and affords little information. There is no reference to rough weather, and, indeed, the state of the vessel's paint and rigging excludes the idea that she was abandoned for any such reason. She is perfectly watertight. No signs of a struggle or of violence are to be detected, and there is absolutely nothing to account for the disappearance of the crew. There are several indications that a lady was present on board, a sewing-machine being found in the cabin and some articles of female attire. These probably belonged to the captain's wife, who is mentioned in the log as having accompanied her husband. As an instance of the mildness of the weather, it may be remarked that a bobbin of silk was found standing, upon the sewing-machine, though the least roll of the vessel would have precipitated it to the floor. The boats were intact and slung upon the davits; and the cargo, consisting of tallow and American clocks, was untouched. An old-fashioned sword of curious workmanship was discovered among some lumber in the forecastle, and this weapon is said to exhibit a longitudinal striation on the steel, as if it had been recently wiped. It has been placed in the hands of the police, and submitted to Dr Monaghan, the analyst, for inspection. The result of his examination has not yet been published. We may remark, in conclusion, that Captain Dalton, of the *Dei Gratia*, an able and intelligent seaman, is of opinion that the *Marie Celeste* may have been abandoned a considerable distance from the spot at which she was picked up, since a powerful current runs up in that latitude from the African coast. He confesses his inability, however, to advance any hypothesis which can reconcile all the facts of the case. In the utter absence of a clue or grain of evidence, it is to be feared that the fate of the crew of the *Marie Celeste* will be added to those numerous mysteries of the deep which will never be solved until the great day when the sea shall give up its dead. If crime has been committed, as is much to be suspected, there is little hope of bringing the perpetrators to justice.'

I shall supplement this extract from the *Gibraltar Gazette* by quoting a telegram from Boston, which went the round of the English papers, and represented the total amount of information which had been collected about the *Marie Celeste*. 'She was,' it said, 'a brigantine of 170 tons burden, and belonged to White, Russell & White, wine importers, of this city. Captain J. W. Tibbs was an old servant of the firm, and was a man of known ability and tried probity. He was accompanied by his wife, aged thirty-one, and their youngest child, five years old. The crew consisted of seven hands, including two coloured seamen, and a boy. There were three passengers, one of whom was the well-known Brooklyn specialist on consumption, Dr Habakuk Jephson, who was a distinguished advocate for Abolition in the early days of the movement, and whose pamphlet, entitled "Where is thy Brother?" exercised a strong influence on public opinion before the war. The other passengers were Mr J. Harton, a writer in the employ of the firm, and Mr Septimius Goring, a half-caste gentleman, from New Orleans. All investigations have failed to throw any light upon the fate of these fourteen human beings. The loss of Dr Jephson will be felt both in political and scientific circles.'

I have here epitomised, for the benefit of the public, all that has been hitherto known concerning the *Marie Celeste* and her crew, for the past ten years have not in any way helped to elucidate the mystery. I have now taken up my pen with the intention of telling all that I know of the ill-fated voyage. I consider that it is a duty which I owe to society, for symptoms which I am familiar with in others lead me to believe that before many months my tongue and hand may be alike incapable of conveying information. Let me remark, as a preface to my narrative, that I am Joseph Habakuk Jephson, Doctor of Medicine of the University of Harvard, and ex-Consulting Physician of the Samaritan Hospital of Brooklyn.

Many will doubtless wonder why I have not proclaimed myself before, and why I have suffered so many conjectures and surmises to pass unchallenged. Could the ends of justice have been served in any way by my revealing the facts in my possession I should unhesitatingly have done so. It seemed to me, however, that there was no possibility of such a result; and when I attempted after the occurrence, to state my case to an English official, I was met with such offensive incredulity that I determined never again to expose myself to the chance of such an indignity. I can excuse the discourtesy of the Liverpool magistrate, however, when I reflect upon the treatment which I received at the hands of my own relatives, who, though they knew my unimpeachable character, listened to my statement with an indulgent smile as if humouring the delusion of a monomaniac. This slur upon my veracity led to a quarrel between myself and John Vanburger, the brother of my wife, and confirmed me in my resolution to let the matter sink into oblivion—a determination which I have only altered through my son's solicitations. In order to make my narrative intelligible, I must run lightly over one or two incidents in my former life which throw light upon subsequent events.

My father, William K. Jephson, was a preacher of the sect called Plymouth Brethren, and was one of the most respected citizens of Lowell. Like most of the other Puritans of New England, he was a determined opponent of slavery, and it was from his lips that I received those lessons which tinged every action of my life. While I was studying medicine at Harvard University, I had already made a mark as an advanced Abolitionist; and when, after taking my degree, I bought a third share of the practice of Dr Willis, of Brooklyn, I managed, in spite of my professional duties, to devote a considerable time to the cause which I had at heart, my pamphlet, 'Where is thy Brother?' (Swarburgh: Lister & Co., 1859) attracting considerable attention.

When the war broke out I left Brooklyn and accompanied the 113th New York Regiment through the campaign. I was present at the second battle of Bull's Run and at the battle of Gettysburg. Finally, I was severely wounded at Antietam, and would probably have perished on the field had it not been for the kindness of a gentleman named Murray, who had me carried to his house and provided me with every comfort. Thanks to his charity, and to the nursing which I received from his black domestics, I was soon able to get about the plantation with the help of a stick. It was during this period of convalescence that an incident occurred which is closely connected with my story.

Among the most assiduous of the negresses who had watched my couch during my illness there was one old crone who appeared to exert considerable authority over the others. She was exceedingly attentive to me, and I gathered from the few words that passed between us that she had heard of me, and that she was grateful to me for championing her oppressed race.

One day as I was sitting alone in the verandah, basking in the sun, and debating whether I should rejoin Grant's army, I was surprised to see this old creature hobbling towards me. After looking cautiously around to see that we were alone, she fumbled in the front of her dress, and produced a small chamois leather bag which was hung round her neck by a white cord.

'Massa,' she said, bending down and croaking the words into my ear, 'me die soon. Me very old woman. Not stay long on Massa Murray's plantation.'

'You may have a long time yet, Martha,' I answered. 'You know I am a doctor. If you feel ill let me know about it, and I will try to cure you.'

'No wish to live—wish to die. I'm gwine to join the heavenly host.' Here she relapsed into one of those half-heathenish rhapsodies in which negroes indulge. 'But, massa, me have one thing must leave behind me when I go. No able to take it with me across the Jordan. That one thing very precious, more precious and more holy than all thing else in the world. Me, a poor old black woman, have this because my people, very great people, 'spose they was back in the old country. But you cannot understand this same as black folk could. My fader give it me, and his fader give it him, but now who shall I give it to? Poor Martha hab no child, no relation, nobody. All round I see black man very bad man. Black woman very stupid woman. Nobody worthy of the stone. And so I say, Here is Massa Jephson who write books and fight for coloured folk— he must be a good man, and he shall have it though he is white man, and nebber can know what it mean or where it came from.' Here the old woman fumbled in the chamois leather bag and pulled out a flattish black stone with a hole through the middle of it. 'Here, take it,' she said, pressing it into my hand; 'take it. No harm nebber come from anything good. Keep it safe—nebber lose it!' and with a warning gesture the old crone hobbled away in the same cautious way as she had come, looking from side to side to see if we had been observed.

I was more amused than impressed by the old woman's earnestness, and was only prevented from laughing during her oration by the fear of hurting her feelings. When she was gone I took a good look at the stone which she had given me. It was intensely black, of extreme hardness, and oval in shape—just such a flat stone as one would pick up on the seashore if one wished to throw a long way. It was about three inches long, and an inch and a half broad at the middle, but rounded off at the extremities. The most curious part about it was several well-marked ridges which ran in semicircles over its surface, and gave it exactly the appearance of a human ear. Altogether I was rather interested in my new possession and determined to submit it, as a geological specimen to my friend Professor Shroeder of the New York Institute upon the earliest opportunity. In the meantime I thrust it into my pocket, and rising from my chair started off for a short stroll in the shrubbery, dismissing the incident from my mind.

As my wound had nearly healed by this time, I took my leave of Mr Murray shortly afterwards. The Union armies were everywhere victorious and converging on Richmond, so that my assistance seemed unnecessary, and I returned to Brooklyn. There I resumed my practice, and married the second daughter of Josiah Vanburger, the well-known wood engraver. In the course of a few years I built up a good connection and acquired considerable reputation in the treatment of pulmonary complaints. I still kept the old black stone in my pocket, and frequently told the story of the dramatic way in which I had become possessed of it. I also kept my resolution of showing it to Professor Shroeder, who was much interested both by the anecdote and the specimen. He pronounced it to be a piece of meteoric stone, and drew my attention to the fact that its resemblance to an ear was not accidental, but that it was most carefully worked into that shape. A dozen little anatomical points showed that the worker had been as accurate as he was skilful. 'I should not wonder,' said the Professor, 'if it were broken off from some larger statue, though how such hard material could be so perfectly worked is more than I can understand. If there is a statue to correspond I should like to see it!' So I thought at the time, but I have changed my opinion since.

The next seven or eight years of my life were quiet and uneventful. Summer followed spring, and spring followed winter, without any variation in my duties. As the practice increased I admitted J. S. Jackson as partner, he to have one-fourth of the profits. The continued strain had told upon my constitution, however, and I became at last so unwell that my wife insisted upon my consulting Dr Kavanagh Smith, who was my colleague at the Samaritan Hospital. That gentleman examined me, and pronounced the apex of my left lung to be in a state of consolidation, recommending me at the same time to go through a course of medical treatment and to take a long sea-voyage.

My own disposition, which is naturally restless, predisposed me strongly in favour of the latter piece of advice, and the matter was clinched by my meeting young Russell, of the firm of White, Russell & White, who offered me a passage in one of his father's ships, the *Marie Celeste*, which was just starting from Boston. 'She is a snug little ship,' he said, 'and Tibbs, the captain, is an excellent fellow. There is nothing like a sailing ship for an invalid.' I was very much of the same opinion myself, so I closed with the offer on the spot.

My original plan was that my wife should accompany me on my travels. She has always been a very poor sailor, however, and there were strong family reasons against her exposing herself to any risk at the time, so we determined that she should remain at home. I am not a religious or an effusive man; but oh, thank God for that! As to leaving my practice, I was easily reconciled to it, as Jackson, my partner, was a reliable and hardworking man.

I arrived in Boston on October 12, 1873, and proceeded immediately to the office of the firm in order to thank them for their courtesy. As I was sitting in the counting-house waiting until they should be at liberty to see me, the words *Marie Celeste* suddenly attracted my attention. I looked round and saw a very tall, gaunt man, who was leaning across the polished mahogany counter asking some questions of the clerk at the other side. His face was turned half towards me, and I could see that he had a strong dash of negro blood in him, being probably a quadroon or even nearer akin to the black. His curved aquiline nose and straight lank hair showed the white strain; but the dark, restless eye, sensuous mouth, and gleaming teeth all told of his African origin. His complexion was of a sickly, unhealthy yellow, and as his face was deeply pitted with small-pox, the general impression was so unfavourable as to be almost revolting. When he spoke, however, it was in a soft, melodious voice, and in well-chosen words, and he was evidently a man of some education.

'I wished to ask a few questions about the *Marie Celeste*,' he repeated, leaning across to the clerk. 'She sails the day after tomorrow, does she not?'

'Yes, sir,' said the young clerk, awed into unusual politeness by the glimmer of a large diamond in the stranger's shirt front.

'Where is she bound for?'

'Lisbon.'

'How many of a crew?'

'Seven, sir.'

'Passengers?'

'Yes, two. One of our young gentlemen, and a doctor from New York.'

'No gentleman from the South?' asked the stranger eagerly.

'No, none, sir.'

'Is there room for another passenger?'

'Accommodation, for three more,' answered the clerk.

'I'll go,' said the quadroon decisively; 'I'll go, I'll engage my passage at once. Put it down, will you—Mr Septimius Goring, of New Orleans.'

The clerk filled up a form and handed it over to the stranger, pointing to a blank space at the bottom. As Mr Goring stooped over to sign it I was horrified to observe that the fingers of his right hand had been lopped off, and that he was holding the pen between his thumb and the palm. I have seen thousands slain in battle, and assisted at every conceivable surgical operation, but I cannot recall any sight which gave me such a thrill of disgust as that great brown sponge-like hand with the single member protruding from it. He used it skilfully enough, however, for, dashing off his signature, he nodded to the clerk and strolled out of the office just as Mr White sent out word that he was ready to receive me.

I went down to the *Marie Celeste* that evening, and looked over my berth, which was extremely comfortable considering the small size of the vessel. Mr Goring, whom I had seen in the morning, was to have the one next mine. Opposite was the captain's cabin and a small berth for Mr John Harton, a gentleman who was going out in the interests of the firm. These little rooms were arranged on each side of the passage which led from the main-deck to the saloon. The latter was a comfortable room, the panelling tastefully done in oak and mahogany, with a rich Brussels carpet and luxurious settees. I was very much pleased with the accommodation, and also with Tibbs the captain, a bluff, sailor-like fellow, with a loud voice and hearty manner, who welcomed me to the ship with effusion, and insisted upon our splitting a bottle of wine in his cabin. He told me that he intended to take his wife and youngest child with him on the voyage, and that he hoped with good luck to make Lisbon in three weeks. We had a pleasant chat and parted the best of friends, he warning me to make the last of my preparations next morning, as he intended to make a start by the mid-day tide, having now shipped all his cargo. I went back to my hotel, where I found a letter from my wife awaiting me, and, after a refreshing night's sleep, returned to the boat in the morning. From this point I am able to quote from the journal which I kept in order to vary the monotony of the long sea-voyage. If it is somewhat bald in places I can at least rely upon its accuracy in details, as it was written conscientiously from day to day.

October 16th—Cast off our warps at half-past two and were towed out into the bay, where the tug left us, and with all sail set we bowled along at about nine knots. I stood upon the poop watching the low land of America sinking gradually upon the horizon until the evening haze hid it from my sight. A single red light, however, continued to blaze balefully behind us, throwing a long track like a trail of blood upon the water, and it is still visible as I write, though reduced to a mere speck. The captain is in a bad humour, for two of his hands disappointed him at the last moment, and he was compelled to ship a couple of negroes who happened to be on the quay. The missing men were steady, reliable fellows, who had been with him several voyages, and their non-appearance puzzled as well as irritated him. Where a crew of seven men have to work a fair-sized ship the loss of two experienced seamen is a serious one, for though the negroes may take a spell at the wheel or swab the decks, they are of little or no use in rough weather. Our cook is also a black man, and Mr Septimius Goring has a little darkie servant, so that we are rather a piebald community. The accountant, John Harton, promises to be an acquisition, for he is a cheery, amusing young fellow. Strange how little wealth has to do with happiness! He has all the world before him and is seeking his fortune in a far land, yet he is as transparently happy as a man can be. Goring is rich, if I am not mistaken, and so am I; but I know that I have a lung, and Goring has some deeper trouble still, to judge by his features. How poorly do we both contrast with the careless, penniless clerk!

October 17th—Mrs Tibbs appeared upon the deck for the first time this morning—a cheerful, energetic woman, with a dear little child just able to walk and prattle. Young Harton pounced on it at once, and carried it away to his cabin, where no doubt he will lay the seeds of future dyspepsia in the child's stomach. Thus medicine doth make cynics of us all! The weather is still all that could be desired, with a fine fresh breeze from the west-sou'-west. The vessel goes so steadily that you would hardly know that she was moving were it not for the creaking of the cordage, the bellying of the sails, and the long white furrow in our wake. Walked the quarter-deck all morning with the captain, and I think the keen fresh air has already done my breathing good, for the exercise did not fatigue me in any way. Tibbs is a remarkably intelligent man, and we had an interesting argument about Maury's observations on ocean currents, which we terminated by going down into his cabin to consult the original work. There we found Goring, rather to the captain's surprise, as it is not usual for passengers to enter that sanctum unless specially invited. He apologised for his intrusion, however, pleading his ignorance of the usages of ship life; and the good-natured sailor simply laughed at the incident, begging him to remain and favour us with his company. Goring pointed to the chronometers, the case of which he had opened, and remarked that he had been admiring them. He has evidently some practical knowledge of mathematical instruments, as he told at a glance which was the most trustworthy of the three, and also named their price within a few dollars. He had a discussion with the captain too upon the variation of the compass, and when we came back to the ocean currents he showed a thorough grasp of the subject. Altogether he rather improves upon acquaintance, and is a man of decided culture and refinement. His voice harmonises with his conversation, and both are the very antithesis of his face and figure.

The noonday observation shows that we have run two hundred and twenty miles. Towards evening the breeze freshened up, and the first mate ordered reefs to be taken in the topsails and top-gallant sails in expectation of a windy night. I observe that the barometer has fallen to twenty-nine. I trust our voyage will not be a rough one, as I am a poor sailor, and my health would probably derive more harm than good from a stormy trip, though I have the greatest confidence in the captain's seamanship and in the soundness of the vessel. Played cribbage with Mrs Tibbs after supper, and Harton gave us a couple of tunes on the violin.

October 18th—The gloomy prognostications of last night were not fulfilled, as the wind died away again and we are lying now in a long greasy swell, ruffled here and there by a fleeting catspaw which is insufficient to fill the sails. The air is colder than it was yesterday, and I have put on one of the thick woollen jerseys which my wife knitted for me. Harton came into my cabin in the morning, and we had a cigar together. He says that he remembers having seen Goring in Cleveland, Ohio, in '69. He was, it appears, a mystery then as now, wandering about without any visible employment, and extremely reticent on his own affairs. The man interests me as a psychological study. At breakfast this morning I suddenly had that vague feeling of uneasiness which comes over some people when closely stared at, and, looking quickly up, I met his eyes bent upon me with an intensity which amounted to ferocity, though their expression instantly softened as he made some conventional remark upon the weather. Curiously enough, Harton says that he had a very similar experience yesterday upon deck. I observe that Goring frequently talks to the coloured seamen as he strolls about—a trait which I rather admire, as it is common to find half-breeds ignore their dark strain and treat their black kinsfolk with greater intolerance than a white man would do. His little page is devoted to him apparently, which speaks well for his treatment of him. Altogether, the man is a curious mixture of incongruous qualities, and unless I am deceived in him will give me food for observation during the voyage.

The captain is grumbling about his chronometers, which do not register exactly the same time. He says it is the first time that they have ever disagreed. We were unable to get a noonday observation on account of the haze. By dead reckoning, we have done about a hundred and seventy miles in the twenty-four hours. The dark seamen have proved, as the skipper prophesied, to be very inferior hands, but as they can both manage the wheel well they are kept steering, and so leave the more experienced men to work the ship. These details are trivial enough, but a small thing serves as food for gossip aboard ship. The appearance of a whale in the evening caused quite a flutter among us. From its sharp back and forked tail, I should pronounce it to have been a rorqual, or 'finner', as they are called by the fishermen.

October 19th—Wind was cold, so I prudently remained in my cabin all day, only creeping out for dinner. Lying in my bunk I can, without moving, reach my books, pipes, or anything else I may want, which is one advantage of a small apartment. My old wound began to ache a little today, probably from the cold. Read Montaigne's *Essays* and nursed myself. Harton came in in the afternoon with Doddy, the captain's child, and the skipper himself followed, so that I held quite a reception.

October 20th and 21st—Still cold, with a continual drizzle of rain, and I have not been able to leave the cabin. This confinement makes me feel weak and depressed. Goring came in to see me, but his company did not tend to cheer me up much, as he hardly uttered a word, but contented himself with staring at me in a peculiar and rather irritating manner. He then got up and stole out of the cabin without saying anything. I am beginning to suspect that the man is a lunatic. I think I mentioned that his cabin is next to mine. The two are simply divided by a thin wooden partition which is cracked in many places, some of the cracks being so large that I can hardly avoid, as I lie in my bunk, observing his motions in the adjoining room. Without any wish to play the spy, I see him continually stooping over what appears to be a chart and working with a pencil and compasses. I have remarked the interest he displays in matters connected with navigation, but I am surprised that he should take the trouble to work out the course of the ship. However, it is a harmless amusement enough, and no doubt he verifies his results by those of the captain.

I wish the man did not run in my thoughts so much. I had a nightmare on the night of the 20th, in which I thought my bunk was a coffin, that I was laid out in it, and that Goring was endeavouring to nail up the lid, which I was frantically pushing away. Even when I woke up, I could hardly persuade myself that I was not in a coffin. As a medical man, I know that a nightmare is simply a vascular derangement of the cerebral hemispheres, and yet in my weak state I cannot shake off the morbid impression which it produces.

October 22nd—A fine day, with hardly a cloud in the sky, and a fresh breeze from the sou'-west which wafts us gaily on our way. There has evidently been some heavy weather near us, as there is a tremendous swell on, and the ship lurches until the end of the fore-yard nearly touches the water. Had a refreshing walk up and down the quarter-deck, though I have hardly found my sea-legs yet. Several small birds—chaffinches, I think—perched in the rigging.

4.40 p.m.—While I was on deck this morning I heard a sudden explosion from the direction of my cabin, and, hurrying down, found that I had very nearly met with a serious accident. Goring was cleaning a revolver, it seems, in his cabin, when one of the barrels which he thought was unloaded went off. The ball passed through the side partition and imbedded itself in the bulwarks in the exact place where my head usually rests. I have been under fire too often to magnify trifles, but there is no doubt that if I had been in the bunk it must have killed me. Goring, poor fellow, did not know that I had gone on deck that day, and must therefore have felt terribly frightened. I never saw such emotion in a man's face as when, on rushing out of his cabin with the smoking pistol in his hand, he met me face to face as I came down from deck. Of course, he was profuse in his apologies, though I simply laughed at the incident.

11 p.m.—A misfortune has occurred so unexpected and so horrible that my little escape of the morning dwindles into insignificance. Mrs Tibbs and her child have disappeared—utterly and entirely disappeared. I can hardly compose myself to write the sad details. About half-past eight Tibbs rushed into my cabin with a very white face and asked me if I had seen his wife. I answered that I had not. He then ran wildly into the saloon and began groping about for any trace of her, while I followed him, endeavouring vainly to persuade him that his fears were ridiculous. We hunted over the ship for an hour and a half without coming on any sign of the missing woman or child. Poor Tibbs lost his voice completely from calling her name. Even the sailors, who are generally stolid enough, were deeply affected by the sight of him as he roamed bareheaded and dishevelled about the deck, searching with feverish anxiety the most impossible places, and returning to them again and again with a piteous pertinacity. The last time she was seen was about seven o'clock, when she took Doddy on to the poop to give him a breath of fresh air before putting him to bed. There was no one there at the time except the black seaman at the wheel, who denies having seen her at all. The whole affair is wrapped in mystery. My own theory is that while Mrs Tibbs was holding the child and standing near the bulwarks it gave a spring and fell overboard, and that in her convulsive attempt to catch, or save it, she followed it. I cannot account for the double disappearance in any other way. It is quite feasible that such a tragedy should be enacted without the knowledge of the man at the wheel, since it was dark at the time, and the peaked skylights of the saloon screen the greater part of the quarter-deck. Whatever the truth may be it is a terrible catastrophe, and has cast the darkest gloom upon our voyage. The mate has put the ship about, but of course there is not the slightest hope of picking them up. The captain is lying in a state of stupor in his cabin. I gave him a powerful dose of opium in his coffee that for a few hours at least his anguish may be deadened.

October 23rd—Woke with a vague feeling of heaviness and misfortune, but it was not until a few moments' reflection that I was able to recall our loss of the night before. When I came on deck I saw the poor skipper standing gazing back at the waste of waters behind us which contains everything dear to him upon earth. I attempted to speak to him, but he turned brusquely away, and began pacing the deck with his head sunk upon his breast. Even now, when the truth is so clear, he cannot pass a boat or an unbent sail without peering under it. He looks ten years older than he did yesterday morning. Harton is terribly cut up, for he was fond of little Doddy, and Goring seems sorry too. At least he has shut himself up in his cabin all day, and when I got a casual glance at him his head was resting on his two hands as if in a melancholy reverie. I fear we are about as dismal a crew as ever sailed. How shocked my wife will be to hear of our disaster! The swell has gone down now, and we are doing about eight knots with all sail set and a nice little breeze. Hyson is practically in command of the ship, as Tibbs, though he does his best to bear up and keep a brave front, is incapable of applying himself to serious work.

October 24th—Is the ship accursed? Was there ever a voyage which began so fairly and which changed so disastrously? Tibbs shot himself through the head during the night. I was awakened about three o'clock in the morning by an explosion, and immediately sprang out of bed and rushed into the captain's cabin to find out the cause, though with a terrible presentiment in my heart. Quickly as I went, Goring went more quickly still, for he was already in the cabin stooping over the dead body of the captain. It was a hideous sight, for the whole front of his face was blown in, and the little room was swimming in blood. The pistol was lying beside him on the floor, just as it had dropped from his hand. He had evidently put it to his mouth before pulling the trigger. Goring and I picked him reverently up and laid him on his bed. The crew had all clustered into his cabin, and the six white men were deeply grieved, for they were old hands who had sailed with him many years. There were dark looks and murmurs among them too, and one of them openly declared that the ship was haunted. Harton helped to lay the poor skipper out, and we did him up in canvas between us. At twelve o'clock the fore-yard was hauled aback, and we committed his body to the deep, Goring reading the Church of England burial service. The breeze has freshened up, and we have done ten knots all day and sometimes twelve. The sooner we reach Lisbon and get away from this accursed ship the better pleased shall I be. I feel as though we were in a floating coffin. Little wonder that the poor sailors are superstitious when I, an educated man, feel it so strongly.

October 25th—Made a good run all day. Feel listless and depressed.

October 26th—Goring, Harton, and I had a chat together on deck in the morning. Harton tried to draw Goring out as to his profession, and his object in going to Europe, but the quadroon parried all his questions and gave us no information. Indeed, he seemed to be slightly offended by Harton's pertinacity, and went down into his cabin. I wonder why we should both take such an interest in this man! I suppose it is his striking appearance, coupled with his apparent wealth, which piques our curiosity. Harton has a theory that he is really a detective, that he is after some criminal who has got away to Portugal, and that he chooses this peculiar way of travelling that he may arrive unnoticed and pounce upon his quarry unawares. I think the supposition is rather a far-fetched one, but Harton bases it upon a book which Goring left on deck, and which he picked up and glanced over. It was a sort of scrap-book, it seems, and contained a large number of newspaper cuttings. All these cuttings related to murders which had been committed at various times in the States during the last twenty years or so. The curious thing which Harton observed about them, however, was that they were invariably murders the authors of which had never been brought to justice. They varied in every detail, he says, as to the manner of execution and the social status of the victim, but they uniformly wound up with the same formula that the murderer was still at large, though, of course, the police had every reason to expect his speedy capture. Certainly the incident seems to support Harton's theory, though it may be a mere whim of Goring's, or, as I suggested to Harton, he may be collecting materials for a book which shall outvie De Quincy. In any case it is no business of ours.

October 27th, 28th—Wind still fair, and we are making good progress. Strange how easily a human unit may drop out of its place and be forgotten! Tibbs is hardly ever mentioned now; Hyson has taken possession of his cabin, and all goes on as before. Were it not for Mrs Tibbs's sewing-machine upon a side-table we might forget that the unfortunate family had ever existed. Another accident occurred on board today, though fortunately not a very serious one. One of our white hands had gone down the afterhold to fetch up a spare coil of rope, when one of the hatches which he had removed came crashing down on the top of him. He saved his life by springing out of the way, but one of his feet was terribly crushed, and he will be of little use for the remainder of the voyage. He attributes the accident to the carelessness of his negro companion, who had helped him to shift the hatches. The latter, however, puts it down to the roll of the ship. Whatever be the cause, it reduces our short-handed crew still further. This run of ill-luck seems to be depressing Harton, for he has lost his usual good spirits and joviality. Goring is the only one who preserves his cheerfulness. I see him still working at his chart in his own cabin. His nautical knowledge would be useful should anything happen to Hyson—which God forbid!

October 29th, 30th—Still bowling along with a fresh breeze. All quiet and nothing of note to chronicle.

October 31st—My weak lungs, combined with the exciting episodes of the voyage, have shaken my nervous system so much that the most trivial incident affects me. I can hardly believe that I am the same man who tied the external iliac artery, an operation requiring the nicest precision, under a heavy rifle fire at Antietam. I am as nervous as a child. I was lying half dozing last night about four bells in the middle watch trying in vain to drop into a refreshing sleep. There was no light inside my cabin, but a single ray of moonlight streamed in through the port-hole, throwing a silvery flickering circle upon the door. As I lay I kept my drowsy eyes upon this circle, and was conscious that it was gradually becoming less well-defined as my senses left me, when I was suddenly recalled to full wakefulness by the appearance of a small dark object in the very centre of the luminous disc. I lay quietly and breathlessly watching it. Gradually it grew larger and plainer, and then I perceived that it was a human hand which had been cautiously inserted through the chink of the half-closed door—a hand which, as I observed with a thrill of horror, was not provided with fingers. The door swung cautiously backwards, and Goring's head followed his hand. It appeared in the centre of the moonlight, and was framed as it were in a ghastly uncertain halo, against which his features showed out plainly. It seemed to me that I had never seen such an utterly fiendish and merciless expression upon a human face. His eyes were dilated and glaring, his lips drawn back so as to show his white fangs, and his straight black hair appeared to bristle over his low forehead like the hood of a cobra. The sudden and noiseless apparition had such an effect upon me that I sprang up in bed trembling in every limb, and held out my hand towards my revolver. I was heartily ashamed of my hastiness when he explained the object of his intrusion, as he immediately did in the most courteous language. He had been suffering from toothache, poor fellow! and had come in to beg some laudanum, knowing that I possessed a medicine chest. As to a sinister expression he is never a beauty, and what with my state of nervous tension and the effect of the shifting moonlight it was easy to conjure up something horrible. I gave him twenty drops, and he went off again, with many expressions of gratitude. I can hardly say how much this trivial incident affected me. I have felt unstrung all day.

A week's record of our voyage is here omitted, as nothing eventful occurred during the time, and my log consists merely of a few pages of unimportant gossip.

November 7th—Harton and I sat on the poop all the morning, for the weather is becoming very warm as we come into southern latitudes. We reckon that we have done two-thirds of our voyage. How glad we shall be to see the green banks of the Tagus, and leave this unlucky ship for ever! I was endeavouring to amuse Harton today and to while away the time by telling him some of the experiences of my past life. Among others I related to him how I came into the possession of my black stone, and as a finale I rummaged in the side pocket of my old shooting coat and produced the identical object in question. He and I were bending over it together, I pointing out to him the curious ridges upon its surface, when we were conscious of a shadow falling between us and the sun, and looking round saw Goring standing behind us glaring over our shoulders at the stone. For some reason or other he appeared to be powerfully excited, though he was evidently trying to control himself and to conceal his emotion. He pointed once or twice at my relic with his stubby thumb before he could recover himself sufficiently to ask what it was and how I obtained it—a question put in such a brusque manner that I should have been offended had I not known the man to be an eccentric. I told him the story very much as I had told it to Harton. He listened with the deepest interest and then asked me if I had any idea what the stone was. I said I had not, beyond that it was meteoric. He asked me if I had ever tried its effect upon a negro. I said I had not. 'Come,' said he, 'we'll see what our black friend at the wheel thinks of it.' He took the stone in his hand and went across to the sailor, and the two examined it carefully. I could see the man gesticulating and nodding his head excitedly as if making some assertion, while his face betrayed the utmost astonishment, mixed, I think, with some reverence. Goring came across the deck to us presently, still holding the stone in his hand. 'He says it is a worthless, useless thing,' he said, 'and fit only to be chucked overboard,' with which he raised his hand and would most certainly have made an end of my relic, had the black sailor behind him not rushed forward and seized him by the wrist. Finding himself secured Goring dropped the stone and turned away with a very bad grace to avoid my angry remonstrances at his breach of faith. The black picked up the stone and handed it to me with a low bow and every sign of profound respect. The whole affair is inexplicable. I am rapidly coming to the conclusion that Goring is a maniac or something very near one. When I compare the effect produced by the stone upon the sailor, however, with the respect shown to Martha on the plantation, and the surprise of Goring on its first production, I cannot but come to the conclusion that I have really got hold of some powerful talisman which appeals to the whole dark race. I must not trust it in Goring's hands again.

November 8th, 9th—What splendid weather we are having! Beyond one little blow, we have had nothing but fresh breezes the whole voyage. These two days we have made better runs than any hitherto. It is a pretty thing to watch the spray fly up from our prow as it cuts through the waves. The sun shines through it and breaks it up into a number of miniature rainbows—'sun-dogs', the sailors call them. I stood on the fo'c'sle-head for several hours today watching the effect, and surrounded by a halo of prismatic colours. The steersman has evidently told the other blacks about my wonderful stone, for I am treated by them all with the greatest respect. Talking about optical phenomena, we had a curious one yesterday evening which was pointed out to me by Hyson. This was the appearance of a triangular well-defined object high up in the heavens to the north of us. He explained that it was exactly like the Peak of Teneriffe as seen from a great distance—the peak was, however, at that moment at least five hundred miles to the south. It may have been a cloud, or it may have been one of those strange reflections of which one reads. The weather is very warm. The mate says that he never knew it so warm in these latitudes. Played chess with Harton in the evening.

November 10th—It is getting warmer and warmer. Some land birds came and perched in the rigging today, though we are still a considerable way from our destination. The heat is so great that we are too lazy to do anything but lounge about the decks and smoke. Goring came over to me today and asked me some more questions about my stone; but I answered him rather shortly, for I have not quite forgiven him yet for the cool way in which he attempted to deprive me of it.

November 11th, 12th—Still making good progress. I had no idea Portugal was ever as hot as this, but no doubt it is cooler on land. Hyson himself seemed surprised at it, and so do the men.

November 13th—A most extraordinary event has happened, so extraordinary as to be almost inexplicable. Either Hyson has blundered wonderfully, or some magnetic influence has disturbed our instruments. Just about daybreak the watch on the fo'c'sle-head shouted out that he heard the sound of surf ahead, and Hyson thought he saw the loom of land. The ship was put about, and, though no lights were seen, none of us doubted that we had struck the Portuguese coast a little sooner than we had expected. What was our surprise to see the scene which was revealed to us at break of day! As far as we could look on either side was one long line of surf, great, green billows rolling in and breaking into a cloud of foam. But behind the surf what was there! Not the green banks nor the high cliffs of the shores of Portugal, but a great sandy waste which stretched away and away until it blended with the skyline. To right and left, look where you would, there was nothing but yellow sand, heaped in some places into fantastic mounds, some of them several hundred feet high, while in other parts were long stretches as level apparently as a billiard board. Harton and I, who had come on deck together, looked at each other in astonishment, and Harton burst out laughing. Hyson is exceedingly mortified at the occurrence, and protests that the instruments have been tampered with. There is no doubt that this is the mainland of Africa, and that it was really the Peak of Teneriffe which we saw some days ago upon the northern horizon. At the time when we saw the land birds we must have been passing some of the Canary Islands. If we continued on the same course, we are now to the north of Cape Blanco, near the unexplored country which skirts the great Sahara. All we can do is to rectify our instruments as far as possible and start afresh for our destination.

8.30 p.m.—Have been lying in a calm all day. The coast is now about a mile and a half from us. Hyson has examined the instruments, but cannot find any reason for their extraordinary deviation.

This is the end of my private journal, and I must make the remainder of my statement from memory. There is little chance of my being mistaken about facts, which have seared themselves into my recollection. That very night the storm which had been brewing so long burst over us, and I came to learn, whither all those little incidents were tending which I had recorded so aimlessly.

Blind fool that I was not to have seen it sooner! I shall tell what occurred as precisely as I can.

I had gone into my cabin about half-past eleven, and was preparing to go to bed, when a tap came at my door. On opening it I saw Goring's little black page, who told me that his master would like to have a word with me on deck. I was rather surprised that he should want me at such a late hour, but I went up without hesitation. I had hardly put my foot on the quarter-deck before I was seized from behind, dragged down upon my back, and a handkerchief slipped round my mouth. I struggled as hard as I could, but a coil of rope was rapidly and firmly wound round me, and I found myself lashed to the davit of one of the boats, utterly powerless to do or say anything, while the point of a knife pressed to my throat warned me to cease my struggles. The night was so dark that I had been unable hitherto to recognize my assailants, but as my eyes became accustomed to the gloom, and the moon broke out through the clouds that obscured it, I made out that I was surrounded by the two negro sailors, the black cook, and my fellow-passenger, Goring. Another man was crouching on the deck at my feet, but he was in the shadow and I could not recognize him.

All this occurred so rapidly that a minute could hardly have elapsed from the time I mounted the companion until I found myself gagged and powerless. It was so sudden that I could scarce bring myself to realize it, or to comprehend what it all meant. I heard the gang round me speaking in short, fierce whispers to each other, and some instinct told me that my life was the question at issue. Goring spoke authoritatively and angrily—the others doggedly and all together, as if disputing his commands. Then they moved away in a body to the opposite side of the deck, where I could still hear them whispering, though they were concealed from my view by the saloon skylights.

All this time the voices of the watch on deck chatting and laughing at the other end of the ship were distinctly audible, and I could see them gathered in a group, little dreaming of the dark doings which were going on within thirty yards of them. Oh! That I could have given them one word of warning, even though I had lost my life in doing it! but it was impossible. The moon was shining fitfully through the scattered clouds, and I could see the silvery gleam of the surge, and beyond it the vast weird desert with its fantastic sand-hills. Glancing down, I saw that the man who had been crouching on the deck was still lying there, and as I gazed at him a flickering ray of moonlight fell full upon his upturned face. Great heaven! even now, when more than twelve years have elapsed, my hand trembles as I write that, in spite of distorted features and projecting eyes, I recognized the face of Harton, the cheery young clerk who had been my companion during the voyage. It needed no medical eye to see that he was quite dead, while the twisted handkerchief round the neck, and the gag in his mouth, showed the silent way in which the hell-hounds had done their work. The clue which explained every event of our voyage came upon me like a flash of light as I gazed on poor Horton's corpse. Much was dark and unexplained, but I felt a great dim perception of the truth.

I heard the striking of a match at the other side of the skylights, and then I saw the tall, gaunt figure of Goring standing up on the bulwarks and holding in his hands what appeared to be a dark lantern. He lowered this for a moment over the side of the ship and, to my inexpressible astonishment, I saw it answered instantaneously by a flash among the sand-hills on shore, which came and went so rapidly, that unless I had been following the direction of Goring's gaze, I should never have detected it. Again he lowered the lantern, and again it was answered from the shore. He then stepped down from the bulwarks, and in doing so slipped, making such a noise, that for a moment my heart bounded with the thought that the attention of the watch would be directed to his proceedings. It was a vain hope. The night was calm and the ship motionless, so that no idea of duty kept them vigilant. Hyson, who after the death of Tibbs was in command of both watches, had gone below to snatch a few hours' sleep, and the boatswain, who was left in charge, was standing with the other two men at the foot of the foremast. Powerless, speechless, with the cords cutting into my flesh and the murdered man at my feet, I awaited the next act in the tragedy.

The four ruffians were standing up now at the other side of the deck. The cook was armed with some sort of a cleaver, the others had knives, and Goring had a revolver. They were all leaning against the rail and looking out over the water as if watching for something. I saw one of them grasp another's arm and point as if at some object, and following the direction I made out the loom of a large moving mass making towards the ship. As it emerged from the gloom I saw that it was a great canoe crammed with men and propelled by at least a score of paddles. As it shot under our stern the watch caught sight of it also, and raising a cry hurried aft. They were too late, however. A swarm of gigantic negroes clambered over the quarter, and led by Goring swept down the deck in an irresistible torrent. All opposition was overpowered in a moment, the unarmed watch were knocked over and bound, and the sleepers dragged out of their bunks and secured in the same manner. Hyson made an attempt to defend the narrow passage leading to his cabin, and I heard a scuffle, and his voice shouting for assistance. There was none to assist, however, and he was brought on to the poop with the blood streaming from a deep cut in his forehead. He was gagged like the others, and a council was held upon our fate by the negroes. I saw our black seamen pointing towards me and making some statement, which was received with murmurs of astonishment and incredulity by the savages. One of them then came over to me, and plunging his hand into my pocket took out my black stone and held it up. He then handed it to a man who appeared to be a chief, who examined it as minutely as the light would permit, and muttering a few words passed it on to the warrior beside him, who also scrutinized it and passed it on until it had gone from hand to hand round the whole circle. The chief then said a few words to Goring in the native tongue, on which the quadroon addressed me in English. At this moment I seem to see the scene. The tall masts of the ship with the moonlight streaming down, silvering the yards and bringing the network of cordage into hard relief; the group of dusky warriors leaning on their spears; the dead man at my feet; the line of white-faced prisoners, and in front of me the loathsome half-breed, looking in his white linen and elegant clothes a strange contrast to his associates.

'You will bear me witness,' he said in his softest accents, 'that I am no party to sparing your life. If it rested with me you would die as these other men are about to do. I have no personal grudge against either you or them, but I have devoted my life to the destruction of the white race, and you are the first that has ever been in my power and has escaped me. You may thank that stone of yours for your life. These poor fellows reverence it, and indeed if it really be what they think it is they have cause. Should it prove when we get ashore that they are mistaken, and that its shape and material is a mere chance, nothing can save your life. In the meantime we wish to treat you well, so if there are any of your possessions which you would like to take with you, you are at liberty to get them.' As he finished he gave a sign, and a couple of the negroes unbound me, though without removing the gag. I was led down into the cabin, where I put a few valuables into my pockets, together with a pocket-compass and my journal of the voyage. They then pushed me over the side into a small canoe, which was lying beside the large one, and my guards followed me, and shoving off began paddling for the shore. We had got about a hundred yards or so from the ship when our steersman held up his hand, and the paddlers paused for a moment and listened. Then on the silence of the night I heard a sort of dull, moaning sound, followed by a succession of splashes in the water. That is all I know of the fate of my poor shipmates. Almost immediately afterwards the large canoe followed us, and the deserted ship was left drifting about—a dreary spectre-like hulk. Nothing was taken from her by the savages. The whole fiendish transaction was carried through as decorously and temperately as though it were a religious rite.

The first grey of daylight was visible in the east as we passed through the surge and reached the shore. Leaving half a dozen men with the canoes, the rest of the negroes set off through the sand-hills, leading me with them, but treating me very gently and respectfully. It was difficult walking, as we sank over our ankles into the loose, shifting sand at every step, and I was nearly dead beat by the time we reached the native village, or town rather, for it was a place of considerable dimensions. The houses were conical structures not unlike bee-hives, and were made of compressed seaweed cemented over with a rude form of mortar, there being neither stick nor stone upon the coast nor anywhere within many hundreds of miles. As we entered the town an enormous crowd of both sexes came swarming out to meet us, beating tom-toms and howling and screaming. On seeing me they redoubled their yells and assumed a threatening attitude, which was instantly quelled by a few words shouted by my escort. A buzz of wonder succeeded the war-cries and yells of the moment before, and the whole dense mass proceeded down the broad central street of the town, having my escort and myself in the centre.

My statement hitherto may seem so strange as to excite doubt in the minds of those who do not know me, but it was the fact which I am now about to relate which caused my own brother-in-law to insult me by disbelief. I can but relate the occurrence in the simplest words, and trust to chance and time to prove their truth. In the centre of this main street there was a large building, formed in the same primitive way as the others, but towering high above them; a stockade of beautifully polished ebony rails was planted all round it, the framework of the door was formed by two magnificent elephant's tusks sunk in the ground on each side and meeting at the top, and the aperture was closed by a screen of native cloth richly embroidered with gold. We made our way to this imposing-looking structure, but on reaching the opening in the stockade, the multitude stopped and squatted down upon their hams, while I was led through into the enclosure by a few of the chiefs and elders of the tribe, Goring accompanying us, and in fact directing the proceedings. On reaching the screen which closed the temple—for such it evidently was—my hat and my shoes were removed, and I was then led in, a venerable old negro leading the way carrying in his hand my stone, which had been taken from my pocket. The building was only lit up by a few long slits in the roof, through which the tropical sun poured, throwing broad golden bars upon the clay floor, alternating with intervals of darkness.

The interior was even larger than one would have imagined from the outside appearance. The walls were hung with native mats, shells, and other ornaments, but the remainder of the great space was quite empty, with the exception of a single object in the centre. This was the figure of a colossal negro, which I at first thought to be some real king or high priest of titanic size, but as I approached it I saw by the way in which the light was reflected from it that it was a statue admirably cut in jet-black stone. I was led up to this idol, for such it seemed to be, and looking at it closer I saw that though it was perfect in every other respect, one of its ears had been broken short off. The grey-haired negro who held my relic mounted upon a small stool, and stretching up his arm fitted Martha's black stone on to the jagged surface on the side of the statue's head. There could not be a doubt that the one had been broken off from the other. The parts dovetailed together so accurately that when the old man removed his hand the ear stuck in its place for a few seconds before dropping into his open palm. The group round me prostrated themselves upon the ground at the sight with a cry of reverence, while the crowd outside, to whom the result was communicated, set up a wild whooping and cheering.

In a moment I found myself converted from a prisoner into a demi-god. I was escorted back through the town in triumph, the people pressing forward to touch my clothing and to gather up the dust on which my foot had trod. One of the largest huts was put at my disposal, and a banquet of every native delicacy was served me. I still felt, however, that I was not a free man, as several spearmen were placed as a guard at the entrance of my hut. All day my mind was occupied with plans of escape, but none seemed in any way feasible. On the one side was the great arid desert stretching away to Timbuctoo, on the other was a sea untraversed by vessels. The more I pondered over the problem the more hopeless did it seem. I little dreamed how near I was to its solution.

Night had fallen, and the clamour of the negroes had died gradually away. I was stretched on the couch of skins which had been provided for me, and was still meditating over my future, when Goring walked stealthily into the hut. My first idea was that he had come to complete his murderous holocaust by making away with me, the last survivor, and I sprang up upon my feet, determined to defend myself to the last. He smiled when he saw the action, and motioned me down again while he seated himself upon the other end of the couch.

'What do you think of me?' was the astonishing question with which he commenced our conversation.

'Think of you!' I almost yelled. 'I think you the vilest, most unnatural renegade that ever polluted the earth. If we were away from these black devils of yours I would strangle you with my hands!'

'Don't speak so loud,' he said, without the slightest appearance of irritation. 'I don't want our chat to be cut short. So you would strangle me, would you!' he went on, with an amused smile. 'I suppose I am returning good for evil, for I have come to help you to escape.'

'You!' I gasped incredulously.

'Yes, I,' he continued. 'Oh, there is no credit to me in the matter. I am quite consistent. There is no reason why I should not be perfectly candid with you. I wish to be king over these fellows—not a very high ambition, certainly, but you know what Caesar said about being first in a village in Gaul. Well, this unlucky stone of yours has not only saved your life, but has turned all their heads so that they think you are come down from heaven, and my influence will be gone until you are out of the way. That is why I am going to help you to escape, since I cannot kill you'—this in the most natural and dulcet voice, as if the desire to do so were a matter of course.

'You would give the world to ask me a few questions,' he went on, after a pause; 'but you are too proud to do it. Never mind, I'll tell you one or two things, because I want your fellow white men to know them when you go back—if you are lucky enough to get back. About that cursed stone of yours, for instance. These negroes, or at least so the legend goes, were Mahometans originally. While Mahomet himself was still alive, there was a schism among his followers, and the smaller party moved away from Arabia, and eventually crossed Africa. They took away with them, in their exile, a valuable relic of their old faith in the shape of a large piece of the black stone of Mecca. The stone was a meteoric one, as you may have heard, and in its fall upon the earth it broke into two pieces. One of these pieces is still at Mecca. The larger piece was carried away to Barbary, where a skilful worker modelled it into the fashion which you saw today. These men are the descendants of the original seceders from Mahomet, and they have brought their relic safely through all their wanderings until they settled in this strange place, where the desert protects them from their enemies.'

'And the ear?' I asked, almost involuntarily.

'Oh, that was the same story over again. Some of the tribe wandered away to the south a few hundred years ago, and one of them, wishing to have good luck for the enterprise, got into the temple at night and carried off one of the ears. There has been a tradition among the negroes ever since that the ear would come back some day. The fellow who carried it was caught by some slaver, no doubt, and that was how it got into America, and so into your hands—and you have had the honour of fulfilling the prophecy.'

He paused for a few minutes, resting his head upon his hands, waiting apparently for me to speak. When he looked up again, the whole expression of his face had changed. His features were firm and set, and he changed the air of half-levity with which he had spoken before for one of sternness and almost ferocity.

'I wish you to carry a message back,' he said, 'to the white race, the great dominating race whom I hate and defy. Tell them that I have battened on their blood for twenty years, that I have slain them until even I became tired of what had once been a joy, that I did this unnoticed and unsuspected in the face of every precaution which their civilization could suggest. There is no satisfaction in revenge when your enemy does not know who has struck him. I am not sorry, therefore, to have you as a messenger. There is no need why I should tell you how this great hate became born in me. See this,' and he held up his mutilated hand; 'that was done by a white man's knife. My father was white, my mother was a slave. When he died she was sold again, and I, a child then, saw her lashed to death to break her of some of the little airs and graces which her late master had encouraged in her. My young wife, too, oh, my young wife!' a shudder ran through his whole frame. 'No matter! I swore my oath, and I kept it. From Maine to Florida, and from Boston to San Francisco, you could track my steps by sudden deaths which baffled the police. I warred against the whole white race as they for centuries had warred against the black one. At last, as I tell you, I sickened of blood. Still, the sight of a white face was abhorrent to me, and I determined to find some bold free black people and to throw in my lot with them, to cultivate their latent powers and to form a nucleus for a great coloured nation. This idea possessed me, and I travelled over the world for two years seeking for what I desired. At last I almost despaired of finding it. There was no hope of regeneration in the slave-dealing Soudanese, the debased Fantee, or the Americanized negroes of Liberia. I was returning from my quest when chance brought me in contact with this magnificent tribe of dwellers in the desert, and I threw in my lot with them. Before doing so, however, my old instinct of revenge prompted me to make one last visit to the United States, and I returned from it in the *Marie Celeste*.

'As to the voyage itself, your intelligence will have told you by this time that, thanks to my manipulation, both compasses and chronometers were entirely untrustworthy. I alone worked out the course with correct instruments of my own, while the steering was done by my black friends under my guidance. I pushed Tibbs's wife overboard. What! You look surprised and shrink away. Surely you had guessed that by this time. I would have shot you that day through the partition, but unfortunately you were not there. I tried again afterwards, but you were awake. I shot Tibbs. I think the idea of suicide was carried out rather neatly. Of course when once we got on the coast the rest was simple. I had bargained that all on board should die; but that stone of yours upset my plans. I also bargained that there should be no plunder. No one can say we are pirates. We have acted from principle, not from any sordid motive.'

I listened in amazement to the summary of his crimes which this strange man gave me, all in the quietest and most composed of voices, as though detailing incidents of everyday occurrence. I still seem to see him sitting like a hideous nightmare at the end of my couch, with the single rude lamp flickering over his cadaverous features.

'And now,' he continued, 'there is no difficulty about your escape. These stupid adopted children of mine will say that you have gone back to heaven from whence you came. The wind blows off the land. I have a boat all ready for you, well stored with provisions and water. I am anxious to be rid of you, so you may rely that nothing is neglected. Rise up and follow me.'

I did what he commanded, and he led me through the door of the hut. The guards had either been withdrawn, or Goring had arranged matters with them. We passed unchallenged through the town and across the sandy plain. Once more I heard the roar of the sea, and saw the long white line of the surge. Two figures were standing upon the shore arranging the gear of a small boat. They were the two sailors who had been with us on the voyage.

'See him safely through the surf,' said Goring. The two men sprang in and pushed off, pulling me in after them. With mainsail and jib we ran out from the land and passed safely over the bar. Then my two companions without a word of farewell sprang overboard, and I saw their heads like black dots on the white foam as they made their way back to the shore, while I scudded away into the blackness of the night. Looking back I caught my last glimpse of Goring. He was standing upon the summit of a sand-hill, and the rising moon behind him threw his gaunt angular figure into hard relief. He was waving his arms frantically to and fro; it may have been to encourage me on my way, but the gestures seemed to me at the time to be threatening ones, and I have often thought that it was more likely that his old savage instinct had returned when he realized that I was out of his power. Be that as it may, it was the last that I ever saw or ever shall see of Septimius Goring.

There is no need for me to dwell upon my solitary voyage. I steered as well as I could for the Canaries, but was picked up upon the fifth day by the British and African Steam Navigation Company's boat *Monrovia*. Let me take this opportunity of tendering my sincerest thanks to Captain Stornoway and his officers for the great kindness, which they showed me from that time till they landed me in Liverpool, where I was enabled to take one of the Guion boats to New York.

From the day on which I found myself once more in the bosom of my family I have said little of what I have undergone. The subject is still an intensely painful one to me, and the little which I have dropped has been discredited. I now put the facts before the public as they occurred, careless how far they may be believed, and simply writing them down because my lung is growing weaker, and I feel the responsibility of holding my peace longer. I make no vague statement. Turn to your map of Africa. There above Cape Blanco, where the land trends away north and south from the westernmost point of the continent, there it is that Septimius Goring still reigns over his dark subjects, unless retribution has overtaken him; and there, where the long green ridges run swiftly in to roar and hiss upon the hot yellow sand, it is there that Harton lies with Hyson and the other poor fellows who were done to death in the *Marie Celeste*.

The Blood-Stone Tragedy

A Druidical Story

'H USH!' SAID MY FELLOW-TRAVELLER, holding up his hand with a warning gesture, and glancing at his wife, who was snugly ensconced amongst her rugs in the corner. 'Hush!'

'My dear sir,' I remonstrated, 'my reference to Doctor Price——'

'Hush!' interrupted my companion, in a more authoritative voice. 'Not a word!'

Now, this was very mysterious conduct. The gentleman who curtailed my remarks so brusquely had entered the carriage at Rugby with his wife, and we had been whiling away an hour or so of our journey by retailing our views upon current subjects to each other. Having chatted over one topic or another, some unlucky impulse had led me to refer to Dr Price and his recent attempt at the revival of Druidism by the cremation of an infant. To my surprise my allusion had a marked effect upon my companion, who became much agitated, and checked me in the decisive manner which I have quoted.

'Ah! it's all right,' he resumed, bending over and looking down at his wife. 'She is asleep. Come over here into the far corner, so that she cannot hear us if she wakes.'

I obeyed this mysterious injunction, with many surmises in my mind as to the cause of so much precaution.

'It's a painful subject to her,' he said, nodding his head in the direction of the sleeping woman. 'I have known her have an attack of acute mania on hearing an allusion made to it.'

'Made to what?'

'To Druidism.'

'What an extraordinary thing!' I ejaculated.

'I have been keeping the papers from her during the last week,' continued my acquaintance, 'so that she should not hear of this escapade of the doctor. I am convinced it would have a very bad effect upon her mind.'

'Indeed!' I remarked, not without a growing conviction that my companion was a little wrong in the upper storey.

'Ah! of course, you don't understand,' he said, smiling at my evident bewilderment. 'The fact is, that just before our marriage—some ten years ago—

my wife had a very terrible experience in connection with Druidism. It did not get into the papers at the time, but there are a good many people alive who can testify to the facts. It shattered her nervous system, and anything which recalls it knocks her over very much.'

With this short preface, my new friend, leaning well forward and speaking in a low voice, with many precautionary glances at his sleeping wife, told me the story of her extraordinary adventure. I have endeavoured to set it down in his own words as far as I can, but I cannot imitate the earnestness of his manner, nor the weird effect produced by the flickering carriage-lamp, and the presence of the unconscious heroine of this strange story.

'I don't know whether you know Wales well,' he began; 'but even if you do, it is not at all likely that you have ever journeyed as far as Llanduran. It is an out-of-the-way little mountain village up in the north, not far from the sea, a place which is hardly marked in the maps, and where no tourist ever goes unless he stumbles upon it by accident. This was our fate in the autumn of '72, and we were so taken by the pretty surroundings and the primitive peasantry, that we made it our resting-place for some time. We were a fairly large party—my brother Stephen and his wife, my present wife, with her two brothers, and three friends of mine from London. Altogether we had a very jolly time of it, and astonished the quiet-living Cymric population not a little, until our holiday was brought to an abrupt and tragic termination.

'I must tell you that my wife—or Miss Madison, as she was in those days—was of a most adventurous disposition. She appeared to be absolutely insensible to fear. I was continually remonstrating with her as to the risks which she ran, and her brothers did all they could to restrain her, but without avail. The more we spoke, the more daring would she become. We were compelled, at last, to leave her behind when we intended to do any serious mountaineering, for fear she should meet with some accident.

'One morning, when we came down to breakfast, we learned to our surprise that Miss Madison had been seen to leave the inn alone at early dawn, in her walking-dress, and to take the direction of the mountains. Her intention, evidently, was to steal a march upon us by visiting alone some of those places which we had gone to without her. We were all rather alarmed by this escapade of the wild girl; but our alarm deepened into positive terror when the whole day passed without our hearing a word of her. The district was a notoriously dangerous one. The mountains, without being remarkably high, were jagged and steep, and intersected by numerous chasms. Several fatal accidents had occurred of late in the vicinity. No wonder, then, that I felt a sinking at my heart when I left the inn that night at the head of a party with torches in search of the woman whom I had already begun to love.

'I will tell you the story now from her point of view, and give you the facts which we heard afterwards from her own lips.

'Leaving the inn, then, and laughing to herself at the way in which she was giving us the slip, she made the best of her way into the mountains. The morning was a beautiful one, and the crisp, bracing air increased her natural activity and endurance, so that she had walked a very long way before the thought of fatigue entered her mind. She had gone on at random, following the little goat-paths from one rugged valley to another, until she had lost sight of all the familiar landmarks, and found herself in a desolate labyrinth, surrounded on every side by precipitous crags, and without the smallest sign of human life. Many women would have been terrified in her position, but, as I have said, she was constitutionally brave; so finding it hopeless to retrace her steps, she pushed on, in the hope of reaching some eminence from which she could catch a glimpse of the outside world.

'As she advanced, the scenery became bleaker and more dismal. The mountains in those regions are always desolate, being hardly picturesque enough to attract tourists, and too barren to allow any one to settle among them. She stumbled along among great boulders, and along the bed of a dried-up stream, with lofty granite walls on each side of her without break or opening. Following the track of the old torrent, she traced it at last to a place where there had evidently been a cascade, as the bed of the stream descended precipitously for thirty or forty feet. Hoping by ascending to obtain some idea of her whereabouts, my wife clambered up this steep incline, and succeeded with some difficulty in reaching the top.

'The sight before her was an extraordinary one. The gap through which the stream had forced its way was the only entrance to a little ravine, surrounded on all sides by high, dark cliffs. This secluded nook formed a cul-de-sac about two hundred yards long and fifty broad, ringed in by fir trees, which sprouted from the base of the rocky walls. In the centre of the clear space in the middle was a large flat slab, round which were placed a number of stones, standing upon their ends, and forming a double circle. This arrangement was evidently artificial, and my wife looked round, in the hope of seeing some signs of human life. To her great delight she perceived among the trees a rough sort of hut, to which she hurried, with the intention of getting some refreshment if possible, and then of inquiring her way homewards.

'The rude door of this wooden dwelling was ajar, and Miss Madison, after knocking several times without receiving an answer, pushed her way in.

'The room in which she found herself was a small one, and furnished in the roughest manner possible. A heap of goat-skins in the corner appeared to have been utilised as a bed, and a large block of wood in the centre was evidently intended as a table, as the remains of a meal, in the shape of a couple of bones, were lying upon it. What struck the young lady most, however, in this extraordinary apartment were the walls, which were thickly covered with curious inscriptions, painted on it in dark letters. These were in some unknown language, which she conjectured to be Welsh; but there were others, especially over the door and in the centre of each wall, which were evidently designed as symbols or charms, consisting of the same letter, repeated a number of times in different shapes and forms.

'My wife was standing in the doorway, regarding all these strange things with natural curiosity, when she became aware of a shadow which intervened between her and the sun. Turning round, she saw behind her the most extraordinary mortal that she had ever beheld. He was an elderly man, with long, floating hair and a grizzled beard, which descended over his breast. He could not have been less than six feet four inches high, and the breadth of his shoulders and length of his arms denoted extraordinary strength, while the great club upon which he leaned might have served him either as a support or as a weapon. His dress was a sort of ragged gown, which had been originally white, but was now weather-stained and dirty. What struck my wife, however, more than either his other features or his strange attire, were his eyes, which were of a light, almost colourless blue, but which projected considerably, and shifted from one object to another without remaining still for an instant.

'"Hail, lady!" he exclaimed, advancing towards Miss Madison, and speaking in a well-modulated voice. "For five moons I have waited for you. Why hast thou tarried so long?"

'Considerably astonished, but more amused than frightened, the young lady took a step or two back from this strange apparition, who walked slowly forwards, waving his hands rhythmically from side to side.

'"The blood-stone is dry!" he cried, "the blood-stone is dry! Shall it be said that in the days of the fifteenth avatar there was no man who would honour the old gods, and no woman who would dare lie down upon the blood-stone? Britain's noblest and fairest have stretched themselves upon that cold couch. You are worthy of the honour, maiden. Thy cheek is unblanched, and thy hand is steady. So should she be whom the high gods select."

'My wife had begun by this time to realise that the man in front of her was a maniac, though she had not yet fathomed the meaning of his strange words. She endeavoured to conceal her fright as much as possible, however, and to conciliate her fierce-looking companion.

'"You must lead a lonely life, sir," she said. "Who are you, and why do you dwell up here alone?"

'"Who am I?' he cried, tossing his long, thin arms in the air. "I am Ap-Griffiths, of the pure blood of Arisdenna, seventieth in descent from the high priest Morla, who was second brother to the great Queen Boadicea. Woman, I am the last of the Druids. All round," he continued, mournfully, "men have left the old creed. None bow to the high gods now. Only we are staunch and true, maiden; you and I—the slayer and the slain."

'Thoroughly alarmed by this time, my wife endeavoured to edge away to the mouth of the little glen, but the maniac, who was wildly excited, caught her by the wrist and dragged her over to the spot where the stones were.

'"Have I not done it well!" he cried. "There have been many larger, but none more complete. What is there wanting? Here is the blood-stone," pointing to the flat slab in the centre; "it has been dry for many years, but when you lie on it, maiden, with the flames roaring around you, and when your life-blood hisses upon the hot stone, then the gods will know that there are believers yet. Nay, do not shudder and shrink. Your vile body may be charred and tortured, but your spirit will soar above the stars, ever exulting in a happiness which no words can depict. Mark my stones. Thirty-four without, and twenty-three within, according to the direction of the learned and holy Morla. I have a trench, too, around the blood-stone, and my instrument is as it should be." Here he drew a long, keen knife from his bosom. "All has been ready for months, save only the victim, and now the great gods have sent me that also."

'My wife was, as I have already told you, a woman of great courage and resource. It was evident to her in a moment that to attempt to escape was impossible, in the presence of so agile and powerful an adversary. Her only hope of safety lay in humouring and outwitting him. She turned towards him, therefore, and assumed as much calmness as she could, while she asked the terrible question:

'"When am I to be sacrificed?"

'"At the middle hour of the night," said the maniac, with decision.

'She felt instinctively that it was useless to plead her sex, her age, or her helplessness to this sanguinary fanatic. The sun was already low down on the horizon, and there would be only a few hours to pass before she should find herself stretched upon the fatal blood-stone. Her last chance lay in the use she might make of that short period.

'"I am ignorant," she said, "of many of the things of which you speak. I have much to learn before I can die."

'"You are right, maiden," he said; "there is much which none can teach in these latter days save those who still have the priestly blood in their veins. Come with me into my dwelling, and I will discourse with you concerning many things, that when thy soul is loosened from its bonds it may know whither it speedeth."

'With these words the Druid, as I will call him, led Miss Madison into the hut, and commanded her to be seated on a rough wooden bench which stood opposite the door. He himself lay down upon a couple of goat-skins at her feet, and began to talk to her with great volubility and earnestness. Much of his conversation was unintelligible to her, and occasionally he would break into rude doggerel verses, but she could understand enough to gather that he was laying down the precepts of the old British faith. Poor girl! her mind was too full of horror to allow her to pay much attention to his disquisition. Certain death seemed to stare her in the face—and death in its most horrible form. Look which way she would, there seemed to be no possibility of escape. Through the half-open door she could see that the night was drawing in. The Druid observed it too, for, suddenly ceasing his harangue, he sprang to his feet, and seized a great chopper which leaned against the wall.

'"I must leave you for a time, maiden," he said. "There is much to be done before the darkness comes. The wood is to be cut for the funeral pyre, for I swear to you that none who ever lay upon that hard bridal couch shall have had a more seemly ending than thine shall be."

'With these words he hurried out of the hut, and Miss Madison could tell by the crashing sound that he was cutting among the fir trees which surrounded the valley.

'For a moment a ray of hope came into her mind. Might she not slip past him while he was engaged in his work, and gain the mouth of the ravine without his detecting her? She rose with the determination to risk everything upon the chance, when, to her unutterable horror, she found that the cunning miscreant had, in some unaccountable way, managed to slip the noose of a rope round her ankles while he lay at her feet, and that she was firmly pinioned to the bench. It was only then that the relentless cruelty and unbending resolution of the monster who had captured her came fully home to her. She screamed piteously for aid, though she knew that her cries were as useless as her struggles would be. She was entirely at the mercy of the maniac.

'He came back upon hearing her cries, and stood in the doorway, looking down at her with a look of melancholy upon his face. It was so dark now that it was difficult for her to distinguish his features.

'"Lady," he said, "this is not what I had hoped. How shall thy courage bear thee up at the supreme moment if thou shrinkest now? You have been honoured above all women by the selection of the gods. Canst thou not prove thyself worthy of the choice? Learn, too, that thy cries are of no avail, for there is no human ear for many a mile. Thou art not the only one on whom death will come tonight. When the red light of thy pyre tinges the crags of Conmorris, and thy holocaust is completed, then Ap-Griffiths, the last of the priestly line, shall pass away with his mission gloriously fulfilled. My life, as well as yours, maiden, terminates at the coming of the fifteenth avatar, which my knowledge teaches me will be at the twelfth hour of this night."

'Driven to desperation, my poor wife prayed and begged for mercy from the madman, using every possible entreaty and expostulation to prevent him from carrying out his murderous design. Her prayers, however, had the exactly opposite effect, for, flying into a paroxysm of rage, the Druid sprang upon her, forcing her down on the bench, to which she was already pinioned.

'"Wicked and ungrateful woman!" he roared, winding a cord round her body, and securing her more firmly than before, "would you persuade the only faithful one to turn false? Not a word more, or I must silence your tongue. You have already committed a grievous sin."

'With these words, he seized his chopper once more, and went back to his work, cutting great faggots, and piling them around the fatal blood-stone.

'Gradually the darkness of night settled down upon the little valley. The poor girl—stretched, more dead than alive, upon the rough bench—could distinguish the gaunt outlines of the madman as he wielded his chopper with demoniacal fury. Then the sound ceased, and she lost sight of him in the gloom. When the moon came out, however, she perceived him once more, kneeling among the perpendicular stones. He was bowing his head, waving his arms, and giving other symptoms of being engaged in religious devotion. Then he stood up, and burst into a rude, wild chant, which reverberated through the little ravine, and was echoed back from the rocky walls.

'During this time, the very possibility of escape had ceased to occur to Miss Madison. Suddenly, however, her senses, strained to an unnatural tension, detected a sound in the distance. She listened once more in a quiver of excitement, and again it seemed to her that the breeze bore a faint note to her ear, not unlike the sound of a horn. Could it be that her friends had hit upon the right track? She lay perfectly still, able to hear the beatings of her own heart. For five minutes all was silence, save the monotonous chant of the maniac. Then again the same long wail struck upon her ear, apparently rather louder and more near than before. The Druid seemed to hear it, too, for he ceased his incantation, and paced uneasily backwards and forwards.

'By her calculation it could not be more than eleven o'clock. She had, therefore, an hour before her if the maniac adhered to his former plan. The suspense was agonising. She lay, with her eyes shut, counting the seconds, and waiting for a repetition of the sound; but all was as silent as the grave.

'Minute passed after minute. Half the hour was gone without any sign of her rescuers. Another quarter passed, and the madman began to take a last look at the pyre, and to make his final preparations. Then he struck a light, and ignited the base of the mound of sticks. The dry, resinous pine-wood crackled and spluttered, while long tongues of flame licked round the borders of the fatal blood-stone. He approached the door of the hut. "The time has come, maiden!" he said.

'It must have been a weird sight—the column of fire shooting up into the air, throwing fantastic shadows among the gaunt fir trees and the Druidical stones—within the circle of light the white-clad maniac, and in front of him the shrinking girl! He was in the very act of undoing the cords which bound her, when from the mouth of the glen came a loud peal from a horn, and a chorus of human voices, all shouting together. The light of the fire had attracted the rescue party.

'The Druid started like a hunted beast. "Too late!" he roared; "too late! Thy doom is sealed! Thou must die!" He caught up the bench and the prostrate woman, and, running with incredible speed, he laid her beside the roaring flames, while he drew his long knife from his bosom. My poor wife's last recollection is of the fierce face looking down at her, the savage, colourless eyes, and the uplifted knife.

* * * * *

'When she came to herself, friendly faces were around her. Her head was pillowed upon my breast, and the first word that passed her dear lips was my name. The Druid was lying on his back, some little way off, with his head cut open. I shall never get such a stick again as the old friend which I broke that night over his crazy skull. It was touch and go, though, for if I had got up one moment later, the fellow's knife would have been in Mary's heart.

'We got her down to the inn at Llanduran, but she developed brain fever next day, and for weeks her life was despaired of. Such an impression has the adventure made upon her that the least incident which may recall it has a very bad effect upon her. That is why I have concealed the episode of Dr Price from her knowledge,'

'And the Druid?' I asked.

'Oh, he turned out to be a very well-known man of science and archaeologist. He had been erratic in his conduct, and was therefore confined in the Merthyr Lunatic Asylum, but he escaped some six months before, and all clue to his whereabouts was lost. He must have spent the whole time in this nook among the mountains, practising his pagan rites, and living on the goats and anything he could pick up.'

'What became of him, then?'

'Oh, that is about the queerest thing in the whole queer story. Whether the crack with my stick depressed some bump, or how it acted, I don't know; but the fact remains that when he had recovered his senses he was as sane as you and I, and has, as far as I know, remained so ever since. They kept him in the asylum for some time for fear of a relapse, but they let him out eventually. Hush! she's waking up. Yes, they will have a lively time at the beginning of the next session, to all appearance. Don't you think so, my dear?'

John Barrington Cowles

I

IT MIGHT SEEM RASH OF ME TO SAY that I ascribe the death of my poor friend, John Barrington Cowles, to any preternatural agency. I am aware that in the present state of public feeling a chain of evidence would require to be strong indeed before the possibility of such a conclusion could be admitted.

I shall therefore merely state the circumstances which led up to this sad event as concisely and as plainly as I can, and leave every reader to draw his own deductions. Perhaps there may be someone who can throw light upon what is dark to me.

I first met Barrington Cowles when I went up to Edinburgh University to take out medical classes there. My landlady in Northumberland Street had a large house, and, being a widow without children, she gained a livelihood by providing accommodation for several students.

Barrington Cowles happened to have taken a bedroom upon the same floor as mine, and when we came to know each other better we shared a small sitting-room, in which we took our meals. In this manner we originated a friendship which was unmarred by the slightest disagreement up to the day of his death.

Cowles' father was the colonel of a Sikh regiment and had remained in India for many years. He allowed his son a handsome income, but seldom gave any other sign of parental affection—writing irregularly and briefly.

My friend, who had himself been born in India, and whose whole disposition was an ardent tropical one, was much hurt by this neglect. His mother was dead, and he had no other relation in the world to supply the blank.

Thus he came in time to concentrate all his affection upon me, and to confide in me in a manner which is rare among men. Even when a stronger and deeper passion came upon him, it never infringed upon the old tenderness between us.

Cowles was a tall, slim young fellow, with an olive, Velasquez-like face, and dark, tender eyes. I have seldom seen a man who was more likely to excite a woman's interest, or to captivate her imagination. His expression was, as a rule, dreamy, and even languid; but if in conversation a subject arose which interested him he would be all animation in a moment. On such occasions his colour would heighten, his eyes gleam, and he could speak with an eloquence which would carry his audience with him.

In spite of these natural advantages he led a solitary life, avoiding female society, and reading with great diligence. He was one of the foremost men of his year, taking the senior medal for anatomy, and the Neil Arnott prize for physics.

How well I can recollect the first time we met her! Often and often I have recalled the circumstances, and tried to remember what the exact impression was which she produced on my mind at the time. After we came to know her my judgment was warped, so that I am curious to recollect what my unbiased instincts were. It is hard, however, to eliminate the feelings which reason or prejudice afterwards raised in me.

It was at the opening of the Royal Scottish Academy in the spring of 1879. My poor friend was passionately attached to art in every form, and a pleasing chord in music or a delicate effect upon canvas would give exquisite pleasure to his highly strung nature. We had gone together to see the pictures, and were standing in the grand central *salon*, when I noticed an extremely beautiful woman standing at the other side of the room. In my whole life I have never seen such a classically perfect countenance. It was the real Greek type—the forehead broad, very low, and as white as marble, with a cloudlet of delicate locks wreathing round it, the nose straight and clean-cut, the lips inclined to thinness, the chin and lower jaw beautifully rounded off, and yet sufficiently developed to promise unusual strength of character.

But those eyes—those wonderful eyes! If I could but give some faint idea of their varying moods, their steely hardness, their feminine softness, their power of command, their penetrating intensity suddenly melting away into an expression of womanly weakness—but I am speaking now of future impressions!

There was a tall, yellow-haired young man with this lady, whom I at once recognised as a law student with whom I had a slight acquaintance.

Archibald Reeves—for that was his name—was a dashing, handsome young fellow, and had at one time been a ringleader in every university escapade; but of late I had seen little of him, and the report was that he was engaged to be married. His companion was, then, I presumed, his fiancée. I seated myself upon the velvet settee in the centre of the room, and furtively watched the couple from behind my catalogue.

The more I looked at her the more her beauty grew upon me. She was somewhat short in stature, it is true; but her figure was perfection, and she bore herself in such a fashion that it was only by actual comparison that one would have known her to be under the medium height.

As I kept my eyes upon them, Reeves was called away for some reason, and the young lady was left alone. Turning her back to the pictures, she passed the time until the return of her escort in taking a deliberate survey of the company, without paying the least heed to the fact that a dozen pair of eyes, attracted by her elegance and beauty, were bent curiously upon her. With one of her hands holding the red silk cord which railed off the pictures, she stood languidly moving her eyes from face to face with as little self-consciousness as if she were looking at the canvas creatures behind her. Suddenly, as I watched her, I saw her gaze become fixed, and, as it were, intense. I followed the direction of her looks, wondering what could have attracted her so strongly.

John Barrington Cowles was standing before a picture—one, I think, by Noel Paton—I know that the subject was a noble and ethereal one. His profile was turned towards us, and never have I seen him to such advantage. I have said that he was a strikingly handsome man, but at that moment he looked absolutely magnificent. It was evident that he had momentarily forgotten his surroundings, and that his whole soul was in sympathy with the picture before him. His eyes sparkled, and a dusky pink shone through his clear olive cheeks. She continued to watch him fixedly, with a look of interest upon her face, until he came out of his reverie with a start, and turned abruptly round, so that his gaze met hers. She glanced away at once, but his eyes remained fixed upon her for some moments. The picture was forgotten already, and his soul had come down to earth once more.

We caught sight of her once or twice before we left, and each time I noticed my friend look after her. He made no remark, however, until we got out into the open air, and were walking arm-in-arm along Princes Street.

'Did you notice that beautiful woman, in the dark dress, with the white fur?' he asked.

'Yes, I saw her,' I answered.

'Do you know her?' he asked eagerly. 'Have you any idea who she is?'

'I don't know her personally,' I replied. 'But I have no doubt I could find out all about her, for I believe she is engaged to young Archie Reeves, and he and I have a lot of mutual friends.'

'Engaged!' ejaculated Cowles.

'Why, my dear boy,' I said, laughing, 'you don't mean to say you are so susceptible that the fact that a girl to whom you never spoke in your life is engaged is enough to upset you?'

'Well, not exactly to upset me,' he answered, forcing a laugh. 'But I don't mind telling you, Armitage, that I never was so taken by any one in my life. It wasn't the mere beauty of the face—though that was perfect enough—but it was the character and the intellect upon it. I hope, if she is engaged, that it is to some man who will be worthy of her.'

'Why,' I remarked, 'you speak quite feelingly. It is a clear case of love at first sight, Jack. However, to put your perturbed spirit at rest, I'll make a point of finding out all about her whenever I meet any fellow who is likely to know.'

Barrington Cowles thanked me, and the conversation drifted off into other channels. For several days neither of us made any allusion to the subject, though my companion was perhaps a little more dreamy and distraught than usual. The incident had almost vanished from my remembrance, when one day young Brodie, who is a second cousin of mine, came up to me on the university steps with the face of a bearer of tidings.

'I say,' he began, 'you know Reeves, don't you?'

'Yes. What of him?'

'His engagement is off.'

'Off!' I cried. 'Why, I only learned the other day that it was on.'

'Oh, yes—it's all off. His brother told me so. Deucedly mean of Reeves, you know, if he has backed out of it, for she was an uncommonly nice girl.'

'I've seen her,' I said; 'but I don't know her name.'

'She is a Miss Northcott, and lives with an old aunt of hers in Abercrombie Place. Nobody knows anything about her people, or where she comes from. Anyhow, she is about the most unlucky girl in the world, poor soul!'

'Why unlucky?'

'Well, you know, this was her second engagement,' said young Brodie, who had a marvellous knack of knowing everything about everybody. 'She was engaged to Prescott—William Prescott, who died. That was a very sad affair. The wedding day was fixed, and the whole thing looked as straight as a die—when the smash came.'

'What smash?' I asked, with some dim recollection of the circumstances.

'Why, Prescott's death. He came to Abercrombie Place one night, and stayed very late. No one knows exactly when he left, but about one in the morning a fellow who knew him met him walking rapidly in the direction of the Queen's Park. He bade him good night, but Prescott hurried on without heeding him, and that was the last time he was ever seen alive. Three days afterwards his body was found floating in St Margaret's Loch, under St Anthony's Chapel. No one could ever understand it, but of course the verdict brought it in as temporary insanity.'

'It was very strange,' I remarked.

'Yes, and deucedly rough on the poor girl,' said Brodie. 'Now that this other blow has come it will quite crush her. So gentle and ladylike she is, too!'

'You know her personally, then!' I asked.

'Oh, yes, I know her. I have met her several times. I could easily manage that you should be introduced to her.'

'Well,' I answered, 'it's not so much for my own sake as for a friend of mine. However, I don't suppose she will go out much for some little time after this. When she does I will take advantage of your offer.'

We shook hands on this, and I thought no more of the matter for some time.

The next incident which I have to relate as bearing at all upon the question of Miss Northcott is an unpleasant one. Yet I must detail it as accurately as possible, since it may throw some light upon the sequel. One cold night, several months after the conversation with my second cousin which I have quoted above, I was walking down one of the lowest streets in the city on my way back from a case which I had been attending. It was very late, and I was picking my way among the dirty loungers who were clustering round the doors of a great gin-palace, when a man staggered out from among them, and held out his hand to me with a drunken leer. The gaslight fell full upon his face, and, to my intense astonishment, I recognised in the degraded creature before me my former acquaintance, young Archibald Reeves, who had once been famous as one of the most dressy and particular men in the whole college. I was so utterly surprised that for a moment I almost doubted the evidence of my own senses; but there was no mistaking those features, which, though bloated with drink, still retained something of their former comeliness. I was determined to rescue him, for one night at least, from the company into which he had fallen.

'Holloa, Reeves!' I said. 'Come along with me. I'm going in your direction.'

He muttered some incoherent apology for his condition, and took my arm. As I supported him towards his lodgings I could see that he was not only suffering from the effects of a recent debauch, but that a long course of intemperance had affected his nerves and his brain. His hand when I touched it was dry and feverish, and he started from every shadow which fell upon the pavement. He rambled in his speech, too, in a manner which suggested the delirium of disease rather than the talk of a drunkard.

When I got him to his lodgings I partially undressed him and laid him upon his bed. His pulse at this time was very high, and he was evidently extremely feverish. He seemed to have sunk into a doze; and I was about to steal out of the room to warn his landlady of his condition, when he started up and caught me by the sleeve of my coat.

'Don't go!' he cried. 'I feel better when you are here. I am safe from her then.'

'From her!' I said. 'From whom?'

'Her! her!' he answered peevishly. 'Ah! you don't know her. She is the devil! Beautiful—beautiful; but the devil!'

'You are feverish and excited,' I said. 'Try and get a little sleep. You will wake better.'

'Sleep!' he groaned. 'How am I to sleep when I see her sitting down yonder at the foot of the bed with her great eyes watching and watching hour after hour? I tell you it saps all the strength and manhood out of me. That's what makes me drink. God help me—I'm half drunk now!'

'You are very ill,' I said, putting some vinegar to his temples; 'and you are delirious. You don't know what you say.'

'Yes, I do,' he interrupted sharply, looking up at me. 'I know very well what I say. I brought it upon myself. It is my own choice. But I couldn't—no, by Heaven! I couldn't—accept the alternative. I couldn't keep my faith to her. It was more than man could do.'

I sat by the side of the bed, holding one of his burning hands in mine, and wondering over his strange words. He lay still for some time, and then, raising his eyes to me, said in a most plaintive voice:

'Why did she not give me warning sooner? Why did she wait until I had learned to love her so?'

He repeated this question several times, rolling his feverish head from side to side, and then he dropped into a troubled sleep. I crept out of the room, and, having seen that he would be properly cared for, left the house. His words, however, rang in my ears for days afterwards, and assumed a deeper significance when taken with what was to come.

My friend, Barrington Cowles, had been away for his summer holidays, and I had heard nothing of him for several months. When the winter session came on, however, I received a telegram from him, asking me to secure the old rooms in Northumberland Street for him, and telling me the train by which he would arrive. I went down to meet him, and was delighted to find him looking wonderfully hearty and well.

'By the way,' he said suddenly, that night, as we sat in our chairs by the fire, talking over the events of the holidays, 'you have never congratulated me yet!'

'On what, my boy?' I asked.

'What! Do you mean to say you have not heard of my engagement?'

'Engagement! No!' I answered. 'However, I am delighted to hear it, and congratulate you with all my heart.'

'I wonder it didn't come to your ears,' he said. 'It was the queerest thing. You remember that girl whom we both admired so much at the Academy?'

'What!' I cried, with a vague feeling of apprehension at my heart. 'You don't mean to say that you are engaged to her?'

'I thought you would be surprised,' he answered. 'When I was staying with an old aunt of mine in Peterhead, in Aberdeenshire, the Northcotts happened to come there on a visit, and as we had mutual friends we soon met. I found out that it was a false alarm about her being engaged, and then—well, you know what it is when you are thrown into the society of such a girl in a place like Peterhead. Not, mind you,' he added, 'that I consider I did a foolish or hasty thing. I have never regretted it for a moment. The more I know Kate the more I admire her and love her. However, you must be introduced to her, and then you will form your own opinion.'

I expressed my pleasure at the prospect, and endeavoured to speak as lightly as I could to Cowles upon the subject, but I felt depressed and anxious at heart. The words of Reeves and the unhappy fate of young Prescott recurred to my recollection, and though I could assign no tangible reason for it, a vague, dim fear and distrust of the woman took possession of me. It may be that this was foolish prejudice and superstition upon my part, and that I involuntarily contorted her future doings and sayings to fit into some half-formed wild theory of my own. This has been suggested to me by others as an explanation of my narrative. They are welcome to their opinion if they can reconcile it with the facts which I have to tell.

I went round with my friend a few days afterwards to call upon Miss Northcott. I remember that, as we went down Abercrombie Place, our attention was attracted by the shrill yelping of a dog, which noise proved eventually to come from the house to which we were bound. We were shown upstairs, where I was introduced to old Mrs Merton, Miss Northcott's aunt, and to the young lady herself. She looked as beautiful as ever, and I could not wonder at my friend's infatuation. Her face was a little more flushed than usual, and she held in her hand a heavy dog-whip, with which she had been chastising a small Scotch terrier, whose cries we had heard in the street. The poor brute was cringing up against the wall, whining piteously, and evidently completely cowed.

'So Kate,' said my friend, after we had taken our seats, 'you have been falling out with Carlo again.'

'Only a very little quarrel this time,' she said, smiling charmingly. 'He is a dear, good old fellow, but he needs correction now and then.' Then, turning to me, 'We all do that, Mr Armitage, don't we? What a capital thing if, instead of receiving a collective punishment at the end of our lives, we were to have one at once, as the dogs do, when we did anything wicked. It would make us more careful, wouldn't it?'

I acknowledged that it would.

'Supposing that every time a man misbehaved himself a gigantic hand were to seize him, and he were lashed with a whip until he fainted'—she clenched her white fingers as she spoke, and cut out viciously with the dog-whip—'it would do more to keep him good than any number of high-minded theories of morality.'

'Why, Kate,' said my friend, 'you are quite savage today.'

'No, Jack,' she laughed. 'I'm only propounding a theory for Mr Armitage's consideration.'

The two began to chat together about some Aberdeenshire reminiscence, and I had time to observe Mrs Merton, who had remained silent during our short conversation. She was a very strange-looking old lady. What attracted attention most in her appearance was the utter want of colour which she exhibited. Her hair was snow-white, and her face extremely pale. Her lips were bloodless, and even her eyes were of such a light tinge of blue that they hardly relieved the general pallor. Her dress was a grey silk, which harmonised with her general appearance. She had a peculiar expression of countenance, which I was unable at the moment to refer to its proper cause. She was working at some old-fashioned piece of ornamental needlework, and as she moved her arms her dress gave forth a dry, melancholy rustling, like the sound of leaves in the autumn. There was something mournful and depressing in the sight of her. I moved my chair a little nearer, and asked her how she liked Edinburgh, and whether she had been there long.

When I spoke to her she started and looked up at me with a scared look on her face. Then I saw in a moment what the expression was which I had observed there. It was one of fear—intense and overpowering fear. It was so marked that I could have staked my life on the woman before me having at some period of her life been subjected to some terrible experience or dreadful misfortune.

'Oh, yes, I like it,' she said, in a soft, timid voice; 'and we have been here long—that is, not very long. We move about a great deal.' She spoke with hesitation, as if afraid of committing herself.

'You are a native of Scotland, I presume?' I said.

'No—that is, not entirely. We are not natives of any place. We are cosmopolitan, you know.' She glanced round in the direction of Miss Northcott as she spoke, but the two were still chatting together near the window. Then she suddenly bent forward to me, with a look of intense earnestness upon her face, and said:

'Don't talk to me any more, please. She does not like it, and I shall suffer for it afterwards. Please, don't do it.'

I was about to ask her the reason for this strange request, but when she saw I was going to address her, she rose and walked slowly out of the room. As she did so I perceived that the lovers had ceased to talk, and that Miss Northcott was looking at me with her keen, grey eyes.

'You must excuse my aunt, Mr Armitage,' she said; 'she is old, and easily fatigued. Come over and look at my album.'

We spent some time examining the portraits. Miss Northcott's father and mother were apparently ordinary mortals enough, and I could not detect in either of them any traces of the character which showed itself in their daughter's face. There was one old daguerreotype, however, which arrested my attention. It represented a man of about the age of forty, and strikingly handsome. He was clean shaven, and extraordinary power was expressed upon his prominent lower jaw and firm, straight mouth. His eyes were somewhat deeply set in his head, however, and there was a snake-like flattening at the upper part of his forehead, which detracted from his appearance. I almost involuntarily, when I saw the head, pointed to it, and exclaimed:

'There is your prototype in your family, Miss Northcott.'

'Do you think so?' she said. 'I am afraid you are paying me a very bad compliment. Uncle Anthony was always considered the black sheep of the family.'

'Indeed,' I answered; 'my remark was an unfortunate one, then.'

'Oh, don't mind that,' she said; 'I always thought myself that he was worth all of them put together. He was an officer in the Forty-first Regiment, and he was killed in action during the Persian War—so he died nobly, at any rate.'

'That's the sort of death I should like to die,' said Cowles, his dark eyes flashing, as they would when he was excited; 'I often wish I had taken to my father's profession instead of this vile pill-compounding drudgery.'

'Come, Jack, you are not going to die any sort of death yet,' she said, tenderly taking his hand in hers.

I could not understand the woman. There was such an extraordinary mixture of masculine decision and womanly tenderness about her, with the consciousness of something all her own in the background, that she fairly puzzled me. I hardly knew, therefore, how to answer Cowles when, as we walked down the street together, he asked the comprehensive question:

'Well, what do you think of her?'

'I think she is wonderfully beautiful,' I answered guardedly.

'That, of course,' he replied irritably. 'You knew that before you came!'

'I think she is very clever too,' I remarked.

Barrington Cowles walked on for some time, and then he suddenly turned on me with the strange question:

'Do you think she is cruel? Do you think she is the sort of girl who would take a pleasure in inflicting pain?'

'Well, really,' I answered, 'I have hardly had time to form an opinion.'

We then walked on for some time in silence.

'She is an old fool,' at length muttered Cowles. 'She is mad.'

'Who is?' I asked.

'Why, that old woman—that aunt of Kate's—Mrs Merton, or whatever her name is.'

Then I knew that my poor colourless friend had been speaking to Cowles, but he never said anything more as to the nature of her communication.

My companion went to bed early that night, and I sat up a long time by the fire, thinking over all that I had seen and heard. I felt that there was some mystery about the girl—some dark fatality so strange as to defy conjecture. I thought of Prescott's interview with her before their marriage, and the fatal termination of it. I coupled it with poor drunken Reeves' plaintive cry, 'Why did she not tell me sooner?' and with the other words he had spoken. Then my mind ran over Mrs Merton's warning to me, Cowles' reference to her, and even the episode of the whip and the cringing dog.

The whole effect of my recollections was unpleasant to a degree, and yet there was no tangible charge which I could bring against the woman. It would be worse than useless to attempt to warn my friend until I had definitely made up my mind what I was to warn him against. He would treat any charge against her with scorn. What could I do? How could I get at some tangible conclusion as to her character and antecedents? No one in Edinburgh knew them except as recent acquaintances. She was an orphan, and as far as I knew she had never disclosed where her former home had been. Suddenly an idea struck me. Among my father's friends there was a Colonel Joyce, who had served a long time in

India upon the staff, and who would be likely to know most of the officers who had been out there since the Mutiny. I sat down at once, and, having trimmed the lamp, proceeded to write a letter to the Colonel. I told him that I was very curious to gain some particulars about a certain Captain Northcott, who had served in the Forty-first Foot, and who had fallen in the Persian War. I described the man as well as I could from my recollection of the daguerreotype, and then, having directed the letter, posted it that very night, after which, feeling that I had done all that could be done, I retired to bed, with a mind too anxious to allow me to sleep.

II

I got an answer from Leicester, where the Colonel resided, within two days. I have it before me as I write, and copy it verbatim.

'DEAR BOB,' it said, 'I remember the man well. I was with him at Calcutta, and afterwards at Hyderabad. He was a curious, solitary sort of mortal; but a gallant soldier enough, for he distinguished himself at Sobraon, and was wounded, if I remember right. He was not popular in his corps—they said he was a pitiless, cold-blooded fellow, with no geniality in him. There was a rumour, too, that he was a devil-worshipper, or something of that sort, and also that he had the evil eye, which, of course, was all nonsense. He had some strange theories, I remember, about the power of the human will and the effects of mind upon matter.

'How are you getting on with your medical studies? Never forget, my boy, that your father's son has every claim upon me, and that if I can serve you in any way I am always at your command.

Ever affectionately yours,

EDWARD JOYCE

'P.S.—By the way, Northcott did not fall in action. He was killed after peace was declared in a crazy attempt to get some of the eternal fire from the sun-worshippers' temple. There was considerable mystery about his death.'

I read this epistle over several times—at first with a feeling of satisfaction, and then with one of disappointment. I had come on some curious information, and yet hardly what I wanted. He was an eccentric man, a devil-worshipper, and rumoured to have the power of the evil eye. I could believe the young lady's eyes, when endowed with that cold, grey shimmer which I had noticed in them once or twice, to be capable of any evil which human eye ever wrought; but still the superstition was an effete one. Was there not more meaning in that sentence which followed—'He had theories of the power of the human will and of the effect of mind upon matter'? I remember having once read a quaint treatise, which I had imagined to be mere charlatanism at the time, of the power of certain human minds, and of effects produced by them at a distance. Was Miss Northcott endowed with some exceptional power of the sort? The idea grew upon me, and very shortly I had evidence which convinced me of the truth of the supposition.

It happened that at the very time when my mind was dwelling upon this subject, I saw a notice in the paper that our town was to be visited by Dr Messinger, the well-known medium and mesmerist. Messinger was a man whose performance, such as it was, had been again and again pronounced to be genuine by competent judges. He was far above trickery, and had the reputation of being the soundest living authority upon the strange pseudo-sciences of animal magnetism and electro-biology. Determined, therefore, to see what the human will could do, even against all the disadvantages of glaring footlights and a public platform, I took a ticket for the first night of the performance, and went with several student friends.

We had secured one of the side boxes, and did not arrive until after the performance had begun. I had hardly taken my seat before I recognised Barrington Cowles, with his fiancée and old Mrs Merton, sitting in the third or fourth row of the stalls. They caught sight of me at almost the same moment, and we bowed to each other. The first portion of the lecture was somewhat commonplace, the lecturer giving tricks of pure legerdemain, with one or two manifestations of mesmerism, performed upon a subject whom he had brought with him. He gave us an exhibition of clairvoyance too, throwing his subject into a trance, and then demanding particulars as to the movements of absent friends, and the whereabouts of hidden objects, all of which appeared to be answered satisfactorily. I had seen all this before, however. What I wanted to see now was the effect of the lecturer's will when exerted upon some independent member of the audience.

He came round to that as the concluding exhibition in his performance. 'I have shown you,' he said, 'that a mesmerised subject is entirely dominated by the will of the mesmeriser. He loses all power of volition, and his very thoughts are such as are suggested to him by the master-mind. The same end may be attained without any preliminary process. A strong will can, simply by virtue of its strength, take possession of a weaker one, even at a distance, and can regulate the impulses and the actions of the owner of it. If there was one man in the world who had a very much more highly-developed will than any of the rest of the human family, there is no reason why he should not be able to rule over them all, and to reduce his fellow-creatures to the condition of automatons. Happily there is such a dead level of mental power, or rather of mental weakness, among us that such a catastrophe is not likely to occur; but still within our small compass there are variations which produce surprising effects. I shall now single out one of the audience, and endeavour "by the mere power of will" to compel him to come upon the platform, and do and say what I wish. Let me assure you that there is no collusion, and that the subject whom I may select is at perfect liberty to resent to the uttermost any impulse which I may communicate to him.'

With these words the lecturer came to the front of the platform, and glanced over the first few rows of the stalls. No doubt Cowles' dark skin and bright eyes marked him out as a man of a highly nervous temperament, for the mesmerist picked him out in a moment, and fixed his eyes upon him. I saw my friend give a start of surprise, and then settle down in his chair, as if to express his determination not to yield to the influence of the operator. Messinger was not a man whose head denoted any great brain-power, but his gaze was singularly intense and penetrating. Under the influence of it Cowles made one or two spasmodic motions of his hands, as if to grasp the sides of his seat, and then half rose, but only to sink down again, though with an evident effort. I was watching the scene with intense interest, when I happened to catch a glimpse of Miss Northcott's face. She was sitting with her eyes fixed intently upon the mesmerist, and with such an expression of concentrated power upon her features as I have never seen on any other human countenance. Her jaw was firmly set, her lips compressed, and her face as hard as if it were a beautiful sculpture cut out of the whitest marble. Her eyebrows were drawn down, however, and from beneath them her grey eyes seemed to sparkle and gleam with a cold light.

I looked at Cowles again, expecting every moment to see him rise and obey the mesmerist's wishes, when there came from the platform a short, gasping cry as of a man utterly worn out and prostrated by a prolonged struggle. Messinger was leaning against the table, his hand to his forehead, and the perspiration pouring down his face. 'I won't go on,' he cried, addressing the audience. 'There is a stronger will than mine acting against me. You must excuse me for tonight.' The man was evidently ill, and utterly unable to proceed, so the curtain was lowered, and the audience dispersed, with many comments upon the lecturer's sudden indisposition.

I waited outside the hall until my friend and the ladies came out. Cowles was laughing over his recent experience.

'He didn't succeed with me, Bob,' he cried triumphantly, as he shook my hand. 'I think he caught a Tartar that time.'

'Yes,' said Miss Northcott, 'I think that Jack ought to be very proud of his strength of mind; don't you, Mr Armitage?'

'It took me all my time, though,' my friend said seriously. 'You can't conceive what a strange feeling I had once or twice. All the strength seemed to have gone out of me—especially just before he collapsed himself.'

I walked round with Cowles in order to see the ladies home. He walked in front with Mrs Merton, and I found myself behind with the young lady. For a minute or so I walked beside her without making any remark, and then I suddenly blurted out, in a manner which must have seemed somewhat brusque to her:

'You did that, Miss Northcott.'

'Did what?' she asked sharply.

'Why, mesmerised the mesmeriser—I suppose that is the best way of describing the transaction.'

'What a strange idea!' she said, laughing. 'You give me credit for a strong will then?'

'Yes,' I said. 'For a dangerously strong one.'

'Why dangerous?' she asked, in a tone of surprise.

'I think,' I answered, 'that any will which can exercise such power is dangerous—for there is always a chance of its being turned to bad uses.'

'You would make me out a very dreadful individual, Mr Armitage,' she said; and then looking up suddenly in my face—'You have never liked me. You are suspicious of me and distrust me, though I have never given you cause.'

The accusation was so sudden and so true that I was unable to find any reply to it. She paused for a moment, and then said in a voice which was hard and cold:

'Don't let your prejudice lead you to interfere with me, however, or say anything to your friend, Mr Cowles, which might lead to a difference between us. You would find that to be very bad policy.'

There was something in the way she spoke which gave an indescribable air of a threat to these few words.

'I have no power,' I said, 'to interfere with your plans for the future. I cannot help, however, from what I have seen and heard, having fears for my friend.'

'Fears!' she repeated scornfully. 'Pray what have you seen and heard. Something from Mr Reeves, perhaps—I believe he is another of your friends?'

'He never mentioned your name to me,' I answered, truthfully enough. 'You will be sorry to hear that he is dying.' As I said it we passed by a lighted window, and I glanced down to see what effect my words had upon her. She was laughing—there was no doubt of it; she was laughing quietly to herself. I could see merriment in every feature of her face. I feared and mistrusted the woman from that moment more than ever.

We said little more that night. When we parted she gave me a quick, warning glance, as if to remind me of what she had said about the danger of interference. Her cautions would have made little difference to me could I have seen my way to benefiting Barrington Cowles by anything which I might say. But what could I say? I might say that her former suitors had been unfortunate. I might say that I believed her to be a cruel-hearted woman. I might say that I considered her to possess wonderful, and almost preternatural powers. What impression would any of these accusations make upon an ardent lover—a man with my friend's enthusiastic temperament? I felt that it would be useless to advance them, so I was silent.

And now I come to the beginning of the end. Hitherto much has been surmise and inference and hearsay. It is my painful task to relate now, as dispassionately and as accurately as I can, what actually occurred under my own notice, and to reduce to writing the events which preceded the death of my friend.

Towards the end of the winter Cowles remarked to me that he intended to marry Miss Northcott as soon as possible—probably some time in the spring. He was, as I have already remarked, fairly well off, and the young lady had some money of her own, so that there was no pecuniary reason for a long engagement. 'We are going to take a little house out at Corstorphine,' he said, 'and we hope to see your face at our table, Bob, as often as you can possibly come.' I thanked him, and tried to shake off my apprehensions, and persuade myself that all would yet be well.

It was about three weeks before the time fixed for the marriage, that Cowles remarked to me one evening that he feared he would be late that night. 'I have had a note from Kate,' he said, 'asking me to call about eleven o'clock tonight, which seems rather a late hour, but perhaps she wants to talk over something quietly after old Mrs Merton retires.'

It was not until after my friend's departure that I suddenly recollected the mysterious interview which I had been told of as preceding the suicide of young Prescott. Then I thought of the ravings of poor Reeves, rendered more tragic by the fact that I had heard that very day of his death. What was the meaning of it all? Had this woman some baleful secret to disclose which must be known before her marriage? Was it some reason which forbade her to marry? Or was it some reason which forbade others to marry her? I felt so uneasy that I would have followed Cowles, even at the risk of offending him, and endeavoured to dissuade him from keeping his appointment, but a glance at the clock showed me that I was too late.

I was determined to wait up for his return, so I piled some coals upon the fire and took down a novel from the shelf. My thoughts proved more interesting than the book, however, and I threw it on one side. An indefinable feeling of anxiety and depression weighed upon me. Twelve o'clock came, and then half-past, without any sign of my friend. It was nearly one when I heard a step in the street outside, and then a knocking at the door. I was surprised, as I knew that my friend always carried a key—however, I hurried down and undid the latch. As the door flew open I knew in a moment that my worst apprehensions had been fulfilled. Barrington Cowles was leaning against the railings outside with his face sunk upon his breast, and his whole attitude expressive of the most intense despondency. As he passed in he gave a stagger, and would have fallen had I not thrown my left arm around him. Supporting him with this, and holding the lamp in my other hand, I led him slowly upstairs into our sitting-room. He sank down upon the sofa without a word. Now that I could get a good view of him, I was horrified to see the change which had come over him. His face was deadly pale, and his very lips were bloodless. His cheeks and forehead were clammy, his eyes glazed, and his whole expression altered. He looked like a man who had gone through some terrible ordeal, and was thoroughly unnerved.

'My dear fellow, what is the matter?' I asked, breaking the silence. 'Nothing amiss, I trust? Are you unwell?'

'Brandy!' he gasped. 'Give me some brandy!'

I took out the decanter, and was about to help him, when he snatched it from me with a trembling hand, and poured out nearly half a tumbler of the spirit. He was usually a most abstemious man, but he took this off at a gulp without adding any water to it. It seemed to do him good, for the colour began to come back to his face, and he leaned upon his elbow.

'My engagement is off, Bob,' he said, trying to speak calmly, but with a tremor in his voice which he could not conceal. 'It is all over.'

'Cheer up!' I answered, trying to encourage him. 'Don't get down on your luck. How was it? What was it all about?'

'About?' he groaned, covering his face with his hands. 'If I did tell you, Bob, you would not believe it. It is too dreadful—too horrible—unutterably awful and incredible! O Kate, Kate!' and he rocked himself to and fro in his grief; 'I pictured you an angel and I find you a——'

'A what?' I asked, for he had paused.

He looked at me with a vacant stare, and then suddenly burst out, waving his arms: 'A fiend!' he cried. 'A ghoul from the pit! A vampire soul behind a lovely face! Now, God forgive me!' he went on in a lower tone, turning his face to the wall; 'I have said more than I should. I have loved her too much to speak of her as she is. I love her too much now.'

He lay still for some time, and I had hoped that the brandy had had the effect of sending him to sleep, when he suddenly turned his face towards me.

'Did you ever read of wehr-wolves?' he asked.

I answered that I had.

'There is a story,' he said thoughtfully, 'in one of Marryat's books, about a beautiful woman who took the form of a wolf at night and devoured her own children. I wonder what put that idea into Marryat's head?'

He pondered for some minutes, and then he cried out for some more brandy. There was a small bottle of laudanum upon the table, and I managed, by insisting upon helping him myself, to mix about half a drachm with the spirits. He drank it off, and sank his head once more upon the pillow. 'Anything better than that,' he groaned. 'Death is better than that. Crime and cruelty; cruelty and crime. Anything is better than that,' and so on, with the monotonous refrain, until at last the words became indistinct, his eyelids closed over his weary eyes, and he sank into a profound slumber. I carried him into his bedroom without arousing him; and making a couch for myself out of the chairs, I remained by his side all night.

In the morning Barrington Cowles was in a high fever. For weeks he lingered between life and death. The highest medical skill of Edinburgh was called in, and his vigorous constitution slowly got the better of his disease. I nursed him during this anxious time; but through all his wild delirium and ravings he never let a word escape him which explained the mystery connected with Miss Northcott. Sometimes he spoke of her in the tenderest words and most loving voice. At others he screamed out that she was a fiend, and stretched out his arms, as if to keep her off. Several times he cried that he would not sell his soul for a beautiful face, and then he would moan in a most piteous voice, 'But I love her—I love her for all that; I shall never cease to love her.'

When he came to himself he was an altered man. His severe illness had emaciated him greatly, but his dark eyes had lost none of their brightness. They shone out with startling brilliancy from under his dark, overhanging brows. His manner was eccentric and variable—sometimes irritable, sometimes recklessly mirthful, but never natural. He would glance about him in a strange, suspicious manner, like one who feared something, and yet hardly knew what it was he dreaded. He never mentioned Miss Northcott's name—never until that fatal evening of which I have now to speak.

In an endeavour to break the current of his thoughts by frequent change of scene, I travelled with him through the highlands of Scotland, and afterwards down the east coast. In one of these peregrinations of ours we visited the Isle of May, an island near the mouth of the Firth of Forth, which, except in the tourist season, is singularly barren and desolate. Beyond the keeper of the lighthouse there are only one or two families of poor fisher-folk, who sustain a precarious existence by their nets, and by the capture of cormorants and solan geese. This grim spot seemed to have such a fascination for Cowles that we engaged a room in one of the fishermen's huts, with the intention of passing a week or two there. I found it very dull, but the loneliness appeared to be a relief to my friend's mind. He lost the look of apprehension which had become habitual to him, and became something like his old self. He would wander round the island all day, looking down from the summit of the great cliffs which gird it round, and watching the long green waves as they came booming in and burst in a shower of spray over the rocks beneath.

One night—I think it was our third or fourth on the island—Barrington Cowles and I went outside the cottage before retiring to rest, to enjoy a little fresh air, for our room was small, and the rough lamp caused an unpleasant odour. How well I remember every little circumstance in connection with that night! It promised to be tempestuous, for the clouds were piling up in the north-west, and the dark wrack was drifting across the face of the moon, throwing alternate belts of light and shade upon the rugged surface of the island and the restless sea beyond.

We were standing talking close by the door of the cottage, and I was thinking to myself that my friend was more cheerful than he had been since his illness, when he gave a sudden, sharp cry, and looking round at him I saw, by the light of the moon, an expression of unutterable horror come over his features. His eyes became fixed and staring, as if riveted upon some approaching object, and he extended his long thin forefinger, which quivered as he pointed.

'Look there!' he cried. 'It is she! It is she! You see her there coming down the side of the brae.' He gripped me convulsively by the wrist as he spoke. 'There she is, coming towards us!'

'Who?' I cried, straining my eyes into the darkness.

'She—Kate—Kate Northcott!' he screamed. 'She has come for me. Hold me fast, old friend. Don't let me go!'

'Hold up, old man,' I said, clapping him on the shoulder. 'Pull yourself together; you are dreaming; there is nothing to fear.'

'She is gone!' he cried, with a gasp of relief. 'No, by heaven! there she is again, and nearer—coming nearer. She told me she would come for me, and she keeps her word.'

'Come into the house,' I said. His hand, as I grasped it, was as cold as ice.

'Ah, I knew it!' he shouted. 'There she is, waving her arms. She is beckoning to me. It is the signal. I must go. I am coming, Kate; I am coming!'

I threw my arms around him, but he burst from me with superhuman strength, and dashed into the darkness of the night. I followed him, calling to him to stop, but he ran the more swiftly. When the moon shone out between the clouds I could catch a glimpse of his dark figure, running rapidly in a straight line, as if to reach some definite goal. It may have been imagination, but it seemed to me that in the flickering light I could distinguish a vague something in front of him—a shimmering form which eluded his grasp and led him onwards. I saw his outlines stand out hard against the sky behind him as he surmounted the brow of a little hill, then he disappeared, and that was the last ever seen by mortal eye of Barrington Cowles.

The fishermen and I walked round the island all that night with lanterns, and examined every nook and corner without seeing a trace of my poor lost friend. The direction in which he had been running terminated in a rugged line of jagged cliffs overhanging the sea. At one place here the edge was somewhat crumbled, and there appeared marks upon the turf which might have been left by human feet. We lay upon our faces at this spot, and peered with our lanterns over the edge, looking down on the boiling surge two hundred feet below. As we lay there, suddenly, above the beating of the waves and the howling of the wind, there rose a strange wild screech from the abyss below. The fishermen—a naturally superstitious race—averred that it was the sound of a woman's laughter, and I could hardly persuade them to continue the search. For my own part I think it may have been the cry of some sea-fowl startled from its nest by the flash of the lantern. However that may be, I never wish to hear such a sound again.

And now I have come to the end of the painful duty which I have undertaken. I have told as plainly and as accurately as I could the story of the death of John Barrington Cowles, and the train of events which preceded it. I am aware that to others the sad episode seemed commonplace enough. Here is the prosaic account which appeared in the *Scotsman* a couple of days afterwards:

Sad Occurrence on the Isle of May—The Isle of May has been the scene of a sad disaster. Mr John Barrington Cowles, a gentleman well known in University circles as a most distinguished student, and the present holder of the Neil Arnott prize for physics, has been recruiting his health in this quiet retreat. The night before last he suddenly left his friend, Mr Robert Armitage, and he has not since been heard of. It is almost certain that he has met his death by falling over the cliffs which surround the island. Mr Cowles' health has been failing for some time, partly from overstudy and partly from worry connected with family affairs. By his death the University loses one of her most promising alumni.

I have nothing more to add to my statement. I have unburdened my mind of all that I know. I can well conceive that many, after weighing all that I have said, will see no ground for an accusation against Miss Northcott. They will say that, because a man of a naturally excitable disposition says and does wild things, and even eventually commits self-murder after a sudden and heavy disappointment, there is no reason why vague charges should be advanced against a young lady. To this, I answer that they are welcome to their opinion. For my own part, I ascribe the death of William Prescott, of Archibald Reeves, and of John Barrington Cowles to this woman with as much confidence as if I had seen her drive a dagger into their hearts.

You ask me, no doubt, what my own theory is which will explain all these strange facts. I have none, or, at best, a dim and vague one. That Miss Northcott possessed extraordinary powers over the minds, and through the minds over the bodies, of others, I am convinced, as well as that her instincts were to use this power for base and cruel purposes. That some even more fiendish and terrible phase of character lay behind this—some horrible trait which it was necessary for her to reveal before marriage—is to be inferred from the experience of her three lovers, while the dreadful nature of the mystery thus revealed can only be surmised from the fact that the very mention of it drove from her those who had loved her so passionately. Their subsequent fate was, in my opinion, the result of her vindictive remembrance of their desertion of her, and that they were forewarned of it at the time was shown by the words of both Reeves and Cowles. Above this, I can say nothing. I lay the facts soberly before the public as they came under my notice. I have never seen Miss Northcott since, nor do I wish to do so. If by the words I have written I can save any one human being from the snare of those bright eyes and that beautiful face, then I can lay down my pen with the assurance that my poor friend has not died altogether in vain.

The Great Keinplatz Experiment

OF ALL THE SCIENCES WHICH HAVE PUZZLED the sons of men, none had such an attraction for the learned Professor Von Baumgarten as those which relate to psychology and the ill-defined relations between mind and matter. A celebrated anatomist, a profound chemist, and one of the first physiologists in Europe, it was a relief for him to turn from these subjects and to bring his varied knowledge to bear upon the study of the soul and the mysterious relationship of spirits. At first, when as a young man he began to dip into the secrets of mesmerism, his mind seemed to be wandering in a strange land where all was chaos and darkness, save that here and there some great unexplainable and disconnected fact loomed out in front of him. As the years passed, however, and as the worthy Professor's stock of knowledge increased, for knowledge begets knowledge as money bears interest, much which had seemed strange and unaccountable began to take another shape in his eyes. New trains of reasoning became familiar to him, and he perceived connecting links where all had been incomprehensible and startling. By experiments which extended over twenty years, he obtained a basis of facts upon which it was his ambition to build up a new, exact science which should embrace mesmerism, spiritualism, and all cognate subjects. In this he was much helped by his intimate knowledge of the more intricate parts of animal physiology which treat of nerve currents and the working of the brain; for Alexis von Baumgarten was Regius Professor of Physiology at the University of Keinplatz, and had all the resources of the laboratory to aid him in his profound researches.

Professor von Baumgarten was tall and thin, with a hatchet face and steel-grey eyes, which were singularly bright and penetrating. Much thought had furrowed his forehead and contracted his heavy eyebrows, so that he appeared to wear a perpetual frown, which often misled people as to his character, for though austere he was tender-hearted. He was popular among the students, who would gather round him after his lectures and listen eagerly to his strange theories. Often he would call for volunteers from amongst them in order to conduct some experiment, so that eventually there was hardly a lad in the class who had not, at one time or another, been thrown into a mesmeric trance by his Professor.

Of all these young devotees of science there was none who equalled in enthusiasm Fritz von Hartmann. It had often seemed strange to his fellow-students that wild, reckless Fritz, as dashing a young fellow as ever hailed from the Rhinelands, should devote the time and trouble which he did in reading up abstruse works and in assisting the Professor in his strange experiments. The fact was, however, that Fritz was a knowing and long-headed fellow. Months before he had lost his heart to young Elise, the blue-eyed, yellow-haired daughter of the lecturer. Although he had succeeded in learning from her lips that she was not indifferent to his suit, he had never dared to announce himself to her family as a formal suitor. Hence he would have found it a difficult matter to see his young lady had he not adopted the expedient of making himself useful to the Professor. By this means he frequently was asked to the old man's house, where he willingly submitted to be experimented upon in any way as long as there was a chance of his receiving one bright glance from the eyes of Elise or one touch of her little hand.

Young Fritz von Hartmann was a handsome lad enough. There were broad acres, too, which would descend to him when his father died. To many he would have seemed an eligible suitor; but Madame frowned upon his presence in the house, and lectured the Professor at times on his allowing such a wolf to prowl around their lamb. To tell the truth, Fritz had an evil name in Keinplatz. Never was there a riot or a duel, or any other mischief afoot, but the young Rhinelander figured as a ringleader in it. No one used more free and violent language, no one drank more, no one played cards more habitually, no one was more idle, save in the one solitary subject. No wonder, then, that the good Frau Professorin gathered her Fräulein under her wing, and resented the attentions of such a *mauvais sujet*. As to the worthy lecturer, he was too much engrossed by his strange studies to form an opinion upon the subject one way or the other.

For many years there was one question which had continually obtruded itself upon his thoughts. All his experiments and his theories turned upon a single point. A hundred times a day the Professor asked himself whether it was possible for the human spirit to exist apart from the body for a time and then to return to it once again. When the possibility first suggested itself to him his scientific mind had revolted from it. It clashed too violently with preconceived ideas and the prejudices of his early training. Gradually, however, as he proceeded farther and farther along the pathway of original research, his mind shook off its old fetters and became ready to face any conclusion which could reconcile the facts. There were many things which made him believe that it was possible for mind to exist apart from matter. At last it occurred to him that by a daring and original experiment the question might be definitely decided.

'It is evident,' he remarked in his celebrated article upon invisible entities, which appeared in the *Keinplatz wochenliche Medicalschrift* about this time, and which surprised the whole scientific world—'it is evident that under certain conditions the soul or mind does separate itself from the body. In the case of a mesmerised person, the body lies in a cataleptic condition, but the spirit has left it. Perhaps you reply that the soul is there, but in a dormant condition. I answer that this is not so, otherwise how can one account for the condition of clairvoyance, which has fallen into disrepute through the knavery of certain scoundrels, but which can easily be shown to be an undoubted fact. I have been able myself, with a sensitive subject, to obtain an accurate description of what was going on in another room or another house. How can such knowledge be accounted for on any hypothesis save that the soul of the subject has left the body and is wandering through space? For a moment it is recalled by the voice of the operator and says what it has seen, and then wings its way once more through the air. Since the spirit is by its very nature invisible, we cannot see these comings and goings, but we see their effect in the body of the subject, now rigid and inert, now struggling to narrate impressions which could never have come to it by natural means. There is only one way which I can see by which the fact can be demonstrated. Although we in the flesh are unable to see these spirits, yet our own spirits, could we separate them from the body, would be conscious of the presence of others. It is my intention, therefore, shortly to mesmerise one of my pupils. I shall then mesmerise myself in a manner which has become easy to me. After that, if my theory holds good, my spirit will have no difficulty in meeting and communing with the spirit of my pupil, both being separated from the body. I hope to be able to communicate the result of this interesting experiment in an early number of the *Keinplatz wochenliche Medicalschrift.*'

When the good Professor finally fulfilled his promise, and published an account of what occurred, the narrative was so extraordinary that it was received with general incredulity. The tone of some of the papers was so offensive in their comments upon the matter that the angry savant declared that he would never open his mouth again or refer to the subject in any way—a promise which he has faithfully kept. This narrative has been compiled, however, from the most authentic sources, and the events cited in it may be relied upon as substantially correct.

It happened, then, that shortly after the time when Professor von Baumgarten conceived the idea of the above-mentioned experiment, he was walking thoughtfully homewards after a long day in the laboratory, when he met a crowd of roistering students who had just streamed out from a beer-house. At the head of them, half-intoxicated and very noisy, was young Fritz von Hartmann. The Professor would have passed them, but his pupil ran across and intercepted him.

'Heh! my worthy master,' he said, taking the old man by the sleeve, and leading him down the road with him. 'There is something that I have to say to you, and it is easier for me to say it now, when the good beer is humming in my head, than at another time.'

'What is it, then, Fritz?' the physiologist asked, looking at him in mild surprise.

'I hear, mein Herr, that you are about to do some wondrous experiment in which you hope to take a man's soul out of his body, and then to put it back again. Is it not so?'

'It is true, Fritz.'

'And have you considered, my dear sir, that you may have some difficulty in finding someone on whom to try this? *Potztausend!* Suppose that the soul went out and would not come back. That would be a bad business. Who is to take the risk?'

'But Fritz,' the Professor cried, very much startled by this view of the matter, 'I had relied upon your assistance in the attempt. Surely you will not desert me. Consider the honour and glory.'

'Consider the fiddlesticks!' the student cried angrily. 'Am I to be paid always thus? Did I not stand two hours upon a glass insulator while you poured electricity into my body? Have you not stimulated my phrenic nerves, besides ruining my digestion with a galvanic current round my stomach? Four-and-thirty times you have mesmerised me, and what have I got from all this? Nothing. And now you wish to take my soul out, as you would take the works from a watch. It is more than flesh and blood can stand.'

'Dear, dear!' the Professor cried in great distress. 'That is very true, Fritz. I never thought of it before. If you can but suggest how I can compensate you, you will find me ready and willing.'

'Then listen,' said Fritz solemnly. 'If you will pledge your word that after this experiment I may have the hand of your daughter, then I am willing to assist you; but if not, I shall have nothing to do with it. These are my only terms.'

'And what would my daughter say to this?' the Professor exclaimed, after a pause of astonishment.

'Elise would welcome it,' the young man replied. 'We have loved each other long.'

'Then she shall be yours,' the physiologist said with decision, 'for you are a good-hearted young man, and one of the best neurotic subjects that I have ever known—that is when you are not under the influence of alcohol. My experiment is to be performed upon the fourth of next month. You will attend at the physiological laboratory at twelve o'clock. It will be a great occasion, Fritz. Von Gruben is coming from Jena, and Hinterstein from Basle. The chief men of science of all South Germany will be there.'

'I shall be punctual,' the student said briefly; and so the two parted. The Professor plodded homeward, thinking of the great coming event, while the young man staggered along after his noisy companions, with his mind full of the blue-eyed Elise, and of the bargain which he had concluded with her father.

The Professor did not exaggerate when he spoke of the widespread interest excited by his novel psychological experiment. Long before the hour had arrived the room was filled by a galaxy of talent. Besides the celebrities whom he had mentioned, there had come from London the great Professor Lurcher, who had just established his reputation by a remarkable treatise upon cerebral centres. Several great lights of the Spiritualistic body had also come a long distance to be present, as had a Swedenborgian minister, who considered that the proceedings might throw some light upon the doctrines of the Rosy Cross.

There was considerable applause from this eminent assembly upon the appearance of Professor von Baumgarten and his subject upon the platform. The lecturer, in a few well-chosen words, explained what his views were, and how he proposed to test them. 'I hold,' he said, 'that when a person is under the influence of mesmerism, his spirit is for the time released from his body, and I challenge anyone to put forward any other hypothesis which will account for the fact of clairvoyance. I therefore hope that upon mesmerising my young friend here, and then putting myself into a trance, our spirits may be able to commune together, though our bodies lie still and inert. After a time nature will resume her sway, our spirits will return into our respective bodies, and all will be as before. With your kind permission, we shall now proceed to attempt the experiment.'

The applause was renewed at this speech, and the audience settled down in expectant silence. With a few rapid passes the Professor mesmerised the young man, who sank back in his chair, pale and rigid. He then took a bright globe of glass from his pocket, and by concentrating his gaze upon it and making a strong mental effort, he succeeded in throwing himself into the same condition. It was a strange and impressive sight to see the old man and the young sitting together in the same cataleptic condition. Whither, then, had their souls fled? That was the question which presented itself to each and every one of the spectators.

Five minutes passed, and then ten, and then fifteen, and then fifteen more, while the Professor and his pupil sat stiff and stark upon the platform. During that time not a sound was heard from the assembled savants, but every eye was bent upon the two pale faces, in search of the first signs of returning consciousness. Nearly an hour had elapsed before the patient watchers were rewarded. A faint flush came back to the cheeks of Professor von Baumgarten. The soul was coming back once more to its earthly tenement. Suddenly he stretched out his long, thin arms, as one awaking from sleep, and rubbing his eyes, stood up from his chair and gazed about him as though he hardly realised where he was. '*Tausend Teufel!*' he exclaimed, rapping out a tremendous South German oath, to the great astonishment of his audience and to the disgust of the Swedenborgian.

'Where the Henker am I then, and what in thunder has occurred? Oh yes, I remember now. One of these nonsensical mesmeric experiments. There is no result this time, for I remember nothing at all since I became unconscious; so you have had all your long journeys for nothing, my learned friends, and a very good joke, too'; at which the Regius Professor of Physiology burst into a roar of laughter and slapped his thigh in a highly indecorous fashion. The audience were so enraged at this behaviour on the part of their host, that there might have been a considerable disturbance, had it not been for the judicious interference of young Fritz von Hartmann, who had now recovered from his lethargy. Stepping to the front of the platform, the young man apologised for the conduct of his companion.

'I am sorry to say,' he said, 'that he is a harum-scarum sort of fellow, although he appeared so grave at the commencement of this experiment. He is still suffering from mesmeric reaction, and is hardly accountable for his words. As to the experiment itself, I do not consider it to be a failure. It is very possible that our spirits may have been communing in space during this hour; but, unfortunately, our gross bodily memory is distinct from our spirit, and we cannot recall what has occurred. My energies shall now be devoted to devising some means by which spirits may be able to recollect what occurs to them in their free state, and I trust that when I have worked this out, I may have the pleasure of meeting you all once again in this hall, and demonstrating to you the result.' This address, coming from so young a student, caused considerable astonishment among the audience, and some were inclined to be offended, thinking that he assumed rather too much importance. The majority, however, looked upon him as a young man of great promise, and many comparisons were made as they left the hall between his dignified conduct and the levity of his professor, who during the above remarks was laughing heartily in a corner, by no means abashed at the failure of the experiment.

Now although all these learned men were filing out of the lecture-room under the impression that they had seen nothing of note, as a matter of fact one of the most wonderful things in the whole history of the world had just occurred before their very eyes. Professor von Baumgarten had been so far correct in his theory that both his spirit and that of his pupil had been, for a time, absent from the body. But here a strange and unforeseen complication had occurred. In their return the spirit of Fritz von Hartmann had entered into the body of Alexis von Baumgarten, and that of Alexis von Baumgarten had taken up its abode in the frame of Fritz von Hartmann. Hence the slang and scurrility which issued from the lips of the serious Professor, and hence also the weighty words and grave statements which fell from the careless student. It was an unprecedented event, yet no one knew of it, least of all those whom it concerned.

The body of the Professor, feeling conscious suddenly of a great dryness about the back of the throat, sallied out into the street, still chuckling to himself over the result of the experiment, for the soul of Fritz within was reckless at the thought of the bride whom he had won so easily. His first impulse was to go up to the house and see her, but on second thoughts he came to the conclusion that it would be best to stay away until Madame Baumgarten should be informed by her husband of the agreement which had been made. He therefore made his way down to the Grüner Mann, which was one of the favourite trysting-places of the wilder students, and ran, boisterously waving his cane in the air, into the little parlour, where sat Spiegel and Müller and half a dozen other boon companions.

'Ha, ha! my boys,' he shouted. 'I knew I should find you here. Drink up, every one of you, and call for what you like, for I'm going to stand treat today.'

Had the green man who is depicted upon the signpost of that well-known inn suddenly marched into the room and called for a bottle of wine, the students could not have been more amazed than they were by this unexpected entry of their revered professor. They were so astonished that for a minute or two they glared at him in utter bewilderment without being able to make any reply to his hearty invitation.

'*Donner und Blitzen!*' shouted the Professor angrily. 'What the deuce is the matter with you, then? You sit there like a set of stuck pigs staring at me. What is it then?'

'It is the unexpected honour,' stammered Spiegel, who was in the chair.

'Honour—rubbish!' said the Professor testily. 'Do you think that just because I happen to have been exhibiting mesmerism to a parcel of old fossils, I am therefore too proud to associate with dear old friends like you? Come out of that chair, Spiegel, my boy, for I shall preside now. Beer, or wine, or schnapps, my lads—call for what you like, and put it all down to me.'

Never was there such an afternoon in the Grüner Mann. The foaming flagons of lager and the green-necked bottles of Rhenish circulated merrily. By degrees the students lost their shyness in the presence of their Professor. As for him, he shouted, he sang, he roared, he balanced a long tobacco-pipe upon his nose, and offered to run a hundred yards against any member of the company. The Kellner and the barmaid whispered to each other outside the door their astonishment at such proceedings on the part of a Regius Professor of the ancient university of Keinplatz. They had still more to whisper about afterwards, for the learned man cracked the Kellner's crown, and kissed the barmaid behind the kitchen door.

'Gentlemen,' said the Professor, standing up, albeit somewhat totteringly, at the end of the table, and balancing his high, old-fashioned wine glass in his bony hand, 'I must now explain to you what is the cause of this festivity.'

'Hear! hear!' roared the students, hammering their beer glasses against the table; 'a speech, a speech!—silence for a speech!'

'The fact is, my friends,' said the Professor, beaming through his spectacles, 'I hope very soon to be married.'

'Married!' cried a student, bolder than the others. 'Is Madame dead, then?'

'Madame who?'

'Why, Madame von Baumgarten, of course.'

'Ha, ha!' laughed the Professor; 'I can see, then, that you know all about my former difficulties. No, she is not dead, but I have reason to believe that she will not oppose my marriage.'

'That is very accommodating of her,' remarked one of the company.

'In fact,' said the Professor, 'I hope that she will now be induced to aid me in getting a wife. She and I never took to each other very much; but now I hope all that may be ended, and when I marry she will come and stay with me.'

'What a happy family!' exclaimed some wag.

'Yes, indeed; and I hope you will come to my wedding, all of you. I won't mention names, but here is to my little bride!' and the Professor waved his glass in the air.

'Here's to his little bride!' roared the roisterers, with shouts of laughter. 'Here's her health. *Sie soll leben—Hoch!*' And so the fun waxed still more fast and furious, while each young fellow followed the Professor's example, and drank a toast to the girl of his heart.

While all this festivity had been going on at the Grüner Mann, a very different scene had been enacted elsewhere. Young Fritz von Hartmann, with a solemn face and a reserved manner, had, after the experiment, consulted and adjusted some mathematical instruments; after which, with a few peremptory words to the janitor, he had walked out into the street and wended his way slowly in the direction of the house of the Professor. As he walked he saw Von Althaus, the professor of anatomy, in front of him, and, quickening his pace, he overtook him.

'I say, Von Althaus,' he exclaimed, tapping him on the sleeve, 'you were asking me for some information the other day concerning the middle coat of the cerebral arteries. Now I find——'

'*Donnerwetter!*' shouted Von Althaus, who was a peppery old fellow. 'What the deuce do you mean by your impertinence! I'll have you up before the Academical Senate for this sir'; with which threat he turned on his heel and hurried away. Von Hartmann was much surprised at this reception. 'It's on account of this failure of my experiment,' he said to himself, and continued moodily on his way.

Fresh surprises were in store for him, however. He was hurrying along when he was overtaken by two students. These youths, instead of raising their caps or showing any other sign of respect, gave a wild whoop of delight the instant that they saw him, and rushing at him seized him by each arm and commenced dragging him along with them.

'*Gott in Himmel!*' roared Von Hartmann. 'What is the meaning of this unparalleled insult? Where are you taking me?'

'To crack a bottle of wine with us,' said the two students. 'Come along! That is an invitation which you have never refused.'

'I never heard of such insolence in my life!' cried Von Hartmann. 'Let go my arms! I shall certainly have you rusticated for this. Let me go, I say!' and he kicked furiously at his captors.

'Oh, if you choose to turn ill-tempered, you may go where you like,' the students said, releasing him. 'We can do very well without you.'

'I know you. I'll pay you out!' said Von Hartmann furiously, and continued in the direction which he imagined to be his own home, much incensed at the two episodes which had occurred to him on the way.

Now, Madame von Baumgarten, who was looking out of the window and wondering why her husband was late for dinner, was considerably astonished to see the young student come stalking down the road. As already remarked, she had a great antipathy to him, and if ever he ventured into the house it was on sufferance, and under the protection of the Professor. Still more astonished was she, therefore, when she beheld him undo the wicket-gate and stride up the garden path with the air of one who is master of the situation. She could hardly believe her eyes, and hastened to the door with all her maternal instincts up in arms. From the upper windows the fair Elise had also observed this daring move upon the part of her lover, and her heart beat quick with mingled pride and consternation.

'Good day, sir,' Madame Baumgarten remarked to the intruder, as she stood in gloomy majesty in the open doorway.

'A very fine day indeed, Martha,' returned the other. 'Now, don't stand there like a statue of Juno, but bustle about and get the dinner ready, for I am wellnigh starved.'

'Martha! Dinner!' ejaculated the lady, falling back in astonishment.

'Yes, dinner, Martha, dinner!' howled Von Hartmann, who was becoming irritable. 'Is there anything wonderful in that request when a man has been out all day? I'll wait in the dining-room. Anything will do. Schinken, and sausage, and prunes—any little thing that happens to be about. There you are, standing staring again. Woman, will you or will you not stir your legs?'

This last address, delivered with a perfect shriek of rage, had the effect of sending good Madame Baumgarten flying along the passage and through the kitchen, where she locked herself up in the scullery and went into violent hysterics. In the meantime Von Hartmann strode into the room and threw himself down upon the sofa in the worst of tempers.

'Elise!' he shouted. 'Confound the girl! Elise!'

Thus roughly summoned, the young lady came timidly downstairs and into the presence of her lover. 'Dearest!' she cried, throwing her arms round him, 'I know this is all done for my sake! It is a *ruse* in order to see me.'

Von Hartmann's indignation at this fresh attack upon him was so great that he became speechless for a minute from rage, and could only glare and shake his fists, while he struggled in her embrace. When he at last regained his utterance, he indulged in such a bellow of passion that the young lady dropped back, petrified with fear, into an armchair.

'Never have I passed such a day in my life,' Von Hartmann cried, stamping upon the floor. 'My experiment has failed. Von Althaus has insulted me. Two students have dragged me along the public road. My wife nearly faints when I ask her for dinner, and my daughter flies at me and hugs me like a grizzly bear.'

'You are ill, dear,' the young lady cried. 'Your mind is wandering. You have not even kissed me once.'

'No, and I don't intend to either,' Von Hartmann said with decision. 'You ought to be ashamed of yourself. Why don't you go and fetch my slippers, and help your mother to dish the dinner?'

'And is it for this,' Elise cried, burying her face in her handkerchief—'is it for this that I have loved you passionately for upwards of ten months? Is it for this that I have braved my mother's wrath? Oh, you have broken my heart; I am sure you have!' and she sobbed hysterically.

'I can't stand much more of this,' roared Von Hartmann furiously. 'What the deuce does the girl mean? What did I do ten months ago which inspired you with such a particular affection for me? If you are really so very fond, you would do better to run away down and find the Schinken and some bread, instead of talking all this nonsense.'

'Oh, my darling!' cried the unhappy maiden, throwing herself into the arms of what she imagined to be her lover: 'you do but joke in order to frighten your little Elise.'

Now it chanced that at the moment of this unexpected embrace Von Hartmann was still leaning back against the end of the sofa, which, like much German furniture, was in a somewhat rickety condition. It also chanced that beneath this end of the sofa there stood a tank full of water in which the physiologist was conducting certain experiments upon the ova of fish, and which he kept in his drawing-room in order to ensure an equable temperature. The additional weight of the maiden combined with the impetus with which she hurled herself upon him, caused the precarious piece of furniture to give way, and the body of the unfortunate student was hurled backwards into the tank, in which his head and shoulders were firmly wedged, while his lower extremities flapped helplessly about in the air. This was the last straw. Extricating himself with some difficulty from his unpleasant position, Von Hartmann gave an inarticulate yell of fury, and dashing out of the room, in spite of the entreaties of Elise, he seized his hat and rushed off into the town, all dripping and dishevelled, with the intention of seeking in some inn the food and comfort which he could not find at home.

As the spirit of Von Baumgarten encased in the body of Von Hartmann strode down the winding pathway which led down to the little town, brooding angrily over his many wrongs, he became aware that an elderly man was approaching him who appeared to be in an advanced state of intoxication. Von Hartmann waited by the side of the road and watched this individual, who came stumbling along, reeling from one side of the road to the other, and singing a student song in a very husky and drunken voice. At first his interest was merely excited by the fact of seeing a man of so venerable an appearance in such a disgraceful condition, but as he approached nearer, he became convinced that he knew the other well, though he could not recall when or where he had met him. This impression became so strong with him, that when the stranger came abreast of him he stepped in front of him and took a good look at his features.

'Well, sonny,' said the drunken man, surveying Von Hartmann and swaying about in front of him, 'where the Henker have I seen you before? I know you as well as I know myself. Who the deuce are you?'

'I am Professor von Baumgarten,' said the student. 'May I ask who you are? I am strangely familiar with your features.'

'You should never tell lies, young man,' said the other. 'You're certainly not the Professor, for he is an ugly, snuffy old chap and you are a big, broad-shouldered young fellow. As to myself, I am Fritz von Hartmann at your service.'

'That you certainly are not,' exclaimed the body of Von Hartmann. 'You might very well be his father. But hullo, sir, are you aware that you are wearing my studs and my watch-chain?'

'*Donnerwetter!*' hiccoughed the other. 'If those are not the trousers for which my tailor is about to sue me, may I never taste beer again.'

Now as Von Hartmann, overwhelmed by the many strange things which had occurred to him that day, passed his hand over his forehead and cast his eyes downwards, he chanced to catch the reflection of his own face in a pool which the rain had left upon the road. To his utter astonishment he perceived that his face was that of a youth, that his dress was that of a fashionable young student, and that in every way he was the antithesis of the grave and scholarly figure in which his mind was wont to dwell. In an instant his active brain ran over the series of events which had occurred and sprang to the conclusion. He fairly reeled under the blow.

'*Himmel!*' he cried, 'I see it all. Our souls are in the wrong bodies. I am you and you are I. My theory is proved—but at what an expense! Is the most scholarly mind in Europe to go about with this frivolous exterior? Oh, the labours of a lifetime are ruined!' and he smote his breast in his despair.

'I say,' remarked the real Von Hartmann from the body of the Professor, 'I quite see the force of your remarks, but don't go knocking my body about like that. You received it in excellent condition, but I perceive that you have wet it and bruised it, and spilled snuff over my ruffled shirt-front.'

'It matters little,' the other said moodily. 'Such as we are so must we stay. My theory is triumphantly proved, but the cost is terrible.'

'If I thought so,' said the spirit of the student, 'it would be hard indeed. What could I do with these stiff old limbs, and how could I woo Elise and persuade her that I was not her father? No, thank Heaven, in spite of the beer which has upset me more than ever it could upset my real self, I can see a way out of it.'

'How?' gasped the Professor.

'Why, by repeating the experiment. Liberate our souls once more, and the chances are that they will find their way back into their respective bodies.'

No drowning man could clutch more eagerly at a straw than did Von Baumgarten's spirit at this suggestion. In feverish haste he dragged his own frame to the side of the road and threw it into a mesmeric trance; he then extracted the crystal ball from the pocket, and managed to bring himself into the same condition.

Some students and peasants who chanced to pass during the next hour were much astonished to see the worthy Professor of Physiology and his favourite student both sitting upon a very muddy bank and both completely insensible. Before the hour was up quite a crowd had assembled, and they were discussing the advisability of sending for an ambulance to convey the pair to hospital, when the learned savant opened his eyes and gazed vacantly around him. For an instant he seemed to forget how he had come there, but next moment he astonished his audience by waving his skinny arms above his head and crying out in a voice of rapture, '*Gott sei gedanket!* I am myself again. I feel I am!' Nor was the amazement lessened when the student, springing to his feet, burst into the same cry, and the two performed a sort of *pas de joie* in the middle of the road.

For some time after that people had some suspicion of the sanity of both the actors in this strange episode. When the Professor published his experiences in the *Medicalschrift* as he had promised, he was met by an intimation, even from his colleagues, that he would do well to have his mind cared for, and that another such publication would certainly consign him to a madhouse. The student also found by experience that it was wisest to be silent about the matter.

When the worthy lecturer returned home that night he did not receive the cordial welcome which he might have looked for after his strange adventures. On the contrary, he was roundly upbraided by both his female relatives for smelling of drink and tobacco, and also for being absent while a young scapegrace invaded the house and insulted its occupants. It was long before the domestic atmosphere of the lecturer's house resumed its normal quiet, and longer still before the genial face of Von Hartmann was seen beneath its roof. Perseverance, however, conquers every obstacle, and the student eventually succeeded in pacifying the enraged ladies and in establishing himself upon the old footing. He has now no longer any cause to fear the enmity of Madame, for he is Hauptmann von Hartmann of the Emperor's own Uhlans, and his loving wife has already presented him with two little Uhlans as a visible sign and token of her affection.

Cyprian Overbeck Wells

[A Literary Mosaic]

FROM MY BOYHOOD I HAVE HAD an intense and overwhelming conviction that my real vocation lay in the direction of literature. I have, however, had a most unaccountable difficulty in getting any responsible person to share my views. It is true that private friends have sometimes after listening to my effusions gone the length of remarking, 'Really, Smith, that's not half bad!' or, 'You take my advice, old boy, and send that to some magazine!' but I have never on these occasions had the moral courage to inform my adviser that the article in question had been sent to well-nigh every publisher in London, and had come back again with a rapidity and precision which spoke well for the efficiency of our postal arrangements.

Had my manuscripts been paper boomerangs they could not have returned with greater accuracy to their unhappy despatcher. Oh, the vileness and utter degradation of the moment when the stale little cylinder of closely written pages, which seemed so fresh and full of promise a few days ago, is handed in by a remorseless postman! And what moral depravity shines through the editor's ridiculous plea of 'want of space!' But the subject is a painful one, and a digression from the plain statement of facts which I originally contemplated.

From the age of seventeen to that of three-and-twenty I was a literary volcano in a constant state of eruption. Poems and tales, articles and reviews, nothing came amiss to my pen. From the great sea-serpent to the nebular hypothesis, I was ready to write on anything or everything, and I can safely say that I seldom handled a subject without throwing new lights upon it. Poetry and romance, however, had always the greatest attractions for me. How I have wept over the pathos of my heroines, and laughed at the comicalities of my buffoons! Alas! I could find no one to join me in my appreciation, and solitary admiration for one's self, however genuine, becomes satiating after a time. My father remonstrated with me too on the score of expense and loss of time, so that I was finally compelled to relinquish my dreams of literary independence and to become a clerk in a wholesale mercantile firm connected with the West African trade.

Even when condemned to the prosaic duties which fell to my lot in the office, I continued faithful to my first love. I have introduced pieces of word-painting into the most commonplace business letters which have, I am told, considerably astonished the recipients. My refined sarcasm has made defaulting creditors writhe and wince. Occasionally, like the great Silas Wegg, I would drop into poetry, and so raise the whole tone of the correspondence. Thus what could be more elegant than my rendering of the firm's instructions to the captain of one of their vessels. It ran in this way:

'From England, Captain, you must steer a
Course directly to Madeira,
Land the casks of salted beef,
Then away to Teneriffe.
Pray be careful, cool, and wary
With the merchants of Canary.
Where you leave them make the most
Of the trade-winds to the coast
Down it you shall sail as far
As the land of Calabar,
And from there you'll onward go
To Bonny and Fernando Po'

and so on for four pages. The captain, instead of treasuring up this little gem, called at the office next day, and demanded with quite unnecessary warmth what the thing meant, and I was compelled to translate it all back into prose. On this, as on other similar occasions, my employer took me severely to task—for he was, you see, a man entirely devoid of all pretensions to literary taste!

All this, however, is a mere preamble, and leads up to the fact that after ten years or so of drudgery I inherited a legacy which, though small, was sufficient to satisfy my simple wants. Finding myself independent, I rented a quiet house removed from the uproar and bustle of London, and there I settled down with the intention of producing some great work which should single me out from the family of the Smiths, and render my name immortal. To this end I laid in several quires of foolscap, a box of quill pens, and a sixpenny bottle of ink, and having given my housekeeper injunctions to deny me to all visitors, I proceeded to look round for a suitable subject.

I was looking round for some weeks. At the end of that time I found that I had by constant nibbling devoured a large number of the quills, and had spread the ink out to such advantage, what with blots, spills, and abortive commencements, that there appeared to be some everywhere except in the bottle. As to the story itself, however, the facility of my youth had deserted me completely, and my mind remained a complete blank; nor could I, do what I would, excite my sterile imagination to conjure up a single incident or character.

In this strait I determined to devote my leisure to running rapidly through the works of the leading English novelists, from Daniel Defoe to the present day, in the hope of stimulating my latent ideas and of getting a good grasp of the general tendency of literature. For some time past I had avoided opening

147

any work of fiction because one of the greatest faults of my youth had been that I invariably and unconsciously mimicked the style of the last author whom I had happened to read. Now, however, I made up my mind to seek safety in a multitude, and by consulting *all* the English classics to avoid the danger of imitating any one too closely. I had just accomplished the task of reading through the majority of the standard novels at the time when my narrative commences.

It was, then, about twenty minutes to ten on the night of the fourth of June, eighteen hundred and eighty-six, that, after disposing of a pint of beer and a Welsh rarebit for my supper, I seated myself in my armchair, cocked my feet upon a stool, and lit my pipe, as was my custom. Both my pulse and my temperature were, as far as I know, normal at the time. I would give the state of the barometer, but that unlucky instrument had experienced an unprecedented fall of forty-two inches—from a nail to the ground—and was not in a reliable condition. We live in a scientific age, and I flatter myself that I move with the times.

Whilst in that comfortable lethargic condition which accompanies both digestion and poisoning by nicotine, I suddenly became aware of the extraordinary fact that my little drawing-room had elongated into a great *salon*, and that my humble table had increased in proportion. Round this colossal mahogany were seated a great number of people who were talking earnestly together, and the surface in front of them was strewn with books and pamphlets. I could not help observing that these persons were dressed in a most extraordinary mixture of costumes, for those at the end nearest to me wore peruke wigs, swords, and all the fashions of two centuries back; those about the centre had tight knee-breeches, high cravats, and heavy bunches of seals; while among those at the far side the majority were dressed in the most modern style, and among them I saw, to my surprise, several eminent men of letters whom I had the honour of knowing. There were two or three women in the company. I should have risen to my feet to greet these unexpected guests, but all power of motion appeared to have deserted me, and I could only lie still and listen to their conversation, which I soon perceived to be all about myself.

'Egad!' exclaimed a rough, weather-beaten man, who was smoking a long churchwarden pipe at my end of the table, 'my heart softens for him. Why, gossips, we've been in the same straits ourselves. Gadzooks, never did mother feel more concern for her eldest born than I when Rory Random went out to make his own way in the world.'

'Right, Tobias, right!' cried another man, seated at my very elbow. 'By my troth, I lost more flesh over poor Robin on his island, than had I the sweating sickness twice told. The tale was well-nigh done when in swaggers my Lord of Rochester—a merry gallant, and one whose word in matters literary might make or mar. "How now, Defoe," quoth he, "Hast a tale on hand?" "Even so, your lordship," I returned. "A right merry one, I trust," quoth he. "Discourse unto me concerning thy heroine, a comely kiss, Dan, or I mistake." "Nay," I replied, "there is no heroine in the matter." "Split not your phrases," quoth he; "thou weighest every word like a scald attorney. Speak to me of thy principal female character, be she heroine or no." "My lord," I answered, "there is no female character." "Then out upon thyself and thy book too!" he cried. "Thou hadst best burn it!"—and so out in great dudgeon, whilst I fell to mourning over my poor romance, which was thus, as it were, sentenced to death before its birth. Yet there are a thousand now who have heard of Robin and his man Friday, to one who has heard of my Lord of Rochester.'

'Very true, Defoe,' said a genial-looking man in a red waistcoat, who was sitting at the modern end of the table. 'But all this won't help our good friend Smith in making a start at his story, which, I believe, was the reason why we assembled.'

'The Dickens it is!' stammered a little man beside him, and everybody laughed, especially the genial man, who cried out, 'Charley Lamb, Charley Lamb, you'll never alter. You would make a pun if you were hanged for it.'

'That would be a case of haltering,' returned the other, on which everybody laughed again.

By this time I had begun to dimly realize in my confused brain the enormous honour which had been done me. The greatest masters of fiction in every age of English letters had apparently made a rendezvous beneath my roof, in order to assist me in my difficulties. There were many faces at the table whom I was unable to identify; but when I looked hard at others I often found them to be very familiar to me, whether from paintings or from mere description. Thus between the first two speakers, who had betrayed themselves as Defoe and Smollett, there sat a dark, saturnine, corpulent old man, with harsh prominent features, who I was sure could be none other than the famous author of Gulliver. There were several others of whom I was not so sure, sitting at the other side of the table, but I conjecture that both Fielding and Richardson were among them, and I could swear to the lantern-jaws and cadaverous visage of Lawrence Sterne. Higher up I could see among the crowd the high forehead of Sir Walter Scott, the masculine features of George Eliot, and the flattened nose of Thackeray; while amongst the living I recognised James Payn, Walter Besant, the lady known as 'Ouida', Robert Louis Stevenson, and several of lesser note. Never before, probably, had such an assemblage of choice spirits gathered under one roof.

'Well,' said Sir Walter Scott, speaking with a very pronounced accent, 'ye ken the auld proverb, sirs, "Ower mony cooks", or as the Border minstrel sang:

> "Black Johnstone wi' his troopers ten
> Might mak' the heart turn cauld,
> But Johnstone when he's a' alane
> Is waur ten thoosand fauld."

The Johntones were one of the Redesdale families, second cousins of the Armstrongs, and connected by marriage to——'

'Perhaps, Sir Walter,' interrupted Thackeray, 'you would take the responsibility off our hands by yourself dictating the commencement of a story to this young literary aspirant.'

'Na, na!' cried Sir Walter; 'I'll do my share, but there's Chairlie over there as full o' wut as a Radical's full o' treason. He's the laddie to give a cheery opening to it.'

Dickens was shaking his head, and apparently about to refuse the honour, when a voice from among the moderns—I could not see who it was for the crowd—said:

'Suppose we begin at the end of the table and work round, anyone contributing a little as the fancy seizes him?'

'Agreed! agreed!' cried the whole company; and every eye was turned on Defoe, who seemed very uneasy, and filled his pipe from a great tobacco-box in front of him.

'Nay, gossips,' he said, 'there are others more worthy——'

But he was interrupted by loud cries of 'No! no!' from the whole table; and Smollett shouted out, 'Stand to it, Dan—stand to it! You and I and the Dean here will make three short tacks just to fetch her out of harbour, and then she may drift where she pleases.' Thus encouraged, Defoe cleared his throat, and began in this way, talking between the puffs of his pipe:

'My father was a well-to-do yeoman of Cheshire, named Cyprian Overbeck, but, marrying about the year 1617, he assumed the name of his wife's family, which was Wells; and thus I, their eldest son, was named Cyprian Overbeck Wells. The farm was a very fertile one, and contained some of the best grazing land in those parts, so that my father was enabled to lay by money to the extent of a thousand crowns, which he laid out in an adventure to the Indies with such surprising success that in less than three years it had increased fourfold. Thus encouraged, he bought a part share of the trader, and, fitting her out once more with such commodities as were most in demand (viz. old muskets, hangars and axes, besides glasses, needles, and the like), he placed me on board as supercargo to look after his interests, and dispatched us upon our voyage.

'We had a fair wind as far as Cape de Verde, and there, getting into the north-west trade-winds, made good progress down the African coast. Beyond sighting a Barbary rover once, whereat our mariners were in sad distress, counting themselves already as little better than slaves, we had good luck until we had come within a hundred leagues of the Cape of Good Hope, when the wind veered round to the southward and blew exceeding hard while the sea rose to such a height that the end of the mainyard dipped into the water, and I heard the master say that though he had been at sea for five-and-thirty years he had never seen the like of it, and that he had little expectation of riding through it. On this I fell to wringing my hands and bewailing myself, until the mast going by the board with a crash, I thought that the ship had struck, and swooned with terror, falling into the scuppers and lying like one dead, which was the saving of me, as will appear in the sequel. For the mariners, giving up all hope of saving the ship, and being in momentary expectation that she would founder, pushed off in the long-boat, whereby I fear that they met the fate which they hoped to avoid, since I have never from that day heard anything of them. For my own part, on recovering from the swoon into which I had fallen, I found that, by the mercy of Providence, the sea had gone down, and that I was alone in the vessel. At which last discovery I was so terror-struck that I could but stand wringing my hands and bewailing my sad fate, until at last taking heart, I fell to comparing my lot with that of my unhappy camerados, on which I became more cheerful, and descending to the cabin, made a meal off such dainties as were in the captain's locker.'

Having got so far, Defoe remarked that he thought he had given them a fair start, and handed over the story to Dean Swift, who, after premising that he feared he would find himself as much at sea as Master Cyprian Overbeck Wells, continued in this way:

'For two days I drifted about in great distress, fearing that there should be a return of the gale, and keeping an eager look-out for my late companions. Upon the third day, towards evening, I observed to my extreme surprise that the ship was under the influence of a very powerful current, which ran to the north with such violence that she was carried, now bows on, now stern on, and occasionally drifting sideways like a crab, at a rate which I cannot compute at less than twelve or fifteen knots. For several weeks I was borne in this manner, until one morning, to my inexpressible joy, I sighted an island upon the starboard quarter. The current would, however, have carried me past it had I not made shift, though single-handed, to set the flying-jib so as to turn her bows, and then clapping on the sprit-sail, studding-sail, and fore-sail, I clewed up the halliards upon the port side, and put the wheel down hard a-starboard, the wind being at the time north-east-half-east.'

At the description of this nautical manoeuvre I observed that Smollett grinned, and a gentleman who was sitting higher up the table in the uniform of the Royal Navy, and who I guessed to be Captain Marryat, became very uneasy and fidgeted in his seat.

'By this means I got clear of the current and was able to steer within a quarter of a mile of the beach, which indeed I might have approached still nearer by making another tack, but being an excellent swimmer, I deemed it best to leave the vessel, which was almost waterlogged, and to make the best of my way to the shore.

'I had had my doubts hitherto as to whether this new-found country was inhabited or no, but as I approached nearer to it, being on the summit of a great wave, I perceived a number of figures on the beach, engaged apparently in watching me and my vessel. My joy, however, was considerably lessened when on reaching the land I found that the figures consisted of a vast concourse of animals of various sorts who were standing about in groups, and who hurried down to the water's edge to meet me. I had scarce put my foot upon the sand before I was surrounded by an eager crowd of deer, dogs, wild boars, buffaloes, and other creatures, none of whom showed the least fear either of me or of each other, but, on the contrary, were animated by a common feeling of curiosity, as well as, it would appear, by some degree of disgust.'

'A second edition,' whispered Lawrence Sterne to his neighbour; 'Gulliver served up cold.'

'Did you speak, sir?' asked the Dean very sternly, having evidently overheard the remark.

'My words were not addressed to you, sir,' answered Sterne, looking rather frightened.

'They were none the less insolent,' roared the Dean. 'Your reverence would fain make a Sentimental Journey of the narrative, I doubt not, and find pathos in a dead donkey—though, faith, no man can blame thee for mourning over thy own kith and kin.'

'Better that than to wallow in all the filth of Yahoo-land,' returned Sterne warmly, and a quarrel would certainly have ensued but for the interposition of the remainder of the company. As it was, the Dean refused indignantly to have any further hand in the story, and Sterne also stood out of it, remarking with a sneer that he was loth to fit a good blade on to a poor handle. Under these circumstances some further unpleasantness might have occurred had not Smollett rapidly taken up the narrative, continuing it in the third person instead of the first:

'Our hero, being considerably alarmed at this strange reception, lost little time in plunging into the sea again and regaining his vessel, being convinced that the worst which might befall him from the elements would be as nothing compared to the dangers of this mysterious island. It was as well that he took this course, for before nightfall his ship was overhauled and he himself picked up by a British man-of-war, the *Lightning* (74), then returning from the West Indies, where it had formed part of the fleet under the command of Admiral Benbow. Young Wells, being a likely lad enough, well-spoken and high-spirited, was at once entered on the books as officer's servant, in which capacity he both gained great popularity on account of the freedom of his manners, and found an opportunity for indulging in those practical pleasantries for which he had all his life been famous.

'Among the quartermasters of the *Lightning* there was one named Jedediah Anchorstock, whose appearance was so remarkable that it quickly attracted the attention of our hero. He was a man of about fifty, dark with exposure to the weather, and so tall that as he came along the 'tween decks he had to bend himself nearly double. The most striking peculiarity of this individual was, however, that in his boyhood some evil-minded person had tattooed eyes all over his countenance with such marvellous skill that it was difficult at a short distance to pick out his real ones among so many counterfeits. On this strange personage Master Cyprian determined to exercise his talents for mischief, the more so as he learned that he was extremely superstitious, and also that he had left behind him in Portsmouth a strong-minded spouse of whom he stood in mortal terror. With this object he secured one of the sheep which were kept on board for the officer's table, and pouring a can of rumbo down its throat, reduced it to a state of utter intoxication. He then conveyed it to Anchorstock's berth, and with the assistance of some other imps, as mischievous as himself, dressed it up in a high nightcap and gown, and covered it over with the bedclothes.

'When the quartermaster came down from his watch our hero met him at the door of his berth with an agitated face. "Mr Anchorstock," said he, "can it be that your wife is on board?" "Wife!" roared the astonished sailor. "Ye white-faced swab, what d'ye mean?" "If she's not here in the ship it must be her ghost," said Cyprian, shaking his head gloomily. "In the ship! How in thunder could she get into the ship? Why, master, I believe as how you're weak in the upper works, d'ye see? to as much as think o' such a thing. My Poll is moored head and starn, behind the point at Portsmouth, more'n two thousand mile away." "Upon my word," said our hero, very earnestly, "I saw a female look out of your cabin not five minutes ago." "Ay, ay, Mr Anchorstock," joined in several of the conspirators. "We all saw her—a spanking-looking craft with a dead-light mounted on one side." "Sure enough," said Anchorstock, staggered by this accumulation of evidence, "my Polly's starboard eye was doused for ever by long Sue Williams of the Hard. But if so be as she be there I must see her, be she ghost or quick"; with which the honest sailor, in much perturbation and trembling in every limb, began to shuffle forward into the cabin, holding the light well in front of him. It chanced, however, that the unhappy sheep, which was quietly engaged in sleeping off the effects of its unusual potations, was awakened by the noise of his approach, and finding herself in such an unusual position, sprang out of bed and rushed furiously for the door, bleating wildly, and rolling about like a brig in a tornado, partly from intoxication and partly from the nightdress which impeded her movements. As Anchorstock saw this extraordinary apparition bearing down upon him, he uttered a yell and fell flat upon his face, convinced that he had to do with a supernatural visitor, the more so as the confederates heightened the effect by a chorus of most ghastly groans and cries. The joke had nearly gone beyond what was originally intended, for the quartermaster lay as one dead, and it was only with the greatest difficulty that he could be brought to his senses. To the end of the voyage he stoutly asserted that he had seen the distant Mrs Anchorstock, remarking with many oaths that though he was too woundily scared to take much note of the features, there was no mistaking the strong smell of rum which was characteristic of his better half.

'It chanced shortly after this to be the king's birthday, an event which was signalised aboard the *Lightning* by the death of the commander under singular circumstances. This officer, who was a real fair-weather Jack, hardly knowing the ship's keel from her ensign, had obtained his position through parliamentary interest, and used it with such tyranny and cruelty that he was universally execrated. So unpopular was he that when a plot was entered into by the whole crew to punish his misdeeds with death, he had not a single friend among six hundred souls to warn him of his danger. It was the custom on board the king's ships that upon his birthday the entire ship's company should be drawn up upon deck, and that at a signal they should discharge their muskets into the air in honour of his Majesty. On this occasion word had been secretly passed round for every man to slip a slug into his firelock, instead of the blank cartridge provided. On the boatswain blowing his whistle the men mustered upon deck and formed line, whilst the captain, standing well in front of them, delivered a few words to them. "When I give the word," he concluded, "you shall discharge your pieces, and by thunder, if any man is a second before or a second after his fellows I shall trice him up to the weather rigging!" With these words he roared "Fire!" on which every man levelled his musket straight at his head and pulled the trigger. So accurate was the aim and so short the distance, that more than five hundred bullets struck him simultaneously, blowing away his head and a large portion of his body. There were so many concerned in this matter, and it was so hopeless to trace it to any individual, that the officers were unable to punish anyone for the affair—the more readily as the captain's haughty ways and heartless conduct had made him quite as hateful to them as to the men whom he commanded.

'By his pleasantries and the natural charm of his manners our hero so far won the good wishes of the ship's company that they parted with infinite regret upon their arrival in England. Filial duty, however, urged him to return home and report himself to his father, with which object he posted from Portsmouth to London, intending to proceed thence to Shropshire. As it chanced, however, one of the horses sprained his off foreleg while passing through Chichester, and as no change could be obtained, Cyprian found himself compelled to put up at The Crown and Bull for the night.

'Ods bodikins!' continued Smollett, laughing, 'I never could pass a comfortable hostel without stopping and so, with your permission, I'll e'en stop here, and whoever wills may lead friend Cyprian to his further adventures. Do you, Sir Walter, give us a touch of the Wizard of the North.'

With these words Smollett produced a pipe, and filling it at Defoe's tobacco-pot, waited patiently for the continuation of the story.

'If I must, I must,' remarked the illustrious Scotchman, taking a pinch of snuff; 'but I must beg leave to put Mr Wells back a few hundred years, for of all things I love the true mediaeval smack. To proceed then:

'Our hero being anxious to continue his journey, and learning that it would be some time before any conveyance would be ready, determined to push on alone mounted on his gallant grey steed. Travelling was particularly dangerous at that time, for besides the usual perils which beset wayfarers, the southern parts of England were in a lawless and disturbed state which bordered on insurrection. The young man, however, having loosened his sword in his sheath, so as to be ready for every eventuality, galloped cheerily upon his way, guiding himself to the best of his ability by the light of the rising moon.

'He had not gone far before he realised that the cautions which had been impressed upon him by the landlord, and which he had been inclined to look upon as self-interested advice, were only too well justified. At a spot where the road was particularly rough, and ran across some marshland, he perceived a short distance from him a dark shadow, which his practised eye detected at once as a body of crouching men. Reining up his horse within a few yards of the ambuscade, he wrapped his cloak round his bridle-arm and summoned the party to stand forth.

'"What ho, my masters!" he cried. "Are beds so scarce, then, that ye must hamper the high road of the king with your bodies? Now, by St Ursula of Alpuxerra, there be those who might think that birds who fly o' nights were after higher game than the moorhen or the woodcock!"

'"Blades and targets, comrades!" exclaimed a tall powerful man, springing into the centre of the road with several companions, and standing in front of the frightened horse. "Who is this swashbuckler who summons his Majesty's lieges from their repose? A very soldado, o' truth. Hark ye, sir, or my lord, or thy grace, or whatsoever title your honour's honour may be pleased to approve, thou must curb thy tongue play, or by the seven witches of Gambleside thou may find thyself in but a sorry plight."

'"I prythee, then, that thou wilt expound to me who and what ye are," quoth our hero, "and whether your purpose be such as an honest man may approve of. As to your threats, they turn from my mind as your caitiffly weapons would shiver upon my hauberk from Milan."

'"Nay, Allen," interrupted one of the party, addressing him who seemed to be their leader; "this is a lad of mettle, and such a one as our honest Jack longs for. But we lure not hawks with empty hands. Look ye, sir, there is game afoot which it may need such bold hunters as thyself to follow. Come with us and take a firkin of canary, and we will find better work for that glaive of thine than getting its owner into broil and bloodshed; for, by my troth! Milan or no Milan, if my curtel axe do but ring against that morion of thine it will be an ill day for thy father's son."

'For a moment our hero hesitated as to whether it would best become his knightly traditions to hurl himself against his enemies, or whether it might not be better to obey their requests. Prudence, mingled with a large share of curiosity, eventually carried the day, and dismounting from his horse, he intimated that he was ready to follow his captors.

'"Spoken like a man!" cried he whom they addressed as Allen. "Jack Cade will be right glad of such a recruit. Blood and carrion! but thou hast the thews of a young ox; and I swear, by the haft of my sword, that it might have gone ill with some of us hadst thou not listened to reason!"

'"Nay, not so, good Allen—not so," squeaked a very small man, who had remained in the background while there was any prospect of a fray, but who now came pushing to the front. "Hadst thou been alone it might indeed have been so, perchance, but an expert swordsman can disarm at pleasure such a one as this young knight. Well I remember in the Palatinate how I clove to the chine even such another—the Baron von Slogstaff. He struck at me, look ye, so; but I, with buckler and blade, did, as one might say, deflect it; and then, countering in carte, I returned in tierce, and so—St Agnes save us! who comes here?"

'The apparition which frightened the loquacious little man was sufficiently strange to cause a qualm even in the bosom of the knight. Through the darkness there loomed a figure which appeared to be of gigantic size, and a hoarse voice, issuing apparently some distance above the heads of the party, broke roughly on the silence of the night.

'"Now out upon thee, Thomas Allen, and foul be thy fate if thou hast abandoned thy post without good and sufficient cause. By St Anselm of the Holy Grove, thou hadst best have never been born than rouse my spleen this night. Wherefore is it that you and your men are trailing over the moor like a flock of geese when Michaelmas is near?"

'"Good captain," said Allen, doffing his bonnet, an example followed by others of the band, "we have captured a goodly youth who was pricking it along the London road. Methought that some word of thanks were meet reward for such service, rather than taunt or threat."

'"Nay, take it not to heart, bold Allen," exclaimed their leader, who was none other than the great Jack Cade himself. "Thou knowest of old that my temper is somewhat choleric, and my tongue not greased with that unguent which oils the mouths of the lip-serving lords of the land. And you," he continued, turning suddenly upon our hero, "are you ready to join the great cause which will make England what it was when the learned Alfred reigned in the land? Zounds, man, speak out, and pick not your phrases."

'"I am ready to do aught which may become a knight and a gentleman," said the soldier stoutly.

'"Taxes shall be swept away!" cried Cade excitedly—"the impost and the anpost—the tithe and the hundred-tax. The poor man's salt-box and flour-bin shall be as free as the nobleman's cellar. Ha! what sayest thou?"

'"It is but just," said our hero.

'"Ay, but they give us such justice as the falcon gives the leveret!" roared the orator. "Down with them, I say—down with every man of them! Noble and judge, priest and king, down with them all!"

'"Nay," said Sir Overbeck Wells, drawing himself up to his full height, and laying his hand upon the hilt of his sword, "there I cannot follow thee, but must rather defy thee as traitor and fainéant, seeing that thou art no true man, but one who would usurp the rights of our master the king whom may the Virgin protect!"

'At these bold words, and the defiance which they conveyed, the rebels seemed for a moment utterly bewildered; but, encouraged by the hoarse shout of their leader they brandished their weapons and prepared to fall upon the knight, who placed himself in a posture for defence and awaited their attack.

'There now!' cried Sir Walter, rubbing his hands and chuckling, 'I've put the chiel in a pretty warm corner, and we'll see which of you moderns can take him oot o't. Neer a word more will ye get frae me to help him one way or the other.'

'You try your hand, James,' cried several voices, and the author in question had got so far as to make an allusion to a solitary horseman who was approaching, when he was interrupted by a tall gentleman a little farther down with a slight stutter and a very nervous manner.

'Excuse me,' he said, 'but I fancy that I may be able to do something here. Some of my humble productions have been said to excel Sir Walter at his best, and I was undoubtedly stronger all round. I could picture modern society as well as ancient; and as to my plays, why Shakespeare never came near *The Lady of Lyons* for popularity. There is this little thing——' (Here he rummaged among a great pile of papers in front of him). 'Ah! that's a report of mine, when I was in India! Here it is. No, this is one of my speeches in the House, and this is my criticism on Tennyson. Didn't I warm him up? I can't find what I wanted, but of course you have read them all—*Rienzi*, and *Harold*, and *The Last of the Barons*. Every schoolboy knows them by heart, as poor Macaulay would have said. Allow me to give you a sample:

'In spite of the gallant knight's valiant resistance the combat was too unequal to be sustained. His sword was broken by a slash from a brown bill, and he was borne to the ground. He expected immediate death, but such did not seem to be the intention of the ruffians who had captured him. He was placed upon the back of his own charger and borne, bound hand and foot, over the trackless moor, in the fastnesses of which the rebels secreted themselves.

'In the depths of these wilds there stood a stone building which had once been a farmhouse, but having been for some reason abandoned had fallen into ruin, and had now become the headquarters of Cade and his men. A large cow-house near the farm had been utilised as sleeping quarters, and some rough attempts had been made to shield the principal room of the main building from the weather by stopping up the gaping apertures in the walls. In this apartment was spread out a rough meal for the returning rebels, and our hero was thrown, still bound, into an empty outhouse, there to await his fate.'

Sir Walter had been listening with the greatest impatience to Bulwer Lytton's narrative, but when it had reached this point he broke in impatiently.

'We want a touch of your own style, man,' he said. 'The animal-magnetico-

157

electro-hysterical-biological mysterious sort of story is all your own, but at present you are just a poor copy of myself, and nothing more.'

There was a murmur of assent from the company, and Defoe remarked, 'Truly, Master Lytton, there is a plaguey resemblance in the style, which may indeed be but a chance, and yet methinks it is sufficiently marked to warrant such words as our friend hath used.'

'Perhaps you will think that this is an imitation also,' said Lytton bitterly, and leaning back in his chair with a morose countenance, he continued the narrative in this way:

'Our unfortunate hero had hardly stretched himself upon the straw with which his dungeon was littered, when a secret door opened in the wall and a venerable old man swept majestically into the apartment. The prisoner gazed upon him with astonishment not unmixed with awe, for on his broad brow was printed the seal of much knowledge—such knowledge as it is not granted to a son of man to know. He was clad in a long white robe, crossed and chequered with mystic devices in the Arabic character, while a high scarlet tiara marked with the square and circle enhanced his venerable appearance. "My son," he said, turning his piercing and yet dreamy gaze upon Sir Overbeck, "all things lead to nothing, and nothing is the foundation of all things. Cosmos is impenetrable. Why then should we exist?"

'Astounded at this weighty query, and at the philosophic demeanour of his visitor, our hero made shift to bid him welcome and to demand his name and quality. As the old man answered him his voice rose and fell in musical cadences, like the sighing of the east wind, while an ethereal and aromatic vapour pervaded the apartment.

'"I am the eternal non-ego," he answered. "I am the concentrated negative—the everlasting essence of nothing. You see in me that which existed before the beginning of matter many years before the commencement of time. I am the algebraic x which represents the infinite divisibility of a finite particle."

'Sir Overbeck felt a shudder as though an ice-cold hand had been placed upon his brow. "What is your message?" he whispered, falling prostrate before his mysterious visitor.

'"To tell you that the eternities beget chaos, and that the immensities are at the mercy of the divine ananke. Infinitude crouches before a personality. The mercurial essence is the prime mover in spirituality, and the thinker is powerless before the pulsating inanity. The cosmical procession is terminated only by the unknowable and unpronounceable——"

'May I ask, Mr Smollett, what you find to laugh at?'

'Gadzooks, master,' cried Smollett, who had been sniggering for some time back. 'It seems to me that there is little danger of anyone venturing to dispute that style with you.'

'It's all your own,' murmured Sir Walter.

'And very pretty, too,' quoth Lawrence Sterne, with a malignant grin. 'Pray, sir, what language do you call it?'

Lytton was so enraged at these remarks, and at the favour with which they appeared to be received, that he endeavoured to stutter out some reply, and then, losing control of himself completely, picked up all his loose papers and strode out of the room, dropping pamphlets and speeches at every step. This incident amused the company so much that they laughed for several minutes without cessation. Gradually the sound of their laughter sounded more and more harshly in my ears, the lights on the table grew dim and the company more misty, until they and their symposium vanished away altogether. I was sitting before the embers of what had been a roaring fire, but was now little more than a heap of grey ashes, and the merry laughter of the august company had changed to the recriminations of my wife, who was shaking me violently by the shoulder and exhorting me to choose some more seasonable spot for my slumbers. So ended the wondrous adventures of Master Cyprian Overbeck Wells, but I still live in the hopes that in some future dream the great masters may themselves finish that which they have begun.

The Ring of Thoth

M R JOHN VANSITTART SMITH, FRS, of 147A Gower Street, was a man whose energy of purpose and clearness of thought might have placed him in the very first rank of scientific observers. He was the victim, however, of a universal ambition which prompted him to aim at distinction in many subjects rather than pre-eminence in one. In his early days he had shown an aptitude for zoology and for botany which caused his friends to look upon him as a second Darwin, but when a professorship was almost within his reach he had suddenly discontinued his studies and turned his whole attention to chemistry. Here his researches upon the spectra of the metals had won him his fellowship in the Royal Society; but again he played the coquette with his subject, and after a year's absence from the laboratory he joined the Oriental Society, and delivered a paper on the Hieroglyphic and Demotic inscriptions of El Kab, thus giving a crowning example both of the versatility and of the inconstancy of his talents.

The most fickle of wooers, however, is apt to be caught at last, and so it was with John Vansittart Smith. The more he burrowed his way into Egyptology the more impressed he became by the vast field which it opened to the inquirer, and by the extreme importance of a subject which promised to throw a light upon the first germs of human civilisation and the origin of the greater part of our arts and sciences. So struck was Mr Smith that he straightway married an Egyptological young lady who had written upon the sixth dynasty, and having thus secured a sound base of operations he set himself to collect materials for a work which should unite the research of Lepsius and the ingenuity of Champollion. The preparation of this *magnum opus* entailed many hurried visits to the magnificent Egyptian collections of the Louvre, upon the last of which, no longer ago than the middle of last October, he became involved in a most strange and noteworthy adventure.

The trains had been slow and the Channel had been rough, so that the student arrived in Paris in a somewhat befogged and feverish condition. On reaching the Hôtel de France, in the Rue Laffitte, he had thrown himself upon a sofa for a couple of hours, but finding that he was unable to sleep, he determined, in spite of his fatigue, to make his way to the Louvre, settle the point which he had come to decide, and take the evening train back to Dieppe.

Having come to his conclusion, he donned his greatcoat, for it was a raw rainy day, and made his way across the Boulevard des Italiens and down the Avenue de l'Opéra. Once in the Louvre he was on familiar ground, and he speedily made his way to the collection of papyri which it was his intention to consult.

The warmest admirers of John Vansittart Smith could hardly claim for him that he was a handsome man. His high-beaked nose and prominent chin had something of the same acute and incisive character which distinguished his intellect. He held his head in a birdlike fashion, and birdlike, too, was the pecking motion with which, in conversation, he threw out his objections and retorts. As he stood, with the high collar of his greatcoat raised to his ears, he might have seen from the reflection in the glass-case before him that his appearance was a singular one. Yet it came upon him as a sudden jar when an English voice behind him exclaimed in very audible tones, 'What a queer-looking mortal!'

The student had a large amount of petty vanity in his composition which manifested itself by an ostentatious and overdone disregard of all personal considerations. He straightened his lips and looked rigidly at the roll of papyrus, while his heart filled with bitterness against the whole race of travelling Britons.

'Yes,' said another voice, 'he really is an extraordinary fellow.'

'Do you know,' said the first speaker, 'one could almost believe that by the continual contemplation of mummies the chap has become half a mummy himself?'

'He has certainly an Egyptian cast of countenance,' said the other.

John Vansittart Smith spun round upon his heel with the intention of shaming his countrymen by a corrosive remark or two. To his surprise and relief, the two young fellows who had been conversing had their shoulders turned towards him, and were gazing at one of the Louvre attendants who was polishing some brass-work at the other side of the room.

'Carter will be waiting for us at the Palais Royal,' said one tourist to the other, glancing at his watch, and they clattered away, leaving the student to his labours.

'I wonder what these chatterers call an Egyptian cast of countenance,' thought John Vansittart Smith, and he moved his position slightly in order to catch a glimpse of the man's face. He started as his eyes fell upon it. It was indeed the very face with which his studies had made him familiar. The regular statuesque features, broad brow, well-rounded chin, and dusky complexion were the exact counterpart of the innumerable statues, mummy-cases, and pictures which adorned the walls of the apartment. The thing was beyond all coincidence. The man must be an Egyptian. The national angularity of the shoulders and narrowness of the hips were alone sufficient to identify him.

John Vansittart Smith shuffled towards the attendant with some intention of addressing him. He was not light of touch in conversation, and found it difficult to strike the happy mean between the brusqueness of the superior and the geniality of the equal. As he came nearer, the man presented his side face to him, but kept his gaze still bent upon his work. Vansittart Smith, fixing his eyes upon the fellow's skin, was conscious of a sudden impression that there was something inhuman and preternatural about its appearance. Over the temple and cheek-bone it was as glazed and as shiny as varnished parchment. There was no suggestion of pores. One could not fancy a drop of moisture upon that arid surface. From brow to chin, however, it was cross-hatched by a million delicate wrinkles, which shot and interlaced as though Nature in some Maori mood had tried how wild and intricate a pattern she could devise.

'*Où est la collection de Memphis?*' asked the student, with the awkward air of a man who is devising a question merely for the purpose of opening a conversation.

'*C'est là,*' replied the man brusquely, nodding his head at the other side of the room.

'*Vous êtes un Egyptien, n'est-ce pas?*' asked the Englishman.

The attendant looked up and turned his strange dark eyes upon his questioner. They were vitreous, with a misty dry shininess, such as Smith had never seen in a human head before. As he gazed into them he saw some strong emotion gather in their depths, which rose and deepened until it broke into a look of something akin both to horror and to hatred.

'*Non, monsieur; je suis français.*' The man turned abruptly and bent low over his polishing. The student gazed at him for a moment in astonishment, and then turning to a chair in a retired corner behind one of the doors he proceeded to make notes of his researches among the papyri. His thoughts, however, refused to return into their natural groove. They would run upon the enigmatical attendant with the sphinx-like face and the parchment skin.

'Where have I seen such eyes?' said Vansittart Smith to himself. 'There is something saurian about them, something reptilian. There's the *membrana nictitans* of the snakes,' he mused, bethinking himself of his zoological studies. 'It gives a shiny effect. But there was something more here. There was a sense of power, of wisdom—so I read them—and of weariness, utter weariness, and ineffable despair. It may be all imagination, but I never had so strong an impression. By Jove, I must have another look at them!' He rose and paced round the Egyptian rooms, but the man who had excited his curiosity had disappeared.

The student sat down again in his quiet corner, and continued to work at his notes. He had gained the information which he required from the papyri, and it only remained to write it down while it was still fresh in his memory. For a time his pencil travelled rapidly over the paper, but soon the lines became less level, the words more blurred, and finally the pencil tinkled down upon the floor, and the head of the student dropped heavily forward upon his chest. Tired out by his journey, he slept so soundly in his lonely post behind the door that neither the clanking civil guard, nor the footsteps of sightseers, nor even the loud hoarse bell which gives the signal for closing, were sufficient to arouse him.

Twilight deepened into darkness, the bustle from the Rue de Rivoli waxed and then waned, distant Notre Dame clanged out the hour of midnight, and still the dark and lonely figure sat silently in the shadow. It was not until close upon one in the morning that, with a sudden gasp and an intaking of the breath, Vansittart Smith returned to consciousness. For a moment it flashed upon him that he had dropped asleep in his study-chair at home. The moon was shining fitfully through the unshuttered window, however, and as his eye ran along the lines of mummies and the endless array of polished cases, he remembered clearly where he was and how he came there. The student was not a nervous man. He possessed that love of a novel situation which is peculiar to his race. Stretching out his cramped limbs, he looked at his watch, and burst into a chuckle as he observed the hour. The episode would make an admirable anecdote to be introduced into his next paper as a relief to the graver and heavier speculations. He was a little cold, but wide awake and much refreshed. It was no wonder that the guardians had overlooked him, for the door threw its heavy black shadow right across him.

The complete silence was impressive. Neither outside nor inside was there a creak or a murmur. He was alone with the dead men of a dead civilisation. What though the outer city reeked of the garish nineteenth century! In all this chamber there was scarce an article, from the shrivelled ear of wheat to the pigment-box of the painter, which had not held its own against four thousand years. Here was the flotsam and jetsam washed up by the great ocean of time from that far-off empire. From stately Thebes, from lordly Luxor, from the great temples of Heliopolis, from a hundred rifled tombs, these relics had been brought. The student glanced round at the long-silent figures who flickered vaguely up through the gloom, at the busy toilers who were now so restful, and he fell into a reverent and thoughtful mood. An unwonted sense of his own youth and insignificance came over him. Leaning back in his chair, he gazed dreamily down the long vista of rooms, all silvery with the moonshine, which extend through the whole wing of the widespread building. His eyes fell upon the yellow glare of a distant lamp.

John Vansittart Smith sat up on his chair with his nerves all on edge. The light was advancing slowly towards him, pausing from time to time, and then coming jerkily onwards. The bearer moved noiselessly. In the utter silence there was no suspicion of the pat of a footfall. An idea of robbers entered the Englishman's head. He snuggled up farther into the corner. The light was two rooms off. Now it was in the next chamber, and still there was no sound. With something approaching to a thrill of fear the student observed a face, floating in the air as it were, behind the flare of the lamp. The figure was wrapped in shadow, but the light fell full upon the strange, eager face. There was no mistaking the metallic, glistening eyes and the cadaverous skin. It was the attendant with whom he had conversed.

Vansittart Smith's first impulse was to come forward and address him. A few words of explanation would set the matter clear, and lead doubtless to his being conducted to some side-door from which he might make his way to his hotel. As the man entered the chamber, however, there was something so stealthy in his movements, and so furtive in his expression, that the Englishman altered his intention. This was clearly no ordinary official walking the rounds. The fellow wore felt-soled slippers, stepped with a rising chest, and glanced quickly from left to right, while his hurried, gasping breathing thrilled the flame of his lamp. Vansittart Smith crouched silently back into the corner and watched him keenly, convinced that his errand was one of secret and probably sinister import.

There was no hesitation in the other's movements. He stepped lightly and swiftly across to one of the great cases, and, drawing a key from his pocket, he unlocked it. From the upper shelf he pulled down a mummy, which he bore away with him, and laid it with much care and solicitude upon the ground. By it he placed his lamp, and then squatting down beside it in Eastern fashion he began with long, quivering fingers to undo the cerecloths and bandages which girt it round. As the crackling rolls of linen peeled off one after the other, a strong aromatic odour filled the chamber, and fragments of scented wood and of spices pattered down upon the marble floor.

It was clear to John Vansittart Smith that this mummy had never been unswathed before. The operation interested him keenly. He thrilled all over with curiosity, and his bird-like head protruded farther and farther from behind the door. When, however, the last roll had been removed from the four-thousand-year-old head, it was all that he could do to stifle an outcry of amazement. First, a cascade of long, black, glossy tresses poured over the workman's hands and arms. A second turn of the bandage revealed a low, white forehead, with a pair of delicately arched eyebrows. A third uncovered a pair of bright, deeply fringed eyes, and a straight, well-cut nose, while a fourth and last showed a sweet, full, sensitive mouth, and a beautifully curved chin. The whole face was one of extraordinary loveliness, save for the one blemish that in the centre of the forehead there was a single irregular, coffee-coloured splotch. It was a triumph of the embalmer's art. Vansittart Smith's eyes grew larger and larger as he gazed upon it, and he chirruped in his throat with satisfaction.

Its effect upon the Egyptologist was as nothing, however, compared with that which it produced upon the strange attendant. He threw his hands up into the air, burst into a harsh clatter of words, and then, hurling himself down upon the ground beside the mummy, he threw his arms round her, and kissed her repeatedly upon the lips and brow. '*Ma petite!*' he groaned in French. '*Ma pauvre petite!*' His voice broke with emotion, and his innumerable wrinkles quivered and writhed, but the student observed in the lamp-light that his shining eyes were still dry and tearless as two beads of steel. For some minutes he lay, with a twitching face, crooning and moaning over the beautiful head. Then he broke into a sudden smile, said some words in an unknown tongue, and sprang to his feet with the vigorous air of one who has braced himself for an effort.

In the centre of the room there was a large, circular case which contained, as the student had frequently remarked, a magnificent collection of early Egyptian rings and precious stones. To this the attendant strode, and, unlocking it, threw it open. On the ledge at the side he placed his lamp, and beside it a small, earthenware jar which he had drawn from his pocket. He then took a handful of rings from the case, and with a most serious and anxious face he proceeded to smear each in turn with some liquid substance from the earthen pot, holding them to the light as he did so. He was clearly disappointed with the first lot, for he threw them petulantly back into the case and drew out some more. One of these, a massive ring with a large crystal set in it, he seized and eagerly tested with the contents of the jar. Instantly he uttered a cry of joy, and threw out his arms in a wild gesture which upset the pot and set the liquid streaming across the floor to the very feet of the Englishman. The attendant drew a red handkerchief from his bosom, and, mopping up the mess, he followed it into the corner, where in a moment he found himself face to face with his observer.

'Excuse me,' said John Vansittart Smith, with all imaginable politeness; 'I have been unfortunate enough to fall asleep behind this door.'

'And you have been watching me?' the other asked in English, with a most venomous look on his corpse-like face.

The student was a man of veracity. 'I confess,' said he, 'that I have noticed your movements, and that they have aroused my curiosity and interest in the highest degree.'

The man drew a long, flamboyant-bladed knife from his bosom. 'You have had a very narrow escape,' he said; 'had I seen you ten minutes ago, I should have driven this through your heart. As it is, if you touch me or interfere with me in any way you are a dead man.'

'I have no wish to interfere with you,' the student answered. 'My presence here is entirely accidental. All I ask is that you will have the extreme kindness to show me out through some side-door.' He spoke with great suavity, for the man was still pressing the tip of his dagger against the palm of his left hand, as though to assure himself of its sharpness, while his face preserved its malignant expression.

'If I thought——' said he. 'But no, perhaps it is as well. What is your name?'

The Englishman gave it.

'Vansittart Smith,' the other repeated. 'Are you the same Vansittart Smith who gave a paper in London upon El Kab? I saw a report of it. Your knowledge of the subject is contemptible.'

'Sir!' cried the Egyptologist.

'Yet it is superior to that of many who make even greater pretensions. The whole keystone of our old life in Egypt was not the inscriptions or monuments of which you make so much, but was our hermetic philosophy and mystic knowledge of which you say little or nothing.'

'Our old life!' repeated the scholar, wide-eyed; and then suddenly, 'Good God, look at the mummy's face!'

The strange man turned and flashed his light upon the dead woman, uttering a long, doleful cry as he did so. The action of the air had already undone all the art of the embalmer. The skin had fallen away, the eyes had sunk inwards, the discoloured lips had writhed away from the yellow teeth, and the brown mark upon the forehead alone showed that it was indeed the same face which had shown such youth and beauty a few short minutes before.

The man flapped his hands together in grief and horror. Then mastering himself by a strong effort he turned his hard eyes once more upon the Englishman.

'It does not matter,' he said, in a shaking voice. 'It does not really matter. I came here tonight with the fixed determination to do something. It is now done. All else is as nothing. I have found my quest. The old curse is broken. I can rejoin her. What matter about her inanimate shell so long as her spirit is awaiting me at the other side of the veil!'

'These are wild words,' said Vansittart Smith. He was becoming more and more convinced that he had to do with a madman.

'Time presses, and I must go,' continued the other. 'The moment is at hand for which I have waited this weary time. But I must show you out first. Come with me.'

Taking up the lamp, he turned from the disordered chamber, and led the student swiftly through the long series of the Egyptian, Assyrian, and Persian apartments. At the end of the latter he pushed open a small door let into the wall and descended a winding, stone stair. The Englishman felt the cold, fresh air of the night upon his brow. There was a door opposite him which appeared to communicate with the street. To the right of this another door stood ajar, throwing a spurt of yellow light across the passage. 'Come in here!' said the attendant shortly.

Vansittart Smith hesitated. He had hoped that he had come to the end of his adventure. Yet his curiosity was strong within him. He could not leave the matter unsolved, so he followed his strange companion into the lighted chamber.

It was a small room, such as is devoted to a *concierge*. A wood fire sparkled in the grate. At one side stood a truckle bed, and at the other a coarse, wooden chair, with a round table in the centre, which bore the remains of a meal. As the visitor's eye glanced round he could not but remark with an ever-recurring thrill that all the small details of the room were of the most quaint design and antique workmanship. The candlesticks, the vases upon the chimney-piece, the fire-irons, the ornaments upon the walls, were all such as he had been wont to associate with the remote past. The gnarled, heavy-eyed man sat himself down upon the edge of the bed, and motioned his guest into the chair.

'There may be design in this,' he said, still speaking excellent English. 'It may be decreed that I should leave some account behind as a warning to all rash mortals who would set their wits up against workings of Nature. I leave it with you. Make such use as you will of it. I speak to you now with my feet upon the threshold of the other world.

'I am, as you surmised, an Egyptian—not one of the down-trodden race of slaves who now inhabit the Delta of the Nile, but a survivor of that fiercer and harder people who tamed the Hebrew, drove the Ethiopian back into the southern deserts, and built those mighty works which have been the envy and the wonder of all after generations. It was in the reign of Tuthmosis, sixteen hundred years before the birth of Christ, that I first saw the light. You shrink away from me. Wait, and you will see that I am more to be pitied than to be feared.

'My name was Sosra. My father had been the chief priest of Osiris in the great temple of Abaris, which stood in those days upon the Bubastic branch of the Nile. I was brought up in the temple and was trained in all those mystic arts which are spoken of in your own Bible. I was an apt pupil. Before I was sixteen I had learned all which the wisest priest could teach me. From that time on I studied Nature's secrets for myself, and shared my knowledge with no man.

'Of all the questions which attracted me there were none over which I laboured so long as over those which concern themselves with the nature of life. I probed deeply into the vital principle. The aim of medicine had been to drive away disease when it appeared. It seemed to me that a method might be devised which should so fortify the body as to prevent weakness or death from ever taking hold of it. It is useless that I should recount my researches. You would scarce comprehend them if I did. They were carried out partly upon animals, partly upon slaves, and partly on myself. Suffice it that their result was to furnish me with a substance which, when injected into the blood, would endow the body with strength to resist the effects of time, of violence, or of disease. It would not indeed confer immortality, but its potency would endure for many thousands of years. I used it upon a cat, and afterwards drugged the creature with the most deadly poisons. That cat is alive in Lower Egypt at the present moment. There was nothing of mystery or magic in the matter. It was simply a chemical discovery, which may well be made again.

'Love of life runs high in the young. It seemed to me that I had broken away from all human care now that I had abolished pain and driven death to such a distance. With a light heart I poured the accursed stuff into my veins. Then I looked round for someone whom I could benefit. There was a young priest of Thoth, Parmes by name, who had won my goodwill by his earnest nature and his devotion to his studies. To him I whispered my secret, and at his request I injected him with my elixir. I should now, I reflected, never be without a companion of the same age as myself.

'After this grand discovery I relaxed my studies to some extent, but Parmes continued his with redoubled energy. Every day I could see him working with his flasks and his distiller in the Temple of Thoth, but he said little to me as to the result of his labours. For my own part, I used to walk through the city and look around me with exultation as I reflected that all this was destined to pass away, and that only I should remain. The people would bow to me as they passed me, for the fame of my knowledge had gone abroad.

'There was war at this time, and the Great King had sent down his soldiers to the eastern boundary to drive away the Hyksos. A Governor, too, was sent to Abaris, that he might hold it for the King. I had heard much of the beauty of the daughter of this Governor, but one day as I walked out with Parmes we met her, borne upon the shoulders of her slaves. I was struck with love as with lightning. My heart went out from me. I could have thrown myself beneath the feet of her bearers. This was my woman. Life without her was impossible. I swore by the head of Horus that she should be mine. I swore it to the Priest of Thoth. He turned away from me with a brow which was as black as midnight.

'There is no need to tell you of our wooing. She came to love me even as I loved her. I learned that Parmes had seen her before I did, and had shown her that he, too, loved her, but I could smile at his passion, for I knew that her heart was mine. The white plague had come upon the city and many were stricken, but I laid my hands upon the sick and nursed them without fear or scathe. She marvelled at my daring. Then I told her my secret, and begged her that she would let me use my art upon her.

'"Your flower shall then be unwithered, Atma," I said. "Other things may pass away, but you and I, and our great love for each other, shall outlive the tomb of King Chefru."

'But she was full of timid, maidenly objections. "Was it right?" she asked, "was it not a thwarting of the will of the gods? If the great Osiris had wished that our years should be so long, would he not himself have brought it about?"

'With fond and loving words I overcame her doubts, and yet she hesitated. It was a great question, she said. She would think it over for this one night. In the morning I should know of her resolution. Surely one night was not too much to ask. She wished to pray to Isis for help in her decision.

'With a sinking heart and a sad foreboding of evil I left her with her tirewomen. In the morning, when the early sacrifice was over, I hurried to her house. A frightened slave met me upon the steps. Her mistress was ill, she said, very ill. In a frenzy I broke my way through the attendants, and rushed through hall and corridor to my Atma's chamber. She lay upon her couch, her head high upon the pillow, with a pallid face and a glazed eye. On her forehead there blazed a single angry, purple patch. I knew that hell-mark of old. It was the scar of the white plague, the sign-manual of death.

'Why should I speak of that terrible time? For months I was mad, fevered, delirious, and yet I could not die. Never did an Arab thirst after the sweet wells as I longed after death. Could poison or steel have shortened the thread of my existence, I should soon have rejoined my love in the land with the narrow portal. I tried, but it was of no avail. The accursed influence was too strong upon me. One night as I lay upon my couch, weak and weary, Parmes, the priest of Thoth, came to my chamber. He stood in the circle of the lamp-light, and he looked down upon me with eyes which were bright with a mad joy.

' "Why did you let the maiden die?" he asked "why did you not strengthen her as you strengthened me?"

' "I was too late," I answered. "But I had forgot. You also loved her. You are my fellow in misfortune. Is it not terrible to think of the centuries which must pass ere we look upon her again? Fools, fools, that we were to take death to be our enemy!"

' "You may say that," he cried with a wild laugh; "the words come well from your lips. For me they have no meaning."

' "What mean you?" I cried, raising myself upon my elbow. "Surely, friend, this grief has turned your brain." His face was aflame with joy, and he writhed and shook like one who hath a devil.

' "Do you know whither I go?" he asked.

' "Nay," I answered, "I cannot tell."

' "I go to her," said he. "She lies embalmed in the farther tomb by the double palm-tree beyond the city wall."

' "Why do you go there?" I asked.

' "To die!" he shrieked, "to die! I am not bound by earthen fetters."

' "But the elixir is in your blood," I cried.

' "I can defy it," said he; "I have found a stronger principle which will destroy it. It is working in my veins at this moment, and in an hour I shall be a dead man. I shall join her, and you shall remain behind."

'As I looked upon him I could see that he spoke words of truth. The light in his eye told me that he was indeed beyond the power of the elixir.

' "You will teach me!" I cried.

' "Never!" he answered.

' "I implore you, by the wisdom of Thoth, by the majesty of Anubis!"

' "It is useless," he said coldly.

' "Then I will find it out," I cried.

' "You cannot," he answered; "it came to me by chance. There is one ingredient which you can never get. Save that which is in the ring of Thoth, none will ever more be made."

' "In the ring of Thoth," I repeated, "where then is the ring of Thoth?"

' "That also you shall never know," he answered. "You won her love. Who has won in the end? I leave you to your sordid earth life. My chains are broken. I must go!" He turned upon his heel and fled from the chamber. In the morning came the news that the Priest of Thoth was dead.

'My days after that were spent in study. I must find this subtle poison which was strong enough to undo the elixir. From early dawn to midnight I bent over the test-tube and the furnace. Above all, I collected the papyri and the chemical flasks of the Priest of Thoth. Alas! they taught me little. Here and there some hint or stray expression would raise hope in my bosom, but no good ever came of it. Still, month after month, I struggled on. When my heart grew faint I would make my way to the tomb by the palm-trees. There, standing by the dead casket from which the jewel had been rifled, I would feel her sweet presence, and would whisper to her that I would rejoin her if mortal wit could solve the riddle.

'Parmes had said that his discovery was connected with the ring of Thoth. I had some remembrance of the trinket. It was a large and weighty circlet, made, not of gold, but of a rarer and heavier metal brought from the mines of Mount Harbal. Platinum, you call it. The ring had, I remembered, a hollow crystal set in it, in which some few drops of liquid might be stored. Now, the secret of Parmes could not have to do with the metal alone, for there were many rings of that metal in the Temple. Was it not more likely that he had stored his precious poison within the cavity of the crystal? I had scarce come to this conclusion before, in hunting through his papers, I came upon one which told me that it was indeed so, and that there was still some of the liquid unused.

'But how to find the ring? It was not upon him when he was stripped for the embalmer. Of that I made sure. Neither was it among his private effects. In vain I searched every room that he had entered, every box and vase and chattel that he had owned. I sifted the very sand of the desert in the places where he had been wont to walk; but, do what I would, I could come upon no traces of the ring of Thoth. Yet it may be that my labours would have overcome all obstacles had it not been for a new and unlooked-for misfortune.

'A great war had been waged against the Hyksos, and the Captains of the Great King had been cut off in the desert with all their bowmen and horsemen. The shepherd tribes were upon us like the locusts in a dry year. From the wilderness of Shur to the great, bitter lake there was blood by day and fire by night. Abaris was the bulwark of Egypt, but we could not keep the savages back. The city fell. The Governor and the soldiers were put to the sword, and I, with many more, was led away into captivity.

'For years and years I tended cattle in the great plains by the Euphrates. My master died, and his son grew old, but I was still as far from death as ever. At last I escaped upon a swift camel, and made my way back to Egypt. The Hyksos had settled in the land which they had conquered, and their own King ruled over the country. Abaris had been torn down, the city had been burned, and of the great Temple there was nothing left save an unsightly mound. Everywhere the tombs had been rifled and the monuments destroyed. Of my Atma's grave no sign was left. It was buried in the sands of the desert, and the palm-trees which marked the spot had long disappeared. The papers of Parmes and the remains of the Temple of Thoth were either destroyed or scattered far and wide over the deserts of Syria. All search after them was vain.

'From that time I gave up all hope of ever finding the ring or discovering the subtle drug. I set myself to live as patiently as might be until the effect of the elixir should wear away. How can you understand how terrible a thing time is, you who have experience only of the narrow course which lies between the cradle and the grave! I know it to my cost, I who have floated down the whole stream of history. I was old when Ilium fell. I was very old when Herodotus came to Memphis. I was bowed down with years when the new gospel came upon earth. Yet you see me much as other men are, with the cursed elixir still sweetening my blood, and guarding me against that which I would court. Now, at last, at last I have come to the end of it!

'I have travelled in all lands and I have dwelt with all nations. Every tongue is the same to me. I learned them all to help pass the weary time. I need not tell you how slowly they drifted by, the long dawn of modern civilization, the dreary middle years, the dark times of barbarism. They are all behind me now. I have never looked with the eyes of love upon another woman. Atma knows that I have been constant to her.

'It was my custom to read all that the scholars had to say upon Ancient Egypt. I have been in many positions, sometimes affluent, sometimes poor, but I have always found enough to enable me to buy the journals which deal with such matters. Some nine months ago I was in San Francisco, when I read an account of some discoveries made in the neighbourhood of Abaris. My heart leapt into my mouth as I read it. It said that the excavator had busied himself in exploring some tombs recently unearthed. In one there had been found an unopened mummy with an inscription upon the outer case setting forth that it contained the body of the daughter of the Governor of the city in the days of Tuthmosis. It added that on removing the outer case there had been exposed a large platinum ring set with a crystal, which had been laid upon the breast of the embalmed woman. This, then, was where Parmes had hid the ring of Thoth. He might well say that it was safe, for no Egyptian would ever stain his soul by moving even the outer case of a buried friend.

'That very night I set off from San Francisco, and in a few weeks I found myself once more at Abaris, if a few sand-heaps and crumbling walls may retain the name of the great city. I hurried to the Frenchmen who were digging there and asked them for the ring. They replied that both the ring and the mummy had been sent to the Boulak Museum at Cairo. To Boulak I went, but only to be told that Mariette Bey had claimed them and had shipped them to the Louvre. I followed them, and there, at last, in the Egyptian chamber, I came, after close upon four thousand years, upon the remains of my Atma, and upon the ring for which I had sought so long.

'But how was I to lay hands upon them? How was I to have them for my very own? It chanced that the office of attendant was vacant. I went to the Director. I convinced him that I knew much about Egypt. In my eagerness I said too much. He remarked that a Professor's chair would suit me better than a seat in the *conciergerie*. I knew more, he said, than he did. It was only by blundering, and letting him think that he had over-estimated my knowledge, that I prevailed upon him to let me move the few effects which I have retained into this chamber. It is my first and my last night here.

'Such is my story, Mr Vansittart Smith. I need not say more to a man of your perception. By a strange chance you have this night looked upon the face of the woman whom I loved in those far-off days. There were many rings with crystals in the case, and I had to test for the platinum to be sure of the one which I wanted. A glance at the crystal has shown me that the liquid is indeed within it, and that I shall at last be able to shake off that accursed health which has been worse to me than the foulest disease. I have nothing more to say to you. I have unburdened myself. You may tell my story or you may withhold it at your pleasure. The choice rests with you. I owe you some amends, for you have had a narrow escape of your life this night. I was a desperate man, and not to be baulked in my purpose. Had I seen you before the thing was done, I might have put it beyond your power to oppose me or to raise an alarm. This is the door. It leads into the Rue de Rivoli. Good night.'

The Englishman glanced back. For a moment the lean figure of Sosra the Egyptian stood framed in the narrow doorway. The next the door had slammed, and the heavy rasping of a bolt broke on the silent night.

It was on the second day after his return to London that Mr John Vansittart Smith saw the following concise narrative in the Paris correspondence of *The Times*.

> *Curious Occurrence in the Louvre.*—Yesterday morning a strange discovery was made in the principal Eastern chamber. The *ouvriers* who are employed to clean out the rooms in the morning found one of the attendants lying dead upon the floor with his arms round one of the mummies. So close was his embrace that it was only with the utmost difficulty that they were separated. One of the cases containing valuable rings had been opened and rifled. The authorities are of opinion that the man was bearing away the mummy with some idea of selling it to a private collector, but that he was struck down in the very act by long-standing disease of the heart. It is said that he was a man of uncertain age and eccentric habits, without any living relations to mourn over his dramatic and untimely end.

A Pastoral Horror

FAR ABOVE THE LEVEL OF THE LAKE OF CONSTANCE, nestling in a little corner of the Tyrolese Alps, lies the quiet town of Feldkirch. It is remarkable for nothing save for the presence of a large and well-conducted Jesuit school and for the extreme beauty of its situation. There is no more lovely spot in the whole of the Vorarlberg. From the hills which rise behind the town, the great lake glimmers some fifteen miles off, like a broad sea of quicksilver. Down below in the plains the Rhine and the Danube prattle along, flowing swiftly and merrily, with none of the dignity which they assume as they grow from brooks into rivers. Five great countries or principalities—Switzerland, Austria, Baden, Wurtemburg, and Bavaria—are visible from the plateau of Feldkirch.

Feldkirch is the centre of a large tract of hilly and pastoral country. The main road runs through the centre of the town, and then on as far as Anspach, where it divides into two branches, one of which is larger than the other. This more important one runs through the valleys across Austrian Tyrol into Tyrol proper, going as far, I believe, as the capital of Innsbruck. The lesser road runs for eight or ten miles amid wild and rugged glens to the village of Laden, where it breaks up into a network of sheeptracks. In this quiet spot, I, John Hudson, spent nearly two years of my life, from the June of '65 to the March of '67, and it was during that time that those events occurred which for some weeks brought the retired hamlet into an unholy prominence, and caused its name for the first, and probably for the last time, to be a familiar word to the European press. The short account of these incidents which appeared in the English papers was, however, inaccurate and misleading, besides which, the rapid advance of the Prussians, culminating in the battle of Sadowa, attracted public attention away from what might have moved it deeply in less troublous times. It seems to me that the facts may be detailed now, and be new to the great majority of readers, especially as I was myself intimately connected with the drama, and am in a position to give many particulars which have never before been made public.

And first a few words as to my own presence in this out of the way spot. When the great city firm of Sprynge, Wilkinson, and Spragge failed, and paid their creditors rather less than eighteen-pence in the pound, a number of humble individuals were ruined, including myself. There was, however, some legal objection which held out a chance of my being made an exception to the other creditors, and being paid in full. While the case was being brought out I was left with a very small sum for my subsistence.

I determined, therefore, to take up my residence abroad in the interim, since I could live more economically there, and be spared the mortification of meeting those who had known me in my more prosperous days. A friend of mine had described Laden to me some years before as being the most isolated place which he had ever come across in all his experience, and as isolation and cheap living are usually synonymous, I bethought use of his words. Besides, I was in a cynical humour with my fellow-man, and desired to see as little of him as possible for some time to come. Obeying, then, the guidances of poverty and of misanthropy, I made my way to Laden, where my arrival created the utmost excitement among the simple inhabitants. The manners and customs of the red-bearded Englander, his long walks, his check suit, and the reasons which had led him to abandon his fatherland, were all fruitful sources of gossip to the topers who frequented the Grüner Mann and the Schwartzer Bar—the two alehouses of the village.

I found myself very happy at Laden. The surroundings were magnificent, and twenty years of Brixton had sharpened my admiration for nature as an olive improves the flavour of wine. In my youth I had been a fair German scholar, and I found myself able, before I had been many months abroad, to converse even on scientific and abstruse subjects with the new curé of the parish.

This priest was a great godsend to me, for he was a most learned man and a brilliant conversationalist. Father Verhagen—for that was his name—though little more than forty years of age, had made his reputation as an author by a brilliant monograph upon the early Popes—a work which eminent critics have compared favourably with Von Ranke's. I shrewdly suspect that it was owing to some rather unorthodox views advanced in this book that Verhagen was relegated to the obscurity of Laden. His opinions upon every subject were ultra-Liberal, and in his fiery youth he had been ready to vindicate them, as was proved by a deep scar across his chin, received from a dragoon's sabre in the abortive insurrection at Berlin. Altogether the man was an interesting one, and though he was by nature somewhat cold and reserved, we soon established an acquaintanceship.

The atmosphere of morality in Laden was a very rarefied one. The position of Intendant Wurms and his satellites had for many years been a sinecure. Non-attendance at church upon a Sunday or feast-day was about the deepest and darkest crime which the most advanced of the villagers had attained to. Occasionally some hulking Fritz or Andreas would come lurching home at ten o'clock at night, slightly under the influence of Bavarian beer, and might even abuse the wife of his bosom if she ventured to remonstrate, but such cases were rare, and when they occurred the Ladeners looked at the culprit for some time in a half admiring, half horrified manner, as one who had committed a gaudy sin and so asserted his individuality.

It was in this peaceful village that a series of crimes suddenly broke out which astonished all Europe, and for atrocity and for the mystery which surrounded them surpassed anything of which I have ever heard or read. I shall endeavour to give a succinct account of these events in the order of their sequence, in which I am much helped by the fact that it has been my custom all my life to keep a journal—to the pages of which I now refer.

It was, then, I find upon the 19th of May in the spring of 1866, that my old landlady, Frau Zimmer, rushed wildly into the room as I was sipping my morning cup of chocolate and informed me that a murder had been committed in the village. At first I could hardly believe the news, but as she persisted in her statement, and was evidently terribly frightened, I put on my hat and went out to find the truth. When I came into the main street of the village I saw several men hurrying along in front of me, and following them I came upon an excited group in front of the little *stadthaus* or town hall—a barn-like edifice which was used for all manner of public gatherings. They were collected round the body of one Maul, who had formerly been a steward upon one of the steamers running between Lindau and Fredericshaven, on the Lake of Constance. He was a harmless, inoffensive little man, generally popular in the village, and, as far as was known, without an enemy in the world. Maul lay upon his face, with his fingers dug into the earth, no doubt in his last convulsive struggles, and his hair all matted together with blood, which had streamed down over the collar of his coat. The body had been discovered nearly two hours, but no one appeared to know what to do or whither to convey it. My arrival, however, together with that of the curé, who came almost simultaneously, infused some vigour into the crowd. Under our direction the corpse was carried up the steps, and laid on the floor of the town hall, where, having made sure that life was extinct, we proceeded to examine the injuries, in conjunction with Lieutenant Wurms, of the police. Maul's face was perfectly placid, showing that he had had no thought of danger until the fatal blow was struck. His watch and purse had not been taken. Upon washing the clotted blood from the back of his head a singular triangular wound was found, which had smashed the bone and penetrated deeply into the brain. It had evidently been inflicted by a heavy blow from a sharp-pointed pyramidal instrument. I believe that it was Father Verhagen, the curé, who suggested the probability of the weapon in question having been a short mattock or small pickaxe, such as are to be found in every Alpine cottage. The Intendant, with praiseworthy promptness, at once obtained one and striking a turnip, produced just such a curious gap as was to be seen in poor Maul's head. We felt that we had come upon the first link of a chain which might guide us to the assassin. It was not long before we seemed to grasp the whole clue.

A sort of inquest was held upon the body that same afternoon, at which Pfiffor, the maire, presided, the curé, the Intendant, Freckler, of the post office, and myself forming ourselves into a sort of committee of investigation. Any villager who could throw a light upon the case or give an account of the movements of the murdered man upon the previous evening was invited to attend. There was a fair muster of witnesses, and we soon gathered a connected series of facts. At half-past eight o'clock Maul had entered the Grüner Mann public-house, and had called for a flagon of beer. At that time there were sitting in the tap-room Waghorn, the butcher of the village, and an Italian pedlar named Cellini, who used to come three times a year to Laden with cheap jewellery and other wares. Immediately after his entrance the landlord had seated himself with his customers, and the four had spent the evening together, the common villagers not being admitted beyond the bar. It seemed from the evidence of the landlord and of Waghorn, both of whom were most respectable and trustworthy men, that shortly after nine o'clock a dispute arose between the deceased and the pedlar. Hot words had been exchanged, and the Italian had eventually left the room, saying that he would not stay any longer to hear his country decried. Maul remained for nearly an hour, and being somewhat elated at having caused his adversary's retreat, he drank rather more than was usual with him. One witness had met him walking towards his home, about ten o'clock, and deposed to his having been slightly the worse for drink. Another had met him just a minute or so before he reached the spot in front of the *stadthaus* where the deed was done. This man's evidence was most important. He swore confidently that while passing the town hall, and before meeting Maul, he had seen a figure standing in the shadow of the building, adding that the person appeared to him, as far as he could make him out, to be not unlike the Italian.

Up to this point we had then established two facts—that the Italian had left the Grüner Mann before Maul, with words of anger on his lips; the second, that some unknown individual had been seen lying in wait on the road which the ex-steward would have to traverse. A third, and most important, was reached when the woman with whom the Italian lodged deposed that he had not returned the night before until half-past ten, an unusually late hour for Laden. How had he employed the time, then, from shortly after nine, when he left the public-house, until half-past ten, when he returned to his rooms? Things were beginning to look very black, indeed, against the pedlar.

It could not be denied, however, that there were points in the man's favour, and that the case against him consisted entirely of circumstantial evidence. In the first place, there was no sign of a mattock or any other instrument which could have been used for such a purpose among the Italian's goods; nor was it easy to understand how he could come by any such a weapon, since he did not go home between the time of the quarrel and his final return. Again, as the curé pointed out, since Cellini was a comparative stranger in the village, it was very unlikely that he would know which road Maul would take in order to reach his home. This objection was weakened, however, by the evidence of the dead man's servant, who deposed that the pedlar had been hawking his wares in front of their house the day before, and might very possibly have seen the owner at one of the windows. As to the prisoner himself, his attitude at first had been one of defiance, and even of amusement; but when he began to realise the weight of evidence against him, his manner became cringing, and he wrung his hands hideously, loudly proclaiming his innocence. His defence was that after leaving the inn, he had taken a long walk down the Anspach-road in order to cool down his excitement, and that this was the cause of his late return. As to the murder of Maul, he knew no more about it than the babe unborn.

I have dwelt at some length upon the circumstances of this case, because there are events in connection with it which makes it peculiarly interesting. I intend now to fall back upon my diary, which was very fully kept during this period, and indeed during my whole residence abroad. It will save me trouble to quote from it, and it will be a teacher for the accuracy of facts.

May 20th—Nothing thought of and nothing talked of but the recent tragedy. A hunt has been made among the woods and along the brook in the hope of finding the weapon of the assassin. The more I think of it, the more convinced I am that Cellini is the man. The fact of the money being untouched proves that the crime was committed from motives of revenge, and who would bear more spite towards poor innocent Maul except the vindictive hot-blooded Italian whom he had just offended. I dined with Pfiffor in the evening, and he entirely agreed with me in my view of the case.

May 21st—Still no word as far as I can hear which throws any light upon the murder. Poor Maul was buried at twelve o'clock in the neat little village churchyard. The curé led the service with great feeling, and his audience, consisting of the whole population of the village, were much moved, interrupting him frequently by sobs and ejaculations of grief. After the painful ceremony was over I had a short walk with our good priest. His naturally excitable nature has been considerably stirred by recent events. His hand trembles and his face is pale.

'My friend,' said he, taking me by the hand as we walked together, 'you know something of medicine.' (I had been two years at Guy's). 'I have been far from well of late.'

'It is this sad affair which has upset you,' I said.

'No,' he answered, 'I have felt it coming on for some time, but it has been worse of late. I have a pain which shoots from here to there,' he put his hand to his temples. 'If I were struck by lightning, the sudden shock it causes me could not be more great. At times when I close my eyes flashes of light dart before them, and my ears are for ever ringing. Often I know not what I do. My fear is lest I faint some time when performing the holy offices.'

'You are overworking yourself,' I said, 'you must have rest and strengthening tonics. Are you writing just now? And how much do you do each day?'

'Eight hours,' he answered. 'Sometimes ten, sometimes even twelve, when the pains in my head do not interrupt me.'

'You must reduce it to four,' I said authoritatively. 'You must also take regular exercise. I shall send you some quinine which I have in my trunk, and you can take as much as would cover a gulden in a glass of milk every morning and night.'

He departed, vowing that he would follow my directions.

I hear from the maire that four policemen are to be sent from Anspach to remove Cellini to a safer gaol.

May 22nd—To say that I was startled would give but a faint idea of my mental state. I am confounded, amazed, horrified beyond all expression. Another and a more dreadful crime has been committed during the night. Freckler has been found dead in his house—the very Freckler who had sat with me on the committee of investigation the day before. I write these notes after a long and anxious day's work, during which I have been endeavouring to assist the officers of the law. The villagers are so paralysed with fear at this fresh evidence of an assassin in their midst that there would be a general panic but for our exertions. It appears that Freckler, who was a man of peculiar habits, lived alone in an isolated dwelling. Some curiosity was aroused this morning by the fact that he had not gone to his work, and that there was no sign of movement about the house. A crowd assembled, and the doors were eventually forced open. The unfortunate Freckler was found in the bedroom upstairs, lying with his head in the fireplace. He had met his death by an exactly similar wound to that which had proved fatal to Maul, save that in this instance the injury was in front. His hands were clenched, and there was an indescribable look of horror, and, as it seemed to me, of surprise upon his features. There were marks of muddy footsteps upon the stairs, which must have been caused by the murderer in his ascent, as his victim had put on his slippers before retiring to his bed-room. These prints, however, were too much blurred to enable us to get a trustworthy outline of the foot. They were only to be found upon every third step, showing with what fiendish swiftness this human tiger had rushed upstairs in search of his victim. There was a considerable sum of money in the house, but not one farthing had been touched, nor had any of the drawers in the bed-room been opened.

As the dismal news became known the whole population of the village assembled in a great crowd in front of the house—rather, I think, from the gregariousness of terror than from mere curiosity. Every man looked with suspicion upon his neighbour. Most were silent, and when they spoke it was in whispers, as if they feared to raise their voices. None of these people were allowed to enter the house, and we, the more enlightened members of the community, made a strict examination of the premises. There was absolutely nothing, however, to give the slightest clue as to the assassin. Beyond the fact that he must be an active man, judging from the manner in which he ascended the stairs, we have gained nothing from this second tragedy. Intendant Wurms pointed out, indeed, that the dead man's rigid right arm was stretched out as if in greeting, and that, therefore, it was probable that this late visitor was someone with whom Freckler was well acquainted. This, however, was, to a large extent, conjecture. If anything could have added to the horror created by the dreadful occurrence, it was the fact that the crime must have been committed at the early hour of half-past eight in the evening—that being the time registered by a small cuckoo clock, which had been carried away by Freckler in his fall.

No one, apparently, heard any suspicious sounds or saw any one enter or leave the house. It was done rapidly, quietly, and completely, though many people must have been about at the time. Poor Pfiffor and our good curé are terribly cut up by the awful occurrence, and, indeed, I feel very much depressed myself now that all the excitement is over and the reaction set in. There are very few of the villagers about this evening, but from every side is heard the sound of hammering—the peasants fitting bolts and bars upon the doors and windows of their houses. Very many of them have been entirely unprovided with anything of the sort, nor were they ever required until now. Frau Zimmer has manufactured a huge fastening which would be ludicrous if we were in a humour for laughter.

I hear tonight that Cellini has been released, as, of course, there is no possible pretext for detaining him now; also that word has been sent to all the villages near for any police that can be spared.

My nerves have been so shaken that I remained awake the greater part of the night, reading Gordon's translation of Tacitus by candlelight. I have got out my navy revolver and cleaned it, so as to be ready for all eventualities.

May 23rd—The police force has been recruited by three more men from Anspach and two from Thalstadt at the other side of the hills. Intendant Wurms has established an efficient system of patrols, so that we may consider ourselves reasonably safe. Today has cast no light upon the murders. The general opinion in the village seems to be that they have been done by some stranger who lies concealed among the woods. They argue that they have all known each other since childhood, and that there is no one of their number who would be capable of such actions. Some of the more daring of them have made a hunt among the pine forests today, but without success.

May 24th—Events crowd on apace. We seem hardly to have recovered from one horror when something else occurs to excite the popular imagination. Fortunately, this time it is not a fresh tragedy, although the news is serious enough.

The murderer has been seen, and that upon the public road, which proves that his thirst for blood has not been quenched yet, and also that our reinforcements of police are not enough to guarantee security. I have just come back from hearing Andreas Murch narrate his experience, though he is still in such a state of trepidation that his story is somewhat incoherent. He was belated among the hills, it seems, owing to mist. It was nearly eleven o'clock before he struck the main road about a couple of miles from the village. He confesses that he felt by no means comfortable at finding himself out so late after the recent occurrences. However, as the fog had cleared away and the moon was shining brightly, he trudged sturdily along. Just about a quarter of a mile from the village the road takes a very sharp bend. Andreas had got as far as this when he suddenly heard in the still night the sound of footsteps approaching rapidly round this curve. Overcome with fear, he threw himself into the ditch which skirts the road, and lay there motionless in the shadow, peering over the side. The steps came nearer and nearer, and then a tall dark figure came round the corner at a swinging pace, and passing the spot where the moon glimmered upon the white face of the frightened peasant, halted in the road about twenty yards further on, and began probing about among the reeds on the roadside with an instrument which Andreas Murch recognised with horror as being a long mattock. After searching about in this way for a minute or so, as if he suspected that someone was concealed there, for he must have heard the sound of the footsteps, he stood still leaning upon his weapon. Murch describes him as a tall, thin man, dressed in clothes of a darkish colour. The lower part of his face was swathed in a wrapper of some sort, and the little which was visible appeared to be of a ghastly pallor. Murch could not see enough of his features to identify him, but thinks that it was no one whom he had ever seen in his life before. After standing for some little time, the man with the mattock had walked swiftly away into the darkness, in the direction in which he imagined the fugitive had gone. Andreas, as may be supposed, lost little time in getting safely into the village, where he alarmed the police. Three of them, armed with carbines, started down the road, but saw no signs of the miscreant. There is, of course, a possibility that Murch's story is exaggerated and that his imagination has been sharpened by fear. Still, the whole incident cannot be trumped up, and this awful demon who haunts us is evidently still active.

There is an ill-conditioned fellow named Hiedler, who lives in a hut on the side of the Spiegelberg, and supports himself by chamois hunting and by acting as guide to the few tourists who find their way here. Popular suspicion has fastened on this man, for no better reason than that he is tall, thin, and known to be rough and brutal. His chalet has been searched today, but nothing of importance found. He has, however, been arrested and confined in the same room which Cellini used to occupy.

At this point there is a gap of a week in my diary, during which time there was an entire cessation of the constant alarms which have harassed us lately. Some explained it by supposing that the terrible unknown had moved on to some fresh and less guarded scene of operations. Others imagine that we have secured the right man in the shape of the vagabond Hiedler. Be the cause what it may, peace and contentment reign once more in the village, and a short seven days have sufficed to clear away the cloud of care from men's brows, though the police are still on the alert. The season for rifle shooting is beginning, and as

Laden has, like every other Tyrolese village, butts of its own, there is a continual pop, pop, all day. These peasants are dead shots up to about four hundred yards. No troops in the world could subdue them among their native mountains.

My friend Verhagen, the curé, and Pfiffor, the maire, used to go down in the afternoon to see the shooting with me. The former says that the quinine has done him much good and that his appetite is improved. We all agree that it is good policy to encourage the amusements of the people so that they may forget all about this wretched business. Vaghorn, the butcher, won the prize offered by the maire. He made five bulls, and what we should call a magpie out of six shots at 100 yards. This is English prize-medal form.

June 2nd—Who could have imagined that a day which opened so fairly could have so dark an ending? The early carrier brought me a letter by which I learned that Spragge and Co. have agreed to pay my claim in full, although it may be some months before the money is forthcoming. This will make a difference of nearly £400 a year to me—a matter of moment when a man is in his seven-and-fortieth year.

And now for the grand events of the hour. My interview with the vampire who haunts us, and his attempt upon Frau Bischoff, the landlady of the Grüner Mann—to say nothing of the narrow escape of our good curé. There seems to be something almost supernatural in the malignity of this unknown fiend, and the impunity with which he continues his murderous course. The real reason of it lies in the badly lit state of the place—or rather the entire absence of light—and also in the fact that thick woods stretch right down to the houses on every side, so that escape is made easy. In spite of this, however, he had two very narrow escapes tonight—one from my pistol, and one from the officers of the law. I shall not sleep much, so I may spend half an hour in jotting down these strange doings in my dairy. I am no coward, but life in Laden is becoming too much for my nerves. I believe the matter will end in the emigration of the whole population.

To come to my story, then. I felt lonely and depressed this evening, in spite of the good news of the morning. About nine o'clock, just as night began to fall, I determined to stroll over and call upon the curé, thinking that a little intellectual chat might cheer me up. I slipped my revolver into my pocket, therefore—a precaution which I never neglected—and went out, very much against the advice of good Frau Zimmer. I think I mentioned some months ago in my diary that the curé's house is some little way out of the village upon the brow of a small hill. When I arrived there I found that he had gone out— which, indeed, I might have anticipated, for he had complained lately of restlessness at night, and I had recommended him to take a little exercise in the evening. His housekeeper made me very welcome, however, and having lit the lamp, left me in the study with some books to amuse me until her master's return.

I suppose I must have sat for nearly half an hour glancing over an odd volume of Klopstock's poems, when some sudden instinct caused me to raise my head and look up. I have been in some strange situations in my life, but never have I felt anything to be compared to the thrill which shot through me at that moment. The recollection of it now, hours after the event, makes me shudder. There, framed in one of the panes of the window, was a human face glaring in, from the darkness, into the lighted room—the face of a man so concealed by a cravat and slouch hat that the only impression I retain of it was a pair of wild-beast eyes and a nose which was whitened by being pressed against the glass. It did not need Andreas Murch's description to tell me that at last I was face to face with the man with the mattock. There was murder in those wild eyes. For a second I was so unstrung as to be powerless; the next I cocked my revolver and fired straight at the sinister face. I was a moment too late. As I pressed the trigger I saw it vanish, but the pane through which it had looked was shattered to pieces. I rushed to the window, and then out through the front door, but everything was silent. There was no trace of my visitor. His intention, no doubt, was to attack the curé, for there was nothing to prevent his coming through the folding window had he not found an armed man inside.

As I stood in the cool night air with the curé's frightened housekeeper beside me, I suddenly heard a great hubbub down in the village. By this time, alas! such sounds were so common in Laden that there was no doubting what it foreboded. Some fresh misfortune had occurred there. Tonight seemed destined to be a night of horror. My presence might be of use in the village, so I set off there, taking with me the trembling woman, who positively refused to remain behind. There was a crowd round the Grüner Mann public-house, and a dozen excited voices were explaining the circumstances to the curé, who had arrived just before us. It was as I had thought, though happily without the result which I had feared. Frau Bischoff, the wife of the proprietor of the inn, had, it seems, gone some twenty minutes before a few yards from her door to draw some water, and had been at once attacked by a tall disguised man, who had cut at her with some weapon. Fortunately he had slipped, so that she was able to seize him by the wrist and prevent his repeating his attempt, while she screamed for help. There were several people about at the time, who came running towards them, on which the stranger wrested himself free, and dashed off into the woods, with two of our police after him. There is little hope of their overtaking or tracing him, however, in such a dark labyrinth. Frau Bischoff had made a bold attempt to hold the assassin, and declares that her nails made deep furrows in his right wrist. This, however, must be mere conjecture, as there was very little light at the time. She knows no more of the man's features than I do. Fortunately she is entirely unhurt. The curé was horrified when I informed him of the incident at his own house. He was returning from his walk, it appears, when hearing cries in the village, he had hurried down to it. I have not told anyone else of my own adventure, for the people are quite excited enough already.

As I said before, unless this mysterious and bloodthirsty villain is captured, the place will become deserted. Flesh and blood cannot stand such a strain. He is either some murderous misanthrope who has declared a vendetta against the whole human race, or else he is an escaped maniac. Clearly after the unsuccessful attempt upon Frau Bischoff he had made at once for the curé's house, bent upon slaking his thirst for blood, and thinking that its lonely situation gave hope of success. I wish I had fired at him through the pocket of my coat. The moment he saw the glitter of the weapon he was off.

June 3rd—Everybody in the village this morning has learned about the attempt upon the curé last night. There was quite a crowd at his house to congratulate him on his escape, and when I appeared they raised a cheer and hailed me as the '*tapferer Englander*'. It seems that his narrow shave must have given the ruffian a great start, for a thick woollen muffler was found lying on the pathway leading down to the village, and later in the day the fatal mattock was discovered close to the same place. The scoundrel evidently threw those things down and then took to his heels. It is possible that he may prove to have been frightened away from the neighbourhood altogether. Let us trust so!

June 4th—A quiet day, which is as remarkable a thing in our annals as an exciting one elsewhere. Wurms has made strict inquiry, but cannot trace the muffler and mattock to any inhabitant. A description of them has been printed, and copies sent to Anspach and neighbouring villages for circulation among the peasants, who may be able to throw some light upon the matter. A thanksgiving service is to be held in the church on Sunday for the double escape of the pastor and of Martha Bischoff. Pfiffer tells me that Herr von Weissendorff, one of the most energetic detectives in Vienna, is on his way to Laden. I see, too, by the English papers sent me, that people at home are interested in the tragedies here, although the accounts which have reached them are garbled and untrustworthy.

How well I can recall the Sunday morning following upon the events which I have described, such a morning as it is hard to find outside the Tyrol! The sky was blue and cloudless, the gentle breeze wafted the balsamic odour of the pine woods through the open windows, and away up on the hills the distant tinkling of the cow bells fell pleasantly upon the ear, until the musical rise and fall which summoned the villagers to prayer drowned their feebler melody. It was hard to believe, looking down that peaceful little street with its quaint top-heavy wooden houses and old-fashioned church, that a cloud of crime hung over it which had horrified Europe. I sat at my window watching the peasants passing with their picturesquely dressed wives and daughters on their way to church. With the kindly reverence of Catholic countries, I saw them cross themselves as they went by the house of Freckler and the spot where Maul had met his fate. When the bell had ceased to toll and the whole population had assembled in the church, I walked up there also, for it has always been my custom to join in the religious exercises of any people among whom I may find myself.

When I arrived at the church I found that the service had already begun. I took my place in the gallery which contained the village organ, from which I had a good view of the congregation. In the front seat of all was stationed Frau Bischoff, whose miraculous escape the service was intended to celebrate, and beside her on one side was her worthy spouse, while the maire occupied the other. There was a hush through the church as the curé turned from the altar and ascended the pulpit. I have seldom heard a more magnificent sermon. Father Verhagen was always an eloquent preacher, but on that occasion he surpassed himself. He chose for his text: 'In the midst of life we are in death', and impressed so vividly upon our minds the thin veil which divides us from eternity, and how unexpectedly it may be rent, that he held his audience spell-bound and horrified. He spoke next with tender pathos of the friends who had been snatched so suddenly and so dreadfully from among us, until his words were almost drowned by the sobs of the women, and, suddenly turning, he compared their peaceful existence in a happier land to the dark fate of the gloomy-minded criminal, steeped in blood and with nothing to hope for either in this world or the next—a man solitary among his fellows, with no woman to love him, no child to prattle at his knee, and an endless torture in his own thoughts. So skilfully and so powerfully did he speak that as he finished I am sure that pity for this merciless demon was the prevailing emotion in every heart.

The service was over, and the priest, with his two acolytes before him, was leaving the altar, when he turned, as was his custom, to give his blessing to the congregation. I shall never forget his appearance. The summer sunshine shining slantwise through the single small stained glass window which adorned the little church threw a yellow lustre upon his sharp intellectual features with their dark haggard lines, while a vivid crimson spot reflected from a ruby-coloured mantle in the window quivered over his uplifted right hand. There was a hush as the villagers bent their heads to receive their pastor's blessing—a hush broken by a wild exclamation of surprise from a woman who staggered to her feet in the front pew and gesticulated frantically as she pointed at Father Verhagen's uplifted arm. No need for Frau Bischoff to explain the cause of that sudden cry, for there—there in full sight of his parishioners, were lines of livid scars upon the cure's white wrist—scars which could be left by nothing on earth but a desperate woman's nails. And what woman save her who had clung so fiercely to the murderer two days before!

That in all this terrible business poor Verhagen was the man most to be pitied I have no manner of doubt. In a town in which there was good medical advice to be had, the approach of the homicidal mania, which had undoubtedly proceeded from overwork and brain worry, and which assumed such a terrible form, would have been detected in time and he would have been spared the awful compunction with which he must have been seized in the lucid intervals between his fits—if, indeed, he had any lucid intervals. How could I diagnose with my smattering of science the existence of such a terrible and insidious form of insanity, especially from the vague symptoms of which he informed me. It is easy now, looking back, to think of many little circumstances which might have put us on the right scent; but what a simple thing is retrospective wisdom! I should be sad indeed if I thought that I had anything with which to reproach myself.

We were never able to discover where he had obtained the weapon with which he had committed his crimes, nor how he managed to secrete it in the interval. My experience proved that it had been his custom to go and come through his study window without disturbing his housekeeper. On the occasion of the attempt on Frau Bischoff he had made a dash for home, and then, finding to his astonishment that his room was occupied, his only resource was to fling away his weapon and muffler, and to mix with the crowd in the village. Being both a strong and an active man, with a good knowledge of the footpaths through the woods, he had never found any difficulty in escaping all observation.

Immediately after his apprehension, Verhagen's disease took an acute form, and he was carried off to the lunatic asylum at Feldkirch. I have heard that some months afterwards he made a determined attempt upon the life of one of his keepers, and afterwards committed suicide. I cannot be positive of this, however, for I heard it quite accidentally during a conversation in a railway carriage.

As for myself, I left Laden within a few months, having received a pleasing intimation from my solicitors that my claim had been paid in full. In spite of my tragic experience there, I had many a pleasing recollection of the little Tyrolese village, and in two subsequent visits I renewed my acquaintance with the maire, the Intendant, and all my old friends, on which occasion, over long pipes and flagons of beer, we have taken a grim pleasure in talking with bated breath of that terrible month in the quiet Vorarlberg hamlet.

The Speckled Band

I N GLANCING OVER MY NOTES of the seventy odd cases in which I have during the last eight years studied the methods of my friend Sherlock Holmes, I find many tragic, some comic, a large number merely strange, but none commonplace; for, working as he did rather for the love of his art than for the acquirement of wealth, he refused to associate himself with any investigation which did not tend towards the unusual, and even the fantastic. Of all these varied cases, however, I cannot recall any which presented more singular features than that which was associated with the well-known Surrey family of the Roylotts of Stoke Moran. The events in question occurred in the early days of my association with Holmes, when we were sharing rooms as bachelors in Baker Street. It is possible that I might have placed them upon record before, but a promise of secrecy was made at the time, from which I have only been freed during the last month by the untimely death of the lady to whom the pledge was given. It is perhaps as well that the facts should now come to light, for I have reasons to know that there are widespread rumours as to the death of Dr Grimesby Roylott which tend to make the matter even more terrible than the truth.

It was early in April in the year '83 that I woke one morning to find Sherlock Holmes standing, fully dressed, by the side of my bed. He was a late riser, as a rule, and, as the clock on the mantelpiece showed me that it was only a quarter-past seven, I blinked up at him in some surprise, and perhaps just a little resentment, for I was myself regular in my habits.

'Very sorry to knock you up, Watson,' said he, 'but it's the common lot this morning. Mrs Hudson has been knocked up, she retorted upon me, and I on you.'

'What is it, then? A fire?'

'No, a client. It seems that a young lady has arrived in a considerable state of excitement, who insists upon seeing me. She is waiting now in the sitting-room. Now, when young ladies wander about the metropolis at this hour of the morning, and knock sleepy people up out of their beds, I presume that it is something very pressing which they have to communicate. Should it prove to be an interesting case, you would, I am sure, wish to follow it from the outset. I thought, at any rate, that I should call you and give you the chance.'

'My dear fellow, I would not miss it for anything.'

I had no keener pleasure than in following Holmes in his professional investigations, and in admiring the rapid deductions, as swift as intuitions, and yet always founded on a logical basis, with which he unravelled the problems which were submitted to him. I rapidly threw on my clothes and was ready in a few minutes to accompany my friend down to the sitting-room. A lady dressed in black and heavily veiled, who had been sitting in the window, rose as we entered.

'Good morning, madam,' said Holmes cheerily. 'My name is Sherlock Holmes. This is my intimate friend and associate, Dr Watson, before whom you can speak as freely as before myself. Ha, I am glad to see that Mrs Hudson has had the good sense to light the fire. Pray draw up to it, and I shall order you a cup of hot coffee, for I observe that you are shivering.'

'It is not cold which makes me shiver,' said the woman in a low voice, changing her seat as requested.

'What, then?'

'It is fear, Mr Holmes. It is terror.' She raised her veil as she spoke, and we could see that she was indeed in a pitiable state of agitation, her face all drawn and grey, with restless, frightened eyes, like those of some hunted animal. Her features and figure were those of a woman of thirty, but her hair was shot with premature grey, and her expression was weary and haggard. Sherlock Holmes ran her over with one of his quick, all-comprehensive glances.

'You must not fear,' said he soothingly, bending forward and patting her forearm. 'We shall soon set matters right, I have no doubt. You have come in by train this morning, I see.'

'You know me, then?'

'No, but I observe the second half of a return ticket in the palm of your left glove. You must have started early, and yet you had a good drive in a dog-cart, along heavy roads, before you reached the station.'

The lady gave a violent start and stared in bewilderment at my companion.

'There is no mystery, my dear madam,' said he, smiling. 'The left arm of your jacket is spattered with mud in no less than seven places. The marks are perfectly fresh. There is no vehicle save a dog-cart which throws up mud in that way, and then only when you sit on the left-hand side of the driver.'

'Whatever your reasons may be, you are perfectly correct,' said she. 'I started from home before six, reached Leatherhead at twenty past, and came in by the first train to Waterloo. Sir, I can stand this strain no longer; I shall go mad if it continues. I have no one to turn to—none, save only one, who cares for me, and he, poor fellow, can be of little aid. I have heard of you, Mr Holmes; I have heard of you from Mrs Farintosh, whom you helped in the hour of her sore need. It was from her that I had your address. Oh, sir, do you not think that you could help me, too, and at least throw a little light through the dense darkness which surrounds me? At present it is out of my power to reward you for your services, but in a month or two I shall be married, with the control of my own income, and then at least you shall not find me ungrateful.'

Holmes turned to his desk and, unlocking it, drew out a small case-book, which he consulted.

'Farintosh,' said he. 'Ah yes, I recall the case; it was concerned with an opal tiara. I think it was before your time, Watson. I can only say, madam, that I shall be happy to devote the same care to your case as I did to that of your friend. As to reward, my profession is its own reward; but you are at liberty to defray whatever expenses I may be put to, at the time which suits you best. And now I beg that you will lay before us everything that may help us in forming an opinion upon the matter.'

'Alas!' replied our visitor. 'The very horror of my situation lies in the fact that my fears are so vague, and my suspicions depend so entirely upon small points, which might seem trivial to another, that even he to whom of all others I have a right to look for help and advice looks upon all that I tell him about it as the fancies of a nervous woman. He does not say so, but I can read it from his soothing answers and averted eyes. But I have heard, Mr Holmes, that you can see deeply into the manifold wickedness of the human heart. You may advise me how to walk amid the dangers which encompass me.'

'I am all attention, madam.'

'My name is Helen Stoner, and I am living with my stepfather, who is the last survivor of one of the oldest Saxon families in England, the Roylotts of Stoke Moran, on the western border of Surrey.'

Holmes nodded his head. 'The name is familiar to me,' said he.

'The family was at one time among the richest in England, and the estate extended over the borders into Berkshire in the north, and Hampshire in the west. In the last century, however, four successive heirs were of a dissolute and wasteful disposition, and the family ruin was eventually completed by a gambler in the days of the Regency. Nothing was left save a few acres of ground, and the two-hundred-year-old house, which is itself crushed under a heavy mortgage. The last squire dragged out his existence there, living the horrible life of an aristocratic pauper; but his only son, my stepfather, seeing that he must adapt himself to the new conditions, obtained an advance from a relative, which enabled him to take a medical degree, and went out to Calcutta, where, by his professional skill and his force of character, he established a large practice. In a fit of anger, however, caused by some robberies which had been perpetrated in the house, he beat his native butler to death and narrowly escaped a capital sentence. As it was, he suffered a long term of imprisonment and afterwards returned to England a morose and disappointed man.

'When Dr Roylott was in India he married my mother, Mrs Stoner, the young widow of Major-General Stoner, of the Bengal Artillery. My sister Julia and I were twins, and we were only two years old at the time of my mother's re-marriage. She had a considerable sum of money—not less than a thousand pounds a year, and this she bequeathed to Dr Roylott entirely while we resided with him, with a provision that a certain annual sum should be allowed to each of us in the event of our marriage. Shortly after our return to England my mother died—she was killed eight years ago in a railway accident near Crewe. Dr Roylott then abandoned his attempts to establish himself in practice in London and took us to live with him in the old ancestral house at Stoke Moran. The money which my mother had left was enough for all our wants, and there seemed no obstacle to our happiness.

'But a terrible change came over our stepfather about this time. Instead of making friends and exchanging visits with our neighbours, who had at first been overjoyed to see a Roylott of Stoke Moran back in the old family seat, he shut himself up in his house and seldom came out save to indulge in ferocious quarrels with whoever might cross his path. Violence of temper approaching to mania has been hereditary in the men of the family, and in my stepfather's case it had, I believe, been intensified by his long residence in the tropics. A series of disgraceful brawls took place, two of which ended in the police-court, until at last he became the terror of the village, and the folks would fly at his approach, for he is a man of immense strength, and absolutely uncontrollable in his anger.

'Last week he hurled the local blacksmith over a parapet into a stream and it was only by paying over all the money that I could gather together that I was able to avert another public exposure. He had no friends at all save the wandering gipsies, and he would give these vagabonds leave to encamp upon the few acres of bramble-covered land which represent the family estate, and would accept in return the hospitality of their tents, wandering away with them sometimes for weeks on end. He has a passion also for Indian animals, which are sent over to him by a correspondent, and he has at this moment a cheetah and a baboon, which wander freely over his grounds, and are feared by the villagers almost as much as their master.

'You can imagine from what I say that my poor sister Julia and I had no great pleasure in our lives. No servant would stay with us, and for a long time we did all the work of the house. She was but thirty at the time of her death, and yet her hair had already begun to whiten, even as mine has.'

'Your sister is dead, then?'

'She died just two years ago, and it is of her death that I wish to speak to you. You can understand that, living the life which I have described, we were little likely to see anyone of our own age and position. We had, however, an aunt, my mother's maiden sister, Miss Honoria Westphail, who lives near Harrow, and we were occasionally allowed to pay short visits at this lady's house. Julia went there at Christmas two years ago, and met there a half-pay Major of Marines, to whom she became engaged. My stepfather learned of the engagement when my sister returned, and offered no objection to the marriage; but within a fortnight of the day which had been fixed for the wedding, the terrible event occurred which has deprived me of my only companion.'

Sherlock Holmes had been leaning back in his chair with his eyes closed and his head sunk in a cushion, but he half opened his lids now and glanced across at his visitor.

'Pray be precise as to details,' said he.

'It is easy for me to be so, for every event of that dreadful time is seared into my memory. The manor house is, as I have already said, very old, and only one wing is now inhabited. The bedrooms in this wing are on the ground floor, the sitting-rooms being in the central block of the buildings. Of these bedrooms, the first is Dr Roylott's, the second my sister's, and the third my own. There is no communication between them, but they all open out into the same corridor. Do I make myself plain?'

'Perfectly so.'

'The windows of the three rooms open out upon the lawn. That fatal night Dr Roylott had gone to his room early, though we knew that he had not retired to rest, for my sister was troubled by the smell of the strong Indian cigars which it was his custom to smoke. She left her room, therefore, and came into mine, where she sat for some time, chatting about her approaching wedding. At eleven o'clock she rose to leave me, but she paused at the door and looked back.

'"Tell me, Helen," said she, "have you ever heard anyone whistle in the dead of the night?"

'"Never," said I.

'"I suppose that you could not possibly whistle, yourself, in your sleep?"

'"Certainly not. But why?"

'"Because during the last few nights I have always, about three in the morning, heard a low, clear whistle. I am a light sleeper, and it has awakened me. I cannot tell where it came from—perhaps from the next room, perhaps from the lawn. I thought that I would just ask you whether you had heard it."

'"No, I have not. It must be those wretched gipsies in the plantation."

'"Very likely. And yet if it were on the lawn, I wonder that you did not hear it also."

'"Ah, but I sleep more heavily than you."

'"Well, it is of no great consequence, at any rate." She smiled back at me, closed my door, and a few moments later I heard her key turn in the lock.'

'Indeed,' said Holmes. 'Was it your custom always to lock yourselves in at night?'

'Always.'

'And why?'

'I think that I mentioned to you that the Doctor kept a cheetah and a baboon. We had no feeling of security unless our doors were locked.'

'Quite so. Pray proceed with your statement.'

'I could not sleep that night. A vague feeling of impending misfortune impressed me. My sister and I, you will recollect, were twins, and you know how subtle are the links which bind two souls which are so closely allied. It was a wild night. The wind was howling outside, and the rain was beating and splashing against the windows. Suddenly, amidst all the hubbub of the gale, there burst forth the wild scream of a terrified woman. I knew that it was my sister's voice. I sprang from my bed, wrapped a shawl round me, and rushed into the corridor. As I opened my door I seemed to hear a low whistle, such as my sister described, and a few moments later a clanging sound, as if a mass of metal had fallen. As I ran down the passage, my sister's door was unlocked, and revolved slowly upon its hinges. I stared at it horror-stricken, not knowing what was about to issue from it. By the light of the corridor-lamp I saw my sister appear at the opening, her face blanched with terror, her hands groping for help, her whole figure swaying to and fro like that of a drunkard. I ran to her and threw my arms round her, but at that moment her knees seemed to give way and she fell to the ground. She writhed as one who is in terrible pain, and her limbs were dreadfully convulsed. At first I thought that she had not recognized me, but as I bent over her she suddenly shrieked out in a voice which I shall never forget, "Oh, my God! Helen! It was the band! The speckled band!" There was something else which she would fain have said, and she stabbed with her finger into the air in the direction of the Doctor's room, but a fresh convulsion seized her and choked her words. I rushed out, calling loudly for my stepfather, and I met him hastening from his room in his dressing-gown. When he reached my sister's side she was unconscious, and though he poured brandy down her throat and sent for medical aid from the village, all efforts were in vain, for she slowly sank and died without having recovered her consciousness. Such was the dreadful end of my beloved sister.'

'One moment,' said Holmes, 'are you sure about this whistle and metallic sound? Could you swear to it?'

'That was what the county coroner asked me at the inquiry. It is my strong impression that I heard it, and yet among the crash of the gale, and the creaking of an old house, I may possibly have been deceived.'

'Was your sister dressed?'

'No, she was in her night-dress. In her right hand was found the charred stump of a match, and in her left a matchbox.'

'Showing that she had struck a light and looked about her when the alarm took place. That is important. And what conclusions did the coroner come to?'

'He investigated the case with great care, for Dr Roylott's conduct had long been notorious in the county, but he was unable to find any satisfactory cause of death. My evidence showed that the door had been fastened upon the inner side, and the windows were blocked by old-fashioned shutters with broad iron bars, which were secured every night. The walls were carefully sounded, and were shown to be quite solid all round, and the flooring was also thoroughly examined, with the same result. The chimney is wide, but is barred up by four large staples. It is certain, therefore, that my sister was quite alone when she met her end. Besides, there were no marks of any violence upon her.'

'How about poison?'

'The doctors examined her for it, but without success.'

'What do you think that this unfortunate lady died of, then?'

'It is my belief that she died of pure fear and nervous shock, though what it was which frightened her I cannot imagine.'

'Were there gipsies in the plantation at the time?'

'Yes, there are nearly always some there.'

'Ah, and what did you gather from this allusion to a band—a speckled band?'

'Sometimes I have thought that it was merely the wild talk of delirium, sometimes that it may have referred to some band of people, perhaps to these very gipsies in the plantation. I do not know whether the spotted handkerchiefs which so many of them wear over their heads might have suggested the strange adjective which she used.'

Holmes shook his head like a man who is far from being satisfied.

'These are very deep waters,' said he; 'pray go on with your narrative.'

'Two years have passed since then, and my life has been until lately lonelier than ever. A month ago, however, a dear friend, whom I have known for many years, has done me the honour to ask my hand in marriage. His name is Armitage—Percy Armitage—the second son of Mr Armitage, of Crane Water, near Reading. My stepfather has offered no opposition to the match, and we are to be married in the course of the spring. Two days ago some repairs were started in the west wing of the building, and my bedroom wall has been pierced, so that I have had to move into the chamber in which my sister died, and to sleep in the very bed in which she slept. Imagine, then, my thrill of terror when last night, as I lay awake, thinking over her terrible fate, I suddenly heard in the silence of the night the low whistle which had been the herald of her own death. I sprang up and lit the lamp, but nothing was to be seen in the room. I was too shaken to go to bed again, however, so I dressed, and as soon as it was daylight I slipped down, got a dog-cart at The Crown Inn, which is opposite, and drove to Leatherhead, from whence I have come on this morning, with the one object of seeing you and asking your advice.'

'You have done wisely,' said my friend. 'But have you told me all?'

'Yes, all.'

'Miss Stoner, you have not. You are screening your stepfather.'

'Why, what do you mean?'

For answer Holmes pushed back the frill of black lace which fringed the hand that lay upon our visitor's knee. Five little livid spots, the marks of four fingers and a thumb, were printed upon the white wrist.

'You have been cruelly used,' said Holmes.

The lady coloured deeply and covered over her injured wrist. 'He is a hard man,' she said, 'and perhaps he hardly knows his own strength.'

There was a long silence, during which Holmes leaned his chin upon his hands and stared into the crackling fire.

'This is a very deep business,' he said at last. 'There are a thousand details which I should desire to know before I decide upon our course of action. Yet we have not a moment to lose. If we were to come to Stoke Moran today, would it be possible for us to see over these rooms without the knowledge of your stepfather?'

'As it happens, he spoke of coming into town today upon some most important business. It is probable that he will be away all day, and that there would be nothing to disturb you. We have a housekeeper now, but she is old and foolish, and I could easily get her out of the way.'

'Excellent. You are not averse to this trip, Watson?'

'By no means.'

'Then we shall both come. What are you going to do yourself?'

'I have one or two things which I would wish to do now that I am in town. But I shall return by the twelve o'clock train, so as to be there in time for your coming.'

'And you may expect us early in the afternoon. I have myself some small business matters to attend to. Will you not wait and breakfast?'

'No, I must go. My heart is lightened already since I have confided my trouble to you. I shall look forward to seeing you again this afternoon.' She dropped her thick black veil over her face and glided from the room.

'And what do you think of it all, Watson?' asked Sherlock Holmes, leaning back in his chair.

'It seems to me to be a most dark and sinister business.'

'Dark enough and sinister enough.'

'Yet if the lady is correct in saying that the flooring and walls are sound, and that the door, window, and chimney are impassable, then her sister must have been undoubtedly alone when she met her mysterious end.'

'What becomes, then, of these nocturnal whistles, and what of the very peculiar words of the dying woman?'

'I cannot think.'

'When you combine the ideas of whistles at night, the presence of a band of gipsies who are on intimate terms with this old doctor, the fact that we have every reason to believe that the doctor has an interest in preventing his stepdaughter's marriage, the dying allusion to a band, and, finally, the fact that Miss Helen Stoner heard a metallic clang, which might have been caused by one of those metal bars which secured the shutters falling back into their place, I think that there is good ground to think that the mystery may be cleared along those lines.'

'But what, then, did the gipsies do?'

'I cannot imagine.'

'I see many objections to any such theory.'

'And so do I. It is precisely for that reason that we are going to Stoke Moran this day. I want to see whether the objections are fatal, or if they may be explained away. But what in the name of the devil!'

The ejaculation had been drawn from my companion by the fact that our door had been suddenly dashed open, and that a huge man framed himself in the aperture. His costume was a peculiar mixture of the professional and of the agricultural, having a black top-hat, a long frock-coat, and a pair of high gaiters, with a hunting-crop swinging in his hand. So tall was he that his hat actually brushed the cross-bar of the doorway, and his breadth seemed to span it across from side to side. A large face, seared with a thousand wrinkles, burned yellow with the sun, and marked with every evil passion, was turned from one to the other of us, while his deep-set, bile-shot eyes, and his high, thin, fleshless nose, gave him somewhat the resemblance to a fierce old bird of prey.

'Which of you is Holmes?' asked this apparition.

'My name, sir; but you have the advantage of me,' said my companion quietly.

'I am Dr Grimesby Roylott, of Stoke Moran.'

'Indeed, Doctor,' said Holmes blandly. 'Pray take a seat.'

'I will do nothing of the kind. My stepdaughter has been here. I have traced her. What has she been saying to you?'

'It is a little cold for the time of the year,' said Holmes.

'What has she been saying to you?' screamed the old man furiously.

'But I have heard that the crocuses promise well,' continued my companion imperturbably.

'Ha! You put me off, do you?' said our new visitor, taking a step forward and shaking his hunting-crop. 'I know you, you scoundrel! I have heard of you before. You are Holmes, the meddler.'

My friend smiled.

'Holmes, the busybody!'

His smile broadened.

'Holmes, the Scotland Yard jack-in-office!'

Holmes chuckled heartily. 'Your conversation is most entertaining,' said he. 'When you go out close the door, for there is a decided draught.'

'I will go when I have said my say. Don't you dare to meddle with my affairs. I know that Miss Stoner has been here. I traced her! I am a dangerous man to fall foul of! See here.' He stepped swiftly forward, seized the poker, and bent it into a curve with his huge brown hands.

'See that you keep yourself out of my grip,' he snarled, and hurling the twisted poker into the fireplace he strode out of the room.

'He seems a very amiable person,' said Holmes, laughing. 'I am not quite so bulky, but if he had remained I might have shown him that my grip was not much more feeble than his own.' As he spoke he picked up the steel poker and, with a sudden effort, straightened it out again.

'Fancy his having the insolence to confound me with the official detective force! This incident gives zest to our investigation, however, and I only trust that our little friend will not suffer from her imprudence in allowing this brute to trace her. And now, Watson, we shall order breakfast, and afterwards I shall walk down to Doctors' Commons, where I hope to get some data which may help us in this matter.'

It was nearly one o'clock when Sherlock Holmes returned from his excursion. He held in his hand a sheet of blue paper, scrawled over with notes and figures.

'I have seen the will of the deceased wife,' said he. 'To determine its exact meaning I have been obliged to work out the present prices of the investments with which it is concerned. The total income, which at the time of the wife's death was little short of £1100, is now through the fall in agricultural prices not more than £750. Each daughter can claim an income of £250, in case of marriage. It is evident, therefore, that if both girls had married, this beauty would have had a mere pittance, while even one of them would cripple him to a serious extent. My morning's work has not been wasted, since it has proved that he has the very strongest motives for standing in the way of anything of the sort. And now, Watson, this is too serious for dawdling, especially as the old man is aware that we are interesting ourselves in his affairs, so if you are ready we shall call a cab and drive to Waterloo. I should be very much obliged if you would slip your revolver into your pocket. An Eley's No. 2 is an excellent argument with gentlemen who can twist steel pokers into knots. That and a tooth-brush are, I think, all that we need.'

At Waterloo we were fortunate in catching a train for Leatherhead, where we hired a trap at the station inn and drove for four or five miles through the lovely Surrey lanes. It was a perfect day, with a bright sun and a few fleecy clouds in the heavens. The trees and wayside hedges were just throwing out their first green shoots, and the air was full of the pleasant smell of the moist earth. To me at least there was a strange contrast between the sweet promise of the spring and this sinister quest upon which we were engaged. My companion sat in the front of the trap, his arms folded, his hat pulled down over his eyes, and his chin sunk upon his breast, buried in the deepest thought. Suddenly, however, he started, tapped me on the shoulder, and pointed over the meadows.

'Look there!' said he.

A heavily timbered park stretched up in a gentle slope, thickening into a grove at the highest point. From amidst the branches there jutted out the grey gables and high roof-tree of a very old mansion.

'Stoke Moran?' said he.

'Yes, sir, that be the house of Dr Grimesby Roylott,' remarked the driver.

'There is some building going on there,' said Holmes; 'that is where we are going.'

'There's the village,' said the driver, pointing to a cluster of roofs some distance to the left; 'but if you want to get to the house, you'll find it shorter to get over this stile, and so by the footpath over the fields. There it is, where the lady is walking.'

'And the lady, I fancy, is Miss Stoner,' observed Holmes, shading his eyes. 'Yes, I think we had better do as you suggest.'

We got off, paid our fare, and the trap rattled back on its way to Leatherhead.

'I thought it as well,' said Holmes, as we climbed the stile, 'that this fellow should think we had come here as architects, or on some definite business. It may stop his gossip. Good afternoon, Miss Stoner. You see that we have been as good as our word.'

Our client of the morning had hurried forward to meet us with a face which spoke her joy. 'I have been waiting so eagerly for you,' she cried, shaking hands with us warmly. 'All has turned out splendidly. Dr Roylott has gone to town, and it is unlikely that he will be back before evening.'

'We have had the pleasure of making the doctor's acquaintance,' said Holmes, and in a few words he sketched out what had occurred. Miss Stoner turned white to the lips as she listened.

'Good heavens!' she cried, 'he has followed me, then.'

'So it appears.'

'He is so cunning that I never know when I am safe from him. What will he say when he returns?'

'He must guard himself, for he may find that there is someone more cunning than himself upon his track. You must lock yourself from him tonight. If he is violent, we shall take you away to your aunt's at Harrow. Now, we must make the best use of our time, so kindly take us at once to the rooms which we are to examine.'

The building was of grey, lichen-blotched stone, with a high central portion and two curving wings, like the claws of a crab, thrown out on each side. In one of these wings the windows were broken, and blocked with wooden boards, while the roof was partly caved in, a picture of ruin. The central portion was in little better repair, but the right-hand block was comparatively modern, and the blinds in the windows, with the blue smoke curling up from the chimneys, showed that this was where the family resided. Some scaffolding had been erected against the end wall, and the stonework had been broken into, but there were no signs of any workmen at the moment of our visit. Holmes walked slowly up and down the ill-trimmed lawn and examined with deep attention the outsides of the windows.

'This, I take it, belongs to the room in which you used to sleep, the centre one to your sister's, and the one next to the main building to Dr Roylott's chamber?'

'Exactly so. But I am now sleeping in the middle one.'

'Pending the alterations, as I understand. By the way, there does not seem to be any very pressing need for repairs at that end wall.'

'There were none. I believe that it was an excuse to move me from my room.'

'Ah! that is suggestive. Now, on the other side of this narrow wing runs the corridor from which these three rooms open. There are windows in it, of course?'

'Yes, but very small ones. Too narrow for anyone to pass through.'

'As you both locked your doors at night, your rooms were unapproachable from that side. Now, would you have the kindness to go into your room, and to bar your shutters?'

Miss Stoner did so, and Holmes, after a careful examination through the open window, endeavoured in every way to force the shutter open, but without success. There was no slit through which a knife could be passed to raise the bar. Then with his lens he tested the hinges, but they were of solid iron, built firmly into the massive masonry. 'Hum!' said he, scratching his chin in some perplexity, 'my theory certainly presents some difficulties. No one could pass these shutters if they were bolted. Well, we shall see if the inside throws any light upon the matter.'

A small side-door led into the whitewashed corridor from which the three bedrooms opened. Holmes refused to examine the third chamber, so we passed at once to the second, that in which Miss Stoner was now sleeping, and in which her sister had met with her fate. It was a homely little room, with a low ceiling and a gaping fireplace, after the fashion of old country-houses. A brown chest of drawers stood in one corner, a narrow white-counterpaned bed in another, and a dressing-table on the left-hand side of the window. These articles, with two small wicker-work chairs, made up all the furniture in the room, save for a square of Wilton carpet in the centre. The boards round and the panelling of the walls were brown, worm-eaten oak, so old and discoloured that it may have dated from the original building of the house. Holmes drew one of the chairs into a corner and sat silent, while his eyes travelled round and round and up and down, taking in every detail of the apartment.

'Where does that bell communicate with?' he asked at last pointing to a thick bell-rope which hung down beside the bed, the tassel actually lying upon the pillow.

'It goes to the housekeeper's room.'

'It looks newer than the other things?'

'Yes, it was only put there a couple of years ago.'

'Your sister asked for it, I suppose?'

'No, I never heard of her using it. We used always to get what we wanted for ourselves.'

'Indeed, it seemed unnecessary to put so nice a bell-pull there. You will excuse me for a few minutes while I satisfy myself as to this floor.' He threw himself down upon his face with his lens in his hand and crawled swiftly backwards and forwards, examining minutely the cracks between the boards.

Then he did the same with the woodwork with which the chamber was panelled. Finally he walked over to the bed and spent some time in staring at it, and in running his eye up and down the wall. Finally he took the bell-rope in his hand and gave it a brisk tug.

'Why, it's a dummy,' said he.

'Won't it ring?'

'No, it is not even attached to a wire. This is very interesting. You can see now that it is fastened to a hook just above where the little opening of the ventilator is.'

'How very absurd! I never noticed that before.'

'Very strange!' muttered Holmes, pulling at the rope. 'There are one or two very singular points about this room. For example, what a fool a builder must be to open a ventilator in another room, when, with the same trouble, he might have communicated with the outside air!'

'That is also quite modern,' said the lady.

'Done about the same time as the bell-rope,' remarked Holmes.

'Yes, there were several little changes carried out about that time.'

'They seem to have been of a most interesting character—dummy bell-ropes, and ventilators which do not ventilate. With your permission, Miss Stoner, we shall now carry our researches into the inner apartment.'

Dr Grimesby Roylott's chamber was larger than that of his stepdaughter, but was as plainly furnished. A camp-bed, a small wooden shelf full of books, mostly of a technical character, an armchair beside the bed, a plain wooden chair against the wall, a round table, and a large iron safe were the principal things which met the eye. Holmes walked slowly round and examined each and all of them with the keenest interest.

'What's in here?' he asked, tapping the safe.

'My stepfather's business papers.'

'Oh! you have seen inside, then?'

'Only once, some years ago. I remember that it was full of papers.'

'There isn't a cat in it, for example?'

'No. What a strange idea!'

'Well, look at this!' He took up a small saucer of milk which stood on the top of it.

'No; we don't keep a cat. But there is a cheetah and a baboon.'

'Ah, yes, of course! Well, a cheetah is just a big cat, and yet a saucer of milk does not go very far in satisfying its wants, I daresay. There is one point which I should wish to determine.' He squatted down in front of the wooden chair and examined the seat of it with the greatest attention.

'Thank you. That is quite settled,' said he, rising and putting his lens in his pocket. 'Hello! Here is something interesting!'

The object which had caught his eye was a small dog lash hung on one corner of the bed. The lash, however, was curled upon itself and tied so as to make a loop of whipcord.

'What do you make of that, Watson?'

'It's a common enough lash. But I don't know why it should be tied.'

'That is not quite so common, is it? Ah, me! it's a wicked world, and when a clever man turns his brain to crime it is the worst of all. I think that I have seen enough now, Miss Stoner, and with your permission we shall walk out upon the lawn.'

I had never seen my friend's face so grim, or his brow so dark, as it was when we turned from the scene of this investigation. We had walked several times up and down the lawn, neither Miss Stoner nor myself liking to break in upon his thoughts before he roused himself from his reverie.

'It is very essential, Miss Stoner,' said he, 'that you should absolutely follow my advice in every respect.'

'I shall most certainly do so.'

'The matter is too serious for any hesitation. Your life may depend upon your compliance.'

'I assure you that I am in your hands.'

'In the first place, both my friend and I must spend the night in your room.'

Both Miss Stoner and I gazed at him in astonishment.

'Yes, it must be so. Let me explain. I believe that that is the village inn over there?'

'Yes, that is The Crown.'

'Very good. Your windows would be visible from there?'

'Certainly.'

'You must confine yourself to your room, on pretence of a headache, when your stepfather comes back. Then when you hear him retire for the night, you must open the shutters of your window, undo the hasp, put your lamp there as a signal to us, and then withdraw with everything which you are likely to want into the room which you used to occupy. I have no doubt that, in spite of the repairs, you could manage there for one night.'

'Oh, yes, easily.'

'The rest you will leave in our hands.'

'But what will you do?'

'We shall spend the night in your room, and we shall investigate the cause of this noise which has disturbed you.'

'I believe, Mr Holmes, that you have already made up your mind,' said Miss Stoner, laying her hand upon my companion's sleeve.

'Perhaps I have.'

'Then for pity's sake tell me what was the cause of my sister's death.'

'I should prefer to have clearer proofs before I speak.'

'You can at least tell me whether my own thought is correct, and if she died from some sudden fright.'

'No, I do not think so. I think that there was probably some more tangible cause. And now, Miss Stoner, we must leave you, for if Dr Roylott returned and saw us, our journey would be in vain. Goodbye, and be brave, for if you will do what I have told you, you may rest assured that we shall soon drive away the dangers that threaten you.'

Sherlock Holmes and I had no difficulty in engaging a bedroom and sitting-room at The Crown Inn. They were on the upper floor, and from our window we could command a view of the avenue gate, and of the inhabited wing of Stoke Moran Manor House. At dusk we saw Dr Grimesby Roylott drive past, his huge form looming up beside the little figure of the lad who drove him. The boy had some slight difficulty in undoing the heavy iron gates, and we heard the hoarse roar of the doctor's voice, and saw the fury with which he shook his clenched fists at him. The trap drove on, and a few minutes later we saw a sudden light spring up among the trees as the lamp was lit in one of the sitting-rooms.

'Do you know, Watson,' said Holmes, as we sat together in the gathering darkness, 'I have really some scruples as to taking you tonight. There is a distinct element of danger.'

'Can I be of assistance?'

'Your presence might be invaluable.'

'Then I shall certainly come.'

'It is very kind of you.'

'You speak of danger. You have evidently seen more in these rooms than was visible to me.'

'No, but I fancy that I may have deduced a little more. I imagine that you saw all that I did.'

'I saw nothing remarkable save the bell-rope, and what purpose that could answer I confess is more than I can imagine.'

'You saw the ventilator, too?'

'Yes, but I do not think that it is such a very unusual thing to have a small opening between two rooms. It was so small that a rat could hardly pass through.'

'I knew that we should find a ventilator before ever we came to Stoke Moran.'

'My dear Holmes!'

'Oh, yes, I did. You remember in her statement she said that her sister could smell Dr Roylott's cigar. Now, of course that suggests at once that there must be a communication between the two rooms. It could only be a small one, or it would have been remarked upon at the coroner's inquiry. I deduced a ventilator.'

'But what harm can there be in that?'

'Well, there is at least a curious coincidence of dates. A ventilator is made, a cord is hung, and a lady who sleeps in the bed dies. Does not that strike you?'

'I cannot as yet see any connection.'

'Did you observe anything very peculiar about that bed?'

'No.'

'It was clamped to the floor. Did you ever see a bed fastened like that before?'

'I cannot say that I have.'

'The lady could not move her bed. It must always be in the same relative position to the ventilator and to the rope—for so we may call it, since it was clearly never meant for a bell-pull.'

'Holmes,' I cried, 'I seem to see dimly what you are hinting at. We are only just in time to prevent some subtle and horrible crime.'

'Subtle enough and horrible enough. When a doctor does go wrong he is the first of criminals. He has nerve and he has knowledge. Palmer and Pritchard were among the heads of their profession. This man strikes even deeper, but I think, Watson, that we shall be able to strike deeper still. But we shall have horrors enough before the night is over: for goodness' sake let us have a quiet pipe and turn our minds for a few hours to something more cheerful.'

About nine o'clock the light among the trees was extinguished, and all was dark in the direction of the Manor House. Two hours passed slowly away, and then, suddenly, just at the stroke of eleven, a single bright light shone out right in front of us.

'That is our signal,' said Holmes, springing to his feet; 'it comes from the middle window.'

As we passed out he exchanged a few words with the landlord, explaining that we were going on a late visit to an acquaintance, and that it was possible that we might spend the night there. A moment later we were out on the dark road, a chill wind blowing in our faces, and one yellow light twinkling in front of us through the gloom to guide us on our sombre errand.

There was little difficulty in entering the grounds, for unrepaired breaches gaped in the old park wall. Making our way among the trees, we reached the lawn, crossed it, and were about to enter through the window, when out from a clump of laurel bushes there darted what seemed to be a hideous and distorted child, who threw itself on the grass with writhing limbs, and then ran swiftly across the lawn into the darkness.

'My God!' I whispered; 'did you see it?'

Holmes was for the moment as startled as I. His hand closed like a vice upon my wrist in his agitation. Then he broke into a low laugh, and put his lips to my ear.

'It is a nice household,' he murmured. 'That is the baboon.'

I had forgotten the strange pets which the doctor affected. There was a cheetah, too; perhaps we might find it upon our shoulders at any moment. I confess that I felt easier in my mind when, after following Holmes's example and slipping off my shoes, I found myself inside the bedroom. My companion noiselessly closed the shutters, moved the lamp on to the table, and cast his eyes round the room. All was as we had seen it in the daytime. Then creeping up to me and making a trumpet of his hand, he whispered into my ear again so gently that it was all that I could do to distinguish the words:

'The least sound would be fatal to our plans.'

I nodded to show that I had heard.

'We must sit without light. He would see it through the ventilator.'

I nodded again.

'Do not go asleep; your very life may depend upon it. Have your pistol ready in case we should need it. I will sit on the side of the bed, and you in that chair.'

I took out my revolver and laid it on the corner of the table.

Holmes had brought up a long thin cane, and this he placed upon the bed beside him. By it he laid the box of matches and the stump of a candle. Then he turned down the lamp, and we were left in darkness.

How shall I ever forget that dreadful vigil? I could not hear a sound, not even the drawing of a breath, and yet I knew that my companion sat open-eyed, within a few feet of me, in the same state of nervous tension in which I was myself. The shutters cut off the least ray of light, and we waited in absolute darkness. From outside came the occasional cry of a night-bird, and once at our very window a long drawn, cat-like whine, which told us that the cheetah was indeed at liberty. Far away we could hear the deep tones of the parish clock, which boomed out every quarter of an hour. How long they seemed, those quarters! Twelve struck, and one, and two, and three, and still we sat waiting silently for whatever might befall.

Suddenly there was the momentary gleam of a light up in the direction of the ventilator, which vanished immediately, but was succeeded by a strong smell of burning oil and heated metal. Someone in the next room had lit a dark-lantern. I heard a gentle sound of movement, and then all was silent once more, though the smell grew stronger. For half an hour I sat with straining ears. Then suddenly another sound became audible—a very gentle, soothing sound, like that of a small jet of steam escaping continually from a kettle. The instant that we heard it, Holmes sprang from the bed, struck a match, and lashed furiously with his cane at the bell-pull.

'You see it, Watson?' he yelled. 'You see it?'

But I saw nothing. At the moment when Holmes struck the light I heard a low, clear whistle, but the sudden glare flashing into my weary eyes made it impossible for me to tell what it was at which my friend lashed so savagely. I could, however, see that his face was deadly pale and filled with horror and loathing.

He had ceased to strike and was gazing up at the ventilator when suddenly there broke from the silence of the night the most horrible cry to which I have ever listened. It swelled up louder and louder, a hoarse yell of pain and fear and anger all mingled in the one dreadful shriek. They say that away down in the village, and even in the distant parsonage, that cry raised the sleepers from their beds. It struck cold to our hearts, and I stood gazing at Holmes, and he at me, until the last echoes of it had died away into the silence from which it rose.

'What can it mean?' I gasped.

'It means that it is all over,' Holmes answered. 'And perhaps, after all, it is for the best. Take your pistol, and we shall enter Dr Roylott's room.'

With a grave face he lit the lamp and led the way down the corridor. Twice he struck at the chamber door without any reply from within. Then he turned the handle and entered, I at his heels, with the cocked pistol in my hand.

It was a singular sight which met our eyes. On the table stood a dark-lantern with the shutter half open, throwing a brilliant beam of light upon the iron safe, the door of which was ajar. Beside this table, on the wooden chair, sat Dr Grimesby Roylott clad in a long grey dressing-gown, his bare ankles protruding beneath, and his feet thrust into red heelless Turkish slippers. Across his lap lay the short stock with the long lash which we had noticed during the day. His chin was cocked upward and his eyes were fixed in a dreadful, rigid stare at the corner of the ceiling. Round his brow he had a peculiar yellow band, with brownish speckles, which seemed to be bound tightly round his head. As we entered he made neither sound nor motion.

'The band! the speckled band!' whispered Holmes.

I took a step forward. In an instant his strange headgear began to move, and there reared itself from among his hair the squat diamond-shaped head and puffed neck of a loathsome serpent.

'It is a swamp adder!' cried Holmes—'the deadliest snake in India. He has died within ten seconds of being bitten. Violence does, in truth, recoil upon the violent, and the schemer falls into the pit which he digs for another. Let us thrust this creature back into its den, and we can then remove Miss Stoner to some place of shelter and let the county police know what has happened.'

As he spoke he drew the dog-whip swiftly from the dead man's lap, and throwing the noose round the reptile's neck he drew it from its horrid perch and, carrying it at arm's length, threw it into the iron safe, which he closed upon it.

Such are the true facts of the death of Dr Grimesby Roylott, of Stoke Moran. It is not necessary that I should prolong a narrative which has already run to too great a length by telling how we broke the sad news to the terrified girl, how we conveyed her by the morning train to the care of her good aunt at Harrow, of how the slow process of official inquiry came to the conclusion that the Doctor met his fate while indiscreetly playing with a dangerous pet. The little which I had yet to learn of the case was told me by Sherlock Holmes as we travelled back next day.

'I had,' said he, 'come to an entirely erroneous conclusion which shows, my dear Watson, how dangerous it always is to reason from insufficient data. The presence of the gipsies, and the use of the word "band", which was used by the poor girl, no doubt to explain the appearance which she had caught a hurried glimpse of by the light of her match, were sufficient to put me upon an entirely wrong scent. I can only claim the merit that I instantly reconsidered my position when, however, it became clear to me that whatever danger threatened an occupant of the room could not come either from the window or the door. My attention was speedily drawn, as I have already remarked to you, to this ventilator, and to the bell-rope which hung down to the bed. The discovery that this was a dummy, and that the bed was clamped to the floor, instantly gave rise to the suspicion that the rope was there as a bridge for something passing through the hole and coming to the bed. The idea of a snake instantly occurred to me, and when I coupled it with my knowledge that the doctor was furnished with a supply of creatures from India, I felt that I was probably on the right track. The idea of using a form of poison which could not possibly be discovered by any chemical test was just such a one as would occur to a clever and ruthless man who had had an Eastern training. The rapidity with which such a poison would take effect would also, from his point of view, be an advantage. It would be a sharp-eyed coroner indeed who could distinguish the two little dark punctures which would show where the poison fangs had done their work. Then I thought of the whistle. Of course, he must recall the snake before the morning light revealed it to the victim. He had trained it, probably by the use of the milk which we saw, to return to him when summoned. He would put it through this ventilator at the hour that he thought best, with the certainty that it would crawl down the rope, and land on the bed. It might or might not bite the occupant, perhaps she might escape every night for a week, but sooner or later she must fall a victim.

'I had come to these conclusions before ever I had entered his room. An inspection of his chair showed me that he had been in the habit of standing on it, which of course would be necessary in order that he should reach the ventilator. The sight of the safe, the saucer of milk, and the loop of whipcord were enough to finally dispel any doubts which may have remained. The metallic clang heard by Miss Stoner was obviously caused by her stepfather hastily closing the door of his safe upon its terrible occupant. Having once made up my mind, you know the steps which I took in order to put the matter to the proof. I heard the creature hiss as I have no doubt that you did also, and I instantly lit the light and attacked it.'

'With the result of driving it through the ventilator.'

'And also with the result of causing it to turn upon its master at the other side. Some of the blows of my cane came home and roused its snakish temper, so that it flew upon the first person it saw. In this way I am no doubt indirectly responsible for Dr Grimesby Roylott's death, and I cannot say that it is likely to weigh very heavily upon my conscience.'

'De Profundis'

S O LONG AS THE OCEANS ARE THE LIGAMENTS which bind together the great, broad-cast British Empire, so long will there be a dash of romance in our minds. For the soul is swayed by the waters, as the waters are by the moon, and when the great highways of an empire are along such roads as these, so full of strange sights and sounds, with danger ever running like a hedge on either side of the course, it is a dull mind indeed which does not bear away with it some trace of such a passage. And now, Britain lies far beyond herself, for the three-mile limit of every seaboard is her frontier, which has been won by hammer and loom and pick rather than by arts of war. For it is written in history that neither king nor army can bar the path to the man who, having twopence in his strong box, and knowing well where he can turn it to threepence, sets his mind to that one end. And as the frontier has broadened, the mind of Britain has broadened, too, spreading out until all men can see that the ways of the island are Continental, even as those of the Continent are insular.

But for this a price must be paid, and the price is a grievous one. As the beast of old must have one young, human life as a tribute every year, so to our Empire we throw from day to day the pick and flower of our youth. The engine is world-wide and strong, but the only fuel that will drive it is the lives of British men. Thus it is that in the grey, old cathedrals as we look round upon the brasses on the walls, we see strange names, such names as they who reared those walls had never heard, for it is in Peshawur, and Umballah, and Korti, and Fort Pearson that the youngsters die, leaving only a precedent and a brass behind them. But if every man had his obelisk, even where he lay, then no frontier line need be drawn, for a cordon of British graves would ever show how high the Anglo-Celtic tide had lapped.

This, then, as well as the waters which join us to the world, has done something to tinge us with romance. For when so many have their loved ones over the seas, walking amid hillmen's bullets, or swamp malaria, where death is sudden and distance great, then mind communes with mind, and strange stories arise of dream, presentiment, or vision, where the mother sees her dying son, and is past the first bitterness of her grief ere the message comes which should have broken the news. The learned have of late looked into the matter and have even labelled it with a name; but what can we know more of it save that a poor, stricken soul, when hard-pressed and driven, can shoot across the earth some ten-thousand-mile-distant picture of its trouble to the mind which is most akin to it. Far be it from me to say that there lies no such power within us, for of all things which the brain will grasp the last will be itself; but yet it is well to be very cautious over such matters, for once at least I have known that which was within the laws of Nature seem to be far upon the further side of them.

John Vansittart was the younger partner of the firm of Hudson and Vansittart, coffee exporters of the Island of Ceylon, three-quarters Dutchman by descent, but wholly English in his sympathies. For years I had been his agent in London, and when in '72 he came over to England for a three months' holiday, he turned to me for the introductions which would enable him to see something of town and country life. Armed with seven letters he left my offices, and for many weeks scrappy notes from different parts of the country let me know that he had found favour in the eyes of my friends. Then came word of his engagement to Emily Lawson, of a cadet branch of the Hereford Lawsons, and at the very tail of the first flying rumour the news of his absolute marriage, for the wooing of a wanderer must be short, and the days were already crowding on towards the date when he must be upon his homeward journey. They were to return together to Colombo in one of the firm's own thousand-ton, barque-rigged sailing ships, and this was to be their princely honeymoon, at once a necessity and a delight.

Those were the royal days of coffee-planting in Ceylon, before a single season and a rotting fungus drove a whole community through years of despair to one of the greatest commercial victories which pluck and ingenuity ever won. Not often is it that men have the heart when their one great industry is withered to rear up, in a few years, another as rich to take its place, and the tea-fields of Ceylon are as true a monument to courage as is the lion at Waterloo. But in '72 there was no cloud yet above the skyline, and the hopes of the planters were as high and as bright as the hill-sides on which they reared their crops. Vansittart came down to London with his young and beautiful wife. I was introduced, dined with them, and it was finally arranged that I, since business called me also to Ceylon, should be a fellow-passenger with them on the *Eastern Star*, which was timed to sail on the following Monday.

It was on the Sunday evening that I saw him again. He was shown up into my rooms about nine o'clock at night, with the air of a man who is bothered and out of sorts. His hand, as I shook it, was hot and dry.

'I wish, Atkinson,' said he, 'that you could give me a little lime-juice and water. I have a beastly thirst upon me, and the more I take the more I seem to want.'

I rang and ordered a carafe and glasses. 'You are flushed,' said I. 'You don't look the thing.'

'No, I'm clean off colour. Got a touch of rheumatism in my back, and don't seem to taste my food. It is this vile London that is choking me. I'm not used to breathing air which has been used up by four million lungs all sucking away on every side of you.' He flapped his crooked hands before his face, like a man who really struggles for his breath.

'A touch of the sea will soon set you right.'

'Yes, I'm of one mind with you there. That's the thing for me. I want no other doctor. If I don't get to sea tomorrow I'll have an illness. There are no two ways about it.' He drank off a tumbler of lime-juice, and clapped his two hands with his knuckles doubled up into the small of his back.

'That seems to ease me,' said he, looking at me with a filmy eye. 'Now I want your help, Atkinson, for I am rather awkwardly placed.'

'As how?'

'This way. My wife's mother got ill and wired for her. I couldn't go—you know best yourself how tied I have been—so she had to go alone. Now I've had another wire to say that she can't come tomorrow, but that she will pick up the ship at Falmouth on Wednesday. We put in there, you know, though I count it hard, Atkinson, that a man should be asked to believe in a mystery, and cursed if he can't do it. Cursed, mind you, no less.' He leaned forward and began to draw a catchy breath like a man who is poised on the very edge of a sob.

Then first it came into my mind that I had heard much of the hard-drinking life of the island, and that from brandy came these wild words and fevered hands. The flushed cheek and the glazing eye were those of one whose drink is strong upon him. Sad it was to see so noble a young man in the grip of that most bestial of all the devils.

'You should lie down,' I said, with some severity.

He screwed up his eyes like a man who is striving to wake himself, and looked up with an air of surprise.

'So I shall presently,' said he, quite rationally. 'I felt quite swimmy just now, but I am my own man again now. Let me see, what was I talking about? Oh ah, of course, about the wife. She joins the ship at Falmouth. Now I want to go round by water. I believe my health depends upon it. I just want a little clean, first-lung air to set me on my feet again. I ask you, like a good fellow, to go to Falmouth by rail, so that in case we should be late you may be there to look after the wife. Put up at the Royal Hotel, and I will wire her that you are there. Her sister will bring her down, so that it will be all plain sailing.'

'I'll do it with pleasure.' said I. 'In fact, I would rather go by rail, for we shall have enough and to spare of the sea before we reach Colombo. I believe, too, that you badly need a change. Now, I should go and turn in, if I were you.'

'Yes, I will. I sleep aboard tonight. You know,' he continued, as the film settled down again over his eyes, 'I've not slept well the last few nights. I've been troubled with theolololog—that is to say, theolological—hang it'—with a desperate effort—'with the doubts of theolologicians. Wondering why the

Almighty made us, you know, and why He made our heads swimmy, and fixed little pains into the small of our backs. Maybe I'll do better tonight.' He rose and steadied himself with an effort against the corner of the chair back.

'Look here, Vansittart,' said I gravely, stepping up to him, and laying my hand upon his sleeve, 'I can give you a shakedown here. You are not fit to go out. You are all over the place. You've been mixing your drinks.'

'Drinks!' He stared at me stupidly.

'You used to carry your liquor better than this.'

'I give you my word, Atkinson, that I have not had a drain for two days. It's not drink. I don't know what it is. I suppose you think this is drink.' He took up my hand in his burning grasp, and passed it over his own forehead.

'Great Lord!' said I.

His skin felt like a thin sheet of velvet beneath which lies a close-packed layer of small shot. It was smooth to the touch at any one place, but to a finger passed along it, rough as a nutmeg-grater.

'It's all right,' said he, smiling at my startled face. 'I've had the prickly heat nearly as bad.'

'But this is never prickly heat.'

'No, it's London. It's breathing bad air. But tomorrow it'll be all right. There's a surgeon aboard, so I shall be in safe hands. I must be off now.'

'Not you,' said I, pushing him back into a chair. 'This is past a joke. You don't move from here until a doctor sees you. Just stay where you are.'

I caught up my hat, and rushing round to the house of a neighbouring physician, I brought him back with me. The room was empty and Vansittart gone. I rang the bell. The servant said that the gentleman had ordered a cab the instant that I had left, and had gone off in it. He had told the cabman to drive to the docks.

'Did the gentleman seem ill?' I asked.

'Ill!' The man smiled. 'No, sir, he was singin' his 'ardest all the time.'

The information was not as reassuring as my servant seemed to think, but I reflected that he was going straight back to the *Eastern Star*, and that there was a doctor aboard of her, so that there was nothing which I could do in the matter. None the less, when I thought of his thirst, his burning hands, his heavy eye, his tripping speech, and lastly, of that leprous forehead, I carried with me to bed an unpleasant memory of my visitor and his visit.

At eleven o'clock next day I was at the docks, but the *Eastern Star* had already moved down the river, and was nearly at Gravesend. To Gravesend I went by train, but only to see her topmasts far off, with a plume of smoke from a tug in front of her. I would hear no more of my friend until I rejoined him at Falmouth. When I got back to my offices, a telegram was awaiting me from Mrs Vansittart, asking me to meet her; and next evening found us both at the Royal Hotel, Falmouth, where we were to wait for the *Eastern Star*. Ten days passed, and there came no news of her.

They were ten days which I am not likely to forget. On the very day that the *Eastern Star* had cleared from the Thames, a furious, easterly gale had sprung up, and blew on from day to day for the greater part of a week without the sign of a lull. Such a screaming, raving, long-drawn storm has never been known on the southern coast. From our hotel windows the sea view was all banked in haze, with a little rain-swept half-circle under our very eyes, churned and lashed into one tossing stretch of foam. So heavy was the wind upon the waves that little sea could rise, for the crest of each billow was torn shrieking from it, and lashed broad-cast over the bay. Clouds, wind, sea, all were rushing to the west, and there, looking down at this mad jumble of elements, I waited on day after day, my sole companion a white, silent woman, with terror in her eyes, her forehead pressed ever against the window, her gaze from early morning to the fall of night fixed upon that wall of grey haze through which the loom of a vessel might come. She said nothing, but that face of hers was one long wail of fear.

On the fifth day I took counsel with an old seaman. I should have preferred to have done so alone, but she saw me speak with him, and was at our side in an instant, with parted lips and a prayer in her eyes.

'Seven days out from London,' said he, 'and five in the gale. Well, the Channel's swept clear by this wind. There's three things for it. She may have popped into port on the French side. That's like enough.'

'No, no; he knew we were here. He would have telegraphed.'

'Ah, yes, so he would. Well, then, he might have run for it, and if he did that he won't be very far from Madeira by now. That'll be it, marm, you may depend.'

'Or else? You said there was a third chance.'

'Did I, marm. No, only two, I think. I don't think I said anything of a third. Your ship's out there, depend upon it, away out in the Atlantic, and you'll hear of it time enough, for the weather is breaking. Now don't you fret, marm, and wait quiet and you'll find a real blue Cornish sky tomorrow.'

The old seaman was right in his surmise, for the next day broke calm and bright, with only a low, dwindling cloud in the west to mark the last trailing wreaths of the storm-wrack. But still there came no word from the sea, and no sign of the ship. Three more weary days had passed, the weariest that I have ever spent, when there came a seafaring man to the hotel with a letter. I gave a shout of joy. It was from the captain of the *Eastern Star*. As I read the first lines of it I whisked my hand over it, but she laid her own upon it and drew it away. 'I have seen it,' said she, in a cold, quiet voice. 'I may as well see the rest, too.'

'DEAR SIR,' said the letter,

'Mr Vansittart is down with the small-pox, and we are blown so far on our course that we don't know what to do, he being off his head and unfit to tell us. By dead reckoning we are but three hundred miles from Funchal, so I take it that it is best that we should push on there, get Mr V. into hospital and wait in the Bay until you come. There's a sailing-ship due from Falmouth to Funchal in a few days' time, as I understand. This goes by the brig *Marian* of Falmouth, and five pounds is due to the master,

Yours respectfully,
'JNO. HINES.'

She was a wonderful woman that, only a chit of a girl fresh from school, but as quiet and strong as a man. She said nothing—only pressed her lips together tight, and put on her bonnet.

'You are going out?' I asked.

'Yes.'

'Can I be of use?'

'No; I am going to the doctor's.'

'To the doctor's?'

'Yes. To learn how to nurse a small-pox case.'

She was busy at that all the evening, and next morning we were off with a fine ten-knot breeze in the barque *Rose of Sharon* for Madeira. For five days we made good time, and were no great way from the island; but on the sixth there fell a calm, and we lay without motion on a sea of oil, heaving slowly, but making not a foot of way.

At ten o'clock that night Emily Vansittart and I stood leaning on the starboard railing of the poop, with a full moon shining at our backs, and casting a black shadow of the barque, and of our own two heads, upon the shining water. From the shadow a broadening path of moonshine stretched away to the lonely skyline, flickering and shimmering in the gentle heave of the swell. We were talking with bent heads, chatting of the calm, of the chances of wind, of the look of the sky, when there came a sudden plop, like a rising salmon, and there, in the clear light, John Vansittart sprang out of the water and looked up at us.

I never saw anything clearer in my life than I saw that man. The moon shone full upon him, and he was but three oars' length away. His face was more puffed than when I had seen him last, mottled here and there with dark scabs, his mouth and eyes open as one who is struck with some overpowering surprise. He had some white stuff streaming from his shoulders, and one hand was raised to his ear, the other crooked across his breast. I saw him leap from the water into the air, and in the dead calm the waves of his coming lapped up against the sides of the vessel. Then his figure sank back into the water again, and I heard a rending, crackling sound like a bundle of brushwood snapping in the fire on a frosty night. There were no signs of him when I looked again, but a swift swirl and eddy on the still sea still marked the spot where he had been. How long I stood there, tingling to my finger-tips, holding up an unconscious woman with one hand, clutching at the rail of the vessel with the other, was more than I could afterwards tell. I had been noted as a man of slow and unresponsive emotions, but this time at least I was shaken to the core. Once and twice I struck my foot upon the deck to be certain that I was indeed the master of my own senses, and that this was not some mad prank of an unruly brain. As I stood still marvelling, the woman shivered, opened her eyes, gasped, and then standing erect with her hands upon the rail, looked out over the moonlit sea with a face which had aged ten years in a summer night.

'You saw his vision?' she murmured.

'I saw something.'

'It was he! It was John! He is dead!'

I muttered some lame words of doubt.

'Doubtless he died at this hour,' she whispered. 'In hospital at Madeira. I have read of such things. His thoughts were with me. His vision came to me. Oh, my John, my dear, dear, lost John!'

She broke out suddenly into a storm of weeping, and I led her down into her cabin, where I left her with her sorrow. That night a brisk breeze blew up from the east, and in the evening of the next day we passed the two islets of Los Desertos, and dropped anchor at sundown in the Bay of Funchal. The *Eastern Star* lay no great distance from us, with the quarantine flag flying from her main, and her Jack half-way up her peak.

'You see,' said Mrs Vansittart quickly. She was dry-eyed now, for she had known how it would be.

At night we received permission from the authorities to move on board the *Eastern Star*. The captain, Hines, was waiting upon deck with confusion and grief contending upon his bluff face as he sought for words with which to break his heavy tidings, but she took the story from his lips.

'I know that my husband is dead,' she said. 'He died yesterday night, about ten o'clock, in hospital at Madeira, did he not?'

The seaman stared aghast. 'No, marm, he died eight days ago at sea, and we had to bury him out there, for we lay in a belt of calm, and could not say when we might make the land.'

Well, those are the main facts about the death of John Vansittart, and his appearance to his wife somewhere about lat. 35 N. and long. 15 W. A clearer case of a wraith has seldom been made out, and since then it has been told as such, and put into print as such, and endorsed by a learned society as such, and so floated off with many others to support the recent theory of telepathy. For myself, I hold telepathy to be proved, but I would snatch this one case from amid the evidence, and say that I do not think that it was the wraith of John Vansittart, but John Vansittart himself whom we saw that night leaping into the moonlight out of the depths of the Atlantic. It has ever been my belief that some strange chance—one of those chances which seem so improbable and yet so constantly occur—had becalmed us over the very spot where the man had been buried a week before. For the rest, the surgeon tells me that the leaden weight was not too firmly fixed, and that seven days bring about changes which fetch a body to the surface. Coming from the depth to which the weight would have sunk it, he explains that it might well attain such a velocity as to carry it clear of the water. Such is my own explanation of the matter, and if you ask me what then became of the body, I must recall to you that snapping, crackling sound, with the swirl in the water. The shark is a surface feeder and is plentiful in those parts.

Lot No. 249

O F THE DEALINGS OF EDWARD BELLINGHAM with William Monkhouse Lee, and of the cause of the great terror of Abercrombie Smith, it may be that no absolute and final judgment will ever be delivered. It is true that we have the full and clear narrative of Smith himself, and such corroboration as he could look for from Thomas Styles the servant, from the Reverend Plumptree Peterson, Fellow of Old's, and from such other people as chanced to gain some passing glance at this or that incident in a singular chain of events. Yet, in the main, the story must rest upon Smith alone, and the most will think that it is more likely that one brain, however outwardly sane, has some subtle warp in its texture, some strange flaw in its workings, than that the path of Nature has been overstepped in open day in so famed a centre of learning and light as the University of Oxford. Yet when we think how narrow and how devious this path of Nature is, how dimly we can trace it, for all our lamps of science, and how from the darkness which girds it round great and terrible possibilities loom ever shadowly upwards, it is a bold and confident man who will put a limit to the strange by-paths into which the human spirit may wander.

In a certain wing of what we will call Old College in Oxford there is a corner turret of an exceeding great age. The heavy arch which spans the open door has bent downwards in the centre under the weight of its years, and the grey, lichen-blotched blocks of stone are bound and knitted together with withes and strands of ivy, as though the old mother had set herself to brace them up against wind and weather. From the door a stone stair curves upward spirally, passing two landings, and terminating in a third one, its steps all shapeless and hollowed by the tread of so many generations of the seekers after knowledge. Life has flowed like water down this winding stair, and, waterlike, has left these smooth-worn grooves behind it. From the long-gowned, pedantic scholars of Plantagenet days down to the young bloods of a later age, how full and strong had been that tide of young, English life. And what was left now of all those hopes, those strivings, those fiery energies, save here and there in some old-world churchyard a few scratches upon a stone, and perchance a handful of dust in a mouldering coffin? Yet here were the silent stair and the grey, old wall, with bend and saltire and many another heraldic device still to be read upon its surface, like grotesque shadows thrown back from the days that had passed.

In the month of May, in the year 1884, three young men occupied the sets of rooms which opened on to the separate landings of the old stair. Each set consisted simply of a sitting-room and of a bedroom, while the two corresponding rooms upon the ground-floor were used, the one as a coal-cellar, and the other as the living-room of the servant, or scout, Thomas Styles, whose duty it was to wait upon the three men above him. To right and to left was a line of lecture-rooms and of offices, so that the dwellers in the old turret enjoyed a certain seclusion, which made the chambers popular among the more studious undergraduates. Such were the three who occupied them now—Abercrombie Smith above, Edward Bellingham beneath him, and William Monkhouse Lee upon the lowest storey.

It was ten o'clock on a bright, spring night, and Abercrombie Smith lay back in his armchair, his feet upon the fender, and his briar-root pipe between his lips. In a similar chair, and equally at his ease, there lounged on the other side of the fireplace his old school friend Jephro Hastie. Both men were in flannels, for they had spent their evening upon the river, but apart from their dress no one could look at their hard-cut, alert faces without seeing that they were open-air men—men whose minds and tastes turned naturally to all that was manly and robust. Hastie, indeed, was stroke of his college boat, and Smith was an even better oar, but a coming examination had already cast its shadow over him and held him to his work, save for the few hours a week which health demanded. A litter of medical books upon the table, with scattered bones, models, and anatomical plates, pointed to the extent as well as the nature of his studies, while a couple of single-sticks and a set of boxing-gloves above the mantelpiece hinted at the means by which, with Hastie's help, he might take his exercise in its most compressed and least-distant form. They knew each other very well—so well that they could sit now in that soothing silence which is the very highest development of companionship.

'Have some whisky,' said Abercrombie Smith at last between two cloudbursts. 'Scotch in the jug and Irish in the bottle.'

'No, thanks. I'm in for the sculls. I don't liquor when I'm training. How about you?'

'I'm reading hard. I think it best to leave it alone.'

Hastie nodded, and they relapsed into a contented silence.

'By the way, Smith,' asked Hastie, presently, 'have you made the acquaintance of either of the fellows on your stair yet?'

'Just a nod when we pass. Nothing more.'

'Hum! I should be inclined to let it stand at that. I know something of them both. Not much, but as much as I want. I don't think I should take them to my bosom if I were you. Not that there's much amiss with Monkhouse Lee.'

'Meaning the thin one?'

'Precisely. He is a gentlemanly little fellow. I don't think there is any vice in him. But then you can't know him without knowing Bellingham.'

'Meaning the fat one?'

'Yes, the fat one. And he's a man whom I, for one, would rather not know.'

Abercrombie Smith raised his eyebrows and glanced across at his companion.

'What's up, then?' he asked. 'Drink? Cards? Cad? You used not to be censorious.'

'Ah! you evidently don't know the man, or you wouldn't ask. There's something damnable about him—something reptilian. My gorge always rises at him. I should put him down as a man with secret vices—an evil liver. He's no fool, though. They say that he is one of the best men in his line that they have ever had in the college.'

'Medicine or classics?'

'Eastern languages. He's a demon at them. Chillingworth met him somewhere above the second cataract last long, and he told me that he just prattled to the Arabs as if he had been born and nursed and weaned among them. He talked Coptic to the Copts, and Hebrew to the Jews, and Arabic to the Bedouins, and they were all ready to kiss the hem of his frock-coat. There are some old hermit Johnnies up in those parts who sit on rocks and scowl and spit at the casual stranger. Well, when they saw this chap Bellingham, before he had said five words they just lay down on their bellies and wriggled. Chillingworth said that he never saw anything like it. Bellingham seemed to take it as his right, too, and strutted about among them and talked down to them like a Dutch uncle. Pretty good for an undergrad. of Old's, wasn't it?'

'Why do you say you can't know Lee without knowing Bellingham?'

'Because Bellingham is engaged to his sister Eveline. Such a bright little girl, Smith! I know the whole family well. It's disgusting to see that brute with her. A toad and a dove, that's what they always remind me of.'

Abercrombie Smith grinned and knocked his ashes out against the side of the grate.

'You show every card in your hand, old chap,' said he. 'What a prejudiced, green-eyed, evil-thinking old man it is! You have really nothing against the fellow except that.'

'Well, I've known her ever since she was as long as that cherry-wood pipe, and I don't like to see her taking risks. And it is a risk. He looks beastly. And he has a beastly temper, a venomous temper. You remember his row with Long Norton?'

'No; you always forget that I am a freshman.'

'Ah, it was last winter. Of course. Well, you know the towpath along by the river. There were several fellows going along it, Bellingham in front, when they came on an old market-woman coming the other way. It had been raining—you know what those fields are like when it has rained—and the path ran between the river and a great puddle that was nearly as broad. Well, what does this swine do but keep the path, and push the old girl into the mud, where she and her marketings came to terrible grief. It was a blackguard thing to do, and Long Norton, who is as gentle a fellow as ever stepped, told him what he thought of it. One word led to another, and it ended in Norton laying his stick across the fellow's shoulders. There was the deuce of a fuss about it, and it's a treat to see the way in which Bellingham looks at Norton when they meet now. By Jove, Smith, it's nearly eleven o'clock!'

'No hurry. Light your pipe again.'

'Not I. I'm supposed to be in training. Here I've been sitting gossiping when I ought to have been safely tucked up. I'll borrow your skull, if you can share it. Williams has had mine for a month. I'll take the little bones of your ear, too, if you are sure you won't need them. Thanks very much. Never mind a bag, I can carry them very well under my arm. Good night, my son, and take my tip as to your neighbour.'

When Hastie, bearing his anatomical plunder, had clattered off down the winding stair, Abercrombie Smith hurled his pipe into the wastepaper basket, and drawing his chair nearer to the lamp, plunged into a formidable, green-covered volume, adorned with great, coloured maps of that strange, internal kingdom of which we are the hapless and helpless monarchs. Though a freshman at Oxford, the student was not so in medicine, for he had worked for four years at Glasgow and at Berlin, and this coming examination would place him finally as a member of his profession. With his firm mouth, broad forehead, and clear-cut, somewhat hard-featured face, he was a man who, if he had no brilliant talent, was yet so dogged, so patient, and so strong that he might in the end overtop a more showy genius. A man who can hold his own among Scotchmen and North Germans is not a man to be easily set back. Smith had left a name at Glasgow and at Berlin, and he was bent now upon doing as much at Oxford, if hard work and devotion could accomplish it.

He had sat reading for about an hour, and the hands of the noisy carriage clock upon the side-table were rapidly closing together upon the twelve, when a sudden sound fell upon the student's ear—a sharp, rather shrill sound, like the hissing intake of a man's breath who gasps under some strong emotion. Smith laid down his book and slanted his ear to listen. There was no one on either side or above him, so that the interruption came certainly from the neighbour beneath—the same neighbour of whom Hastie had given so unsavoury an account. Smith knew him only as a flabby, pale-faced man of silent and studious habits, a man whose lamp threw a golden bar from the old turret even after he had extinguished his own. This community in lateness had formed a certain silent bond between them. It was soothing to Smith when the hours stole on towards dawning to feel that there was another so close who set as small a value upon his sleep as he did. Even now, as his thoughts turned towards him, Smith's feelings were kindly. Hastie was a good fellow, but he was rough, strong-fibred, with no imagination or sympathy. He could not tolerate departures from what he looked upon as the model type of manliness. If a man could not be measured by a public-school standard, then he was beyond the pale with Hastie. Like so many who are themselves robust, he was apt to confuse the constitution with the character, to ascribe to want of principle what was really a want of circulation. Smith, with his stronger mind, knew his friend's habit, and made allowance for it now as his thoughts turned towards the man beneath him.

There was no return of the singular sound, and Smith was about to turn to his work once more, when suddenly there broke out in the silence of the night a hoarse cry, a positive scream—the call of a man who is moved and shaken beyond all control. Smith sprang out of his chair and dropped his book. He was a man of fairly firm fibre, but there was something in this sudden, uncontrollable shriek of horror which chilled his blood and pringled in his skin. Coming in such a place and at such an hour, it brought a thousand fantastic possibilities into his head. Should he rush down, or was it better to wait? He had all the national hatred of making a scene, and he knew so little of his neighbour that he would not lightly intrude upon his affairs. For a moment he stood in doubt and even as he balanced the matter there was a quick rattle of footsteps upon the stairs, and young Monkhouse Lee, half-dressed and as white as ashes, burst into his room.

'Come down!' he gasped. 'Bellingham's ill.'

Abercrombie Smith followed him closely downstairs into the sitting-room which was beneath his own, and intent as he was upon the matter in hand, he could not but take an amazed glance around him as he crossed the threshold. It was such a chamber as he had never seen before—a museum rather than a study. Walls and ceiling were thickly covered with a thousand strange relics from Egypt and the East. Tall, angular figures bearing burdens or weapons stalked in an uncouth frieze round the apartments. Above were bull-headed, stork-headed, cat-headed, owl-headed statues, with viper-crowned, almond-eyed monarchs, and strange, beetle-like deities cut out of the blue Egyptian lapis lazuli. Horus and Isis and Osiris peeped down from every niche and shelf, while across the ceiling a true son of Old Nile, a great, hanging-jawed crocodile, was slung in a double noose.

In the centre of this singular chamber was a square table, littered with papers, bottles, and the dried leaves of some graceful, palm-like plant. These varied objects had all been heaped together in order to make room for a mummy case, which had been conveyed from the wall, as was evident from the gap there, and laid across the front of the table. The mummy itself, a horrid, black, withered thing, like a charred head on a gnarled bush, was lying half out of the case, with its claw-like hand and bony forearm resting upon the table. Propped up against the sarcophagus was an old, yellow scroll of papyrus, and in front of it, in a wooden armchair, sat the owner of the room, his head thrown back, his widely opened eyes directed in a horrified stare to the crocodile above him, and his blue, thick lips puffing loudly with every expiration.

'My God! he's dying!' cried Monkhouse Lee, distractedly.

He was a slim, handsome young fellow, olive-skinned and dark-eyed, of a Spanish rather than of an English type, with a Celtic intensity of manner which contrasted with the Saxon phlegm of Abercrombie Smith.

'Only a faint, I think,' said the medical student. 'Just give me a hand with him. You take his feet. Now on to the sofa. Can you kick all those little wooden devils off? What a litter it is! Now he will be all right if we undo his collar and give him some water. What has he been up to at all?'

'I don't know. I heard him cry out. I ran up. I know him pretty well, you know. It is very good of you to come down.'

'His heart is going like a pair of castanets,' said Smith, laying his hand on the breast of the unconscious man. 'He seems to me to be frightened all to pieces. Chuck the water over him! What a face he has got on him!'

It was indeed a strange and most repellent face, for colour and outline were equally unnatural. It was white, not with the ordinary pallor of fear, but with an absolutely bloodless white, like the under side of a sole. He was very fat, but gave the impression of having at some time been considerably fatter, for his skin hung loosely in creases and folds, and was shot with a meshwork of wrinkles. Short, stubbly brown hair bristled up from his scalp, with a pair of thick, wrinkled ears protruding at the sides. His light-grey eyes were still open, the pupils dilated and the balls projecting in a fixed and horrid stare. It seemed to Smith as he looked down upon him that he had never seen Nature's danger signals flying so plainly upon a man's countenance, and his thoughts turned more seriously to the warning which Hastie had given him an hour before.

'What the deuce can have frightened him so?' he asked.

'It's the mummy.'

'The mummy? How, then?'

'I don't know. It's beastly and morbid. I wish he would drop it. It's the second fright he has given me. It was the same last winter. I found him just like this, with that horrid thing in front of him.'

'What does he want with the mummy, then?'

'Oh, he's a crank, you know. It's his hobby. He knows more about these things than any man in England. But I wish he wouldn't. Ah, he's beginning to come to.'

A faint tinge of colour had begun to steal back into Bellingham's ghastly cheeks, and his eyelids shivered like a sail after a calm. He clasped and unclasped his hands, drew a long, thin breath between his teeth, and suddenly jerking up his head, threw a glance of recognition around him. As his eyes fell upon the mummy, he sprang off the sofa, seized the roll of papyrus, thrust it into a drawer, turned the key, and then staggered back on to the sofa.

'What's up?' he asked. 'What do you chaps want?'

'You've been shrieking out and making no end of a fuss,' said Monkhouse Lee. 'If our neighbour here from above hadn't come down, I'm sure I don't know what I should have done with you.'

'Ah, it's Abercrombie Smith,' said Bellingham, glancing up at him. 'How very good of you to come in! What a fool I am! Oh, my God, what a fool I am!'

He sank his head on to his hands, and burst into peal after peal of hysterical laughter.

'Look here! Drop it!' cried Smith, shaking him roughly by the shoulder.

'Your nerves are all in a jangle. You must drop these little midnight games with mummies, or you'll be going off your chump. You're all on wires now.'

'I wonder,' said Bellingham, 'whether you would be as cool as I am if you had seen——'

'What then?'

'Oh, nothing. I meant that I wonder if you could sit up at night with a mummy without trying your nerves. I have no doubt that you are quite right. I dare say that I have been taking it out of myself too much lately. But I am all right now. Please don't go, though. Just wait for a few minutes until I am quite myself.'

'The room is very close,' remarked Lee, throwing open the window and letting in the cool night air.

'It's balsamic resin,' said Bellingham. He lifted up one of the dried palmate leaves from the table and frizzled it over the chimney of the lamp. It broke away into heavy smoke wreaths, and a pungent, biting odour filled the chamber. 'It's the sacred plant—the plant of the priests,' he remarked. 'Do you know anything of Eastern languages, Smith?'

'Nothing at all. Not a word.'

The answer seemed to lift a weight from the Egyptologist's mind.

'By the way,' he continued, 'how long was it from the time that you ran down, until I came to my senses?'

'Not long. Some four or five minutes.'

'I thought it could not be very long,' said he, drawing a long breath. 'But what a strange thing unconsciousness is! There is no measurement to it. I could not tell from my own sensations if it were seconds or weeks. Now that gentleman on the table was packed up in the days of the eleventh dynasty, some forty centuries ago, and yet if he could find his tongue, he would tell us that this lapse of time has been but a closing of the eyes and a reopening of them. He is a singularly fine mummy, Smith.'

Smith stepped over to the table and looked down with a professional eye at the black and twisted form in front of him. The features, though horribly discoloured, were perfect, and two little nut-like eyes still lurked in the depths of the black, hollow sockets. The blotched skin was drawn tightly from bone to bone, and a tangled wrap of black, coarse hair fell over the ears. Two thin teeth, like those of a rat, overlay the shrivelled lower lip. In its crouching position, with bent joints and craned head, there was a suggestion of energy about the horrid thing which made Smith's gorge rise. The gaunt ribs, with their parchment-like covering, were exposed, and the sunken, leaden-hued abdomen, with the long slit where the embalmer had left his mark; but the lower limbs were wrapped round with coarse, yellow bandages. A number of little clove-like pieces of myrrh and of cassia were sprinkled over the body, and lay scattered on the inside of the case.

'I don't know his name,' said Bellingham, passing his hand over the shrivelled head. 'You see the outer sarcophagus with the inscriptions is missing. Lot 249 is all the title he has now. You see it printed on his case. That was his number in the auction at which I picked him up.'

'He has been a very pretty sort of fellow in his day,' remarked Abercrombie Smith.

'He has been a giant. His mummy is six feet seven in length, and that would be a giant over there, for they were never a very robust race. Feel these great, knotted bones, too. He would be a nasty fellow to tackle.'

'Perhaps these very hands helped to build the stones into the pyramids,' suggested Monkhouse Lee, looking down with disgust in his eyes at the crooked, unclean talons.

'No fear. This fellow has been pickled in natron, and looked after in the most approved style. They did not serve hodsmen in that fashion. Salt or bitumen was enough for them. It has been calculated that this sort of thing cost about seven hundred and thirty pounds in our money. Our friend was a noble at the least. What do you make of that small inscription near his feet, Smith?'

'I told you that I know no Eastern tongue.'

'Ah, so you did. It is the name of the embalmer, I take it. A very conscientious worker he must have been. I wonder how many modern works will survive four thousand years?'

He kept on speaking lightly and rapidly, but it was evident to Abercrombie Smith that he was still palpitating with fear. His hands shook, his lower lip trembled and look where he would, his eye always came sliding round to his gruesome companion. Through all his fear, however, there was a suspicion of triumph in his tone and manner. His eyes shone, and his footstep, as he paced the room, was brisk and jaunty. He gave the impression of a man who has gone through an ordeal, the marks of which he still bears upon him, but which has helped him to his end.

'You're not going yet?' he cried, as Smith rose from the sofa.

At the prospect of solitude, his fears seemed to crowd back upon him, and he stretched out a hand to detain him.

'Yes, I must go. I have my work to do. You are all right now. I think that with your nervous system you should take up some less morbid study.'

'Oh, I am not nervous as a rule; and I have unwrapped mummies before.'

'You fainted last time,' observed Monkhouse Lee.

'Ah, yes, so I did. Well, I must have a nerve tonic or a course of electricity. You are not going, Lee?'

'I'll do whatever you wish, Ned.'

'Then I'll come down with you and have a shakedown on your sofa. Good night, Smith. I am so sorry to have disturbed you with my foolishness.'

They shook hands, and as the medical student stumbled up the spiral and irregular stair he heard a key turn in a door, and the steps of his two new acquaintances as they descended to the lower floor.

In this strange way began the acquaintance between Edward Bellingham and Abercrombie Smith, an acquaintance which the latter, at least, had no desire to push further. Bellingham, however, appeared to have taken a fancy to his rough-spoken neighbour, and made his advances in such a way that he could hardly be repulsed without absolute brutality. Twice he called to thank Smith for his assistance, and many times afterwards he looked in with books, papers, and such other civilities as two bachelor neighbours can offer each other. He was, as Smith soon found, a man of wide reading, with catholic tastes and an extraordinary memory. His manner, too, was so pleasing and suave that one came, after a time, to overlook his repellent appearance. For a jaded and wearied man he was no unpleasant companion, and Smith found himself, after a time, looking forward to his visits, and even returning them.

Clever as he undoubtedly was, however, the medical student seemed to detect a dash of insanity in the man. He broke out at times into a high, inflated style of talk which was in contrast with the simplicity of his life.

'It is a wonderful thing,' he cried, 'to feel that one can command powers of good and of evil—a ministering angel or a demon of vengeance.' And again, of Monkhouse Lee, he said, 'Lee is a good fellow, an honest fellow, but he is without strength or ambition. He would not make a fit partner for a man with a great enterprise. He would not make a fit partner for me.'

At such hints and innuendoes stolid Smith, puffing solemnly at his pipe, would simply raise his eyebrows and shake his head, with little interjections of medical wisdom as to earlier hours and fresher air.

One habit Bellingham had developed of late which Smith knew to be a frequent herald of a weakening mind. He appeared to be for ever talking to himself. At late hours of the night, when there could be no visitor with him, Smith could still hear his voice beneath him in a low, muffled monologue, sunk almost to a whisper, and yet very audible in the silence. This solitary babbling annoyed and distracted the student, so that he spoke more than once to his neighbour about it. Bellingham, however, flushed up at the charge, and denied curtly that he had uttered a sound; indeed, he showed more annoyance over the matter than the occasion seemed to demand.

Had Abercrombie Smith had any doubt as to his own ears he had not to go far to find corroboration. Tom Styles, the little wrinkled man-servant who had attended to the wants of the lodgers in the turret for a longer time than any man's memory could carry him, was sorely put to it over the same matter.

'If you please, sir,' said he, as he tidied down the top chamber one morning, 'do you think Mr Bellingham is all right, sir?'

'All right, Styles?'

'Yes, sir. Right in his head, sir.'

'Why should he not be, then?'

'Well, I don't know, sir. His habits has changed of late. He's not the same man he used to be, though I make free to say that he was never quite one of my gentlemen, like Mr Hastie or yourself, sir. He's took to talkin' to himself something awful. I wonder it don't disturb you. I don't know what to make of him, sir.'

'I don't know what business it is of yours, Styles.'

'Well, I takes an interest, Mr Smith. It may be forward of me, but I can't help it. I feel sometimes as if I was mother and father to my young gentlemen. It all falls on me when things go wrong and the relations come. But Mr Bellingham, sir. I want to know what it is that walks about his room sometimes when he's out and when the door's locked on the outside.'

'Eh? you're talking nonsense, Styles.'

'Maybe so, sir; but I heard it more'n once with my own ears.'

'Rubbish, Styles.'

'Very good, sir. You'll ring the bell if you want me.'

Abercrombie Smith gave little heed to the gossip of the old man-servant, but a small incident occurred a few days later which left an unpleasant effect upon his mind, and brought the words of Styles forcibly to his memory.

Bellingham had come up to see him late one night, and was entertaining him with an interesting account of the rock tombs of Beni Hassan in Upper Egypt, when Smith, whose hearing was remarkably acute, distinctly heard the sound of a door opening on the landing below.

'There's some fellow gone in or out of your room,' he remarked.

Bellingham sprang up and stood helpless for a moment, with the expression of a man who is half-incredulous and half-afraid.

'I surely locked it. I am almost positive that I locked it,' he stammered. 'No one could have opened it.'

'Why, I hear someone coming up the steps now,' said Smith.

Bellingham rushed out through the door, slammed it loudly behind him, and hurried down the stairs. About halfway down Smith heard him stop, and thought he caught the sound of whispering. A moment later the door beneath him shut, a key creaked in a lock, and Bellingham, with beads of moisture upon his pale face, ascended the stairs once more, and re-entered the room.

'It's all right,' he said, throwing himself down in a chair. 'It was that fool of a dog. He had pushed the door open. I don't know how I came to forget to lock it.'

'I didn't know you kept a dog,' said Smith, looking very thoughtfully at the disturbed face of his companion.

'Yes, I haven't had him long. I must get rid of him. He's a great nuisance.'

'He must be, if you find it so hard to shut him up. I should have thought that shutting the door would have been enough, without locking it.'

'I want to prevent old Styles from letting him out. He's of some value, you know, and it would be awkward to lose him.'

'I am a bit of a dog-fancier myself,' said Smith, still gazing hard at his companion from the corner of his eyes. 'Perhaps you'll let me have a look at it.'

'Certainly. But I am afraid it cannot be tonight; I have an appointment. Is that clock right? Then I am a quarter of an hour late already. You'll excuse me, I am sure.'

He picked up his cap and hurried from the room. In spite of his appointment, Smith heard him re-enter his own chamber and lock his door upon the inside.

This interview left a disagreeable impression upon the medical student's mind. Bellingham had lied to him, and lied so clumsily that it looked as if he had desperate reasons for concealing the truth. Smith knew that his neighbour had no dog. He knew, also, that the step which he had heard upon the stairs was not the step of an animal. But if it were not, then what could it be? There was old Style's statement about the something which used to pace the room at times when the owner was absent. Could it be a woman? Smith rather inclined to the view. If so, it would mean disgrace and expulsion to Bellingham if it were discovered by the authorities, so that his anxiety and falsehoods might be accounted for. And yet it was inconceivable that an undergraduate could keep a woman in his rooms without being instantly detected. Be the explanation what it might, there was something ugly about it, and Smith determined, as he turned to his books, to discourage all her attempts at intimacy on the part of his soft spoken and ill-favoured neighbour.

But his work was destined to interruption that night. He had hardly caught up the broken threads when a firm, heavy footfall came three steps at a time from below, and Hastie, in blazer and flannels, burst into the room.

'Still at it!' said he, plumping down into his wonted armchair. 'What a chap you are to stew! I believe an earthquake might come and knock Oxford into a cocked hat, and you would sit perfectly placid with your books among the ruins. However, I won't bore you long. Three whiffs of baccy, and I am off.'

'What's the news, then?' asked Smith, cramming a plug of bird's-eye into his briar with his forefinger.

'Nothing very much. Wilson made 70 for the freshmen against the eleven. They say that they will play him instead of Buddicomb, for Buddicomb is clean off colour. He used to be able to bowl a little, but it's nothing but half-volleys and long hops now.'

'Medium right,' suggested Smith, with the intense gravity which comes upon a 'varsity man when he speaks of athletics.

'Inclining to fast, with a work from leg. Comes with the arm about three inches or so. He used to be nasty on a wet wicket. Oh, by the way, have you heard about Long Norton?'

'What's that?'

'He's been attacked.'

'Attacked?'

'Yes, just as he was turning out of the High Street, and within a hundred yards of the gate of Old's.'

'But who——'

'Ah, that's the rub! If you said "what", you would be more grammatical. Norton swears that it was not human, and, indeed, from the scratches on his throat, I should be inclined to agree with him.'

'What, then? Have we come down to spooks?'

Abercrombie Smith puffed his scientific contempt.

'Well, no; I don't think that is quite the idea, either. I am inclined to think that if any showman has lost a great ape lately, and the brute is in these parts, a jury would find a true bill against it. Norton passes that way every night, you know, about the same hour. There's a tree that hangs low over the path—the big elm from Rainy's garden. Norton thinks the thing dropped on him out of the tree. Anyhow, he was nearly strangled by two arms, which, he says, were as strong and as thin as steel bands. He saw nothing; only those beastly arms that tightened and tightened on him. He yelled his head nearly off, and a couple of chaps came running, and the thing went over the wall like a cat. He never got a fair sight of it the whole time. It gave Norton a shake up, I can tell you. I tell him it has been as good as a change at the seaside for him.'

'A garrotter, most likely,' said Smith.

'Very possibly. Norton says not; but we don't mind what he says. The garrotter had long nails, and was pretty smart at swinging himself over walls. By the way, your beautiful neighbour would be pleased if he heard about it. He had a grudge against Norton, and he's not a man, from what I know of him, to forget his little debts. But hallo, old chap, what have you got in your noddle?'

'Nothing,' Smith answered curtly.

He had started in his chair, and the look had flashed over his face which comes upon a man who is struck suddenly by some unpleasant idea.

'You looked as if something I had said had taken you on the raw. By the way, you have made the acquaintance of Master B. since I looked in last, have you not? Young Monkhouse Lee told me something to that effect.'

'Yes; I know him slightly. He has been up here once or twice.'

'Well, you're big enough and ugly enough to take care of yourself. He's not what I should call exactly a healthy sort of Johnny, though, no doubt, he's very clever, and all that. But you'll soon find out for yourself. Lee is all right; he's a very decent little fellow. Well, so long, old chap! I row Mullins for the Vice-Chancellor's pot on Wednesday week, so mind you come down, in case I don't see you before.'

Bovine Smith laid down his pipe and turned stolidly to his books once more. But with all the will in the world, he found it very hard to keep his mind upon his work. It would slip away to brood upon the man beneath him, and upon the little mystery which hung round his chambers. Then his thoughts turned to this singular attack of which Hastie had spoken, and to the grudge which Bellingham was said to owe the object of it. The two ideas would persist in rising together in his mind, as though there were some close and intimate connection between them. And yet the suspicion was so dim and vague that it could not be put down in words.

'Confound the chap!' cried Smith, as he shied his book on pathology across the room. 'He has spoiled my night's reading, and that's reason enough, if there were no other, why I should steer clear of him in the future.'

For ten days the medical student confined himself so closely to his studies that he neither saw nor heard anything of either of the men beneath him. At the hours when Bellingham had been accustomed to visit him, he took care to sport his oak, and though he more than once heard a knocking at his outer door, he resolutely refused to answer it. One afternoon, however, he was descending the stairs when, just as he was passing it, Bellingham's door flew open, and young Monkhouse Lee came out with his eyes sparkling and a dark flush of anger upon his olive cheeks. Close at his heels followed Bellingham, his fat, unhealthy face all quivering with malignant passion.

'You fool!' he hissed. 'You'll be sorry.'

'Very likely,' cried the other. 'Mind what I say. It's off! I won't hear of it!'

'You've promised, anyhow.'

'Oh, I'll keep that! I won't speak. But I'd rather little Eva was in her grave. Once for all, it's off. She'll do what I say. We don't want to see you again.'

So much Smith could not avoid hearing, but he hurried on, for he had no wish to be involved in their dispute. There had been a serious breach between them, that was clear enough, and Lee was going to cause the engagement with his sister to be broken off. Smith thought of Hastie's comparison of the toad and the dove, and was glad to think that the matter was at an end. Bellingham's face when he was in a passion was not pleasant to look upon. He was not a man to whom an innocent girl could be trusted for life. As he walked, Smith wondered languidly what could have caused the quarrel, and what the promise might be which Bellingham had been so anxious that Monkhouse Lee should keep.

It was the day of the sculling match between Hastie and Mullins, and a stream of men were making their way down to the banks of the Isis. A May sun was shining brightly, and the yellow path was barred with the black shadows of the tall elm-trees. On either side the grey colleges lay back from the road, the hoary old mothers of minds looking out from their high, mullioned windows at the tide of young life which swept so merrily past them. Black-clad tutors, prim officials, pale, reading men, brown-faced, straw-hatted young athletes in white sweaters or many-coloured blazers, all were hurrying towards the blue, winding river which curves through the Oxford meadows.

Abercrombie Smith, with the intuition of an old oarsman, chose his position at the point where he knew that the struggle, if there were a struggle, would come. Far off he heard the hum which announced the start, the gathering roar of the approach, the thunder of running feet, and the shouts of the men in the boats beneath him. A spray of half-clad, deep-breathing runners shot past him, and craning over their shoulders, he saw Hastie pulling a steady thirty-six, while his opponent, with a jerky forty, was a good boat's length behind him. Smith gave a cheer for his friend, and pulling out his watch, was starting off again for his chambers, when he felt a touch upon his shoulder, and found that young Monkhouse Lee was beside him.

'I saw you there,' he said, in a timid, deprecating way. 'I wanted to speak to you, if you could spare me a half-hour. This cottage is mine. I share it with Harrington of King's. Come in and have a cup of tea.'

'I must be back presently,' said Smith. 'I am hard on the grind at present. But I'll come in for a few minutes with pleasure. I wouldn't have come out only Hastie is a friend of mine.'

'So he is of mine. Hasn't he a beautiful style? Mullins wasn't in it. But come into the cottage. It's a little den of a place, but it is pleasant to work in during the summer months.'

It was a small, square, white building, with green doors and shutters, and a rustic trellis-work porch, standing back some fifty yards from the river's bank. Inside, the main room was roughly fitted up as a study—deal table, unpainted shelves with books, and a few cheap oleographs upon the wall. A kettle sang upon a spirit-stove, and there were tea things upon a tray on the table.

'Try that chair and have a cigarette,' said Lee. 'Let me pour you out a cup of tea. It's so good of you to come in, for I know that your time is a good deal taken up. I wanted to say to you that, if I were you, I should change my rooms at once.'

'Eh?'

Smith sat staring with a lighted match in one hand and his unlit cigarette in the other.

'Yes; it must seem very extraordinary, and the worst of it is that I cannot give my reasons, for I am under a solemn promise—a very solemn promise. But I may go so far as to say that I don't think Bellingham is a very safe man to live near. I intend to camp out here as much as I can for a time.'

'Not safe! What do you mean?'

'Ah, that's what I mustn't say. But do take my advice and move your rooms. We had a grand row today. You must have heard us, for you came down the stairs.'

'I saw that you had fallen out.'

'He's a horrible chap, Smith. That is the only word for him. I have had doubts about him ever since that night when he fainted—you remember, when you came down. I taxed him today, and he told me things that made my hair rise, and wanted me to stand in with him. I'm not straight-laced, but I am a clergyman's son, you know, and I think there are some things which are quite beyond the pale. I only thank God that I found him out before it was too late, for he was to have married into my family.'

'This is all very fine, Lee,' said Abercrombie Smith curtly. 'But either you are saying a great deal too much or a deal too little.'

'I give you a warning.'

'If there is real reason for warning, no promise can bind you. If I see a rascal about to blow a place up with dynamite no pledge will stand in my way of preventing him.'

'Ah, but I cannot prevent him, and I can do nothing but warn you.'

'Without saying what you warn me against.'

'Against Bellingham.'

'But that is childish. Why should I fear him, or any man?'

'I can't tell you. I can only entreat you to change your rooms. You are in danger where you are. I don't even say that Bellingham would wish to injure you. But it might happen, for he is a dangerous neighbour just now.'

'Perhaps I know more than you think,' said Smith, looking keenly at the young man's boyish, earnest face. 'Suppose I tell you that someone else shares Bellingham's rooms.'

Monkhouse Lee sprang from his chair in uncontrollable excitement.

'You know, then?' he gasped.

'A woman.'

Lee dropped back again with a groan.

'My lips are sealed,' he said. 'I must not speak.'

'Well, anyhow,' said Smith, rising, 'it is not likely that I should allow myself to be frightened out of rooms which suit me very nicely. It would be a little too feeble for me to move out all my goods and chattels because you say that Bellingham might in some unexplained way do me an injury. I think that I'll just take my chance, and stay where I am, and as I see that it's nearly five o'clock, I must ask you to excuse me.'

He bade the young student adieu in a few curt words, and made his way homeward through the sweet spring evening feeling half-ruffled, half-amused, as any other strong, unimaginative man might who has been menaced by a vague and shadowy danger.

There was one little indulgence which Abercrombie Smith always allowed himself, however closely his work might press upon him. Twice a week, on the Tuesday and the Friday, it was his invariable custom to walk over to Farlingford, the residence of Doctor Plumptree Peterson, situated about a mile and a half out of Oxford. Peterson had been a close friend of Smith's elder brother, Francis, and as he was a bachelor, fairly well-to-do, with a good cellar and a better library, his house was a pleasant goal for a man who was in need of a brisk walk. Twice a week, then, the medical student would swing out there along the dark country roads and spend a pleasant hour in Peterson's comfortable study, discussing, over a glass of old port, the gossip of the 'varsity or the latest developments of medicine or of surgery.

On the day which followed his interview with Monkhouse Lee, Smith shut up his books at a quarter past eight, the hour when he usually started for his friend's house. As he was leaving his room, however, his eyes chanced to fall upon one of the books which Bellingham had lent him, and his conscience pricked him for not having returned it. However repellent the man might be, he should not be treated with discourtesy. Taking the book, he walked downstairs and knocked at his neighbour's door. There was no answer; but on turning the handle he found that it was unlocked. Pleased at the thought of avoiding an interview, he stepped inside, and placed the book with his card upon the table.

The lamp was turned half down, but Smith could see the details of the room plainly enough. It was all much as he had seen it before—the frieze, the animal-headed gods, the hanging crocodile, and the table littered over with papers and dried leaves. The mummy case stood upright against the wall, but the mummy itself was missing. There was no sign of any second occupant of the room, and he felt as he withdrew that he had probably done Bellingham an injustice. Had he a guilty secret to preserve, he would hardly leave his door open so that all the world might enter.

The spiral stair was as black as pitch, and Smith was slowly making his way down its irregular steps, when he was suddenly conscious that something had passed him in the darkness. There was a faint sound, a whiff of air, a light brushing past his elbow, but so slight that he could scarcely be certain of it. He stopped and listened, but the wind was rustling among the ivy outside, and he could hear nothing else.

'Is that you, Styles?' he shouted.

There was no answer, and all was still behind him. It must have been a sudden gust of air, for there were crannies and cracks in the old turret. And yet he could almost have sworn that he heard a footfall by his very side. He had emerged into the quadrangle, still turning the matter over in his head, when a man came running swiftly across the smooth-cropped lawn.

'Is that you, Smith?'

'Hullo, Hastie!'

'For God's sake come at once! Young Lee is drowned! Here's Harrington of King's with the news. The doctor is out. You'll do, but come along at once. There may be life in him.'

'Have you brandy?'

'No.'

'I'll bring some. There's a flask on my table.'

Smith bounded up the stairs, taking three at a time, seized the flask, and was rushing down with it, when, as he passed Bellingham's room, his eyes fell upon something which left him gasping and staring upon the landing.

The door, which he had closed behind him, was now open, and right in front of him, with the lamp-light shining upon it, was the mummy case. Three minutes ago it had been empty. He could swear to that. Now it framed the lank body of its horrible occupant, who stood, grim and stark, with his black, shrivelled face towards the door. The form was lifeless and inert, but it seemed to Smith as he gazed that there still lingered a lurid spark of vitality, some faint sign of consciousness in the little eyes which lurked in the depths of the hollow sockets. So astounded and shaken was he that he had forgotten his errand, and was still staring at the lean, sunken figure when the voice of his friend below recalled him to himself.

'Come on, Smith!' he shouted. 'It's life and death, you know. Hurry up! Now, then,' he added, as the medical student reappeared, 'let us do a sprint. It is well under a mile, and we should do it in five minutes. A human life is better worth running for than a pot.'

Neck and neck they dashed through the darkness, and did not pull up until panting and spent, they had reached the little cottage by the river. Young Lee, limp and dripping like a broken water-plant, was stretched upon the sofa, the green scum of the river upon his black hair, and a fringe of white foam upon his leaden-hued lips. Beside him knelt his fellow-student, Harrington, endeavouring to chafe some warmth back into his rigid limbs.

'I think there's life in him,' said Smith, with his hand to the lad's side. 'Put your watch glass to his lips. Yes, there's dimming on it. You take one arm, Hastie. Now work it as I do, and we'll soon pull him round.'

For ten minutes they worked in silence, inflating and depressing the chest of the unconscious man. At the end of that time a shiver ran through his body, his lips trembled, and he opened his eyes. The three students burst out into an irrepressible cheer.

'Wake up, old chap. You've frightened us quite enough.'

'Have some brandy. Take a sip from the flask.'

'He's all right now,' said his companion Harrington. 'Heavens, what a fright I got! I was reading here, and he had gone out for a stroll as far as the river when I heard a scream and a splash. Out I ran, and by the time I could find him and fish him out, all life seemed to have gone. Then Simpson couldn't get a doctor, for he has a game-leg, and I had to run, and I don't know what I'd have done without you fellows. That's right, old chap. Sit up.'

Monkhouse Lee had raised himself on his hands, and looked wildly about him.

'What's up?' he asked. 'I've been in the water. Ah, yes; I remember.'

A look of fear came into his eyes, and he sank his face into his hands.

'How did you fall in?'

'I didn't fall in.'

'How then?'

'I was thrown in. I was standing by the bank, and something from behind picked me up like a feather and hurled me in. I heard nothing, and I saw nothing. But I know what it was, for all that.'

'And so do I,' whispered Smith.

Lee looked up with a quick glance of surprise.

'You've learned, then?' he said. 'You remember the advice I gave you?'

'Yes, and I begin to think that I shall take it.'

'I don't know what the deuce you fellows are talking about,' said Hastie, 'but I think, if I were you, Harrington, I should get Lee to bed at once. It will be time enough to discuss the why and the wherefore when he is a little stronger. I think, Smith, you and I can leave him alone now. I am walking back to college; if you are coming in that direction, we can have a chat.'

But it was little chat that they had upon their homeward path. Smith's mind was too full of the incidents of the evening, the absence of the mummy from his neighbour's rooms, the step that passed him on the stair, the reappearance—the extraordinary, inexplicable reappearance of the grisly thing—and then this attack upon Lee, corresponding so closely to the previous outrage upon another man against whom Bellingham bore a grudge. All this settled in his thoughts, together with the many little incidents which had previously turned him against his neighbour, and the singular circumstances under which he was first called in to him. What had been a dim suspicion, a vague, fantastic conjecture, had suddenly taken form, and stood out in his mind as a grim fact, a thing not to be denied. And yet, how monstrous it was! how unheard of! how entirely beyond all bounds of human experience. An impartial judge, or even the friend who walked by his side, would simply tell him that his eyes had deceived him, that the mummy had been there all the time, that young Lee had tumbled into the river as any other man tumbles into a river, and the blue pill was the best thing for a disordered liver. He felt that he would have said as much if the positions had been reversed. And yet he could swear that Bellingham was a murderer at heart, and that he wielded a weapon such as no man had ever used in all the grim history of crime.

Hastie had branched off to his rooms with a few crisp and emphatic comments upon his friend's unsociability, and Abercrombie Smith crossed the quadrangle to his corner turret with a strong feeling of repulsion for his chambers and their associations. He would take Lee's advice, and move his quarters as soon as possible, for how could a man study when his ear was ever straining for every murmur or footstep in the room below? He observed, as he crossed over the lawn, that the light was still shining in Bellingham's window, and as he passed up the staircase the door opened, and the man himself looked out at him. With his fat, evil face he was like some bloated spider fresh from the weaving of his poisonous web.

'Good evening,' said he. 'Won't you come in?'

'No,' cried Smith fiercely.

'No? You are as busy as ever? I wanted to ask you about Lee. I was sorry to hear that there was a rumour that something was amiss with him.'

His features were grave, but there was the gleam of a hidden laugh in his eyes as he spoke. Smith saw it, and he could have knocked him down for it.

'You'll be sorrier still to hear that Monkhouse Lee is doing very well, and is out of all danger,' he answered. 'Your hellish tricks have not come off this time. Oh, you needn't try to brazen it out. I know all about it.'

Bellingham took a step back from the angry student, and half-closed the door as if to protect himself.

'You are mad,' he said. 'What do you mean? Do you assert that I had anything to do with Lee's accident?'

'Yes,' thundered Smith. 'You and that bag of bones behind you; you worked it between you. I tell you what it is, Master B., they have given up burning folk like you, but we still keep a hangman, and, by George! if any man in this college meets his death while you are here, I'll have you up, and if you don't swing for it, it won't be my fault. You'll find that your filthy Egyptian tricks won't answer in England.'

'You're a raving lunatic,' said Bellingham.

'All right. You just remember what I say, for you'll find that I'll be better than my word.'

The door slammed, and Smith went fuming up to his chamber, where he locked the door upon the inside, and spent half the night in smoking his old briar and brooding over the strange events of the evening.

Next morning Abercrombie Smith heard nothing of his neighbour, but Harrington called upon him in the afternoon to say that Lee was almost himself again. All day Smith stuck fast to his work, but in the evening he determined to pay the visit to his friend Doctor Peterson upon which he had started the night before. A good walk and a friendly chat would be welcome to his jangled nerves.

Bellingham's door was shut as he passed, but glancing back when he was some distance from the turret, he saw his neighbour's head at the window outlined against the lamp-light, his face pressed apparently against the glass as he gazed out into the darkness. It was a blessing to be away from all contact with him, if but for a few hours, and Smith stepped out briskly, and breathed the soft spring air into his lungs. The half-moon lay in the west between two Gothic pinnacles, and threw upon the silvered street a dark tracery from the stonework above. There was a brisk breeze, and light, fleecy clouds drifted swiftly across the sky. Old's was on the very border of the town, and in five minutes Smith found himself beyond the houses and between the hedges of a May-scented, Oxfordshire lane.

It was a lonely and little-frequented road which led to his friend's house. Early as it was, Smith did not meet a single soul upon his way. He walked briskly along until he came to the avenue gate, which opened into the long, gravel drive leading up to Farlingford. In front of him he could see the cosy, red light of the windows glimmering through the foliage. He stood with his hand upon the iron latch of the swinging gate, and he glanced back at the road along which he had come. Something was coming swiftly down it.

It moved in the shadow of the hedge, silently and furtively, a dark, crouching figure, dimly visible against the black background. Even as he gazed back at it, it had lessened its distance by twenty paces, and was fast closing upon him. Out of the darkness he had a glimpse of a scraggy neck, and of two eyes that will ever haunt him in his dreams. He turned, and with a cry of terror he ran for his life up the avenue. There were the red lights, the signals of safety, almost within a stone's-throw of him. He was a famous runner, but never had he run as he ran that night.

The heavy gate had swung into place behind him but he heard it dash open again before his pursuer. As he rushed madly and wildly through the night, he could hear a swift, dry patter behind him, and could see, as he threw back a glance, that this horror was bounding like a tiger at his heels, with blazing eyes and one stringy arm out-thrown. Thank God, the door was ajar. He could see the thin bar of light which shot from the lamp in the hall. Nearer yet sounded the clatter from behind. He heard a hoarse gurgling at his very shoulder. With a shriek he flung himself against the door, slammed and bolted it behind him, and sank half-fainting on to the hall chair.

'My goodness, Smith, what's the matter?' asked Peterson, appearing at the door of his study.

'Give me some brandy.'

Peterson disappeared, and came rushing out again with a glass and a decanter.

'You need it,' he said, as his visitor drank off what he poured out for him. 'Why, man, you are as white as a cheese.'

Smith laid down his glass, rose up, and took a deep breath.

'I am my own man again now,' said he. 'I was never so unmanned before. But, with your leave, Peterson, I will sleep here tonight, for I don't think I could face that road again except by daylight. It's weak, I know, but I can't help it.'

Peterson looked at his visitor with a very questioning eye.

'Of course you shall sleep here if you wish. I'll tell Mrs Burney to make up the spare bed. Where are you off to now?'

'Come up with me to the window that overlooks the door. I want you to see what I have seen.'

They went up to the window of the upper hall whence they could look down upon the approach to the house. The drive and the fields on either side lay quiet and still, bathed in the peaceful moonlight.

'Well, really, Smith,' remarked Peterson, 'it is well that I know you to be an abstemious man. What in the world can have frightened you?'

'I'll tell you presently. But where can it have gone? Ah, now, look, look! See the curve of the road just beyond your gate.'

'Yes, I see; you needn't pinch my arm off. I saw someone pass. I should say a man, rather thin, apparently, and tall, very tall. But what of him? And what of yourself? You are still shaking like an aspen leaf.'

'I have been within hand-grip of the devil, that's all. But come down to your study, and I shall tell you the whole story.'

He did so. Under the cheery lamp-light with a glass of wine on the table beside him, and the portly form and florid face of his friend in front, he narrated, in their order, all the events, great and small, which had formed so singular a chain, from the night on which he had found Bellingham fainting in front of the mummy case until this horrid experience of an hour ago.

'There now,' he said as he concluded, 'that's the whole, black business. It is monstrous and incredible, but it is true.'

Doctor Plumptree Peterson sat for some time in silence with a very puzzled expression upon his face.

'I never heard of such a thing in my life, never!' he said at last. 'You have told me the facts. Now tell me your inferences.'

'You can draw your own.'

'But I should like to hear yours. You have thought over the matter, and I have not.'

'Well, it must be a little vague in detail, but the main points seem to me to be clear enough. This fellow Bellingham, in his Eastern studies, has got hold of some infernal secret by which a mummy—or possibly only this particular mummy—can be temporarily brought to life. He was trying this disgusting business on the night when he fainted. No doubt the sight of the creature moving had shaken his nerve, even though he had expected it. You remember that almost the first words he said were to call out upon himself as a fool. Well, he got more hardened afterwards, and carried the matter through without fainting. The vitality which he could put into it was evidently only a passing thing, for I have seen it continually in its case as dead as this table. He has some elaborate process, I fancy, by which he brings the thing to pass. Having done it, he naturally bethought him that he might use the creature as an agent. It has intelligence and it has strength. For some purpose he took Lee into his confidence; but Lee, like a decent Christian, would have nothing to do with such a business. Then they had a row, and Lee vowed that he would tell his sister of Bellingham's true character. Bellingham's game was to prevent him, and he nearly managed it, by setting this creature of his on his track. He had already tried its powers upon another man—Norton—towards whom he had a grudge. It is the merest chance that he has not two murders upon his soul. Then, when I taxed him with the matter, he had the strongest reasons for wishing to get me out of the way before I could convey my knowledge to anyone else. He got his chance when I went out, for he knew my habits and where I was bound for. I have had a narrow shave, Peterson, and it is mere luck you didn't find me on your doorstep in the morning. I'm not a nervous man as a rule, and I never thought to have the fear of death put upon me as it was tonight.'

'My dear boy, you take the matter too seriously,' said his companion. 'Your nerves are out of order with your work, and you make too much of it. How could such a thing as this stride about the streets of Oxford, even at night, without being seen?'

'It has been seen. There is quite a scare in the town about an escaped ape, as they imagine the creature to be. It is the talk of the place.'

'Well, it's a striking chain of events. And yet, my dear fellow, you must allow that each incident in itself is capable of a more natural explanation.'

'What! even my adventure of tonight?'

'Certainly. You come out with your nerves all unstrung, and your head full of this theory of yours. Some gaunt, half-famished tramp steals after you, and seeing you run, is emboldened to pursue you. Your fears and imagination do the rest.'

'It won't do, Peterson; it won't do.'

'And again, in the instance of your finding the mummy case empty, and then a few moments later with an occupant, you know that it was lamp-light, that the lamp was half turned down, and that you had no special reason to look hard at the case. It is quite possible that you may have overlooked the creature in the first instance.'

'No, no; it is out of the question.'

'And then Lee may have fallen into the river, and Norton been garrotted. It is certainly a formidable indictment that you have against Bellingham; but if you were to place it before a police magistrate, he would simply laugh in your face.'

'I know he would. That is why I mean to take the matter into my own hands.'

'Eh?'

'Yes; I feel that a public duty rests upon me, and, besides, I must do it for my own safety, unless I choose to allow myself to be hunted by this beast out of the college, and that would be a little too feeble. I have quite made up my mind what I shall do. And first of all, may I use your paper and pens for an hour?'

'Most certainly. You will find all that you want upon that side-table.'

Abercrombie Smith sat down before a sheet of foolscap, and for an hour, and then for a second hour his pen travelled swiftly over it. Page after page was finished and tossed aside while his friend leaned back in his armchair, looking across at him with patient curiosity. At last, with an exclamation of satisfaction, Smith sprang to his feet, gathered his papers up into order, and laid the last one upon Peterson's desk.

'Kindly sign this as a witness,' he said.

'A witness? Of what?'

'Of my signature, and of the date. The date is the most important. Why, Peterson, my life might hang upon it.'

'My dear Smith, you are talking wildly. Let me beg you to go to bed.'

'On the contrary, I never spoke so deliberately in my life. And I will promise to go to bed the moment you have signed it.'

'But what is it?'

'It is a statement of all that I have been telling you tonight. I wish you to witness it.'

'Certainly,' said Peterson, signing his name under that of his companion. 'There you are! But what is the idea?'

'You will kindly retain it, and produce it in case I am arrested.'

'Arrested? For what?'

'For murder. It is quite on the cards. I wish to be ready for every event. There is only one course open to me, and I am determined to take it.'

'For Heaven's sake, don't do anything rash!'

'Believe me, it would be far more rash to adopt any other course. I hope that we won't need to bother you, but it will ease my mind to know that you have this statement of my motives. And now I am ready to take your advice and to go to roost, for I want to be at my best in the morning.'

Abercrombie Smith was not an entirely pleasant man to have as an enemy. Slow and easy-tempered, he was formidable when driven to action. He brought to every purpose in life the same deliberate resoluteness which had distinguished him as a scientific student. He had laid his studies aside for a day, but he intended that the day should not be wasted. Not a word did he say to his host as to his plans, but by nine o'clock he was well on his way to Oxford.

In the High Street he stopped at Clifford's, the gun-maker's, and bought a heavy revolver, with a box of central-fire cartridges. Six of them he slipped into the chambers, and half-cocking the weapon, placed it in the pocket of his coat. He then made his way to Hastie's rooms, where the big oarsman was lounging over his breakfast, with the *Sporting Times* propped up against the coffee-pot.

'Hullo! What's up?' he asked. 'Have some coffee?'

'No, thank you. I want you to come with me, Hastie, and do what I ask you.'

'Certainly, my boy.'

'And bring a heavy stick with you.'

'Hullo!' Hastie stared. 'Here's a hunting crop that would fell an ox.'

'One other thing. You have a box of amputating knives. Give me the longest of them.'

'There you are. You seem to be fairly on the war trail. Anything else?'

'No; that will do.' Smith placed the knife inside his coat, and led the way to the quadrangle. 'We are neither of us chickens, Hastie,' said he. 'I think I can do this job alone, but I take you as a precaution. I am going to have a little talk with Bellingham. If I have only him to deal with, I won't, of course, need you. If I shout, however, up you come, and lam out with your whip as hard as you can lick. Do you understand?'

'All right. I'll come if I hear you bellow.'

'Stay here, then. I may be a little time, but don't budge until I come down.'

'I'm a fixture.'

Smith ascended the stairs, opened Bellingham's door, and stepped in. Bellingham was seated behind his table, writing. Beside him, among his litter of strange possessions, towered the mummy case, with its sale number 249 still stuck upon its front, and its hideous occupant stiff and stark within it. Smith looked very deliberately round him, closed the door, and then, stepping across to the fireplace, struck a match and set the fire alight. Bellingham sat staring, with amazement and rage upon his bloated face.

'Well, really now, you make yourself at home,' he gasped.

Smith sat himself deliberately down, placing his watch upon the table, drew out his pistol, cocked it, and laid it in his lap. Then he took the long amputating knife from his bosom, and threw it down in front of Bellingham.

'Now, then,' said he, 'just get to work and cut up that mummy.'

'Oh, is that it?' said Bellingham with a sneer.

'Yes, that is it. They tell me that the law can't touch you. But I have a law that will set matters straight. If in five minutes you have not set to work, I swear by the God who made me that I will put a bullet through your brain!'

'You would murder me?'

Bellingham had half-risen, and his face was the colour of putty.

'Yes.'

'And for what?'

'To stop your mischief. One minute has gone.'

'But what have I done?'

'I know and you know.'

'This is mere bullying.'

'Two minutes are gone.'

'But you must give reasons. You are a madman—a dangerous madman. Why should I destroy my own property? It is a valuable mummy.'

'You must cut it up, and you must burn it.'

'I will do no such thing.'

'Four minutes are gone.'

Smith took up the pistol and he looked towards Bellingham with an inexorable face. As the second-hand stole round, he raised his hand, and the finger twitched upon the trigger.

'There! there! I'll do it!' screamed Bellingham.

In frantic haste he caught up the knife and hacked at the figure of the mummy, ever glancing round to see the eye and the weapon of his terrible visitor bent upon him. The creature crackled and snapped under every stab of the keen blade. A thick, yellow dust rose up from it. Spices and dried essences rained down upon the floor. Suddenly, with a rending crack, its backbone snapped asunder, and it fell, a brown heap of sprawling limbs, upon the floor.

'Now into the fire!' said Smith.

The flames leaped and roared as the dried and tinder-like debris was piled upon it. The little room was like the stoke-hole of a steamer and the sweat ran down the faces of the two men; but still the one stooped and worked, while the other sat watching him with a set face. A thick, fat smoke oozed out from the fire, and a heavy smell of burned resin and singed hair filled the air. In a quarter of an hour a few charred and brittle sticks were all that was left of Lot No. 249.

'Perhaps that will satisfy you,' snarled Bellingham, with hate and fear in his little grey eyes as he glanced back at his tormentor.

'No; I must make a clean sweep of all your materials. We must have no more devil's tricks. In with all these leaves! They may have something to do with it.'

'And what now?' asked Bellingham, when the leaves also had been added to the blaze.

'Now the roll of papyrus which you had on the table that night. It is in that drawer, I think.'

'No, no,' shouted Bellingham. 'Don't burn that! Why, man, you don't know what you do. It is unique; it contains wisdom which is nowhere else to be found.'

'Out with it!'

'But look here, Smith, you can't really mean it. I'll share the knowledge with you. I'll teach you all that is in it. Or, stay, let me only copy it before you burn it!'

Smith stepped forward and turned the key in the drawer. Taking out the yellow, curled roll of paper, he threw it into the fire, and pressed it down with his heel. Bellingham screamed, and grabbed at it; but Smith pushed him back and stood over it until it was reduced to a formless, grey ash.

'Now, Master B.,' said he, 'I think I have pretty well drawn your teeth. You'll hear from me again, if you return to your old tricks. And now good morning, for I must go back to my studies.'

And such is the narrative of Abercrombie Smith as to the singular events which occurred in Old College, Oxford, in the spring of '84. As Bellingham left the university immediately afterwards, and was last heard of in the Soudan, there is no one who can contradict his statement. But the wisdom of men is small, and the ways of Nature are strange, and who shall put a bound to the dark things which may be found by those who seek for them?

The Los Amigos Fiasco

I USED TO BE THE LEADING PRACTITIONER OF LOS AMIGOS. Of course, every one has heard of the great electrical generating gear there. The town is widespread, and there are dozens of little townlets and villages all around, which receive their supply from the same centre, so that the works are on a very large scale. The Los Amigos folk say that they are the largest upon earth, but then we claim that for everything in Los Amigos except the gaol and the death-rate. Those are said to be the smallest.

Now, with so fine an electrical supply, it seemed to be a sinful waste of hemp that the Los Amigos criminals should perish in the old-fashioned manner. And then came the news of the electrocutions in the East, and how the results had not after all been so instantaneous as had been hoped. The Western engineers raised their eyebrows when they read of the puny shocks by which these men had perished, and they vowed in Los Amigos that when an irreclaimable came their way he should be dealt handsomely by, and have the run of all the big dynamos. There should be no reserve, said the engineers, but he should have all that they had got. And what the result of that would be none could predict, save that it must be absolutely blasting and deadly. Never before had a man been so charged with electricity as they would charge him. He was to be smitten by the essence of ten thunderbolts. Some prophesied combustion, and some disintegration and disappearance. They were waiting eagerly to settle the question by actual demonstration, and it was just at that moment that Duncan Warner came that way.

Warner had been wanted by the law, and by nobody else, for many years. Desperado, murderer, train robber, and road agent, he was a man beyond the pale of human pity. He had deserved a dozen deaths, and the Los Amigos folk grudged him so gaudy a one as that. He seemed to feel himself to be unworthy of it, for he made two frenzied attempts at escape. He was a powerful, muscular man, with a lion head, tangled black locks, and a sweeping beard which covered his broad chest. When he was tried, there was no finer head in all the crowded court. It's no new thing to find the best face looking from the dock. But his good looks could not balance his bad deeds. His advocate did all he knew, but the cards lay against him, and Duncan Warner was handed over to the mercy of the big Los Amigos dynamos.

I was there at the committee meeting when the matter was discussed. The town council had chosen four experts to look after the arrangements. Three of them were admirable. There was Joseph M'Connor, the very man who had designed the dynamos, and there was Joshua Westmacott, the chairman of the Los Amigos Electrical Supply Company, Limited. Then there was myself as the chief medical man, and lastly an old German of the name of Peter Stulpnagel. The Germans were a strong body at Los Amigos, and they all voted for their man. That was how he got on the committee. It was said that he had been a wonderful electrician at home, and he was eternally working with wires and insulators and Leyden jars; but, as he never seemed to get any further, or to have any results worth publishing, he came at last to be regarded as a harmless crank, who had made science his hobby. We three practical men smiled when we heard that he had been elected as our colleague, and at the meeting we fixed it all up very nicely among ourselves without much thought of the old fellow who sat with his ears scooped forward in his hands, for he was a trifle hard of hearing, taking no more part in the proceedings than the gentlemen of the press who scribbled their notes on the back benches.

We did not take long to settle it all. In New York a strength of some two thousand volts had been used, and death had not been instantaneous. Evidently their shock had been too weak. Los Amigos should not fall into that error. The charge should be six times greater, and therefore, of course, it would be six times more effective. Nothing could possibly be more logical. The whole concentrated force of the great dynamos should be employed on Duncan Warner.

So we three settled it, and had already risen to break up the meeting, when our silent companion opened his mouth for the first time.

'Gentlemen,' said he, 'you appear to me to show an extraordinary ignorance upon the subject of electricity. You have not mastered the first principles of its actions upon a human being.'

The committee was about to break into an angry reply to this brusque comment, but the chairman of the Electrical Company tapped his forehead to claim its indulgence for the crankiness of the speaker.

'Pray tell us, sir,' said he, with an ironical smile, 'what is there in our conclusions with which you find fault?'

'With your assumption that a large dose of electricity will merely increase the effect of a small dose. Do you not think it possible that it might have an entirely different result? Do you know anything, by actual experiment, of the effect of such powerful shocks?'

'We know it by analogy,' said the chairman pompously. 'All drugs increase their effect when they increase their dose; for example—for example——'

'Whisky,' said Joseph M'Connor.

'Quite so. Whisky. You see it there.'

Peter Stulpnagel smiled and shook his head.

'Your argument is not very good,' said he. 'When I used to take whisky, I used to find that one glass would excite me, but that six would send me to sleep, which is just the opposite. Now, suppose that electricity were to act in just the opposite way also, what then?'

We three practical men burst out laughing. We had known that our colleague was queer, but we never had thought that he would be as queer as this.

'What then?' repeated Peter Stulpnagel.

'We'll take our chances,' said the chairman.

'Pray consider,' said Peter, 'that workmen who have touched the wires, and who have received shocks of only a few hundred volts, have died instantly. The fact is well known. And yet when a much greater force was used upon a criminal at New York, the man struggled for some little time. Do you not clearly see that the smaller dose is the more deadly?'

'I think, gentlemen, that this discussion has been carried on quite long enough,' said the chairman, rising again. 'The point, I take it, has already been decided by the majority of the committee, and Duncan Warner shall be electrocuted on Tuesday by the full strength of the Los Amigos dynamos. Is it not so?'

'I agree,' said Joseph M'Connor.

'I agree,' said I.

'And I protest,' said Peter Stulpnagel.

'Then the motion is carried, and your protest will be duly entered in the minutes,' said the chairman, and so the sitting was dissolved.

The attendance at the electrocution was a very small one. We four members of the committee were, of course, present with the executioner, who was to act under their orders. The others were the United States Marshal, the governor of the gaol, the chaplain, and three members of the press. The room was a small, brick chamber, forming an out-house to the Central Electrical station. It had been used as a laundry, and had an oven and copper at one side, but no other furniture save a single chair for the condemned man. A metal plate for his feet was placed in front of it, to which ran a thick, insulated wire. Above, another wire depended from the ceiling, which could be connected with a small, metallic rod projecting from a cap which was to be placed upon his head. When this connection was established Duncan Warner's hour was come.

There was a solemn hush as we waited for the coming of the prisoner. The practical engineers looked a little pale, and fidgeted nervously with the wires. Even the hardened Marshal was ill at ease, for a mere hanging was one thing, and this blasting of flesh and blood a very different one. As to the pressmen, their faces were whiter than the sheets which lay before them. The only man who appeared to feel none of the influence of these preparations was the little German crank, who strolled from one to the other with a smile on his lips and mischief in his eyes. More than once he even went so far as to burst into a shout of laughter, until the chaplain sternly rebuked him for his ill-timed levity.

'How can you so far forget yourself, Mr Stulpnagel,' said he, 'as to jest in the presence of death?'

But the German was quite unabashed.

'If I were in the presence of death I should not jest,' said he, 'but since I am not I may do what I choose.'

This flippant reply was about to draw another and a sterner reproof from the chaplain, when the door was swung open and two warders entered leading Duncan Warner between them. He glanced round him with a set face, stepped resolutely forward, and seated himself upon the chair.

'Touch her off!' said he.

It was barbarous to keep him in suspense. The chaplain murmured a few words in his ear, the attendant placed the cap upon his head, and then, while we all held our breath, the wire and the metal were brought in contact.

'Great Scott!' shouted Duncan Warner.

He had bounded in his chair as the frightful shock crashed through his system. But he was not dead. On the contrary, his eyes gleamed far more brightly than they had done before. There was only one change, but it was a singular one. The black had passed from his hair and beard as the shadow passes from a landscape. They were both as white as snow. And yet there was no other sign of decay. His skin was smooth and plump and lustrous as a child's.

The Marshal looked at the committee with a reproachful eye.

'There seems to be some hitch here, gentlemen,' said he.

We three practical men looked at each other.

Peter Stulpnagel smiled pensively.

'I think that another one should do it,' said I.

Again the connection was made, and again Duncan Warner sprang in his chair and shouted, but, indeed, were it not that he still remained in the chair none of us would have recognised him. His hair and his beard had shredded off in an instant, and the room looked like a barber's shop on a Saturday night. There he sat, his eyes still shining, his skin radiant with the glow of perfect health, but with a scalp as bald as a Dutch cheese, and a chin without so much as a trace of down. He began to revolve one of his arms, slowly and doubtfully at first, but with more confidence as he went on.

'That jint,' said he, 'has puzzled half the doctors on the Pacific Slope. It's as good as new, and as limber as a hickory twig.'

'You are feeling pretty well?' asked the old German.

'Never better in my life,' said Duncan Warner cheerily.

The situation was a painful one. The Marshal glared at the committee. Peter Stulpnagel grinned and rubbed his hands. The engineers scratched their heads. The bald-headed prisoner revolved his arm and looked pleased.

'I think that one more shock——' began the chairman.

'No, sir,' said the Marshal; 'we've had foolery enough for one morning. We are here for an execution, and an execution we'll have.'

'What do you propose?'

'There's a hook handy upon the ceiling. Fetch a rope, and we'll soon set this matter straight.'

There was another awkward delay while the warders departed for the cord. Peter Stulpnagel bent over Duncan Warner, and whispered something in his ear. The desperado stared in surprise.

'You don't say?' he asked.

The German nodded.

'What! No ways?'

Peter shook his head, and the two began to laugh as though they shared some huge joke between them.

The rope was brought, and the Marshal himself slipped the noose over the criminal's neck. Then the two warders, the assistant, and he swung their victim into the air. For half an hour he hung—a dreadful sight—from the ceiling. Then in solemn silence they lowered him down, and one of the warders went out to order the shell to be brought round. But as he touched ground again what was our amazement when Duncan Warner put his hands up to his neck, loosened the noose, and took a long, deep breath.

'Paul Jefferson's sale is goin' well,' he remarked. 'I could see the crowd from up yonder,' and he nodded at the hook in the ceiling.

'Up with him again!' shouted the Marshal, 'we'll get the life out of him somehow.'

In an instant the victim was up at the hook once more.

They kept him there for an hour, but when he came down he was perfectly garrulous.

'Old man Plunket goes too much to the Arcady Saloon,' said he. 'Three times he's been there in an hour; and him with a family. Old man Plunket would do well to swear off.'

It was monstrous and incredible, but there it was. There was no getting round it. The man was there talking when he ought to have been dead. We all sat staring in amazement, but United States Marshal Carpenter was not a man to be euchred so easily. He motioned the others to one side, so that the prisoner was left standing alone.

'Duncan Warner,' said he slowly, 'you are here to play your part, and I am here to play mine. Your game is to live if you can, and my game is to carry out the sentence of the law. You've beat us on electricity. I'll give you one there. And you've beat us on hanging, for you seem to thrive on it. But it's my turn to beat you now, for my duty has to be done.'

He pulled a six-shooter from his coat as he spoke, and fired all the shots through the body of the prisoner. The room was so filled with smoke that we could see nothing, but when it cleared the prisoner was still standing there, looking down in disgust at the front of his coat.

'Coats must be cheap where you come from,' said he. 'Thirty dollars it cost me, and look at it now. The six holes in front are bad enough, but four of the balls have passed out, and a pretty fine state the back must be in.'

The Marshal's revolver fell from his hand, and he dropped his arms to his sides, a beaten man.

'Maybe some of you gentlemen can tell me what this means,' said he, looking helplessly at the committee.

Peter Stulpnagel took a step forward.

'I'll tell you all about it,' said he.

'You seem to be the only person who knows anything.'

'I *am* the only person who knows anything. I should have warned these gentlemen; but, as they would not listen to me, I have allowed them to learn by experience. What you have done with your electricity is that you have increased the man's vitality until he can defy death for centuries.'

'Centuries!'

'Yes, it will take the wear of hundreds of years to exhaust the enormous nervous energy with which you have drenched him. Electricity is life, and you have charged him with it to the utmost. Perhaps in fifty years you might execute him, but I am not sanguine about it.'

'Great Scott! What shall I do with him?' cried the unhappy Marshal.

Peter Stulpnagel shrugged his shoulders.

'It seems to me that it does not much matter what you do with him now,' said he.

'Maybe we could drain the electricity out of him again. Suppose we hang him up by the heels?'

'No, no, it's out of the question.'

'Well, well, he shall do no more mischief in Los Amigos, anyhow,' said the Marshal, with decision. 'He shall go into the new gaol. The prison will wear him out.'

'On the contrary,' said Peter Stulpnagel, 'I think that it is much more probable that he will wear out the prison.'

It was rather a fiasco, and for years we didn't talk more about it than we could help, but it's no secret now, and I thought you might like to jot down the facts in your case-book.

The Case of Lady Sannox

T HE RELATIONS BETWEEN DOUGLAS STONE and the notorious Lady Sannox were very well known both among the fashionable circles of which she was a brilliant member, and the scientific bodies which numbered him among their most illustrious *confrères*. There was naturally, therefore, a very widespread interest when it was announced one morning that the lady had absolutely and for ever taken the veil, and that the world would see her no more. When, at the very tail of this rumour, there came the assurance that the celebrated operating surgeon, the man of steel nerves, had been found in the morning by his valet, seated on one side of his bed, smiling pleasantly upon the universe, with both legs jammed into one side of his breeches and his great brain about as valuable as a cap full of porridge, the matter was strong enough to give quite a little thrill of interest to folk who had never hoped that their jaded nerves were capable of such a sensation.

Douglas Stone in his prime was one of the most remarkable men in England. Indeed, he could hardly be said to have ever reached his prime, for he was but nine-and-thirty at the time of this little incident. Those who knew him best were aware that famous as he was as a surgeon, he might have succeeded with even greater rapidity in any of a dozen lines of life. He could have cut his way to fame as a soldier, struggled to it as an explorer, bullied for it in the courts, or built it out of stone and iron as an engineer. He was born to be great, for he could plan what another man dare not do, and he could do what another man dare not plan. In surgery none could follow him. His nerve, his judgment, his intuition, were things apart. Again and again his knife cut away death, but grazed the very springs of life in doing it, until his assistants were as white as the patient. His energy, his audacity, his full-blooded self-confidence—does not the memory of them still linger to the south of Marylebone Road and the north of Oxford Street?

His vices were as magnificent as his virtues, and infinitely more picturesque. Large as was his income, and it was the third largest of all professional men in London, it was far beneath the luxury of his living. Deep in his complex nature lay a rich vein of sensualism, at the sport of which he placed all the prizes of his life. The eye, the ear, the touch, the palate, all were his masters. The bouquet of old vintages, the scent of rare exotics, the curves and tints of the daintiest potteries of Europe, it was to these that the quick-running stream of gold was transformed. And then there came his sudden mad passion for Lady Sannox, when a single interview with two challenging glances and a whispered word set him ablaze. She was the loveliest woman in London and the only one to him. He was one of the handsomest men in London, but not the only one to her. She had a liking for new experiences, and was gracious to most men who wooed her. It may have been cause or it may have been effect that Lord Sannox looked fifty, though he was but six-and-thirty.

He was a quiet, silent, neutral-tinted man, this lord, with thin lips and heavy eyelids, much given to gardening and full of home-like habits. He had at one time been fond of acting, had even rented a theatre in London, and on its boards had first seen Miss Marion Dawson, to whom he had offered his hand, his title, and the third of a county. Since his marriage this early hobby had become distasteful to him. Even in private theatricals it was no longer possible to persuade him to exercise the talent which he had often shown that he possessed. He was happier with a spud and a watering-can among his orchids and chrysanthemums.

It was quite an interesting problem whether he was absolutely devoid of sense, or miserably wanting in spirit. Did he know his lady's ways and condone them, or was he a mere blind, doting fool? It was a point to be discussed over the teacups in snug little drawing-rooms, or with the aid of a cigar in the bow windows of clubs. Bitter and plain were the comments among men upon his conduct. There was but one who had a good word to say for him, and he was the most silent member in the smoking-room. He had seen him break in a horse at the University, and it seemed to have left an impression upon his mind.

But when Douglas Stone became the favourite all doubts as to Lord Sannox's knowledge or ignorance were set for ever at rest. There was no subterfuge about Stone. In his high-handed, impetuous fashion, he set all caution and discretion at defiance. The scandal became notorious. A learned body intimated that his name had been struck from the list of its vice-presidents. Two friends implored him to consider his professional credit. He cursed them all three, and spent forty guineas on a bangle to take with him to the lady. He was at her house every evening, and she drove in his carriage in the afternoons. There was not an attempt on either side to conceal their relations; but there came at last a little incident to interrupt them.

It was a dismal winter's night, very cold and gusty, with the wind whooping in the chimneys and blustering against the window-panes. A thin spatter of rain tinkled on the glass with each fresh sough of the gale, drowning for the instant the dull gurgle and drip from the eaves. Douglas Stone had finished his dinner, and sat by his fire in the study, a glass of rich port upon the malachite table at his elbow. As he raised it to his lips, he held it up against the lamplight, and watched with the eye of a connoisseur the tiny scales of beeswing which floated in its rich ruby depths. The fire, as it spurted up, threw fitful lights upon his bold, clear-cut face with its widely opened grey eyes, its thick and yet firm lips, and the deep, square jaw, which had something Roman in its strength and its animalism. He smiled from time to time as he nestled back in his luxurious chair. Indeed, he had a right to feel well pleased, for, against the advice of six colleagues, he had performed an operation that day of which only two cases were on record, and the result had been brilliant beyond all expectation. No other man in London would have had the daring to plan, or the skill to execute, such a heroic measure.

But he had promised Lady Sannox to see her that evening and it was already half-past eight. His hand was outstretched to the bell to order the carriage when he heard the dull thud of the knocker. An instant later there was the shuffling of feet in the hall, and the sharp closing of a door.

'A patient to see you, sir, in the consulting-room,' said the butler.

'About himself?'

'No, sir; I think he wants you to go out.'

'It is too late,' cried Douglas Stone peevishly. 'I won't go.'

'This is his card, sir.'

The butler presented it upon the gold salver which had been given to his master by the wife of a Prime Minister.

'"Hamil Ali, Smyrna." Hum! The fellow is a Turk, I suppose.'

'Yes, sir. He seems as if he came from abroad, sir. And he's in a terrible way.'

'Tut, tut! I have an engagement. I must go somewhere else. But I'll see him. Show him in here, Pim.'

A few moments later the butler swung open the door and ushered in a small and decrepit man, who walked with a bent back and with the forward push of the face and blink of the eyes which goes with extreme short sight. His face was swarthy, and his hair and beard of the deepest black. In one hand he held a turban of white muslin striped with red, in the other a small chamois leather bag.

'Good evening,' said Douglas Stone, when the butler had closed the door. 'You speak English, I presume?'

'Yes, sir. I am from Asia Minor, but I speak English when I speak slow.'

'You wanted me to go out, I understand?'

'Yes, sir. I wanted very much that you should see my wife.'

'I could come in the morning, but I have an engagement which prevents me from seeing your wife tonight.'

The Turk's answer was a singular one. He pulled the string which closed the mouth of the chamois leather bag, and poured a flood of gold on to the table.

'There are one hundred pounds there,' said he, 'and I promise you that it will not take you an hour. I have a cab ready at the door.'

Douglas Stone glanced at his watch. An hour would not make it too late to visit Lady Sannox. He had been there later. And the fee was an extraordinarily high one. He had been pressed by his creditors lately, and he could not afford to let such a chance pass. He would go.

'What is the case?' he asked.

'Oh, it is so sad a one! So sad a one! You have not, perhaps, heard of the daggers of the Almohades?'

'Never.'

'Ah, they are Eastern daggers of a great age and of a singular shape, with the hilt like what you call a stirrup. I am a curiosity dealer, you understand, and that is why I have come to England from Smyrna, but next week I go back once more. Many things I brought with me, and I have a few things left, but among them, to my sorrow, is one of these daggers.'

'You will remember that I have an appointment, sir,' said the surgeon, with some irritation; 'pray confine yourself to the necessary details.'

'You will see that it is necessary. Today my wife fell down in a faint in the room in which I keep my wares, and she cut her lower lip upon this cursed dagger of Almohades.'

'I see,' said Douglas Stone, rising. 'And you wish me to dress the wound?'

'No, no, it is worse than that.'

'What then?'

'These daggers are poisoned.'

'Poisoned!'

'Yes, and there is no man, East or West, who can tell now what is the poison or what the cure. But all that is known I know, for my father was in this trade before me, and we have had much to do with these poisoned weapons.'

'What are the symptoms?'

'Deep sleep, and death in thirty-hours.'

'And you say there is no cure. Why then should you pay me this considerable fee?'

'No drug can cure, but the knife may.'

'And how?'

'The poison is slow of absorption. It remains for hours in the wound.'

'Washing, then, might cleanse it?'

'No more than in a snake bite. It is too subtle and too deadly.'

'Excision of the wound, then?'

'That is it. If it be on the finger, take the finger off. So said my father always. But think of where this wound is, and that it is my wife. It is dreadful!'

But familiarity with such grim matters may take the finer edge from a man's sympathy. To Douglas Stone this was already an interesting case, and he brushed aside as irrelevant the feeble objections of the husband.

'It appears to be that or nothing,' said he brusquely. 'It is better to lose a lip than a life.'

'Ah, yes, I know that you are right. Well, well, it is kismet, and it must be faced. I have the cab, and you will come with me and do this thing.'

Douglas Stone took his case of bistouries from a drawer, and placed it with a roll of bandage and a compress of lint in his pocket. He must waste no more time if he were to see Lady Sannox.

'I am ready,' said he, pulling on his overcoat. 'Will you take a glass of wine before you go out into this cold air?'

His visitor shrank away, with a protesting hand upraised.

'You forget that I am a Mussulman, and a true follower of the Prophet,' said he. 'But tell me what is the bottle of green glass which you have placed in your pocket?'

'It is chloroform.'

'Ah, that also is forbidden to us. It is a spirit, and we make no use of such things.'

'What! You would allow your wife to go through an operation without an anaesthetic?'

'Ah! she will feel nothing, poor soul. The deep sleep has already come on, which is the first working of the poison. And then I have given her of our Smyrna opium. Come, sir, for already an hour has passed.'

As they stepped out into the darkness, a sheet of rain was driven in upon their faces, and the hall lamp, which dangled from the arm of a marble Caryatid, went out with a fluff. Pim, the butler, pushed the heavy door to, straining hard with his shoulder against the wind, while the two men groped their way towards the yellow glare which showed where the cab was waiting. An instant later they were rattling upon their journey.

'Is it far?' asked Douglas Stone.

'Oh, no. We have a very little quiet place off the Euston Road.'

The surgeon pressed the spring of his repeater and listened to the little tings which told him the hour. It was a quarter past nine. He calculated the distances, and the short time which it would take him to perform so trivial an operation. He ought to reach Lady Sannox by ten o'clock. Through the fogged windows he saw the blurred gas lamps dancing past, with occasionally the broader glare of a shop front. The rain was pelting and rattling upon the leathern top of the carriage, and the wheels swashed as they rolled through puddle and mud. Opposite to him the white headgear of his companion gleamed faintly through the obscurity. The surgeon felt in his pockets and arranged his needles, his ligatures, and his safety-pins, that no time might be wasted when they arrived. He chafed with impatience and drummed his foot upon the floor.

But the cab slowed down at last and pulled up. In an instant Douglas Stone was out, and the Smyrna merchant's toe was at his very heel.

'You can wait,' said he to the driver.

It was a mean-looking house in a narrow and sordid street. The surgeon, who knew his London well, cast a swift glance into the shadows, but there was nothing distinctive—no shop, no movement, nothing but a double line of dull, flat-faced houses, a double stretch of wet flagstones which gleamed in the lamplight, and a double rush of water in the gutters which swirled and gurgled towards the sewer gratings. The door which faced them was blotched and discoloured, and a faint light in the fan pane above it served to show the dust and the grime which covered it. Above, in one of the bedroom windows, there was a dull yellow glimmer. The merchant knocked loudly, and, as he turned his dark face towards the light, Douglas Stone could see that it was contracted with anxiety. A bolt was drawn, and an elderly woman with a taper stood in the doorway, shielding the thin flame with her gnarled hand.

'Is all well?' gasped the merchant.

'She is as you left her, sir.'

'She has not spoken?'

'No, she is in a deep sleep.'

The merchant closed the door, and Douglas Stone walked down the narrow passage, glancing about him in some surprise as he did so. There was no oil-cloth, no mat, no hat-rack. Deep grey dust and heavy festoons of cobwebs met his eyes everywhere. Following the old woman up the winding stair, his firm footfall echoed harshly through the silent house. There was no carpet.

The bedroom was on the second landing. Douglas Stone followed the old nurse into it, with the merchant at his heels. Here, at least, there was furniture and to spare. The floor was littered and the corners piled with Turkish cabinets, inlaid tables, coats of chain mail, strange pipes, and grotesque weapons. A single small lamp stood upon a bracket on the wall. Douglas Stone took it down, and picking his way among the lumber, walked over to a couch in the corner, on which lay a woman dressed in the Turkish fashion, with yashmak and veil. The lower part of the face was exposed, and the surgeon saw a jagged cut which zigzagged along the border of the under lip.

'You will forgive the yashmak,' said the Turk. 'You know our views about woman in the East.'

But the surgeon was not thinking about the yashmak. This was no longer a woman to him. It was a case. He stooped and examined the wound carefully.

'There are no signs of irritation,' said he. 'We might delay the operation until local symptoms develop.'

The husband wrung his hands in uncontrollable agitation.

'Oh! sir, sir,' he cried. 'Do not trifle. You do not know. It is deadly. I know, and I give you my assurance that an operation is absolutely necessary. Only the knife can save her.'

'And yet I am inclined to wait,' said Douglas Stone.

'That is enough,' the Turk cried, angrily. 'Every minute is of importance, and I cannot stand here and see my wife allowed to sink. It only remains for me to give you my thanks for having come, and to call in some other surgeon before it is too late.'

Douglas Stone hesitated. To refund that hundred pounds was no pleasant matter. But of course if he left the case he must return the money. And if the Turk were right and the woman died, his position before a coroner might be an embarrassing one.

'You have had personal experience of this poison?' he asked.

'I have.'

'And you assure me that an operation is needful.'

'I swear it by all that I hold sacred.'

'The disfigurement will be frightful.'

'I can understand that the mouth will not be a pretty one to kiss.'

Douglas Stone turned fiercely upon the man. The speech was a brutal one. But the Turk has his own fashion of talk and of thought, and there was no time for wrangling. Douglas Stone drew a bistoury from his case, opened it, and felt the keen straight edge with his forefinger. Then he held the lamp closer to the bed. Two dark eyes were gazing up at him through the slit in the yashmak. They were all iris, and the pupil was hardly to be seen.

'You have given her a very heavy dose of opium.'

'Yes, she has had a good dose.'

He glanced again at the dark eyes which looked straight at his own. They were dull and lustreless, but, even as he gazed, a little shifting sparkle came into them, and the lips quivered.

'She is not absolutely unconscious,' said he.

'Would it not be well to use the knife while it will be painless?'

The same thought had crossed the surgeon's mind. He grasped the wounded lip with his forceps, and with two swift cuts he took out a broad V-shaped piece. The woman sprang up on the couch with a dreadful gurgling scream. Her covering was torn from her face. It was a face that he knew. In spite of that protruding upper lip and that slobber of blood, it was a face that he knew. She kept on putting her hand up to the gap and screaming. Douglas Stone sat down at the foot of the couch with his knife and his forceps. The room was whirling round, and he had felt something go like a ripping seam behind his ear. A bystander would have said, that his face was the more ghastly of the two. As in a dream, or as if he had been looking at something at the play, he was conscious that the Turk's hair and beard lay upon the table, and that Lord Sannox was leaning against the wall with his hand to his side, laughing silently. The screams had died away now, and the dreadful head had dropped back again upon the pillow, but Douglas Stone still sat motionless, and Lord Sannox still chuckled quietly to himself.

'It was really very necessary for Marion, this operation,' said he 'not physically, but morally, you know, morally.'

Douglas Stone stooped forwards and began to play with the fringe of the coverlet. His knife tinkled down upon the ground, but he still held the forceps and something more.

'I had long intended to make a little example,' said Lord Sannox, suavely.

'Your note of Wednesday miscarried, and I have it here in my pocket-book. I took some pains in carrying out my idea. The wound, by the way, was from nothing more dangerous than my signet ring.'

He glanced keenly at his silent companion, and cocked the small revolver which he held in his coat pocket. But Douglas Stone was still picking at the coverlet.

'You see you have kept your appointment after all,' said Lord Sannox.

And at that Douglas Stone began to laugh. He laughed long and loudly. But Lord Sannox did not laugh now. Something like fear sharpened and hardened his features. He walked from the room, and he walked on tiptoe. The old woman was waiting outside.

'Attend to your mistress when she awakes,' said Lord Sannox.

Then he went down to the street. The cab was at the door, and the driver raised his hand to his hat.

'John,' said Lord Sannox, 'you will take the doctor home first. He will want leading downstairs, I think. Tell his butler that he has been taken ill at a case.'

'Very good, sir.'

'Then you can take Lady Sannox home.'

'And how about yourself, sir?'

'Oh, my address for the next few months will be Hotel di Roma, Venice. Just see that the letters are sent on. And tell Stevens to exhibit all the purple chrysanthemums next Monday, and to wire me the result.'

The Lord of Château Noir

IT WAS IN THE DAYS WHEN THE GERMAN ARMIES had broken their way across France, and when the shattered forces of the young Republic had been swept away to the north of the Aisne and to the south of the Loire. Three broad streams of armed men had rolled slowly but irresistibly from the Rhine, now meandering to the north, now to the south, dividing, coalescing, but all uniting to form one great lake round Paris. And from this lake there welled out smaller streams, one to the north, one southward to Orleans, and a third westward to Normandy. Many a German trooper saw the sea for the first time when he rode his horse girth-deep into the waves at Dieppe.

Black and bitter were the thoughts of Frenchmen when they saw this weal of dishonour slashed across the fair face of their country. They had fought and they had been overborne. That swarming cavalry, those countless footmen, the masterful guns—they had tried and tried to make head against them. In battalions their invaders were not to be beaten; but man to man, or ten to ten, they were their equals. A brave Frenchman might still make a single German rue the day that he had left his own bank of the Rhine. Thus, unchronicled amid the battles and the sieges, there broke out another war, a war of individuals, with foul murder upon the one side and brutal reprisal on the other.

Colonel von Gramm, of the 24th Posen Infantry, had suffered severely during this new development. He commanded in the little Norman town of Les Andelys, and his outposts stretched amid the hamlets and farm-houses of the district round. No French force was within fifty miles of him, and yet morning after morning he had to listen to a black report of sentries found dead at their posts, or of foraging parties which had never returned. Then the Colonel would go forth in his wrath, and farmsteadings would blaze and villages tremble; but next morning there was still that same dismal tale to be told. Do what he might, he could not shake off his invisible enemies. And yet, it should not have been so hard, for from certain signs in common, in the plan and in the deed, it was certain that all these outrages came from a single source.

Colonel von Gramm had tried violence and it had failed. Gold might be more successful. He published it abroad over the countryside that five hundred francs would be paid for information. There was no response. Then eight hundred. The peasants were incorruptible. Then, goaded on by a murdered corporal, he rose to a thousand, and so bought the soul of François Rejane, farm labourer, whose Norman avarice was a stronger passion than his French hatred.

'You say that you know who did these crimes?' asked the Prussian Colonel, eyeing with loathing the blue-bloused, rat-faced creature before him.

'Yes, Colonel.'

'And it was——?'

'Those thousand francs, Colonel——'

'Not a sou until your story has been tested. Come! Who is it who has murdered my men?'

'It is Count Eustace of Château Noir.'

'You lie!' cried the Colonel, angrily. 'A gentleman and a nobleman could not have done such crimes.'

The peasant shrugged his shoulders.

'It is evident to me that you do not know the Count. It is this way, Colonel. What I tell you is the truth, and I am not afraid that you should test it. The Count of Château Noir is a hard man: even at the best time he was a hard man. But of late he has been terrible. It was his son's death, you know. His son was under Douay, and he was taken, and then in escaping from Germany he met his death. It was the Count's only child, and indeed we all think that it has driven him mad. With his peasants he follows the German armies. I do not know how many he has killed, but it is he who cuts the cross upon the foreheads, for it is the badge of his house.'

It was true. The murdered sentries had each had a saltire cross slashed across their brows, as by a hunting-knife. The Colonel bent his stiff back and ran his forefinger over the map which lay upon the table.

'The Château Noir is not more than four leagues,' he said.

'Three and a kilometre, Colonel.'

'You know the place?'

'I used to work there.'

Colonel von Gramm rang the bell.

'Give this man food and detain him,' said he to the sergeant.

'Why detain me, Colonel? I can tell you no more.'

'We shall need you as guide.'

'As guide! But the Count? If I were to fall into his hands? Ah, Colonel——'

The Prussian commander waved him away.

'Send Captain Baumgarten to me at once,' said he.

The officer who answered the summons was a man of middle age, heavy-jawed, blue-eyed, with a curving yellow moustache and a brick-red face which turned to an ivory white where his helmet had sheltered it. He was bald, with a shining, tightly-stretched scalp, at the back of which, as in a mirror, it was a favourite mess-joke of the subalterns to trim their moustaches. As a soldier he was slow, but reliable and brave. The Colonel could trust him where a more dashing officer might be in danger.

'You will proceed to Château Noir tonight, Captain,' said he. 'A guide has been provided. You will arrest the Count and bring him back. If there is an attempt at rescue, shoot him at once.'

'How many men shall I take, Colonel?'

'Well, we are surrounded by spies, and our only chance is to pounce upon him before he knows that we are on the way. A large force will attract attention. On the other hand, you must not risk being cut off.'

'I might march north, Colonel, as if to join General Goeben. Then I could turn down this road which I see upon your map, and get to Château Noir before they could hear of us. In that case, with twenty men——'

'Very good, Captain. I hope to see you with your prisoner tomorrow morning.'

It was a cold December night when Captain Baumgarten marched out of Les Andelys with his twenty Poseners, and took the main road to the north-west. Two miles out he turned suddenly down a narrow, deeply-rutted track, and made swiftly for his man. A thin, cold rain was falling, swishing among the tall poplar trees and rustling in the fields on either side. The Captain walked first with Moser, a veteran sergeant, beside him. The sergeant's wrist was fastened to that of the French peasant, and it had been whispered in his ear that in case of an ambush the first bullet fired would be through his head. Behind them the twenty infantrymen plodded along through the darkness with their faces sunk to the rain, and their boots squeaking in the soft, wet clay. They knew where they were going and why, and the thought upheld them, for they were bitter at the loss of their comrades. It was a cavalry job, they knew, but the cavalry were all on with the advance, and, besides, it was more fitting that the regiment should avenge its own dead men.

It was nearly eight when they left Les Andelys. At half-past eleven their guide stopped at a place where two high pillars, crowned with some heraldic stonework, flanked a huge iron gate. The wall in which it had been the opening had crumbled away, but the great gate still towered above the brambles and weeds which had overgrown its base. The Prussians made their way round it, and advanced stealthily, under the shadow of a tunnel of oak branches, up the long avenue, which was still cumbered by the leaves of last autumn. At the top they halted and reconnoitred.

The black château lay in front of them. The moon had shone out between two rain-clouds, and threw the old house into silver and shadow. It was shaped like an L, with a low arched door in front, and lines of small windows like the open ports of a man-of-war. Above was a dark roof breaking at the corners into little round overhanging turrets, the whole lying silent in the moonshine, with a drift of ragged clouds blackening the heavens behind it. A single light gleamed in one of the lower windows.

The Captain whispered his orders to his men. Some were to creep to the front door, some to the back. Some were to watch the east, and some the west. He and the sergeant stole on tiptoe to the lighted window.

It was a small room into which they looked, very meanly furnished. An elderly man in the dress of a menial was reading a tattered paper by the light of a guttering candle. He leaned back in his wooden chair with his feet upon a box, while a bottle of white wine stood with a half-filled tumbler upon a stool beside him. The sergeant thrust his needle-gun through the glass, and the man sprang to his feet with a shriek.

'Silence, for your life! The house is surrounded and you cannot escape. Come round and open the door, or we will show you no mercy when we come in.'

'For God's sake, don't shoot! I will open it! I will open it!' He rushed from the room with his paper still crumpled up in his hand. An instant later, with a groaning of old locks and a rasping of bars, the low door swung open, and the Prussians poured into the stone-flagged passage.

'Where is Count Eustace de Château Noir?'

'My master! He is out, sir.'

'Out at this time of night? Your life for a lie.'

'It is true, sir. He is out!'

'Where?'

'I do not know.'

'Doing what?'

'I cannot tell. No, it is no use your cocking your pistol, sir. You may kill me, but you cannot make me tell you that which I do not know.'

'Is he often out at this hour?'

'Frequently.'

'And when does he come home?'

'Before daybreak.'

Captain Baumgarten rasped out a German oath. He had had his journey for nothing, then. The man's answers were only too likely to be true. It was what he might have expected. But at least he would search the house and make sure. Leaving a picket at the front door and another at the back, the sergeant and he drove the trembling butler in front of them—his shaking candle sending strange, flickering shadows over the old tapestries and the low, oak-raftered ceilings. They searched the whole house, from the huge, stone-flagged kitchen below to the dining-hall on the second floor with its gallery for musicians, and its panelling black with age, but nowhere was there a living creature. Up above in an attic they found Marie, the elderly wife of the butler; but the owner kept no other servants, and of his own presence there was no trace.

It was long, however, before Captain Baumgarten had satisfied himself upon the point. It was a difficult house to search. Thin stairs, which only one man could ascend at a time, connected lines of tortuous corridors. The walls were so thick that each room was cut off from its neighbour. Huge fireplaces yawned in each, while the windows were six feet deep in the wall. Captain Baumgarten stamped with his feet, and tore down curtains, and struck with the pommel of his sword. If there were secret hiding-places, he was not fortunate enough to find them.

'I have an idea,' said he, at last speaking in German to the sergeant. 'You will place a guard over this fellow, and make sure that he communicates with no one.'

'Yes, Captain.'

'And you will place four men in ambush at the front and at the back. It is likely enough that about daybreak our bird may return to the nest.'

'And the others, Captain?'

'Let them have their suppers in the kitchen. This fellow will serve you with meat and wine. It is a wild night, and we shall be better here than on the country road.'

'And yourself, Captain?'

'I will take my supper up here in the dining-hall. The logs are laid and we can light the fire. You will call me if there is any alarm. What can you give me for supper—you?'

'Alas, monsieur, there was a time when I might have answered, "What you wish!" but now it is all that we can do to find a bottle of new claret and a cold pullet.'

'That will do very well. Let a guard go about with him, sergeant, and let him feel the end of a bayonet if he plays us any tricks.'

Captain Baumgarten was an old campaigner. In the Eastern provinces, and before that in Bohemia, he had learned the art of quartering himself upon the enemy. While the butler brought his supper he occupied himself in making his preparations for a comfortable night. He lit the candelabrum of ten candles upon the centre table. The fire was already burning up, crackling merrily, and sending spurts of blue, pungent smoke into the room. The Captain walked to the window and looked out. The moon had gone in again, and it was raining heavily. He could hear the deep sough of the wind and see the dark loom of the trees, all swaying in the one direction. It was a sight which gave a zest to his comfortable quarters, and to the cold fowl and the bottle of wine which the butler had brought up for him. He was tired and hungry after his long tramp, so he threw his sword, his helmet, and his revolver-belt down upon a chair, and fell to eagerly upon his supper. Then, with his glass of wine before him and his cigar between his lips, he tilted his chair back and looked about him.

He sat within a small circle of brilliant light which gleamed upon his silver shoulder-straps, and threw out his terra-cotta face, his heavy eyebrows, and his yellow moustache. But outside that circle things were vague and shadowy in the old dining-hall. Two sides were oak-panelled and two were hung with faded tapestry, across which huntsmen and dogs and stags were still dimly streaming. Above the fireplace were rows of heraldic shields with the blazonings of the family and of its alliances, the fatal saltire cross breaking out on each of them.

Four paintings of old seigneurs of Château Noir faced the fireplace, all men with hawk noses and bold, high features, so like each other that only the dress could distinguish the Crusader from the Cavalier of the Fronde. Captain Baumgarten, heavy with his repast, lay back in his chair looking up at them through the clouds of his tobacco smoke, and pondering over the strange chance which had sent him, a man from the Baltic coast, to eat his supper in the ancestral hall of these proud Norman chieftains. But the fire was hot, and the Captain's eyes were heavy. His chin sank slowly upon his chest, and the ten candles gleamed upon the broad white scalp.

Suddenly a slight noise brought him to his feet. For an instant it seemed to his dazed senses that one of the pictures opposite had walked from its frame. There, beside the table, and almost within arm's length of him, was standing a huge man, silent, motionless, with no sign of life save his fierce, glinting eyes. He was black-haired, olive-skinned, with a pointed tuft of black beard, and a great, fierce nose, towards which all his features seemed to run. His cheeks were wrinkled like a last year's apple, but his sweep of shoulder, and bony, corded hands, told of a strength which was unsapped by age. His arms were folded across his arching chest, and his mouth was set in a fixed smile.

'Pray do not trouble yourself to look for your weapons,' he said, as the Prussian cast a swift glance at the empty chair in which they had been laid. 'You have been, if you will allow me to say so, a little indiscreet to make yourself so much at home in a house every wall of which is honeycombed with secret passages. You will be amused to hear that forty men were watching you at your supper. Ah! what then?'

Captain Baumgarten had taken a step forward with clenched fists. The Frenchman held up the revolver which he grasped in his right hand, while with the left he hurled the German back into his chair.

'Pray keep your seat,' said he. 'You have no cause to trouble about your men. They have already been provided for. It is astonishing with these stone floors how little one can hear what goes on beneath. You have been relieved of your command, and have now only to think of yourself. May I ask what your name is?'

'I am Captain Baumgarten, of the 24th Posen Regiment.'

'Your French is excellent, though you incline, like most of your countrymen, to turn the "p" into a "b". I have been amused to hear them cry "*avez biti, sur moi!*" You know, doubtless, who it is who addresses you?'

'The Count of Château Noir.'

'Precisely. It would have been a misfortune if you had visited my château and I had been unable to have a word with you. I have had to do with many German soldiers, but never with an officer before. I have much to talk to you about.'

Captain Baumgarten sat still in his chair. Brave as he was, there was something in this man's manner which made his skin creep with apprehension. His eyes glanced to right and to left, but his weapons were gone, and in a struggle he saw that he was but a child to this gigantic adversary. The Count had picked up the claret bottle, and held it to the light:

'Tut! tut!' said he. 'And was this the best that Pierre could do for you? I am ashamed to look you in the face, Captain Baumgarten. We must improve upon this.'

He blew a call upon a whistle, which hung from his shooting-jacket. The old manservant was in the room in an instant.

'Chambertin from bin 15!' he cried, and a minute later a grey bottle streaked with cobwebs was carried in as a nurse bears an infant. The Count filled two glasses to the brim.

'Drink!' said he. 'It is the very best in my cellars, and not to be matched between Rouen and Paris. Drink, sir, and be happy! There are cold joints below. There are two lobsters fresh from Honfleur. Will you not venture upon a second and more savoury supper?'

The German officer shook his head. He drained the glass, however, and his host filled it once more, pressing him to give an order for this or that dainty.

'There is nothing in my house which is not at your disposal. You have but to say the word. Well, then, you will allow me to tell you a story while you drink your wine. I have so longed to tell it to some German officer. It is about my son, my only child, Eustace, who was taken and died in escaping. It is a curious little story, and I think that I can promise you that you will never forget it.

'You must know, then, that my boy was in the artillery, a fine young fellow, Captain Baumgarten, and the pride of his mother. She died within a week of the news of his death reaching us. It was brought by a brother officer who was at his side throughout, and who escaped while my lad died. I want to tell you all that he told me.

'Eustace was taken at Weissenburg on the 4th of August. The prisoners were broken up into parties, and sent back into Germany by different routes. Eustace was taken upon the 5th to a village called Lauterburg, where he met with kindness from the German officer in command. This good Colonel had the hungry lad to supper, offered him the best he had, opened a bottle of good wine, as I have tried to do for you, and gave him a cigar from his own case. Might I entreat you to take one from mine?'

The German again shook his head. His horror of his companion had increased as he sat watching the lips that smiled and the eyes that glared.

'The Colonel, as I say, was good to my boy. But, unluckily, the prisoners were moved next day across the Rhine to Ettlingen. They were not equally fortunate there. The officer who guarded them was a ruffian and a villain, Captain Baumgarten. He took a pleasure in humiliating and ill-treating the brave men who had fallen into his power. That night, upon my son answering fiercely back to some taunt of his, he struck him in the eye, like this!'

The crash of the blow rang through the hall. The German's face fell forward, his hand up, and blood oozing through his fingers. The Count settled down in his chair once more.

'My boy was disfigured by the blow, and this villain made his appearance the object of his jeers. By the way, you look a little comical yourself at the present moment, Captain, and your Colonel would certainly say that you had been getting into mischief. To continue, however, my boy's youth and his destitution—for his pockets were empty—moved the pity of a kind-hearted major, and he advanced him ten Napoleons from his own pocket without security of any kind. Into your hands, Captain Baumgarten, I return these ten gold pieces, since I cannot learn the name of the lender. I am grateful from my heart for this kindness shown to my boy.

'The vile tyrant who commanded the escort accompanied the prisoners to Durlach, and from there to Carlsruhe. He heaped every outrage upon my lad, because the spirit of the Châteaux Noirs would not stoop to turn away his wrath by a feigned submission. Ay, this cowardly villain, whose heart's blood shall yet clot upon this hand, dared to strike my son with his open hand, to kick him, to tear hairs from his moustache—to use him thus—and thus—and thus!'

The German writhed and struggled. He was helpless in the hands of this huge giant whose blows were raining upon him. When at last, blinded and half senseless, he staggered to his feet, it was only to be hurled back again into the great oaken chair. He sobbed in his impotent anger and shame.

'My boy was frequently moved to tears by the humiliation of his position,' continued the Count. 'You will understand me when I say that it is a bitter thing to be helpless in the hands of an insolent and remorseless enemy. On arriving at Carlsruhe, however, his face, which had been wounded by the brutality of his guard, was bound up by a young Bavarian subaltern who was touched by his appearance. I regret to see that your eye is bleeding so. Will you permit me to bind it with my silk handkerchief?'

He leaned forward, but the German dashed his hand aside.

'I am in your power, you monster!' he cried; 'I can endure your brutalities, but not your hypocrisy.'

The Count shrugged his shoulders. 'I am taking things in their order, just as they occurred,' said he. 'I was under vow to tell it to the first German officer with whom I could talk *tête-à-tête*. Let me see, I had got as far as the young Bavarian at Carlsruhe. I regret extremely that you will not permit me to use such slight skill in surgery as I possess. At Carlsruhe, my lad was shut up in the old caserne, where he remained for a fortnight. The worst pang of his captivity was that some unmannerly curs in the garrison would taunt him with his position as he sat by his window in the evening. That reminds me, Captain, that you are not quite situated upon a bed of roses yourself, are you, now? You came to trap a wolf, my man, and now the beast has you down with his fangs in your throat. A family man, too, I should judge, by that well-filled tunic. Well, a widow the more will make little matter, and they do not usually remain widows long. Get back into the chair, you dog!

'Well, to continue my story—at the end of a fortnight my son and his friend escaped. I need not trouble you with the dangers which they ran, or with the privations which they endured. Suffice it that to disguise themselves they had to take the clothes of two peasants, whom they waylaid in a wood. Hiding by day and travelling by night, they had got as far into France as Remilly, and were within a mile—a single mile, Captain—of crossing the German lines when a patrol of Uhlans came right upon them. Ah! it was hard, was it not, when they had come so far and were so near to safety?'

The Count blew a double call upon his whistle, and three hard-faced peasants entered the room.

'These must represent my Uhlans,' said he. 'Well, then, the Captain in command, finding that these men were French soldiers in civilian dress within the German lines, proceeded to hang them without trial or ceremony. I think, Jean, that the centre beam is the strongest.'

The unfortunate soldier was dragged from his chair to where a noosed rope had been flung over one of the huge oaken rafters which spanned the room. The cord was slipped over his head, and he felt its harsh grip round his throat. The three peasants seized the other end, and looked to the Count for his orders. The officer, pale, but firm, folded his arms and stared defiantly at the man who tortured him.

'You are now face to face with death, and I perceive from your lips that you are praying. My son was also face to face with death, and he prayed, also. It happened that a general officer came up, and he heard the lad praying for his mother, and it moved him so—he being himself a father—that he ordered his Uhlans away, and he remained with his aide-de-camp only, beside the condemned men. And when he heard all the lad had to tell, that he was the only child of an old family, and that his mother was in failing health, he threw off the rope as I throw off this, and he kissed him on either cheek, as I kiss you, and he bade him go, as I bid you go, and may every kind wish of that noble General, though it could not stave off the fever which slew my son, descend now upon your head.'

And so it was that Captain Baumgarten, disfigured, blinded, and bleeding, staggered out into the wind and the rain of that wild December dawn.

The Parasite

M ARCH 24TH—The spring is fairly with us now. Outside my laboratory window the great chestnut-tree is all covered with the big, glutinous, gummy buds, some of which have already begun to break into little green shuttle-cocks. As you walk down the lanes you are conscious of the rich, silent forces of nature working all around you. The wet earth smells fruitful and luscious. Green shoots are peeping out everywhere. The twigs are stiff with their sap; and the moist, heavy English air is laden with a faintly resinous perfume. Buds in the hedges, lambs beneath them—everywhere the work of reproduction going forward!

I can see it without, and I can feel it within. We also have our spring when the little arterioles dilate, the lymph flows in a brisker stream, the glands work harder, winnowing and straining. Every year nature readjusts the whole machine. I can feel the ferment in my blood at this very moment, and as the cool sunshine pours through my window I could dance about in it like a gnat. So I should, only that Charles Sadler would rush upstairs to know what was the matter. Besides, I must remember that I am Professor Gilroy. An old professor may afford to be natural, but when fortune has given one of the first chairs in the university to a man of four-and-thirty he must try and act the part consistently.

What a fellow Wilson is! If I could only throw the same enthusiasm into physiology that he does into psychology, I should become a Claude Bernard at the least. His whole life and soul and energy work to one end. He drops to sleep collating his results of the past day, and he wakes to plan his researches for the coming one. And yet, outside the narrow circle who follow his proceedings, he gets so little credit for it. Physiology is a recognised science. If I add even a brick to the edifice, every one sees and applauds it. But Wilson is trying to dig the foundations for a science of the future. His work is underground and does not show. Yet he goes on uncomplainingly, corresponding with a hundred semi-maniacs in the hope of finding one reliable witness, sifting a hundred lies on the chance of gaining one little speck of truth, collating old books, devouring new ones, experimenting, lecturing, trying to light up in others the fiery interest which is consuming him. I am filled with wonder and admiration when I think of him; and yet, when he asks me to associate myself with his researches, I am compelled to tell him that, in their present state, they offer little attraction to a man who is devoted to exact science. If he could show me something positive and objective, I might then be tempted to approach the question from its physiological side. So long as half his subjects are tainted with charlatanry and the other half with hysteria we physiologists must content ourselves with the body and leave the mind to our descendants.

No doubt I am a materialist. Agatha says that I am a rank one. I tell her that is an excellent reason for shortening our engagement, since I am in such urgent need of her spirituality. And yet I may claim to be a curious example of the effect of education upon temperament, for by nature I am, unless I deceive myself, a highly psychic man. I was a nervous, sensitive boy, a dreamer, a somnambulist, full of impressions and intuitions. My black hair, my dark eyes, my thin, olive face, my tapering fingers are all characteristic of my real temperament, and cause experts like Wilson to claim me as their own. But my brain is soaked with exact knowledge. I have trained myself to deal only with fact and with proof. Surmise and fancy have no place in my scheme of thought. Show me what I can see with my microscope, cut with my scalpel, weigh in my balance, and I will devote a lifetime to its investigation. But when you ask me to study feelings, impressions, suggestions, you ask me to do what is distasteful and even demoralising. A departure from pure reason affects me like an evil smell or a musical discord.

Which is a very sufficient reason why I am a little loth to go to Professor Wilson's tonight. Still I feel that I could hardly get out of the invitation without positive rudeness—and, now that Mrs Marden and Agatha are going, of course I would not if I could. But I had rather meet them anywhere else. I know that Wilson would draw me into this nebulous semi-science of his if he could. In his enthusiasm he is perfectly impervious to hints or remonstrances. Nothing short of a positive quarrel will make him realize my aversion to the whole business. I have no doubt that he has some new mesmerist, or clairvoyant, or medium, or trickster of some sort whom he is going to exhibit to us, for even his entertainments bear upon his hobby. Well, it will be a treat for Agatha at any rate. She is interested in it, as woman usually is in whatever is vague and mystical and indefinite.

10.50 p.m.—This diary-keeping of mine is, I fancy, the outcome of that scientific habit of mind about which I wrote this morning. I like to register impressions while they are fresh. Once a day at least I endeavour to define my own mental position. It is a useful piece of self-analysis, and has, I fancy, a steadying effect upon the character. Frankly, I must confess that my own needs what stiffening I can give it. I fear that, after all, much of my neurotic temperament survives, and that I am far from that cool, calm precision which characterizes Murdoch or Pratt-Haldane. Otherwise, why should the tomfoolery which I have witnessed this evening have set my nerves thrilling so that even now I am all unstrung? My only comfort is that neither Wilson, nor Miss Penclosa, nor even Agatha could have possibly known my weakness.

And what in the world was there to excite me? Nothing, or so little that it will seem ludicrous when I set it down.

The Mardens got to Wilson's before me. In fact I was one of the last to arrive, and found the room crowded. I had hardly time to say a word to Mrs Marden and to Agatha, who was looking charming in white and pink with glittering wheat-ears in her hair, when Wilson came twitching at my sleeve.

'You want something positive, Gilroy,' said he, drawing me apart into a corner. 'My dear fellow, I have a phenomenon—a phenomenon!'

I should have been more impressed had I not heard the same before. His sanguine spirit turns every firefly into a star.

'No possible question about the bona fides this time,' said he, in answer, perhaps, to some little gleam of amusement in my eyes. 'My wife has known her for many years. They both come from Trinidad, you know. Miss Penclosa has only been in England a month or two, and knows no one outside the university circle; but I assure you that the things she has told us suffice in themselves to establish clairvoyance upon an absolutely scientific basis. There is nothing like her, amateur or professional. Come and be introduced!'

I like none of these mystery-mongers, but the amateur least of all. With the paid performer you may pounce upon him and expose him the instant that you have seen through his trick. He is there to deceive you, and you are there to find him out. But what are you to do with the friend of your host's wife? Are you to turn on a light suddenly and expose her slapping a surreptitious banjo? Or are you to hurl cochineal over her evening frock when she steals round with her phosphorus bottle and her supernatural platitude? There would be a scene, and you would be looked upon as a brute. So you have your choice of being that or a dupe. I was in no very good humour as I followed Wilson to the lady.

Any one less like my idea of a West Indian could not be imagined. She was a small, frail creature, well over forty, I should say, with a pale, peaky face, and hair of a very light shade of chestnut. Her presence was insignificant and her manner retiring. In any group of ten women she would have been the last whom one would have picked out. Her eyes were perhaps her most remarkable, and also, I am compelled to say, her least pleasant, feature. They were grey in colour—grey with a shade of green—and their expression struck me as being decidedly furtive. I wonder if furtive is the word, or should I have said fierce? On second thoughts, feline would have expressed it better. A crutch leaning against the wall told me what was painfully evident when she rose: that one of her legs was crippled.

So I was introduced to Miss Penclosa, and it did not escape me that as my name was mentioned she glanced across at Agatha. Wilson had evidently been talking. And presently, no doubt, thought I, she will inform me by occult means that I am engaged to a young lady with wheat-ears in her hair. I wondered how much more Wilson had been telling her about me.

'Professor Gilroy is a terrible sceptic,' said he; 'I hope, Miss Penclosa, that you will be able to convert him.'

She looked keenly up at me.

'Professor Gilroy is quite right to be sceptical if he has not seen any thing convincing,' said she. 'I should have thought,' she added, 'that you would yourself have been an excellent subject.'

'For what, may I ask?' said I.

'Well, for mesmerism, for example.'

'My experience has been that mesmerists go for their subjects to those who are mentally unsound. All their results are vitiated, as it seems to me, by the fact that they are dealing with abnormal organisms.'

'Which of these ladies would you say possessed a normal organism?' she asked. 'I should like you to select the one who seems to you to have the best-balanced mind. Should we say the girl in pink and white—Miss Agatha Marden, I think the name is?'

'Yes, I should attach weight to any results from her.'

'I have never tried how far she is impressionable. Of course some people respond much more rapidly than others. May I ask how far your scepticism extends? I suppose that you admit the mesmeric sleep and the power of suggestion.'

'I admit nothing, Miss Penclosa.'

'Dear me, I thought science had got further than that. Of course I know nothing about the scientific side of it. I only know what I can do. You see the girl in red, for example, over near the Japanese jar. I shall will that she come across to us.'

She bent forward as she spoke and dropped her fan upon the floor. The girl whisked round and came straight toward us, with an enquiring look upon her face, as if some one had called her.

'What do you think of that, Gilroy?' cried Wilson, in a kind of ecstasy.

I did not dare to tell him what I thought of it. To me it was the most barefaced, shameless piece of imposture that I had ever witnessed. The collusion and the signal had really been too obvious.

'Professor Gilroy is not satisfied,' said she, glancing up at me with her strange little eyes. 'My poor fan is to get the credit of that experiment. Well, we must try something else. Miss Marden, would you have any objection to my putting you off?'

'Oh, I should love it!' cried Agatha.

By this time all the company had gathered round us in a circle, the shirt-fronted men, and the white-throated women, some awed, some critical, as though it were something between a religious ceremony and a conjurer's entertainment. A red velvet armchair had been pushed into the centre, and Agatha lay back in it, a little flushed and trembling slightly from excitement. I could see it from the vibration of the wheat-ears. Miss Penclosa rose from her seat and stood over her, leaning upon her crutch.

And there was a change in the woman. She no longer seemed small or insignificant. Twenty years were gone from her age. Her eyes were shining, a tinge of colour had come into her sallow cheeks, her whole figure had expanded. So I have seen a dull-eyed, listless lad change in an instant into briskness and life when given a task of which he felt himself master. She looked down at Agatha with an expression which I resented from the bottom of my soul—the expression with which a Roman empress might have looked at her kneeling slave. Then with a quick, commanding gesture she tossed up her arms and swept them slowly down in front of her.

I was watching Agatha narrowly. During three passes she seemed to be simply amused. At the fourth I observed a slight glazing of her eyes, accompanied by some dilation of her pupils. At the sixth there was a momentary rigor. At the seventh her lids began to droop. At the tenth her eyes were closed, and her breathing was slower and fuller than usual. I tried as I watched to preserve my scientific calm, but a foolish, causeless agitation convulsed me. I trust that I hid it, but I felt as a child feels in the dark. I could not have believed that I was still open to such weakness.

'She is in the trance,' said Miss Penclosa.

'She is sleeping!' I cried.

'Wake her, then!'

I pulled her by the arm and shouted in her ear. She might have been dead for all the impression that I could make. Her body was there on the velvet chair. Her organs were acting—her heart, her lungs. But her soul! It had slipped from beyond our ken. Whither had it gone? What power had dispossessed it? I was puzzled and disconcerted.

'So much for the mesmeric sleep,' said Miss Penclosa. 'As regards suggestion, whatever I may suggest Miss Marden will infallibly do, whether it be now or after she has awakened from her trance. Do you demand proof of it?'

'Certainly,' said I.

'You shall have it.'

I saw a smile pass over her face, as though an amusing thought had struck her. She stooped and whispered earnestly into her subject's ear. Agatha, who had been so deaf to me, nodded her head as she listened.

'Awake!' cried Miss Penclosa, with a sharp tap of her crutch upon the floor. The eyes opened, the glazing cleared slowly away, and the soul looked out once more after its strange eclipse.

We went away early. Agatha was none the worse for her strange excursion, but I was nervous and unstrung, unable to listen to or answer the stream of comments which Wilson was pouring out for my benefit. As I bade her goodnight Miss Penclosa slipped a piece of paper into my hand.

'Pray forgive me,' said she, 'if I take means to overcome your scepticism. Open this note at ten o'clock tomorrow morning. It is a little private test.'

I can't imagine what she means, but there is the note, and it shall be opened as she directs. My head is aching, and I have written enough for tonight. Tomorrow I dare say that what seems so inexplicable will take quite another complexion. I shall not surrender my convictions without a struggle.

March 25th—I am amazed—confounded. It is clear that I must reconsider my opinion upon this matter. But first, let me place on record what has occurred.

I had finished breakfast, and was looking over some diagrams with which my lecture is to be illustrated, when my housekeeper entered to tell me that Agatha was in my study and wished to see me immediately. I glanced at the clock, and saw with surprise that it was only half-past nine.

When I entered the room, she was standing on the hearthrug facing me. Something in her pose chilled me and checked the words which were rising to my lips. Her veil was half down, but I could see that she was pale and that her expression was constrained.

'Austin,' she said, 'I have come to tell you that our engagement is at an end.'

I staggered. I believe that I literally did stagger. I know that I found myself leaning against the bookcase for support.

'But—but——' I stammered, 'this is very sudden, Agatha.'

'Yes, Austin, I have come here to tell you that our engagement is at an end.'

'But surely,' I cried, 'you will give me some reason! This is unlike you, Agatha. Tell me how I have been unfortunate enough to offend you.'

'It is all over, Austin.'

'But why? You must be under some delusion, Agatha. Perhaps you have been told some falsehood about me. Or you may have misunderstood something that I have said to you. Only let me know what it is, and a word may set it all right.'

'We must consider it all at an end.'

'But you left me last night without a hint at any disagreement. What could have occurred in the interval to change you so? It must have been something that happened last night. You have been thinking it over and you have disapproved of my conduct. Was it the mesmerism? Did you blame me for letting that woman exercise her power over you? You know that at the least sign I should have interfered.'

'It is useless, Austin. All is over.'

Her voice was cold and measured; her manner strangely formal and hard. It seemed to me that she was absolutely resolved not to be drawn into any argument or explanation. As for me, I was shaking with agitation, and I turned my face aside, so ashamed was I that she should see my want of control.

'You must know what this means to me,' I cried. 'It is the blasting of all my hopes and the ruin of my life. You surely will not inflict such a punishment upon me unheard. You will let me know what is the matter. Consider how impossible it would be for me, under any circumstances, to treat you so. For God's sake, Agatha, let me know what I have done.'

She walked past me without a word and opened the door.

'It is quite useless, Austin,' said she. 'You must consider our engagement at an end.' An instant later she was gone, and before I could recover myself sufficiently to follow her I heard the hall-door close behind her.

I rushed into my room to change my coat, with the idea of hurrying round to Mrs Marden's to learn from her what the cause of my misfortune might be. So shaken was I that I could hardly lace my boots. Never shall I forget those horrible ten minutes. I had just pulled on my overcoat when the clock upon the mantel-piece struck ten.

Ten! I associated the idea with Miss Penclosa's note. It was lying before me on the table, and I tore it open. It was scribbled in pencil in a peculiarly angular handwriting.

'My dear Professor Gilroy,' it said, 'Pray excuse the personal nature of the test which I am giving you. Professor Wilson happened to mention the relations between you and my subject of this evening, and it struck me that nothing could be more convincing to you than if I were to suggest to Miss Marden that she should call upon you at half-past nine tomorrow morning and suspend your engagement for half an hour or so. Science is so exacting that it is difficult to give a satisfying test, but I am convinced that this at least will be an action which she would be most unlikely to do of her own free will. Forget anything that she may have said, as she has really nothing whatever to do with it, and will certainly not recollect any thing about it. I write this note to shorten your anxiety, and to beg you to forgive me for the momentary unhappiness which my suggestion must have caused you.—Yours faithfully, Helen Penclosa.'

Really, when I had read the note, I was too relieved to be angry. It was a liberty. Certainly it was a very great liberty indeed on the part of a lady whom I had only met once. But, after all, I had challenged her by my scepticism. It may have been, as she said, a little difficult to devise a test which would satisfy me.

And she had done that. There could be no question at all upon the point. For me hypnotic suggestion was finally established. It took its place from now onward as one of the facts of life. That Agatha, who of all women of my acquaintance has the best balanced mind, had been reduced to a condition of automatism appeared to be certain. A person at a distance had worked her as an engineer on the shore might guide a Brennan torpedo. A second soul had stepped in, as it were, had pushed her own aside, and had seized her nervous mechanism, saying, 'I will work this for half an hour.' And Agatha must have been unconscious as she came and as she returned. Could she make her way in safety through the streets in such a state? I put on my hat and hurried round to see if all was well with her.

Yes. She was at home. I was shown into the drawing-room and found her sitting with a book upon her lap.

'You are an early visitor, Austin,' said she, smiling.

'And you have been an even earlier one,' I answered.

She looked puzzled. 'What do you mean?' she asked.

'You have not been out today?'

'No, certainly not.'

'Agatha,' said I seriously, 'would you mind telling me exactly what you have done this morning?'

She laughed at my earnestness.

'You've got on your professional look, Austin. See what comes of being engaged to a man of science. However, I will tell you, though I can't imagine what you want to know for. I got up at eight. I breakfasted at half-past. I came into this room at ten minutes past nine and began to read the *Memoirs of Mme de Rémusat*. In a few minutes I did the French lady the bad compliment of dropping to sleep over her pages and I did you, sir, the very flattering one of dreaming about you. It is only a few minutes since I woke up.'

'And found yourself where you had been before?'

'Why, where else should I find myself?'

'Would you mind telling me, Agatha, what it was that you dreamed about me? It really is not mere curiosity on my part.'

'I merely had a vague impression that you came into it. I cannot recall any thing definite.'

'If you have not been out today, Agatha, how is it that your shoes are dusty?'

A pained look came over her face.

'Really, Austin, I do not know what is the matter with you this morning. One would almost think that you doubted my word. If my boots are dusty, it must be, of course, that I have put on a pair which the maid had not cleaned.'

It was perfectly evident that she knew nothing whatever about the matter, and I reflected that after all perhaps it was better that I should not enlighten her. It might frighten her, and could serve no good purpose that I could see. I said no more about it, therefore, and left shortly afterwards to give my lecture.

But I am immensely impressed. My horizon of scientific possibilities has suddenly been enormously extended. I no longer wonder at Wilson's demoniac energy and enthusiasm. Who would not work hard who had a vast virgin field ready to his hand? Why, I have known the novel shape of a nucleolus, or a trifling peculiarity of striped muscular fibre seen under a 300-diameter lens fill me with exultation. How petty do such researches seem when compared with this one which strikes at the very roots of life, and the nature of the soul! I had always looked upon spirit as a product of matter. The brain, I thought, secreted the mind, as the liver does the bile. But how can this be when I see mind working from a distance, and playing upon matter as a musician might upon a violin? The body does not give rise to the soul then, but is rather the rough instrument by which the spirit manifests itself. The windmill does not give rise to the wind, but only indicates it. It was opposed to my whole habit of thought, and yet it was undeniably possible and worthy of investigation.

And why should I not investigate it? I see that under yesterday's date I said, 'If I could see something positive and objective, I might be tempted to approach it from the physiological aspect.' Well, I have got my test. I shall be as good as my word. The investigation would, I am sure, be of immense interest. Some of my colleagues might look askance at it, for science is full of unreasoning prejudices, but if Wilson has the courage of his convictions, I can afford to have it also. I shall go to him tomorrow morning—to him and to Miss Penclosa. If she can show us so much, it is probable that she can show us more.

March 26th—Wilson was, as I had anticipated, very exultant over my conversion, and Miss Penclosa was also demurely pleased at the result of her experiment. Strange what a silent, colourless creature she is, save only when she exercises her power! Even talking about it gives her colour and life. She seems to take a singular interest in me. I cannot help observing how her eyes follow me about the room.

We had the most interesting conversation about her own powers. It is just as well to put her views on record, though they cannot of course claim any scientific weight.

'You are on the very fringe of the subject,' said she, when I had expressed wonder at the remarkable instance of suggestion which she had shown me. 'I had no direct influence upon Miss Marden when she came round to you. I was not even thinking of her that morning. What I did was to set her mind as I might set the alarum of a clock so that at the hour named it would go off of its own accord. If six months instead of twelve hours had been suggested, it would have been the same.'

'And if the suggestion had been to assassinate me?'

'She would most inevitably have done so.'

'But this is a terrible power!' I cried.

'It is, as you say, a terrible power,' she answered gravely. 'And the more you know of it the more terrible will it seem to you.'

'May I ask,' said I, 'what you meant when you said that this matter of suggestion is only at the fringe of it? What do you consider the essential?'

'I had rather not tell you.'

I was surprised at the decision of her answer.

'You understand,' said I, 'that it is not out of curiosity I ask, but in the hope that I may find some scientific explanation for the facts with which you furnish me.'

'Frankly, Professor Gilroy,' said she, 'I am not at all interested in science, nor do I care whether it can or cannot classify these powers.'

'But I was hoping——'

'Ah, that is quite another thing. If you make it a personal matter,' said she, with the pleasantest of smiles, 'I shall be only too happy to tell you anything you wish to know. Let me see! What was it you asked me? Oh, about the further powers. Professor Wilson won't believe in them, but they are quite true all the same. For example, it is possible for an operator to gain complete command over his subject—presuming that the latter is a good one. Without any previous suggestion he may make him do whatever he likes.'

'Without the subject's knowledge?'

'That depends. If the force were strongly excited, he would know no more about it than Miss Marden did when she came round and frightened you so. Or, if the influence were less powerful, he might be conscious of what he was doing but be quite unable to prevent himself from doing it.'

'Would he have lost his own will-power, then?'

'It would be overridden by another stronger one.'

'Have you ever exercised this power yourself?'

'Several times.'

'Is your own will so strong, then?'

'Well, it does not entirely depend upon that. Many have strong wills which are not detachable from themselves. The thing is to have the gift of projecting it into another person, and superseding their own. I find that the power varies with my own strength and health.'

'Practically, you send your soul into another person's body.'

'Well, you might put it that way.'

'And what does your own body do?'

'It merely feels lethargic.'

'Well, but is there no danger to your own health?' I asked.

'There might be a little. You have to be careful never to let your own consciousness absolutely go; otherwise you might experience some difficulty in finding your way back again. You must always preserve the connection, as it were. I am afraid I express myself very badly, Professor Gilroy, but of course I don't know how to put these things in a scientific way. I am just giving you my own experiences and my own explanations.'

Well, I read this over now at my leisure, and I marvel at myself! Is this Austin Gilroy, the man who has won his way to the front by his hard reasoning power and by his devotion to fact? Here I am gravely retailing the gossip of a woman who tells me how her soul may be projected from her body, and how, while she lies in a lethargy, she can control the actions of people at a distance! Do I accept it? Certainly not. She must prove and re-prove before I yield a point. But if I am still a sceptic, I have at least ceased to be a scoffer. We are to have a sitting this evening, and she is to try if she can produce any mesmeric effect upon me. If she can, it will make an excellent starting-point for our investigation. No one can accuse me, at any rate, of complicity. If she cannot, we must try and find some subject who will be like Caesar's wife. Wilson is perfectly impervious.

10 p.m.—I believe that I am on the threshold of an epoch-making investigation. To have the power of examining these phenomena from inside— to have an organism which will respond, and, at the same time, a brain which will appreciate and criticise—that is surely a unique advantage. I am quite sure that Wilson would give five years of his life to be as susceptible as I have proved myself to be.

There was no one present except Wilson and his wife. I was seated with my head leaning back, and Miss Penclosa, standing in front and a little way to the left, used the same long, sweeping strokes as with Agatha. At each of them a warm current of air seemed to strike me, and to suffuse a thrill and glow all through me from head to foot. My eyes were fixed upon Miss Penclosa's face, but as I gazed the features seemed to blur and to fade away. I was conscious only of her own eyes looking down at me, grey, deep, inscrutable. Larger they grew and larger, until they changed suddenly into two mountain lakes towards which I seemed to be falling with horrible rapidity. I shuddered, and as I did so some deeper stratum of thought told me that the shudder represented the rigor which I had observed in Agatha. An instant later I struck the surface of the lakes, now joined into one, and down I went beneath the water with a fullness in my head and a buzzing in my ears. Down I went, down, down, and then with a swoop up again until I could see the light streaming brightly through the green water. I was almost at the surface when the word 'Awake!' rang through my head, and, with a start, I found myself back in the armchair, with Miss Penclosa leaning on her crutch, and Wilson, his note-book in his hand, peeping over her shoulder. No heaviness or weariness was left behind. On the contrary, though it is only an hour or so since the experiment, I feel so wakeful that I am more inclined for my study than my bedroom. I see quite a vista of interesting experiments extending before us, and am all impatience to begin upon them.

March 27th—A blank day, as Miss Penclosa goes with Wilson and his wife to the Suttons. Have begun Binet and Ferré's *Animal Magnetism*. What strange, deep waters these are! Results, results, results—and the cause an absolute mystery. It is stimulating to the imagination, but I must be on my guard against that. Let us have no inferences nor deductions, and nothing but solid facts. I know that the mesmeric trance is true, I know that mesmeric suggestion is true; I know that I am myself sensitive to this force. That is my present position. I have a large new note-book, which shall be devoted entirely to scientific detail.

Long talk with Agatha and Mrs Marden in the evening about our marriage. We think that the summer vac. (the beginning of it) would be the best time for the wedding. Why should we delay? I grudge even those few months. Still, as

Mrs Marden says, there are a good many things to be arranged.

March 28th—Mesmerised again by Miss Penclosa. Experience much the same as before, save that insensibility came on more quickly. See Note-book A for temperature of room, barometric pressure, pulse, and respiration as taken by Professor Wilson.

March 29th—Mesmerised again. Details in Note-book A.

March 30th—Sunday, and a blank day. I grudge any interruption of our experiments. At present they merely embrace the physical signs which go with slight, with complete, and with extreme insensibility. Afterward we hope to pass on to the phenomena of suggestion and of lucidity. Professors have demonstrated these things upon women at Nancy and at the Salpêtrière. It will be more convincing when a woman demonstrates it upon a professor, with a second professor as a witness. And that I should be the subject, I the sceptic, the materialist! At least, I have shown that my devotion to science is greater than to my own personal consistency. The eating of our own words is the greatest sacrifice which truth ever requires of us.

My neighbour, Charles Sadler, the handsome young demonstrator of Anatomy, came in this evening to return a volume of Virchow's *Archives* which I had lent him. I call him young, but, as a matter of fact, he is a year older than I am.

'I understand, Gilroy,' said he, 'that you are being experimented upon by Miss Penclosa.

'Well,' he went on, when I had acknowledged it, 'if I were you, I should not let it go any further. You will think me very impertinent, no doubt, but none the less I feel it to be my duty to advise you to have no more to do with her.'

Of course I asked him why.

'I am so placed that I cannot enter into particulars as freely as I could wish,' said he. 'Miss Penclosa is the friend of my friend, and my position is a delicate one. I can only say this, that I have myself been the subject of some of the woman's experiments, and that they have left a most unpleasant impression upon my mind.'

He could hardly expect me to be satisfied with that, and I tried hard to get something more definite out of him, but without success. Is it conceivable that he could be jealous at my having superseded him? Or is he one of those men of science who feel personally injured when facts run counter to their preconceived opinions? He cannot seriously suppose that because he has some vague grievance I am therefore to abandon a series of experiments which promise to be so fruitful of results. He appeared to be annoyed at the light way in which I treated his shadowy warnings, and we parted with some little coldness on both sides.

March 31st—Mesmerised by Miss P.

April 1st—Mesmerised by Miss P. (Note-book A.)

April 2nd—Mesmerised by Miss P. (Sphygmographic chart taken by Professor Wilson.)

April 3rd—It is possible that this course of mesmerism may be a little trying to the general constitution. Agatha says that I am thinner and darker under the eyes. I am conscious of a nervous irritability which I had not observed in myself before. The least noise, for example, makes me start, and the stupidity of a student causes me exasperation instead of amusement. Agatha wishes me to stop, but I tell her that every course of study is trying, and that one can never attain a result without paying some price for it. When she sees the sensation which my forthcoming paper on 'The Relation between Mind and Matter' may make, she will understand that it is worth a little nervous wear-and-tear. I should not be surprised if I got my FRS over it.

Mesmerised again in the evening. The effect is produced more rapidly now, and the subjective visions are less marked. I keep full notes of each sitting. Wilson is leaving for town for a week or ten days, but we shall not interrupt the experiments, which depend for their value as much upon my sensations as on his observations.

April 4th—I must be carefully on my guard. A complication has crept into our experiments which I had not reckoned upon. In my eagerness for scientific facts I have been foolishly blind to the human relations between Miss Penclosa and myself. I can write here what I would not breathe to a living soul. The unhappy woman appears to have formed an attachment for me.

I should not say such a thing, even in the privacy of my own intimate journal if it had not come to such a pass that it is impossible to ignore it. For some time—that is, for the last week—there have been signs which I have brushed aside and refused to think of. Her brightness when I come, her dejection when I go, her eagerness that I should come often, the expression of her eyes, the tone of her voice—I tried to think that they meant nothing and were, perhaps, only her ardent West Indian manner. But last night, as I awoke from the mesmeric sleep, I put out my hand, unconsciously, involuntarily, and clasped hers. When I came fully to myself, we were sitting with them locked, she looking up at me with an expectant smile. And the horrible thing was that I felt impelled to say what she expected me to say. What a false wretch I should have been! How I should have loathed myself today had I yielded to the temptation of that moment! But, thank God, I was strong enough to spring up and hurry from the room. I was rude, I fear, but I could not—no, I could not, trust myself another moment. I, a gentleman, a man of honour, engaged to one of the sweetest girls in England—and yet in a moment of reasonless passion I nearly professed love for this woman whom I hardly know! She is far older than myself, and a cripple. It is monstrous—odious—and yet the impulse was so strong that, had I stayed another minute in her presence, I should have committed myself. What was it? I have to teach others the workings of our organism, and what do I know of it myself? Was it the sudden upcropping of

273

some lower stratum in my nature—a brutal primitive instinct suddenly asserting itself? I could almost believe the tales of obsession by evil spirits, so overmastering was the feeling.

Well, the incident places me in a most unfortunate position. On the one hand, I am very loth to abandon a series of experiments which have already gone so far, and which promise such brilliant results. On the other, if this unhappy woman has conceived a passion for me—but surely even now I must have made some hideous mistake. She, with her age and her deformity! It is impossible. And then she knew about Agatha. She understood how I was placed. She only smiled out of amusement, perhaps, when in my dazed state I seized her hand. It was my half-mesmerised brain which gave it a meaning, and sprang with such bestial swiftness to meet it. I wish I could persuade myself that it was indeed so. On the whole, perhaps, my wisest plan would be to postpone our other experiments until Wilson's return. I have written a note to Miss Penclosa, therefore, making no allusion to last night, but saying that a press of work would cause me to interrupt our sittings for a few days. She has answered, formally enough, to say that if I should change my mind I should find her at home at the usual hour.

10 p.m.—Well, well, what a thing of straw I am! I am coming to know myself better of late, and the more I know the lower I fall in my own estimation. Surely I was not always so weak as this. At four o'clock I should have smiled had any one told me that I should go to Miss Penclosa's tonight; and yet at eight I was at Wilson's door as usual. I don't know how it occurred. The influence of habit, I suppose. Perhaps there is a mesmeric craze as there is an opium craze, and I am a victim to it. I only know that as I worked in my study I became more and more uneasy. I fidgeted. I worried. I could not concentrate my mind upon the papers in front of me. And then, at last, almost before I knew what I was doing, I seized my hat and hurried round to keep my usual appointment.

We had an interesting evening. Mrs Wilson was present during most of the time, which prevented the embarrassment which one at least of us must have felt. Miss Penclosa's manner was quite the same as usual, and she expressed no surprise at my having come in spite of my note. There was nothing in her bearing to show that yesterday's incident had made any impression upon her, and so I am inclined to hope that I overrated it.

April 6th (evening)—No, no, no, I did not overrate it. I can no longer attempt to conceal from myself that this woman has conceived a passion for me. It is monstrous, but it is true. Again, tonight, I awoke from the mesmeric trance to find my hand in hers, and to suffer that odious feeling which urges me to throw away my honour, my career, everything, for the sake of this creature who, as I can plainly see when I am away from her influence, possesses no single charm upon earth. But when I am near her, I do not feel this. She rouses something in me, something evil, something I had rather not think of. She paralyses my better nature, too, at the moment when she stimulates my worse. Decidedly it is not good for me to be near her.

Last night was worse than before. Instead of flying I actually sat for some time with my hand in hers talking over the most intimate subjects with her. We spoke of Agatha among other things. What could I have been dreaming of! Miss Penclosa said that she was conventional, and I agreed with her. She spoke once or twice in a disparaging way of her, and I did not protest. What a creature I have been!

Weak as I have proved myself to be, I am still strong enough to bring this sort of thing to an end. It shall not happen again. I have sense enough to fly when I cannot fight. From this Sunday night onwards I shall never sit with Miss Penclosa again. Never! Let the experiments go, let the research come to an end; anything is better than facing this monstrous temptation which drags me so low. I have said nothing to Miss Penclosa, but I shall simply stay away. She can tell the reason without any words of mine.

April 7th—Have stayed away as I said. It is a pity to ruin such an interesting investigation, but it would be a greater pity still to ruin my life, and I know that I cannot trust myself with that woman.

11 p.m.—God help me! What is the matter with me? Am I going mad? Let me try and be calm and reason with myself. First of all I shall set down exactly what occurred.

It was nearly eight when I wrote the lines with which this day begins. Feeling strangely restless and uneasy, I left my rooms and walked round to spend the evening with Agatha and her mother. They both remarked that I was pale and haggard. About nine Professor Pratt-Haldane came in, and we played a game of whist. I tried hard to concentrate my attention upon the cards, but the feeling of restlessness grew and grew until I found it impossible to struggle against it. I simply *could* not sit still at the table. At last, in the very middle of a hand, I threw my cards down and, with some sort of an incoherent apology about having an appointment, I rushed from the room. As if in a dream, I have a vague recollection of tearing through the hall, snatching my hat from the stand, and slamming the door behind me. As in a dream, too, I have the impression of the double line of gas-lamps, and my bespattered boots tell me that I must have run down the middle of the road. It was all misty and strange and unnatural. I came to Wilson's house; I saw Mrs Wilson and I saw Miss Penclosa. I hardly recall what we talked about, but I do remember that Miss P. shook the head of her crutch at me in a playful way, and accused me of being late and of losing interest in our experiments. There was no mesmerism, but I stayed some time and have only just returned.

My brain is quite clear again, now, and I can think over what has occurred. It is absurd to suppose that it is merely weakness and force of habit. I tried to explain it in that way the other night, but it will no longer suffice. It is something much deeper and more terrible than that. Why, when I was at the Marden's whist-table I was dragged away, as if the noose of a rope had been cast round me. I can no longer disguise it from myself. The woman has her grip upon me. I am in her clutch. But I must keep my head and reason it out, and see what is best to be done.

But what a blind fool I have been! In my enthusiasm over my research I have walked straight into the pit, although it lay gaping before me. Did she not herself warn me? Did she not tell me, as I can read in my own journal, that when she has acquired power over a subject she can make him do her will? And she has acquired that power over me. I am for the moment at the beck and call of this creature with the crutch. I must come when she wills it. I must do as she wills. Worst of all, I must feel as she wills. I loathe her and fear her, yet, while I am under the spell, she can doubtless make me love her.

There is some consolation in the thought, then, that those odious impulses for which I have blamed myself do not really come from me at all. They are all transferred from her, little as I could have guessed it at the time. I feel cleaner and lighter for the thought.

April 8th—Yes, now, in broad daylight, writing coolly and with time for reflection, I am compelled to confirm everything which I find in my journal last night. I am in a horrible position, but, above all, I must not lose my head. I must pit my intellect against her powers. After all, I am no silly puppet, to dance at the end of a string. I have energy, brains, courage. For all her devil's tricks I may beat her yet. May! I must, or what is to become of me?

Let me try to reason it out! This woman, by her own explanation, can dominate my nervous organism. She can project herself into my body and take command of it. She has a parasite soul. Yes, she is a parasite, a monstrous parasite. She creeps into my frame as the hermit crab does into the whelk's shell. I am powerless! What can I do? I am dealing with forces of which I know nothing. And I can tell no one of my trouble. They would set me down as a madman. Certainly, if it got noised abroad, the university would say that they had no need of a devil-ridden professor. And Agatha! No, no, I must face it alone.

I read over my notes of what the woman said when she spoke about her powers. There is one point which fills me with dismay. She implies that when the influence is slight the subject knows what he is doing, but cannot control himself, whereas, when it is strongly exerted, he is absolutely unconscious. Now, I have always known what I did, though less so last night than on the previous occasions. That seems to mean that she has never yet exerted her full powers upon me. Was ever a man so placed before!

Yes, perhaps there was, and very near me, too. Charles Sadler must know something of this! His vague words of warning take a meaning now. Oh, if I had only listened to him then, before I helped by these repeated sittings to forge the links of the chain which binds me. But I will see him today. I will apologise to him for having treated his warning so lightly. I will see if he can advise me.

4 p.m.—Sadler cannot advise me. I have talked with him, and he showed such surprise at the first words in which I tried to express my unspeakable secret that I went no further. As far as I can gather (by hints and inferences rather than by any statement), his own experience was limited to some words or looks such as I have myself endured. His abandonment of Miss Penclosa is in itself a sign that he was never really in her toils. Oh, if he only knew his escape! He has to thank his phlegmatic Saxon temperament for it. I am black and Celtic, and this hag's clutch is deep in my nerves. Shall I ever get it out? Shall I ever be the same man that I was just one short fortnight ago?

Let me consider what I had better do. I cannot leave the university in the middle of the term. If I were free my course would be obvious. I should start at once and travel in Persia. But would she allow me to start? And could her influence not reach me in Persia, and bring me back to within touch of her crutch? I can only find out the limits of this hellish power by my own bitter experience. I will fight and fight and fight—and what can I do more?

I know very well that about eight o'clock tonight that craving for her society—that irresistible restlessness—will come upon me. How shall I overcome it? What shall I do? I must make it impossible for me to leave the room. I shall lock the door and throw the key out of the window. But, then, what am I to do in the morning? Never mind about the morning. I must at all costs break this chain which holds me.

April 9th—Victory! I have done splendidly! At seven o'clock last night I took a hasty dinner, and then locked myself up in my bedroom and dropped the key into the garden. I chose a cheery novel and lay in bed for three hours trying to read it, but really in a horrible state of trepidation, expecting every instant that I should become conscious of the impulse. Nothing of the sort occurred, however, and I awoke this morning with the feeling that a black nightmare had been lifted off me. Perhaps the creature realized what I had done, and understood that it was useless to try to influence me. At any rate, I have beaten her once, and if I can do it once I can do it again.

It was most awkward about the key in the morning. Luckily, there was an under-gardener below, and I asked him to throw it up. No doubt he thought I had just dropped it. I will have doors and windows screwed up and six stout men to hold me down in my bed before I will surrender myself to be hag-ridden in this way.

I had a note from Mrs Marden this afternoon asking me to go round and see her. I intended to do so in any case, but had not excepted to find bad news waiting for me. It seems that the Armstrongs, from whom Agatha has expectations, are due home from Adelaide in the *Aurora*, and that they have written to Mrs Marden and her to meet them in town. They will probably be away for a month or six weeks, and, as the *Aurora* is due on Wednesday, they must go at once—tomorrow, if they are ready in time. My consolation is that when we meet again there will be no more parting between Agatha and me.

'I want you to do one thing, Agatha,' said I, when we were alone together. 'If you should happen to meet Miss Penclosa, either in town or here, you must promise me never again to allow her to mesmerise you.'

Agatha opened her eyes.

'Why, it was only the other day that you were saying how interesting it all was, and how determined you were to finish your experiments.'

'I know, but I have changed my mind since then.'

'And you won't have it any more?'

'No.'

'I am so glad, Austin. You can't think how pale and worn you have been lately. It was really our principal objection to going to London now, that we did not wish to leave you when you were so pulled down. And your manner has been so strange occasionally—especially that night when you left poor Professor Pratt-Haldane to play dummy. I am convinced that these experiments are very bad for your nerves.'

'I think so, too, dear.'

'And for Miss Penclosa's nerves as well. You have heard that she is ill?'

'No.'

'Mrs Wilson told us so last night. She described it as a nervous fever. Professor Wilson is coming back this week, and of course Mrs Wilson is very anxious that Miss Penclosa should be well again then, for he has quite a programme of experiments which he is anxious to carry out.'

I was glad to have Agatha's promise, for it was enough that this woman should have one of us in her clutch. On the other hand, I was disturbed to hear about Miss Penclosa's illness. It rather discounts the victory which I appeared to win last night. I remember that she said that loss of health interfered with her power. That may be why I was able to hold my own so easily. Well, well, I must take the same precautions tonight and see what comes of it. I am childishly frightened when I think of her.

April 10th—All went very well last night. I was amused at the gardener's face when I had again to hail him this morning and to ask him to throw up my key. I shall get a name among the servants if this sort of thing goes on. But the great point is that I stayed in my room without the slightest inclination to leave it. I do believe that I am shaking myself clear of this incredible bond—or is it only that the woman's power is in abeyance until she recovers her strength? I can but pray for the best.

The Mardens left this morning, and the brightness seems to have gone out of the spring sunshine. And yet it is very beautiful also as it gleams on the green chestnuts opposite my windows, and gives a touch of gaiety to the heavy, lichen-mottled walls of the old colleges. How sweet and gentle and soothing is Nature! Who would think that there lurked in her also such vile forces, such odious possibilities! For of course I understand that this dreadful thing which has sprung out at me is neither supernatural nor even preternatural. No, it is a natural force which this woman can use and society is ignorant of. The mere fact that it ebbs with her strength shows how entirely it is subject to physical laws. If I had time, I might probe it to the bottom and lay my hands upon its antidote. But you cannot tame the tiger when you are beneath his claws. You can but try to writhe away from him. Ah, when I look in the glass and see my own dark eyes and clear-cut Spanish face, I long for a vitriol splash or a bout of the small-pox. One or the other might have saved me from this calamity.

I am inclined to think that I may have trouble tonight. There are two things which make me fear so. One is that I met Mrs Wilson in the street, and that she tells me that Miss Penclosa is better, though still weak. I find myself wishing in my heart that the illness had been her last. The other is that Professor Wilson comes back in a day or two, and his presence would act as a constraint upon her. I should not fear our interviews if a third person were present. For both these reasons I have a presentiment of trouble tonight, and I shall take the same precautions as before.

April 10th—No, thank God, all went well last night. I really could not face the gardener again. I locked my door and thrust the key underneath it, so that I had to ask the maid to let me out in the morning. But the precaution was really not needed, for I never had any inclination to go out at all. Three evenings in succession at home! I am surely near the end of my troubles, for Wilson will be home again either today or tomorrow. Shall I tell him of what I have gone through or not? I am convinced that I should not have the slightest sympathy from him. He would look upon me as an interesting case, and read a paper about me at the next meeting of the Psychical Society, in which he would gravely discuss the possibility of my being a deliberate liar, and weigh it against the chances of my being in an early stage of lunacy. No, I shall get no comfort out of Wilson.

I am feeling wonderfully fit and well. I don't think I ever lectured with greater spirit. Oh, if I could only get this shadow off my life, how happy I should be! Young, fairly wealthy, in the front rank of my profession, engaged to a beautiful and charming girl—have I not every thing which a man could ask for? Only one thing to trouble me, but what a thing it is!

Midnight—I shall go mad. Yes, that will be the end of it. I shall go mad. I am not far from it now. My head throbs as I rest it on my hot hand. I am quivering all over like a scared horse. Oh, what a night I have had! And yet I have some cause to be satisfied also.

At the risk of becoming the laughing-stock of my own servant, I again slipped my key under the door, imprisoning myself for the night. Then, finding it too early to go to bed, I lay down with my clothes on and began to read one of Dumas' novels. Suddenly I was gripped—gripped and dragged from the couch. It is only thus that I can describe the overpowering nature of the force which pounced upon me. I clawed at the coverlet. I clung to the woodwork. I believe that I screamed out in my frenzy. It was all useless—hopeless. I must go. There was no way out of it. It was only at the outset that I resisted. The force soon became too overmastering for that. I thank goodness that there were no watchers there to interfere with me. I could not have answered for myself if there had been. And besides the determination to get out, there came to me also the keenest and coolest judgment in choosing my means. I lit a candle and endeavoured, kneeling in front of the door, to pull the key through with the feather-end of a quill pen. It was just too short and pushed it further away. Then with quiet persistence I got a paper-knife out of one of the drawers, and with that I managed to draw the key back. I opened the door, stepped into my study, took a photograph of myself from the bureau, wrote something across it, placed it in the inside pocket of my coat, and then started off for Wilson's.

It was all wonderfully clear, and yet disassociated from the rest of my life, as the incidents of even the most vivid dream might be. A peculiar double consciousness possessed me. There was the predominant alien will, which was bent upon drawing me to the side of its owner, and there was the feebler protesting personality, which I recognized as being myself, tugging feebly at the overmastering impulse as a led terrier might at its chain. I can remember recognizing these two conflicting forces, but I recall nothing of my walk, nor of how I was admitted to the house.

Very vivid, however, is my recollection of how I met Miss Penclosa. She was reclining on the sofa in the little boudoir in which our experiments had usually been carried out. Her head was rested on her hand, and a tiger-skin rug had been partly drawn over her. She looked up expectantly as I entered, and, as the lamplight fell upon her face, I could see that she was very pale and thin, with dark hollows under her eyes. She smiled at me and pointed to a stool beside her. It was with her left hand that she pointed, and I, running eagerly forward, seized it—I loathe myself as I think of it—and pressed it passionately to my lips. Then, seating myself upon the stool, and still retaining her hand, I gave her the photograph which I had brought with me, and talked and talked and talked, of my love for her, of my grief over her illness, of my joy at her recovery, of the misery it was to me to be absent a single evening from her side. She lay quietly looking down at me with imperious eyes and her provocative smile. Once I remember that she passed her hand over my hair as one caresses a dog. And it gave me pleasure, the caress. I thrilled under it. I was her slave, body and soul, and for the moment I rejoiced in my slavery.

And then came the blessed change. Never tell me that there is not a Providence. I was on the brink of perdition. My feet were on the edge. Was it a coincidence that at that very instant help should come? No, no, no! There is a Providence, and its hand has drawn me back. There is something in the universe stronger than this devil woman with her tricks. Ah, what a balm to my heart it is to think so!

As I looked up at her I was conscious of a change in her. Her face, which had been pale before, was now ghastly. Her eyes were dull, and the lids drooped heavily over them. Above all, the look of serene confidence had gone from her features. Her mouth had weakened. Her forehead had puckered. She was frightened and undecided. And as I watched the change my own spirit fluttered and struggled, trying hard to tear itself from the grip which held it—a grip which, from moment to moment, grew less secure.

'Austin,' she whispered, 'I have tried to do too much. I was not strong enough. I have not recovered yet from my illness. But I could not live longer without seeing you. You won't leave me, Austin. This is only a passing weakness. If you will only give me five minutes, I shall be myself again. Give me the small decanter from the table in the window.'

But I had regained my soul. With her waning strength the influence had cleared away from me and left me free. And I was aggressive—bitterly, fiercely aggressive. For once at least I could make this woman understand what my real feelings towards her were. My soul was filled with a hatred as bestial as the love against which it was a reaction. It was the savage, murderous passion of the revolted serf. I could have taken the crutch from her side and beaten her face in with it. She threw her hands up, as if to avoid a blow, and cowered away from me into the corner of the settee.

'The brandy!' she gasped. 'The brandy!'

I took the decanter and poured it over the roots of a palm in the window. Then I snatched the photograph from her hand and tore it into a hundred pieces.

'You vile woman,' I said, 'if I did my duty to society, you would never leave this room alive!'

'I love you, Austin; I love you,' she wailed.

'Yes,' I cried, 'and Charles Sadler before. And how many others before that?'

'Charles Sadler!' she gasped. 'He has spoken to you? So, Charles Sadler, Charles Sadler!' Her voice came through her white lips like a snake's hiss.

'Yes, I know you, and others shall know you, too. You shameless creature! You knew how I stood. And yet you used your vile power to bring me to your side. You may perhaps do so again, but at least you will remember that you have heard me say that I love Miss Marden from the bottom of my soul, and that I loathe you, abhor you. The very sight of you and the sound of your voice fill me with horror and disgust. The thought of you is repulsive. That is how I feel towards you, and if it pleases you by your tricks to draw me again to your side as you have done tonight, you will at least, I should think, have little satisfaction in trying to make a lover out of a man who has told you his real opinion of you. You may put what words you will into my mouth, but you cannot help remembering——'

I stopped, for the woman's head had fallen back, and she had fainted. She could not bear to hear what I had to say to her. What a glow of satisfaction it gives me to think that, come what may, in the future she can never misunderstand my true feelings towards her. But what will occur in the future? What will she do next? I dare not think of it. Oh, if only I could hope that she will leave me alone! But when I think of what I said to her—Never mind; I have been stronger than she for once.

April 11th—I hardly slept last night, and found myself in the morning so unstrung and feverish that I was compelled to ask Pratt-Haldane to do my lecture for me. It is the first that I have ever missed. I rose at mid-day, but my head is aching, my hands quivering, and my nerves in a pitiable state.

Who should come round this evening but Wilson. He has just come back from London, where he has lectured, read papers, convened meetings, exposed a medium, conducted a series of experiments on thought transference, entertained Professor Richet of Paris, spent hours gazing into a crystal, and obtained some evidence as to the passage of matter through matter. All this he poured into my ears in a single gust.

'But you!' he cried at last; 'you are not looking well. And Miss Penclosa is quite prostrated today. How about the experiments?'

'I have abandoned them.'

'Tut, tut! Why?'

'The subject seems to me to be a dangerous one.'

Out came his big brown note-book.

'This is of great interest,' said he. 'What are your grounds for saying that it is a dangerous one? Please give your facts in chronological order, with approximate dates and names of reliable witnesses with their permanent addresses.'

'First of all,' I asked, 'would you tell me whether you have collected any cases where the mesmerist has gained a command over the subject and has used it for evil purposes?'

'Dozens!' he cried exultantly. 'Crime by suggestion——'

'I don't mean suggestion. I mean where a sudden impulse comes from a person at a distance—an uncontrollable impulse.'

'Obsession!' he shrieked, in an ecstasy of delight. 'It is the rarest condition. We have eight cases, five well attested. You don't mean to say——' His exultation made him hardly articulate.

'No, I don't,' said I. 'Good evening! You will excuse me, but I am not very well tonight.' And so at last I got rid of him, still brandishing his pencil and his note-book. My troubles may be bad to bear, but at least it is better to hug them to myself than to have myself exhibited by Wilson like a freak at a fair. He has lost sight of human beings. Everything to him is a case and a phenomenon. I will die before I speak to him again upon the matter.

April 12th—Yesterday was a blessed day of quiet, and I enjoyed an uneventful night. Wilson's presence is a great consolation. What can the woman do now? Surely, when she has heard me say what I have said, she will conceive the same disgust for me which I have for her. She could not, no, she *could* not, desire to have a lover who had insulted her so. No, I believe I am free from her love—but how about her hate? Might she not use these powers of hers for revenge? Tut! why should I frighten myself over shadows? She will forget about me, and I shall forget about her, and all will be well.

April 13th—My nerves have quite recovered their tone. I really believe that I have conquered the creature. But I must confess to living in some suspense. She is well again, for I hear that she was driving with Mrs Wilson in the High Street in the afternoon.

April 14th—I do wish I could get away from the place altogether. I shall fly to Agatha's side the very day that the term closes. I suppose it is pitiably weak of me, but this woman gets upon my nerves most terribly. I have seen her again, and I have spoken with her.

It was just after lunch, and I was smoking a cigarette in my study, when I heard the step of my servant Murray in the passage. I was languidly conscious that a second step was audible behind, and had hardly troubled myself to speculate who it might be, when suddenly a slight noise brought me out of my chair with my skin creeping with apprehension. I had never particularly observed before what sort of sound the tapping of a crutch was, but my quivering nerves told me that I heard it now in the sharp wooden clack which alternated with the muffled thud of the footfall. Another instant and my servant had shown her in.

I did not attempt the usual conventions of society, nor did she. I simply stood with the smouldering cigarette in my hand, and gazed at her. She in her turn looked silently at me, and at her look I remembered how in these very pages I had tried to define the expression of her eyes, whether they were furtive or fierce. Today they were fierce—coldly and inexorably so.

'Well' said she at last, 'are you still of the same mind as when I saw you last?'

'I have always been of the same mind.'

'Let us understand each other, Professor Gilroy,' said she slowly. 'I am not a very safe person to trifle with, as you should realise by now. It was you who asked me to enter into a series of experiments with you, it was you who won my affections, it was you who professed your love for me, it was you who brought me your own photograph with words of affection upon it, and, finally, it was you who on the very same evening thought fit to insult me most outrageously, addressing me as no man has ever dared to speak to me yet. Tell me that those words came from you in a moment of passion and I am prepared to forget and to forgive them. You did not mean what you said, Austin? You do not really hate me?'

I might have pitied this deformed woman—such a longing for love broke suddenly through the menace of her eyes. But then I thought of what I had gone through, and my heart set like flint.

'If ever you heard me speak of love,' said I, 'you know very well that it was your voice which spoke and not mine. The only words of truth which I have ever been able to say to you are those which you heard when last we met.'

'I know. Someone has set you against me. It was he.' She tapped with her crutch upon the floor. 'Well, you know very well that I could bring you this instant crouching like a spaniel to my feet. You will not find me again in my hour of weakness, when you can insult me with impunity. Have a care what you are doing, Professor Gilroy. You stand in a terrible position. You have not yet realised the hold which I have upon you.'

I shrugged my shoulders and turned away.

'Well,' said she, after a pause, 'if you despise my love, I must see what can be done with fear. You smile, but the day will come when you will come screaming to me for pardon. Yes, you will grovel on the ground before me, proud as you are, and you will curse the day that ever you turned me from your best friend into your most bitter enemy. Have a care, Professor Gilroy!' I saw a white hand shaking in the air, and a face which was scarcely human, so convulsed was it with passion. An instant later she was gone, and I heard the quick hobble and tap receding down the passage.

But she has left a weight upon my heart. Vague presentiments of coming misfortune lie heavy upon me. I try in vain to persuade myself that these are only words of empty anger. I can remember those relentless eyes too clearly to think so. What shall I do—ah, what shall I do? I am no longer master of my own soul. At any moment this loathsome parasite may creep into me, and then—— I must tell someone my hideous secret. I must tell it or go mad. If I had someone to sympathize and advise! Wilson is out of the question. Charles Sadler would understand me only so far as his own experience carries him. Pratt-Haldane! He is a well-balanced man, a man of great common-sense and resource. I will go to him. I will tell him every thing. God grant that he may be able to advise me!

6.45 p.m.—No, it is useless. There is no human help for me. I must fight this out single-handed. Two courses lie before me. I might become this woman's lover; or I must endure such persecutions as she can inflict upon me. Even if none come, I shall live in a hell of apprehension. But she may torture me, she may drive me mad, she may kill me—I will never, never, never give in. What can she inflict which would be worse than the loss of Agatha, and the knowledge that I am a perjured liar, and have forfeited the name of gentleman?

Pratt-Haldane was most amiable, and listened with all politeness to my story. But when I looked at his heavy set features, his slow eyes, and the ponderous study furniture which surrounded him, I could hardly tell him what I had come to say. It was all so substantial, so material. And, besides, what would I myself have said a short month ago if one of my colleagues had come to me with a story of demonic possession? Perhaps I should have been less patient than he was. As it was, he took notes of my statement, asked me how much tea I drank, how many hours I slept, whether I had been overworking much, had I had sudden pains in the head, evil dreams, singing in the ears, flashes before the eyes—all questions which pointed to his belief that brain congestion was at the bottom of my trouble. Finally he dismissed me with a great many platitudes about open-air exercise, and avoidance of nervous excitement. His prescription, which was for chloral and bromide, I rolled up and threw into the gutter.

No, I can look for no help from any human being. If I consult any more, they may put their heads together and I may find myself in an asylum. I can but grip my courage with both hands, and pray that an honest man may not be abandoned.

April 15th—It is the sweetest spring within the memory of man. So green, so mild, so beautiful! Ah, what a contrast between nature without and my own soul so torn with doubt and terror! It has been an uneventful day, but I know that I am on the edge of an abyss. I know it, and yet I go on with the routine of my life. The one bright spot is that Agatha is happy and well and out of all danger. If this creature had a hand on each of us, what might she not do?

April 16th—The woman is ingenious in her torments. She knows how fond I am of my work, and how highly my lectures are thought of. So it is from that point that she now attacks me. It will end, I can see, in my losing my professorship, but I will fight to the finish. She shall not drive me out of it without a struggle.

I was not conscious of any change during my lecture this morning, save that for a minute or two I had a dizziness and swimminess which rapidly passed away. On the contrary, I congratulated myself upon having made my subject (the functions of the red corpuscles) both interesting and clear. I was surprised, therefore, when a student came into my laboratory immediately after the lecture, and complained of being puzzled by the discrepancy between my statements and those in the text-books. He showed me his note-book, in which I was reported as having in one portion of the lecture championed the most outrageous and unscientific heresies. Of course I denied it, and declared that he had misunderstood me; but on comparing his notes with those of his companions, it became clear that he was right, and that I really had made some most preposterous statements. Of course I shall explain it away as being the result of a moment of aberration, but I feel only too sure that it will be the first of a series. It is but a month now to the end of the session, and I pray that I may be able to hold out until then.

April 26th—Ten days have elapsed since I have had the heart to make any entry in my journal. Why should I record my own humiliation and degradation? I had vowed never to open it again. And yet the force of habit is strong, and here I find myself taking up once more the record of my own dreadful experiences, in much the same spirit in which a suicide has been known to take notes of the effects of the poison which killed him.

Well, the crash which I had foreseen has come—and that no further back than yesterday. The university authorities have taken my lectureship from me. It has been done in the most delicate way, purporting to be a temporary measure to relieve me from the effects of overwork and to give me the opportunity of recovering my health. None the less, it has been done, and I am no longer Professor Gilroy. The laboratory is still in my charge, but I have little doubt that that also will soon go.

The fact is that my lectures had become the laughing-stock of the university. My class was crowded with students who came to see and hear what the eccentric professor would do or say next. I cannot go into the detail of my humiliation. Oh, that devilish woman! There is no depth of buffoonery and imbecility to which she has not forced me. I would begin my lecture clearly and well—but always with the sense of a coming eclipse. Then as I felt the influence I would struggle against it, striving with clenched hands and beads of sweat upon my brow to get the better of it, while the students, hearing my incoherent words and watching my contortions, would roar with laughter at the antics of their professor. And then, when she had once fairly mastered me, out would come the most outrageous things—silly jokes, sentiments as though I were proposing a toast, snatches of ballads, personal abuse even against some member of my class. And then in a moment my brain would clear again, and my lecture would proceed decorously to the end. No wonder that my conduct has been the talk of the colleges. No wonder that the University Senate has been compelled to take official notice of such a scandal. Oh, that devilish woman!

And the most dreadful part of it all is my own loneliness. Here I sit in a commonplace English bow-window, looking out upon a commonplace English street with its garish 'buses and its lounging policeman, and behind me there hangs a shadow which is out of all keeping with the age and place. In the home of knowledge I am weighed down and tortured by a power of which science knows nothing. No magistrate would listen to me. No paper would discuss my case. No doctor would believe my symptoms. My own most intimate friends would only look upon it as a sign of brain derangement. I am out of all touch with my kind. Oh, that devilish woman! Let her have a care! She may push me too far. When the law cannot help a man, he may make a law for himself.

She met me in the High Street yesterday evening and spoke to me. It was as well for her, perhaps, that it was not between the hedges of a lonely country road. She asked me with her cold smile whether I had been chastened yet. I did not deign to answer her. 'We must try another turn of the screw,' said she. Have a care, my lady, have a care! I had her at my mercy once. Perhaps another chance may come.

April 28th—The suspension of my lectureship has had the effect also of taking away her means of annoying me, and so I have enjoyed two blessed days of peace. After all, there is no reason to despair. Sympathy pours in to me from all sides, and every one agrees that it is my devotion to science and the arduous nature of my researches which have shaken my nervous system. I have had the kindest message from the council advising me to travel abroad, and expressing the confident hope that I may be able to resume all my duties by the beginning of the summer term. Nothing could be more flattering than their allusions to my career and to my services to the university. It is only in misfortune that one can test one's own popularity. This creature may weary of tormenting me, and then all may yet be well. May God grant it!

April 29th—Our sleepy little town has had a small sensation. The only knowledge of crime which we ever have is when a rowdy undergraduate breaks a few lamps or comes to blows with a policeman. Last night, however, there was an attempt made to break into the branch of the Bank of England, and we are all in a flutter in consequence.

Parkenson, the manager, is an intimate friend of mine, and I found him very much excited when I walked round there after breakfast. Had the thieves broken into the counting-house they would still have had the safes to reckon with, so that the defence was considerably stronger than the attack. Indeed, the latter does not appear to have ever been very formidable. Two of the lower windows have marks as if a chisel or some such instrument had been pushed under them to force them open. The police should have a good clue, for the woodwork had been done with green paint only the day before, and from the smears it is evident that some of it has found its way on to the criminal's hands or clothes.

4.30 p.m.—Ah, that accursed woman! That thrice accursed woman! Never mind! She shall not beat me! No, she shall not! But, oh, the she-devil! She has taken my professorship. Now she would take my honour. Is there nothing I can do against her, nothing save—ah, but, hard pushed as I am, I cannot bring myself to think of that!

It was about an hour ago that I went into my bedroom, and was brushing my hair before the glass, when suddenly my eyes lit upon something which left me so sick and cold that I sat down upon the edge of the bed and began to cry. It is many a long year since I shed tears, but all my nerve was gone, and I could but sob and sob in impotent grief and anger. There was my house jacket, the coat I usually wear after dinner, hanging on its peg by the wardrobe, with the right sleeve thickly crusted from wrist to elbow with daubs of green paint.

So this was what she meant by another turn of the screw! She had made a public imbecile of me. Now she would brand me as a criminal. This time she has failed. But how about the next? I dare not think of it—and of Agatha and my poor old mother! I wish that I were dead!

Yes, this is the other turn of the screw. And this is also what she meant, no doubt, when she said that I had not realised yet the power she has over me. I look back at my account of my conversation with her, and I see how she declared that with a slight exertion of her will her subject would be conscious, and with a stronger one unconscious. Last night I was unconscious. I could have sworn that I slept soundly in my bed without so much as a dream. And yet those stains tell me that I dressed, made my way out, attempted to open the bank windows, and returned. Was I observed? Is it possible that someone saw me do it and followed me home? Ah, what a hell my life has become! I have no peace, no rest. But my patience is nearing its end.

10 p.m.—I have cleaned my coat with turpentine. I do not think that any one could have seen me. It was with my screw-driver that I made the marks. I found it all crusted with paint, and I have cleaned it. My head aches as if it would burst, and I have taken five grains of antipyrine. If it were not for Agatha, I should have taken fifty and had an end of it.

May 3rd—Three quiet days. This hell fiend is like a cat with a mouse. She lets me loose only to pounce upon me again. I am never so frightened as when everything is still. My physical state is deplorable—perpetual hiccough and ptosis of the left eyelid.

I have heard from the Mardens that they will be back the day after tomorrow. I do not know whether I am glad or sorry. They were safe in London. Once here they may be drawn into the miserable network in which I am myself struggling. And I must tell them of it. I cannot marry Agatha so long as I know that I am not responsible for my own actions. Yes, I must tell them, even if it brings everything to an end between us.

Tonight is the university ball, and I must go. God knows I never felt less in the humour for festivity, but I must not have it said that I am unfit to appear in public. If I am seen there, and have speech with some of the elders of the university it will go a long way towards showing them that it would be unjust to take my chair away from me.

11.30 p.m.—I have been to the ball. Charles Sadler and I went together, but I have come away before him. I shall wait up for him, however, for indeed I fear to go to sleep these nights. He is a cheery, practical fellow, and a chat with him will steady my nerves. On the whole, the evening was a great success. I talked to everyone who has influence, and I think that I made them realise that my chair is not vacant quite yet. The creature was at the ball—unable to dance, of course, but sitting with Mrs Wilson. Again and again her eyes rested upon me. They were almost the last things I saw before I left the room. Once, as I sat sideways to her, I watched her and saw that her gaze was following someone else. It was Sadler, who was dancing at the time with the second Miss Thurston. To judge by her expression it is well for him that he is not in her grip as I am. He does not know the escape he has had. I think I hear his step in the street now, and I will go down and let him in. If he will——

May 4th—Why did I break off in this way last night? I never went downstairs, after all—at least, I have no recollection of doing so. But, on the other hand, I cannot remember going to bed. One of my hands is greatly swollen this morning, and yet I have no remembrance of injuring it yesterday. Otherwise, I am feeling all the better for last night's festivity. But I cannot understand how it is that I did not meet Charles Sadler when I so fully intended to do so. Is it possible? My God, it is only too probable! Has she been leading me some devil's dance again? I will go down to Sadler and ask him.

Mid-day—The thing has come to a crisis. My life is not worth living. But if I am to die, then she shall come also. I will not leave her behind to drive some other man mad as she has me. No, I have come to the limit of my endurance. She has made me as desperate and dangerous a man as walks the earth. God knows I have never had the heart to hurt a fly, and yet, if I had my hands now upon that woman, she should never leave this room alive. I shall see her this very day, and she shall learn what she has to expect from me.

I went to Sadler and found him, to my surprise, in bed. As I entered he sat up and turned a face towards me which sickened me as I looked at it.

'Why, Sadler, what has happened?' I cried, but my heart turned cold as I said it.

'Gilroy,' he answered, mumbling with his swollen lips, 'I have for some weeks been under the impression that you are a madman. Now I know it, and that you are a dangerous one as well. If it were not that I am unwilling to make a scandal in the college, you would now be in the hands of the police.'

'Do you mean——' I cried.

'I mean that, as I opened the door last night you rushed out upon me, struck me with both your fists in the face, knocked me down, kicked me furiously in the side, and left me lying almost unconscious in the street. Look at your own hand bearing witness against you.'

Yes, there it was, puffed up, with sponge-like knuckles as after some terrific blow. What could I do? Though he put me down as a madman, I must tell him all. I sat by his bed and went over all my troubles from the beginning. I poured them out with quivering hands and burning words which might have carried conviction to the most sceptical. 'She hates you and she hates me,' I cried. 'She revenged herself last night on both of us at once. She saw me leave the ball and she must have seen you also. She knew how long it would take you to reach home. Then she had but to use her wicked will. Ah, your bruised face is a small thing beside my bruised soul!'

He was struck by my story. That was evident. 'Yes, yes, she watched me out of the room,' he muttered. 'She is capable of it. But is it possible that she has really reduced you to this? What do you intend to do?'

'To stop it!' I cried. 'I am perfectly desperate; I shall give her fair warning today, and the next time will be the last.'

'Do nothing rash,' said he.

'Rash!' I cried. 'The only rash thing is that I should postpone it another hour.' With that I rushed to my room, and here I am on the eve of what may be the great crisis of my life. I shall start at once. I have gained one thing today, for I have made one man, at least, realize the truth of this monstrous experience of mine. And, if the worst should happen, this diary remains as a proof of the goad that has driven me.

Evening—When I came to Wilson's, I was shown up, and found that he was sitting with Miss Penclosa. For half an hour I had to endure his fussy talk about his recent research into the exact nature of the spiritualistic rap, while the creature and I sat in silence looking across the room at each other. I read a sinister amusement in her eyes, and she must have seen hatred and menace in mine. I had almost despaired of having speech with her when he was called from the room, and we were left for a few moments together.

'Well, Professor Gilroy—or is it Mr Gilroy?' said she, with that bitter smile of hers, 'how is your friend Mr Charles Sadler after the ball?'

'You fiend!' I cried. 'You have come to the end of your tricks now. I will have no more of them. Listen to what I say'—I strode across and shook her roughly by the shoulder—'as sure as there is a God in heaven, I swear that if you try another of your deviltries upon me I will have your life for it. Come what may, I will have your life. I have come to the end of what a man can endure.'

'Accounts are not quite settled between us,' said she, with a passion that equalled my own. 'I can love, and I can hate. You had your choice. You chose to spurn the first; now you must test the other. It will take a little more to break your spirit, I see, but broken it shall be. Miss Marden comes back tomorrow, as I understand.'

'What has that to do with you?' I cried. 'It is a pollution that you should dare even to think of her. If I thought that you would harm her——'

She was frightened, I could see, though she tried to brazen it out. She read the black thought in my mind, and cowered away from me.

'She is fortunate in having such a champion,' said she. 'He actually dares to threaten a lonely woman. I must really congratulate Miss Marden upon her protector.'

The words were bitter, but the voice and manner were more acid still.

'There is no use talking,' said I. 'I only came here to tell you—and to tell you most solemnly—that your next outrage upon me will be your last.' With that, as I heard Wilson's step upon the stair, I walked from the room. Ay, she may look venomous and deadly, but for all that she is beginning to see now that she has as much to fear from me as I can have from her. Murder! It has an ugly sound. But you don't talk of murdering a snake or of murdering a tiger. Let her have a care now.

May 5th—I met Agatha and her mother at the station at eleven o'clock. She is looking so bright, so happy, so beautiful. And she was so overjoyed to see me. What have I done to deserve such love? I went back home with them, and we lunched together. All the troubles seem in a moment to have been shredded back from my life. She tells me that I am looking pale and worried and ill. The dear child puts it down to my loneliness and the perfunctory attentions of a housekeeper. I pray that she may never know the truth! May the shadow, if shadow there must be, lie ever black across my life and leave hers in the sunshine. I have just come back from them, feeling a new man. With her by my side I think that I could show a bold face to any thing which life might send.

5 p.m.—Now, let me try to be accurate. Let me try to say exactly how it occurred. It is fresh in my mind, and I can set it down correctly, though it is not likely that the time will ever come when I shall forget the doings of today.

I had returned from the Mardens' after lunch, and was cutting some microscopic sections in my freezing microtome, when in an instant I lost consciousness in the sudden hateful fashion which has become only too familiar to me of late.

When my senses came back to me I was sitting in a small chamber, very different from the one in which I had been working. It was cosy and bright, with chintz-covered settees, coloured hangings, and a thousand pretty little trifles upon the wall. A small ornamental clock ticked in front of me, and the hands pointed to half-past three. It was all quite familiar to me, and yet I stared about for a moment in a half-dazed way until my eyes fell upon a cabinet photograph of myself upon the top of the piano. At the other side stood one of Mrs Marden. Then, of course, I remembered where I was. It was Agatha's boudoir.

But how came I there, and what did I want? A horrible sinking came to my heart. Had I been sent here on some devilish errand? Had that errand already been done? Surely it must be, otherwise why should I be allowed to come back to consciousness? Oh, the agony of that moment! What had I done? I sprang to my feet in my despair, and as I did so a small glass bottle fell from my knees on to the carpet.

It was unbroken, and I picked it up. Outside was written 'Sulphuric Acid. Fort.' When I drew the round glass stopper, a thick fume rose slowly up, and a pungent, choking smell pervaded the room. I recognized it as one which I kept for chemical testing in my chambers. But why had I brought a bottle of vitriol into Agatha's chamber? Was it not this thick, reeking liquid with which jealous women had been known to mar the beauty of their rivals? My heart stood still as I held the bottle to the light. Thank God, it was full! No mischief had been done as yet. But had Agatha come in a minute sooner, was it not certain that the hellish parasite within me would have dashed the stuff on to her—ah, it will not bear to be thought of. But it must have been for that. Why else should I have brought it? At the thought of what I might have done my worn nerves broke down, and I sat shivering and twitching, the pitiable wreck of a man.

It was the sound of Agatha's voice and the rustle of her dress which restored me. I looked up, and saw her blue eyes, so full of tenderness and pity, gazing down at me.

'We must take you away to the country, Austin,' she said. 'You want rest and quiet. You look wretchedly ill.'

'Oh, it is nothing!' said I, trying to smile. 'It was only a momentary weakness. I am all right again now.'

'I am so sorry to keep you waiting. Poor boy, you must have been here for quite half an hour! The vicar was in the drawing-room, and as I knew that you did not care for him I thought it better that Jane should show you up here. I thought the man would never go.'

'Thank God he stayed! Thank God he stayed!' I cried hysterically.

'Why, what is the matter with you, Austin?' she asked, holding my arm as I staggered up from the chair. 'Why are you glad that the vicar stayed? And what is this little bottle in your hand?'

'Nothing,' I cried, thrusting it into my pocket. 'But I must go. I have something important to do.'

'How stern you look, Austin! I have never seen your face like that. You are angry?'

'Yes, I am angry.'

'But not with me?'

'No, no, my darling. You would not understand.'

'But you have not told me why you came.'

'I came to ask you whether you would always love me—no matter what I did, or what shadow might fall on my name. Would you believe in me and trust me however black appearances might be against me?'

'You know that I would, Austin.'

'Yes, I know that you would. What I do I shall do for you. I am driven to it. There is no other way out, my darling!' I kissed her and rushed from the room.

The time for indecision was at an end. As long as the creature threatened my own prospects and my honour there might be a question as to what I should do. But now, when Agatha—my innocent Agatha—was endangered, my duty lay before me like a turnpike road. I had no weapon, but I never paused for that. What weapon should I need when I felt every muscle quivering with the strength of a frenzied man? I ran through the streets, so set upon what I had to do that I was only dimly conscious of the faces of friends whom I met—dimly conscious also that Professor Wilson met me, running with equal precipitance in the opposite direction. Breathless but resolute I reached the house and rang the bell. A white-cheeked maid opened the door, and turned whiter yet when she saw the face that looked in at her.

'Show me up at once to Miss Penclosa,' I demanded.

'Sir,' she gasped, 'Miss Penclosa died this afternoon at half-past three!'

The Striped Chest

'WHAT DO YOU MAKE OF HER, Allardyce?' I asked.

My second mate was standing beside me upon the poop, with his short, thick legs astretch, for the gale had left a considerable swell behind it, and our two quarter-boats nearly touched the water with every roll. He steadied his glass against the mizzen-shrouds, and he looked long and hard at this disconsolate stranger every time she came reeling up on to the crest of a roller and hung balanced for a few seconds before swooping down upon the other side. She lay so low in the water that I could only catch an occasional glimpse of a pea-green line of bulwark.

She was a brig, but her mainmast had been snapped short off some ten feet above the deck, and no effort seemed to have been made to cut away the wreckage, which floated, sails and yards, like the broken wing of a wounded gull, upon the water beside her. The foremast was still standing, but the fore-topsail was flying loose, and the headsails were streaming out in long white pennons in front of her. Never have I seen a vessel which appeared to have gone through rougher handling.

But we could not be surprised at that, for there had been times during the last three days when it was a question whether our own barque would ever see land again. For thirty-six hours we had kept her nose to it, and if the *Mary Sinclair* had not been as good a sea-boat as ever left the Clyde, we could not have gone through. And yet here we were at the end of it with the loss only of our gig and of part of the starboard bulwark. It did not astonish us, however, when the smother had cleared away, to find that others had been less lucky, and that this mutilated brig, staggering about upon a blue sea, and under a cloudless sky, had been left, like a blinded man after a lightning flash, to tell of the terror which is past.

Allardyce, who was a slow and methodical Scotchman, stared long and hard at the little craft, while our seamen lined the bulwark or clustered upon the fore shrouds to have a view of the stranger. In latitude 20° and longitude 10°, which were about our bearings, one becomes a little curious as to whom one meets, for one has left the main lines of Atlantic commerce to the north. For ten days we had been sailing over a solitary sea.

'She's derelict, I'm thinking,' said the second mate.

I had come to the same conclusion, for I could see no sign of life upon her deck, and there was no answer to the friendly wavings from our seamen. The crew had probably deserted her under the impression that she was about to founder.

'She can't last long,' continued Allardyce, in his measured way. 'She may put her nose down and her tail up any minute. The water's lipping up to the edge of her rail.'

'What's her flag?' I asked.

'I'm trying to make out. It's got all twisted and tangled with the halyards. Yes, I've got it now, clear enough. It's the Brazilian flag, but it's wrong side up.'

She had hoisted a signal of distress, then, before her people had abandoned her. Perhaps they had only just gone. I took the mate's glass and looked round over the tumultuous face of the deep blue Atlantic, still veined and starred with white lines and spoutings of foam. But nowhere could I see anything human beyond ourselves.

'There may be living men aboard,' said I.

'There may be salvage,' muttered the second mate.

'Then we will run down upon her lee side, and lie to.'

We were not more than a hundred yards from her when we swung our foreyard aback, and there we were, the barque and the brig, ducking and bowing like two clowns in a dance.

'Drop one of the quarter-boats,' said I. 'Take four men, Mr Allardyce, and see what you can learn of her.'

But just at that moment my first officer, Mr Armstrong, came on deck, for seven bells had struck, and it was but a few minutes off his watch. It would interest me to go myself to this abandoned vessel and to see what there might be aboard of her. So, with a word to Armstrong, I swung myself over the side, slipped down the falls, and took my place in the sheets of the boat.

It was but a little distance, but it took some time to traverse, and so heavy was the roll, that often, when we were in the trough of the sea, we could not see either the barque which we had left or the brig which we were approaching. The sinking sun did not penetrate down there, and it was cold and dark in the hollows of the waves, but each passing billow heaved us up into the warmth and the sunshine once more. At each of these moments, as we hung upon a white-capped ridge between the two dark valleys, I caught a glimpse of the long, pea-green line, and the nodding foremast of the brig, and I steered so as to come round by her stern, so that we might determine which was the best way of boarding her. As we passed her we saw the name *Nossa Sehnora da Vittoria* painted across her dripping counter.

'The weather side, sir,' said the second mate. 'Stand by with the boathook, carpenter!' An instant later we had jumped over the bulwarks, which were hardly higher than our boat, and found ourselves upon the deck of the abandoned vessel.

Our first thought was to provide for our own safety in case—as seemed very probable—the vessel should settle down beneath our feet. With this object two of our men held on to the painter of the boat, and fended her off from the vessel's side, so that she might be ready in case we had to make a hurried retreat. The carpenter was sent to find out how much water there was, and whether it was still gaining, while the other seaman, Allardyce, and myself, made a rapid inspection of the vessel and her cargo.

The deck was littered with wreckage and with hencoops, in which the dead birds were washing about. The boats were gone, with the exception of one, the bottom of which had been stove, and it was certain that the crew had abandoned the vessel. The cabin was in a deck house, one side of which had been beaten in by a heavy sea. Allardyce and I entered it, and found the captain's table as he had left it, his books and papers—all Spanish or Portuguese—scattered over it, with piles of cigarette ash everywhere. I looked about for the log, but could not find it.

'As likely as not he never kept one,' said Allardyce. 'Things are pretty slack aboard a South American trader, and they don't do more than they can help. If there was one it must have been taken away with him in the boat.'

'I should like to take all these books and papers,' said I. 'Ask the carpenter how much time we have.'

His report was reassuring. The vessel was full of water, but some of the cargo was buoyant, and there was no immediate danger of her sinking. Probably she would never sink, but would drift about as one of those terrible, unmarked reefs which have sent so many stout vessels to the bottom.

'In that case there is no danger in your going below, Mr Allardyce,' said I. 'See what you can make of her, and find out how much of her cargo may be saved. I'll look through these papers while you are gone.'

The bills of lading, and some notes and letters which lay upon the desk, sufficed to inform me that the Brazilian brig *Nossa Sehnora da Vittoria* had cleared from Bahia a month before. The name of the captain was Texeira, but there was no record as to the number of the crew. She was bound for London, and a glance at the bills of lading was sufficient to show me that we were not likely to profit much in the way of salvage. Her cargo consisted of nuts, ginger, and wood, the latter in the shape of great logs of valuable tropical growths. It was these, no doubt, which had prevented the ill-fated vessel from going to the bottom, but they were of such a size as to make it impossible for us to extract them. Besides these, there were a few fancy goods, such as a number of ornamental birds for millinery purposes, and a hundred cases of preserved fruits. And then, as I turned over the papers, I came upon a short note in English, which arrested my attention.

'It is requested,' said the note, 'that the various old Spanish and Indian curiosities, which came out of the Santarem collection, and which are consigned to Prontfoot and Neuman, of Oxford Street, London, should be put in some place where there may be no danger of these very valuable and unique articles being injured or tampered with. This applies most particularly to the treasure-chest of Don Ramirez di Leyra, which must on no account be placed where anyone can get at it.'

The treasure-chest of Don Ramirez! Unique and valuable articles! Here was a chance of salvage after all! I had risen to my feet with the paper in my hand, when my Scotch mate appeared in the doorway.

'I'm thinking all isn't quite as it should be aboard of this ship, sir,' said he. He was a hard-faced man, and yet I could see that he had been startled.

'What's the matter?'

'Murder's the matter, sir. There's a man here with his brains beaten out.'

'Killed in the storm?' said I.

'Maybe so, sir. But I'll be surprised if you think so after you have seen him.'

'Where is he, then?'

'This way, sir; here in the main-deck house.'

There appeared to have been no accommodation below in the brig, for there was the afterhouse for the captain, another by the main hatchway with the cook's galley attached to it, and a third in the forecastle for the men. It was to this middle one that the mate led me. As you entered, the galley, with its litter of tumbled pots and dishes, was upon the right, and upon the left was a small room with two bunks for the officers. Then beyond there was a place about twelve feet square, which was littered with flags and spare canvas. All round the walls were a number of packets done up in coarse cloth and carefully lashed to the woodwork. At the other end was a great box, striped red and white, though the red was so faded and the white so dirty that it was only where the light fell directly upon it that one could see the colouring. The box was, by subsequent measurement, four feet three inches in length, three feet two inches in height, and three feet across—considerably larger than a seaman's chest.

But it was not to the box that my eyes or my thoughts were turned as I entered the store-room. On the floor, lying across the litter of bunting, there was stretched a small, dark man with a short, curling beard. He lay as far as it was possible from the box, with his feet towards it and his head away. A crimson patch was printed upon the white canvas on which his head was resting, and little red ribbons wreathed themselves round his swarthy neck and trailed away on to the floor, but there was no sign of a wound that I could see, and his face was as placid as that of a sleeping child.

It was only when I stooped that I could perceive his injury, and then I turned away with an exclamation of horror. He had been pole-axed; apparently by some person standing behind him. A frightful blow had smashed in the top of his head and penetrated deeply into his brain. His face might well be placid, for death must have been absolutely instantaneous, and the position of the wound showed that he could never have seen the person who had inflicted it.

'Is that foul play or accident, Captain Barclay?' asked my second mate, demurely.

'You are quite right, Mr Allardyce. The man has been murdered, struck down from above by a sharp and heavy weapon. But who was he, and why did they murder him?'

'He was a common seaman, sir,' said the mate. 'You can see that if you look at his fingers.' He turned out his pockets as he spoke and brought to light a pack of cards, some tarred string, and a bundle of Brazilian tobacco.

'Hullo, look at this!' said he.

It was a large, open knife with a stiff spring blade which he had picked up from the floor. The steel was shining and bright, so that we could not associate it with the crime, and yet the dead man had apparently held it in his hand when he was struck down, for it still lay within his grasp.

'It looks to me, sir, as if he knew he was in danger, and kept his knife handy,' said the mate. 'However, we can't help the poor beggar now. I can't make out these things that are lashed to the wall. They seem to be idols and weapons and curios of all sorts done up in old sacking.'

'That's right,' said I. 'They are the only things of value that we are likely to get from the cargo. Hail the barque and tell them to send the other quarter-boat to help us to get the stuff aboard.'

While he was away I examined this curious plunder which had come into our possession. The curiosities were so wrapped up that I could only form a general idea as to their nature, but the striped box stood in a good light where I could thoroughly examine it. On the lid, which was clamped and cornered with metal-work, there was engraved a complex coat of arms, and beneath it was a line of Spanish which I was able to decipher as meaning, 'The treasure-chest of Don Ramirez di Leyra, Knight of the Order of Saint James, Governor and Captain-General of Terra Firma and of the Province of Veraquas.' In one corner was the date 1606, and on the other a large white label, upon which was written in English, 'You are earnestly requested, upon no account, to open this box.' The same warning was repeated underneath in Spanish. As to the lock, it was a very complex and heavy one of engraved steel, with a Latin motto, which was above a seaman's comprehension.

By the time I had finished this examination of the peculiar box, the other quarter-boat with Mr Armstrong, the first officer, had come alongside, and we began to carry out and place in her the various curiosities which appeared to be the only objects worth moving from the derelict ship. When she was full I sent her back to the barque, and then Allardyce and I, with a carpenter and one seaman, shifted the striped box, which was the only thing left, to our boat, and lowered it over, balancing it upon the two middle thwarts, for it was so heavy that it would have given the boat a dangerous tilt had we placed it at either end. As to the dead man, we left him where we had found him.

The mate had a theory that, at the moment of the desertion of the ship, this fellow had started plundering, and that the captain in an attempt to preserve discipline, had struck him down with a hatchet or some other heavy weapon. It seemed more probable than any other explanation, and yet it did not entirely satisfy me either. But the ocean is full of mysteries, and we were content to leave the fate of the dead seaman of the Brazilian brig to be added to that long list which every sailor can recall.

The heavy box was slung up by ropes on to the deck of the *Mary Sinclair*, and was carried by four seamen into the cabin, where, between the table and the after-lockers, there was just space for it to stand. There it remained during supper, and after that meal the mates remained with me, and discussed over a glass of grog the event of the day. Mr Armstrong was a long, thin, vulture-like man, an excellent seaman, but famous for his nearness and cupidity. Our treasure-trove had excited him greatly, and already he had begun with glistening eyes to reckon up how much it might be worth to each of us when the shares of the salvage came to be divided.

'If the paper said that they were unique, Mr Barclay, then they may be worth anything that you like to name. You wouldn't believe the sums that the rich collectors give. A thousand pounds is nothing to them. We'll have something to show for our voyage, or I am mistaken.'

'I don't think that,' said I. 'As far as I can see they are not very different from any other South American curios.'

'Well, sir, I've traded there for fourteen voyages, and I have never seen anything like that chest before. That's worth a pile of money, just as it stands. But it's so heavy, that surely there must be something valuable inside it. Don't you think that we ought to open it and see?'

'If you break it open you will spoil it, as likely as not,' said the second mate.

Armstrong squatted down in front of it, with his head on one side, and his long, thin nose within a few inches of the lock.

'The wood is oak,' said he, 'and it has shrunk a little with age. If I had a chisel or a strong-bladed knife I could force the lock back without doing any damage at all.'

The mention of a strong-bladed knife made me think of the dead seaman upon the brig.

'I wonder if he could have been on the job when someone came to interfere with him,' said I.

'I don't know about that, sir, but I am perfectly certain that I could open the box. There's a screwdriver here in the locker. Just hold the lamp, Allardyce, and I'll have it done in a brace of shakes.'

'Wait a bit,' said I, for already, with eyes which gleamed with curiosity and with avarice, he was stooping over the lid. 'I don't see that there is any hurry over this matter. You've read that card which warns us not to open it. It may mean anything or it may mean nothing, but somehow I feel inclined to obey it. After all, whatever is in it will keep, and if it is valuable it will be worth as much if it is opened in the owner's offices as in the cabin of the *Mary Sinclair*.'

The first officer seemed bitterly disappointed at my decision.

'Surely, sir, you are not superstitious about it,' said he, with a slight sneer upon his thin lips. 'If it gets out of our own hands, and we don't see for ourselves what is inside it, we may be done out of our rights; besides——'

'That's enough, Mr Armstrong,' said I, abruptly. 'You may have every confidence that you will get your rights, but I will not have that box opened tonight.'

'Why, the label itself shows that the box has been examined by Europeans,' Allardyce added. 'Because a box is a treasure-box is no reason that it has treasures inside it now. A good many folk have had a peep into it since the days of the old Governor of Terra Firma.'

Armstrong threw the screwdriver down upon the table and shrugged his shoulders.

'Just as you like,' said he; but for the rest of the evening, although we spoke upon many subjects, I noticed that his eyes were continually coming round, with the same expression of curiosity and greed, to the old striped box.

And now I come to that portion of my story which fills me even now with a shuddering horror when I think of it. The main cabin had the rooms of the officers round it, but mine was the farthest away from it at the end of the little passage which led to the companion. No regular watch was kept by me, except in cases of emergency, and the three mates divided the watches among them. Armstrong had the middle watch, which ends at four in the morning, and he was relieved by Allardyce. For my part I have always been one of the soundest of sleepers, and it is rare for anything less than a hand upon my shoulder to arouse me.

And yet I was aroused that night, or rather in the early grey of the morning. It was just half-past four by my chronometer when something caused me to sit up in my berth wide awake and with every nerve tingling. It was a sound of some sort, a crash with a human cry at the end of it, which still jarred upon my ears. I sat listening, but all was now silent. And yet it could not have been imagination, that hideous cry, for the echo of it still rang in my head, and it seemed to have come from some place quite close to me. I sprang from my bunk, and, pulling on some clothes, I made my way into the cabin.

At first I saw nothing unusual there. In the cold, grey light I made out the red-clothed table, the six rotating chairs, the walnut lockers, the swinging barometer, and there, at the end, the big striped chest. I was turning away with the intention of going upon deck and asking the second mate if he had heard anything, when my eyes fell suddenly upon something which projected from under the table. It was the leg of a man—a leg with a long sea-boot upon it. I stooped, and there was a figure sprawling upon his face, his arms thrown forward and his body twisted. One glance told me that it was Armstrong, the first officer, and a second that he was a dead man. For a few moments I stood gasping. Then I rushed on to the deck, called Allardyce to my assistance, and came back with him into the cabin.

Together we pulled the unfortunate fellow from under the table, and as we looked at his dripping head we exchanged glances, and I do not know which was the paler of the two.

'The same as the Spanish sailor,' said I.

'The very same. God preserve us! It's that infernal chest! Look at Armstrong's hand!'

He held up the mate's right hand, and there was the screwdriver which he had wished to use the night before.

'He's been at the chest, sir. He knew that I was on deck and you asleep. He knelt down in front of it, and he pushed the lock back with that tool. Then something happened to him, and he cried out so that you heard him.'

'Allardyce,' I whispered, 'what *could* have happened to him?'

The second mate put his hand upon my sleeve and drew me into his cabin.

'We can talk here, sir, and we don't know who may be listening to us in there. What do you suppose is in that box, Captain Barclay?'

'I give you my word, Allardyce, that I have no idea.'

'Well, I can only find one theory which will fit all the facts. Look at the size of the box. Look at all the carving and metal-work which may conceal any number of holes. Look at the weight of it; it took four men to carry it. On the top of that, remember that two men have tried to open it, and both have come to their end through it. Now, sir, what can it mean except one thing?'

'You mean there is a man in it?'

'Of course there is a man in it. You know how it is in these South American States, sir. A man may be President one week and hunted like a dog the next. They are for ever flying for their lives. My idea is that there is some fellow in hiding there, who is armed and desperate, and who will fight to the death before he is taken.'

'But his food and drink?'

'It's a roomy chest, sir, and he may have some provisions stowed away. As to his drink, he had a friend among the crew upon the brig who saw that he had what he needed.'

'You think, then, that the label asking people not to open the box was simply written in his interest?'

'Yes, sir, that is my idea. Have you any other way of explaining the facts?'

I had to confess that I had not.

'The question is what are we to do?' I asked.

'The man's a dangerous ruffian who sticks at nothing. I'm thinking it wouldn't be a bad thing to put a rope round the chest and tow it alongside for half an hour; then we could open it at our ease. Or if we just tied the box up and kept him from getting any water maybe that would do as well. Or the carpenter could put a coat of varnish over it and stop all the blowholes.'

'Come, Allardyce,' said I, angrily. 'You don't seriously mean to say that a whole ship's company are going to be terrorized by a single man in a box. If he's there, I'll engage to fetch him out!' I went to my room and came back with my revolver in my hand. 'Now, Allardyce,' said I. 'Do you open the lock, and I'll stand on guard.'

'For God's sake, think what you are doing, sir!' cried the mate. 'Two men have lost their lives over it, and the blood of one not yet dry upon the carpet.'

'The more reason why we should revenge him.'

'Well sir, at least let me call the carpenter. Three are better than two, and he is a good stout man.'

He went off in search of him, and I was left alone with the striped chest in the cabin. I don't think that I'm a nervous man, but I kept the table between me and this solid old relic of the Spanish Main. In the growing light of morning the red and white striping was beginning to appear, and the curious scrolls and wreaths of metal and carving which showed the loving pains which cunning craftsmen had expended upon it. Presently the carpenter and the mate came back together, the former with a hammer in his hand.

'It's a bad business, this, sir,' said he, shaking his head, as he looked at the body of the mate. 'And you think there's someone hiding in the box?'

'There's no doubt about it,' said Allardyce, picking up the screwdriver and setting his jaw like a man who needs to brace his courage. 'I'll drive the lock back if you will both stand by. If he rises let him have it on the head with your hammer, carpenter! Shoot at once, sir, if he raises his hand. Now!'

He had knelt down in front of the striped chest, and passed the blade of the tool under the lid. With a sharp snick the lock flew back. 'Stand by!' yelled the mate, and with a heave he threw open the massive top of the box. As it swung up, we all three sprang back, I with my pistol levelled, and the carpenter with the hammer above his head. Then, as nothing happened, we each took a step forward and peeped in. The box was empty.

Not quite empty either, for in one corner was lying an old yellow candlestick, elaborately engraved, which appeared to be as old as the box itself. Its rich yellow tone and artistic shape suggested that it was an object of value. For the rest there was nothing more weighty or valuable than dust in the old striped treasure-chest.

'Well, I'm blessed!' cried Allardyce, staring blankly into it. 'Where does the weight come in, then?'

'Look at the thickness of the sides and look at the lid. Why, it's five inches through. And see that great metal spring across it.'

'That's for holding the lid up,' said the mate. 'You see, it won't lean back. What's that German printing on the inside?'

'It means that it was made by Johann Rothstein of Augsburg, in 1606.'

'And a solid bit of work, too. But it doesn't throw much light on what has passed, does it, Captain Barclay? That candlestick looks like gold. We shall have something for our trouble after all.'

He leant forward to grasp it, and from that moment I have never doubted as to the reality of inspiration, for on the instant I caught him by the collar and pulled him straight again. It may have been some story of the Middle Ages which had come back to my mind, or it may have been that my eye had caught some red which was not that of rust upon the upper part of the lock, but to him and to me it will always seem an inspiration, so prompt and sudden was my action.

'There's devilry here,' said I. 'Give me the crooked stick from the corner.'

It was an ordinary walking-cane with a hooked top. I passed it over the candlestick and gave it a pull. With a flash a row of polished steel fangs shot out from below the upper lip, and the great striped chest snapped at us like a wild animal. Clang came the huge lid into its place, and the glasses on the swinging rack sang and tinkled with the shock. The mate sat down on the edge of the table and shivered like a frightened horse.

'You've saved my life, Captain Barclay!' said he.

So this was the secret of the striped treasure-chest of old Don Ramirez di Leyra, and this was how he preserved his ill-gotten gains from the Terra Firma and the Province of Veraquas. Be the thief ever so cunning he could not tell that golden candlestick from the other articles of value, and the instant that he laid hand upon it the terrible spring was unloosed and the murderous steel spikes were driven into his brain, while the shock of the blow sent the victim backwards and enabled the chest to automatically close itself. How many, I wondered, had fallen victims to the ingenuity of the Mechanic of Augsburg. And as I thought of the possible history of that grim striped chest my resolution was very quickly taken.

'Carpenter, bring three men and carry this on deck.'

'Going to throw it overboard, sir?'

'Yes, Mr Allardyce. I'm not superstitious as a rule, but there are some things which are more than a sailor can be called upon to stand.'

'No wonder that brig made heavy weather, Captain Barclay, with such a thing on board. The glass is dropping fast, sir, and we are only just in time.'

So we did not even wait for the three sailors, but we carried it out, the mate, the carpenter, and I, and we pushed it with our own hands over the bulwarks. There was a white spout of water, and it was gone. There it lies, the striped chest, a thousand fathoms deep, and if, as they say, the sea will some day be dry land, I grieve for the man who finds that old box and tries to penetrate into its secret.

The Fiend of the Cooperage

I T WAS NO EASY MATTER TO BRING the *Gamecock* up to the island, for the river
had swept down so much silt that the banks extended for many miles out
into the Atlantic. The coast was hardly to be seen when the first white curl
of the breakers warned us of our danger, and from there onwards we made our
way very carefully under mainsail and jib, keeping the broken water well to the
left, as is indicated on the chart. More than once her bottom touched the sand
(we were drawing something under six feet at the time), but we had always way
enough and luck enough to carry us through. Finally, the water shoaled very
rapidly, but they had sent a canoe from the factory, and the Krooboy pilot
brought us within two hundred yards of the island. Here we dropped our
anchor, for the gestures of the negro indicated that we could not hope to get
any farther. The blue of the sea had changed to the brown of the river, and
even under the shelter of the island the current was singing and swirling round
our bows. The stream appeared to be in spate, for it was over the roots of the
palm trees, and everywhere upon its muddy, greasy surface we could see logs of
wood and debris of all sorts which had been carried down by the flood.

When I had assured myself that we swung securely at our moorings, I
thought it best to begin watering at once, for the place looked as if it reeked
with fever. The heavy river, the muddy, shining banks, the bright poisonous
green of the jungle, the moist steam in the air, they were all so many danger
signals to one who could read them. I sent the long-boat off, therefore, with
two large hogsheads, which should be sufficient to last us until we made St
Paul de Loanda. For my own part I took the dinghy and rowed for the island,
for I could see the Union Jack fluttering above the palms to mark the position
of Armitage and Wilson's trading station.

When I had cleared the grove, I could see the place, a long, low,
whitewashed building, with a deep verandah in front, and an immense pile of
palm-oil barrels heaped upon either flank of it. A row of surf boats and canoes
lay along the beach, and a single small jetty projected into the river. Two men
in white suits with red cummerbunds round their waists were waiting upon the
end of it to receive me. One was a large portly fellow with a greyish beard. The
other was slender and tall, with a pale, pinched face, which was half-concealed
by a great mushroom-shaped hat.

'Very glad to see you,' said the latter, cordially. 'I am Walker, the agent of Armitage and Wilson. Let me introduce Dr Severall of the same company. It is not often we see a private yacht in these parts.'

'She's the *Gamecock*,' I explained. 'I'm owner and captain—Meldrum is the name.'

'Exploring?' he asked.

'I'm a lepidopterist—a butterfly catcher. I've been doing the west coast from Senegal downwards.'

'Good sport?' asked the doctor, turning a slow, yellow-shot eye upon me.

'I have forty cases full. We came in here to water, and also to see what you have in my line.'

These introductions and explanations had filled up the time whilst my two Krooboys were making the dinghy fast. Then I walked down the jetty with one of my new acquaintances upon either side, each plying me with questions, for they had seen no white man for months.

'What do we do?' said the Doctor, when I had begun asking questions in my turn. 'Our business keeps us pretty busy, and in our leisure time we talk politics.'

'Yes, by the special mercy of Providence Severall is a rank Radical and I am a good stiff Unionist, and we talk Home Rule for two solid hours every evening.'

'And drink quinine cocktails,' said the Doctor. 'We're both pretty well salted now, but our normal temperature was about 103 last year. I shouldn't, as an impartial adviser, recommend you to stay here very long unless you are collecting bacilli as well as butterflies. The mouth of the Ogowai River will never develop into a health resort.'

There is nothing finer than the way in which these outlying pickets of civilization distil a grim humour out of their desolate situation, and turn not only a bold, but a laughing face upon the chances which their lives may bring. Everywhere from Sierra Leone downwards I had found the same reeking swamps, the same isolated fever-racked communities, and the same bad jokes. There is something approaching to the divine in that power of man to rise above his conditions and to use his mind for the purpose of mocking at the miseries of his body.

'Dinner will be ready in about half an hour, Captain Meldrum,' said the Doctor. 'Walker has gone in to see about it; he's the housekeeper this week. Meanwhile, if you like, we'll stroll round and I'll show you the sights of the island.'

The sun had already sunk beneath the line of palm trees, and the great arch of the heaven above our head was like the inside of a huge shell, shimmering with dainty pinks and delicate iridescence. No one who has not lived in a land where the weight and heat of a napkin become intolerable upon the knees can imagine the blessed relief which the coolness of evening brings along with it. In this sweeter and purer air the Doctor and I walked round the little island, he pointing out the stores, and explaining the routine of his work.

'There's a certain romance about the place,' said he, in answer to some remark of mine about the dullness of their lives. 'We are living here just upon the edge of the great unknown. Up there,' he continued, pointing to the north-east, 'Du Chaillu penetrated, and found the home of the gorilla. That is the Gaboon country—the land of the great apes. In this direction,' pointing to the south-east, 'no one has been very far. The land which is drained by this river is practically unknown to Europeans. Every log which is carried past us by the current has come from an undiscovered country. I've often wished that I was a better botanist when I have seen the singular orchids and curious-looking plants which have been cast up on the eastern end of the island.'

The place which the Doctor indicated was a sloping brown beach, freely littered with the flotsam of the stream. At each end was a curved point, like a little natural breakwater, so that a small shallow bay was left between. This was full of floating vegetation, with a single huge splintered tree lying stranded in the middle of it, the current rippling against its high black side.

'These are all from up country,' said the Doctor. 'They get caught in our little bay, and then when some extra freshet comes they are washed out again and carried out to sea.'

'What is the tree?' I asked.

'Oh, some kind of teak I should imagine, but pretty rotten by the look of it. We get all sorts of big hardwood trees floating past here, to say nothing of the palms. Just come in here, will you?'

He led the way into a long building with an immense quantity of barrel staves and iron hoops littered about in it.

'This is our cooperage,' said he. 'We have the staves sent out in bundles, and we put them together ourselves. Now, you don't see anything particularly sinister about this building, do you?'

I looked round at the high corrugated iron roof, the white wooden walls, and the earthen floor. In one corner lay a mattress and a blanket.

'I see nothing very alarming,' said I.

'And yet there's something out of the common, too,' he remarked. 'You see that bed? Well, I intend to sleep there tonight. I don't want to buck, but I think it's a bit of a test for nerve.'

'Why?'

'Oh, there have been some funny goings on. You were talking about the monotony of our lives, but I assure you that they are sometimes quite as exciting as we wish them to be. You'd better come back to the house now, for after sundown we begin to get the fever-fog up from the marshes. There, you can see it coming across the river.'

I looked and saw long tentacles of white vapour writhing out from among the thick green underwood and crawling at us over the broad swirling surface of the brown river. At the same time the air turned suddenly dank and cold.

'There's the dinner gong,' said the Doctor. 'If this matter interests you I'll tell you about it afterwards.'

It did interest me very much, for there was something earnest and subdued in his manner as he stood in the empty cooperage, which appealed very forcibly to my imagination. He was a big, bluff, hearty man, this Doctor, and yet I had detected a curious expression in his eyes as he glanced about him—an expression which I would not describe as one of fear, but rather that of a man who is alert and on his guard.

'By the way,' said I, as we returned to the house, 'you have shown me the huts of a good many of your native assistants, but I have not seen any of the natives themselves.'

'They sleep in the hulk over yonder,' the Doctor answered, pointing over to one of the banks.

'Indeed. I should not have thought in that case that they would need the huts.'

'Oh, they used the huts until quite recently. We've put them on the hulk until they recover their confidence a little. They were all half mad with fright, so we let them go, and nobody sleeps on the island except Walker and myself.'

'What frightened them?' I asked.

'Well, that brings us back to the same story. I suppose Walker has no objection to your hearing all about it. I don't know why we should make any secret about it, though it is certainly a pretty bad business.'

He made no further allusion to it during the excellent dinner which had been prepared in my honour. It appeared that no sooner had the little white topsail of the *Gamecock* shown round Cape Lopez than these kind fellows had begun to prepare their famous pepper pot—which is the pungent stew peculiar to the West Coast—and to boil their yams and sweet potatoes. We sat down to as good a native dinner as one could wish, served by a smart Sierra Leone waiting boy. I was just remarking to myself that he at least had not shared in the general flight when, having laid the dessert and wine upon the table, he raised his hand to his turban.

'Anything else I do, Massa Walker?' he asked.

'No, I think that is all right, Moussa,' my host answered. 'I am not feeling very well tonight, though, and I should much prefer if you would stay on the island.'

I saw a struggle between his fears and his duty upon the swarthy face of the African. His skin had turned of that livid purplish tint which stands for pallor in a negro, and his eyes looked furtively about him.

'No, no, Massa Walker,' he cried, at last, 'you better come to the hulk with me, sah. Look after you much better in the hulk, sah!'

'That won't do, Moussa. White men don't run away from the posts where they are placed.'

Again I saw the passionate struggle in the negro's face, and again his fears prevailed.

'No use, Massa Walker, sah!' he cried. 'S'elp me, I can't do it. If it was yesterday or if it was tomorrow, but this is the third night, sah, an' it's more than I can face.'

Walker shrugged his shoulders.

'Off with you then!' said he. 'When the mail boat comes you can get back to Sierra Leone, for I'll have no servant who deserts me when I need him most. I suppose this is all mystery to you, or has the Doctor told you, Captain Meldrum?'

'I showed Captain Meldrum the cooperage, but I did not tell him anything,' said Dr Severall. 'You're looking bad, Walker,' he added, glancing at his companion. 'You have a strong touch coming on you.'

'Yes, I've had the shivers all day, and now my head is like a cannonball. I took ten grains of quinine, and my ears are singing like a kettle. But I want to sleep with you in the cooperage tonight.'

'No, no, my dear chap. I won't hear of such a thing. You must get to bed at once, and I am sure Meldrum will excuse you. I shall sleep in the cooperage, and I promise you that I'll be round with your medicine before breakfast.'

It was evident that Walker had been struck by one of those sudden and violent attacks of remittent fever which are the curse of the West Coast. His sallow cheeks were flushed and his eyes shining with fever, and suddenly as he sat there he began to croon out a song in the high-pitched voice of delirium.

'Come, come, we must get you to bed, old chap,' said the Doctor, and with my aid he led his friend into his bedroom. There we undressed him, and presently, after taking a strong sedative, he settled down into a deep slumber.

'He's right for the night,' said the Doctor, as we sat down and filled our glasses once more. 'Sometimes it is my turn and sometimes his, but, fortunately, we have never been down together. I should have been sorry to be out of it tonight, for I have a little mystery to unravel. I told you that I intended to sleep in the cooperage.'

'Yes, you said so.'

'When I said sleep I meant watch, for there will be no sleep for me. We've had such a scare here that no native will stay after sundown, and I mean to find out tonight what the cause of it all may be. It has always been the custom for a native watchman to sleep in the cooperage, to prevent the barrel hoops being stolen. Well, six days ago the fellow who slept there disappeared, and we have never seen a trace of him since. It was certainly singular, for no canoe had been taken, and these waters are too full of crocodiles for any man to swim to shore. What became of the fellow, or how he could have left the island is a complete mystery. Walker and I were merely surprised, but the blacks were badly scared, and queer Voodoo tales began to get about amongst them. But the real stampede broke out three nights ago, when the new watchman in the cooperage also disappeared.'

'What became of him?' I asked.

'Well, we not only don't know, but we can't even give a guess which would fit the facts. The niggers swear there is a fiend in the cooperage who claims a man every third night. They wouldn't stay in the island—nothing could persuade them. Even Moussa, who is a faithful boy enough, would, as you have seen, leave his master in a fever rather than remain for the night. If we are to continue to run this place we must reassure our niggers, and I don't know any better way of doing it than by putting in a night there myself. This is the third night, you see, so I suppose the thing is due, whatever it may be.'

'Have you no clue?' I asked. 'Was there no mark of violence, no blood-stain, no footprints, nothing to give a hint as to what kind of danger you may have to meet?'

'Absolutely nothing. The man was gone and that was all. Last time it was old Ali, who has been wharf tender here since the place was started. He was always as steady as a rock, and nothing but foul play would take him from his work.'

'Well,' said I, 'I really don't think that this is a one-man job. Your friend is full of laudanum, and come what might he can be of no assistance to you. You must let me stay and put in a night with you at the cooperage.'

'Well, now, that's very good of you, Meldrum,' said he heartily, shaking my hand across the table. 'It's not a thing that I should have ventured to propose, for it is asking a good deal of a casual visitor, but if you really mean it——'

'Certainly I mean it. If you will excuse me a moment, I will hail the *Gamecock* and let them know that they need not expect me.'

As we came back from the other end of the little jetty we were both struck by the appearance of the night. A huge blue-black pile of clouds had built itself up upon the landward side, and the wind came from it in little hot pants, which beat upon our faces like the draught from a blast furnace. Under the jetty the river was swirling and hissing, tossing little white spurts of spray over the planking.

'Confound it!' said Doctor Severall. 'We are likely to have a flood on the top of all our troubles. That rise in the river means heavy rain up-country, and when it once begins you never know how far it will go. We've had the island nearly covered before now. Well, we'll just go and see that Walker is comfortable, and then if you like we'll settle down in our quarters.'

The sick man was sunk in a profound slumber, and we left him with some crushed limes in a glass beside him in case he should awake with the thirst of fever upon him. Then we made our way through the unnatural gloom thrown by that menacing cloud. The river had risen so high that the little bay which I have described at the end of the island had become almost obliterated through the submerging of its flanking peninsula. The great raft of driftwood, with the huge black tree in the middle, was swaying up and down in the swollen current.

'That's one good thing a flood will do for us,' said the Doctor. 'It carries away all the vegetable stuff which is brought down on the east end of the island. It came down with the freshet the other day, and here it will stay until a flood sweeps it out into the main stream. Well, here's our room, and here are some books, and here is my tobacco pouch, and we must try and put in the night as best we may.'

By the light of our single lantern the great lonely room looked very gaunt and dreary. Save for the piles of staves and heaps of hoops there was absolutely nothing in it, with the exception of the mattress for the Doctor, which had been laid in the corner. We made a couple of seats and a table out of the staves, and settled down together for a long vigil. Severall had brought a revolver for me, and was himself armed with a double-barrelled shotgun. We loaded our weapons and laid them cocked within reach of our hands. The little circle of light and the black shadows arching over us were so melancholy that he went off to the house, and returned with two candles. One side of the cooperage was pierced, however, by several open windows, and it was only by screening our lights behind staves that we could prevent them from being extinguished. The Doctor, who appeared to be a man of iron nerves, had settled down to a book, but I observed that every now and then he laid it upon his knee, and took an earnest look all round him. For my part, although I tried once or twice to read, I found it impossible to concentrate my thoughts upon the book. They would always wander back to this great empty silent room, and to the sinister mystery which overshadowed it. I racked my brains for some possible theory which would explain the disappearance of these two men. There was the black fact that they were gone, and not the least tittle of evidence as to why or whither. And here we were waiting in the same place—waiting without an idea as to what we were waiting for. I was right in saying that it was not a one-man job. It was trying enough as it was, but no force upon earth would have kept me there without a comrade.

What an endless, tedious night it was! Outside we heard the lapping and gurgling of the great river, and the soughing of the rising wind. Within, save for our breathing, the turning of the Doctor's pages, and the high, shrill ping of an occasional mosquito there was a heavy silence. Once my heart sprang into my mouth as Severall's book suddenly fell to the ground and he sprang to his feet with his eyes on one of the windows.

'Did you see anything, Meldrum?'

'No. Did you?'

'Well, I had a vague sense of movement outside that window.' He caught up his gun and approached it. 'No, there's nothing to be seen, and yet I could have sworn that something passed slowly across it.'

'A palm leaf, perhaps,' said I, for the wind was growing stronger every instant.

'Very likely,' said he, and settled down to his book again, but his eyes were forever darting little suspicious glances up at the window. I watched it also, but all was quiet outside.

And then suddenly our thoughts were turned into a new direction by the bursting of the storm. A blinding flash was followed by a clap which shook the building. Again and again came the vivid white glare with thunder at the same instant, like the flash and roar of a monstrous piece of artillery. And then down came the tropical rain, crashing and rattling on the corrugated iron roofing of the cooperage. The big hollow room boomed like a drum. From the darkness arose a strange mixture of noises, a gurgling, splashing, tinkling, bubbling, washing, dripping—every liquid sound that nature can produce from the thrashing and swishing of the rain to the deep steady boom of the river. Hour after hour the uproar grew louder and more sustained.

'My word,' said Severall, 'we are going to have the father of all the floods this time. Well, here's the dawn coming at last and that is a blessing. We've about exploded the third night superstition anyhow.'

A grey light was stealing through the room, and there was the day upon us in an instant. The rain had eased off, but the coffee-coloured river was roaring past like a waterfall. Its power made me fear for the anchor of the *Gamecock*.

'I must get aboard,' said I. 'If she drags she'll never be able to beat up the river again.'

'The island is as good as a breakwater,' the Doctor answered. 'I can give you a cup of coffee if you will come up to the house.'

I was chilled and miserable, so the suggestion was a welcome one. We left the ill-omened cooperage with its mystery still unsolved, and we splashed our way up to the house.

'There's the spirit lamp,' said Severall. 'If you would just put a light to it, I will see how Walker feels this morning.

He left me, but was back in an instant with a dreadful face.

'He's gone!' he cried hoarsely.

The words sent a shrill of horror through me. I stood with the lamp in my hand, glaring at him.

'Yes, he's gone!' he repeated. 'Come and look!'

I followed him without a word, and the first thing that I saw as I entered the bedroom was Walker himself lying huddled on his bed in the grey flannel sleeping suit in which I had helped to dress him on the night before.

'Not dead, surely!' I gasped.

The Doctor was terribly agitated. His hands were shaking like leaves in the wind.

'He's been dead some hours.'

'Was it fever?'

'Fever! Look at his foot!'

I glanced down and a cry of horror burst from my lips. One foot was not merely dislocated, but was turned completely round in a most grotesque contortion.

'Good God!' I cried. 'What can have done this?'

Severall had laid his hand upon the dead man's chest.

'Feel here,' he whispered.

I placed my hand at the same spot. There was no resistance. The body was absolutely soft and limp. It was like pressing a sawdust doll.

'The breast-bone is gone,' said Severall in the same awed whisper. 'He's broken to bits. Thank God that he had the laudanum. You can see by his face that he died in his sleep.'

'But who can have done this?'

'I've had about as much as I can stand,' said the Doctor, wiping his forehead. 'I don't know that I'm a greater coward than my neighbours, but this gets beyond me. If you're going out to the *Gamecock*——'

'Come on!' said I, and off we started. If we did not run it was because each of us wished to keep up the last shadow of his self-respect before the other. It was dangerous in a light canoe on that swollen river, but we never paused to give the matter a thought. He bailing and I paddling we kept her above water, and gained the deck of the yacht. There, with two hundred yards of water between us and this cursed island, we felt that we were our own men once more.

'We'll go back in an hour or so,' said he. 'But we need a little time to steady ourselves. I wouldn't have had the niggers see me as I was just now for a year's salary.'

'I've told the steward to prepare breakfast Then we shall go back,' said I. 'But in God's name, Doctor Severall, what do you make of it all?'

'It beats me—beats me clean. I've heard of Voodoo devilry, and I've laughed at it with the others. But that poor old Walker, a decent, God-fearing, nineteenth-century, Primrose-League Englishman, should go under like this without a whole bone in his body—it's given me a shake, I won't deny it. But look there, Meldrum, is that hand of yours mad or drunk, or what is it?'

Old Patterson, the oldest man of my crew, and as steady as the Pyramids, had been stationed in the bows with a boathook to fend off the drifting logs which came sweeping down with the current. Now he stood with crooked knees, glaring out in front of him, and one forefinger stabbing furiously at the air.

'Look at it!' he yelled. 'Look at it!'

And at the same instant we saw it.

A huge black tree trunk was coming down the river, its broad glistening back just lapped by the water. And in front of it—about three feet in front—arching upwards like the figurehead of a ship, there hung a dreadful face, swaying slowly from side to side. It was flattened, malignant, as large as a small beer-barrel, of a faded fungoid colour, but the neck which supported it was mottled with a dull yellow and black. As it flew past the *Gamecock* in the swirl of the waters I saw two immense coils roll up out of some great hollow in the tree, and the villainous head rose suddenly to the height of eight or ten feet, looking with dull, skin-covered eyes at the yacht. An instant later the tree had shot past us and was plunging with its horrible passenger towards the Atlantic.

'What was it?' I cried.

'It is our fiend of the cooperage,' said Doctor Severall, and he had become in an instant the same bluff, self-confident man that he had been before. 'Yes, that is the devil who has been haunting our island. It is the great python of the Gaboon.'

I thought of the stories which I had heard all down the coast of the monstrous constrictors of the interior, of their periodical appetite, and of the murderous effects of their deadly squeeze. Then it all took shape in my mind. There had been a freshet the week before. It had brought down this huge hollow tree with its hideous occupant. Who knows from what far distant tropical forest it may have come! It had been stranded on the little east bay of the island. The cooperage had been the nearest house. Twice with the return of its appetite it had carried off the watchman. Last night it had doubtless come again, when Severall had thought he saw something move at the window, but our lights had driven it away. It had writhed onwards and had slain poor Walker in his sleep.

'Why did it not carry him off?' I asked.

'The thunder and lightning must have scared the brute away. There's your steward, Meldrum. The sooner we have breakfast and get back to the island the better, or some of those niggers might think that we had been frightened.'

The New Catacomb

L OOK HERE, BURGER,' SAID KENNEDY, 'I do wish that you would confide in me.'

The two famous students of Roman remains sat together in Kennedy's comfortable room overlooking the Corso. The night was cold, and they had both pulled up their chairs to the unsatisfactory Italian stove which threw out a zone of stuffiness rather than of warmth. Outside under the bright winter stars lay the modern Rome, the long, double chain of the electric lamps, the brilliantly lighted cafés, the rushing carriages, and the dense throng upon the footpaths. But inside, in the sumptuous chamber of the rich young English archaeologist, there was only old Rome to be seen. Cracked and timeworn friezes hung upon the walls, grey old busts of senators and soldiers with their fighting heads and their hard, cruel faces peered out from the corners. On the centre table, amidst a litter of inscriptions, fragments, and ornaments, there stood the famous reconstruction by Kennedy of the Baths of Caracalla, which excited such interest and admiration when it was exhibited in Berlin. Amphorae hung from the ceiling, and a litter of curiosities strewed the rich red Turkey carpet. And of them all there was not one which was not of the most unimpeachable authenticity, and of the utmost rarity and value; for Kennedy, though little more than thirty, had a European reputation in this particular branch of research, and was, moreover, provided with that long purse which either proves to be a fatal handicap to the student's energies, or, if his mind is still true to its purpose, gives him an enormous advantage in the race for fame. Kennedy had often been seduced by whim and pleasure from his studies, but his mind was an incisive one, capable of long and concentrated efforts which ended in sharp reactions of sensuous languor. His handsome face, with its high, white forehead, its aggressive nose, and its somewhat loose and sensual mouth, was a fair index of the compromise between strength and weakness in his nature.

Of a very different type was his companion, Julius Burger. He came of a curious blend, a German father and an Italian mother, with the robust qualities of the North mingling strangely with the softer graces of the South. Blue Teutonic eyes lightened his sun-browned face, and above them rose a square, massive forehead, with a fringe of close yellow curls lying round it. His strong, firm jaw was clean-shaven, and his companion had frequently remarked how

313

much it suggested those old Roman busts which peered out from the shadows in the corners of his chamber. Under its bluff German strength there lay always a suggestion of Italian subtlety, but the smile was so honest, and the eyes so frank, that one understood that this was only an indication of his ancestry, with no actual bearing upon his character. In age and in reputation, he was on the same level as his English companion, but his life and his work had both been far more arduous. Twelve years before, he had come as a poor student to Rome, and had lived ever since upon some small endowment for research which had been awarded to him by the University of Bonn. Painfully, slowly, and doggedly, with extraordinary tenacity and single-mindedness, he had climbed from rung to rung of the ladder of fame, until now he was a member of the Berlin Academy, and there was every reason to believe that he would shortly be promoted to the Chair of the greatest of German Universities. But the singleness of purpose which had brought him to the same high level as the rich and brilliant Englishman, had caused him in everything outside their work to stand infinitely below him. He had never found a pause in his studies in which to cultivate the social graces. It was only when he spoke of his own subject that his face was filled with life and soul. At other times he was silent and embarrassed, too conscious of his own limitations in larger subjects, and impatient of that small talk which is the conventional refuge of those who have no thoughts to express.

And yet for some years there had been an acquaintanceship which appeared to be slowly ripening into a friendship between these two very different rivals. The base and origin of this lay in the fact that in their own studies each was the only one of the younger men who had knowledge and enthusiasm enough to properly appreciate the other. Their common interests and pursuits had brought them together, and each had been attracted by the other's knowledge. And then gradually something had been added to this. Kennedy had been amused by the frankness and simplicity of his rival, while Burger in turn had been fascinated by the brilliancy and vivacity which had made Kennedy such a favourite in Roman society. I say 'had', because just at the moment the young Englishman was somewhat under a cloud. A love affair, the details of which had never quite come out, had indicated a heartlessness and callousness upon his part which shocked many of his friends. But in the bachelor circles of students and artists in which he preferred to move there is no very rigid code of honour in such matters, and though a head might be shaken or a pair of shoulders shrugged over the flight of two and the return of one, the general sentiment was probably one of curiosity and perhaps of envy rather than of reprobation.

'Look here, Burger,' said Kennedy, looking hard at the placid face of his companion, 'I do wish that you would confide in me.'

As he spoke he waved his hand in the direction of a rug which lay upon the floor. On the rug stood a long, shallow fruit-basket of the light wicker-work which is used in the Campagna, and this was heaped with a litter of objects, inscribed tiles, broken inscriptions, cracked mosaics, torn papyri, rusty metal

314

ornaments, which to the uninitiated might have seemed to have come straight from a dustman's bin, but which a specialist would have speedily recognized as unique of their kind. The pile of odds and ends in the flat wicker-work basket supplied exactly one of those missing links of social development which are of such interest to the student. It was the German who had brought them in, and the Englishman's eyes were hungry as he looked at them.

'I won't interfere with your treasure-trove, but I should very much like to hear about it,' he continued, while Burger very deliberately lit a cigar. 'It is evidently a discovery of the first importance. These inscriptions will make a sensation throughout Europe.'

'For every one here there are a million there!' said the German. 'There are so many that a dozen savants might spend a lifetime over them, and build up a reputation as solid as the Castle of St Angelo.'

Kennedy sat thinking with his fine forehead wrinkled and his fingers playing with his long, fair moustache.

'You have given yourself away, Burger!' said he at last. 'Your words can only apply to one thing. You have discovered a new catacomb.'

'I had no doubt that you had already come to that conclusion from an examination of these objects.'

'Well, they certainly appeared to indicate it, but your last remarks make it certain. There is no place except a catacomb which could contain so vast a store of relics as you describe.'

'Quite so. There is no mystery about that. I have discovered a new catacomb.'

'Where?'

'Ah, that is my secret, my dear Kennedy. Suffice it that it is so situated that there is not one chance in a million of anyone else coming upon it. Its date is different from that of any known catacomb, and it has been reserved for the burial of the highest Christians, so that the remains and the relics are quite different from anything which has ever been seen before. If I was not aware of your knowledge and of your energy, my friend, I would not hesitate, under the pledge of secrecy, to tell you everything about it. But as it is I think that I must certainly prepare my own report of the matter before I expose myself to such formidable competition.'

Kennedy loved his subject with a love which was almost a mania—a love which held him true to it, amidst all the distractions which come to a wealthy and dissipated young man. He had ambition, but his ambition was secondary to his mere abstract joy and interest in everything which concerned the old life and history of the city. He yearned to see this new underworld which his companion had discovered.

'Look here, Burger,' said he, earnestly, 'I assure you that you can trust me most implicitly in the matter. Nothing would induce me to put pen to paper about anything which I see until I have your express permission. I quite understand your feeling and I think it is most natural, but you have really nothing whatever to fear from me. On the other hand, if you don't tell me I shall make a systematic search, and I shall most certainly discover it. In that case, of course, I should make what use I liked of it, since I should be under no obligation to you.'

Burger smiled thoughtfully over his cigar.

'I have noticed, friend Kennedy,' said he, 'that when I want information over any point you are not always so ready to supply it.'

'When did you ever ask me anything that I did not tell you? You remember, for example, my giving you the material for your paper about the temple of the Vestals.'

'Ah, well, that was not a matter of much importance. If I were to question you upon some intimate thing would you give me an answer, I wonder! This new catacomb is a very intimate thing to me, and I should certainly expect some sign of confidence in return.'

'What you are driving at I cannot imagine,' said the Englishman, 'but if you mean that you will answer my question about the catacomb if I answer any question which you may put to me I can assure you that I will certainly do so.'

'Well, then,' said Burger, leaning luxuriously back in his settee, and puffing a blue tree of cigar-smoke into the air, 'tell me all about your relations with Miss Mary Saunderson.'

Kennedy sprang up in his chair and glared angrily at his impassive companion.

'What the devil do you mean?' he cried. 'What sort of a question is this? You may mean it as a joke, but you never made a worse one.'

'No, I don't mean it as a joke,' said Burger, simply. 'I am really rather interested in the details of the matter. I don't know much about the world and women and social life and that sort of thing, and such an incident has the fascination of the unknown for me. I know you, and I knew her by sight—I had even spoken to her once or twice. I should very much like to hear from your own lips exactly what it was which occurred between you.'

'I won't tell you a word.'

'That's all right. It was only my whim to see if you would give up a secret as easily as you expected me to give up my secret of the new catacomb. You wouldn't, and I didn't expect you to. But why should you expect otherwise of me? There's Saint John's clock striking ten. It is quite time that I was going home.'

'No; wait a bit, Burger,' said Kennedy; 'this is really a ridiculous caprice of yours to wish to know about an old love-affair which has burned out months ago. You know we look upon a man who kisses and tells as the greatest coward and villain possible.'

'Certainly,' said the German, gathering up his basket of curiosities, 'when he tells anything about a girl which is previously unknown he must be so. But in this case, as you must be aware, it was a public matter which was the common talk of Rome, so that you are not really doing Miss Mary Saunderson any injury by discussing her case with me. But still, I respect your scruples, and so good night!'

'Wait a bit, Burger,' said Kennedy, laying his hand upon the other's arm; 'I am very keen upon this catacomb business, and I can't let it drop quite so easily. Would you mind asking me something else in return—something not quite so eccentric this time?'

'No, no; you have refused, and there is an end of it,' said Burger, with his basket on his arm. 'No doubt you are quite right not to answer, and no doubt I am quite right also—and so again, my dear Kennedy, good night!'

The Englishman watched Burger cross the room, and he had his hand on the handle of the door before his host sprang up with the air of a man who is making the best of that which cannot be helped.

'Hold on, old fellow,' said he; 'I think you are behaving in a most ridiculous fashion; but still, if this is your condition, I suppose that I must submit to it. I hate saying anything about a girl, but, as you say, it is all over Rome, and I don't suppose I can tell you anything which you do not know already. What was it you wanted to know?'

The German came back to the stove, and, laying down his basket, he sank into his chair once more.

'May I have another cigar?' said he. 'Thank you very much! I never smoke when I work, but I enjoy a chat much more when I am under the influence of tobacco. Now, as regards this young lady, with whom you had this little adventure. What in the world has become of her?'

'She is at home with her own people.'

'Oh, really—in England?'

'Yes.'

'What part of England—London?'

'No, Twickenham.'

'You must excuse my curiosity, my dear Kennedy, and you must put it down to my ignorance of the world. No doubt it is quite a simple thing to persuade a young lady to go off with you for three weeks or so, and then to hand her over to her own family at—what did you call the place?'

'Twickenham.'

'Quite so—at Twickenham. But it is something so entirely outside my own experience that I cannot even imagine how you set about it. For example, if you had loved this girl your love could hardly disappear in three weeks, so I presume that you could not have loved her at all. But if you did not love her why should you make this great scandal which has damaged you and ruined her?'

Kennedy looked moodily into the red eye of the stove.

'That's a logical way of looking at it, certainly,' said he. 'Love is a big word, and it represents a good many different shades of feeling. I liked her, and—well, you say you've seen her—you know how charming she could look. But still I am willing to admit, looking back, that I could never have really loved her.'

'Then, my dear Kennedy, why did you do it?'

'The adventure of the thing had a great deal to do with it.'

'What! You are so fond of adventures!'

'Where would the variety of life be without them? It was for an adventure that I first began to pay my attentions to her. I've chased a good deal of game in my time, but there's no chase like that of a pretty woman. There was the piquant difficulty of it also, for, as she was the companion of Lady Emily Rood, it was almost impossible to see her alone. On the top of all the other obstacles which attracted me, I learned from her own lips very early in the proceedings that she was engaged.'

'Mein Gott! To whom?'

'She mentioned no names.'

'I do not think that anyone knows that. So that made the adventure more alluring, did it?'

'Well, it did certainly give a spice to it. Don't you think so?'

'I tell you that I am very ignorant about these things.'

'My dear fellow, you can remember that the apple you stole from your neighbour's tree was always sweeter than that which fell from your own. And then I found that she cared for me.'

'What—at once?'

'Oh, no, it took about three months of sapping and mining. But at last I won her over. She understood that my judicial separation from my wife made it impossible for me to do the right thing by her—but she came all the same, and we had a delightful time, as long as it lasted.'

'But how about the other man?'

Kennedy shrugged his shoulders.

'I suppose it is the survival of the fittest,' said he. 'If he had been the better man she would not have deserted him. Let's drop the subject, for I have had enough of it!'

'Only one other thing. How did you get rid of her in three weeks?'

'Well, we had both cooled down a bit, you understand. She absolutely refused, under any circumstances, to come back to face the people she had known in Rome. Now, of course, Rome is necessary to me, and I was already pining to be back at my work—so there was one obvious cause of separation. Then, again, her old father turned up at the hotel in London, and there was a scene, and the whole thing became so unpleasant that really—though I missed her dreadfully at first—I was very glad to slip out of it. Now, I rely upon you not to repeat anything of what I have said.'

'My dear Kennedy, I should not dream of repeating it. But all that you say interests me very much, for it gives me an insight into your way of looking at things, which is entirely different from mine, for I have seen so little of life. And now you want to know about my new catacomb. There's no use my trying to describe it, for you would never find it by that. There is only one thing, and that is for me to take you there.'

'That would be splendid.'

'When would you like to come?'

'The sooner the better. I am all impatience to see it.'

'Well, it is a beautiful night—though a trifle cold. Suppose we start in an hour. We must be very careful to keep the matter to ourselves. If anyone saw us hunting in couples they would suspect that there was something going on.'

'We can't be too cautious,' said Kennedy. 'Is it far?'

'Some miles.'

'Not too far to walk?'

'Oh, no, we could walk there easily.'

'We had better do so, then. A cabman's suspicions would be aroused if he dropped us both at some lonely spot in the dead of the night.'

'Quite so. I think it would be best for us to meet at the Gate of the Appian Way at midnight. I must go back to my lodgings for the matches and candles and things.'

'All right, Burger! I think it is very kind of you to let me into this secret, and I promise you that I will write nothing about it until you have published your report. Goodbye for the present! You will find me at the Gate at twelve.'

The cold, clear air was filled with the musical chimes from that city of clocks as Burger, wrapped in an Italian overcoat, with a lantern hanging from his hand, walked up to the rendezvous. Kennedy stepped out of the shadow to meet him.

'You are ardent in work as well as in love!' said the German, laughing.

'Yes; I have been waiting here for nearly half an hour.'

'I hope you left no clue as to where we were going.'

'Not such a fool! By Jove, I am chilled to the bone! Come on, Burger, let us warm ourselves by a spurt of hard walking.'

Their footsteps sounded loud and crisp upon the rough stone paving of the disappointing road which is all that is left of the most famous highway of the world. A peasant or two going home from the wine-shop, and a few carts of country produce coming up to Rome, were the only things which they met. They swung along, with the huge tombs looming up through the darkness upon each side of them, until they had come as far as the Catacombs of St Calixtus, and saw against a rising moon the great circular bastion of Cecilia Metella in front of them. Then Burger stopped with his hand to his side.

'Your legs are longer than mine, and you are more accustomed to walking,' said he, laughing. 'I think that the place where we turn off is somewhere here.

Yes, this is it, round the corner of the trattoria. Now, it is a very narrow path, so perhaps I had better go in front and you can follow.'

He had lit his lantern, and by its light they were enabled to follow a narrow and devious track which wound across the marshes of the Campagna. The great Aqueduct of old Rome lay like a monstrous caterpillar across the moonlit landscape, and their road led them under one of its huge arches, and past the circle of crumbling bricks which marks the old arena. At last Burger stopped at a solitary wooden cow-house, and he drew a key from his pocket.

'Surely your catacomb is not inside a house!' cried Kennedy.

'The entrance to it is. That is just the safeguard which we have against anyone else discovering it.'

'Does the proprietor know of it?'

'Not he. He had found one or two objects which made me almost certain that his house was built on the entrance to such a place. So I rented it from him, and did my excavations for myself. Come in, and shut the door behind you.'

It was a long, empty building, with the mangers of the cows along one wall. Burger put his lantern down on the ground, and shaded its light in all directions save one by draping his overcoat round it.

'It might excite remark if anyone saw a light in this lonely place,' said he. 'Just help me to move this boarding.'

The flooring was loose in the corner, and plank by plank the two savants raised it and leaned it against the wall. Below there was a square aperture and a stair of old stone steps which led away down into the bowels of the earth.

'Be careful!' cried Burger, as Kennedy, in his impatience, hurried down them. 'It is a perfect rabbits'-warren below, and if you were once to lose your way there the chances would be a hundred to one against your ever coming out again. Wait until I bring the light.'

'How do you find your own way if it is so complicated?'

'I had some very narrow escapes at first, but I have gradually learned to go about. There is a certain system to it, but it is one which a lost man, if he were in the dark, could not possibly find out. Even now I always spin out a ball of string behind me when I am going far into the catacomb. You can see for yourself that it is difficult, but every one of these passages divides and subdivides a dozen times before you go a hundred yards.'

They had descended some twenty feet from the level of the byre, and they were standing now in a square chamber cut out of the soft tufa. The lantern cast a flickering light, bright below and dim above, over the cracked brown walls. In every direction were the black openings of passages which radiated from this common centre.

'I want you to follow me closely, my friend,' said Burger. 'Do not loiter to look at anything upon the way, for the place to which I will take you contains all that you can see, and more. It will save time for us to go there direct.'

He led the way down one of the corridors, and the Englishman followed closely at his heels. Every now and then the passage bifurcated, but Burger was evidently following some secret marks of his own, for he neither stopped nor hesitated. Everywhere along the walls, packed like the berths upon an emigrant ship, lay the Christians of old Rome. The yellow light flickered over the shrivelled features of the mummies, and gleamed upon rounded skulls and long, white armbones crossed over fleshless chests. And everywhere as he passed Kennedy looked with wistful eyes upon inscriptions, funeral vessels, pictures, vestments, utensils, all lying as pious hands had placed them so many centuries ago. It was apparent to him, even in those hurried, passing glances, that this was the earliest and finest of the catacombs, containing such a storehouse of Roman remains as had never before come at one time under the observation of the student.

'What would happen if the light went out?' he asked, as they hurried onwards.

'I have a spare candle and a box of matches in my pocket. By the way, Kennedy, have you any matches?'

'No; you had better give me some.'

'Oh, that is all right. There is no chance of our separating.'

'How far are we going? It seems to me that we have walked at least a quarter of a mile.'

'More than that, I think. There is really no limit to the tombs—at least, I have never been able to find any. This is a very difficult place, so I think that I will use our ball of string.'

He fastened one end of it to a projecting stone and he carried the coil in the breast of his coat, paying it out as he advanced. Kennedy saw that it was no unnecessary precaution, for the passages had become more complex and tortuous than ever, with a perfect network of intersecting corridors. But these all ended in one large circular hall with a square pedestal of tufa topped with a slab of marble at one end of it.

'By Jove!' cried Kennedy in an ecstasy, as Burger swung his lantern over the marble. 'It is a Christian altar—probably the first one in existence. Here is the little consecration cross cut upon the corner of it. No doubt this circular space was used as a church.'

'Precisely,' said Burger. 'If I had more time I should like to show you all the bodies which are buried in these niches upon the walls, for they are the early popes and bishops of the Church, with their mitres, their croziers, and full canonicals. Go over to that one and look at it!'

Kennedy went across, and stared at the ghastly head which lay loosely on the shredded and mouldering mitre.

'This is most interesting,' said he, and his voice seemed to boom against the concave vault. 'As far as my experience goes, it is unique. Bring the lantern over, Burger, for I want to see them all.'

But the German had strolled away, and was standing in the middle of a yellow circle of light at the other side of the hall.

'Do you know how many wrong turnings there are between this and the stairs?' he asked. 'There are over two thousand. No doubt it was one of the means of protection which the Christians adopted. The odds are two thousand to one against a man getting out, even if he had a light; but if he were in the dark it would, of course, be far more difficult.'

'So I should think.'

'And the darkness is something dreadful. I tried it once for an experiment. Let us try it again!' He stooped to the lantern, and in an instant it was as if an invisible hand was squeezed tightly over each of Kennedy's eyes. Never had he known what such darkness was. It seemed to press upon him and to smother him. It was a solid obstacle against which the body shrank from advancing. He put his hands out to push it back from him.

'That will do, Burger,' said he, 'let's have the light again.'

But his companion began to laugh, and in that circular room the sound seemed to come from every side at once.

'You seem uneasy, friend Kennedy,' said he.

'Go on, man, light the candle!' said Kennedy impatiently.

'It's very strange, Kennedy, but I could not in the least tell by the sound in which direction you stand. Could you tell where I am?'

'No; you seem to be on every side of me.'

'If it were not for this string which I hold in my hand I should not have a notion which way to go.'

'I dare say not. Strike a light, man, and have an end of this nonsense.'

'Well, Kennedy, there are two things which I understand that you are very fond of. The one is an adventure, and the other is an obstacle to surmount. The adventure must be the finding of your way out of this catacomb. The obstacle will be the darkness and the two thousand wrong turns which make the way a little difficult to find. But you need not hurry, for you have plenty of time, and when you halt for a rest now and then, I should like you just to think of Miss Mary Saunderson, and whether you treated her quite fairly.'

'You devil, what do you mean?' roared Kennedy. He was running about in little circles and clasping at the solid blackness with both hands.

'Goodbye,' said the mocking voice, and it was already at some distance. 'I really do not think, Kennedy, even by your own showing that you did the right thing by that girl. There was only one little thing which you appeared not to know, and I can supply it. Miss Saunderson was engaged to a poor ungainly devil of a student, and his name was Julius Burger.'

There was a rustle somewhere, the vague sound of a foot striking a stone, and then there fell silence upon that old Christian church—a stagnant, heavy silence which closed round Kennedy and shut him in like water round a drowning man.

Some two months afterwards the following paragraph made the round of the European Press:

> One of the most interesting discoveries of recent years is that of the new catacomb in Rome, which lies some distance to the east of the well-known vaults of St Calixtus. The finding of this important burial-place, which is exceeding rich in most interesting early Christian remains, is due to the energy and sagacity of Dr Julius Burger, the young German specialist, who is rapidly taking the first place as an authority upon ancient Rome. Although the first to publish his discovery, it appears that a less fortunate adventurer had anticipated Dr Burger. Some months ago Mr Kennedy, the well-known English student, disappeared suddenly from his rooms in the Corso, and it was conjectured that his association with a recent scandal had driven him to leave Rome. It appears now that he had in reality fallen a victim to that fervid love of archaeology which had raised him to a distinguished place among living scholars. His body was discovered in the heart of the new catacomb, and it was evident from the condition of his feet and boots that he had tramped for days through the tortuous corridors which make these subterranean tombs so dangerous to explorers. The deceased gentleman had, with inexplicable rashness, made his way into this labyrinth without, as far as can be discovered, taking with him either candles or matches, so that his sad fate was the natural result of his own temerity. What makes the matter more painful is that Dr Julius Burger was an intimate friend of the deceased. His joy at the extraordinary find which he has been so fortunate as to make has been greatly marred by the terrible fate of his comrade and fellow-worker.

The Sealed Room

SOLICITOR OF AN ACTIVE HABIT and athletic tastes who is compelled by his hopes of business to remain within the four walls of his office from ten till five must take what exercise he can in the evenings. Hence it was that I was in the habit of indulging in very long nocturnal excursions, in which I sought the heights of Hampstead and Highgate in order to cleanse my system from the impure air of Abchurch Lane. It was in the course of one of these aimless rambles that I first met Felix Stanniford, and so led up to what has been the most extraordinary adventure of my lifetime.

One evening—it was in April or early May of the year 1894—I made my way to the extreme northern fringe of London, and was walking down one of those fine avenues of high brick villas which the huge city is for ever pushing farther and farther out into the country. It was a fine, clear spring night, the moon was shining out of an unclouded sky, and I, having already left many miles behind me, was inclined to walk slowly and look about me. In this contemplative mood, my attention was arrested by one of the houses which I was passing.

It was a very large building, standing in its own grounds, a little back from the road. It was modern in appearance, and yet it was far less so than its neighbours, all of which were crudely and painfully new. Their symmetrical line was broken by the gap caused by the laurel-studded lawn, with the great, dark, gloomy house looming at the back of it. Evidently it had been the country retreat of some wealthy merchant, built perhaps when the nearest street was a mile off, and now gradually overtaken and surrounded by the red brick tentacles of the London octopus. The next stage, I reflected, would be its digestion and absorption, so that the cheap builder might rear a dozen eighty-pound-a-year villas upon the garden frontage. And then, as all this passed vaguely through my mind, an incident occurred which brought my thoughts into quite another channel.

A four-wheeled cab, that opprobrium of London, was coming jolting and creaking in one direction, while in the other there was a yellow glare from the lamp of a cyclist. They were the only moving objects in the whole long, moonlit road, and yet they crashed into each other with that malignant accuracy which brings two ocean liners together in the broad waste of the Atlantic. It was the cyclist's fault. He tried to cross in front of the cab, miscalculated his distance, and was knocked sprawling by the horse's shoulder. He rose, snarling; the cabman swore back at him, and then, realizing that his number had not yet been taken, lashed his horse and lumbered off. The cyclist caught at the handles of his prostrate machine, and then suddenly sat down with a groan. 'Oh, Lord!' he said.

I ran across the road to his side. 'Any harm done?' I asked.

'It's my ankle,' said he. 'Only a twist, I think; but it's pretty painful. Just give me your hand, will you?'

He lay in the yellow circle of the cycle lamp, and I noted as I helped him to his feet that he was a gentlemanly young fellow, with a slight dark moustache and large, brown eyes, sensitive and nervous in appearance, with indications of weak health upon his sunken cheeks. Work or worry had left its traces upon his thin, yellow face. He stood up when I pulled his hand, but he held one foot in the air, and he groaned as he moved it.

'I can't put it to the ground,' said he.

'Where do you live?'

'Here!' He nodded his head towards the big, dark house in the garden. 'I was cutting across to the gate when that confounded cab ran into me. Could you help me so far?'

It was easily done. I put his cycle inside the gate, and then I supported him down the drive, and up the steps to the hall door. There was not a light anywhere, and the place was as black and silent as if no one had ever lived in it.

'That will do. Thank you very much,' said he, fumbling with his key in the lock.

'No, you must allow me to see you safe.'

He made some feeble, petulant protest, and then realised that he could really do nothing without me. The door had opened into a pitch-dark hall. He lurched forward, with my hand still on his arm.

'This door to the right,' said he, feeling about in the darkness.

I opened the door, and at the same moment he managed to strike a light. There was a lamp upon the table, and we lit it between us. 'Now, I'm all right. You can leave me now! Goodbye!' said he, and with the words he sat down in the armchair and fainted dead away.

It was a queer position for me. The fellow looked so ghastly, that really I was not sure that he was not dead. Presently his lips quivered and his breast heaved, but his eyes were two white slits and his colour was horrible. The responsibility was more than I could stand. I pulled at the bell-rope, and heard the bell ringing furiously far away. But no one came in response. The bell tinkled away into silence which no murmur or movement came to break. I waited, and rang again, with the same result. There must be someone about. This young gentleman could not live all alone in that huge house. His people ought to know of his condition. If they would not answer the bell, I must hunt them out myself. I seized the lamp and rushed from the room.

What I saw outside amazed me. The hall was empty. The stairs were bare, and yellow with dust. There were three doors opening into spacious rooms, and each was uncarpeted and undraped, save for the grey webs which drooped from the cornice, and rosettes of lichen which had formed upon the walls. My feet reverberated in those empty and silent chambers. Then I wandered on down the passage, with the idea that the kitchens, at least, might be tenanted. Some caretaker might lurk in some secluded room. No, they were all equally desolate.

Despairing of finding any help, I ran down another corridor, and came on something which surprised me more than ever.

The passage ended in a large, brown door, and the door had a seal of red wax the size of a five-shilling piece over the keyhole. This seal gave me the impression of having been there for a long time, for it was dusty and discoloured. I was still staring at it, and wondering what that door might conceal, when I heard a voice calling behind me, and, running back, found my young man sitting up in his chair and very much astonished at finding himself in darkness.

'Why on earth did you take the lamp away?' he asked.

'I was looking for assistance.'

'You might look for some time,' said he. 'I am alone in the house.'

'Awkward if you get an illness.'

'It was foolish of me to faint. I inherit a weak heart from my mother, and pain or emotion has that effect upon me. It will carry me off someday, as it did her. You're not a doctor, are you?'

'No, a lawyer. Frank Alder is my name.'

'Mine is Felix Stanniford. Funny that I should meet a lawyer, for my friend, Mr Perceval, was saying that we should need one soon.'

'Very happy, I am sure.'

'Well, that will depend upon him, you know. Did you say that you had run with that lamp all over the ground floor?'

'Yes.'

'*All* over it?' he asked, with emphasis, and he looked at me very hard.

'I think so. I kept on hoping that I should find someone.'

'Did you enter *all* the rooms?' he asked, with the same intent gaze.

'Well, all that I could enter.'

'Oh, then you *did* notice it!' said he, and he shrugged his shoulders with the air of a man who makes the best of a bad job.

'Notice what?'

'Why, the door with the seal on it.'

'Yes, I did.'

'Weren't you curious to know what was in it?'

'Well, it did strike me as unusual.'

'Do you think you could go on living alone in this house, year after year, just longing all the time to know what is at the other side of that door, and yet not looking?'

'Do you mean to say,' I cried, 'that you don't know yourself?'

'No more than you do.'

'Then why don't you look?'

'I mustn't,' said he.

He spoke in a constrained way, and I saw that I had blundered on to some delicate ground. I don't know that I am more inquisitive than my neighbours, but there certainly was something in the situation which appealed very strongly to my curiosity. However, my last excuse for remaining in the house was gone now that my companion had recovered his senses. I rose to go.

'Are you in a hurry?' he asked.

'No; I have nothing to do.'

'Well, I should be very glad if you would stay with me a little. The fact is that I live a very retired and secluded life here. I don't suppose there is a man in London who leads such a life as I do. It is quite unusual for me to have anyone to talk with.'

I looked round at the little room, scantily furnished, with a sofa bed at one side. Then I thought of the great, bare house, and the sinister door with the discoloured red seal upon it. There was something queer and grotesque in the situation, which made me long to know a little more. Perhaps I should, if I waited. I told him that I should be very happy.

'You will find the spirits and a siphon upon the side-table. You must forgive me if I cannot act as host, but I can't get across the room. Those are cigars in the tray there. I'll take one myself, I think. And so you are a solicitor, Mr Alder?'

'Yes.'

'And I am nothing. I am that most helpless of living creatures, the son of a millionaire. I was brought up with the expectation of great wealth; and here I am, a poor man, without any profession at all. And then, on the top of it all, I am left with this great mansion on my hands, which I cannot possibly keep up. Isn't it an absurd situation? For me to use this as my dwelling is like a coster drawing his barrow with a thoroughbred. A donkey would be more useful to him, and a cottage to me.'

'But why not sell the house?' I asked.

'I mustn't.'

'Let it, then?'

'No, I mustn't do that either.'

I looked puzzled, and my companion smiled.

'I'll tell you how it is, if it won't bore you,' said he.

'On the contrary, I should be exceedingly interested.'

'I think, after your kind attention to me, I cannot do less than relieve any curiosity that you may feel. You must know that my father was Stanislaus Stanniford, the banker.'

Stanniford, the banker! I remembered the name at once. His flight from the country some seven years before had been one of the scandals and sensations of the time.

'I see that you remember,' said my companion. 'My poor father left the country to avoid numerous friends, whose savings he had invested in an unsuccessful speculation. He was a nervous, sensitive man, and the responsibility quite upset his reason. He had committed no legal offence. It was purely a matter of sentiment. He would not even face his own family, and he died among strangers without ever letting us know where he was.'

'He died!' said I.

'We could not prove his death, but we know that it must be so, because the speculations came right again, and so there was no reason why he should not look any man in the face. He would have returned if he were alive. But he must have died in the last two years.'

'Why in the last two years?'

'Because we heard from him two years ago.'

'Did he not tell you then where he was living?'

'The letter came from Paris, but no address was given. It was when my poor mother died. He wrote to me then, with some instructions and some advice, and I have never heard from him since.'

'Had you heard before?'

'Oh, yes, we had heard before, and that's where our mystery of the sealed door, upon which you stumbled tonight, has its origin. Pass me that desk, if you please. Here I have my father's letters, and you are the first man except Mr Perceval who has seen them.'

'Who is Mr Perceval, may I ask?'

'He was my father's confidential clerk, and he has continued to be the friend and adviser of my mother and then of myself. I don't know what we should have done without Perceval. He saw the letters, but no one else. This is the first one, which came on the very day when my father fled, seven years ago. Read it to yourself.'

This is the letter which I read:

> My Ever Dearest Wife,
> Since Sir William told me how weak your heart is, and how harmful any shock might be, I have never talked about my business affairs to you. The time has come when at all risks I can no longer refrain from telling you that things have been going badly with me. This will cause me to leave you for a little time, but it is with the absolute assurance that we shall see each other very soon. On this you can thoroughly rely. Our parting is only for a very short time, my own darling, so don't let it fret you, and above all don't let it impair your health, for that is what I want above all things to avoid.

Now, I have a request to make, and I implore you by all that binds us together to fulfil it exactly as I tell you. There are some things which I do not wish to be seen by anyone in my dark room—the room which I use for photographic purposes at the end of the garden passage. To prevent any painful thoughts, I may assure you once for all, dear, that it is nothing of which I need be ashamed. But still I do not wish you or Felix to enter that room. It is locked, and I implore you when you receive this to at once place a seal over the lock, and leave it so. Do not sell or let the house, for in either case my secret will be discovered. As long as you or Felix are in the house, I know that you will comply with my wishes. When Felix is twenty-one he may enter the room—not before.

And now, goodbye, my own best of wives. During our short separation you can consult Mr Perceval on any matters which may arise. He has my complete confidence. I hate to leave Felix and you—even for a time—but there is really no choice.

Ever and always your loving husband,
Stanislaus Stanniford.
June 4th, 1887.

'These are very private family matters for me to inflict upon you,' said my companion, apologetically. 'You must look upon it as done in your professional capacity. I have wanted to speak about it for years.'

'I am honoured by your confidence,' I answered, 'and exceedingly interested by the facts.'

'My father was a man who was noted for his almost morbid love of truth. He was always pedantically accurate. When he said, therefore, that he hoped to see my mother very soon, and when he said that he had nothing to be ashamed of in that dark room, you may rely upon it that he meant it.'

'Then what can it be?' I ejaculated.

'Neither my mother nor I could imagine. We carried out his wishes to the letter, and placed the seal upon the door; there it has been ever since. My mother lived for five years after my father's disappearance, although at the time all the doctors said that she could not survive long. Her heart was terribly diseased. During the first few months she had two letters from my father. Both had the Paris post-mark, but no address. They were short and to the same effect: that they would soon be reunited, and that she should not fret. Then there was a silence, which lasted until her death; and then came a letter to me of so private a nature that I cannot show it to you, begging me never to think evil of him, giving me much good advice, and saying that the sealing of the room was of less importance now than during the lifetime of my mother, but that the opening might still cause pain to others, and that, therefore, he thought it best that it should be postponed until my twenty-first year, for the lapse of time would make things easier. In the meantime, he committed the care of the room to me; so now you can understand how it is that, although I am a very poor man, I can neither let nor sell this great house.'

'You could mortgage it.'

'My father had already done so.'

'It is a most singular state of affairs.'

'My mother and I were gradually compelled to sell the furniture and to dismiss the servants, until now, as you see, I am living unattended in a single room. But I have only two more months.'

'What do you mean?'

'Why, that in two months I come of age. The first thing that I do will be to open that door; the second, to get rid of the house.'

'Why should your father have continued to stay away when these investments had recovered themselves?'

'He must be dead.'

'You say that he had not committed any legal offence when he fled the country?'

'None.'

'Why should he not take your mother with him?'

'I do not know.'

'Why should he conceal his address?'

'I do not know.'

'Why should he allow your mother to die and be buried without coming back?'

'I do not know.'

'My dear sir,' said I, 'if I may speak with the frankness of a professional adviser, I should say that it is very clear that your father had the strongest reasons for keeping out of the country, and that, if nothing has been proved against him, he at least thought that something might be, and refused to put himself within the power of the law. Surely that must be obvious, for in what other possible way can the facts be explained?'

My companion did not take my suggestion in good part.

'You had not the advantage of knowing my father, Mr Alder,' he said, coldly. 'I was only a boy when he left us, but I shall always look upon him as my ideal man. His only fault was that he was too sensitive and too unselfish. That anyone should lose money through him would cut him to the heart. His sense of honour was most acute, and any theory of his disappearance which conflicts with that is a mistaken one.'

It pleased me to hear the lad speak out so roundly, and yet I knew that the facts were against him, and that he was incapable of taking an unprejudiced view of the situation.

'I only speak as an outsider,' said I. 'And now I must leave you, for I have a long walk before me. Your story has interested me so much that I should be glad if you could let me know the sequel.'

'Leave me your card,' said he; and so, having bade him 'Good night,' I left him.

I heard nothing more of the matter for some time, and had almost feared that it would prove to be one of those fleeting experiences which drift away from our direct observation and end only in a hope or a suspicion. One afternoon, however, a card bearing the name of Mr J. H. Perceval was brought up to my office in Abchurch Lane, and its bearer, a small, dry, bright-eyed fellow of fifty, was ushered in by the clerk.

'I believe, sir,' said he, 'that my name has been mentioned to you by my young friend, Mr Felix Stanniford?'

'Of course,' I answered, 'I remember.'

'He spoke to you, I understand, about the circumstances in connection with the disappearance of my former employer, Mr Stanislaus Stanniford, and the existence of a sealed room in his former residence.'

'He did.'

'And you expressed an interest in the matter.'

'It interested me extremely.'

'You are aware that we hold Mr Stanniford's permission to open the door on the twenty-first birthday of his son?'

'I remember.'

'The twenty-first birthday is today.'

'Have you opened it?' I asked, eagerly.

'Not yet, sir,' said he, gravely. 'I have reason to believe that it would be well to have witnesses present when that door is opened. You are a lawyer, and you are acquainted with the facts. Will you be present on the occasion?'

'Most certainly.'

'You are employed during the day, and so am I. Shall we meet at nine o'clock at the house?'

'I will come with pleasure.'

'Then you will find us waiting for you. Goodbye, for the present.' He bowed solemnly, and took his leave.

I kept my appointment that evening, with a brain which was weary with fruitless attempts to think out some plausible explanation of the mystery which we were about to solve. Mr Perceval and my young acquaintance were waiting for me in the little room. I was not surprised to see the young man looking pale and nervous, but I was rather astonished to find the dry little City man in a state of intense, though partially suppressed, excitement. His cheeks were flushed, his hands twitching, and he could not stand still for an instant.

Stanniford greeted me warmly, and thanked me many times for having come. 'And now, Perceval,' said he to his companion, 'I suppose there is no obstacle to our putting the thing through without delay? I shall be glad to get it over.'

The banker's clerk took up the lamp and led the way. But he paused in the passage outside the door, and his hand was shaking, so that the light flickered up and down the high, bare walls.

'Mr Stanniford,' said he, in a cracking voice, 'I hope you will prepare yourself in case any shock should be awaiting you when that seal is removed and the door is opened.'

'What could there be, Perceval? You are trying to frighten me.'

'No, Mr Stanniford; but I should wish you to be ready . . . to be braced up . . . not to allow yourself . . .' He had to lick his dry lips between every jerky sentence, and I suddenly realized, as clearly as if he had told me, that he knew what was behind that closed door, and that it *was* something terrible. 'Here are the keys, Mr Stanniford, but remember my warning!'

He had a bunch of assorted keys in his hand, and the young man snatched them from him. Then he thrust a knife under the discoloured red seal and jerked it off. The lamp was rattling and shaking in Perceval's hands, so I took it from him and held it near the keyhole, while Stanniford tried key after key. At last one turned in the lock, the door flew open, he took one step into the room, and then, with a horrible cry, the young man fell senseless at our feet.

If I had not given heed to the clerk's warning, and braced myself for a shock, I should certainly have dropped the lamp. The room, windowless and bare, was fitted up as a photographic laboratory, with a tap and sink at the side of it. A shelf of bottles and measures stood at one side, and a peculiar, heavy smell, partly chemical, partly animal, filled the air. A single table and chair were in front of us, and at this, with his back turned towards us, a man was seated in the act of writing. His outline and attitude were as natural as life; but as the light fell upon him, it made my hair rise to see that the nape of his neck was black and wrinkled, and no thicker than my wrist. Dust lay upon him—thick, yellow dust—upon his hair, his shoulders, his shrivelled, lemon-coloured hands. His head had fallen forward upon his breast. His pen still rested upon a discoloured sheet of paper.

'My poor master! My poor, poor master!' cried the clerk, and the tears were running down his cheeks.

'What!' I cried, 'Mr Stanislaus Stanniford!'

'Here he has sat for seven years. Oh, why would he do it? I begged him, I implored him, I went on my knees to him, but he would have his way. You see the key on the table. He had locked the door upon the inside. And he has written something. We must take it.'

'Yes, yes, take it, and for God's sake, let us get out of this,' I cried; 'the air is poisonous. Come, Stanniford, come!' Taking an arm each, we half led and half carried the terrified man back to his own room.

'It was my father!' he cried, as he recovered his consciousness. 'He is sitting there dead in his chair. You knew it, Perceval! This was what you meant when you warned me.'

'Yes, I knew it, Mr Stanniford. I have acted for the best all long, but my position has been a terribly difficult one. For seven years I have known that your father was dead in that room.'

'You knew it, and never told us!'

'Don't be harsh with me, Mr Stanniford, sir! Make allowance for a man who has had a hard part to play.'

'My head is swimming round. I cannot grasp it!' He staggered up, and helped himself from the brandy bottle. 'These letters to my mother and to myself—were they forgeries?'

'No, sir; your father wrote them and addressed them, and left them in my keeping to be posted. I have followed his instructions to the very letter in all things. He was my master, and I have obeyed him.'

The brandy had steadied the young man's shaken nerves. 'Tell me about it. I can stand it now,' said he.

'Well, Mr Stanniford, you know that at one time there came a period of great trouble upon your father, and he thought that many poor people were about to lose their savings through his fault. He was a man who was so tender-hearted that he could not bear the thought. It worried him and tormented him, until he determined to end his life. Oh, Mr Stanniford, if you knew how I have prayed him and wrestled with him over it, you would never blame me! And he in turn prayed me as no man has ever prayed me before. He had made up his mind, and he would do it in any case, he said; but it rested with me whether his death should be happy and easy or whether it should be most miserable. I read in his eyes that he meant what he said. And at last I yielded to his prayers, and I consented to do his will.

'What was troubling him was this. He had been told by the first doctor in London that his wife's heart would fail at the slightest shock. He had a horror of accelerating her end, and yet his own existence had become unendurable to him. How could he end himself without injuring her?

'You know now the course that he took. He wrote the letter which she received. There was nothing in it which was not literally true. When he spoke of seeing her again so soon, he was referring to her own approaching death, which he had been assured could not be delayed more than a very few months. So convinced was he of this, that he only left two letters to be forwarded at intervals after his death. She lived five years, and I had no letters to send.

'He left another letter with me to be sent to you, sir, upon the occasion of the death of your mother. I posted all these in Paris to sustain the idea of his being abroad. It was his wish that I should say nothing, and I have said nothing. I have been a faithful servant. Seven years after his death, he thought no doubt that the shock to the feelings of his surviving friends would be lessened. He was always considerate for others.'

There was silence for some time. It was broken by young Stanniford.

'I cannot blame you, Perceval. You have spared my mother a shock, which would certainly have broken her heart. What is that paper?'

'It is what your father was writing, sir. Shall I read it to you?'

'Do so.'

' "I have taken the poison, and I feel it working in my veins. It is strange, but not painful. When these words are read I shall, if my wishes have been faithfully carried out, have been dead many years. Surely no one who has lost money through me will still bear me animosity. And you, Felix, you will forgive me this family scandal. May God find rest for a sorely wearied spirit!" '

'Amen!' we cried, all three.

The Retirement of Signor Lambert

Sir William Sparter was a man who had raised himself in the course of a quarter of a century from earning four-and-twenty shillings a week as a fitter in Portsmouth Dockyard to being the owner of a yard and a fleet of his own. The little house in Lake Road, Landport, where he, an obscure mechanic, had first conceived the idea of the boilers which are associated with his name, is still pointed out to the curious. But now, at the age of fifty, he owned a mansion in Leinster Gardens, a country house at Taplow, and a shooting in Argyleshire, with the best stable, the choicest cellars, and the prettiest wife in town.

As untiring and inflexible as one of his own engines, his life had been directed to the one purpose of attaining the very best which the world had to give. Square-headed and round-shouldered, with massive, clean-shaven face and slow deep-set eyes, he was the very embodiment of persistency and strength. Never once from the beginning of his career had public failure of any sort tarnished its brilliancy.

And yet he had failed in one thing, and that the most important of all. He had never succeeded in gaining the affection of his wife. She was the daughter of a surgeon and the belle of a northern town when he married her. Even then he was rich and powerful, which made her overlook the twenty years which divided them. But he had come on a long way since then. His great Brazilian contract, his conversion into a company, his baronetcy—all these had been since his marriage. Only in the one thing he had never progressed. He could frighten his wife, he could dominate her, he could make her admire his strength and respect his consistency, he could mould her to his will in every other direction, but, do what he would he could not make her love him.

But it was not for want of trying. With the unrelaxing patience which made him great in business, he had striven, year in and year out, to win her affection. But the very qualities which had helped him in his public life made him unendurable in private. He was tactless, unsympathetic, overbearing, almost brutal sometimes, and utterly unable to think out those small attentions in word and deed which women value far more than the larger material benefits. The hundred pound cheque tossed across a breakfast table is a much smaller thing to a woman than the five-shilling charm which represents some thought and some trouble upon the part of the giver.

Sparter failed to understand this. With his mind full of the affairs of his firm, he had little time for the delicacies of life, and he endeavoured to atone by periodical munificence. At the end of five years he found that he had lost rather than gained in the lady's affections. Then at this unwonted sense of failure the evil side of the man's nature began to stir, and he became dangerous. But he was more dangerous still when a letter of his wife came, through the treachery of a servant, into his hands, and he realised that if she was cold to him she had passion enough for another. His firm, his ironclads, his patents, everything was dropped, and he turned his huge energies to the undoing of the man who had wronged him.

He had been cold and silent during dinner that evening, and she had wondered vaguely what had occurred to change him. He had said nothing while they sat together over their coffee in the drawing-room. Once or twice she had glanced at him in surprise, and had found those deep-set grey eyes fixed upon her with an expression which was new to her. Her mind had been full of someone else, but gradually her husband's silence and the inscrutable expression of his face forced themselves upon her attention.

'You don't seem yourself, tonight, William. What is the matter?' she asked. 'I hope there has been nothing to trouble you.'

He was still silent, and leant back in his armchair watching her beautiful face, which had turned pale with the sense of some impending catastrophe.

'Can I do anything for you, William?'

'Yes, you can write a letter.'

'What is the letter?'

'I will tell you presently.'

The last murmur died away in the house, and they heard the discreet step of Peterson, the butler, and the snick of the lock as he made all secure for the night. Sir William Sparter sat listening for a little. Then he rose.

'Come into my study,' said he.

The room was dark, but he switched on the green-shaded electric lamp which stood upon the writing-table.

'Sit here at the table,' said he. He closed the door and seated himself beside her. 'I only wanted to tell you, Jacky, that I know all about Lambert and the Warburton Street studio.'

She gasped and shivered, flinching away from him with her hands out as if she feared a blow.

'Yes, I know everything,' said he, and his quiet tone carried such conviction with it that she could not question what he said. She made no reply, but sat with her eyes fixed upon his grave, impassive face. A clock ticked loudly upon the mantelpiece, but everything else was silent in the house. She had never noticed that ticking before, but now it was like the hammering of a nail into her head. He rose and put a sheet of paper before her. Then he drew one from his own pocket and flattened it out upon the corner of the table.

'I have a rough draft here of the letter which I wish you to copy,' said he. 'I will read it to you if you like. "My own dearest Cecil— I will be at No. 29 at half-past six, and I particularly wish you to come before you go down to the Opera. Don't fail me, for I have the very strongest reasons for wishing to see you. Ever yours, Jacqueline." Take up a pen, and copy that letter.'

'William, you are plotting some revenge. Oh, Willie, if I have wronged you, I am so sorry——'

'Copy that letter!'

'How can you be so harsh to me, William. You know very well——'

'Copy that letter!'

'I begin to hate you, William. I believe that it is a fiend, not a man, that I have married.'

'Copy that letter!'

Gradually the inflexible will and the unfaltering purpose began to prevail over the creature of nerves and moods. Reluctantly, mutinously, she took the pen in her hand.

'You wouldn't harm him, William!'

'Copy the letter!'

'Will you promise to forgive me, if I do?'

'Copy it!'

She looked at him with the intention of defying him, but those masterful grey eyes dominated her. She was like a half-hypnotised creature, resentful, and yet obedient.

'There, will that satisfy you?'

He took the note from her and placed it in an envelope.

'Now address it to him!'

She wrote 'Cecil Lambert, Esq., 133B, Half Moon Street, W.', in a straggling agitated hand. Her husband very deliberately blotted it and placed it carefully in his pocket-book.

'I hope that you are satisfied now,' said she with weak petulance.

'Quite,' said he gravely. 'You can go to your room. Mrs McKay has my orders to sleep with you, and to see that you write no letters.'

'Mrs McKay! Do you expose me to the humiliation of being watched by my own servants!'

'Go to your room.'

'If you imagine that I am going to be under the orders of the house-keeper——'

'Go to your room.'

'Oh, William, who would have thought in the old days that you could ever have treated me like this. If my mother had ever dreamed——'

He took her by the arm, and led her to the door.

'Go to your room!' said he, and she passed out into the darkened hall. He closed the door and returned to the writing-table. Out of a drawer he took two things which he had purchased that day, the one a paper and the other a book. The former was a recent number of the *Musical Record*, and it contained a biography and picture of the famous Signor Lambert, whose wonderful tenor voice had been the delight of the public and the despair of his rivals. The picture was that of a good-natured, self-satisfied creature, young and handsome, with a full eye, a curling moustache, and a bull neck. The biography explained that he was only in his twenty-seventh year, that his career had been one continued triumph, that he was devoted to his art, and that his voice was worth to him, at a very moderate computation, some twenty thousand pounds a year. All this Sir William Sparter read very carefully, with his great brows drawn down, and a furrow like a gash between them, as his way was when his attention was concentrated. Then he folded the paper up again, and he opened the book.

It was a curious work for such a man to select for his reading—a technical treatise upon the organs of speech and voice-production. There were numerous coloured illustrations, to which he paid particular attention. Most of them were of the internal anatomy of the larynx, with the silvery vocal chords shining from under the pink aretenoid cartilages. Far into the night Sir William Sparter, with those great virile eyebrows still bunched together, pored over these irrelevant pictures, and read and re-read the text in which they were explained.

Dr Manifold Ormonde, the famous throat specialist, of Cavendish Square, was surprised next morning when his butler brought the card of Sir William Sparter into his consulting-room. He had met him at dinner at the table of Lord Marvin a few nights before, and it had struck him at the time that he had seldom seen a man who looked such a type of rude, physical health. So he thought again, as the square, thick-set figure of the shipbuilder was ushered in to him.

'Glad to meet you again, Sir William,' said the specialist. 'I hope there is nothing wrong with your health.'

'Nothing, thank you.'

'Or with Lady Sparter's?'

'She is quite well.'

He sat down in the chair which the Doctor had indicated, and he ran his eyes slowly and deliberately round the room. Dr Ormonde watched him with some curiosity, for he had the air of a man who looks for something which he had expected to see.

'No, I didn't come about my health,' said he at last. 'I came for information.'

'Whatever I can give you is entirely at your disposal.'

'I have been studying the throat a little of late. I read McIntyre's book about it. I suppose that is all right.'

'An elementary treatise, but accurate as far as it goes.'

'I had an idea that you would be likely to have a model or something of the kind.'

For answer the Doctor unclasped the lid of a yellow, shining box upon his consulting-room table, and turned it back upon the hinge. Within was a very complete model of the human vocal organs.

'You are right, you see,' said he.

Sir William Sparter stood up, and bent over the model.

'It's a neat little bit of work,' said he, looking at it with the critical eyes of an engineer. 'This is the glottis, is it not? And here is the epiglottis.'

'Precisely. And here are the cords.'

'What would happen if you cut them?'

'Cut what?'

'These things—the vocal cords.'

'But you could not cut them. They are out of the reach of all accident.'

'But if such a thing did happen?'

'There is no such case upon record, but of course, the person would become dumb—for the time, at any rate.'

'You have a large practice among singers, have you not?'

'The largest in London.'

'I suppose you agree with what this man McIntyre says, that a fine voice depends partly upon the cords.'

'The volume of sound would depend upon the lung capacity, but the clearness of the note would correspond with the complete control which the singer exercised over the cords.'

'Any roughness or notching of the cords would ruin the voice?'

'For singing purposes, undoubtedly—but your researches seem to be taking a very curious direction.'

'Yes,' said Sir William, as he picked up his hat, and laid a fee upon the corner of the table. 'They *are* a little out of the common, are they not?'

Warburton Street is one of the network of thoroughfares which connect Chelsea with Kensington, and it is chiefly remarkable for a number of studios, in which it is rumoured that other arts besides that of painting are occasionally cultivated. The possession of a comfortable room, easily accessible and at a moderate rent, may be useful to other people besides artists amid the publicity of London. At any rate, Signor Cecil Lambert, the famous tenor, owned such an apartment, and his neat little dark green brougham might have been seen several times a week waiting at the head of the long passage which led down to the chambers in question.

When Sir William Sparter, muffled in his overcoat, and carrying a small black leather bag in his hand, turned the corner he saw the lamps of the carriage against the kerb, and knew that the man whom he had come to see was already at the place of assignation. He passed the empty brougham, and walked up the tile-paved passage with the yellow gas lamp shining at the far end of it.

The door was open, and led into a large empty hall, laid down with cocoa-nut matting and stained with many footmarks. The place was a rabbit warren by daylight, but now, when the working hours were over, it was deserted. A housekeeper in the basement was the only permanent resident. Sir William paused, but everything was silent and everything was dark, save for one door which was outlined in thin yellow slashes. He pushed it open and entered. Then he locked it upon the inside and put the key in his pocket.

It was a large room, scantily furnished, and lit by a single oil lamp upon a centre table. A gaunt easel kept up appearances in the corner, and three studies of antique figures hung upon unpapered walls. For the rest a couple of comfortable chairs, a cupboard, and a settee made up the whole of the furniture. There was no carpet, but the windows were discreetly draped. On one of the chairs at the further side of a table a man had been sitting, who had sprung to his feet with an exclamation of joy, which had changed into one of surprise, and culminated in an oath.

'What the devil do you mean by locking that door? Unlock it again, sir, this instant!'

Sir William did not even answer him. He took off his overcoat and laid it over the back of a chair. Then he advanced to the table, opened his bag, and began to take out all sorts of things—a green bottle, a dentist's gag, an inhaler, a pair of forceps, a curved bistoury, and a curious pair of scissors. Signor Lambert stood staring at him in a paralysis of rage and astonishment.

'You infernal scoundrel; who are you, and what do you want?'

Sir William had emptied his bag, and now for the first time he turned his eyes upon the singer. He was a taller man than himself, but far slighter and weaker. The engineer, though short, was exceedingly powerful, with muscles which had been roughened by hard, physical work. His broad shoulders, arching chest, and great gnarled hands gave him the outline of a gorilla. Lambert shrunk away from him, frightened by his sinister figure and by his cold, inexorable eyes.

'Have you come to rob me?' he gasped.

'I have come to speak to you. My name is Sparter.'

Lambert tried to retain his grasp upon the self-possession which was rapidly slipping away from him.

'Sparter!' said he, with an attempt at jauntiness. 'Sir William Sparter, I presume? I have had the pleasure of meeting Lady Sparter, and I have heard her mention you. May I ask the object of this visit?' He buttoned up his coat with twitching fingers, and tried to look fierce over his high collar.

'I've come,' said Sparter, jerking some fluid from the green bottle into the inhaler, 'to treat your voice.'

'To treat my voice?'

'Precisely.'

'You are a madman! What do you mean?'

'Kindly lie back upon the settee.'

'You are raving! I see it all. You wish to bully me. You have some motive in this. You imagine that there are relations between Lady Sparter and me. I do assure you that your wife——'

'My wife has nothing to do with the matter either now or hereafter. Her name does not appear at all. My motives are musical—purely musical, you understand. I don't like your voice. It wants treatment. Lie back upon the settee!'

'Sir William, I give you my word of honour——'

'Lie back!'

'You're choking me! It's chloroform! Help, help, help! You brute! Let me go! let me go, I say! Oh please! Lemme— Lemme Lem——!' His head had fallen back, and he muttered into the inhaler. Sir William pulled up the table which held the lamp and the instruments.

It was some minutes after the gentleman with the overcoat and the bag had emerged that the coachman outside heard a voice shouting, and shouting very hoarsely and angrily, within the building. Presently came the sounds of unsteady steps, and his master, crimson with rage, stumbled out into the yellow circle thrown by the carriage lamps.

'You, Holden!' he cried, 'you leave my service tonight. Did you not hear me calling? Why did you not come?'

The man looked at him in bewilderment, and shuddered at the colour of his shirt-front.

'Yes, sir, I heard someone calling,' he answered, 'but it wasn't you sir. *It was a voice that I had never heard before.*'

'Considerable disappointment was caused at the Opera last week,' said one of the best informed of our musical critics, 'by the fact that Signor Cecil Lambert was unable to appear in the various roles which had been announced. On Tuesday night it was only at the very last instant that the management learned of the grave indisposition which had overtaken him, and had it not been for the presence of Jean Caravatti, who had understudied the part, the piece must have been abandoned. Since then we regret to hear that Signor Lambert's seizure was even more severe than was originally thought, and that it consists of an acute form of laryngitis, spreading to the vocal cords, and involving changes which may permanently affect the quality of his voice. All lovers of music will hope that these reports may prove to be pessimistic, and that we may soon be charmed once more by the finest tenor which we have heard for many a year upon the London operatic stage.'

The Brazilian Cat

I T IS HARD LUCK ON A YOUNG FELLOW to have expensive tastes, great
expectations, aristocratic connections, but no actual money in his pocket,
and no profession by which he may earn any. The fact was that my father,
a good, sanguine, easy-going man, had such confidence in the wealth and
benevolence of his bachelor elder brother, Lord Southerton, that he took it for
granted that I, his only son, would never be called upon to earn a living for
myself. He imagined that if there were not a vacancy for me on the great
Southerton Estates, at least there would be found some post in that diplomatic
service which still remains the special preserve of our privileged classes. He
died too early to realize how false his calculations had been. Neither my uncle
nor the State took the slightest notice of me, or showed any interest in my
career. An occasional brace of pheasants, or basket of hares, was all that ever
reached me to remind me that I was heir to Otwell House and one of the
richest estates in the country. In the meantime, I found myself a bachelor and
man about town, living in a suite of apartments in Grosvenor Mansions, with
no occupation save that of pigeon shooting and polo playing at Hurlingham.
Month by month I realized that it was more and more difficult to get the
brokers to renew my bills, or to cash any further post-obits upon an unentailed
property. Ruin lay right across my path, and every day I saw it clearer, nearer,
and more absolutely unavoidable.

What made me feel my own poverty the more was that, apart from the
great wealth of Lord Southerton, all my other relations were fairly well-to-do.
The nearest of these was Everard King, my father's nephew and my own first
cousin, who had spent an adventurous life in Brazil, and had now returned to
this country to settle down on his fortune. We never knew how he made his
money, but he appeared to have plenty of it, for he bought the estate of
Greylands, near Clipton-on-the-Marsh, in Suffolk. For the first year of his
residence in England he took no more notice of me than my miserly uncle; but
at last one summer morning, to my very great relief and joy, I received a letter
asking me to come down that very day and spend a short visit at Greylands
Court. I was expecting a rather long visit to Bankruptcy Court at the time, and
this interruption seemed almost providential. If I could only get on terms with
this unknown relative of mine, I might pull through yet. For the family credit

he could not let me go entirely to the wall. I ordered my valet to pack my valise, and I set off the same evening for Clipton-on-the-Marsh.

After changing at Ipswich, a little local train deposited me at a small, deserted station lying amidst a rolling grassy country, with a sluggish and winding river curving in and out amidst the valleys, between high, silted banks, which showed that we were within reach of the tide. No carriage was awaiting me (I found afterwards that my telegram had been delayed), so I hired a dogcart at the local inn. The driver, an excellent fellow, was full of my relative's praises, and I learned from him that Mr Everard King was already a name to conjure with in that part of the country. He had entertained the school-children, he had thrown his grounds open to visitors, he had subscribed to charities—in short, his benevolence had been so universal that my driver could only account for it on the supposition that he had Parliamentary ambitions.

My attention was drawn away from my driver's panegyric by the appearance of a very beautiful bird which settled on a telegraph-post beside the road. At first I thought that it was a jay, but it was larger, with a brighter plumage. The driver accounted for its presence at once by saying that it belonged to the very man whom we were about to visit. It seems that the acclimatization of foreign creatures was one of his hobbies, and that he had brought with him from Brazil a number of birds and beasts which he was endeavouring to rear in England. When once we had passed the gates of Greylands Park we had ample evidence of this taste of his. Some small spotted deer, a curious wild pig known, I believe, as a peccary, a gorgeously feathered oriole, some sort of armadillo, and a singular lumbering intoed beast like a very fat badger, were among the creatures which I observed as we drove along the winding avenue.

Mr Everard King, my unknown cousin, was standing in person upon the steps of his house, for he had seen us in the distance, and guessed that it was I. His appearance was very homely and benevolent, short and stout, forty-five years old perhaps, with a round, good-humoured face, burned brown with the tropical sun, and shot with a thousand wrinkles. He wore white linen clothes, in true planter style, with a cigar between his lips, and a large Panama hat upon the back of his head. It was such a figure as one associates with a verandahed bungalow, and it looked curiously out of place in front of this broad, stone English mansion, with its solid wings and its Palladio pillars before the doorway.

'My dear!' he cried, glancing over his shoulder; 'my dear, here is our guest! Welcome, welcome to Greylands! I am delighted to make your acquaintance, Cousin Marshall, and I take it as a great compliment that you should honour this sleepy little country place with your presence.'

Nothing could be more hearty than his manner, and he set me at my ease in an instant. But it needed all his cordiality to atone for the frigidity and even rudeness of his wife, a tall, haggard woman, who came forward at his summons. She was, I believe, of Brazilian extraction, though she spoke excellent English, and I excused her manners on the score of her ignorance of our customs. She did not attempt to conceal, however, either then or afterwards, that I was no very welcome visitor at Greylands Court. Her actual words were, as a rule, courteous, but she was the possessor of a pair of particularly expressive dark eyes, and I read in them very clearly from the first that she heartily wished me back in London once more.

However, my debts were too pressing and my designs upon my wealthy relative were too vital for me to allow them to be upset by the ill-temper of his wife, so I disregarded her coldness and reciprocated the extreme cordiality of his welcome. No pains had been spared by him to make me comfortable. My room was a charming one. He implored me to tell him anything which could add to my happiness. It was on the tip of my tongue to inform him that a blank cheque would materially help towards that end, but I felt that it might be premature in the present state of our acquaintance. The dinner was excellent, and as we sat together afterwards over his Havanas and coffee, which latter he told me was specially prepared upon his own plantation, it seemed to me that all my driver's eulogies were justified, and that I had never met a more large-hearted and hospitable man.

But, in spite of his cheery good nature, he was a man with a strong will and a fiery temper of his own. Of this I had an example upon the following morning. The curious aversion which Mrs Everard King had conceived towards me was so strong, that her manner at breakfast was almost offensive. But her meaning became unmistakable when her husband had quitted the room.

'The best train in the day is at twelve-fifteen,' said she.

'But I was not thinking of going today,' I answered, frankly—perhaps even defiantly, for I was determined not to be driven out by this woman.

'Oh, if it rests with you——' said she, and stopped, with a most insolent expression in her eyes.

'I am sure,' I answered, 'that Mr Everard King would tell me if I were outstaying my welcome.'

'What's this? What's this?' said a voice, and there he was in the room. He had overheard my last words, and a glance at our faces had told him the rest. In an instant his chubby, cheery face set into an expression of absolute ferocity.

'Might I trouble you to walk outside, Marshall,' said he. (I may mention that my own name is Marshall King.)

He closed the door behind me, and then, for an instant, I heard him talking in a low voice of concentrated passion to his wife. This gross breach of hospitality had evidently hit upon his tenderest point. I am no eavesdropper, so I walked out on to the lawn. Presently I heard a hurried step behind me, and there was the lady, her face pale with excitement, and her eyes red with tears.

'My husband has asked me to apologize to you, Mr Marshall King,' said she, standing with downcast eyes before me.

'Please do not say another word, Mrs King.'

Her dark eyes suddenly blazed out at me.

'You fool!' she hissed, with frantic vehemence, and turning on her heel swept back to the house.

The insult was so outrageous, so insufferable, that I could only stand staring after her in bewilderment. I was still there when my host joined me. He was his cheery, chubby self once more.

'I hope that my wife has apologized for her foolish remarks,' said he.

'Oh, yes—yes, certainly!'

He put his hand through my arm and walked with me up and down the lawn.

'You must not take it seriously,' said he. 'It would grieve me inexpressibly if you curtailed your visit by one hour. The fact is—there is no reason why there should be any concealment between relatives—that my poor dear wife is incredibly jealous. She hates that anyone—male or female—should for an instant come between us. Her ideal is a desert island and an eternal *tête-à-tête*. That gives you the clue to her actions, which are, I confess, upon this particular point, not very far removed from mania. Tell me that you will think no more of it.'

'No, no; certainly not.'

'Then light this cigar and come round with me and see my little menagerie.'

The whole afternoon was occupied by this inspection, which included all the birds, beasts, and even reptiles which he had imported. Some were free, some in cages, a few actually in the house. He spoke with enthusiasm of his successes and his failures, his births and his deaths, and he would cry out in his delight, like a schoolboy, when, as we walked, some gaudy bird would flutter up from the grass, or some curious beast slink into the cover. Finally he led me down a corridor which extended from one wing of the house. At the end of this there was a heavy door with a sliding shutter in it, and beside it there projected from the wall an iron handle attached to a wheel and a drum. A line of stout bars extended across the passage.

'I am about to show you the jewel of my collection,' said he. 'There is only one other specimen in Europe, now that the Rotterdam cub is dead. It is a Brazilian cat.'

'But how does that differ from any other cat?'

'You will soon see that,' said he, laughing. 'Will you kindly draw that shutter and look through?'

I did so, and found that I was gazing into a large, empty room, with stone flags, and small, barred windows upon the farther wall.

In the centre of this room, lying in the middle of a golden patch of sunlight, there was stretched a huge creature, as large as a tiger, but as black and sleek as ebony. It was simply a very enormous and very well-kept black cat, and it cuddled up and basked in that yellow pool of light exactly as a cat would do. It was so graceful, so sinewy, and so gently and smoothly diabolical, that I could not take my eyes from the opening.

'Isn't he splendid?' said my host, enthusiastically.

'Glorious! I never saw such a noble creature.'

'Some people call it a black puma, but really it is not a puma at all. That fellow is nearly eleven feet from tail to tip. Four years ago he was a little ball of black fluff, with two yellow eyes staring out of it. He was sold me as a new-born cub up in the wild country at the headwaters of the Rio Negro. They speared his mother to death after she had killed a dozen of them.'

'They are ferocious, then?'

'The most absolutely treacherous and bloodthirsty creatures upon earth. You talk about a Brazilian cat to an up-country Indian, and see him get the jumps. They prefer humans to game. This fellow has never tasted living blood yet, but when he does he will be a terror. At present he won't stand anyone but me in his den. Even Baldwin, the groom, dare not go near him. As to me, I am his mother and father in one.'

As he spoke he suddenly, to my astonishment, opened the door and slipped in, closing it instantly behind him. At the sound of his voice the huge, lithe creature rose, yawned, and rubbed its round, black head affectionately against his side, while he patted and fondled it.

'Now, Tommy, into your cage!' said he.

The monstrous cat walked over to one side of the room and coiled itself up under a grating. Everard King came out, and taking the iron handle which I have mentioned, he began to turn it. As he did so the line of bars in the corridor began to pass through a slot in the wall and closed up the front of this grating, so as to make an effective cage. When it was in position he opened the door once more and invited me into the room, which was heavy with the pungent, musty smell peculiar to the great carnivora.

'That's how we work it,' said he. 'We give him the run of the room for exercise, and then at night we put him in his cage. You can let him out by turning the handle from the passage, or you can, as you have seen, coop him up in the same way. No, no, you should not do that!'

I had put my hand between the bars to pat the glossy, heaving flank. He pulled it back, with a serious face.

'I assure you that he is not safe. Don't imagine that because I can take liberties with him anyone else can. He is very exclusive in his friends—aren't you, Tommy? Ah, he hears his lunch coming to him! Don't you, boy?'

A step sounded in the stone-flagged passage, and the creature had sprung to his feet, and was pacing up and down the narrow cage, his yellow eyes gleaming, and his scarlet tongue rippling and quivering over the white line of his jagged teeth. A groom entered with a coarse joint upon a tray and thrust it through the bars to him. He pounced lightly upon it, carried it off to the corner, and there, holding it between his paws, tore and wrenched at it, raising his bloody muzzle every now and then to look at us. It was a malignant and yet fascinating sight.

'You can't wonder that I am fond of him, can you?' said my host, as we left the room, 'especially when you consider that I have had the rearing of him. It was no joke bringing him over from the centre of South America; but here he is safe and sound—and, as I have said, far the most perfect specimen in Europe. The people at the Zoo are dying to have him, but I really can't part with him. Now, I think that I have inflicted my hobby upon you long enough, so we cannot do better than follow Tommy's example, and go to our lunch.'

My South American relative was so engrossed by his grounds and their curious occupants, that I hardly gave him credit at first for having any interests outside them. That he had some, and pressing ones, was soon borne in upon me by the number of telegrams which he received. They arrived at all hours, and were always opened by him with the utmost eagerness and anxiety upon his face. Sometimes I imagined that it must be the turf, and sometimes the Stock Exchange, but certainly he had some very urgent business going forward which was not transacted upon the Downs of Suffolk. During the six days of my visit he had never fewer than three or four telegrams a day, and sometimes as many as seven or eight.

I had occupied these six days so well, that by the end of them I had succeeded in getting upon the most cordial terms with my cousin. Every night we had sat up late in the billiard-room, he telling me the most extraordinary stories of his adventures in America—stories so desperate and reckless, that I could hardly associate them with the brown little chubby man before me. In return, I ventured upon some of my own reminiscences of London life, which interested him so much, that he vowed he would come up to Grosvenor Mansions and stay with me. He was anxious to see the faster side of city life, and certainly, though I say it, he could not have chosen a more competent guide. It was not until the last day of my visit that I ventured to approach that which was on my mind. I told him frankly about my pecuniary difficulties and my impending ruin, and I asked his advice—though I hoped for something more solid. He listened attentively, puffing hard at his cigar.

'But surely,' said he, 'you are the heir of our relative, Lord Southerton?'

'I have every reason to believe so, but he would never make me any allowance.'

'No, no, I have heard of his miserly ways. My poor Marshall, your position has been a very hard one. By the way, have you heard any news of Lord Southerton's health lately?'

'He has always been in a critical condition ever since my childhood.'

'Exactly—a creaking hinge, if ever there was one. Your inheritance may be a long way off. Dear me, how awkwardly situated you are!'

'I had some hopes, sir, that you, knowing all the facts, might be inclined to advance——'

'Don't say another word, my dear boy,' he cried, with the utmost cordiality;

'we shall talk it over tonight, and I give you my word that whatever is in my power shall be done.'

I was not sorry that my visit was drawing to a close, for it is unpleasant to feel that there is one person in the house who eagerly desires your departure. Mrs King's sallow face and forbidding eyes had become more and more hateful to me. She was no longer actively rude—her fear of her husband prevented her—but she pushed her insane jealousy to the extent of ignoring me, never addressing me, and in every way making my stay at Greylands as uncomfortable as she could. So offensive was her manner during that last day that I should certainly have left had it not been for that interview with my host in the evening which would, I hoped, retrieve my broken fortunes.

It was very late when it occurred, for my relative, who had been receiving even more telegrams than usual during the day, went off to his study after dinner, and only emerged when the household had retired to bed. I heard him go round locking the doors, as his custom was of a night, and finally he joined me in the billiard-room. His stout figure was wrapped in a dressing-gown, and he wore a pair of red Turkish slippers without any heels. Settling down into an armchair, he brewed himself a glass of grog, in which I could not help noticing that the whisky considerably predominated over the water.

'My word!' said he, 'what a night!'

It was, indeed. The wind was howling and screaming round the house, and the latticed windows rattled and shook as if they were coming in. The glow of the yellow lamps and the flavour of our cigars seemed the brighter and more fragrant for the contrast.

'Now, my boy,' said my host, 'we have the house and the night to ourselves. Let me have an idea of how your affairs stand, and I will see what can be done to set them in order. I wish to hear every detail.'

Thus encouraged, I entered into a long exposition, in which all my tradesmen and creditors, from my landlord to my valet, figured in turn. I had notes in my pocketbook, and I marshalled my facts, and gave, I flatter myself, a very business-like statement of my own unbusiness-like ways and lamentable position. I was depressed, however, to notice that my companion's eyes were vacant and his attention elsewhere. When he did occasionally throw out a remark it was so entirely perfunctory and pointless, that I was sure he had not in the least followed my remarks. Every now and then he roused himself and put on some show of interest, asking me to repeat or to explain more fully, but it was always to sink once more into the same brown study. At last he rose and threw the end of his cigar into the grate.

'I'll tell you what, my boy,' said he. 'I never had a head for figures, so you will excuse me. You must jot it all down upon paper, and let me have a note of the amount. I'll understand it when I see it in black and white.'

The proposal was encouraging. I promised to do so.

'And now it's time we were in bed. By jove, there's one o'clock striking in the hall.'

The tingling of the chiming clock broke through the deep roar of the gale. The wind was sweeping past with the rush of a great river.

'I must see my cat before I go to bed,' said my host. 'A high wind excites him. Will you come?'

'Certainly,' said I.

'Then tread softly and don't speak, for everyone is asleep.'

We passed quietly down the lamp-lit Persian-rugged hall, and through the door at the farther end. All was dark in the stone corridor, but a stable lantern hung on a hook, and my host took it down and lit it. There was no grating visible in the passage, so I knew that the beast was in its cage.

'Come in!' said my relative, and opened the door.

A deep growling as we entered showed that the storm had really excited the creature. In the flickering light of the lantern, we saw it, a huge black mass coiled in the corner of its den and throwing a squat, uncouth shadow upon the whitewashed wall. Its tail switched angrily among the straw.

'Poor Tommy is not in the best of tempers,' said Everard King, holding up the lantern and looking in at him. 'What a black devil he looks, doesn't he? I must give him a little supper to put him in a better humour. Would you mind holding the lantern for a moment?'

I took it from his hand and he stepped to the door.

'His larder is just outside here,' said he. 'You will excuse me for an instant, won't you?' He passed out, and the door shut with a sharp metallic click behind him.

That hard crisp sound made my heart stand still. A sudden wave of terror passed over me. A vague perception of some monstrous treachery turned me cold. I sprang to the door, but there was no handle upon the inner side.

'Here,' I cried. 'Let me out!'

'All right! Don't make a row!' said my host from the passage. 'You've got the light all right.'

'Yes, but I don't care about being locked in alone like this.'

'Don't you?' I heard his hearty, chuckling laugh. 'You won't be alone long.'

'Let me out, sir!' I repeated angrily. 'I tell you I don't allow practical jokes of this sort.'

'Practical is the word,' said he, with another hateful chuckle. And then suddenly I heard, amidst the roar of the storm, the creak and whine of the winch-handle turning, and the rattle of the grating as it passed through the slot. Great God, he was letting loose the Brazilian cat!

In the light of the lantern I saw the bars sliding slowly before me. Already there was an opening a foot wide at the farther end. With a scream I seized the last bar with my hands and pulled with the strength of a madman. I *was a* madman with rage and horror. For a minute or more I held the thing motionless. I knew that he was straining with all his force upon the handle, and that the leverage was sure to overcome me. I gave inch by inch, my feet sliding along the stones, and all the time I begged and prayed this inhuman monster to save me from this horrible death. I conjured him by his kinship. I reminded him that I was his guest; I begged to know what harm I had ever done him. His only answers were the tugs and jerks upon the handle, each of which, in spite of all my struggles, pulled another bar through the opening. Clinging and clutching, I was dragged across the whole front of the cage, until at last, with aching wrists and lacerated fingers, I gave up the hopeless struggle. The grating clanged back as I released it, and an instant later I heard the shuffle of the Turkish slippers in the passage, and the slam of the distant door. Then everything was silent.

The creature had never moved during this time. He lay still in the corner, and his tail had ceased switching. This apparition of a man adhering to his bars and dragged screaming across him had apparently filled him with amazement. I saw his great eyes staring steadily at me. I had dropped the lantern when I seized the bars, but it still burned upon the floor, and I made a movement to grasp it, with some idea that its light might protect me. But the instant I moved, the beast gave a deep and menacing growl. I stopped and stood still, quivering with fear in every limb. The cat (if one may call so fearful a creature by so homely a name) was not more than ten feet from me. The eyes glimmered like two disks of phosphorus in the darkness. They appalled and yet fascinated me. I could not take my own eyes from them. Nature plays strange tricks with us at such moments of intensity, and those glimmering lights waxed and waned with a steady rise and fall. Sometimes they seemed to be tiny points of extreme brilliancy—little electric sparks in the black obscurity—then they would widen and widen until all that corner of the room was filled with their shifting and sinister light. And then suddenly they went out altogether.

The beast had closed its eyes. I do not know whether there may be any truth in the old idea of the dominance of the human gaze, or whether the huge cat was simply drowsy, but the fact remains that, far from showing any symptom of attacking me, it simply rested its sleek, black head upon its huge forepaws and seemed to sleep. I stood, fearing to move lest I should rouse it into malignant life once more. But at least I was able to think clearly now that the baleful eyes were off me. Here I was shut up for the night with the ferocious beast. My own instincts, to say nothing of the words of the plausible villain who laid this trap for me, warned me that the animal was as savage as its master. How could I stave it off until morning? The door was hopeless, and so were the narrow, barred windows. There was no shelter anywhere in the bare, stone-flagged room. To cry for assistance was absurd. I knew that this den was an outhouse, and that the corridor which connected it with the house was at least a hundred feet long. Besides, with that gale thundering outside, my cries were not likely to be heard. I had only my own courage and my own wits to trust to.

And then, with a fresh wave of horror, my eyes fell upon the lantern. The candle had burned low, and was already beginning to gutter. In ten minutes it would be out. I had only ten minutes then in which to do something, for I felt that if I were once left in the dark with that fearful beast I should be incapable of action. The very thought of it paralysed me. I cast my despairing eyes round this chamber of death, and they rested upon one spot which seemed to promise— I will not say safety, but less immediate and imminent danger than the open floor.

I have said that the cage had a top as well as a front, and this top was left standing when the front was wound through the slot in the wall. It consisted of bars at a few inches' interval, with stout wire netting between, and it rested upon a strong stanchion at each end. It stood now as a great barred canopy over the crouching figure in the corner. The space between this iron shelf and the roof may have been from two to three feet. If I could only get there, squeezed in between bars and ceiling, I should have only one vulnerable side. I should be safe from below, from behind, and from each side. Only on the open face of it could I be attacked. There, it is true, I had no protection whatever; but, at least, I should be out of the brute's path when he began to pace about his den. He would have to come out of his way to reach me. It was now or never, for if once the light were out it would be impossible. With a gulp in my throat I sprang up, seized the iron edge of the top, and swung myself panting onto it. I writhed in face downwards, and found myself looking straight into the terrible eyes and yawning jaws of the cat. Its fetid breath came up into my face like the steam from some foul pot.

It appeared, however, to be rather curious than angry. With a sleek ripple of its long, black back it rose, stretched itself, and then rearing itself on its hind legs, with one forepaw against the wall, it raised the other, and drew its claws across the wire meshes beneath me. One sharp, white hook tore through my trousers—for I may mention that I was still in evening dress—and dug a furrow in my knee. It was not meant as an attack, but rather as an experiment, for upon my giving a sharp cry of pain he dropped down again, and springing lightly into the room, he began walking swiftly round it, looking up every now and again in my direction. For my part I shuffled backwards until I lay with my back against the wall, screwing myself into the smallest space possible. The farther I got the more difficult it was for him to attack me.

He seemed more excited now that he had begun to move about, and he ran swiftly and noiselessly round and round the den, passing continually underneath the iron couch upon which I lay. It was wonderful to see so great a bulk passing like a shadow, with hardly the softest thudding of velvety pads. The candle was burning low—so low that I could hardly see the creature. And then, with a last flare and splutter it went out altogether. I was alone with the cat in the dark!

It helps one to face a danger when one knows that one has done all that possibly can be done. There is nothing for it then but to quietly await the result. In this case, there was no chance of safety anywhere except the precise spot where I was. I stretched myself out, therefore, and lay silently, almost breathlessly, hoping that the beast might forget my presence if I did nothing to remind him. I reckoned that it must already be two o'clock. At four it would be full dawn. I had not more than two hours to wait for daylight.

Outside, the storm was still raging, and the rain lashed continually against the little windows. Inside, the poisonous and fetid air was overpowering. I could neither hear nor see the cat. I tried to think about other things—but only one had power enough to draw my mind from my terrible position. That was the contemplation of my cousin's villainy, his unparalleled hypocrisy, his malignant hatred of me. Beneath that cheerful face there lurked the spirit of a mediaeval assassin. And as I thought of it I saw more clearly how cunningly the thing had been arranged. He had apparently gone to bed with the others. No doubt he had his witnesses to prove it. Then, unknown to them, he had slipped down, had lured me into this den, and abandoned me. His story would be so simple. He had left me to finish my cigar in the billiard-room. I had gone down on my own account to have a last look at the cat. I had entered the room without observing that the cage was opened, and I had been caught. How could such a crime be brought home to him? Suspicion, perhaps—but proof, never!

How slowly those dreadful two hours went by! Once I heard a low, rasping sound, which I took to be the creature licking its own fur. Several times those greenish eyes gleamed at me through the darkness, but never in a fixed stare, and my hopes grew stronger that my presence had been forgotten or ignored. At last the least faint glimmer of light came through the windows—I first dimly saw them as two grey squares upon the black wall, then grey turned to white, and I could see my terrible companion once more. And he, alas, could see me!

It was evident to me at once that he was in a much more dangerous and aggressive mood than when I had seen him last. The cold of the morning had irritated him, and he was hungry as well. With a continual growl he paced swiftly up and down the side of the room which was farthest from my refuge, his whiskers bristling angrily and his tail switching and lashing. As he turned at the corners his savage eyes always looked upwards at me with a dreadful menace. I knew then that he meant to kill me. Yet I found myself even at that moment admiring the sinuous grace of the devilish thing, its long, undulating, rippling movements, the gloss of its beautiful flanks, the vivid, palpitating scarlet of the glistening tongue which hung from the jet-black muzzle. And all the time that deep, threatening growl was rising and rising in an unbroken crescendo. I knew that the crisis was at hand.

It was a miserable hour to meet such a death—so cold, so comfortless, shivering in my light dress clothes upon this gridiron of torment upon which I was stretched. I tried to brace myself to it, to raise my soul above it, and at the same time, with the lucidity which comes to a perfectly desperate man, I cast round for some possible means of escape. One thing was clear to me. If that front of the cage was only back in its position once more, I could find a sure refuge behind it. Could I possibly pull it back? I hardly dared to move for fear of bringing the creature upon me. Slowly, very slowly, I put my hand forward until it grasped the edge of the front, the final bar which protruded through the wall. To my surprise it came quite easily to my jerk. Of course the difficulty of drawing it out arose from the fact that I was clinging to it. I pulled again, and three inches of it came through. It ran apparently on wheels. I pulled again . . . and then the cat sprang.

It was so quick, so sudden, that I never saw it happen. I simply heard the savage snarl, and in an instant afterwards the blazing yellow eyes, the flattened black head with its red tongue and flashing teeth, were within reach of me. The impact of the creature shook the bars upon which I lay, until I thought (as far as I could think of anything at such a moment) that they were coming down. The cat swayed there for an instant, the head and front paws quite close to me, the hind paws clawing to find a grip upon the edge of the grating. I heard the claws rasping as they clung to the wire netting, and the breath of the beast made me sick. But its bound had been miscalculated. It could not retain its position. Slowly, grinning with rage and scratching madly at the bars, it swung backwards and dropped heavily upon the floor. With a growl it instantly faced round to me and crouched for another spring.

I knew that the next few moments would decide my fate. The creature had learned by experience. It would not miscalculate again. I must act promptly, fearlessly, if I were to have a chance for life. In an instant I had formed my plan. Pulling off my dress coat, I threw it down over the head of the beast. At the same moment I dropped over the edge, seized the end of the front grating, and pulled it frantically out of the wall.

It came more easily than I could have expected. I rushed across the room, bearing it with me; but, as I rushed, the accident of my position put me upon the outer side. Had it been the other way, I might have come off scathless. As it was, there was a moment's pause as I stopped it and tried to pass in through the opening which I had left. That moment was enough to give time to the creature to toss off the coat with which I had blinded him and to spring upon me. I hurled myself through the gap and pulled the rails to behind me, but he seized my leg before I could entirely withdraw it. One stroke of that huge paw tore off my calf as a shaving of wood curls off before a plane. The next moment, bleeding and fainting, I was lying among the foul straw with a line of friendly bars between me and the creature which ramped so frantically against them.

Too wounded to move, and too faint to be conscious of fear, I could only lie, more dead than alive, and watch it. It pressed its broad, black chest against the bars and angled for me with its crooked paws as I have seen a kitten do before a mousetrap. It ripped my clothes, but, stretch as it would, it could not quite reach me. I have heard of the curious numbing effect produced by wounds from the great carnivora, and now I was destined to experience it, for I had lost all sense of personality, and was as interested in the cat's failure or success as if it were some game which I was watching. And then gradually my mind drifted away into strange, vague dreams, always with that black face and red tongue coming back into them, and so I lost myself in the nirvana of delirium, the blessed relief of those who are too sorely tried.

Tracing the course of events afterwards, I conclude that I must have been insensible for about two hours. What roused me to consciousness once more was that sharp metallic click which had been the precursor of my terrible experience. It was the shooting back of the spring lock. Then, before my senses were clear enough to entirely apprehend what they saw, I was aware of the round, benevolent face of my cousin peering in through the opened door. What he saw evidently amazed him. There was the cat crouching on the floor. I was stretched upon my back in my shirt-sleeves within the cage, my trousers torn to ribbons and a great pool of blood all round me. I can see his amazed face now, with the morning sunlight upon it. He peered at me, and peered again. Then he closed the door behind him, and advanced to the cage to see if I were really dead.

I cannot undertake to say what happened. I was not in a fit state to witness or to chronicle such events. I can only say that I was suddenly conscious that his face was away from me—that he was looking towards the animal.

'Good old Tommy!' he cried. 'Good old Tommy!'

Then he came near the bars, with his back still towards me.

'Down, you stupid beast!' he roared. 'Down, sir! Don't you know your master?'

Suddenly even in my bemuddled brain a remembrance came of those words of his when he had said that the taste of blood would turn the cat into a fiend. My blood had done it, but he was to pay the price.

'Get away!' he screamed. 'Get away, you devil! Baldwin! Baldwin! Oh, my God!'

And then I heard him fall, and rise, and fall again, with a sound like the ripping of sacking. His screams grew fainter until they were lost in the worrying snarl. And then, after I thought that he was dead, I saw, as in a nightmare, a blinded, tattered, blood-soaked figure running wildly round the room—and that was the last glimpse which I had of him before I fainted once again.

I was many months in my recovery—in fact, I cannot say that I have ever recovered, for to the end of my days I shall carry a stick as a sign of my night with the Brazilian cat. Baldwin, the groom, and the other servants could not tell what had occurred when, drawn by the death cries of their master, they found me behind the bars, and his remains—or what they afterwards discovered to be his remains—in the clutch of the creature which he had reared. They stalled him off with hot irons, and afterwards shot him through the loophole of the door before they could finally extricate me. I was carried to my bedroom, and there, under the roof of my would-be murderer, I remained between life and death for several weeks. They had sent for a surgeon from Clipton and a nurse from London, and in a month I was able to be carried to the station, and so conveyed back once more to Grosvenor Mansions.

I have one remembrance of that illness, which might have been part of the ever-changing panorama conjured up by a delirious brain were it not so definitely fixed in my memory. One night, when the nurse was absent, the door of my chamber opened, and a tall woman in blackest mourning slipped into the room. She came across to me, and as she bent her sallow face I saw by the faint gleam of the night-light that it was the Brazilian woman whom my cousin had married. She stared intently into my face, and her expression was more kindly than I had ever seen it.

'Are you conscious?' she asked.

I feebly nodded—for I was still very weak.

'Well, then, I only wished to say to you that you have yourself to blame. Did I not do all I could for you? From the beginning I tried to drive you from the house. By every means, short of betraying my husband, I tried to save you from him. I knew that he had a reason for bringing you here. I knew that he would never let you get away again. No one knew him as I knew him, who had suffered from him so often. I did not dare to tell you all this. He would have killed me. But I did my best for you. As things have turned out, you have been the best friend that I have ever had. You have set me free, and I fancied that nothing but death would do that. I am sorry if you are hurt, but I cannot reproach myself. I told you that you were a fool—and a fool you have been.'

She crept out of the room, the bitter, singular woman, and I was never destined to see her again. With what remained from her husband's property she went back to her native land, and I have heard that she afterwards took the veil at Pernambuco.

It was not until I had been back in London for some time that the doctors pronounced me to be well enough to do business. It was not a very welcome permission to me, for I feared that it would be the signal for an inrush of creditors; but it was Summers, my lawyer, who first took advantage of it.

'I am very glad to see that your lordship is so much better,' said he. 'I have been waiting a long time to offer my congratulations.'

'What do you mean, Summers? This is no time for joking.'

'I mean what I say,' he answered. 'You have been Lord Southerton for the last six weeks, but we feared that it would retard your recovery if you were to learn it.'

Lord Southerton! One of the richest peers in England! I could not believe my ears. And then suddenly I thought of the time which had elapsed, and how it coincided with my injuries.

'Then Lord Southerton must have died about the same time that I was hurt?'

'His death occurred upon that very day.' Summers looked hard at me as I spoke, and I am convinced—for he was a very shrewd fellow—that he had guessed the true state of the case. He paused for a moment as if awaiting a confidence from me, but I could not see what was to be gained by exposing such a family scandal.

'Yes, a very curious coincidence,' he continued, with the same knowing look. 'Of course, you are aware that your cousin Everard King was the next heir to the estates. Now, if it had been you instead of him who had been torn to pieces by this tiger, or whatever it was, then of course he would have been Lord Southerton at the present moment.'

'No doubt,' said I.

'And he took such an interest in it,' said Summers. 'I happen to know that the late Lord Southerton's valet was in his pay, and that he used to have telegrams from him every few hours to tell him how he was getting on. That would be about the time when you were down there. Was it not strange that he should wish to be so well informed, since he knew that he was not the direct heir?'

'Very strange,' said I. 'And now, Summers, if you will bring me my bills and a new cheque-book, we will begin to get things into order.'

The Brown Hand

EVERYONE KNOWS THAT SIR DOMINIC HOLDEN, the famous Indian surgeon, made me his heir, and that his death changed me in an hour from a hard-working and impecunious medical man to a well-to-do landed proprietor. Many know also that there were at least five people between the inheritance and me, and that Sir Dominick's selection appeared to be altogether arbitrary and whimsical. I can assure them, however, that they are quite mistaken, and that although I only knew Sir Dominick in the closing years of his life, there were none the less very real reasons why he should show his goodwill towards me. As a matter of fact, though I say it myself, no man ever did more for another than I did for my Indian uncle. I cannot expect the story to be believed, but it is so singular that I should feel that it was a breach of duty if I did not put it upon record—so here it is, and your belief or incredulity is your own affair.

Sir Dominick Holden, CB, KCSI, and I don't know what besides, was the most distinguished Indian surgeon of his day. In the Army originally, he afterwards settled down into civil practice in Bombay, and visited as a consultant every part of India. His name is best remembered in connection with the Oriental Hospital, which he founded and supported. The time came, however, when his iron constitution began to show signs of the long strain to which he had subjected it, and his brother practitioners (who were not, perhaps, entirely disinterested upon the point) were unanimous in recommending him to return to England. He held on so long as he could, but at last he developed nervous symptoms of a very pronounced character, and so came back, a broken man, to his native county of Wiltshire. He bought a considerable estate with an ancient manor house upon the edge of Salisbury Plain, and devoted his old age to the study of Comparative Pathology, which had been his learned hobby all his life, and in which he was a foremost authority.

We of the family were, as may be imagined, much excited by the news of the return of this rich and childless uncle to England. On his part, although by no means exuberant in his hospitality, he showed some sense of his duty to his relations, and each of us in turn had an invitation to visit him. From the accounts of my cousins it appeared to be a melancholy business, and it was with mixed feelings that I at last received my own summons to appear at Rodenhurst. My wife was so carefully excluded in the invitation that my first impulse was to refuse it, but the interests of the children had to be considered, and so, with her consent, I set out one October afternoon upon my visit to Wiltshire, with little thought of what that visit was to entail.

My uncle's estate was situated where the arable land of the plains begins to swell upwards into the rounded chalk hills which are characteristic of the county. As I drove from Dinton Station in the waning light of that autumn day, I was impressed by the weird nature of the scenery. The few scattered cottages of the peasants were so dwarfed by the huge evidences of prehistoric life, that the present appeared to be a dream and the past to be the obtrusive and masterful reality. The road wound through the valleys, formed by a succession of grassy hills, and the summit of each was cut and carved into the most elaborate fortifications, some circular and some square, but all on a scale which has defied the winds and the rains of many centuries. Some call them Roman and some British, but their true origin and the reasons for this particular tract of country being so interlaced with entrenchments have never been finally made clear. Here and there on the long, smooth, olive-coloured slopes there rose small rounded barrows or tumuli. Beneath them lie the cremated ashes of the race which cut so deeply into the hills, but their graves tell us nothing save that a jar full of dust represents the man who once laboured under the sun.

It was through this weird country that I approached my uncle's residence of Rodenhurst, and the house was, as I found, in due keeping with its surroundings. Two broken and weather-stained pillars, each surmounted by a mutilated heraldic emblem, flanked the entrance to a neglected drive. A cold wind whistled through the elms which lined it, and the air was full of the drifting leaves. At the far end, under the gloomy arch of trees, a single yellow lamp burned steadily. In the dim half-light of the coming night I saw a long, low building stretching out two irregular wings, with deep eaves, a sloping gambrel roof, and walls which were criss-crossed with timber balks in the fashion of the Tudors. The cheery light of a fire flickered in the broad, latticed window to the left of the low-porched door, and this, as it proved, marked the study of my uncle, for it was thither that I was led by his butler in order to make my host's acquaintance.

He was cowering over his fire, for the moist chill of an English autumn had set him shivering. His lamp was unlit, and I only saw the red glow of the embers beating upon a huge, craggy face, with a Red Indian nose and cheek, and deep furrows and seams from eye to chin, the sinister marks of hidden volcanic fires. He sprang up at my entrance with something of an old-world courtesy and welcomed me warmly to Rodenhurst. At the same time I was conscious, as the lamp was carried in, that it was a very critical pair of light blue eyes which looked out at me from under shaggy eyebrows, like scouts beneath a bush, and that this outlandish uncle of mine was carefully reading off my character with all the ease of a practised observer and an experienced man of the world.

For my part I looked at him, and looked again, for I had never seen a man whose appearance was more fitted to hold one's attention. His figure was the framework of a giant, but he had fallen away until his coat dangled straight down in a shocking fashion from a pair of broad and bony shoulders. All his limbs were huge and yet emaciated, and I could not take my gaze from his knobby wrists, and long, gnarled hands. But his eyes—those peering light blue eyes—they were the most arrestive of any of his peculiarities. It was not their colour alone, nor was it the ambush of hair in which they lurked; but it was the expression which I read in them. For the appearance and bearing of the man were masterful, and one expected a certain corresponding arrogance in his eyes, but instead of that I read the look which tells of a spirit cowed and crushed, the furtive, expectant look of the dog whose master has taken the whip from the rack. I formed my own medical diagnosis upon one glance at those critical and yet appealing eyes. I believed that he was stricken with some mortal ailment, that he knew himself to be exposed to sudden death, and that he lived in terror of it. Such was my judgment—a false one, as the event showed; but I mention it that it may help you to realize the look which I read in his eyes.

My uncle's welcome was, as I have said, a courteous one, and in an hour or so I found myself seated between him and his wife at a comfortable dinner, with curious, pungent delicacies upon the table, and a stealthy, quick-eyed Oriental waiter behind his chair. The old couple had come round to that tragic imitation of the dawn of life when husband and wife, having lost or scattered all those who were their intimates, find themselves face to face and alone once more, their work done, and the end nearing fast. Those who have reached that stage in sweetness and love, who can change their winter into a gentle Indian summer, have come as victors through the ordeal of life. Lady Holden was a small, alert woman with a kindly eye, and her expression as she glanced at him was a certificate of character to her husband. And yet, though I read a mutual love in their glances, I read also a mutual horror, and recognized in her face some reflection of that stealthy fear which I detected in his. Their talk was sometimes merry and sometimes sad, but there was a forced note in their merriment and a naturalness in their sadness which told me that a heavy heart beat upon either side of me.

We were sitting over our first glass of wine, and the servants had left the room, when the conversation took a turn which produced a remarkable effect upon my host and hostess. I cannot recall what it was which started the topic of the supernatural, but it ended in my showing them that the abnormal in psychical experiences was a subject to which I had, like many neurologists, devoted a great deal of attention. I concluded by narrating my experiences when, as a member of the Psychical Research Society, I had formed one of a committee of three who spent the night in a haunted house. Our adventures were neither exciting nor convincing, but, such as it was, the story appeared to interest my auditors in a remarkable degree. They listened with an eager silence, and I caught a look of intelligence between them which I could not understand. Lady Holden immediately afterwards rose and left the room.

Sir Dominick pushed the cigar box over to me, and we smoked for some little time in silence. That huge bony hand of his was twitching as he raised it with his cheroot to his lips, and I felt that the man's nerves were vibrating like fiddle strings. My instincts told me that he was on the verge of some intimate confidence, and I feared to speak lest I should interrupt it. At last he turned towards me with a spasmodic gesture like a man who throws his last scruple to the winds.

'From the little that I have seen of you it appears to me, Dr Hardacre,' said he, 'that you are the very man I have wanted to meet.'

'I am delighted to hear it, sir.'

'Your head seems to be cool and steady. You will acquit me of any desire to flatter you, for the circumstances are too serious to permit of insincerities. You have some special knowledge upon these subjects, and you evidently view them from that philosophical standpoint which robs them of all vulgar terror. I presume that the sight of an apparition would not seriously discompose you?'

'I think not, sir.'

'Would even interest you, perhaps?'

'Most intensely.'

'As a psychical observer, you would probably investigate it in as impersonal a fashion as an astronomer investigates a wandering comet?'

'Precisely.'

He gave a heavy sigh.

'Believe me, Dr Hardacre, there was a time when I could have spoken as you do now. My nerve was a byword in India. Even the Mutiny never shook it for an instant. And yet you see what I am reduced to—the most timorous man, perhaps, in all this county of Wiltshire. Do not speak too bravely upon this subject, or you may find yourself subjected to as long-drawn a test as I am—a test which can only end in the madhouse or the grave.'

I waited patiently until he should see fit to go farther in his confidence. His preamble had, I need not say, filled me with interest and expectation.

'For some years, Dr Hardacre,' he continued, 'my life and that of my wife have been made miserable by a cause which is so grotesque that it borders upon the ludicrous. And yet familiarity has never made it more easy to bear— on the contrary, as time passes my nerves become more worn and shattered by the constant attrition. If you have no physical fears, Dr Hardacre, I should very much value your opinion upon this phenomenon which troubles us so.'

'For what it is worth my opinion is entirely at your service. May I ask the nature of the phenomenon?'

'I think that your experiences will have a higher evidential value if you are not told in advance what you may expect to encounter. You are yourself aware of the quibbles of unconscious cerebration and subjective impressions with which a scientific sceptic may throw a doubt upon your statement. It would be as well to guard against them in advance.'

'What shall I do, then?'

'I will tell you. Would you mind following me this way?' He led me out of the dining-room and down a long passage until we came to a terminal door. Inside there was a large, bare room fitted as a laboratory, with numerous scientific instruments and bottles. A shelf ran along one side, upon which there stood a long line of glass jars containing pathological and anatomical specimens.

'You see that I still dabble in some of my old studies,' said Sir Dominick. 'These jars are the remains of what was once a most excellent collection, but unfortunately I lost the greater part of them when my house was burned down in Bombay in '92. It was a most unfortunate affair for me—in more ways than one. I had examples of many rare conditions, and my splenic collection was probably unique. These are the survivors.'

I glanced over them, and saw that they really were of a very great value and rarity from a pathological point of view: bloated organs, gaping cysts, distorted bones, odious parasites—a singular exhibition of the products of India.

'There is, as you see, a small settee here,' said my host. 'It was far from our intention to offer a guest so meagre an accommodation, but since affairs have taken this turn, it would be a great kindness upon your part if you would consent to spend the night in this apartment. I beg that you will not hesitate to let me know if the idea should be at all repugnant to you.'

'On the contrary,' I said, 'it is most acceptable.'

'My own room is the second on the left, so that if you should feel that you are in need of company a call would always bring me to your side.'

'I trust that I shall not be compelled to disturb you.'

'It is unlikely that I shall be asleep. I do not sleep much. Do not hesitate to summon me.'

And so with this agreement we joined Lady Holden in the drawing-room and talked of lighter things.

It was no affectation upon my part to say that the prospect of my night's adventure was an agreeable one. I have no pretence to greater physical courage than my neighbours, but familiarity with a subject robs it of those vague and undefined terrors which are the most appalling to the imaginative mind. The human brain is capable of only one strong emotion at a time, and if it be filled with curiosity or scientific enthusiasm, there is no room for fear. It is true that I had my uncle's assurance that he had himself originally taken this point of view, but I reflected that the breakdown of his nervous system might be due to his forty years in India as much as to any psychical experiences which had befallen him. I at least was sound in nerve and brain, and it was with something of the pleasurable thrill of anticipation with which the sportsman takes his position beside the haunt of his game that I shut the laboratory door behind me, and partially undressing, lay down upon the rug-covered settee.

It was not an ideal atmosphere for a bedroom. The air was heavy with many chemical odours, that of methylated spirit predominating. Nor were the decorations of my chamber very sedative. The odious line of glass jars with their relics of disease and suffering stretched in front of my very eyes. There was no blind to the window, and a three-quarter moon streamed its white light into the room, tracing a silver square with filigree lattices upon the opposite wall. When I had extinguished my candle this one bright patch in the midst of the general gloom had certainly an eerie and discomposing aspect. A rigid and absolute silence reigned throughout the old house, so that the low swish of the branches in the garden came softly and soothingly to my ears. It may have been the hypnotic lullaby of this gentle susurrus, or it may have been the result of my tiring day, but after many dozings and many efforts to regain my clearness of perception, I fell at last into a deep and dreamless sleep.

I was awakened by some sound in the room, and I instantly raised myself upon my elbow on the couch. Some hours had passed, for the square patch upon the wall had slid downwards and sideways until it lay obliquely at the end of my bed. The rest of the room was in deep shadow. At first I could see nothing; presently, as my eyes became accustomed to the faint light, I was aware, with a thrill which all my scientific absorption could not entirely prevent, that something was moving slowly along the line of the wall. A gentle, shuffling sound, as of soft slippers, came to my ears, and I dimly discerned a human figure walking stealthily from the direction of the door. As it emerged into the patch of moonlight I saw very clearly what it was and how it was employed. It was a man, short and squat, dressed in some sort of dark grey gown, which hung straight from his shoulders to his feet. The moon shone upon the side of his face, and I saw that it was chocolate brown in colour, with a ball of black hair like a woman's at the back of his head. He walked slowly, and his eyes were cast upwards towards the line of bottles which contained those gruesome remnants of humanity. He seemed to examine each jar with attention, and then to pass on to the next. When he had come to the end of the line, immediately opposite my bed, he stopped, faced me, threw up his hands with a gesture of despair, and vanished from my sight.

I have said that he threw up his hands, but I should have said his arms, for as he assumed that attitude of despair. I observed a singular peculiarity about his appearance. He had only one hand! As the sleeves drooped down from the upflung arms I saw the left plainly, but the right ended in a knobby and unsightly stump. In every other way his appearance was so natural, and I had both seen and heard him so clearly, that I could easily have believed that he was an Indian servant of Sir Dominick's who had come into my room in search of something. It was only his sudden disappearance which suggested anything more sinister to me. As it was I sprang from my couch, lit a candle, and examined the whole room carefully. There were no signs of my visitor, and I was forced to conclude that there had really been something outside the normal laws of Nature in his appearance. I lay awake for the remainder of the night, but nothing else occurred to disturb me.

I am an early riser, but my uncle was an even earlier one, for I found him pacing up and down the lawn at the side of the house. He ran towards me in his eagerness when he saw me come out from the door.

'Well, well!' he cried. 'Did you see him?'

'An Indian with one hand?'

'Precisely.'

'Yes, I saw him'—and I told him all that occurred. When I had finished, he led the way into his study.

'We have a little time before breakfast,' said he. 'It will suffice to give you an explanation of this extraordinary affair—so far as I can explain that which is essentially inexplicable. In the first place, when I tell you that for four years I have never passed one single night, either in Bombay, aboard ship, or here in England without my sleep being broken by this fellow, you will understand why it is that I am a wreck of my former self. His programme is always the same. He appears by my bedside, shakes me roughly by the shoulder, passes from my room into the laboratory, walks slowly along the line of my bottles, and then vanishes. For more than a thousand times he has gone through the same routine.'

'What does he want?'

'He wants his hand.'

'His hand?'

'Yes, it came about in this way. I was summoned to Peshawur for a consultation some ten years ago, and while there I was asked to look at the hand of a native who was passing through with an Afghan caravan. The fellow came from some mountain tribe living away at the back of beyond somewhere on the other side of Kaffiristan. He talked a bastard Pushtoo, and it was all I could do to understand him. He was suffering from a soft sarcomatous swelling of one of the metacarpal joints, and I made him realize that it was only by losing his hand that he could hope to save his life. After much persuasion he consented to the operation, and he asked me, when it was over, what fee I demanded. The poor fellow was almost a beggar, so that the idea of a fee was absurd, but I answered in jest that my fee should be his hand, and that I proposed to add it to my pathological collection.

'To my surprise he demurred very much to the suggestion, and he explained that according to his religion it was an all-important matter that the body should be reunited after death, and so make a perfect dwelling for the spirit. The belief is, of course, an old one, and the mummies of the Egyptians arose from an analogous superstition. I answered him that his hand was already off, and asked him how he intended to preserve it. He replied that he would pickle it in salt and carry it about with him. I suggested that it might be safer in my keeping than in his, and that I had better means than salt for preserving it. On realizing that I really intended to carefully keep it, his opposition vanished instantly. 'But remember, sahib,' said he, 'I shall want it back when I am dead.' I laughed at the remark, and so the matter ended. I returned to my practice, and he no doubt in the course of time was able to continue his journey to Afghanistan.

'Well, as I told you last night, I had a bad fire in my house at Bombay. Half of it was burned down, and, among other things, my pathological collection was largely destroyed. What you see are the poor remains of it. The hand of the hillman went with the rest, but I gave the matter no particular thought at the time. That was six years ago.

'Four years ago—two years after the fire—I was awakened one night by a furious tugging at my sleeve. I sat up under the impression that my favourite mastiff was trying to arouse me. Instead of this, I saw my Indian patient of long ago, dressed in the long, grey gown which was the badge of his people. He was holding up his stump and looking reproachfully at me. He then went over to my bottles, which at the time I kept in my room, and he examined them carefully, after which he gave a gesture of anger and vanished. I realized that he had just died, and that he had come to claim my promise that I should keep his limb in safety for him.

'Well, there you have it all, Dr Hardacre. Every night at the same hour for four years this performance has been repeated. It is a simple thing in itself, but it has worn me out like water dropping on a stone. It has brought a vile insomnia with it, for I cannot sleep now for the expectation of his coming. It has poisoned my old age and that of my wife, who has been the sharer in this great trouble. But there is the breakfast gong, and she will be waiting impatiently to know how it fared with you last night. We are both much indebted to you for your gallantry, for it takes something from the weight of our misfortune when we share it, even for a single night, with a friend, and it reassures us as to our sanity, which we are sometimes driven to question.'

This was the curious narrative which Sir Dominick confided to me—a story which to many would have appeared to be a grotesque impossibility, but which, after my experience of the night before, and my previous knowledge of such things, I was prepared to accept as an absolute fact. I thought deeply over the matter, and brought the whole range of my reading and experience to bear upon it. After breakfast, I surprised my host and hostess by announcing that I was returning to London by the next train.

'My dear doctor,' cried Sir Dominick in great distress, 'you make me feel that I have been guilty of a gross breach of hospitality in intruding this unfortunate matter upon you. I should have borne my own burden.'

'It is, indeed, that matter which is taking me to London,' I answered; 'but you are mistaken, I assure you, if you think that my experience of last night was an unpleasant one to me. On the contrary, I am about to ask your permission to return in the evening and spend one more night in your laboratory. I am very eager to see this visitor once again.'

My uncle was exceedingly anxious to know what I was about to do, but my fears of raising false hopes prevented me from telling him. I was back in my own consulting-room a little after luncheon, and was confirming my memory of a passage in a recent book upon occultism which had arrested my attention when I read it.

'In the case of earthbound spirits,' said my authority, 'some one dominant idea obsessing them at the hour of death is sufficient to hold them in this material world. They are the amphibia of this life and of the next, capable of passing from one to the other as the turtle passes from land to water. The causes which may bind a soul so strongly to a life which its body has abandoned are any violent emotion. Avarice, revenge, anxiety, love, and pity have all been known to have this effect. As a rule it springs from some unfulfilled wish, and when the wish has been fulfilled the material bond relaxes. There are many cases upon record which show the singular persistence of these visitors, and also their disappearance when their wishes have been fulfilled, or in some cases when a reasonable compromise has been effected.'

'*A reasonable compromise effected*'—those were the words which I had brooded over all the morning, and which I now verified in the original. No actual atonement could be made here—but a reasonable compromise! I made my way as fast as a train could take me to the Shadwell Seamen's Hospital, where my old friend Jack Hewett was house surgeon. Without explaining the situation I made him understand exactly what it was that I wanted.

'A brown man's hand!' said he, in amazement. 'What in the world do you want that for?'

'Never mind. I'll tell you some day. I know that your wards are full of Indians.'

'I should think so. But a hand——' He thought a little and then struck a bell.

'Travers,' said he to a student dresser, 'what became of the hands of the Lascar which we took off yesterday? I mean the fellow from the East India Dock who got caught in the steam winch.'

'They are in the post-mortem room, sir.'

'Just pack one of them in antiseptics and give it to Dr Hardacre.'

And so I found myself back at Rodenhurst before dinner with this curious outcome of my day in town. I still said nothing to Sir Dominick, but I slept that night in the laboratory, and I placed the Lascar's hand in one of the glass jars at the end of my couch.

So interested was I in the result of my experiment that sleep was out of the question. I sat with a shaded lamp beside me and waited patiently for my visitor. This time I saw him clearly from the first. He appeared beside the door, nebulous for an instant, and then hardening into as distinct an outline as any living man. The slippers beneath his gray gown were red and heelless, which accounted for the low, shuffling sound which he made as he walked. As on the previous night he passed slowly along the line of bottles until he paused before that which contained the hand. He reached up to it, his whole figure quivering with expectation, took it down, examined it eagerly, and then, with a face which was convulsed with fury and disappointment, he hurled it down on the floor. There was a crash which resounded through the house, and when I looked up the mutilated Indian had disappeared. A moment later my door flew open and Sir Dominick rushed in.

'You are not hurt?' he cried.

'No—but deeply disappointed.'

He looked in astonishment at the splinters of glass, and the brown hand lying upon the floor.

'Good God!' he cried. 'What is this?'

I told him my idea and its wretched sequel. He listened intently, but shook his head.

'It was well thought of,' said he, 'but I fear that there is no such easy end to my sufferings. But one thing I now insist upon. It is that you shall never again upon any pretext occupy this room. My fears that something might have happened to you—when I heard that crash—have been the most acute of all the agonies which I have undergone. I will not expose myself to a repetition of it.'

He allowed me, however, to spend the remainder of that night where I was, and I lay there worrying over the problem and lamenting my own failure. With the first light of morning there was the Lascar's hand still lying upon the floor to remind me of my fiasco. I lay looking at it—and as I lay suddenly an idea flew like a bullet through my head and brought me quivering with excitement out of my couch. I raised the grim relic from where it had fallen. Yes, it was indeed so. The hand was the *left* hand of the Lascar.

By the first train I was on my way to town, and hurried at once to the Seamen's Hospital. I remembered that both hands of the Lascar had been amputated, but I was terrified lest the precious organ which I was in search of might have been already consumed in the crematory. My suspense was soon ended. It had still been preserved in the post-mortem room. And so I returned to Rodenhurst in the evening with my mission accomplished and the material for a fresh experiment.

But Sir Dominick Holden would not hear of my occupying the laboratory again. To all my entreaties he turned a deaf ear. It offended his sense of hospitality, and he could no longer permit it. I left the hand, therefore, as I had done its fellow the night before, and I occupied a comfortable bedroom in another portion of the house, some distance from the scene of my adventures.

But in spite of that my sleep was not destined to be uninterrupted. In the dead of night my host burst into my room, a lamp in his hand. His huge gaunt figure was enveloped in a loose dressing-gown, and his whole appearance might certainly have seemed more formidable to a weak-nerved man than that of the Indian of the night before. But it was not his entrance so much as his expression which amazed me. He had turned suddenly younger by twenty years at the least. His eyes were shining, his features radiant, and he waved one hand in triumph over his head. I sat up astounded, staring sleepily at this extraordinary visitor. But his words soon drove the sleep from my eyes.

'We have done it! We have succeeded!' he shouted. 'My dear Hardacre, how can I ever in this world repay you?'

'You don't mean to say that it is all right?'

'Indeed I do. I was sure that you would not mind being awakened to hear such blessed news.'

'Mind! I should think not indeed. But is it really certain?'

'I have no doubt whatever upon the point. I owe you such a debt, my dear nephew, as I have never owed a man before, and never expected to. What can I possibly do for you that is commensurate? Providence must have sent you to my rescue. You have saved both my reason and my life, for another six months of this must have seen me either in a cell or a coffin. And my wife—it was wearing her out before my eyes. Never could I have believed that any human being could have lifted this burden off me.' He seized my hand and wrung it in his bony grip.

'It was only an experiment—a forlorn hope—but I am delighted from my heart that it has succeeded. But how do you know that it is all right? Have you seen something?'

He seated himself at the foot of my bed.

'I have seen enough,' said he. 'It satisfies me that I shall be troubled no more. What has passed is easily told. You know that at a certain hour this creature always comes to me. Tonight he arrived at the usual time, and aroused me with even more violence than is his custom. I can only surmise that his disappointment of last night increased the bitterness of his anger against me. He looked angrily at me, and then went on his usual round. But in a few minutes I saw him, for the first time since this persecution began, return to my chamber. He was smiling. I saw the gleam of his white teeth through the dim light. He stood facing me at the end of my bed, and three times he made the low Eastern salaam, which is their solemn leave-taking. And the third time that he bowed he raised his arms over his head, and I saw his *two* hands outstretched in the air. So he vanished, and, as I believe, forever.'

So that is the curious experience which won me the affection and the gratitude of my celebrated uncle, the famous Indian surgeon. His anticipations were realized, and never again was he disturbed by the visits of the restless hillman in search of his lost member. Sir Dominick and Lady Holden spent a very happy old age, unclouded, so far as I know, by any trouble, and they finally died during the great influenza epidemic within a few weeks of each other. In his lifetime he always turned to me for advice in everything which concerned that English life of which he knew so little; and I aided him also in the purchase and development of his estates. It was no great surprise to me, therefore, that I found myself eventually promoted over the heads of five exasperated cousins, and changed in a single day from a hard-working country doctor into the head of an important Wiltshire family. I, at least, have reason to bless the memory of the man with the brown hand, and the day when I was fortunate enough to relieve Rodenhurst of his unwelcome presence.

Playing with Fire

I CANNOT PRETEND TO SAY WHAT OCCURRED on the 14th of April last at No. 17, Badderly Gardens. Put down in black and white, my surmise might seem too crude, too grotesque, for serious consideration. And yet that something did occur, and that it was of a nature which will leave its mark upon every one of us for the rest of our lives, is as certain as the unanimous testimony of five witnesses can make it. I will not enter into any argument or speculation. I will only give a plain statement, which will be submitted to John Moir, Harvey Deacon, and Mrs Delamere, and withheld from publication unless they are prepared to corroborate every detail. I cannot obtain the sanction of Paul Le Duc, for he appears to have left the country.

It was John Moir (the well-known senior partner of Moir, Moir, and Sanderson) who had originally turned our attention to occult subjects. He had, like many very hard and practical men of business, a mystic side to his nature, which had led him to the examination, and eventually to the acceptance, of those elusive phenomena which are grouped together with much that is foolish, and much that is fraudulent, under the common heading of spiritualism. His researches, which had begun with an open mind, ended unhappily in dogma, and he became as positive and fanatical as any other bigot. He represented in our little group the body of men who have turned these singular phenomena into a new religion.

Mrs Delamere, our medium, was his sister, the wife of Delamere, the rising sculptor. Our experience had shown us that to work on these subjects without a medium was as futile as for an astronomer to make observations without a telescope. On the other hand, the introduction of a paid medium was hateful to all of us. Was it not obvious that he or she would feel bound to return some result for money received, and that the temptation to fraud would be an overpowering one? No phenomena could be relied upon which were produced at a guinea an hour. But, fortunately, Moir had discovered that his sister was mediumistic—in other words, that she was a battery of that animal magnetic force which is the only form of energy which is subtle enough to be acted upon from the spiritual plane as well as from our own material one. Of course, when I say this, I do not mean to beg the question; but I am simply indicating the theories upon which we were ourselves, rightly or wrongly, explaining what we saw. The lady came, not altogether with the approval of her husband, and though she never gave indications of any very great psychic force, we were able, at least, to obtain those usual phenomena of message-tilting which are at the same time so puerile and so inexplicable. Every Sunday evening we met in Harvey Deacon's studio at Badderly Gardens, the next house to the corner of Merton Park Road.

Harvey Deacon's imaginative work in art would prepare anyone to find that he was an ardent lover of everything which was *outré* and sensational. A certain picturesqueness in the study of the occult had been the quality which had originally attracted him to it, but his attention was speedily arrested by some of those phenomena to which I have referred, and he was coming rapidly to the conclusion that what he had looked upon as an amusing romance and an after-dinner entertainment was really a very formidable reality. He is a man with a remarkably clear and logical brain—a true descendant of his ancestor, the well-known Scotch professor—and he represented in our small circle the critical element, the man who has no prejudices, is prepared to follow facts as far as he can see them, and refuses to theorise in advance of his data. His caution annoyed Moir as much as the latter's robust faith amused Deacon, but each in his own way was equally keen upon the matter.

And I? What am I to say that I represented? I was not the devotee. I was not the scientific critic. Perhaps the best that I can claim for myself is that I was the dilettante man about town, anxious to be in the swim of every fresh movement, thankful for any new sensation which would take me out of myself and open up fresh possibilities of existence. I am not an enthusiast myself, but I like the company of those who are. Moir's talk, which made me feel as if we had a private pass-key through the door of death, filled me with a vague contentment. The soothing atmosphere of the séance with the darkened lights was delightful to me. In a word, the thing amused me, and so I was there.

It was, as I have said, upon the 14th of April last that the very singular event which I am about to put upon record took place. I was the first of the men to arrive at the studio, but Mrs Delamere was already there, having had afternoon tea with Mrs Harvey Deacon. The two ladies and Deacon himself were standing in front of an unfinished picture of his upon the easel. I am not an expert in art, and I have never professed to understand what Harvey Deacon meant by his pictures; but I could see in this instance that it was all very clever and imaginative, fairies and animals and allegorical figures of all sorts. The ladies were loud in their praises, and indeed the colour effect was a remarkable one.

'What do you think of it, Markham?' he asked.

'Well, it's above me,' said I. 'These beasts—what are they?'

'Mythical monsters, imaginary creatures, heraldic emblems—a sort of weird, bizarre procession of them.'

'With a white horse in front!'

'It's not a horse,' said he, rather testily—which was surprising, for he was a very good-humoured fellow as a rule, and hardly ever took himself seriously.

'What is it, then?'

'Can't you see the horn in front? It's a unicorn. I told you they were heraldic beasts. Can't you recognize one?'

'Very sorry, Deacon,' said I, for he really seemed to be annoyed.

He laughed at his own irritation.

'Excuse me, Markham!' said he; 'the fact is that I have had an awful job over the beast. All day I have been painting him in and painting him out, and trying to imagine what a real live, ramping unicorn would look like. At last I got him, as I hoped; so when you failed to recognize it, it took me on the raw.'

'Why, of course it's a unicorn,' said I, for he was evidently depressed at my obtuseness. 'I can see the horn quite plainly, but I never saw a unicorn except beside the Royal Arms, and so I never thought of the creature. And these others are griffins and cockatrices and dragons of sorts?'

'Yes, I had no difficulty with them. It was the unicorn which bothered me. However, there's an end of it until tomorrow.' He turned the picture round upon the easel, and we all chatted about other subjects.

Moir was late that evening, and when he did arrive he brought with him, rather to our surprise, a small, stout Frenchman, whom he introduced as Monsieur Paul Le Duc. I say to our surprise, for we held a theory that any intrusion into our spiritual circle deranged the conditions, and introduced an element of suspicion. We knew that we could trust each other, but all our results were vitiated by the presence of an outsider. However, Moir soon reconciled us to the innovation. Monsieur Paul Le Duc was a famous student of occultism, a seer, a medium, and a mystic. He was travelling in England with a letter of introduction to Moir from the President of the Parisian brothers of the Rosy Cross. What more natural than that he should bring him to our little séance, or that we should feel honoured by his presence?

He was, as I have said, a small, stout man, undistinguished in appearance, with a broad, smooth, clean-shaven face, remarkable only for a pair of large, brown, velvety eyes, staring vaguely out in front of him. He was well dressed, with the manners of a gentleman, and his curious little turns of English speech set the ladies smiling. Mrs Deacon had a prejudice against our researches and left the room, upon which we lowered the lights, as was our custom, and drew up our chairs to the square mahogany table which stood in the centre of the studio. The light was subdued, but sufficient to allow us to see each other quite plainly. I remember that I could even observe the curious, podgy little square-topped hands which the Frenchman laid upon the table.

'What a fun!' said he. 'It is many years since I have sat in this fashion, and it is to me amusing. Madame is medium. Does madame make the trance?'

'Well, hardly that,' said Mrs Delamere. 'But I am always conscious of extreme sleepiness.'

'It is the first stage. Then you encourage it, and there comes the trance. When the trance comes, then out jumps your little spirit and in jumps another little spirit, and so you have direct talking or writing. You leave your machine to be worked by another. *Hein?* But what have unicorns to do with it?'

Harvey Deacon started in his chair. The Frenchman was moving his head slowly round and staring into the shadows which draped the walls.

'What a fun!' said he. 'Always unicorns. Who has been thinking so hard upon a subject so bizarre?'

'This is wonderful!' cried Deacon. 'I have been trying to paint one all day. But how could you know it?'

'You have been thinking of them in this room.'

'Certainly.'

'But thoughts are things, my friend. When you imagine a thing you make a thing. You did not know it, *hein?* But I can see your unicorns because it is not only with my eye that I can see.'

'Do you mean to say that I create a thing which has never existed by merely thinking of it?'

'But certainly. It is the fact which lies under all other facts. That is why an evil thought is also a danger.'

'They are, I suppose, upon the astral plane?' said Moir.

'Ah, well, these are but words, my friends. They are there—somewhere—everywhere—I cannot tell myself. I see them. I could touch them.'

'You could not make *us* see them.'

'It is to materialize them. Hold! It is an experiment. But the power is wanting. Let us see what power we have, and then arrange what we shall do. May I place you as I wish?'

'You evidently know a great deal more about it than we do,' said Harvey Deacon; 'I wish that you would take complete control.'

'It may be that the conditions are not good. But we will try what we can do. Madame will sit where she is, I next, and this gentleman beside me. Meester Moir will sit next to madame, because it is well to have blacks and blondes in turn. So! And now with your permission I will turn the lights all out.'

'What is the advantage of the dark?' I asked.

'Because the force with which we deal is a vibration of ether and so also is light. We have the wires all for ourselves now—*hein?* You will not be frightened in the darkness, madame? What a fun is such a séance!'

At first the darkness appeared to be absolutely pitchy, but in a few minutes our eyes became so far accustomed to it that we could just make out each other's presence—very dimly and vaguely, it is true. I could see nothing else in the room—only the black loom of the motionless figures. We were all taking the matter much more seriously than we had ever done before.

'You will place your hands in front. It is hopeless that we touch, since we are so few round so large a table. You will compose yourself, madame, and if sleep should come to you you will not fight against it. And now we sit in silence and we expect—*hein?*'

So we sat in silence and expected, staring out into the blackness in front of us. A clock ticked in the passage. A dog barked intermittently far away. Once or twice a cab rattled past in the street, and the gleam of its lamps through the chink in the curtains was a cheerful break in that gloomy vigil. I felt those physical symptoms with which previous séances had made me familiar—the coldness of the feet, the tingling in the hands, the glow of the palms, the feeling of a cold wind upon the back. Strange little shooting pains came in my forearms, especially as it seemed to me in my left one, which was nearest to our visitor— due no doubt to disturbance of the vascular system, but worthy of some attention all the same. At the same time I was conscious of a strained feeling of expectancy which was almost painful. From the rigid, absolute silence of my companions I gathered that their nerves were as tense as my own.

And then suddenly a sound came out of the darkness—a low, sibilant sound, the quick, thin breathing of a woman. Quicker and thinner yet it came, as between clenched teeth, to end in a loud gasp with a dull rustle of cloth.

'What's that? Is all right?' someone asked in the darkness.

'Yes, all is right,' said the Frenchman. 'It is madame. She is in her trance. Now, gentlemen, if you will wait quiet you will see something, I think, which will interest you much.'

Still the ticking in the hall. Still the breathing, deeper and fuller now, from the medium. Still the occasional flash, more welcome than ever, of the passing lights of the hansoms. What a gap we were bridging, the half-raised veil of the eternal on the one side and the cabs of London on the other. The table was throbbing with a mighty pulse. It swayed steadily, rhythmically, with an easy swooping, scooping motion under our fingers. Sharp little raps and cracks came from its substance, file-firing, volley-firing, the sounds of a fagot burning briskly on a frosty night.

'There is much power,' said the Frenchman. 'See it on the table!'

I had thought it was some delusion of my own, but all could see it now. There was a greenish-yellow phosphorescent light—or I should say a luminous vapour rather than a light—which lay over the surface of the table. It rolled and wreathed and undulated in dim glimmering folds, turning and swirling like clouds of smoke. I could see the white, square-ended hands of the French medium in this baleful light.

'What a fun!' he cried. 'It is splendid!'

'Shall we call the alphabet?' asked Moir.

'But no—for we can do much better,' said our visitor. 'It is but a clumsy thing to tilt the table for every letter of the alphabet, and with such a medium as madame we should do better than that.'

'Yes, you will do better,' said a voice.

'Who was that? Who spoke? Was that you, Markham?'

'No, I did not speak.'

'It was madame who spoke.'

'But it was not her voice.'

'Is that you, Mrs Delamere?'

'It is not the medium, but it is the power which uses the organs of the medium,' said the strange, deep voice.

'Where is Mrs Delamere? It will not hurt her, I trust.'

'The medium is happy in another plane of existence. She has taken my place, as I have taken hers.'

'Who are you?'

'It cannot matter to you who I am. I am one who has lived as you are living, and who has died as you will die.'

We heard the creak and grate of a cab pulling up next door. There was an argument about the fare, and the cabman grumbled hoarsely down the street. The green-yellow cloud still swirled faintly over the table, dull elsewhere, but glowing into a dim luminosity in the direction of the medium. It seemed to be piling itself up in front of her. A sense of fear and cold struck into my heart. It seemed to me that lightly and flippantly we had approached the most real and august of sacraments, that communion with the dead of which the fathers of the Church had spoken.

'Don't you think we are going too far? Should we not break up this séance?' I cried.

But the others were all earnest to see the end of it. They laughed at my scruples.

'All the powers are made for use,' said Harvey Deacon. 'If we *can* do this, we *should* do this. Every new departure of knowledge has been called unlawful in its inception. It is right and proper that we should inquire into the nature of death.'

'It is right and proper,' said the voice.

'There, what more could you ask?' cried Moir, who was much excited. 'Let us have a test. Will you give us a test that you are really there?'

'What test do you demand?'

'Well, now—I have some coins in my pocket. Will you tell me how many?'

'We come back in the hope of teaching and of elevating, and not to guess childish riddles.'

'Ha, ha, Meester Moir, you catch it that time,' cried the Frenchman. 'But surely this is very good sense what the Control is saying.'

'It is a religion, not a game,' said the cold, hard voice.

'Exactly—the very view I take of it,' cried Moir. 'I am sure I am very sorry if I have asked a foolish question. You will not tell me who you are?'

'What does it matter?'

'Have you been a spirit long?'

'Yes.'

'How long?'

'We cannot reckon time as you do. Our conditions are different.'

'Are you happy?'

'Yes.'

'You would not wish to come back to life?'

'No—certainly not.'

'Are you busy?'

'We could not be happy if we were not busy.'

'What do you do?'

'I have said that the conditions are entirely different.'

'Can you give us no idea of your work?'

'We labour for our own improvement and for the advancement of others.'

'Do you like coming here tonight?'

'I am glad to come if I can do any good by coming.'

'Then to do good is your object?'

'It is the object of all life on every plane.'

'You see, Markham, that should answer your scruples.'

It did, for my doubts had passed and only interest remained.

'Have you pain in your life?' I asked.

'No; pain is a thing of the body.'

'Have you mental pain?'

'Yes; one may always be sad or anxious.'

'Do you meet the friends whom you have known on earth?'

'Some of them.'

'Why only some of them?'

'Only those who are sympathetic.'

'Do husbands meet wives?'

'Those who have truly loved.'

'And the others?'

'They are nothing to each other.'

'There must be a spiritual connection?'

'Of course.'

'Is what we are doing right?'

'If done in the right spirit.'

'What is the wrong spirit?'

'Curiosity and levity.'

'May harm come of that?'

'Very serious harm.'

'What sort of harm?'

'You may call up forces over which you have no control.'

'Evil forces?'

'Undeveloped forces.'

'You say they are dangerous. Dangerous to body or mind?'

'Sometimes to both.'

There was a pause, and the blackness seemed to grow blacker still, while the yellow-green fog swirled and smoked upon the table.

'Any questions you would like to ask, Moir?' said Harvey Deacon.

'Only this—do you pray in your world?'

'One should pray in every world.'

'Why?'

'Because it is the acknowledgment of forces outside ourselves.'

'What religion do you hold over there?'

'We differ exactly as you do.'

'You have no certain knowledge?'

'We have only faith.'

'These question of religion,' said the Frenchman, 'they are of interest to you serious English people, but they are not so much fun. It seems to me that with this power here we might be able to have some great experience—*hein?* Something of which we could talk.'

'But nothing could be more interesting than this,' said Muir.

'Well, if you think so, that is very well,' the Frenchman answered, peevishly. 'For my part, it seems to me that I have heard all this before, and that tonight I should weesh to try some experiment with all this force which is given to us. But if you have other questions, then ask them, and when you are finish we can try something more.'

But the spell was broken. We asked and asked, but the medium sat silent in her chair. Only her deep, regular breathing showed that she was there. The mist still swirled upon the table.

'You have disturbed the harmony. She will not answer.'

'But we have learned already all that she can tell—*hein?* For my part I wish to see something that I have never seen before.'

'What then?'

'You will let me try?'

'What would you do?'

'I have said to you that thoughts are things. Now I wish to *prove* it to you, and to show you that which is only a thought. Yes, yes, I can do it and you will see. Now I ask you only to sit still and say nothing, and keep ever your hands quiet upon the table.'

The room was blacker and more silent than ever. The same feeling of apprehension which had lain heavily upon me at the beginning of the séance was back at my heart once more. The roots of my hair were tingling.

'It is working! It is working!' cried the Frenchman, and there was a crack in his voice as he spoke which told me that he also was strung to his tightest.

The luminous fog drifted slowly off the table and wavered and flickered across the room. There in the farther and darkest corner it gathered and glowed, hardening down into a shining core—a strange, shifty, luminous, and yet non-illuminating patch of radiance, bright itself, but throwing no rays into the darkness. It had changed from a greenish-yellow to a dusky sullen red. Then round this centre there coiled a dark, smoky substance, thickening, hardening, growing denser and blacker. And then the light went out, smothered in that which had grown round it.

'It has gone.'

'Hush—there's something in the room.'

We heard it in the corner where the light had been, something which breathed deeply and fidgeted in the darkness.

'What is it? Le Duc, what have you done?'

'It is all right. No harm will come.' The Frenchman's voice was treble with agitation.

'Good heavens, Moir, there's a large animal in the room. Here it is, close by my chair! Go away! Go away!'

It was Harvey Deacon's voice, and then came the sound of a blow upon some hard object. And then . . . And then . . . how can I tell you what happened then?

Some huge thing hurtled against us in the darkness, rearing, stamping, smashing, springing, snorting. The table was splintered. We were scattered in every direction. It clattered and scrambled amongst us, rushing with horrible energy from one corner of the room to another. We were all screaming with fear, grovelling upon our hands and knees to get away from it. Something trod upon my left hand, and I felt the bones splinter under the weight.

'A light! A light!' someone yelled.

'Moir, you have matches, matches!'

'No, I have none. Deacon, where are the matches? For God's sake, the matches!'

'I can't find them. Here, you Frenchman, stop it!'

'It is beyond me. Oh, *mon Dieu*, I cannot stop it. The door! Where is the door?'

My hand, by good luck, lit upon the handle as I groped about in the darkness. The hard-breathing, snorting, rushing creature tore past me and butted with a fearful crash against the oaken partition. The instant that it had passed I turned the handle, and next moment we were all outside, and the door shut behind us. From within came a horrible crashing and rending and stamping.

'What is it? In Heaven's name, what is it?'

'A horse. I saw it when the door opened. But Mrs Delamere——?'

'We must fetch her out. Come on, Markham; the longer we wait the less we shall like it.'

He flung open the door and we rushed in. She was there on the ground amidst the splinters of her chair. We seized her and dragged her swiftly out, and as we gained the door I looked over my shoulder into the darkness. There were two strange eyes glowing at us, a rattle of hoofs, and I had just time to slam the door when there came a crash upon it which split it from top to bottom.

'It's coming through! It's coming!'

'Run, run for your lives!' cried the Frenchman.

Another crash, and something shot through the riven door. It was a long white spike, gleaming in the lamp-light. For a moment it shone before us, and then with a snap it disappeared again.

'Quick! Quick! This way!' Harvey Deacon shouted. 'Carry her in! Here! Quick!'

We had taken refuge in the dining-room, and shut the heavy oak door. We laid the senseless woman upon the sofa, and as we did so, Moir, the hard man of business, drooped and fainted across the hearthrug. Harvey Deacon was as white as a corpse, jerking and twitching like an epileptic. With a crash we heard the studio door fly to pieces, and the snorting and stamping were in the passage, up and down, up and down, shaking the house with their fury. The Frenchman had sunk his face on his hands, and sobbed like a frightened child.

'What shall we do?' I shook him roughly by the shoulder. 'Is a gun any use?'

'No, no. The power will pass. Then it will end.'

'You might have killed us all—you unspeakable fool—with your infernal experiments.'

'I did not know. How could I tell that it would be frightened? It is mad with terror. It was his fault. He struck it.'

Harvey Deacon sprang up. 'Good heavens!' he cried.

A terrible scream sounded through the house.

'It's my wife! Here, I'm going out. If it's the Evil One himself, I am going out!'

He had thrown open the door and rushed out into the passage. At the end of it, at the foot of the stairs, Mrs Deacon was lying senseless, struck down by the sight which she had seen. But there was nothing else.

With eyes of horror we looked about us, but all was perfectly quiet and still. I approached the black square of the studio door, expecting with every slow step that some atrocious shape would hurl itself out of it. But nothing came, and all was silent inside the room. Peeping and peering, our hearts in our mouths, we came to the very threshold, and stared into the darkness. There was still no sound, but in one direction there was also no darkness. A luminous, glowing cloud, with an incandescent centre, hovered in the corner of the room. Slowly it dimmed and faded, growing thinner and fainter, until at last the same dense, velvety blackness filled the whole studio. And with the last flickering gleam of that baleful light the Frenchman broke into a shout of joy.

'What a fun!' he cried. 'No one is hurt, and only the door broken, and the ladies frightened. But, my friends, we have done what has never been done before.'

'And as far as I can help,' said Harvey Deacon, 'it will certainly never be done again.'

And that was what befell on the 14th of April last at No. 17, Badderly Gardens. I began by saying that it would seem too grotesque to dogmatise as to what it was which actually did occur; but I give my impressions, *our* impressions (since they are corroborated by Harvey Deacon and John Moir), for what they are worth. You may, if it pleases you, imagine that we were the victims of an elaborate and extraordinary hoax. Or you may think with us that we underwent a very real and a very terrible experience. Or perhaps you may know more than we do of such occult matters, and can inform us of some similar occurrence. In this latter case a letter to William Markham, 146M, The Albany, would help to throw a light upon that which is very dark to us.

The Legend of
the Hound of the Baskervilles

O F THE ORIGIN OF THE HOUND OF THE BASKERVILLES there have been many
statements, yet as I come in a direct line from Hugo Baskerville, and
as I had the story from my father, who also had it from his, I have set
it down with all belief that it occurred even as is here set forth. And I would
have you believe, my sons, that the same Justice which punishes sin may also
most graciously forgive it, and that no ban is so heavy but that by prayer and
repentance it may be removed. Learn then from this story not to fear the fruits
of the past, but rather to be circumspect in the future, that those foul passions
whereby our family has suffered so grievously may not again be loosed to our
undoing.

Know then that in the time of the Great Rebellion (the history of which by
the learned Lord Clarendon I most earnestly commend to your attention) this
Manor of Baskerville was held by Hugo of that name, nor can it be gainsaid
that he was a most wild, profane, and godless man. This, in truth, his neighbours
might have pardoned, seeing that saints have never flourished in those parts,
but there was in him a certain wanton and cruel humour which made his name
a by-word through the West. It chanced that this Hugo came to love (if, indeed,
so dark a passion may be known under so bright a name) the daughter of a
yeoman who held lands near the Baskerville estate. But the young maiden,
being discreet and of good repute, would ever avoid him, for she feared his evil
name. So it came to pass that one Michaelmas this Hugo, with five or six of his
idle and wicked companions, stole down upon the farm and carried off the
maiden, her father and brothers being from home, as he well knew. When they
had brought her to the Hall the maiden was placed in an upper chamber, while
Hugo and his friends sat down to a long carouse, as was their nightly custom.
Now, the poor lass upstairs was like to have her wits turned at the singing and
shouting and terrible oaths which came up to her from below, for they say that
the words used by Hugo Baskerville, when he was in wine, were such as might
blast the man who said them. At last in the stress of her fear she did that which
might have daunted the bravest or most active man, for by the aid of the growth
of ivy which covered (and still covers) the south wall she came down from

under the eaves, and so homeward across the moor, there being three leagues betwixt the Hall and her father's farm.

It chanced that some little time later Hugo left his guests to carry food and drink—with other worse things, perchance—to his captive, and so found the cage empty and the bird escaped. Then, as it would seem, he became as one that hath a devil, for, rushing down the stairs into the dining-hall, he sprang upon the great table, flagons and trenchers flying before him, and he cried aloud before all the company that he would that very night render his body and soul to the Powers of Evil if he might but overtake the wench. And while the revellers stood aghast at the fury of the man, one more wicked or, it may be, more drunken than the rest, cried out that they should put the hounds upon her. Whereat Hugo ran from the house, crying to his grooms that they should saddle his mare and unkennel the pack, and giving the hounds a kerchief of the maid's, he swung them to the line, and so off full cry in the moonlight over the moor.

Now, for some space the revellers stood agape, unable to understand all that had been done in such haste. But anon their bemused wits awoke to the nature of the deed which was like to be done upon the moorlands. Everything was now in an uproar, some calling for their pistols, some for their horses, and some for another flask of wine. But at length some sense came back to their crazed minds, and the whole of them, thirteen in number, took horse and started in pursuit. The moon shone clear above them, and they rode swiftly abreast, taking that course which the maid must needs have taken if she were to reach her own home.

They had gone a mile or two when they passed one of the night shepherds upon the moorlands, and they cried to him to know if he had seen the hunt. And the man, as the story goes, was so crazed with fear that he could scarce speak, but at last he said that he had indeed seen the unhappy maiden, with the hounds upon her track. 'But I have seen more than that,' said he, 'for Hugo Baskerville passed me upon his black mare, and there ran mute behind him such a hound of hell as God forbid should ever be at my heels.'

So the drunken squires cursed the shepherd and rode onward. But soon their skins turned cold, for there came a sound of galloping across the moor, and the black mare, dabbled with white froth, went past with trailing bridle and empty saddle. Then the revellers rode close together, for a great fear was on them, but they still followed over the moor, though each, had he been alone, would have been right glad to have turned his horse's head. Riding slowly in this fashion, they came at last upon the hounds. These, though known for their valour and their breed, were whimpering in a cluster at the head of a deep dip or goyal, as we call it, upon the moor, some slinking away and some, with starting hackles and staring eyes, gazing down the narrow valley before them.

The company had come to a halt, more sober men, as you may guess, than when they started. The most of them would by no means advance, but three of them, the boldest, or it may be the most drunken, rode forward down the goyal. Now, it opened into a broad space in which stood two of those great stones, still to be seen there, which were set by certain forgotten peoples in the days of old. The moon was shining bright upon the clearing, and there in the centre lay the unhappy maid where she had fallen, dead of fear and of fatigue. But it was not the sight of her body, nor yet was it that of the body of Hugo Baskerville lying near her, which raised the hair upon the heads of these three dare-devil roysterers, but it was that, standing over Hugo, and plucking at his throat, there stood a foul thing, a great, black beast, shaped like a hound, yet larger than any hound that ever mortal eye has rested upon. And even as they looked the thing tore the throat out of Hugo Baskerville, on which, as it turned its blazing eyes and dripping jaws upon them, the three shrieked with fear and rode for dear life, still screaming, across the moor. One, it is said, died that very night of what he had seen, and the other twain were but broken men for the rest of their days.

Such is the tale, my sons, of the coming of the hound which is said to have plagued the family so sorely ever since. If I have set it down it is because that which is clearly known hath less terror than that which is but hinted at and guessed. Nor can it be denied that many of the family have been unhappy in their deaths, which have been sudden, bloody, and mysterious. Yet may we shelter ourselves in the infinite goodness of Providence, which would not forever punish the innocent beyond that third or fourth generation which is threatened in Holy Writ. To that Providence, my sons, I hereby commend you, and I counsel you by way of caution to forbear from crossing the moor in those dark hours when the powers of evil are exalted.

[This from Hugo Baskerville to his sons Rodger and John, with instructions that they say nothing thereof to their sister Elizabeth.]

The Leather Funnel

MY FRIEND, LIONEL DACRE, lived in the Avenue de Wagram, Paris. His house was that small one, with the iron railings and grass plot in front of it, on the left-hand side as you pass down from the Arc de Triomphe. I fancy that it had been there long before the avenue was constructed, for the grey tiles were stained with lichens, and the walls were mildewed and discoloured with age. It looked a small house from the street, five windows in front, if I remember right, but it deepened into a single long chamber at the back. It was here that Dacre had that singular library of occult literature, and the fantastic curiosities which served as a hobby for himself, and an amusement for his friends. A wealthy man of refined and eccentric tastes, he had spent much of his life and fortune in gathering together what was said to be a unique private collection of Talmudic, cabalistic, and magical works, many of them of great rarity and value. His tastes leaned towards the marvellous and the monstrous, and I have heard that his experiments in the direction of the unknown have passed all the bounds of civilization and of decorum. To his English friends he never alluded to such matters, and took the tone of the student and *virtuoso*; but a Frenchman whose tastes were of the same nature has assured me that the worst excesses of the black mass have been perpetrated in that large and lofty hall, which is lined with the shelves of his books, and the cases of his museum.

Dacre's appearance was enough to show that his deep interest in these psychic matters was intellectual rather than spiritual. There was no trace of asceticism upon his heavy face, but there was much mental force in his huge dome-like skull, which curved upwards from amongst his thinning locks, like a snow peak above its fringe of fir trees. His knowledge was greater than his wisdom, and his powers were far superior to his character. The small bright eyes, buried deeply in his fleshy face, twinkled with intelligence and an unabated curiosity of life, but they were the eyes of a sensualist and an egotist. Enough of the man, for he is dead now, poor devil, dead at the very time that he had made sure that he had at last discovered the elixir of life. It is not with his complex character that I have to deal, but with the very strange and inexplicable incident which had its rise in my visit to him in the early spring of the year '82.

I had known Dacre in England, for my researches in the Assyrian Room of the British Museum had been conducted at the time when he was endeavouring to establish a mystic and esoteric meaning in the Babylonian tablets, and this community of interests had brought us together. Chance remarks had led to daily conversation, and that to something verging upon friendship. I had promised him that on my next visit to Paris I would call upon him. At the time when I was able to fulfil my compact I was living in a cottage at Fontainebleau, and as the evening trains were inconvenient, he asked me to spend the night in his house.

'I have only that one spare couch,' said he, pointing to a broad sofa in his large salon; 'I hope that you will manage to be comfortable there.'

It was a singular bedroom, with its high walls of brown volumes, but there could be no more agreeable furniture to a bookworm like myself, and there is no scent so pleasant to my nostrils as that faint, subtle reek which comes from an ancient book. I assured him that I could desire no more charming chamber, and no more congenial surroundings.

'If the fittings are neither convenient nor conventional, they are at least costly,' said he, looking round at his shelves. 'I have expended nearly a quarter of a million of money upon these objects which surround you. Books, weapons, gems, carvings, tapestries, images—there is hardly a thing here which has not its history, and it is generally one worth telling.'

He was seated as he spoke at one side of the open fireplace, and I at the other. His reading-table was on his right, and the strong lamp above it ringed it with a very vivid circle of golden light. A half-rolled palimpsest lay in the centre, and around it were many quaint articles of bric-à-brac. One of these was a large funnel, such as is used for filling wine casks. It appeared to be made of black wood, and to be rimmed with discoloured brass.

'That is a curious thing,' I remarked. 'What is the history of that?'

'Ah!' said he, 'it is the very question which I have had occasion to ask myself. I would give a good deal to know. Take it in your hands and examine it.'

I did so, and found that what I had imagined to be wood was in reality leather, though age had dried it into an extreme hardness. It was a large funnel, and might hold a quart when full. The brass rim encircled the wide end, but the narrow was also tipped with metal.

'What do you make of it?' asked Dacre.

'I should imagine that it belonged to some vintner or maltster in the middle ages,' said I. 'I have seen in England leathern drinking flagons of the seventeenth century—"black jacks" as they were called—which were of the same colour and hardness as this filler.'

'I dare say the date would be about the same,' said Dacre, 'and no doubt, also, it was used for filling a vessel with liquid. If my suspicions are correct, however, it was a queer vintner who used it, and a very singular cask which was filled. Do you observe nothing strange at the spout end of the funnel.'

As I held it to the light I observed that at a spot some five inches above the brass tip the narrow neck of the leather funnel was all haggled and scored, as if someone had notched it round with a blunt knife. Only at that point was there any roughening of the dead black surface.

'Someone has tried to cut off the neck.'

'Would you call it a cut?'

'It is torn and lacerated. It must have taken some strength to leave these marks on such tough material, whatever the instrument may have been. But what do you think of it? I can tell that you know more than you say.'

Dacre smiled, and his little eyes twinkled with knowledge.

'Have you included the psychology of dreams among your learned studies?' he asked.

'I did not even know that there was such a psychology.'

'My dear sir, that shelf above the gem case is filled with volumes, from Albertus Magnus onwards, which deal with no other subject. It is a science in itself.'

'A science of charlatans.'

'The charlatan is always the pioneer. From the astrologer came the astronomer, from the alchemist the chemist, from the mesmerist the experimental psychologist. The quack of yesterday is the professor of tomorrow. Even such subtle and elusive things as dreams will in time be reduced to system and order. When that time comes the researches of our friends on the bookshelf yonder will no longer be the amusement of the mystic, but the foundations of a science.'

'Supposing that is so, what has the science of dreams to do with a large black brass-rimmed funnel?'

'I will tell you. You know that I have an agent who is always on the lookout for rarities and curiosities for my collection. Some days ago he heard of a dealer upon one of the Quais who had acquired some old rubbish found in a cupboard in an ancient house at the back of the Rue Mathurin, in the Quartier Latin. The dining-room of this old house is decorated with a coat of arms, chevrons, and bars rouge upon a field argent, which prove, upon inquiry, to be the shield of Nicholas de la Reynie, a high official of King Louis XIV. There can be no doubt that the other articles in the cupboard date back to the early days of that king. The inference is, therefore, that they were all the property of this Nicholas de la Reynie, who was, as I understand, the gentleman specially concerned with the maintenance and execution of the Draconic laws of that epoch.'

'What then?'

'I would ask you now to take the funnel into your hands once more and to examine the upper brass rim. Can you make out any lettering upon it?'

There were certainly some scratches upon it, almost obliterated by time. The general effect was of several letters, the last of which bore some resemblance to a B.

'You make it a B?'

'Yes, I do.'

'So do I. In fact, I have no doubt whatever that it is a B.'

'But the nobleman you mentioned would have had R for his initial.'

'Exactly! That's the beauty of it. He owned this curious object, and yet he had someone else's initials upon it. Why did he do this?'

'I can't imagine; can you?'

'Well, I might, perhaps, guess. Do you observe something drawn a little farther along the rim?'

'I should say it was a crown.'

'It is undoubtedly a crown; but if you examine it in a good light, you will convince yourself that it is not an ordinary crown. It is a heraldic crown—a badge of rank, and it consists of an alternation of four pearls and strawberry leaves, the proper badge of a marquis. We may infer, therefore, that the person whose initials end in B was entitled to wear that coronet.'

'Then this common leather filler belonged to a marquis?'

Dacre gave a peculiar smile.

'Or to some member of the family of a marquis,' said he. 'So much we have clearly gathered from this engraved rim.'

'But what has all this to do with dreams?' I do not know whether it was from a look upon Dacre's face, or from some subtle suggestion in his manner, but a feeling of repulsion, of unreasoning horror, came upon me as I looked at the gnarled old lump of leather.

'I have more than once received important information through my dreams,' said my companion, in the didactic manner which he loved to affect. 'I make it a rule now when I am in doubt upon any material point to place the article in question beside me as I sleep, and to hope for some enlightenment. The process does not appear to me to be very obscure, though it has not yet received the blessing of orthodox science. According to my theory, any object which has been intimately associated with any supreme paroxysm of human emotion, whether it be joy or pain, will retain a certain atmosphere or association which it is capable of communicating to a sensitive mind. By a sensitive mind I do not mean an abnormal one, but such a trained and educated mind as you or I possess.'

'You mean, for example, that if I slept beside that old sword upon the wall, I might dream of some bloody incident in which that very sword took part?'

'An excellent example, for, as a matter of fact, that sword was used in that fashion by me, and I saw in my sleep the death of its owner, who perished in a brisk skirmish, which I have been unable to identify, but which occurred at the time of the wars of the Frondists. If you think of it, some of our popular observances show that the fact has already been recognized by our ancestors, although we, in our wisdom, have classed it among superstitions.'

'For example?'

'Well, the placing of the bride's cake beneath the pillow in order that the sleeper may have pleasant dreams. That is one of several instances which you will find set forth in a small *brochure* which I am myself writing upon the subject. But to come back to the point, I slept one night with this funnel beside me, and I had a dream which certainly throws a curious light upon its use and origin.'

'What did you dream?'

'I dreamed——' He paused, and an intent look of interest came over his massive face. 'By Jove that's well thought of,' said he. 'This really will be an exceedingly interesting experiment. You are yourself a psychic subject—with nerves which respond readily to any impression.'

'I have never tested myself in that direction.'

'Then we shall test you tonight. Might I ask you as a very great favour, when you occupy that couch, tonight, to sleep with this old funnel placed by the side of your pillow?'

The request seemed to me a grotesque one; but I have myself, in my complex nature, a hunger after all which is bizarre and fantastic. I had not the faintest belief in Dacre's theory, nor any hopes for success in such an experiment; yet it amused me that the experiment should be made. Dacre, with great gravity, drew a small stand to the head of my settee, and placed the funnel upon it. Then, after a short conversation, he wished me good night and left me.

I sat for some little time smoking by the smouldering fire, and turning over in my mind the curious incident which had occurred, and the strange experience which might lie before me. Sceptical as I was, there was something impressive in the assurance of Dacre's manner, and my extraordinary surroundings, the huge room with the strange and often sinister objects which were hung round it, struck solemnity into my soul. Finally I undressed, and turning out the lamp, I lay down. After long tossing I fell asleep. Let me try to describe as accurately as I can the scene which came to me in my dreams. It stands out now in my memory more clearly than anything which I have seen with my waking eyes.

There was a room which bore the appearance of a vault. Four spandrels from the corners ran up to join a sharp cup-shaped roof. The architecture was rough, but very strong. It was evidently part of a great building.

Three men in black, with curious top-heavy, black velvet hats, sat in a line upon a red-carpeted dais. Their faces were very solemn and sad. On the left stood two long-gowned men with portfolios in their hands, which seemed to be stuffed with papers. Upon the right, looking towards me, was a small woman with blonde hair and singular, light blue eyes—the eyes of a child. She was past her first youth, but could not yet be called middle-aged. Her figure was inclined to stoutness, and her bearing was proud and confident. Her face was pale, but serene. It was a curious face, comely and yet feline, with a subtle suggestion of cruelty about the straight, strong little mouth and chubby jaw. She was draped in some sort of loose, white gown. Beside her stood a thin, eager priest, who whispered in her ear, and continually raised a crucifix before her eyes. She turned her head and looked fixedly past the crucifix at the three men in black, who were, I felt, her judges.

As I gazed the three men stood up and said something, but I could distinguish no words, though I was aware that it was the central one who was speaking. They then swept out of the room, followed by the two men with the papers. At the same instant several rough-looking fellows in stout jerkins came bustling in and removed first the red carpet, and then the boards which formed the dais, so as to entirely clear the room. When this screen was removed I saw some singular articles of furniture behind it. One looked like a bed with wooden rollers at each end, and a winch handle to regulate its length. Another was a wooden horse. There were several other curious objects, and a number of swinging cords which played over pulleys. It was not unlike a modern gymnasium.

When the room had been cleared there appeared a new figure upon the scene. This was a tall, thin person clad in black, with a gaunt and austere face. The aspect of the man made me shudder. His clothes were all shining with grease and mottled with stains. He bore himself with a slow and impressive dignity, as if he took command of all things from the instant of his entrance. In spite of his rude appearance and sordid dress, it was now *his* business, *his* room, his to command. He carried a coil of light ropes over his left forearm. The lady looked him up and down with a searching glance, but her expression was unchanged. It was confident—even defiant. But it was very different with the priest. His face was ghastly white, and I saw the moisture glisten and run on his high, sloping forehead. He threw up his hands in prayer, and he stooped continually to mutter frantic words in the lady's ear.

The man in black now advanced, and taking one of the cords from his left arm, he bound the woman's hands together. She held them meekly towards him as he did so. Then he took her arm with a rough grip and led her towards the wooden horse, which was little higher than her waist. On to this she was lifted and laid, with her back upon it, and her face to the ceiling, while the priest, quivering with horror, had rushed out of the room. The woman's lips were moving rapidly, and though I could hear nothing, I knew that she was praying. Her feet hung down on either side of the horse, and I saw that the rough varlets in attendance had fastened cords to her ankles and secured the other ends to iron rings in the stone floor.

My heart sank within me as I saw these ominous preparations, and yet I was held by the fascination of horror, and I could not take my eyes from the strange spectacle. A man had entered the room with a bucket of water in either hand. Another followed with a third bucket. They were laid beside the wooden horse. The second man had a wooden dipper—a bowl with a straight handle—in his other hand. This he gave to the man in black. At the same moment one of the varlets approached with a dark object in his hand, which even in my dream filled me with a vague feeling of familiarity. It was a leathern filler. With horrible energy he thrust it—but I could stand no more. My hair stood on end with horror. I writhed, I struggled, I broke through the bonds of sleep, and I burst with a shriek into my own life, and found myself lying shivering with terror in the huge library, with the moonlight flooding through the window and throwing strange silver and black traceries upon the opposite wall. Oh, what a blessed relief to feel that I was back in the nineteenth century—back out of that mediaeval vault into a world where men had human hearts within their bosoms. I sat up on my couch, trembling in every limb, my mind divided between thankfulness and horror. To think that such things were ever done— that they *could* be done without God striking the villains dead. Was it all a fantasy, or did it really stand for something which had happened in the black, cruel days of the world's history? I sank my throbbing head upon my shaking hands. And then, suddenly, my heart seemed to stand still in my bosom, and I could not even scream, so great was my terror. Something was advancing towards me through the darkness of the room.

It is a horror coming upon a horror which breaks a man's spirit. I could not reason, I could not pray; I could only sit like a frozen image, and glare at the dark figure which was coming down the great room. And then it moved out into the white lane of moonlight, and I breathed once more. It was Dacre, and his face showed that he was as frightened as myself.

'Was that you? For God's sake what's the matter?' he asked in a husky voice.

'Oh, Dacre, I am glad to see you! I have been down into hell. It was dreadful.'

'Then it was you who screamed?'

'I dare say it was.'

'It rang through the house. The servants are all terrified.' He struck a match and lit the lamp. 'I think we may get the fire to burn up again,' he added, throwing some logs upon the embers. 'Good God, my dear chap, how white you are! You look as if you had seen a ghost.'

'So I have—several ghosts.'

'The leather funnel has acted, then?'

'I wouldn't sleep near the infernal thing again for all the money you could offer me.'

Dacre chuckled.

'I expected that you would have a lively night of it,' said he. 'You took it out of me in return, for that scream of yours wasn't a very pleasant sound at two in the morning. I suppose from what you say that you have seen the whole dreadful business.'

'What dreadful business?'

'The torture of the water—the "Extraordinary Question", as it was called in the genial days of "Le Roi Soleil". Did you stand it out to the end?'

'No, thank God, I awoke before it really began.'

'Ah! it is just as well for you. I held out till the third bucket. Well, it is an old story, and they are all in their graves now anyhow, so what does it matter how they got there. I suppose that you have no idea what it was that you have seen?'

'The torture of some criminal. She must have been a terrible malefactor indeed if her crimes are in proportion to her penalty.'

'Well, we have that small consolation,' said Dacre, wrapping his dressing-gown round him and crouching closer to the fire. 'They *were* in proportion to her penalty. That is to say, if I am correct in the lady's identity.'

'How could you possibly know her identity?'

For answer Dacre took down an old vellum-covered volume from the shelf.

'Just listen to this,' said he; 'it is in the French of the seventeenth century, but I will give a rough translation as I go. You will judge for yourself whether I have solved the riddle or not:

' "The prisoner was brought before the Grand Chambers and Tournelles of Parliament sitting as a court of justice, charged with the murder of Master Dreux d'Aubray, her father, and of her two brothers, MM. d'Aubray, one being civil lieutenant, and the other a counsellor of Parliament. In person it seemed hard to believe that she had really done such wicked deeds, for she was of a mild appearance, and of short stature, with a fair skin and blue eyes. Yet the Court, having found her guilty, condemned her to the ordinary and to the extraordinary question in order that she might be forced to name her accomplices, after which she should be carried in a cart to the Place de Grève, there to have her head cut off, her body being afterwards burned and her ashes scattered to the winds."

'The date of this entry is July 16, 1676.'

'It is interesting,' said I, 'but not convincing. How do you prove the two women to be the same?'

'I am coming to that. The narrative goes on to tell of the woman's behaviour when questioned. "When the executioner approached her she recognized him by the cords which he held in his hands, and she at once held out her own hands to him, looking at him from head to foot without uttering a word." How's that?'

'Yes, it was so.'

' "She gazed without wincing upon the wooden horse and rings which had twisted so many limbs and caused so many shrieks of agony. When her eyes fell upon the three pails of water, which were all ready for her, she said with a smile, 'All that water must have been brought here for the purpose of drowning me, Monsieur. You have no idea, I trust, of making a person of my small stature swallow it all.' " Shall I read the details of the torture?'

'No, for Heaven's sake, don't.'

'Here is a sentence which must surely show you that what is here recorded is the very scene which you have gazed upon tonight: "The good Abbé Pirot, unable to contemplate the agonies which were suffered by his penitent, had hurried from the room." Does that convince you?'

'It does entirely. There can be no question that it is indeed the same event. But who, then, is this lady whose appearance was so attractive and whose end was so horrible?'

For answer Dacre came across to me, and placed the small lamp upon the table which stood by my bed. Lifting up the ill-omened filler, he turned the brass rim so that the light fell upon it. Seen in this way the engraving seemed clearer than on the night before.

'We have already agreed that this is the badge of a marquis or of a marquise,' said he. 'We have also settled that the last letter is B.'

'It is undoubtedly so.'

'I now suggest to you that the other letters from left to right are, M, M, a small d, A, a small d, and then the final B.'

'Yes, I am sure that you are right. I can make out the two small d's quite plainly.'

'What I have read to you tonight,' said Dacre, 'is the official record of the trial of Marie Madeleine d'Aubray, Marquise de Brinvilliers, one of the most famous poisoners and murderers of all time.'

I sat in silence, overwhelmed at the extraordinary nature of the incident, and at the completeness of the proof with which Dacre had exposed its real meaning. In a vague way I remembered some details of the woman's career, her unbridled debauchery, the cold-blooded and protracted torture of her sick father, the murder of her brothers for motives of petty gain. I recollected also that the bravery of her end had done something to atone for the horror of her life, and that all Paris had sympathised with her last moments, and blessed her as a martyr within a few days of the time when they had cursed her as a murderess. One objection, and one only, occurred to my mind.

'How came her initials and her badge of rank upon the filler? Surely they did not carry their mediaeval homage to the nobility to the point of decorating instruments of torture with their titles?'

'I was puzzled with the same point,' said Dacre, 'but it admits of a simple explanation. The case excited extraordinary interest at the time, and nothing could be more natural than that La Reynie, the head of the police, should retain this filler as a grim souvenir. It was not often that a marchioness of France underwent the extraordinary question. That he should engrave her initials upon it for the information of others was surely a very ordinary proceeding upon his part.'

'And this?' I asked, pointing to the marks upon the leathern neck.

'She was a cruel tigress,' said Dacre, as he turned away. 'I think it is evident that like other tigresses her teeth were both strong and sharp.'

The Silver Mirror

JAN. 3RD—This affair of White and Wotherspoon's accounts proves to be a gigantic task. There are twenty thick ledgers to be examined and checked. Who would be a junior partner? However, it is the first big bit of business which has been left entirely in my hands. I must justify it. But it has to be finished so that the lawyers may have the result in time for the trial. Johnson said this morning that I should have to get the last figure out before the twentieth of the month. Good Lord! Well, have at it, and if human brain and nerve can stand the strain, I'll win out at the other side. It means office-work from ten to five, and then a second sitting from about eight to one in the morning. There's drama in an accountant's life. When I find myself in the still early hours, while all the world sleeps, hunting through column after column for those missing figures which will turn a respected alderman into a felon, I understand that it is not such a prosaic profession after all.

On Monday I came on the first trace of defalcation. No heavy game hunter ever got a finer thrill when first he caught sight of the trail of his quarry. But I look at the twenty ledgers and think of the jungle through which I have to follow him before I get my kill. Hard work—but rare sport, too, in a way! I saw the fat fellow once at a City dinner, his red face glowing above a white napkin. He looked at the little pale man at the end of the table. He would have been pale, too, if he could have seen the task that would be mine.

Jan. 6th—What perfect nonsense it is for doctors to prescribe rest when rest is out of the question! Asses! They might as well shout to a man who has a pack of wolves at his heels that what he wants is absolute quiet. My figures must be out by a certain date; unless they are so, I shall lose the chance of my lifetime, so how on earth am I to rest? I'll take a week or so after the trial.

Perhaps I was myself a fool to go to the doctor at all. But I get nervous and highly strung when I sit alone at my work at night. It's not a pain—only a sort of fullness of the head with an occasional mist over the eyes. I thought perhaps some bromide, or chloral, or something of the kind might do me good. But stop work? It's absurd to ask such a thing. It's like a long-distance race. You feel queer at first and your heart thumps and your lungs pant, but if you have only the pluck to keep on, you get your second wind. I'll stick to my work and wait for my second wind. If it never comes—all the same, I'll stick to my work.

Two ledgers are done, and I am well on in the third. The rascal has covered his tracks well, but I pick them up for all that.

Jan. 9th—I had not meant to go to the doctor again. And yet I have had to. 'Straining my nerves, risking a complete breakdown, even endangering my sanity.' That's a nice sentence to have fired off at one. Well, I'll stand the strain and I'll take the risk, and so long as I can sit in my chair and move a pen I'll follow the old sinner's slot.

By the way, I may as well set down here the queer experience which drove me this second time to the doctor. I'll keep an exact record of my symptoms and sensations, because they are interesting in themselves—'a curious psycho-physiological study,' says the doctor—and also because I am perfectly certain that when I am through with them they will all seem blurred and unreal, like some queer dream betwixt sleeping and waking. So now, while they are fresh, I will just make a note of them if only as a change of thought after the endless figures.

There's an old silver-framed mirror in my room. It was given me by a friend who had a taste for antiquities, and he, as I happen to know, picked it up at a sale and had no notion where it came from. It's a large thing—three feet across and two feet high—and it leans at the back of a side-table on my left as I write. The frame is flat, about three inches across, and very old; far too old for hall-marks or other methods of determining its age. The glass part projects, with a bevelled edge, and has the magnificent reflecting power which is only, as it seems to me, to be found in very old mirrors. There's a feeling of perspective when you look into it such as no modern glass can ever give.

The mirror is so situated that as I sit at the table I can usually see nothing in it but the reflection of the red window curtains. But a queer thing happened last night. I had been working for some hours, very much against the grain, with continual bouts of that mistiness of which I had complained. Again and again I had to stop and clear my eyes. Well, on one of these occasions I chanced to look at the mirror. It had the oddest appearance. The red curtains which should have been reflected in it were no longer there, but the glass seemed to be clouded and steamy, not on the surface, which glittered like steel, but deep down in the very grain of it. This opacity, when I stared hard at it, appeared to slowly rotate this way and that, until it was a thick, white cloud swirling in heavy wreaths. So real and solid was it, and so reasonable was I, that I remember turning, with the idea that the curtains were on fire. But everything was deadly still in the room—no sound save the ticking of the clock, no movement save the slow gyration of that strange woolly cloud deep in the heart of the old mirror.

Then, as I looked, the mist, or smoke, or cloud, or whatever one may call it, seemed to coalesce and solidify at two points quite close together, and I was aware, with a thrill of interest rather than of fear, that these were two eyes looking out into the room. A vague outline of a head I could see—a woman's by the hair, but this was very shadowy. Only the eyes were quite distinct; such eyes—dark, luminous, filled with some passionate emotion, fury or horror, I could not say which. Never have I seen eyes which were so full of intense, vivid life. They were not fixed upon me, but stared out into the room. Then as I sat erect, passed my hand over my brow, and made a strong conscious effort to pull myself together, the dim head faded into the general opacity, the mirror slowly cleared, and there were the red curtains once again.

A sceptic would say, no doubt, that I had dropped asleep over my figures, and that my experience was a dream. As a matter of fact, I was never more vividly awake in my life. I was able to argue about it even as I looked at it, and to tell myself that it was a subjective impression—a chimera of the nerves—begotten by worry and insomnia. But why this particular shape? And who is the woman, and what is the dreadful emotion which I read in those wonderful brown eyes? They come between me and my work. For the first time I have done less than the daily tally which I had marked out. Perhaps that is why I have had no abnormal sensations tonight. Tomorrow I must wake up, come what may.

Jan. 11th—All well, and good progress with my work. I wind the net, coil after coil, round that bulky body. But the last smile may remain with him if my own nerves break over it. The mirror would seem to be a sort of barometer which marks my brain pressure. Each night I have observed that it had clouded before I reached the end of my task.

Dr Sinclair (who is, it seems, a bit of a psychologist) was so interested in my account that he came round this evening to have a look at the mirror. I had observed that something was scribbled in crabbed old characters upon the metal work at the back. He examined this with a lens, but could make nothing of it. 'Sanc. X. Pal.' was his final reading of it, but that did not bring us any further. He advised me to put it away into another room; but, after all, whatever I may see in it is, by his own account, only a symptom. It is in the cause that the danger lies. The twenty ledgers—not the silver mirror—should be packed away if I could only do it. I'm at the eighth now, so I progress.

Jan. 13th—Perhaps it would have been wiser after all if I had packed away the mirror. I had an extraordinary experience with it last night. And yet I find it so interesting, so fascinating, that even now I will keep it in its place. What on earth is the meaning of it all?

I suppose it was about one in the morning, and I was closing my books preparatory to staggering off to bed, when I saw her there in front of me. The stage of mistiness and development must have passed unobserved, and there she was in all her beauty and passion and distress, as clear-cut as if she were really in the flesh before me. The figure was small, but very distinct—so much so that every feature, and every detail of dress, are stamped in my memory. She is seated on the extreme left of the mirror. A sort of shadowy figure crouches down beside her—I can dimly discern that it is a man—and then behind them is cloud, in which I see figures—figures which move. It is not a mere picture upon which I look. It is a scene in life, an actual episode. She crouches and quivers. The man beside her cowers down. The vague figures make abrupt movements and gestures. All my fears were swallowed up in my interest. It was maddening to see so much and not to see more.

But I can at least describe the woman to the smallest point. She is very beautiful and quite young—not more than five-and-twenty, I should judge. Her hair is of a very rich brown, with a warm chestnut shade fining into gold at the edges. A little flat-pointed cap comes to an angle in front and is made of lace edged with pearls. The forehead is high, too high perhaps for perfect beauty; but one would not have it otherwise, as it gives a touch of power and strength to what would otherwise be a softly feminine face. The brows are most delicately curved over heavy eyelids, and then come those wonderful eyes—so large, so dark, so full of overmastering emotion, of rage and horror, contending with a pride of self-control which holds her from sheer frenzy! The cheeks are pale, the lips white with agony, the chin and throat most exquisitely rounded. The figure sits and leans forward in the chair, straining and rigid, cataleptic with horror. The dress is black velvet, a jewel gleams like a flame in the breast, and a golden crucifix smoulders in the shadow of a fold. This is the lady whose image still lives in the old silver mirror. What dire deed could it be which has left its impress there, so that now, in another age, if the spirit of a man be but worn down to it, he may be conscious of its presence?

One other detail: On the left side of the skirt of the black dress was, as I thought at first, a shapeless bunch of white ribbon. Then, as I looked more intently or as the vision defined itself more clearly, I perceived what it was. It was the hand of a man, clenched and knotted in agony, which held on with a convulsive grasp to the fold of the dress. The rest of the crouching figure was a mere vague outline, but that strenuous hand shone clear on the dark background, with a sinister suggestion of tragedy in its frantic clutch. The man is frightened—horribly frightened. That I can clearly discern. What has terrified him so? Why does he grip the woman's dress? The answer lies amongst those moving figures in the background. They have brought danger both to him and to her. The interest of the thing fascinated me. I thought no more of its relation to my own nerves. I stared and stared as if in a theatre. But I could get no further. The mist thinned. There were tumultuous movements in which all the figures were vaguely concerned. Then the mirror was clear once more.

The doctor says I must drop work for a day, and I can afford to do so, for I have made good progress lately. It is quite evident that the visions depend entirely upon my own nervous state, for I sat in front of the mirror for an hour tonight, with no result whatever. My soothing day has chased them away. I wonder whether I shall ever penetrate what they all mean? I examined the mirror this evening under a good light, and besides the mysterious inscription 'Sanc. X. Pal.,' I was able to discern some signs of heraldic marks, very faintly visible upon the silver. They must be very ancient, as they are almost obliterated. So far as I could make out, they were three spear-heads, two above and one below. I will show them to the doctor when he calls tomorrow.

Jan. 14th—Feel perfectly well again, and I intend that nothing else shall stop me until my task is finished. The doctor was shown the marks on the mirror and agreed that they were armorial bearings. He is deeply interested in all that I have told him, and cross-questioned me closely on the details. It amuses me to notice how he is torn in two by conflicting desires—the one that his patient should lose his symptoms, the other that the medium—for so he regards me—should solve this mystery of the past. He advised continued rest, but did not oppose me too violently when I declared that such a thing was out of the question until the ten remaining ledgers have been checked.

Jan. 17th—For three nights I have had no experiences—my day of rest has borne fruit. Only a quarter of my task is left, but I must make a forced march, for the lawyers are clamouring for their material. I will give them enough and to spare. I have him fast on a hundred counts. When they realise what a slippery, cunning rascal he is, I should gain some credit from the case. False trading accounts, false balance-sheets, dividends drawn from capital, losses written down as profits, suppression of working expenses, manipulation of petty cash—it is a fine record!

Jan. 18th—Headaches, nervous twitches, mistiness, fullness of the temples—all the premonitions of trouble, and the trouble came sure enough. And yet my real sorrow is not so much that the vision should come as that it should cease before all is revealed.

But I saw more tonight. The crouching man was as visible as the lady whose gown he clutched. He is a little swarthy fellow, with a black, pointed beard. He has a loose gown of damask trimmed with fur. The prevailing tints of his dress are red. What a fright the fellow is in, to be sure! He cowers and shivers and glares back over his shoulder. There is a small knife in his other hand, but he is far too tremulous and cowed to use it. Dimly now I begin to see the figures in the background. Fierce faces, bearded and dark, shape themselves out of the mist. There is one terrible creature, a skeleton of a man, with hollow cheeks and eyes sunk in his head. He also has a knife in his hand. On the right of the woman stands a tall man, very young, with flaxen hair, his face sullen and dour. The beautiful woman looks up at him in appeal. So does the man on the ground. This youth seems to be the arbiter of their fate. The crouching man draws closer and hides himself in the woman's skirts. The tall youth bends and tries to drag her away from him. So much I saw last night before the mirror cleared. Shall I never know what it leads to and whence it comes? It is not a mere imagination, of that I am very sure. Somewhere, some time, this scene has been acted, and this old mirror has reflected it. But when—where?

Jan. 20th—My work draws to a close, and it is time. I feel a tenseness within my brain, a sense of intolerable strain, which warns me that something must give. I have worked myself to the limit. But tonight should be the last night. With a supreme effort I should finish the final ledger and complete the case before I rise from my chair. I will do it. I will.

Feb 7th—I did. My God, what an experience! I hardly know if I am strong enough yet to set it down.

Let me explain in the first instance that I am writing this in Dr Sinclair's private hospital some three weeks after the last entry in my diary. On the night of January 20th my nervous system finally gave way, and I remembered nothing afterwards until I found myself, three days ago, in the home of rest. And I can rest with a good conscience. My work was done before I went under. My figures are in the solicitors' hands. The hunt is over.

And now I must describe that last night. I had sworn to finish my work, and so intently did I stick to it, though my head was bursting, that I would never look up until the last column had been added. And yet it was fine self-restraint, for all the time I knew that wonderful things were happening in the mirror. Every nerve in my body told me so. If I looked up there was an end of my work. So I did not look up till all was finished. Then, when at last with throbbing temples I threw down my pen and raised my eyes, what a sight was there!

The mirror in its silver frame was like a stage, brilliantly lit, in which a drama was in progress. There was no mist now. The oppression of my nerves had wrought this amazing clarity. Every feature, every movement, was as clear-cut as in life. To think that I, a tired accountant, the most prosaic of mankind, with the account-books of a swindling bankrupt before me, should be chosen of all the human race to look upon such a scene!

It was the same scene and the same figures, but the drama had advanced a stage. The tall young man was holding the woman in his arms. She strained away from him and looked up at him with loathing in her face. They had torn the crouching man away from his hold upon the skirt of her dress. A dozen of them were round him—savage men, bearded men. They hacked at him with knives. All seemed to strike him together. Their arms rose and fell. The blood did not flow from him—it squirted. His red dress was dabbled in it. He threw himself this way and that, purple upon crimson, like an over-ripe plum. Still they hacked, and still the jets shot from him. It was horrible—horrible! They dragged him kicking to the door. The woman looked over her shoulder at him and her mouth gaped. I heard nothing, but I knew that she was screaming. And then whether it was this nerve-racking vision before me, or whether, my task finished, all the overwork of the past weeks came in one crushing weight upon me, the room danced round me, the floor seemed to sink away beneath my feet, and I remembered no more. In the early morning my landlady found me stretched senseless before the silver mirror, but I knew nothing myself until three days ago I awoke in the deep peace of the doctor's nursing home.

Feb. 9th—Only today have I told Dr Sinclair my full experience. He had not allowed me to speak of such matters before. He listened with an absorbed interest. 'You don't identify this with any well-known scene in history?' he asked, with suspicion in his eyes. I assured him that I knew nothing of history. 'Have you no idea whence that mirror came and to whom it once belonged?' he continued. 'Have you?' I asked, for he spoke with meaning. 'It's incredible,' said he, 'and yet how else can one explain it? The scenes which you described before suggested it, but now it has gone beyond all range of coincidence. I will bring you some notes in the evening.'

Later—He has just left me. Let me set down his words as closely as I can recall them. He began by laying several musty volumes upon my bed.

'These you can consult at your leisure,' said he. 'I have some notes here which you can confirm. There is not a doubt that what you have seen is the murder of Rizzio by the Scottish nobles in the presence of Mary, which occurred in March 1566. Your description of the woman is accurate. The high forehead and heavy eyelids combined with great beauty could hardly apply to two women. The tall young man was her husband, Darnley. Rizzio, says the chronicle, "was dressed in a loose dressing-gown of furred damask, with hose of russet velvet". With one hand he clutched Mary's gown, with the other he held a dagger. Your fierce, hollow-eyed man was Ruthven, who was new-risen from a bed of sickness. Every detail is exact.'

'But why to me?' I asked, in bewilderment. 'Why of all the human race to me?'

'Because you were in the fit mental state to receive the impression. Because you chanced to own the mirror which gave the impression.'

'The mirror! You think, then, that it was Mary's mirror—that it stood in the room where the deed was done?'

'I am convinced that it was Mary's mirror. She had been Queen of France. Her personal property would be stamped with the Royal arms. What you took to be three spear-heads were really the lilies of France.'

'And the inscription?'

'"Sanc. X. Pal." You can expand it into Sanctae Crucis Palatium. Someone has made a note upon the mirror as to whence it came. It was the Palace of the Holy Cross.'

'Holyrood!' I cried.

'Exactly. Your mirror came from Holyrood. You have had one very singular experience, and have escaped. I trust that you will never put yourself into the way of having such another.'

The Terror of Blue John Gap

THE FOLLOWING NARRATIVE WAS FOUND among the papers of Dr James Hardcastle, who died of phthisis on February 4, 1908, at 36, Upper Coventry Flats, South Kensington. Those who knew him best, while refusing to express an opinion upon this particular statement, are unanimous in asserting that he was a man of a sober and scientific turn of mind, absolutely devoid of imagination, and most unlikely to invent any abnormal series of events. The paper was contained in an envelope, which was docketed, 'A Short Account of the Circumstances which occurred near Miss Allerton's Farm in North-West Derbyshire in the Spring of Last Year'. The envelope was sealed, and on the other side was written in pencil:

> DEAR SEATON—It may interest, and perhaps pain you to know that the incredulity with which you met my story has prevented me from ever opening my mouth upon the subject again. I leave this record after my death, and perhaps strangers may be found to have more confidence in me than my friend.

Inquiry has failed to elicit who this Seaton may have been. I may add that the visit of the deceased to Allerton's Farm, and the general nature of the alarm there, apart from his particular explanation, have been absolutely established. With this foreword I append his account exactly as he left it. It is in the form of a diary, some entries in which have been expanded, while a few have been erased.

April 17th—Already I feel the benefit of this wonderful upland air. The farm of the Allertons lies fourteen hundred and twenty feet above sea-level, so it may well be a bracing climate. Beyond the usual morning cough I have very little discomfort, and, what with the fresh milk and the home-grown mutton, I have every chance of putting on weight. I think Saunderson will be pleased.

The two Miss Allertons are charmingly quaint and kind, two dear little hard-working old maids, who are ready to lavish all the heart which might have gone out to husband and to children upon an invalid stranger. Truly, the old maid is a most useful person, one of the reserve forces of the community. They talk of the superfluous woman, but what would the poor superfluous man do without her kindly presence? By the way, in their simplicity they very quickly let out the reason why Saunderson recommended their farm. The Professor rose from the ranks himself, and I believe that in his youth he was not above scaring crows in these very fields.

It is a most lonely spot, and the walks are picturesque in the extreme. The farm consists of grazing land lying at the bottom of an irregular valley. On each side are the fantastic limestone hills, formed of rock so soft that you can break it away with your hands. All this country is hollow. Could you strike it with some gigantic hammer it would boom like a drum, or possibly cave in altogether and expose some huge subterranean sea. A great sea there must surely be, for on all sides the streams run into the mountain itself, never to reappear. There are gaps everywhere amid the rocks, and when you pass through them you find yourself in great caverns, which wind down into the bowels of the earth. I have a small bicycle lamp, and it is a perpetual joy to me to carry it into these weird solitudes, and to see the wonderful silver and black effects when I throw its light upon the stalactites which drape the lofty roofs. Shut off the lamp, and you are in the blackest darkness. Turn it on, and it is a scene from the Arabian Nights.

But there is one of these strange openings in the earth which has a special interest, for it is the handiwork, not of nature, but of man. I had never heard of Blue John when I came to these parts. It is the name given to a peculiar mineral of a beautiful purple shade, which is only found at one or two places in the world. It is so rare that an ordinary vase of Blue John would be valued at a great price. The Romans, with that extraordinary instinct of theirs, discovered that it was to be found in this valley, and sank a horizontal shaft deep into the mountain side. The opening of their mine has been called Blue John Gap, a clean-cut arch in the rock, the mouth all overgrown with bushes. It is a goodly passage which the Roman miners have cut, and it intersects some of the great water-worn caves, so that if you enter Blue John Gap you would do well to mark your steps and to have a good store of candles, or you may never make your way back to the daylight again. I have not yet gone deeply into it, but this very day I stood at the mouth of the arched tunnel, and peering down into the black recesses beyond, I vowed that when my health returned I would devote some holiday to exploring those mysterious depths and finding out for myself how far the Roman had penetrated into the Derbyshire hills.

Strange how superstitious these countrymen are! I should have thought better of young Armitage, for he is a man of some education and character, and a very fine fellow for his station in life. I was standing at the Blue John Gap when he came across the field to me.

'Well, doctor,' said he, 'you're not afraid, anyhow.'

'Afraid!' I answered. 'Afraid of what?'

'Of it,' said he, with a jerk of his thumb towards the black vault, 'of the Terror that lives in the Blue John Cave.'

How absurdly easy it is for a legend to arise in a lonely countryside! I examined him as to the reasons for his weird belief. It seems that from time to time sheep have been missing from the fields, carried bodily away, according to Armitage. That they could have wandered away of their own accord and disappeared among the mountains was an explanation to which he would not listen. On one occasion a pool of blood had been found, and some tufts of wool. That also, I pointed out, could be explained in a perfectly natural way. Further, the nights upon which sheep disappeared were invariably very dark, cloudy nights with no moon. This I met with the obvious retort that those were the nights which a commonplace sheep-stealer would naturally choose for his work. On one occasion a gap had been made in a wall, and some of the stones scattered for a considerable distance. Human agency again, in my opinion. Finally, Armitage clinched all his arguments by telling me that he had actually heard the Creature—indeed, that anyone could hear it who remained long enough at the Gap. It was a distant roaring of an immense volume. I could not but smile at this, knowing, as I do, the strange reverberations which come out of an underground water system running amid the chasms of a limestone formation. My incredulity annoyed Armitage so that he turned and left me with some abruptness.

And now comes the queer point about the whole business. I was still standing near the mouth of the cave turning over in my mind the various statements of Armitage, and reflecting how readily they could be explained away, when suddenly, from the depth of the tunnel beside me, there issued a most extraordinary sound. How shall I describe it? First of all, it seemed to be a great distance away, far down in the bowels of the earth. Secondly, in spite of this suggestion of distance, it was very loud. Lastly, it was not a boom, nor a crash, such as one would associate with falling water or tumbling rock, but it was a high whine, tremulous and vibrating, almost like the whinnying of a horse. It was certainly a most remarkable experience, and one which for a moment, I must admit, gave a new significance to Armitage's words. I waited by the Blue John Gap for half an hour or more, but there was no return of the sound, so at last I wandered back to the farmhouse, rather mystified by what had occurred. Decidedly I shall explore that cavern when my strength is restored. Of course, Armitage's explanation is too absurd for discussion, and yet that sound was certainly very strange. It still rings in my ears as I write.

April 20th—In the last three days I have made several expeditions to the Blue John Gap, and have even penetrated some short distance, but my bicycle lantern is so small and weak that I dare not trust myself very far. I shall do the thing more systematically. I have heard no sound at all, and could almost believe that I had been the victim of some hallucination suggested, perhaps, by Armitage's conversation. Of course, the whole idea is absurd, and yet I must confess that those bushes at the entrance of the cave do present an appearance as if some heavy creature had forced its way through them. I begin to be keenly interested. I have said nothing to the Miss Allertons, for they are quite superstitious enough already, but I have bought some candles, and mean to investigate for myself.

I observed this morning that among the numerous tufts of sheep's wool which lay among the bushes near the cavern there was one which was smeared with blood. Of course, my reason tells me that if sheep wander into such rocky places they are likely to injure themselves, and yet somehow that splash of crimson gave me a sudden shock, and for a moment I found myself shrinking back in horror from the old Roman arch. A fetid breath seemed to ooze from the black depths into which I peered. Could it indeed be possible that some nameless thing, some dreadful presence, was lurking down yonder? I should have been incapable of such feelings in the days of my strength, but one grows more nervous and fanciful when one's health is shaken.

For the moment I weakened in my resolution, and was ready to leave the secret of the old mine, if one exists, for ever unsolved. But tonight my interest has returned and my nerves grown more steady. Tomorrow I trust that I shall have gone more deeply into this matter.

April 22nd—Let me try and set down as accurately as I can my extraordinary experience of yesterday. I started in the afternoon, and made my way to the Blue John Gap. I confess that my misgivings returned as I gazed into its depths, and I wished that I had brought a companion to share my exploration. Finally, with a return of resolution, I lit my candle, pushed my way through the briars, and descended into the rocky shaft.

It went down at an acute angle for some fifty feet, the floor being covered with broken stone. Thence there extended a long, straight passage cut in the solid rock. I am no geologist, but the lining of this corridor was certainly of some harder material than limestone, for there were points where I could actually see the tool-marks which the old miners had left in their excavation, as fresh as if they had been done yesterday. Down this strange, old-world corridor I stumbled, my feeble flame throwing a dim circle of light around me, which made the shadows beyond the more threatening and obscure. Finally, I came to a spot where the Roman tunnel opened into a water-worn cavern—a huge hall, hung with long white icicles of lime deposit. From this central chamber I could dimly perceive that a number of passages worn by the subterranean streams wound away into the depths of the earth. I was standing there wondering whether I had better return, or whether I dare venture farther into this dangerous labyrinth, when my eyes fell upon something at my feet which strongly arrested my attention.

The greater part of the floor of the cavern was covered with boulders of rock or with hard encrustations of lime, but at this particular point there had been a drip from the distant roof, which had left a patch of soft mud. In the very centre of this there was a huge mark—an ill-defined blotch, deep, broad, and irregular, as if a great boulder had fallen upon it. No loose stone lay near, however, nor was there anything to account for the impression. It was far too large to be caused by any possible animal, and besides, there was only the one, and the patch of mud was of such a size that no reasonable stride could have covered it. As I rose from the examination of that singular mark and then looked round into the black shadows which hemmed me in, I must confess that I felt for a moment a most unpleasant sinking of my heart, and that, do what I could, the candle trembled in my outstretched hand.

I soon recovered my nerve, however, when I reflected how absurd it was to associate so huge and shapeless a mark with the track of any known animal. Even an elephant could not have produced it. I determined, therefore, that I would not be scared by vague and senseless fears from carrying out my exploration. Before proceeding, I took good note of a curious rock formation in the wall by which I could recognise the entrance of the Roman tunnel. The precaution was very necessary, for the great cave, so far as I could see it, was intersected by passages. Having made sure of my position, and reassured myself by examining my spare candles and my matches, I advanced slowly over the rocky and uneven surface of the cavern.

And now I come to the point where I met with such sudden and desperate disaster. A stream, some twenty feet broad, ran across my path, and I walked for some little distance along the bank to find a spot where I could cross dry-shod. Finally, I came to a place where a single flat boulder lay near the centre, which I could reach in a stride. As it chanced, however, the rock had been cut away and made top-heavy by the rush of the stream, so that it tilted over as I landed on it and shot me into the ice-cold water. My candle went out, and I found myself floundering about in utter and absolute darkness.

I staggered to my feet again, more amused than alarmed by my adventure. The candle had fallen from my hand, and was lost in the stream, but I had two others in my pocket, so that it was of no importance. I got one of them ready, and drew out my box of matches to light it. Only then did I realize my position. The box had been soaked in my fall into the river. It was impossible to strike the matches.

A cold hand seemed to close round my heart as I realized my position. The darkness was opaque and horrible. It was so utter that one put one's hand up to one's face as if to press off something solid. I stood still, and by an effort I steadied myself. I tried to reconstruct in my mind a map of the floor of the cavern as I had last seen it. Alas! the bearings which had impressed themselves upon my mind were high on the wall, and not to be found by touch. Still, I remembered in a general way how the sides were situated, and I hoped that by groping my way along them I should at last come to the opening of the Roman tunnel. Moving very slowly, and continually striking against the rocks, I set out on this desperate quest.

But I very soon realized how impossible it was. In that black, velvety darkness one lost all one's bearings in an instant. Before I had made a dozen paces, I was utterly bewildered as to my whereabouts. The rippling of the stream, which was the one sound audible, showed me where it lay, but the moment that I left its bank I was utterly lost. The idea of finding my way back in absolute darkness through that limestone labyrinth was clearly an impossible one.

I sat down upon a boulder and reflected upon my unfortunate plight. I had not told anyone that I proposed to come to the Blue John mine, and it was unlikely that a search party would come after me. Therefore I must trust to my own resources to get clear of the danger. There was only one hope, and that was that the matches might dry. When I fell into the river, only half of me had got thoroughly wet. My left shoulder had remained above the water. I took the box of matches, therefore, and put it into my left armpit. The moist air of the cavern might possibly be counteracted by the heat of my body, but even so, I knew that I could not hope to get a light for many hours. Meanwhile there was nothing for it but to wait.

By good luck I had slipped several biscuits into my pocket before I left the farm-house. These I now devoured, and washed them down with a draught from that wretched stream which had been the cause of all my misfortunes. Then I felt about for a comfortable seat among the rocks, and, having discovered a place where I could get a support for my back, I stretched out my legs and settled myself down to wait. I was wretchedly damp and cold, but I tried to cheer myself with the reflection that modern science prescribed open windows and walks in all weather for my disease. Gradually, lulled by the monotonous gurgle of the stream and by the absolute darkness, I sank into an uneasy slumber.

How long this lasted I cannot say. It have been for an hour, it may have been for several. Suddenly I sat up on my rock couch, with every nerve thrilling and every sense acutely on the alert. Beyond all doubt I had heard a sound— some sound very distinct from the gurgling of the waters. It had passed, but the reverberation of it still lingered in my ear. Was it a search party? They would most certainly have shouted, and vague as this sound was which had wakened me, it was very distinct from the human voice. I sat palpitating and hardly daring to breathe. There it was again! And again! Now it had become continuous. It was a tread—yes, surely it was the tread of some living creature. But what a tread it was! It gave one the impression of enormous weight carried upon sponge-like feet, which gave forth a muffled but ear-filling sound. The darkness was as complete as ever, but the tread was regular and decisive. And it was coming beyond all question in my direction.

My skin grew cold, and my hair stood on end as I listened to that steady and ponderous footfall. There was some creature there, and surely by the speed of its advance, it was one which could see in the dark. I crouched low on my rock and tried to blend myself into it. The steps grew nearer still, then stopped, and presently I was aware of a loud lapping and gurgling. The creature was drinking at the stream. Then again there was silence, broken by a succession of long sniffs and snorts of tremendous volume and energy. Had it caught the scent of me? My own nostrils were filled by a low fetid odour, mephitic and abominable. Then I heard the steps again. They were on my side of the stream now. The stones rattled within a few yards of where I lay. Hardly daring to breathe, I crouched upon my rock. Then the steps drew away. I heard the splash as it returned across the river, and the sound died away into the distance in the direction from which it had come.

For a long time I lay upon the rock, too much horrified to move. I thought of the sound which I had heard coming from the depths of the cave, of Armitage's fears, of the strange impression in the mud, and now came this final and absolute proof that there was indeed some inconceivable monster, something utterly unearthly and dreadful, which lurked in the hollow of the mountain. Of its nature or form I could frame no conception, save that it was both light-footed and gigantic. The combat between my reason, which told me that such things could not be, and my senses, which told me that they were, raged within me as I lay. Finally, I was almost ready to persuade myself that this experience had been part of some evil dream, and that my abnormal condition might have conjured up an hallucination. But there remained one final experience which removed the last possibility of doubt from my mind.

I had taken my matches from my armpit and felt them. They seemed perfectly hard and dry. Stooping down into a crevice of the rocks, I tried one of them. To my delight it took fire at once. I lit the candle, and, with a terrified backward glance into the obscure depths of the cavern, I hurried in the direction of the Roman passage. As I did so I passed the patch of mud on which I had seen the huge imprint. Now I stood astonished before it, for there were three similar imprints upon its surface, enormous in size, irregular in outline, of a depth which indicated the ponderous weight which had left them. Then a great terror surged over me. Stooping and shading my candle with my hand, I ran in a frenzy of fear to the rocky archway, hastened up it, and never stopped until, with weary feet and panting lungs, I rushed up the final slope of stones, broke through the tangle of briars, and flung myself exhausted upon the soft grass under the peaceful light of the stars. It was three in the morning when I reached the farm-house, and today I am all unstrung and quivering after my terrific adventure. As yet I have told no one. I must move warily in the matter. What would the poor lonely women, or the uneducated yokels here think of it if I were to tell them my experience? Let me go to someone who can understand and advise.

April 25th—I was laid up in bed for two days after my incredible adventure in the cavern. I use the adjective with a very definite meaning, for I have had an experience since which has shocked me almost as much as the other. I have said that I was looking round for someone who could advise me. There is a Dr Mark Johnson who practises some few miles away, to whom I had a note of recommendation from Professor Saunderson. To him I drove, when I was strong enough to get about, and I recounted to him my whole strange experience. He listened intently, and then carefully examined me, paying special attention to my reflexes and to the pupils of my eyes. When he had finished, he refused to discuss my adventure, saying that it was entirely beyond him, but he gave me the card of a Mr Picton at Castleton, with the advice that I should instantly go to him and tell him the story exactly as I had done to himself. He was, according to my adviser, the very man who was pre-eminently suited to help me. I went on to the station, therefore, and made my way to the little town, which is some ten miles away. Mr Picton appeared to be a man of importance, as his brass plate was displayed upon the door of a considerable building on the outskirts of the town. I was about to ring his bell, when some misgiving came into my mind, and, crossing to a neighbouring shop, I asked the man behind the counter if he could tell me anything of Mr Picton. 'Why,' said he, 'he is the best mad doctor in Derbyshire, and yonder is his asylum.' You can imagine that it was not long before I had shaken the dust of Castleton from my feet and returned to the farm, cursing all unimaginative pedants who cannot conceive that there may be things in creation which have never yet chanced to come across their mole's vision. After all, now that I am cooler, I can afford to admit that I have been no more sympathetic to Armitage than Dr Johnson has been to me.

April 27th—When I was a student I had the reputation of being a man of courage and enterprise. I remember that when there was a ghost-hunt at Coltbridge it was I who sat up in the haunted house. Is it advancing years (after all, I am only thirty-five), or is it this physical malady which has caused degeneration? Certainly my heart quails when I think of that horrible cavern in the hill, and the certainty that it has some monstrous occupant. What shall I do? There is not an hour in the day that I do not debate the question. If I say nothing, then the mystery remains unsolved. If I do say anything, then I have the alternative of mad alarm over the whole countryside, or of absolute incredulity which may end in consigning me to an asylum. On the whole, I think that my best course is to wait, and to prepare for some expedition which shall be more deliberate and better thought out than the last. As a first step I have been to Castleton and obtained a few essentials—a large acetylene lantern for one thing, and a good double-barrelled sporting rifle for another. The latter I have hired, but I have bought a dozen heavy game cartridges, which would bring down a rhinoceros. Now I am ready for my troglodyte friend. Give me better health and a little spate of energy, and I shall try conclusions with him yet. But who and what is he? Ah! there is the question which stands between me and my sleep. How many theories do I form, only to discard each in turn! It is all so utterly unthinkable. And yet the cry, the footmark, the tread in the cavern—no reasoning can get past these. I think of the old-world legends of dragons and of other monsters. Were they, perhaps, not such fairy-tales as we have thought? Can it be that there is some fact which underlies them, and am I, of all mortals, the one who is chosen to expose it?

May 3rd—For several days I have been laid up by the vagaries of an English spring, and during those days there have been developments, the true and sinister meaning of which no one can appreciate save myself. I may say that we have had cloudy and moonless nights of late, which according to my information were the seasons upon which sheep disappeared. Well, sheep *have* disappeared. Two of Miss Allerton's, one of old Pearson's of the Cat Walk, and one of Mrs Moulton's. Four in all during three nights. No trace is left of them at all, and the countryside is buzzing with rumours of gipsies and of sheep-stealers.

But there is something more serious than that. Young Armitage has disappeared also. He left his moorland cottage early on Wednesday night and has never been heard of since. He was an unattached man, so there is less sensation than would otherwise be the case. The popular explanation is that he owes money, and has found a situation in some other part of the country, whence he will presently write for his belongings. But I have grave misgivings. Is it not much more likely that the recent tragedy of the sheep has caused him to take some steps which may have ended in his own destruction? He may, for example, have lain in wait for the creature and been carried off by it into the recesses of the mountains. What an inconceivable fate for a civilized Englishman of the twentieth century! And yet I feel that it is possible and even probable. But in that case, how far am I answerable both for his death and for any other mishap which may occur? Surely with the knowledge I already possess it must be my duty to see that something is done, or if necessary to do it myself. It must be the latter, for this morning I went down to the local police-station and told my story. The inspector entered it all in a large book and bowed me out with commendable gravity, but I heard a burst of laughter before I had got down his garden path. No doubt he was recounting my adventure to his family.

June 10th—I am writing this, propped up in bed, six weeks after my last entry in this journal. I have gone through a terrible shock both to mind and body, arising from such an experience as has seldom befallen a human being before. But I have attained my end. The danger from the Terror which dwells in the Blue John Gap has passed never to return. Thus much at least I, a broken invalid, have done for the common good. Let me now recount what occurred as clearly as I may.

The night of Friday, May 3rd, was dark and cloudy—the very night for the monster to walk. About eleven o'clock I went from the farm-house with my lantern and my rifle, having first left a note upon the table of my bedroom in which I said that, if I were missing, search should be made for me in the direction of the Gap. I made my way to the mouth of the Roman shaft, and, having perched myself among the rocks close to the opening, I shut off my lantern and waited patiently with my loaded rifle ready to my hand.

It was a melancholy vigil. All down the winding valley I could see the scattered lights of the farm-houses, and the church clock of Chapel-le-Dale tolling the hours came faintly to my ears. These tokens of my fellow men served only to make my own position seem the more lonely, and to call for a greater effort to overcome the terror which tempted me continually to get back to the farm, and abandon for ever this dangerous quest. And yet there lies deep in every man a rooted self-respect which makes it hard for him to turn back from that which he has once undertaken. This feeling of personal pride was my salvation now, and it was that alone which held me fast when every instinct of my nature was dragging me away. I am glad now that I had the strength. In spite of all that it has cost me, my manhood is at least above reproach.

Twelve o'clock struck in the distant church, then one, then two. It was the darkest hour of the night. The clouds were drifting low, and there was not a star in the sky. An owl was hooting somewhere among the rocks, but no other sound, save the gentle sough of the wind, came to my ears. And then suddenly I heard it! From far away down the tunnel came those muffled steps, so soft and yet so ponderous. I heard also the rattle of stones as they gave way under that giant tread. They drew nearer. They were close upon me. I heard the crashing of the bushes round the entrance, and then dimly through the darkness I was conscious of the loom of some enormous shape, some monstrous inchoate creature, passing swiftly and very silently out from the tunnel. I was paralysed with fear and amazement. Long as I had waited, now that it had actually come I was unprepared for the shock. I lay motionless and breathless, whilst the great dark mass whisked by me and was swallowed up in the night.

But now I nerved myself for its return. No sound came from the sleeping countryside to tell of the horror which was loose. In no way could I judge how far off it was, what it was doing, or when it might be back. But not a second time should my nerve fail me, not a second time should it pass unchallenged. I swore it between my clenched teeth as I laid my cocked rifle across the rock.

And yet it nearly happened. There was no warning of approach now as the creature passed over the grass. Suddenly, like a dark, drifting shadow, the huge bulk loomed up once more before me, making for the entrance of the cave. Again came that paralysis of volition which held my crooked forefinger impotent upon the trigger. But with a desperate effort I shook it off. Even as the brushwood rustled, and the monstrous beast blended with the shadow of the Gap, I fired at the retreating form. In the blaze of the gun I caught a glimpse of a great shaggy mass, something with rough and bristling hair of a withered grey colour, fading away to white in its lower parts, the huge body supported upon short, thick, curving legs. I had just that glance, and then I heard the rattle of the stones as the creature tore down into its burrow. In an instant, with a triumphant revulsion of feeling, I had cast my fears to the wind, and uncovering my powerful lantern, with my rifle in my hand, I sprang down from my rock and rushed after the monster down the old Roman shaft.

My splendid lamp cast a brilliant flood of vivid light in front of me, very different from the yellow glimmer which had aided me down the same passage only twelve days before. As I ran, I saw the great beast lurching along before me, its huge bulk filling up the whole space from wall to wall. Its hair looked like coarse faded oakum, and hung down in long, dense masses which swayed as it moved. It was like an enormous unclipped sheep in its fleece, but in size it was far larger than the largest elephant, and its breadth seemed to be nearly as great as its height. It fills me with amazement now to think that I should have dared to follow such a horror into the bowels of the earth, but when one's blood is up, and when one's quarry seems to be flying, the old primeval hunting-spirit awakes and prudence is cast to the wind. Rifle in hand, I ran at the top of my speed upon the trail of the monster.

I had seen that the creature was swift. Now I was to find out to my cost that it was also very cunning. I had imagined that it was in panic flight, and that I had only to pursue it. The idea that it might turn upon me never entered my excited brain. I have already explained that the passage down which I was racing opened into a great central cave. Into this I rushed, fearful lest I should lose all trace of the beast. But he had turned upon his own traces, and in a moment we were face to face.

That picture, seen in the brilliant white light of the lantern, is etched for ever upon my brain. He had reared up on his hind legs as a bear would do, and stood above me, enormous, menacing—such a creature as no nightmare had ever brought to my imagination. I have said that he reared like a bear, and there was something bear-like—if one could conceive a bear which was ten-fold the bulk of any bear seen upon earth—in his whole pose and attitude, in his great crooked forelegs with their ivory-white claws, in his rugged skin, and in his red, gaping mouth, fringed with monstrous fangs. Only in one point did he differ from the bear, or from any other creature which walks the earth, and even at that supreme moment a shudder of horror passed over me as I observed that the eyes which glistened in the glow of my lantern were huge, projecting bulbs, white and sightless. For a moment his great paws swung over my head. The next he fell forward upon me, I and my broken lantern crashed to the earth, and I remember no more.

When I came to myself I was back in the farm-house of the Allertons. Two days had passed since my terrible adventure in the Blue John Gap. It seems that I had lain all night in the cave insensible from concussion of the brain, with my left arm and two ribs badly fractured. In the morning my note had been found, a search party of a dozen farmers assembled, and I had been tracked down and carried back to my bedroom, where I had lain in high delirium ever since. There was, it seems, no sign of the creature, and no bloodstain which would show that my bullet had found him as he passed. Save for my own plight and the marks upon the mud, there was nothing to prove that what I said was true.

Six weeks have now elapsed, and I am able to sit out once more in the sunshine. Just opposite me is the steep hillside, grey with shaly rock, and yonder on its flank is the dark cleft which marks the opening of the Blue John Gap. But it is no longer a source of terror. Never again through that ill-omened tunnel shall any strange shape flit out into the world of men. The educated and the scientific, the Dr Johnsons and the like, may smile at my narrative, but the poorer folk of the countryside had never a doubt as to its truth. On the day after my recovering consciousness they assembled in their hundreds round the Blue John Gap. As the *Castleton Courier* said:

> It was useless for our correspondent, or for any of the adventurous gentlemen who had come from Matlock, Buxton, and other parts, to offer to descend, to explore the cave to the end, and to finally test the extraordinary narrative of Dr James Hardcastle. The country people had taken the matter into their own hands, and from an early hour of the morning they had worked hard in stopping up the entrance of the tunnel. There is a sharp slope where the shaft begins, and great boulders, rolled along by many willing hands, were thrust down it until the Gap was absolutely sealed. So ends the episode which has caused such excitement throughout the country. Local opinion is fiercely divided upon the subject. On the one hand are those who point to Dr Hardcastle's impaired health, and to the possibility of cerebral lesions of tubercular origin giving rise to strange hallucinations. Some *idée fixe*, according to these gentlemen, caused the doctor to wander down the tunnel, and a fall among the rocks was sufficient to account for his injuries. On the other hand, a legend of a strange creature in the Gap has existed for some months back, and the farmers look upon Dr Hardcastle's narrative and his personal injuries as a final corroboration. So the matter stands, and so the matter will continue to stand, for no definite solution seems to us to be now possible. It transcends human wit to give any scientific explanation which could cover the alleged facts.

Perhaps before the *Courier* published these words they would have been wise to send their representative to me. I have thought the matter out, as no one else has occasion to do, and it is possible that I might have removed some of the more obvious difficulties of the narrative and brought it one degree nearer to scientific acceptance. Let me then write down the only explanation which seems to me to elucidate what I know to my cost to have been a series of facts. My theory may seem to be wildly improbable, but at least no one can venture to say that it is impossible.

My view is—and it was formed, as is shown by my diary, before my personal adventure—that in this part of England there is a vast subterranean lake or sea, which is fed by the great number of streams which pass down through the limestone. Where there is a large collection of water there must also be some evaporation, mists or rain, and a possibility of vegetation. This in turn suggests that there may be animal life, arising, as the vegetable life would also do, from those seeds and types which had been introduced at an early period of the world's history, when communication with the outer air was more easy. This place had then developed a fauna and flora of its own, including such monsters as the one which I had seen, which may well have been the old cave-bear, enormously enlarged and modified by its new environment. For countless aeons the internal and the external creation had kept apart, growing steadily away from each other. Then there had come some rift in the depths of the mountain which had enabled one creature to wander up and, by means of the Roman tunnel, to reach the open air. Like all subterranean life, it had lost the power of sight, but this had no doubt been compensated for by nature in other directions. Certainly it had some means of finding its way about, and of hunting down the sheep upon the hillside. As to its choice of dark nights, it is part of my theory that light was painful to those great white eyeballs, and that it was only a pitch-black world which it could tolerate. Perhaps, indeed, it was the glare of my lantern which saved my life at that awful moment when we were face to face. So I read the riddle. I leave these facts behind me, and if you can explain them, do so; or if you choose to doubt them, do so. Neither your belief nor your incredulity can alter them, nor affect one whose task is nearly over.

So ended the strange narrative of Dr James Hardcastle.

The Blighting of Sharkey

SHARKEY, THE ABOMINABLE SHARKEY, was out again. After two years of the Coromandel coast, his black barque of death, the *Happy Delivery*, was prowling off the Spanish Main, while trader and fisher flew for dear life at the menace of that patched fore-topsail, rising slowly over the violet rim of the tropical sea.

As the birds cower when the shadow of the hawk falls athwart the field, or as the jungle folk crouch and shiver when the coughing cry of the tiger is heard in the night-time, so through all the busy world of ships, from the whalers of Nantucket to the tobacco ships of Charleston, and from the Spanish supply ships of Cadiz to the sugar merchants of the Main, there spread the rumour of the black curse of the ocean.

Some hugged the shore, ready to make for the nearest port, while others struck far out beyond the known lines of commerce, but none were so stout-hearted that they did not breathe more freely when their passengers and cargoes were safe under the guns of some mothering fort.

Through all the islands there ran tales of charred derelicts at sea, of sudden glares seen afar in the night-time, and of withered bodies stretched upon the sand of waterless Bahama Keys. All the old signs were there to show that Sharkey was at his bloody game once more.

These fair waters and yellow-rimmed palm-nodding islands are the traditional home of the sea rover. First it was the gentleman adventurer, the man of family and honour, who fought as a patriot, though he was ready to take his payment in Spanish plunder.

Then, within a century, his debonair figure had passed to make room for the buccaneers, robbers pure and simple, yet with some organized code of their own, commanded by notable chieftains, and taking in hand great concerted enterprises.

They, too, passed with their fleets and their sacking of cities, to make room for the worst of all, the lonely, outcast pirate, the bloody Ishmael of the seas, at war with the whole human race. This was the vile brood which the early eighteenth century had spawned forth, and of them all there was none who could compare in audacity, wickedness, and evil repute with the unutterable Sharkey.

It was early in May, in the year 1720, that the *Happy Delivery* lay with her fore-yard aback some five leagues west of the Windward Passage, waiting to see what rich, helpless craft the trade-wind might bring down to her.

Three days she had lain there, a sinister black speck, in the centre of the great sapphire circle of the ocean. Far to the south-east the low blue hills of Hispaniola showed up on the skyline.

Hour by hour as he waited without avail, Sharkey's savage temper had risen, for his arrogant spirit chafed against any contradiction, even from Fate itself. To his quartermaster, Ned Galloway, he had said that night, with his odious neighing laugh, that the crew of the next captured vessel should answer to him for having kept him waiting so long.

The cabin of the pirate barque was a good-sized room, hung with much tarnished finery, and presenting a strange medley of luxury and disorder. The panelling of carved and polished sandal-wood was blotched with foul smudges and chipped with bullet-marks fired in some drunken revelry.

Rich velvets and laces were heaped upon the brocaded settees, while metal-work and pictures of great price filled every niche and corner, for anything which caught the pirate's fancy in the sack of a hundred vessels was thrown haphazard into his chamber. A rich, soft carpet covered the floor, but it was mottled with wine-stains and charred with burned tobacco.

Above, a great brass hanging-lamp threw a brilliant yellow light upon this singular apartment, and upon the two men who sat in their shirt-sleeves with the wine between them, and the cards in their hands, deep in a game of piquet. Both were smoking long pipes, and the thin blue reek filled the cabin and floated through the skylight above them, which, half opened, disclosed a slip of deep violet sky spangled with great silver stars.

Ned Galloway, the quartermaster, was a huge New England wastrel, the one rotten branch upon a goodly Puritan family tree. His robust limbs and giant frame were the heritage of a long line of God-fearing ancestors, while his black savage heart was all his own. Bearded to the temples, with fierce blue eyes, a tangled lion's mane of coarse, dark hair, and huge gold rings in his ears, he was the idol of the women in every waterside hell from the Tortugas to Maracaibo on the Main. A red cap, a blue silken shirt, brown velvet breeches with gaudy knee-ribbons, and high sea-boots made up the costume of the rover Hercules.

A very different figure was Captain John Sharkey. His thin, drawn, clean-shaven face was corpse-like in its pallor, and all the suns of the Indies could but turn it to a more deathly parchment tint. He was part bald, with a few lank locks of tow-like hair, and a steep, narrow forehead. His thin nose jutted sharply forth, and near-set on either side of it were those filmy blue eyes, red-rimmed like those of a white bull-terrier, from which strong men winced away in fear and loathing. His bony hands, with long, thin fingers which quivered ceaselessly like the antennae of an insect, were toying constantly with the cards and the heap of gold moidores which lay before him. His dress was of some sober drab material, but, indeed, the men who looked upon that fearsome face had little thought for the costume of its owner.

The game was brought to a sudden interruption, for the cabin door was swung rudely open, and two rough fellows—Israel Martin, the boatswain, and Red Foley, the gunner—rushed into the cabin. In an instant Sharkey was on his feet with a pistol in either hand and murder in his eyes.

'Sink you for villains!' he cried. 'I see well that if I do not shoot one of you from time to time you will forget the man I am. What mean you by entering my cabin as though it were a Wapping alehouse?'

'Nay, Captain Sharkey,' said Martin with a sullen frown upon his brick-red face, 'it is even such talk as this which has set us by the ears. We have had enough of it.'

'And more than enough,' said Red Foley, the gunner. 'There be no mates aboard a pirate craft, and so the boatswain, the gunner, and the quartermaster are the officers.'

'Did I gainsay it?' asked Sharkey with an oath.

'You have miscalled us and mishandled us before the men, and we scarce know at this moment why we should risk our lives in fighting for the cabin and against the fo'c'sle.'

Sharkey saw that something serious was in the wind. He laid down his pistols and leaned back in his chair with a flash of his yellow fangs.

'Nay, this is sad talk,' said he, 'that two stout fellows who have emptied many a bottle and cut many a throat with me, should now fall out over nothing. I know you to be roaring boys who would go with me against the devil himself if I bid you. Let the steward bring cups and drown all unkindness between us.'

'It is no time for drinking, Captain Sharkey,' said Martin. 'The men are holding council round the main-mast, and may be aft at any minute. They mean mischief, Captain Sharkey, and we have come to warn you.'

Sharkey sprang for the brass-handled sword which hung from the wall.

'Sink them for rascals!' he cried. 'When I have gutted one or two of them they may hear reason.'

But the others barred his frantic way to the door.

'There are forty of them under the lead of Sweetlocks, the master,' said Martin, 'and on the open deck they would surely cut you to pieces. Here within the cabin it may be that we can hold them off at the points of our pistols.'

He had hardly spoken when there came the tread of many heavy feet upon the deck. Then there was a pause with no sound but the gentle lapping of the water against the sides of the pirate vessel. Finally, a crashing blow as from a pistol-butt fell upon the door, and an instant afterwards Sweetlocks himself, a tall, dark man, with a deep red birth-mark blazing upon his cheek, strode into the cabin. His swaggering air sank somewhat as he looked into those pale and filmy eyes.

'Captain Sharkey,' said he, 'I come as spokesman of the crew.'

'So I have heard, Sweetlocks,' said the captain, softly. 'I may live to rip you the length of your vest for this night's work.'

'That is as it may be, Captain Sharkey,' the master answered, 'but if you will look up you will see that I have those at my back who will not see me mishandled.'

'Cursed if we do!' growled a deep voice from above, and glancing upwards the officers in the cabin were aware of a line of fierce, bearded, sun-blackened faces looking down at them through the open skylight.

'Well, what would you have?' asked Sharkey. 'Put it in words, man, and let us have an end of it.'

'The men think,' said Sweetlocks, 'that you are the devil himself, and that there will be no luck for them whilst they sail the sea in such company. Time was when we did our two or three craft a day, and every man had women and dollars to his liking, but now for a long week we have not raised a sail, and save for three beggarly sloops, have taken never a vessel since we passed the Bahama Bank. Also, they know that you killed Jack Bartholomew, the carpenter, by beating his head in with a bucket, so that each of us goes in fear of his life. Also, the rum has given out and we are hard put to it for liquor. Also, you sit in your cabin whilst it is in the articles that you should drink and roar with the crew. For all these reasons it has been this day in general meeting decreed——'

Sharkey had stealthily cocked a pistol under the table, so it may have been as well for the mutinous master that he never reached the end of his discourse, for even as he came to it there was a swift patter of feet upon the deck, and a ship lad, wild with his tidings, rushed into the room.

'A craft!' he yeered. 'A great craft, and close aboard us!'

In a flash the quarrel was forgotten, and the pirates were rushing to quarters. Sure enough, surging slowly down before the gentle trade-wind, a great full-rigged ship, with all sail set, was close beside them.

It was clear that she had come from afar and knew nothing of the ways of the Caribbean Sea, for she made no effort to avoid the low, dark craft which lay so close upon her bow, but blundered on as if her mere size would avail her.

So daring was she, that for an instant the rovers, as they flew to loose the tackles of their guns, and hoisted their battle-lanterns, believed that a man-of-war had caught them napping.

But at the sight of her bulging, portless sides and merchant rig a shout of exultation broke from amongst them, and in an instant they had swung round their foreyard, and darting alongside they had grappled with her and flung a spray of shrieking, cursing ruffians upon her deck.

Half a dozen seamen of the night-watch were cut down where they stood, the mate was felled by Sharkey and tossed overboard by Ned Galloway, and before the sleepers had time to sit up in their berths, the vessel was in the hands of the pirates.

The prize proved to be the full-rigged ship *Portobello*—Captain Hardy, master—bound from London to Kingston in Jamaica, with a cargo of cotton goods and hoop-iron.

Having secured their prisoners, all huddled together in a dazed, distracted group, the pirates spread over the vessel in search of plunder, handing all that was found to the giant quartermaster, who in turn passed it over the side of the *Happy Delivery* and laid it under guard at the foot of her mainmast.

The cargo was useless, but there were a thousand guineas in the ship's strong-box, and there were some eight or ten passengers, three of them wealthy Jamaica merchants, all bringing home well-filled boxes from their London visit.

When all the plunder was gathered, the passengers and crew were dragged to the waist, and under the cold smile of Sharkey each in turn was thrown over the side—Sweetlocks standing by the rail and ham-stringing them with his cutlass as they passed over, lest some strong swimmer should rise in judgment against them. A portly, grey-haired woman, the wife of one of the planters, was among the captives, but she also was thrust screaming and clutching over the side.

'Mercy, you hussy!' neighed Sharkey, 'you are surely a good twenty years too old for that.'

The captain of the *Portobello*, a hale, blue-eyed grey-beard, was the last upon the deck. He stood, a thick-set resolute figure, in the glare of the lanterns, while Sharkey bowed and smirked before him.

'One skipper should show courtesy to another,' said he, 'and sink me if Captain Sharkey would be behind in good manners! I have held you to the last, as you see, where a brave man should be; so now, my bully, you have seen the end of them, and may step over with an easy mind.'

'So I shall, Captain Sharkey,' said the old seaman, 'for I have done my duty so far as my power lay. But before I go over I would say a word in your ear.'

'If it be to soften me, you may save your breath. You have kept us waiting here for three days, and curse me if one of you shall live!'

'Nay, it is to tell you what you should know. You have not yet found what is the true treasure aboard of this ship.'

'Not found it? Sink me, but I will slice your liver, Captain Hardy, if you do not make good your words! Where is this treasure you speak of?'

'It is not a treasure of gold, but it is a fair maid, which may be no less welcome.'

'Where is she, then? And why was she not with the others?'

'I will tell you why she was not with the others. She is the only daughter of the Count and Countess Ramirez, who are amongst those whom you have murdered. Her name is Inez Ramirez, and she is of the best blood of Spain, her father being Governor of Chagre, to which he was now bound. It chanced that she was found to have formed an attachment, as maids will, to one far beneath her in rank aboard this ship; so her parents, being people of great power, whose word is not to be gainsaid, constrained me to confine her close in a special cabin aft of my own. Here she was held straitly, all food being carried to her, and she allowed to see no one. This I tell you as a last gift, though why I should make it to you I do not know, for indeed you are a most bloody rascal, and it comforts me in dying to think that you will surely be gallow's-meat in this world, and hell's-meat in the next.'

At the words he ran to the rail, and vaulted over into the darkness, praying as he sank into the depths of the sea, that the betrayal of this maid might not be counted too heavily against his soul.

The body of Captain Hardy had not yet settled upon the sand forty fathoms deep before the pirates had rushed along the cabin gangway. There, sure enough, at the farther end, was a barred door, overlooked in the previous search. There was no key, but they beat it in with their gunstocks, whilst shriek after shriek came from within. In the light of their outstretched lanterns they saw a young woman, in the very prime and fullness of her youth, crouching in a corner, her unkempt hair hanging to the ground, her dark eyes glaring with fear, her lovely form straining away in horror from this inrush of savage blood-stained men. Rough hands seized her, she was jerked to her feet, and dragged with scream on scream to where John Sharkey awaited her. He held the light long and fondly to her face, then, laughing loudly, he bent forward and left his red handprint upon her cheek.

' 'Tis the Rovers' brand, lass, that he marks his ewes. Take her to the cabin and use her well. Now, hearties, get her under water, and out to our luck once more.'

Within an hour the good ship *Portobello* had settled down to her doom, till she lay beside her murdered passengers upon the Caribbean sand, while the pirate barque, her deck littered with plunder, was heading northward in search of another victim.

There was a carouse that night in the cabin of the *Happy Delivery*, at which three men drank deep. They were the captain, the quartermaster, and Baldy Stable, the surgeon, a man who had held the first practice in Charleston, until, misusing a patient, he fled from justice, and took his skill over to the pirates. A bloated fat man he was, with a creased neck and a great shining scalp, which gave him his name. Sharkey had put for the moment all thought of the mutiny out of his head, knowing that no animal is fierce when it is over-fed, and that whilst the plunder of the great ship was new to them he need fear no trouble from his crew. He gave himself up, therefore, to the wine and the riot, shouting and roaring with his boon companions. All three were flushed and mad, ripe for any devilment, when the thought of the woman crossed the pirate's evil mind. He yelled to the negro steward that he should bring her on the instant.

Inez Ramirez had now realized it all—the death of her father and mother, and her own position in the hands of their murderers. Yet calmness had come with the knowledge, and there was no sign of terror in her proud, dark face as she was led into the cabin, but rather a strange, firm set of the mouth and an exultant gleam of the eyes, like one who sees great hopes in the future. She smiled at the pirate captain as he rose and seized her by the waist.

''Fore God! this is a lass of spirit,' cried Sharkey; passing his arm round her. 'She was born to be a Rover's bride. Come, my bird, and drink to our better friendship.'

'Article Six!' hiccoughed the doctor. 'All *bona robas* in common.'

'Aye! we hold you to that, Captain Sharkey,' said Galloway. 'It is so writ in Article Six.'

'I will cut the man into ounces who comes betwixt us!' cried Sharkey, as he turned his fish-like eyes from one to the other. 'Nay, lass, the man is not born that will take you from John Sharkey. Sit here upon my knee, and place your arm round me so. Sink me, if she has not learned to love me at sight! Tell me, my pretty, why you were so mishandled and laid in the bilboes aboard yonder craft?'

The woman shook her head and smiled. 'No Inglese—no Inglese,' she lisped. She had drunk off the bumper of wine which Sharkey held to her, and her dark eyes gleamed more brightly than before. Sitting on Sharkey's knee, her arm encircled his neck, and her hand toyed with his hair, his ear, his cheek. Even the strange quartermaster and the hardened surgeon felt a horror as they watched her, but Sharkey laughed in his joy. 'Curse me, if she is not a lass of metal!' he cried, as he pressed her to him and kissed her unresisting lips.

But a strange intent look of interest had come into the surgeon's eyes as he watched her, and his face set rigidly, as if a fearsome thought had entered his mind. There stole a grey pallor over his bull face, mottling all the red of the tropics and the flush of the wine.

'Look at her hand, Captain Sharkey!' he cried. 'For the Lord's sake, look at her hand!'

Sharkey stared down at the hand which had fondled him. It was of a strange dead-pallor, with a yellow shiny web betwixt the fingers. All over it was a white fluffy dust, like the flour of a new-baked loaf. It lay thick on Sharkey's neck and cheek. With a cry of disgust he flung the woman from his lap; but in an instant, with a wild-cat bound, and a scream of triumphant malice, she had sprung at the surgeon, who vanished yelling under the table. One of her clawing hands grasped Galloway by the beard, but he tore himself away, and snatching a pike, held her off from him as she gibbered and mowed with the blazing eyes of a maniac.

The black steward had run in on the sudden turmoil, and among them they forced the mad creature back into a cabin and turned the key upon her. Then the three sank panting into their chairs and looked with eyes of horror upon each other. The same word was in the mind of each, but Galloway was the first to speak it.

'A leper!' he cried. 'She has us all, curse her!'

'Not me,' said the surgeon; 'she never laid her finger on me.'

'For that matter,' cried Galloway, 'it was but my beard that she touched. I will have every hair of it off before morning.'

'Dolts that we were!' the surgeon shouted, beating his head with his hand. 'Tainted or no, we shall never know a moment's peace till the year is up and the time of danger past. 'Fore God, that merchant skipper has left his mark on us, and pretty fools we were to think that such a maid would be quarantined for the cause he gave. It is easy to see now that her corruption broke forth in the journey, and that save throwing her over they had no choice but to board her up until they should come to some port with a lazarette.'

Sharkey had sat leaning back in his chair with a ghastly face while he listened to the surgeon's words. He mopped himself with his red handkerchief, and wiped away the fatal dust with which he was smeared.

'What of me?' he croaked. 'What say you, Baldy Stable? Is there a chance for me? Curse you for a villain! speak out, or I will drub you within an inch of your life, and that inch also! Is there a chance for me, I say!'

But the surgeon shook his head. 'Captain Sharkey,' said he, 'it would be an ill deed to speak you false. The taint is on you. No man on whom the leper scales have rested is ever clean again.'

Sharkey's head fell forward on his chest, and he sat motionless, stricken by this great and sudden horror, looking with his smouldering eyes into his fearsome future. Softly the mate and the surgeon rose from their places, and stealing out from the poisoned air of the cabin, came forth into the freshness of the early dawn, with the soft, scent-laden breeze in their faces and the first red feathers of cloud catching the earliest gleam of the rising sun as it shot its golden rays over the palm-clad ridges of distant Hispaniola.

That morning a second council of the Rovers was held at the base of the mainmast, and a deputation chosen to see the captain. They were approaching the after-cabins when Sharkey came forth, the old devil in his eyes, and his bandolier with a pair of pistols over his shoulder.

'Sink you all for villains!' he cried. 'Would you dare to cross my hawse? Stand out Sweetlocks, and I will lay you open! Here, Galloway, Martin, Foley, stand by me and lash the dogs to their kennel!'

But his officers had deserted him, and there was none to come to his aid. There was a rush of the pirates. One was shot through the body, but an instant afterwards Sharkey had been seized and was triced to his own mainmast. His filmy eyes looked round from face to face, and there was none who felt the happier for having met them.

'Captain Sharkey,' said Sweetlocks, 'you have mishandled many of us, and you have now pistolled John Masters, besides killing Bartholomew, the carpenter, by braining him with a bucket. All this might have been forgiven you, in that you have been our leader for years, and that we have signed articles to serve under you while the voyage lasts. But now we have heard of this *bona roba* on board, and we know that you are poisoned to the marrow, and that while you rot there will be no safety for any of us, but that we shall all be turned into filth and corruption. Therefore, John Sharkey, we Rovers of the *Happy Delivery*, in council assembled, have decreed that while there be yet time, before the plague spreads, you shall be set adrift in a boat to find such a fate as Fortune may be pleased to send you.'

John Sharkey said nothing, but slowly circling his head, he cursed them all with his baleful gaze. The ship's dinghy had been lowered, and he, with his hands still tied, was dropped into it on the bight of a rope.

'Cast her off!' cried Sweetlocks.

'Nay, hold hard a moment, Master Sweetlocks!' shouted one of the crew. 'What of the wench? Is she to bide aboard and poison us all?'

'Send her off with her mate!' cried another, and the Rovers roared their approval. Driven forth at the end of pikes, the girl was pushed towards the boat. With all the spirit of Spain in her rotting body she flashed triumphant glances at her captors.

'Perros! Perros Ingleses! Lepero, Lepero!' she cried in exultation, as they thrust her over into the boat.

'Good luck, captain! God speed you on your honeymoon!' cried a chorus of mocking voices, as the painter was unloosed, and the *Happy Delivery*, running full before the trade-wind, left the little boat astern, a tiny dot upon the vast expanse of the lonely sea.

EXTRACT FROM THE LOG OF H.M. 50-GUN SHIP HECATE
IN HER CRUISE OFF THE AMERICAN MAIN.

Jan. 26th, 1721—This day, the junk having become unfit for food, and five of the crew down with scurvy, I ordered that we send two boats ashore at the nor'western point of Hispaniola, to seek for fresh fruit, and perchance shoot some of the wild oxen with which the island abounds.

7 p.m.—The boats have returned with good store of green stuff and two bullocks. Mr Woodruff, the master, reports that near the landing-place at the edge of the forest was found the skeleton of a woman, clad in European dress, of such sort as to show that she may have been a person of quality. Her head had been crushed by a great stone which lay beside her. Hard by was a grass hut, and signs that a man had dwelt therein for some time, as was shown by charred wood, bones, and other traces. There is a rumour upon the coast that Sharkey, the bloody pirate, was marooned in these parts last year, but whether he has made his way into the interior, or whether he has been picked up by some craft, there is no means of knowing. If he be once again afloat, then I pray that God send him under our guns.

Through the Veil

H E WAS A GREAT SHOCK-HEADED, freckle-faced Borderer, the lineal descendant of a cattle-thieving clan in Liddesdale. In spite of his ancestry he was as solid and sober a citizen as one would wish to see, a town councillor of Melrose, an elder of the Church, and the chairman of the local branch of the Young Men's Christian Association. Brown was his name—and you saw it printed up as 'Brown and Handiside' over the great grocery stores in the High Street. His wife, Maggie Brown, was an Armstrong before her marriage, and came from an old farming stock in the wilds of Teviothead. She was small, swarthy, and dark-eyed, with a strangely nervous temperament for a Scotch woman. No greater contrast could be found than the big, tawny man and the dark little woman, but both were of the soil as far back as any memory could extend.

One day—it was the first anniversary of their wedding—they had driven over together to see the excavations of the Roman Fort at Newstead. It was not a particularly picturesque spot. From the northern bank of the Tweed, just where the river forms a loop, there extends a gentle slope of arable land. Across it run the trenches of the excavators, with here and there an exposure of old stonework to show the foundations of the ancient walls. It had been a huge place, for the camp was fifty acres in extent, and the fort fifteen. However, it was all made easy for them since Mr Brown knew the farmer to whom the land belonged. Under his guidance they spent a long summer evening inspecting the trenches, the pits, the ramparts, and all the strange variety of objects which were waiting to be transported to the Edinburgh Museum of Antiquities. The buckle of a woman's belt had been dug up that very day, and the farmer was discoursing upon it when his eyes fell upon Mrs Brown's face.

'Your good leddy's tired,' said he. 'Maybe you'd best rest a wee before we gang further.'

Brown looked at his wife. She was certainly very pale, and her dark eyes were bright and wild.

'What is it, Maggie? I've wearied you. I'm thinkin' it's time we went back.'

'No, no, John, let us go on. It's wonderful! It's like a dreamland place. It all seems so close and so near to me. How long were the Romans here, Mr Cunningham?'

'A fair time, mam. If you saw the kitchen middenpits you would guess it took a long time to fill them.'

'And why did they leave?'

'Well, mam, by all accounts they left because they had to. The folk round could thole them no longer, so they just up and burned the fort aboot their lugs. You can see the fire marks on the stanes.'

The woman gave a quick little shudder. 'A wild night—a fearsome night,' said she. 'The sky must have been red that night—and these grey stones, they may have been red also.'

'Aye, I think they were red,' said her husband. 'It's a queer thing, Maggie, and it may be your words that have done it; but I seem to see that business aboot as clear as ever I saw anything in my life. The light shone on the water.'

'Aye, the light shone on the water. And the smoke gripped you by the throat. And all the savages were yelling.'

The old farmer began to laugh. 'The leddy will be writin' a story aboot the old fort,' said he. 'I've shown many a one ower it, but I never heard it put so clear afore. Some folk have the gift.'

They had strolled along the edge of the foss, and a pit yawned upon the right of them.

'That pit was fourteen foot deep,' said the farmer. 'What d'ye think we dug oot from the bottom o't? Weel, it was just the skeleton of a man wi' a spear by his side. I'm thinkin' he was grippin' it when he died. Now, how cam' a man wi' a spear doon a hole fourteen foot deep. He wasna' buried there, for they aye burned their dead. What make ye o' that, mam?'

'He sprang doon to get clear of the savages,' said the woman.

'Weel, it's likely enough, and a' the professors from Edinburgh couldna gie a better reason. I wish you were aye here, mam, to answer a' oor deeficulties sae readily. Now, here's the altar that we foond last week. There's an inscreeption. They tell me it's Latin, and it means that the men o' this fort give thanks to God for their safety.'

They examined the old worn stone. There was a large, deeply cut 'VV' upon the top of it.

'What does "VV" stand for?' asked Brown.

'Naebody kens,' the guide answered.

'*Valeria Victrix*,' said the lady softly. Her face was paler than ever, her eyes far away, as one who peers down the dim aisles of over-arching centuries.

'What's that?' asked her husband sharply.

She started as one who wakes from sleep. 'What were we talking about?' she asked.

'About this "VV" upon the stone.'

'No doubt it was just the name of the Legion which put the altar up.'

'Aye, but you gave some special name.'

'Did I? How absurd! How should I ken what the name was?'

'You said something—"*Victrix*", I think.'

'I suppose I was guessing. It gives me the queerest feeling, this place, as if I were not myself, but someone else.'

'Aye, it's an uncanny place,' said her husband, looking round with an expression almost of fear in his bold grey eyes. 'I feel it mysel'. I think we'll just be wishin' you good evenin', Mr Cunningham, and get back to Melrose before the dark sets in.'

Neither of them could shake off the strange impression which had been left upon them by their visit to the excavations. It was as if some miasma had risen from those damp trenches and passed into their blood. All the evening they were silent and thoughtful, but such remarks as they did make showed that the same subject was in the mind of each. Brown had a restless night, in which he dreamed a strange, connected dream, so vivid that he woke sweating and shivering like a frightened horse. He tried to convey it all to his wife as they sat together at breakfast in the morning.

'It was the clearest thing, Maggie,' said he. 'Nothing that has ever come to me in my waking life has been more clear than that. I feel as if these hands were sticky with blood.'

'Tell me of it—tell me slow,' said she.

'When it began, I was oot on a braeside. I was laying flat on the ground. It was rough, and there were clumps of heather. All round me was just darkness, but I could hear the rustle and the breathin' of men. There seemed a great multitude on every side of me, but I could see no one. There was a low chink of steel sometimes, and then a number of voices would whisper, "Hush!" I had a ragged club in my hand, and it had spikes o' iron near the end of it. My heart was beaten' quickly, and I felt that a moment of great danger and excitement was at hand. Once I dropped my club, and again from all round me the voices in the darkness cried, "Hush!" I put oot my hand, and it touched the foot of another man lying in front of me. There was someone at my very elbow on either side. But they said nothin'.

'Then we all began to move. The whole braeside seemed to be crawlin' downwards. There was a river at the bottom and a high-arched wooden bridge. Beyond the bridge were many lights—torches on a wall. The creepin' men all flowed towards the bridge. There had been no sound of any kind, just a velvet stillness. And then there was a cry in the darkness, the cry of a man who had been stabbed suddenly to the hairt. That one cry swelled out for a moment, and then the roar of a thoosand furious voices. I was runnin'. Everyone was runnin'. A bright red light shone out, and the river was a scarlet streak. I could see my companions now. They were more like devils than men, wild figures clad in skins, with their hair and beards streamin'. They were all mad with rage, jumpin' as they ran, their mouths open, their arms wavin', the red light beatin' on their faces. I ran, too, and yelled out curses like the rest. Then I heard a great cracklin' of wood, and I knew that the palisades were doon. There was a loud whistlin' in my ears, and I was aware that arrows were flying past me. I got to the bottom of a dyke, and I saw a hand stretched doon from above. I took it, and was dragged to the top. We looked doon, and there were silver men beneath us holdin' up their spears. Some of our folk sprang on to the spears. Then we others followed, and we killed the soldiers before they could draw the spears oot again. They shouted loud in some foreign tongue, but no mercy was shown them. We went ower them like a wave, and trampled them doon into the mud, for they were few, and there was no end to our numbers.

'I found myself among buildings, and one of them was on fire. I saw the flames spoutin' through the roof. I ran on, and then I was alone among the buildings. Someone ran across in front o' me. It was a woman. I caught her by the arm, and I took her chin and turned her face so as the light of the fire would strike it. Whom think you that it was, Maggie?'

His wife moistened her dry lips. 'It was I,' she said.

He looked at her in surprise. 'That's a good guess,' said he. 'Yes, it was just you. Not merely like you, you understand. It was you—you yourself. I saw the same soul in your frightened eyes. You looked white and bonnie and wonderful in the firelight. I had just one thought in my head—to get you awa' with me; to keep you all to mysel' in my own home somewhere beyond the hills. You clawed at my face with your nails. I heaved you over my shoulder, and I tried to find a way oot of the light of the burning hoose and back into the darkness.

'Then came the thing that I mind best of all. You're ill, Maggie. Shall I stop? My God! you have the very look on your face that you had last night in my dream. You screamed. He came runnin' in the firelight. His head was bare; his hair was black and curled; he had a naked sword in his hand, short and broad, little more than a dagger. He stabbed at me, but he tripped and fell. I held you with one hand, and with the other——'

His wife had sprung to her feet with writhing features.

'Marcus!' she cried. 'My beautiful Marcus! Oh, you brute! you brute! you brute!' There was a clatter of tea-cups as she fell forward senseless upon the table.

They never talk about that strange, isolated incident in their married life. For an instant the curtain of the past had swung aside, and some strange glimpse of a forgotten life had come to them. But it closed down, never to open again. They live their narrow round—he in his shop, she in her household—and yet new and wider horizons have vaguely formed themselves around them since that summer evening by the crumbling Roman fort.

How It Happened

S HE WAS A WRITING MEDIUM. This is what she wrote:

I can remember some things upon that evening most distinctly, and others are like some vague, broken dreams. That is what makes it so difficult to tell a connected story. I have no idea now what it was that had taken me to London and brought me back so late. It just merges into all my other visits to London. But from the time that I got out at the little country station everything is extraordinarily clear. I can live it again—every instant of it.

I remember so well walking down the platform and looking at the illuminated clock at the end which told me that it was half-past eleven. I remember also my wondering whether I could get home before midnight. Then I remember the big motor, with its glaring head-lights and glitter of polished brass, waiting for me outside. It was my new thirty-horsepower Robur, which had only been delivered that day. I remember also asking Perkins, my chauffeur, how she had gone, and his saying that he thought she was excellent.

'I'll try her myself,' said I, and I climbed into the driver's seat.

'The gears are not the same,' said he. 'Perhaps, sir, I had better drive.'

'No; I should like to try her,' said I.

And so we started on the five-mile drive for home.

My old car had the gears as they used always to be in notches on a bar. In this car you passed the gear-lever through a gate to get on the higher ones. It was not difficult to master, and soon I thought that I understood it. It was foolish, no doubt, to begin to learn a new system in the dark, but one often does foolish things, and one has not always to pay the full price for them. I got along very well until I came to Claystall Hill. It is one of the worst hills in England, a mile and a half long and one in six in places, with three fairly sharp curves. My park gate stands at the very foot of it upon the main London road.

We were just over the brow of this hill, where the grade is steepest, when the trouble began. I had been on the top speed, and wanted to get her on the free; but she stuck between gears, and I had to get her back on the top again. By this time she was going at a great rate, so I clapped on both brakes, and one after the other they gave way. I didn't mind so much when I felt my footbrake snap, but when I put all my weight on my side-brake, and the lever clanged to its full limit without a catch, it brought a cold sweat out of me. By this time we were fairly tearing down the slope. The lights were brilliant, and I brought her round the first curve all right. Then we did the second one, though it was a close shave for the ditch. There was a mile of straight then with the third curve beneath it, and after that the gate of the park. If I could shoot into that harbour all would be well, for the slope up to the house would bring her to a stand.

Perkins behaved splendidly. I should like that to be known. He was perfectly cool and alert. I had thought at the very beginning of taking the bank, and he read my intention.

'I wouldn't do it, sir,' said he. 'At this pace it must go over and we should have it on the top of us.'

Of course he was right. He got to the electric switch and had it off, so we were in the free; but we were still running at a fearful pace. He laid his hands on the wheel.

'I'll keep her steady,' said he, 'if you care to jump and chance it. We can never get round that curve. Better jump, sir.'

'No,' said I; 'I'll stick it out. You can jump if you like.'

'I'll stick it with you, sir,' said he.

If it had been the old car I should have jammed the gear-lever into the reverse, and seen what would happen. I expect she would have stripped her gears or smashed up somehow, but it would have been a chance. As it was, I was helpless. Perkins tried to climb across, but you couldn't do it going at that pace. The wheels were whirring like a high wind and the big body creaking and groaning with the strain. But the lights were brilliant, and one could steer to an inch. I remember thinking what an awful and yet majestic sight we should appear to anyone who met us. It was a narrow road, and we were just a great, roaring, golden death to anyone who came in our path.

We got round the corner with one wheel three feet high upon the bank. I thought we were surely over, but after staggering for a moment she righted and darted onwards. That was the third corner and the last one. There was only the park gate now. It was facing us, but, as luck would have it, not facing us directly. It was about twenty yards to the left up the main road into which we ran. Perhaps I could have done it, but I expect that the steering-gear had been jarred when we ran on the bank. The wheel did not turn easily. We shot out of the lane. I saw the open gate on the left. I whirled round my wheel with all the strength of my wrists. Perkins and I threw our bodies across, and then the next instant, going at fifty miles an hour, my right wheel struck full on the right-hand pillar of my own gate. I heard the crash. I was conscious of flying through the air, and then—and then——!

When I became aware of my own existence once more I was among some brushwood in the shadow of the oaks upon the lodge side of the drive. A man was standing beside me. I imagined at first that it was Perkins, but when I looked again I saw that it was Stanley, a man whom I had known at college some years before, and for whom I had a really genuine affection. There was always something peculiarly sympathetic to me in Stanley's personality; and I was proud to think that I had some similar influence upon him. At the present moment I was surprised to see him, but I was like a man in a dream, giddy and shaken and quite prepared to take things as I found them without questioning them.

'What a smash!' I said. 'Good Lord, what an awful smash!'

He nodded his head, and even in the gloom I could see that he was smiling the gentle, wistful smile which I connected with him.

I was quite unable to move. Indeed, I had not any desire to try to move. But my senses were exceedingly alert. I saw the wreck of the motor lit up by the moving lanterns. I saw the little group of people and heard the hushed voices. There were the lodge-keeper and his wife, and one or two more. They were taking no notice of me, but were very busy round the car. Then suddenly I heard a cry of pain.

'The weight is on him. Lift it easy,' cried a voice.

'It's only my leg!' said another one, which I recognised as Perkins's. 'Where's master?' he cried.

'Here I am,' I answered, but they did not seem to hear me. They were all bending over something which lay in front of the car.

Stanley laid his hand upon my shoulder, and his touch was inexpressibly soothing. I felt light and happy, in spite of all.

'No pain, of course?' said he.

'None,' said I.

'There never is,' said he.

And then suddenly a wave of amazement passed over me. Stanley! Stanley! Why, Stanley had surely died of enteric at Bloemfontein in the Boer War!

'Stanley!' I cried, and the words seemed to choke my throat—'Stanley, you are dead.'

He looked at me with the same old gentle, wistful smile.

'So are you,' he answered.

The Horror of the Heights

(WHICH INCLUDES THE MANUSCRIPT KNOWN AS
THE JOYCE-ARMSTRONG FRAGMENT)

THE IDEA THAT THE EXTRAORDINARY NARRATIVE which has been called the Joyce-Armstrong Fragment is an elaborate practical joke evolved by some unknown person, cursed by a perverted and sinister sense of humour, has now been abandoned by all who have examined the matter. The most macabre and imaginative of plotters would hesitate before linking his morbid fancies with the unquestioned and tragic facts which reinforce the statement. Though the assertions contained in it are amazing and even monstrous, it is none the less forcing itself upon the general intelligence that they are true, and that we must readjust our ideas to the new situation. This world of ours appears to be separated by a slight and precarious margin of safety from a most singular and unexpected danger. I will endeavour in this narrative, which reproduces the original document in its necessarily somewhat fragmentary form, to lay before the reader the whole of the facts up to date, prefacing my statement by saying that, if there be any who doubt the narrative of Joyce-Armstrong, there can be no question at all as to the facts concerning Lieutenant Myrtle, R.N., and Mr Hay Connor, who undoubtedly met their end in the manner described.

The Joyce-Armstrong Fragment was found in the field which is called Lower Haycock, lying one mile to the westward of the village of Withyham, upon the Kent and Sussex border. It was on the fifteenth of September last that an agricultural labourer, James Flynn, in the employment of Mathew Dodd, farmer, of the Chauntry Farm, Withyham, perceived a briar pipe lying near the footpath which skirts the hedge in Lower Haycock. A few paces farther on he picked up a pair of broken binocular glasses. Finally, among some nettles in the ditch, he caught sight of a flat, canvas-backed book, which proved to be a note-book with detachable leaves, some of which had come loose and were fluttering along the base of the hedge. These he collected, but some, including the first, were never recovered, and leave a deplorable hiatus in this all-important statement. The note-book was taken by the labourer to his master, who in turn showed it to Dr J. H. Atherton, of Hartfield. This gentleman at once recognized the need for an expert examination, and the manuscript was forwarded to the Aero Club in London, where it now lies.

The first two pages of the manuscript are missing. There is also one torn away at the end of the narrative, though none of these affect the general coherence of the story. It is conjectured that the missing opening is concerned with the record of Mr Joyce-Armstrong's qualifications as an aeronaut, which can be gathered from other sources and are admitted to be unsurpassed among the air-pilots of England. For many years he has been looked upon as among the most daring and the most intellectual of flying men, a combination which has enabled him to both invent and test several new devices, including the common gyroscopic attachment which is known by his name. The main body of the manuscript is written neatly in ink, but the last few lines are in pencil and are so ragged as to be hardly legible—exactly, in fact, as they might be expected to appear if they were scribbled off hurriedly from the seat of a moving aeroplane. There are, it may be added, several stains, both on the last page and on the outside cover which have been pronounced by the Home Office experts to be blood—probably human and certainly mammalian. The fact that something closely resembling the organism of malaria was discovered in this blood, and that Joyce-Armstrong is known to have suffered from intermittent fever, is a remarkable example of the new weapons which modern science has placed in the hands of our detectives.

And now a word as to the personality of the author of this epoch-making statement. Joyce-Armstrong, according to the few friends who really knew something of the man, was a poet and a dreamer, as well as a mechanic and an inventor. He was a man of considerable wealth, much of which he had spent in the pursuit of his aeronautical hobby. He had four private aeroplanes in his hangars near Devizes, and is said to have made no fewer than one hundred and seventy ascents in the course of last year. He was a retiring man with dark moods, in which he would avoid the society of his fellows. Captain Dangerfield, who knew him better than anyone, says that there were times when his eccentricity threatened to develop into something more serious. His habit of carrying a shot-gun with him in his aeroplane was one manifestation of it.

Another was the morbid effect which the fall of lieutenant Myrtle had upon his mind. Myrtle, who was attempting the height record, fell from an altitude of something over thirty thousand feet. Horrible to narrate, his head was entirely obliterated, though his body and limbs preserved their configuration. At every gathering of airmen, Joyce-Armstrong, according to Dangerfield, would ask, with an enigmatic smile: 'And where, pray, is Myrtle's head?'

On another occasion after dinner, at the mess of the Flying School on Salisbury Plain, he started a debate as to what will be the most permanent danger which airmen will have to encounter. Having listened to successive opinions as to air-pockets, faulty construction, and overbanking, he ended by shrugging his shoulders and refusing to put forward his own views, though he gave the impression that they differed from any advanced by his companions.

It is worth remarking that after his own complete disappearance it was found that his private affairs were arranged with a precision which may show that he had a strong premonition of disaster. With these essential explanations I will now give the narrative exactly as it stands, beginning at page three of the blood-soaked note-book:

'Nevertheless, when I dined at Rheims with Coselli and Gustav Raymond I found that neither of them was aware of any particular danger in the higher layers of the atmosphere. I did not actually say what was in my thoughts, but I got so near to it that if they had any corresponding idea they could not have failed to express it. But then they are two empty, vainglorious fellows with no thought beyond seeing their silly names in the newspaper. It is interesting to note that neither of them had ever been much beyond the twenty-thousand-foot level. Of course, men have been higher than this both in balloons and in the ascent of mountains. It must be well above that point that the aeroplane enters the danger zone—always presuming that my premonitions are correct.

'Aeroplaning has been with us now for more than twenty years, and one might well ask: Why should this peril be only revealing itself in our day? The answer is obvious. In the old days of weak engines, when a hundred horse-power Gnome or Green was considered ample for every need, the flights were very restricted. Now that three hundred horse-power is the rule rather than the exception, visits to the upper layers have become easier and more common. Some of us can remember how, in our youth, Garros made a world-wide reputation by attaining nineteen thousand feet, and it was considered a remarkable achievement to fly over the Alps. Our standard now has been immeasurably raised, and there are twenty high flights for one in former years. Many of them have been undertaken with impunity. The thirty-thousand-foot level has been reached time after time with no discomfort beyond cold and asthma. What does this prove? A visitor might descend upon this planet a thousand times and never see a tiger. Yet tigers exist, and if he chanced to come down into a jungle he might be devoured. There are jungles of the upper air, and there are worse things than tigers which inhabit them. I believe in time they will map these jungles accurately out. Even at the present moment I could name two of them. One of them lies over the Pau-Biarritz district of France. Another is just over my head as I write here in my house in Wiltshire. I rather think there is a third in the Homburg-Wiesbaden district.

'It was the disappearance of the airmen that first set me thinking. Of course, everyone said that they had fallen into the sea, but that did not satisfy me at all. First, there was Verrier in France; his machine was found near Bayonne, but they never got his body. There was the case of Baxter also, who vanished, though his engine and some of the iron fixings were found in a wood in Leicestershire.

In that case, Dr Middleton, of Amesbury, who was watching the flight with a telescope, declares that just before the clouds obscured the view he saw the machine, which was at an enormous height, suddenly rise perpendicularly upwards in a succession of jerks in a manner that he would have thought to be impossible. That was the last seen of Baxter. There was a correspondence in the papers, but it never led to anything. There were several other similar cases, and then there was the death of Hay Connor. What a cackle there was about an unsolved mystery of the air, and what columns in the halfpenny papers, and yet how little was ever done to get to the bottom of the business! He came down in a tremendous vol-plané from an unknown height. He never got off his machine and died in his pilot's seat. Died of what? "Heart disease," said the doctors. Rubbish! Hay Connor's heart was as sound as mine is. What did Venables say? Venables was the only man who was at his side when he died. He said that he was shivering and looked like a man who had been badly scared. "Died of fright," said Venables, but could not imagine what he was frightened about. Only said one word to Venables, which sounded like "Monstrous". They could make nothing of that at the inquest. But I could make something of it. Monsters! That was the last word of poor Harry Hay Connor. And he *did* die of fright, just as Venables thought.

'And then there was Myrtle's head. Do you really believe—does anybody really believe—that a man's head could be driven clean into his body by the force of a fall? Well, perhaps it may be possible, but I, for one, have never believed that it was so with Myrtle. And the grease upon his clothes—"all slimy with grease," said somebody at the inquest. Queer that nobody got thinking after that! I did—but, then, I had been thinking for a good long time. I've made three ascents—how Dangerfield used to chaff me about my shot-gun— but I've never been high enough. Now, with this new, light Paul Veroner machine and its one hundred and seventy-five Robur, I should easily touch the thirty thousand tomorrow. I'll have a shot at the record. Maybe I shall have a shot at something else as well. Of course, it's dangerous. If a fellow wants to avoid danger he had best keep out of flying altogether and subside finally into flannel slippers and a dressing-gown. But I'll visit the air-jungle tomorrow—and if there's anything there I shall know it. If I return, I'll find myself a bit of a celebrity. If I don't, this note-book may explain what I am trying to do, and how I lost my life in doing it. But no drivel about accidents or mysteries, if *you* please.

'I chose my Paul Veroner monoplane for the job. There's nothing like a monoplane when real work is to be done. Beaumont found that out in very early days. For one thing it doesn't mind damp, and the weather looks as if we should be in the clouds all the time. It's a bonny little model and answers my hand like a tender-mouthed horse. The engine is a ten-cylinder rotary Robur working up to one hundred and seventy-five. It has all the modern improvements—enclosed fuselage, high-curved landing skids, brakes, gyroscopic steadiers, and three speeds, worked by an alteration of the angle of the planes upon the Venetian-blind principle. I took a shot-gun with me and a dozen cartridges filled with buck-shot. You should have seen the face of Perkins, my old mechanic, when I directed him to put them in. I was dressed like an Arctic explorer, with two jerseys under my overalls, thick socks inside my padded boots, a storm-cap with flaps, and my talc goggles. It was stifling outside the hangars, but I was going for the summit of the Himalayas, and had to dress for the part. Perkins knew there was something on and implored me to take him with me. Perhaps I should if I were using the biplane, but a monoplane is a one-man show—if you want to get the last foot of lift out of it. Of course, I took an oxygen bag; the man who goes for the altitude record without one will either be frozen or smothered—or both.

'I had a good look at the planes, the rudder-bar, and the elevating lever before I got in. Everything was in order so far as I could see. Then I switched on my engine and found that she was running sweetly. When they let her go she rose almost at once upon the lowest speed. I circled my home field once or twice just to warm her up, and then, with a wave to Perkins and the others, I flattened out my planes and put her on her highest. She skimmed like a swallow down wind for eight or ten miles until I turned her nose up a little and she began to climb in a great spiral for the cloud-bank above me. It's all-important to rise slowly and adapt yourself to the pressure as you go.

'It was a close, warm day for an English September, and there was the hush and heaviness of impending rain. Now and then there came sudden puffs of wind from the south-west—one of them so gusty and unexpected that it caught me napping and turned me half-round for an instant. I remember the time when gusts and whirls and air-pockets used to be things of danger—before we learned to put an overmastering power into our engines. Just as I reached the cloud-banks, with the altimeter marking three thousand, down came the rain. My word, how it poured! It drummed upon my wings and lashed against my face, blurring my glasses so that I could hardly see. I got down on to a low speed, for it was painful to travel against it. As I got higher it became hail, and I had to turn tail to it. One of my cylinders was out of action—a dirty plug, I should imagine, but still I was rising steadily with plenty of power. After a bit the trouble passed, whatever it was, and I heard the full, deep-throated purr— the ten singing as one. That's where the beauty of our modern silencers comes in. We can at last control our engines by ear. How they squeal and squeak and sob when they are in trouble! All those cries for help were wasted in the old days, when every sound was swallowed up by the monstrous racket of the machine. If only the early aviators could come back to see the beauty and perfection of the mechanism which have been bought at the cost of their lives!

'About nine-thirty I was nearing the clouds. Down below me, all blurred and shadowed with rain, lay the vast expanse of Salisbury Plain. Half a dozen flying machines were doing hackwork at the thousand-foot level, looking like little black swallows against the green background. I dare say they were wondering what I was doing up in cloud-land. Suddenly a grey curtain drew across beneath me and the wet folds of vapours were swirling round my face. It was clammily cold and miserable. But I was above the hail-storm, and that was something gained. The cloud was as dark and thick as a London fog. In my anxiety to get clear, I cocked her nose up until the automatic alarm-bell rang, and I actually began to slide backwards. My sopped and dripping wings had made me heavier than I thought, but presently I was in lighter cloud, and soon had cleared the first layer. There was a second—opal-coloured and fleecy—at a great height above my head, a white, unbroken ceiling above, and a dark, unbroken floor below, with the monoplane labouring upwards upon a vast spiral between them. It is deadly lonely in these cloud-spaces. Once a great flight of some small water-birds went past me, flying very fast to the westwards. The quick whir of their wings and their musical cry were cheery to my ear. I fancy that they were teal, but I am a wretched zoologist. Now that we humans have become birds we must really learn to know our brethren by sight.

'The wind down beneath me whirled and swayed the broad cloud-plain. Once a great eddy formed in it, a whirlpool of vapour, and through it, as down a funnel, I caught sight of the distant world. A large white biplane was passing at a vast depth beneath me. I fancy it was the morning mail service betwixt Bristol and London. Then the drift swirled inwards again and the great solitude was unbroken.

'Just after ten I touched the lower edge of the upper cloud-stratum. It consisted of fine diaphanous vapour drifting swiftly from the westward. The wind had been steadily rising all this time and it was now blowing a sharp breeze—twenty-eight an hour by my gauge. Already it was very cold, though my altimeter only marked nine thousand. The engines were working beautifully, and we went droning steadily upwards. The cloud-bank was thicker than I had expected, but at last it thinned out into a golden mist before me, and then in an instant I had shot out from it, and there was an unclouded sky and a brilliant sun above my head—all blue and gold above, all shining silver below, one vast, glimmering plain as far as my eyes could reach. It was a quarter past ten o'clock, and the barograph needle pointed to twelve thousand eight hundred. Up I went and up, my ears concentrated upon the deep purring of my motor, my eyes busy always with the watch, the revolution indicator, the petrol lever, and the oil pump. No wonder aviators are said to be a fearless race. With so many things to think of there is no time to trouble about oneself. About this time I noted how unreliable is the compass when above a certain height from earth. At fifteen thousand feet mine was pointing east and a point south. The sun and the wind gave me my true bearings.

'I had hoped to reach an eternal stillness in these high altitudes, but with every thousand feet of ascent the gale grew stronger. My machine groaned and trembled in every joint and rivet as she faced it, and swept away like a sheet of paper when I banked her on the turn, skimming down wind at a greater pace, perhaps, than ever mortal man has moved. Yet I had always to turn again and tack up in the wind's eye, for it was not merely a height record that I was after. By all my calculations it was above little Wiltshire that my air-jungle lay, and all my labour might be lost if I struck the outer layers at some farther point.

'When I reached the nineteen-thousand-foot level, which was about midday, the wind was so severe that I looked with some anxiety to the stays of my wings, expecting momentarily to see them snap or slacken. I even cast loose the parachute behind me, and fastened its hook into the ring of my leathern belt, so as to be ready for the worst. Now was the time when a bit of scamped work by the mechanic is paid for by the life of the aeronaut. But she held together bravely. Every cord and strut was humming and vibrating like so many harp-strings, but it was glorious to see how, for all the beating and the buffeting, she was still the conqueror of Nature and the mistress of the sky. There is surely something divine in man himself that he should rise so superior to the limitations which Creation seemed to impose—rise, too, by such unselfish, heroic devotion as this air-conquest has shown. Talk of human degeneration! When has such a story as this been written in the annals of our race?

'These were the thoughts in my head as I climbed that monstrous, inclined plane with the wind sometimes beating in my face and sometimes whistling behind my ears, while the cloud-land beneath me fell away to such a distance that the folds and hummocks of silver had all smoothed out into one flat, shining plain. But suddenly I had a horrible and unprecedented experience. I have known before what it is to be in what our neighbours have called a *tourbillon*, but never on such a scale as this. That huge, sweeping river of wind of which I have spoken had, as it appears, whirlpools within it which were as monstrous as itself. Without a moment's warning I was dragged suddenly into the heart of one. I spun round for a minute or two with such velocity that I almost lost my senses, and then fell suddenly, left wing foremost, down the vacuum funnel in the centre. I dropped like a stone, and lost nearly a thousand feet. It was only my belt that kept me in my seat, and the shock and breathlessness left me hanging half-insensible over the side of the fuselage. But I am always capable of a supreme effort—it is my one great merit as an aviator. I was conscious that the descent was slower. The whirlpool was a cone rather than a funnel, and I had come to the apex. With a terrific wrench, throwing my weight all to one side, I levelled my planes and brought her head away from the wind. In an instant I had shot out of the eddies and was skimming down the sky. Then, shaken but victorious, I turned her nose up and began once more my steady grind on the upward spiral. I took a large sweep to avoid the danger-spot of the whirlpool, and soon I was safely above it. Just after one o'clock I was twenty-one thousand feet above the sea-level. To my great joy I had topped the gale, and with every hundred feet of ascent the air grew stiller. On the other hand, it was very cold, and I was conscious of that peculiar nausea which goes with rarefaction of the air. For the first time I unscrewed the mouth of my oxygen bag and took an occasional whiff of the glorious gas. I could feel it running like a cordial through my veins, and I was exhilarated almost to the point of drunkenness. I shouted and sang as I soared upwards into the cold, still outer world.

'It is very clear to me that the insensibility which came upon Glaisher, and in a lesser degree upon Coxwell, when, in 1862, they ascended in a balloon to the height of thirty thousand feet, was due to the extreme speed with which a perpendicular ascent is made. Doing it at an easy gradient and accustoming oneself to the lessened barometric pressure by slow degrees, there are no such dreadful symptoms. At the same great height I found that even without my oxygen inhaler I could breathe without undue distress. It was bitterly cold, however, and my thermometer was at zero, Fahrenheit. At one-thirty I was nearly seven miles above the surface of the earth, and still ascending steadily. I found, however, that the rarefied air was giving markedly less support to my planes, and that my angle of ascent had to be considerably lowered in consequence. It was already clear that even with my light weight and strong engine-power there was a point in front of me where I should be held. To make matters worse, one of my sparking-plugs was in trouble again and there was intermittent misfiring in the engine. My heart was heavy with the fear of failure.

'It was about that time that I had a most extraordinary experience. Something whizzed past me in a trail of smoke and exploded with a loud, hissing sound, sending forth a cloud of steam. For the instant I could not imagine what had happened. Then I remembered that the earth is for ever being bombarded by meteor stones, and would be hardly inhabitable were they not in nearly every case turned to vapour in the outer layers of the atmosphere. Here is a new danger for the high-altitude man, for two others passed me when I was nearing the forty-thousand-foot mark. I cannot doubt that at the edge of the earth's envelope the risk would be a very real one.

'My barograph needle marked forty-one thousand three hundred when I became aware that I could go no farther. Physically, the strain was not as yet greater than I could bear, but my machine had reached its limit. The attenuated air gave no firm support to the wings, and the least tilt developed into side-slip, while she seemed sluggish on her controls. Possibly, had the engine been at its best, another thousand feet might have been within our capacity, but it was still misfiring, and two out of the ten cylinders appeared to be out of action. If I had not already reached the zone for which I was searching then I should never see it upon this journey. But was it not possible that I had attained it? Soaring in circles like a monstrous hawk upon the forty-thousand-foot level I let the monoplane guide herself, and with my Mannheim glass I made a careful observation of my surroundings. The heavens were perfectly clear; there was no indication of those dangers which I had imagined.

'I have said that I was soaring in circles. It struck me suddenly that I would do well to take a wider sweep and open up a new air-tract. If the hunter entered an earth-jungle he would drive through it if he wished to find his game. My reasoning had led me to believe that the air-jungle which I had imagined lay somewhere over Wiltshire. This should be to the south and west of me. I took my bearings from the sun, for the compass was hopeless and no trace of earth was to be seen—nothing but the distant, silver cloud-plain. However, I got my direction as best I might and kept her head straight to the mark. I reckoned that my petrol supply would not last for more than another hour or so, but I could afford to use it to the last drop, since a single magnificent vol-plané could at any time take me to the earth.

'Suddenly I was aware of something new. The air in front of me had lost its crystal clearness. It was full of long, ragged wisps of something which I can only compare to very fine cigarette-smoke. It hung about in wreaths and coils, turning and twisting slowly in the sunlight. As the monoplane shot through it, I was aware of a faint taste of oil upon my lips, and there was a greasy scum upon the woodwork of the machine. Some infinitely fine organic matter appeared to be suspended in the atmosphere. There was no life there. It was inchoate and diffuse, extending for many square acres and then fringing off into the void. No, it was not life. But might it not be the remains of life? Above all, might it not be the food of life, of monstrous life, even as the humble grease of the ocean is the food for the mighty whale? The thought was in my mind when my eyes looked upwards and I saw the most wonderful vision that ever man has seen. Can I hope to convey it to you even as I saw it myself last Thursday?

'Conceive a jelly-fish such as sails in our summer seas, bell-shaped and of enormous size—far larger, I should judge, than the dome of St Paul's. It was of a light pink colour veined with a delicate green, but the whole huge fabric so tenuous that it was but a fairy outline against the dark blue sky. It pulsated with a delicate and regular rhythm. From it there depended two long, drooping, green tentacles, which swayed slowly backwards and forwards. This gorgeous vision passed gently with noiseless dignity over my head, as light and fragile as a soap-bubble, and drifted upon its stately way.

'I had half-turned my monoplane, that I might look after this beautiful creature, when, in a moment, I found myself amidst a perfect fleet of them, of all sizes, but none so large as the first. Some were quite small, but the majority about as big as an average balloon, and with much the same curvature at the top. There was in them a delicacy of texture and colouring which reminded me of the finest Venetian glass. Pale shades of pink and green were the prevailing tints, but all had a lovely iridescence where the sun shimmered through their dainty forms. Some hundreds of them drifted past me, a wonderful fairy squadron of strange, unknown argosies of the sky—creatures whose forms and substance were so attuned to these pure heights that one could not conceive anything so delicate within actual sight or sound of earth.

'But soon my attention was drawn to a new phenomenon—the serpents of the outer air. These were long, thin, fantastic coils of vapour-like material, which turned and twisted with great speed, flying round and round at such a pace that the eyes could hardly follow them. Some of these ghost-like creatures were twenty or thirty feet long, but it was difficult to tell their girth, for their outline was so hazy that it seemed to fade away into the air around them. These air-snakes were of a very light grey or smoke colour, with some darker lines within, which gave the impression of a definite organism. One of them whisked past my very face, and I was conscious of a cold, clammy contact, but their composition was so unsubstantial that I could not connect them with any thought of physical danger, any more than the beautiful bell-like creatures which had preceded them. There was no more solidity in their frames than in the floating spume from a broken wave.

'But a more terrible experience was in store for me. Floating downwards from a great height there came a purplish patch of vapour, small as I saw it first, but rapidly enlarging as it approached me, until it appeared to be hundreds of square feet in size. Though fashioned of some transparent, jelly-like substance, it was none the less of much more definite outline and solid consistence than anything which I had seen before. There were more traces, too, of a physical organization, especially two vast, shadowy, circular plates upon either side, which may have been eyes, and a perfectly solid white projection between them which was as curved and cruel as the beak of a vulture.

'The whole aspect of this monster was formidable and threatening, and it kept changing its colour from a very light mauve to a dark, angry purple so thick that it cast a shadow as it drifted between my monoplane and the sun. On the upper curve of its huge body there were three great projections which I can only describe as enormous bubbles, and I was convinced as I looked at them that they were charged with some extremely light gas which served to buoy up the misshapen and semi-solid mass in the rarefied air. The creature moved swiftly along, keeping pace easily with the monoplane, and for twenty miles or more it formed my horrible escort, hovering over me like a bird of prey which is waiting to pounce. Its method of progression—done so swiftly that it was not easy to follow—was to throw out a long, glutinous streamer in front of it, which in turn seemed to draw forward the rest of the writhing body. So elastic and gelatinous was it that never for two successive minutes was it the same shape, and yet each change made it more threatening and loathsome than the last.

'I knew that it meant mischief. Every purple flush of its hideous body told me so. The vague, goggling eyes which were turned always upon me were cold and merciless in their viscid hatred. I dipped the nose of my monoplane downwards to escape it. As I did so, as quick as a flash there shot out a long tentacle from this mass of floating blubber, and it fell as light and sinuous as a whip-lash across the front of my machine. There was a loud hiss as it lay for a moment across the hot engine, and it whisked itself into the air again, while the huge, flat body drew itself together as if in sudden pain. I dipped to a volpiqué, but again a tentacle fell over the monoplane and was shorn off by the propeller as easily as it might have cut through a smoke wreath. A long, gliding, sticky, serpent-like coil came from behind and caught me round the waist, dragging me out of the fuselage. I tore at it, my fingers sinking into the smooth, glue-like surface, and for an instant I disengaged myself, but only to be caught round the boot by another coil, which gave me a jerk that tilted me almost on to my back.

'As I fell over I blazed off both barrels of my gun, though, indeed, it was like attacking an elephant with a pea-shooter to imagine that any human weapon could cripple that mighty bulk. And yet I aimed better than I knew, for, with a loud report, one of the great blisters upon the creature's back exploded with the puncture of the buck-shot. It was very clear that my conjecture was right, and that these vast, clear bladders were distended with some lifting gas, for in an instant the huge, cloud-like body turned sideways, writhing desperately to find its balance, while the white beak snapped and gaped in horrible fury. But already I had shot away on the steepest glide that I dared to attempt, my engine still full on, the flying propeller and the force of gravity shooting me downwards like an aerolite. Far behind me I saw a dull, purplish smudge growing swiftly smaller and merging into the blue sky behind it. I was safe out of the deadly jungle of the outer air.

'Once out of danger I throttled my engine, for nothing tears a machine to pieces quicker than running on full power from a height. It was a glorious, spiral vol-plané from nearly eight miles of altitude—first, to the level of the silver cloud-bank, then to that of the storm-cloud beneath it, and finally, in beating rain, to the surface of the earth. I saw the Bristol Channel beneath me as I broke from the clouds, but, having still some petrol in my tank, I got twenty miles inland before I found myself stranded in a field half a mile from the village of Ashcombe. There I got three tins of petrol from a passing motor-car, and at ten minutes past six that evening I alighted gently in my own home meadow at Devizes, after such a journey as no mortal upon earth has ever yet taken and lived to tell the tale. I have seen the beauty and I have seen the horror of the heights—and greater beauty or greater horror than that is not within the ken of man.

'And now it is my plan to go once again before I give my results to the world. My reason for this is that I must surely have something to show by way of proof before I lay such a tale before my fellow-men. It is true that others will soon follow and will confirm what I have said, and yet I should wish to carry conviction from the first. Those lovely iridescent bubbles of the air should not be hard to capture. They drift slowly upon their way, and the swift monoplane could intercept their leisurely course. It is likely enough that they would dissolve in the heavier layers of the atmosphere, and that some small heap of amorphous jelly might be all that I should bring to earth with me. And yet something there would surely be by which I could substantiate my story. Yes, I will go, even if I run a risk by doing so. These purple horrors would not seem to be numerous. It is probable that I shall not see one. If I do I shall dive at once. At the worst there is always the shot-gun and my knowledge of . . .'

Here a page of the manuscript is unfortunately missing. On the next page is written, in large, straggling writing:

'Forty-three thousand feet. I shall never see earth again. They are beneath me, three of them. God help me; it is a dreadful death to die!'

Such in its entirety is the Joyce-Armstrong Statement. Of the man nothing has since been seen. Pieces of his shattered monoplane have been picked up in the preserves of Mr Budd-Lushington upon the borders of Kent and Sussex, within a few miles of the spot where the note-book was discovered. If the unfortunate aviator's theory is correct that this air-jungle, as he called it, existed only over the south-west of England, then it would seem that he had fled from it at the full speed of his monoplane, but had been overtaken and devoured by these horrible creatures at some spot in the outer atmosphere above the place where the grim relics were found. The picture of that monoplane skimming down the sky, with the nameless terrors flying as swiftly beneath it and cutting it off always from the earth while they gradually closed in upon their victim, is one upon which a man who valued his sanity would prefer not to dwell. There are many, as I am aware, who still jeer at the facts which I have here set down, but even they must admit that Joyce-Armstrong has disappeared, and I would commend to them his own words: 'This note-book may explain what I am trying to do, and how I lost my life in doing it. But no drivel about accidents or mysteries, if *you* please.'

The Bully of Brocas Court

A Legend of the Ring

THAT YEAR—IT WAS IN 1878—the South Midland Yeomanry were out near Luton, and the real question which appealed to every man in the great camp was not how to prepare for a possible European war, but the far more vital one how to get a man who could stand up for ten rounds to Farrier-Sergeant Burton. Slogger Burton was a fine upstanding fourteen stone of bone and brawn, with a smack in either hand which would leave any ordinary mortal senseless. A match must be found for him somewhere or his head would outgrow his dragoon helmet. Therefore Sir Fred. Milburn, better known as Mumbles, was dispatched to London to find if among the fancy there was no one who would make a journey in order to take down the number of the bold dragoon.

They were bad days, those, in the prize-ring. The old knuckle-fighting had died out in scandal and disgrace, smothered by the pestilent crowd of betting men and ruffians of all sorts who hung upon the edge of the movement and brought disgrace and ruin upon the decent fighting men, who were often humble heroes whose gallantry has never been surpassed. An honest sportsman who desired to see a fight was usually set upon by villains, against whom he had no redress, since he was himself engaged on what was technically an illegal action. He was stripped in the open street, his purse taken, and his head split open if he ventured to resist. The ringside could only be reached by men who were prepared to fight their way there with cudgels and hunting-crops. No wonder that the classic sport was attended now by those only who had nothing to lose.

On the other hand, the era of the reserved building and the legal glove-fight had not yet arisen, and the cult was in a strange intermediate condition. It was impossible to regulate it, and equally impossible to abolish it, since nothing appeals more directly and powerfully to the average Briton. Therefore there were scrambling contests in stableyards and barns, hurried visits to France, secret meetings at dawn in wild parts of the country, and all manner of evasions and experiments. The men themselves became as unsatisfactory as their surroundings. There could be no honest open contest, and the loudest bragger talked his way to the top of the list. Only across the Atlantic had the huge figure of John Lawrence Sullivan appeared, who was destined to be the last of the earlier system and the first of the later one.

Things being in this condition, the sporting Yeomanry Captain found it no easy matter among the boxing saloons and sporting pubs of London to find a man who could be relied upon to give a good account of the huge Farrier-Sergeant. Heavy-weights were at a premium. Finally his choice fell upon Alf Stevens of Kentish Town, an excellent rising middle-weight who had never yet known defeat and had indeed some claims to the championship. His professional experience and craft would surely make up for the three stone of weight which separated him from the formidable dragoon. It was in this hope that Sir Fred. Milburn engaged him, and proceeded to convey him in his dog-cart behind a pair of spanking greys to the camp of the Yeomen. They were to start one evening, drive up the Great North Road, sleep at St Albans, and finish their journey next day.

The prize-fighter met the sporting Baronet at The Golden Cross, where Bates, the little groom, was standing at the head of the spirited horses. Stevens, a pale-faced, clean-cut young fellow, mounted beside his employer and waved his hand to a little knot of fighting men, rough, collarless, reefer-coated fellows who had gathered to bid their comrade goodbye. 'Good luck, Alf!' came in a hoarse chorus as the boy released the horses' heads and sprang in behind, while the high dog-cart swung swiftly round the curve into Trafalgar Square.

Sir Frederick was so busy steering among the traffic in Oxford Street and the Edgware Road that he had little thought for anything else, but when he got into the edges of the country near Hendon, and the hedges had at last taken the place of that endless panorama of brick dwellings, he let his horses go easy with a loose rein while he turned his attention to the young man at his side. He had found him by correspondence and recommendation, so that he had some curiosity now in looking him over. Twilight was already falling and the light dim, but what the Baronet saw pleased him well. The man was a fighter every inch, clean-cut, deep-chested, with the long straight cheek and deep-set eye which goes with an obstinate courage. Above all, he was a man who had never yet met his master and was still upheld by the deep sustaining confidence which is never quite the same after a single defeat. The Baronet chuckled as he realized what a surprise packet was being carried north for the Farrier-Sergeant.

'I suppose you are in some sort of training, Stevens?' he remarked, turning to his companion.

'Yes, sir; I am fit to fight for my life.'

'So I should judge by the look of you.'

'I live regular all the time, sir, but I was matched against Mike Connor for this last weekend and scaled down to eleven four. Then he paid forfeit, and here I am at the top of my form.'

'That's lucky. You'll need it all against a man who has a pull of three stone and four inches.'

The young man smiled.

'I have given greater odds than that, sir.'

'I dare say. But he's a game man as well.'

'Well, sir, one can but do one's best.'

The Baronet liked the modest but assured tone of the young pugilist. Suddenly an amusing thought struck him, and he burst out laughing.

'By Jove!' he cried. 'What a lark if the Bully is out tonight!'

Alf Stevens pricked up his ears.

'Who might he be, sir?'

'Well, that's what the folk are asking. Some say they've seen him, and some say he's a fairy-tale, but there's good evidence that he is a real man with a pair of rare good fists that leave their marks behind him.'

'And where might he live?'

'On this very road. It's between Finchley and Elstree, as I've heard. There are two chaps, and they come out on nights when the moon is at full and challenge the passers-by to fight in the old style. One fights and the other picks up. By George! the fellow *can* fight, too, by all accounts. Chaps have been found in the morning with their faces all cut to ribbons to show that the Bully had been at work upon them.'

Alf Stevens was full of interest.

'I've always wanted to try an old-style battle, sir, but it never chanced to come my way. I believe it would suit me better than the gloves.'

'Then you won't refuse the Bully?'

'Refuse him! I'd go ten mile to meet him.'

'By George! it would be great!' cried the Baronet. 'Well, the moon is at the full, and the place should be about here.'

'If he's as good as you say,' Stevens remarked, 'he should be known in the ring, unless he is just an amateur who amuses himself like that.'

'Some think he's an ostler, or maybe a racing man from the training stables over yonder. Where there are horses there is boxing. If you can believe the accounts, there is something a bit queer and outlandish about the fellow. Hi! Look out, damn you, look out!'

The Baronet's voice had risen to a sudden screech of surprise and of anger. At this point the road dips down into a hollow, heavily shaded by trees, so that at night it arches across like the mouth of a tunnel. At the foot of the slope there stand two great stone pillars, which, as viewed by daylight, are lichen-stained and weathered, with heraldic devices on each which are so mutilated by time that they are mere protuberances of stone. An iron gate of elegant design, hanging loosely upon rusted hinges, proclaims both the past glories and the present decay of Brocas Old Hall, which lies at the end of the weed-encumbered avenue. It was from the shadow of this ancient gateway that an active figure had sprung suddenly into the centre of the road and had, with great dexterity, held up the horses, who ramped and pawed as they were forced back upon their haunches.

'Here, Rowe, you 'old the tits, will ye?' cried a high strident voice. 'I've a little word to say to this 'ere slap-up Corinthian before 'e goes any farther.'

A second man had emerged from the shadows and without a word took hold of the horses' heads. He was a short, thick fellow, dressed in a curious brown many-caped overcoat, which came to his knees, with gaiters and boots beneath it. He wore no hat, and those in the dog-cart had a view, as he came in front of the side-lamps, of a surly red face with an ill-fitting lower lip clean shaven, and a high black cravat swathed tightly under the chin. As he gripped the leathers his more active comrade sprang forward and rested a bony hand upon the side of the splashboard while he looked keenly up with a pair of fierce blue eyes at the faces of the two travellers, the light beating full upon his own features. He wore a hat low upon his brow, but in spite of its shadow both the Baronet and the pugilist could see enough to shrink from him, for it was an evil face, evil but very formidable, stern, craggy, high-nosed, and fierce, with an inexorable mouth which bespoke a nature which would neither ask for mercy nor grant it. As to his age, one could only say for certain that a man with such a face was young enough to have all his virility and old enough to have experienced all the wickedness of life. The cold, savage eyes took a deliberate survey, first of the Baronet and then of the young man beside him.

'Aye, Rowe, it's a slap-up Corinthian, same as I said,' he remarked over his shoulder to his companion. 'But this other is a likely chap. If 'e isn't a millin' cove 'e ought to be. Any'ow, we'll try 'im out.'

'Look here,' said the Baronet, 'I don't know who you are, except that you are a damned impertinent fellow. I'd put the lash of my whip across your face for two pins!'

'Stow that gammon, gov'nor! It ain't safe to speak to me like that.'

'I've heard of you and your ways!' cried the angry soldier. 'I'll teach you to stop my horses on the Queen's high road! You've got the wrong men this time, my fine fellow, as you will soon learn.'

'That's as it may be,' said the stranger. 'May'ap, master, we may all learn something before we part. One or other of you 'as got to get down and put up your 'ands before you get any farther.'

Stevens had instantly sprung down into the road.

'If you want a fight you've come to the right shop,' said he; 'it's my trade, so don't say I took you unawares.'

The stranger gave a cry of satisfaction.

'Blow my dickey!' he shouted. 'It *is* a millin' cove, Joe, same as I said. No more chaw-bacons for us, but the real thing. Well, young man, you've met your master tonight. Happen you never 'eard what Lord Longmore said o' me? "A man must be made special to beat you," says 'e. That's wot Lord Longmore said.'

'That was before the Bull came along,' growled the man in front, speaking for the first time.

'Stow your chaffing, Joe! A little more about the Bull and you and me will quarrel. 'E bested me once, but it's all betters and no takers that I glut 'im if ever we meet again. Well, young man, what d'ye think of me?'

'I think you've got your share of cheek.'

'Cheek. Wot's that?'

'Impudence, bluff—gas, if you like.'

The last word had a surprising effect upon the stranger. He smote his leg with his hand and broke out into a high neighing laugh, in which he was joined by his gruff companion.

'You've said the right word, my beauty,' cried the latter, '"Gas" is the word and no error. Well, there's a good moon, but the clouds are comin' up. We had best use the light while we can.'

Whilst this conversation had been going on the Baronet had been looking with an ever-growing amazement at the attire of the stranger. A good deal of it confirmed his belief that he was connected with some stables, though making every allowance for this his appearance was very eccentric and old-fashioned. Upon his head he wore a yellowish-white top-hat of long-haired beaver, such as is still affected by some drivers of four-in-hands, with a bell crown and a curling brim. His dress consisted of a short-waisted swallow-tail coat, snuff-coloured, with steel buttons. It opened in front to show a vest of striped silk, while his legs were encased in buff knee-breeches with blue stockings and low shoes. The figure was angular and hard, with a great suggestion of wiry activity. This Bully of Brocas was clearly a very great character, and the young dragoon officer chuckled as he thought what a glorious story he would carry back to the mess of this queer old-world figure and the thrashing which he was about to receive from the famous London boxer.

Billy, the little groom, had taken charge of the horses, who were shivering and sweating.

'This way!' said the stout man, turning towards the gate. It was a sinister place, black and weird, with the crumbling pillars and the heavy arching trees. Neither the Baronet nor the pugilist liked the look of it.

'Where are you going, then?'

'This is no place for a fight,' said the stout man. 'We've got as pretty a place as ever you saw inside the gate here. You couldn't beat it on Molesey Hurst.'

'The road is good enough for me,' said Stevens.

'The road is good enough for two Johnny Raws,' said the man with the beaver hat. 'It ain't good enough for two slap-up millin' coves like you an' me. You ain't afeard, are you?'

'Not of you or ten like you,' said Stevens, stoutly.

'Well, then, come with me and do it as it ought to be done.'

Sir Frederick and Stevens exchanged glances.

'I'm game,' said the pugilist.

'Come on, then.'

The little party of four passed through the gateway. Behind them in the darkness the horses stamped and reared, while the voice of the boy could be heard as he vainly tried to soothe them. After walking fifty yards up the grass-grown drive the guide turned to the right through a thick belt of trees, and they came out upon a circular plot of grass, white and clear in the moonlight. It had a raised bank, and on the farther side was one of those little pillared stone summer-houses beloved by the early Georgians.

'What did I tell you?' cried the stout man, triumphantly. 'Could you do better than this within twenty mile of town? It was made for it. Now, Tom, get to work upon him, and show us what you can do.'

It had all become like an extraordinary dream. The strange men, their odd dress, their queer speech, the moonlit circle of grass, and the pillared summer-house all wove themselves into one fantastic whole. It was only the sight of Alf Stevens's ill-fitting tweed suit, and his homely English face surmounting it, which brought the Baronet back to the workaday world. The thin stranger had taken off his beaver hat, his swallow-tailed coat, his silk waistcoat, and finally his shirt had been drawn over his head by his second. Stevens in a cool and leisurely fashion kept pace with the preparations of his antagonist. Then the two fighting men turned upon each other.

But as they did so Stevens gave an exclamation of surprise and horror. The removal of the beaver hat had disclosed a horrible mutilation of the head of his antagonist. The whole upper forehead had fallen in, and there seemed to be a broad red weal between his close-cropped hair and his heavy brows.

'Good Lord,' cried the young pugilist. 'What's amiss with the man?'

The question seemed to rouse a cold fury in his antagonist.

'You look out for your own head, master,' said he. 'You'll find enough to do, I'm thinkin', without talkin' about mine.'

This retort drew a shout of hoarse laughter from his second. 'Well said, my Tommy!' he cried. 'It's Lombard Street to a China orange on the one and only.'

The man whom he called Tom was standing with his hands up in the centre of the natural ring. He looked a big man in his clothes, but he seemed bigger in the buff, and his barrel chest, sloping shoulders, and loosely-slung muscular arms were all ideal for the game. His grim eyes gleamed fiercely beneath his misshapen brows, and his lips were set in a fixed hard smile, more menacing than a scowl. The pugilist confessed, as he approached him, that he had never seen a more formidable figure. But his bold heart rose to the fact that he had never yet found the man who could master him, and that it was hardly credible that he would appear as an old-fashioned stranger on a country road. Therefore, with an answering smile, he took up his position and raised his hands.

But what followed was entirely beyond his experience. The stranger feinted quickly with his left, and sent in a swinging hit with his right, so quick and hard that Stevens had barely time to avoid it and to counter with a short jab as his opponent rushed in upon him. Next instant the man's bony arms were round him, and the pugilist was hurled into the air in a whirling cross-buttock, coming down with a heavy thud upon the grass. The stranger stood back and folded his arms while Stevens scrambled to his feet with a red flush of anger upon his cheeks.

'Look here,' he cried. 'What sort of game is this?'

'We claim foul!' the Baronet shouted.

'Foul be damned! As clean a throw as ever I saw!' said the stout man. 'What rules do you fight under?'

'Queensberry, of course.'

'I never heard of it. It's London prize-ring with us.'

'Come on, then!' cried Stevens, furiously. 'I can wrestle as well as another. You won't get me napping again.'

Nor did he. The next time that the stranger rushed in Stevens caught him in as strong a grip, and after swinging and swaying they came down together in a dog-fall. Three times this occurred, and each time the stranger walked across to his friend and seated himself upon the grassy bank before he recommenced.

'What d'ye make of him?' the Baronet asked, in one of these pauses.

Stevens was bleeding from the ear, but otherwise showed no sign of damage.

'He knows a lot,' said the pugilist. 'I don't know where he learned it, but he's had a deal of practice somewhere. He's as strong as a lion and as hard as a board, for all his queer face.'

'Keep him at out-fighting. I think you are his master there.'

'I'm not so sure that I'm his master anywhere, but I'll try my best.'

It was a desperate fight, and as round followed round it became clear, even to the amazed Baronet, that the middle-weight champion had met his match. The stranger had a clever draw and a rush which, with his springing hits, made him a most dangerous foe. His head and body seemed insensible to blows, and the horribly malignant smile never for one instant flickered from his lips. He hit very hard with fists like flints, and his blows whizzed up from every angle. He had one particularly deadly lead, an uppercut at the jaw, which again and again nearly came home, until at last it did actually fly past the guard and brought Stevens to the ground. The stout man gave a whoop of triumph.

'The whisker hit, by George! It's a horse to a hen on my Tommy! Another like that, lad, and you have him beat.'

'I say, Stevens, this is going too far,' said the Baronet, as he supported his weary man. 'What will the regiment say if I bring you up all knocked to pieces in a bye-battle! Shake hands with this fellow and give him best, or you'll not be fit for your job.'

'Give him best? Not I!' cried Stevens, angrily. 'I'll knock that dammed smile off his ugly mug before I've done.'

'What about the Sergeant?'

'I'd rather go back to London and never see the Sergeant than have my number taken down by this chap.'

'Well, 'ad enough?' his opponent asked, in a sneering voice, as he moved from his seat on the bank.

For answer young Stevens sprang forward and rushed at his man with all the strength that was left to him. By the fury of his onset he drove him back, and for a long minute had all the better of the exchanges. But this iron fighter seemed never to tire. His step was as quick and his blow as hard as ever when this long rally had ended. Stevens had eased up from pure exhaustion. But his opponent did not ease up. He came back on him with a shower of furious blows which beat down the weary guard of the pugilist. Alf Stevens was at the end of his strength and would in another instant have sunk to the ground but for a singular intervention.

It has been said that in their approach to the ring the party had passed through a grove of trees. Out of these there came a peculiar shrill cry, a cry of agony, which might be from a child or from some small woodland creature in distress. It was inarticulate, high-pitched, and inexpressibly melancholy. At the sound the stranger, who had knocked Stevens on to his knees, staggered back and looked round him with an expression of helpless horror upon his face. The smile had left his lips and there only remained the loose-lipped weakness of a man in the last extremity of terror.

'It's after me again, mate!' he cried.

'Stick it out, Tom! You have him nearly beat! It can't hurt you.'

'It can 'urt me! It will 'urt me!' screamed the fighting man. 'My God! I can't face it! Ah, I see it! I see it!'

With a scream of fear he turned and bounded off into the brushwood. His companion, swearing loudly, picked up the pile of clothes and darted after him, the dark shadows swallowing up their flying figures.

Stevens, half-senselessly, had staggered back and lay upon the grassy bank, his head pillowed upon the chest of the young Baronet, who was holding his flask of brandy to his lips. As they sat there they were both aware that the cries had become louder and shriller. Then from among the bushes there ran a small white terrier, nosing about as if following a trail and yelping most piteously. It squattered across the grassy sward, taking no notice of the two young men. Then it also vanished into the shadows. As it did so the two spectators sprang to their feet and ran as hard as they could tear for the gateway and the trap. Terror had seized them—a panic terror far above reason or control. Shivering and shaking, they threw themselves into the dog-cart, and it was not until the willing horses had put two good miles between that ill-omened hollow and themselves that they at last ventured to speak.

'Did you ever see such a dog?' asked the Baronet.

'No,' cried Stevens. 'And, please God, I never may again.'

Late that night the two travellers broke their journey at The Swan Inn, near Harpenden Common. The landlord was an old acquaintance of the Baronet's, and gladly joined him in a glass of port after supper. A famous old sport was Mr Joe Horner, of The Swan, and he would talk by the hour of the legends of the ring, whether new or old. The name of Alf Stevens was well known to him, and he looked at him with the deepest interest.

'Why, sir, you have surely been fighting,' said he. 'I hadn't read of any engagement in the papers.'

'Enough said of that,' Stevens answered, in a surly voice.

'Well, no offence! I suppose'—his smiling face became suddenly very serious—'I suppose you didn't, by chance, see anything of him they call the Bully of Brocas as you came north?'

'Well, what if we did?'

The landlord was tense with excitement.

'It was him that nearly killed Bob Meadows. It was at the very gate of Brocas Old Hall that he stopped him. Another man was with him. Bob was game to the marrow, but he was found hit to pieces on the lawn inside the gate where the summer-house stands.'

The Baronet nodded.

'Ah, you've been there!' cried the landlord.

'Well, we may as well make a clean breast of it,' said the Baronet, looking at Stevens. 'We have been there, and we met the man you speak of—an ugly customer he is, too!'

'Tell me!' said the landlord, in a voice that sank to a whisper. 'Is it true what Bob Meadows says, that the men are dressed like our grandfathers, and that the fighting man has his head all caved in?'

'Well, he was old-fashioned, certainly, and his head was the queerest ever I saw.'

'God in Heaven!' cried the landlord. 'Do you know, sir, that Tom Hickman, the famous prize-fighter, together with his pal, Joe Rowe, a silversmith of the City, met his death at that very point in the year 1822, when he was drunk, and tried to drive on the wrong side of a wagon? Both were killed and the wheel of the wagon crushed in Hickman's forehead.'

'Hickman! Hickman!' said the Baronet. 'Not the gasman?'

'Yes, sir, they called him Gas. He won his fights with what they called the "whisker hit", and no one could stand against him until Neate—him that they called the Bristol Bull—brought him down.'

Stevens had risen from the table as white as cheese.

'Let's get out of this, sir. I want fresh air. Let us get on our way.'

The landlord clapped him on the back.

'Cheer up, lad! You've held him off, anyhow, and that's more than anyone else has ever done. Sit down and have another glass of wine, for if a man in England has earned it this night it is you. There's many a debt you would pay if you gave the Gasman a welting, whether dead or alive. Do you know what he did in this very room?'

The two travellers looked round with startled eyes at the lofty room, stone-flagged and oak-panelled, with great open grate at the farther end.

'Yes, in this very room. I had it from old Squire Scotter, who was here that very night. It was the day when Shelton beat Josh Hudson out St Albans way, and Gas had won a pocketful of money on the fight. He and his pal Rowe came in here upon their way, and he was mad-raging drunk. The folk fairly shrunk into the corners and under the tables, for he was stalkin' round with the great kitchen poker in his hand, and there was murder behind the smile upon his face. He was like that when the drink was in him—cruel, reckless, and a terror to the world. Well, what think you that he did at last with the poker? There was a little dog, a terrier as I've heard, coiled up before the fire, for it was a bitter December night. The Gasman broke its back with one blow of the poker. Then he burst out laughin', flung a curse or two at the folk that shrunk away from him, and so out to his high gig that was waiting outside. The next we heard was that he was carried down to Finchley with his head ground to a jelly by the wagon wheel. Yes, they do say the little dog with its bleeding skin and its broken back has been seen since then, crawlin' and yelpin' about Brocas Corner, as if it were lookin' for the swine that killed it. So you see, Mr Stevens, you were fightin' for more than yourself when you put it across the Gasman.'

'Maybe so,' said the young prize-fighter, 'but I want no more fights like that. The Farrier-Sergeant is good enough for me, sir, and if it is the same to you we'll take a railway train back to town.'

The Lift

FLIGHT-COMMANDER STANGATE SHOULD HAVE BEEN HAPPY. He had come safely through the war without a hurt, and with a good name in the most heroic of services. He had only just turned thirty, and a great career seemed to lie ahead of him. Above all, beautiful Mary MacLean was walking by his side, and he had her promise that she was there for life. What could a young man ask for more? And yet there was a heavy load upon his heart.

He could not explain it himself, and endeavoured to reason himself out of it. There was the blue sky above him, the blue sea in front, the beautiful gardens with their throngs of happy pleasure-seekers around. Above all, there was that sweet face turned upon his with questioning concern. Why could he not raise himself to so joyful an environment? He made effort after effort, but they were not convincing enough to deceive the quick instinct of a loving woman.

'What is it, Tom?' she asked anxiously. 'I can see that something is clouding you. Do tell me if I can help you in any way.'

He laughed in shamefaced fashion.

'It is such a sin to spoil our little outing,' he said. 'I could kick myself round these gardens when I think of it. Don't worry, my darling, for I know the cloud will roll off. I suppose I am a creature of nerves, though I should have got past that by now. The Flying Service is supposed either to break you or to warrant you for life.'

'It is nothing definite, then?'

'No, it is nothing definite. That's the worst of it. You could fight it more easily if it was. It's just a dead, heavy depression here in my chest and across my forehead. But do forgive me, dear girl! What a brute I am to shadow you like this.'

'But I love to share even the smallest trouble.'

'Well, it's gone—vamosed—vanished. We will talk about it no more.'

She gave him a swift, penetrating glance.

'No, no, Tom; your brow shows, as well as feels. Tell me, dear, have you often felt like this? You really look very ill. Sit here, dear, in the shade and tell me of it.'

They sat together in the shadow of the great, latticed Tower which reared itself six hundred feet high beside them.

'I have an absurd faculty,' said he; 'I don't know that I have ever mentioned it to anyone before. But when imminent danger is threatening me I get these strange forebodings. Of course it is absurd today in these peaceful surroundings. It only shows how queerly these things work. But it is the first time that it has deceived me.'

'When had you it before?'

'When I was a lad it seized me one morning. I was nearly drowned that afternoon. I had it when the burglar came to Morton Hall and I got a bullet through my coat. Then twice in the war when I was overmatched and escaped by a miracle, I had this strange feeling before ever I climbed into my machine. Then it lifts quite suddenly, like a mist in the sunshine. Why, it is lifting now. Look at me! Can't you see that it is so?'

She could indeed. He had turned in a minute from a haggard man to a laughing boy. She found herself laughing in sympathy. A rush of high spirits and energy had swept away his strange foreboding and filled his whole soul with the vivid, dancing joy of youth.

'Thank goodness!' he cried. 'I think it is your dear eyes that have done it. I could not stand that wistful look in them. What a silly, foolish nightmare it all has been! There's an end for ever in my belief in presentiments. Now, dear girl, we have just time for one good turn before luncheon. After that the gardens get so crowded that it is hopeless to do anything. Shall we have a side-show, or the great wheel, or the flying boat, or what?'

'What about the Tower?' she asked, glancing upwards. 'Surely that glorious air and the view from the top would drive the last wisps of cloud out of your mind.'

He looked at his watch.

'Well, it's past twelve, but I suppose we could do it all in an hour. But it doesn't seem to be working. What about it, conductor?'

The man shook his head and pointed to a little knot of people who were assembled at the entrance.

'They've all been waiting, sir. It's hung up, but the gear is being overhauled, and I expect the signal every minute. If you join the others I promise it won't be long.'

They had hardly reached the group when the steel face of the lift rolled aside—a sign that there was hope in the future. The motley crowd drifted through the opening and waited expectantly upon the wooden platform. They were not numerous, for the gardens are not crowded until the afternoon, but they were fair samples of the kindly, good-humoured north-country folk who take their annual holiday at Northam. Their faces were all upturned now, and they were watching with keen interest a man who was descending the steel framework. It seemed a dangerous, precarious business, but he came as swiftly as an ordinary mortal upon a staircase.

'My word!' said the conductor, glancing up. 'Jim has got a move on this morning.'

'Who is he?' asked Commander Stangate.

'That's Jim Barnes, sir, the best workman that ever went on a scaffold. He fair lives up there. Every bolt and rivet are under his care. He's a wonder, is Jim.'

'But don't argue religion with him,' said one of the group.

The attendant laughed.

'Ah, you know him, then,' said he. 'No, don't argue religion with him.'

'Why not?' asked the officer.

'Well, he takes it very hard, he does. He's the shining light of his sect.'

'It ain't hard to be that,' said the knowing one. 'I've heard there are only six folk in the fold. He's one of those who picture heaven as the exact size of their own back street conventicle and everyone else left outside it.'

'Better not tell him so while he's got that hammer in his hand,' said the conductor, in a hurried whisper. 'Hallo, Jim, how goes it this morning?'

The man slid swiftly down the last thirty feet, and then balanced himself on a cross-bar while he looked at the little group in the lift. As he stood there, clad in a leather suit, with his pliers and other tools dangling from his brown belt, he was a figure to please the eye of an artist. The man was very tall and gaunt, with great, straggling limbs and every appearance of giant strength. His face was a remarkable one, noble and yet sinister, with dark eyes and hair, a prominent, hooked nose, and a beard which flowed over his chest. He steadied himself with one knotted hand, while the other held a steel hammer dangling by his knee.

'It's all ready aloft,' said he. 'I'll go up with you if I may.' He sprang down from his perch and joined the others in the lift.

'I suppose you are always watching it,' said the young lady.

'That is what I am engaged for, miss. From morning to night, and often from night to morning, I am up here. There are times when I feel as if I were not a man at all, but a fowl of the air. They fly round me, the creatures, as I lie out on the girders, and they cry to me until I find myself crying back to the poor, soulless things.'

'It's a great charge,' said the Commander, glancing up at the wonderful tracery of steel outlined against the deep blue sky.

'Aye, sir, and there is not a nut nor a screw that is not in my keeping. Here's my hammer to ring them true and my spanner to wrench them tight. As the Lord over the earth, so am I—even I—over the Tower, with power of life and power of death, aye of death and of life.'

The hydraulic machinery had begun to work and the lift very slowly ascended. As it mounted, the glorious panorama of the coast and bay gradually unfolded itself. So engrossing was the view that the passengers hardly noticed it when the platform stopped abruptly between stages at the five hundred foot level. Barnes, the workman, muttered that something must be amiss, and springing like a cat across the gap which separated them from the trellis-work of metal he clambered out of sight. The motley little party, suspended in mid-air, lost something of their British shyness under such unwonted conditions and began to compare notes with each other. One couple, who addressed each other as Dolly and Billy, announced to the company that they were the particular stars of the Hippodrome bill, and kept their neighbours tittering with their rather obvious wit. A buxom mother, her precocious son, and two married couples upon holiday formed an appreciative audience.

'You'd like to be a sailor, would you?' said Billy the comedian, in answer to some remark of the boy. 'Look 'ere, my nipper, you'll end up as a blooming corpse if you ain't careful. See 'im standin' at the edge. At this hour of the morning I can't bear to watch it.'

'What's the hour got to do with it?' asked a stout commercial traveller.

'My nerves are worth nothin' before midday. Why, lookin' down there, and seein' those folk like dots, puts me all in a twitter. My family is all alike in the mornin'.'

'I expect,' said Dolly, a high-coloured young woman, 'that they're all alike the evening before.'

There was a general laugh, which was led by the comedian.

'You got it across that time, Dolly. It's K.O. for Battling Billy—still senseless when last heard of. If my family is laughed at I'll leave the room.'

'It's about time we did,' said the commercial traveller, who was a red-faced, choleric person. 'It's a disgrace the way they hold us up. I'll write to the company.'

'Where's the bell-push?' said Billy. 'I'm goin' to ring.'

'What for—the waiter?' asked the lady.

'For the conductor, the chauffeur, whoever it is that drives the old bus up and down. Have they run out of petrol, or broke the mainspring, or what?'

'We have a fine view, anyhow,' said the Commander.

'Well, I've had that,' remarked Billy. 'I'm done with it, and I'm for getting on.'

'I'm getting nervous,' cried the stout mother. 'I do hope there is nothing wrong with the lift.'

'I say, hold on to the slack of my coat, Dolly. I'm going to look over and chance it. Oh, Lord, it makes me sick and giddy! There's a horse down under, and it ain't bigger than a mouse. I don't see anyone lookin' after us. Where's old Isaiah the prophet who came up with us?'

'He shinned out of it mighty quick when he thought trouble was coming.'

'Look here,' said Dolly, looking very perturbed, 'this is a nice thing, I don't think. Here we are five hundred foot up, and stuck for the day as like as not. I'm due for the *matinée* at the Hippodrome. I'm sorry for the company if they don't get me down in time for that. I'm billed all over the town for a new song.'

'A new one! What's that, Dolly?'

'A real pot o' ginger, I tell you. It's called "On the Road to Ascot". I've got a hat four foot across to sing it in.'

'Come on, Dolly, let's have a rehearsal while we wait.'

'No, no; the young lady here wouldn't understand.'

'I'd be very glad to hear it,' cried Mary MacLean. 'Please don't let me prevent you.'

'The words were written to the hat. I couldn't sing the verses without the hat. But there's a nailin' good chorus to it:

> ' "If you want a little mascot
> When you're on the way to Ascot,
> Try the lady with the cartwheel hat." '

She had a tuneful voice and a sense of rhythm which set everyone nodding. 'Try it now all together,' she cried; and the strange little haphazard company sang it with all their lungs.

'I say,' said Billy, 'that ought to wake somebody up. What? Let's try a shout all together.'

It was a fine effort, but there was no response. It was clear that the management down below was quite ignorant or impotent. No sound came back to them.

The passengers became alarmed. The commercial traveller was rather less rubicund. Billy still tried to joke, but his efforts were not well received. The officer in his blue uniform at once took his place as rightful leader in a crisis. They all looked to him and appealed to him.

'What would you advise, sir? You don't think there's any danger of it coming down, do you?'

'Not the least. But it's awkward to be stuck here all the same. I think I could jump across on to that girder. Then perhaps I could see what is wrong.'

'No, no, Tom; for goodness' sake, don't leave us!'

'Some people have a nerve,' said Billy. 'Fancy jumping across a five-hundred-foot drop!'

'I dare say the gentleman did worse things in the war.'

'Well, I wouldn't do it myself—not if they starred me in the bills. It's all very well for old Isaiah. It's his job, and I wouldn't do him out of it.'

Three sides of the lift were shut in with wooden partitions, pierced with windows for the view. The fourth side, facing the sea, was clear. Stangate leaned over as far as he could and looked upwards. As he did so there came from above him a peculiar, sonorous, metallic twang, as if a mighty harp-string had been struck. Some distance up—a hundred feet, perhaps—he could see a long, brown, corded arm, which was working furiously among the wire cordage above.

The form was beyond his view, but he was fascinated by this bare, sinewy arm which tugged and pulled and sagged and stabbed.

'It's all right,' he said, and a general sigh of relief broke from his strange comrades at his words. 'There is someone above us setting things right.'

'It's old Isaiah,' said Billy, stretching his neck round the corner. 'I can't see him, but it's his arm for a dollar. What's he got in his hand? Looks like a screwdriver or something. No, by George, it's a file.'

As he spoke there came another sonorous twang from above. There was a troubled frown upon the officer's brow.

'I say, dash it all, that's the very sound our steel hawser made when it parted, strand by strand, at Dixmude. What the deuce is the fellow about? Heh, there! what are you trying to do?'

The man had ceased his work and was now slowly descending the iron trellis.

'All right, he's coming,' said Stangate to his startled companions. 'It's all right, Mary. Don't be frightened, any of you. It's absurd to suppose he would really weaken the cord that holds us.'

A pair of high boots appeared from above. Then came the leathern breeches, the belt with its dangling tools, the muscular form, and, finally, the fierce, swarthy, eagle face of the workman. His coat was off and his shirt open showing the hairy chest. As he appeared there came another sharp, snapping vibration from above. The man made his way down in leisurely fashion, and then, balancing himself upon the cross-girder and leaning against the side-piece, he stood with folded arms, looking from under his heavy black brows at the huddled passengers upon the platform.

'Hallo!' said Stangate. 'What's the matter?'

The man stood impassive and silent, with something indescribably menacing in his fixed, unwinking stare.

The flying officer grew angry.

'Hallo! Are you deaf?' he cried. 'How long do you mean to have us stuck here?'

The man stood silent. There was something devilish in his appearance.

'I'll complain of you, my lad,' said Billy, in a quivering voice. 'This won't stop here, I can promise you.'

'Look here!' cried the officer. 'We have ladies here and you are alarming them. Why are we stuck here? Has the machinery gone wrong?'

'You are here,' said the man, 'because I have put a wedge against the hawser above you.'

'You fouled the line! How dared you do such a thing! What right have you to frighten the women and put us all to this inconvenience? Take that wedge out this instant, or it will be the worse for you.'

The man was silent.

'Do you hear what I say? Why the devil don't you answer? Is this a joke or what? We've had about enough of it, I tell you.'

Mary MacLean had gripped her lover by the arm in an agony of sudden panic.

'Oh, Tom!' she cried. 'Look at his eyes—look at his horrible eyes! The man is a maniac.'

The workman stirred suddenly into sinister life. His dark face broke into writhing lines of passion, and his fierce eyes glowed like embers, while he shook one long arm in the air.

'Behold,' he cried, 'those who are mad to the children of this world are in very truth the Lord's anointed and the dwellers in the inner temple. Lo, I am one who is prepared to testify even to the uttermost, for of a verity the day has now come when the humble will be exalted and the wicked will be cut off in their sins!'

'Mother! Mother!' cried the little boy, in terror.

'There, there! It's all right, Jack,' said the buxom woman, and then, in a burst of womanly wrath, 'What d'you want to make the child cry for? You're a pretty man, you are!'

'Better he should cry now than in the outer darkness. Let him seek safety while there is yet time.'

The officer measured the gap with a practised eye. It was a good eight feet across, and the fellow could push him over before he could steady himself. It would be a desperate thing to attempt. He tried soothing words once more.

'See here, my lad, you've carried this joke too far. Why should you wish to injure us? Just shin up and get that wedge out, and we will agree to say no more about it.'

Another rending snap came from above.

'By George, the hawser is going!' cried Stangate. 'Here! Stand aside! I'm coming over to see to it.'

The workman had plucked the hammer from his belt, and waved it furiously in the air.

'Stand back, young man! Stand back! Or come—if you would hasten your end.'

'Tom, Tom, for God's sake, don't spring! Help! Help!'

The passengers all joined in the cry for aid. The man smiled malignly as he watched them.

'There is no one to help. They could not come if they would. You would be wiser to turn to your own souls that ye be not cast to the burning. Lo, strand by strand the cable snaps which holds you. There is yet another, and with each that goes there is more strain upon the rest. Five minutes of time, and all eternity beyond.'

A moan of fear rose from the prisoners in the lift. Stangate felt a cold sweat upon his brow as he passed his arm round the shrinking girl. If this vindictive devil could only be coaxed away for an instant he would spring across and take his chance in a hand-to-hand fight.

'Look here, my friend! We give you best!' he cried. 'We can do nothing. Go up and cut the cable if you wish. Go on—do it now, and get it over!'

'That you may come across unharmed. Having set my hand to the work, I will not draw back from it.'

Fury seized the young officer.

'You devil!' he cried. 'What do you stand there grinning for? I'll give you something to grin about. Give me a stick, one of you.'

The man waved his hammer.

'Come, then! Come to judgment!' he howled.

'He'll murder you, Tom! Oh, for God's sake, don't! If we must die, let us die together.'

'I wouldn't try it, sir,' cried Billy. 'He'll strike you down before you get a footing. Hold up, Dolly, my dear! Faintin' won't 'elp us. You speak to him, miss. Maybe he'll listen to you.'

'Why should you wish to hurt us?' said Mary. 'What have we ever done to you? Surely you will be sorry afterwards if we are injured. Now do be kind and reasonable and help us to get back to the ground.'

For a moment there may have been some softening in the man's fierce eyes as he looked at the sweet face which was upturned to him. Then his features set once more into their grim lines of malice.

'My hand is set to the work, woman. It is not for the servant to look back from his task.'

'But why should this be your task?'

'Because there is a voice within me which tells me so. In the night-time I have heard it, and in the day-time, too, when I have lain out alone upon the girders and seen the wicked dotting the streets beneath me, each busy on his own evil intent. "John Barnes, John Barnes," said the voice. "You are here that you may give a sign to a sinful generation—such a sign as shall show them that the Lord liveth and that there is a judgment upon sin." Who am I that I should disobey the voice of the Lord?'

'The voice of the devil,' said Stangate. 'What is the sin of this lady, or of these others, that you should seek their lives?'

'You are as the others, neither better nor worse. All day they pass me, load by load, with foolish cries and empty songs and vain babble of voices. Their thoughts are set upon the things of the flesh. Too long have I stood aside and watched and refused to testify. But now the day of wrath is come and the sacrifice is ready. Think not that a woman's tongue can turn me from my task.'

'It is useless!' Mary cried. 'Useless! I read death in his eyes.'

Another cord had snapped.

'Repent! Repent!' cried the madman. 'One more, and it is over!'

Commander Stangate felt as if it were all some extraordinary dream—

some monstrous nightmare. Could it be possible that he, after all his escapes of death in warfare, was now, in the heart of peaceful England, at the mercy of a homicidal lunatic, and that his dear girl, the one being whom he would shield from the very shadow of danger, was helpless before this horrible man? All his energy and manhood rose up in him for one last effort.'

'Here, we won't be killed like sheep in the shambles!' he cried, throwing himself against the wooden wall of the lift and kicking with all his force. 'Come on, boys! Kick it! Beat it! It's only match-boarding, and it is giving. Smash it down! Well done! Once more all together! There she goes! Now for the side! Out with it! Splendid!'

First the back and then the side of the little compartment had been knocked out, and the splinters dropped down into the abyss. Barnes danced upon his girder, his hammer in the air.

'Strive not!' he shrieked. 'It avails not. The day is surely come.'

'It's not two feet from the side-girder,' cried the officer. 'Get across! Quick! Quick! All of you. I'll hold this devil off!' He had seized a stout stick from the commercial traveller and faced the madman, daring him to spring across.

'Your turn now, my friend!' he hissed. 'Come on, hammer and all! I'm ready for you.'

Above him he heard another snap, and the frail platform began to rock. Glancing over his shoulder, he saw that his companions were all safe upon the side-girder. A strange line of terrified castaways they appeared as they clung in an ungainly row to the trellis-work of steel. But their feet were on the iron support. With two quick steps and a spring he was at their side. At the same instant the murderer, hammer in hand, jumped the gap. They had one vision of him there—a vision which will haunt their dreams—the convulsed face, the blazing eyes, the wind-tossed, raven locks. For a moment he balanced himself upon the swaying platform. The next, with a rending crash, he and it were gone. There was a long silence and then, far down, the thud and clatter of a mighty fall.

With white faces, the forlorn group clung to the cold steel bars and gazed down into the terrible abyss. It was the Commander who broke the silence.

'They'll send for us now. It's all safe,' he cried, wiping his brow. 'But, by Jove, it was a close call!'

Sources

'The Haunted Grange of Goresthorpe': submitted to *Blackwood's Magazine*, c.1877 and retained in their archives, which are now deposited with the National Library of Scotland, Edinburgh. First published by The Arthur Conan Doyle Society, 2000.

'The American's Tale': *London Society*, Christmas 1880; Collected in *Mysteries and Adventures* (1889).

'The Captain of the "Pole-Star"': *Temple Bar*, January 1883; Collected in *The Captain of the Polestar and Other Tales* (1890).

'The Winning Shot': *Bow Bells*, 11 July 1883; not collected.

'The Silver Hatchet': *London Society*, Christmas 1883; Collected in *Mysteries and Adventures* (1889).

'Selecting A Ghost': *London Society*, December 1883; Collected in *Mysteries and Adventures* (1889).

'J. Habakuk Jephson's Statement': *Cornhill Magazine*, January 1884; Collected in *The Captain of the Polestar and Other Tales* (1890).

'The Blood-Stone Tragedy': *Cassell's Saturday Journal*, February 1884; First published in book form by The Arthur Conan Doyle Society, 1995.

'John Barrington Cowles': *Cassell's Saturday Journal*, April 1884; Collected in *The Captain of the Polestar and Other Tales* (1890).

'The Great Keinplatz Experiment': *Belgravia Magazine*, July 1885; Collected in *The Captain of the Polestar and Other Tales* (1890).

'Cyprian Overbeck Wells': *Boy's Own Paper* (as 'A Literary Mosaic'), Christmas 1886; Collected in *The Captain of the Polestar and Other Tales* (1890).

'The Ring of Thoth': *Cornhill Magazine*, January 1890; Collected in *The Captain of the Polestar and Other Tales* (1890).

'A Pastoral Horror': *People*, December 1890; not collected.

'The Speckled Band': *Strand Magazine*, February 1892; Collected in *The Adventures of Sherlock Holmes* (1892).

'De Profundis': *Idler*, March 1892; Collected in *The Last Galley* (1911).

'Lot No. 249': *Harper's Monthly Magazine*, September 1892; Collected in *Round the Red Lamp* (1894).

'The Los Amigos Fiasco': *Idler*, December 1892; Collected in *Round the Red Lamp* (1894).

'The Case of Lady Sannox': *Idler*, November 1893; Collected in *Round the Red Lamp* (1894).

'The Lord of Château Noir': *Strand Magazine*, July 1894; Collected in *The Green Flag and Other Stories of War and Sport* (1900).

'The Parasite': *Lloyds Weekly Newspaper*, 11 November–2 December 1894; First book publication, December 1894.

'The Striped Chest': *Pearson's Magazine*, July 1897; Collected in *The Green Flag and Other Stories of War and Sport* (1900).

'The Fiend of the Cooperage': *Manchester Weekly Times*, 1 October 1897; Collected in *Round the Fire Stories* (1908).

'The New Catacomb': *Sunlight Year Book*, 1898 (as 'Burger's Secret'); Collected in *The Green Flag and Other Stories of War and Sport* (1900).

'The Sealed Room': *Strand Magazine*, September 1898; Collected in *Round the Fire Stories* (1908).

'The Retirement of Signor Lambert': *Pearson's Magazine*, December 1898; not collected.

'The Brazilian Cat': *Strand Magazine*, December 1898; Collected in *Round the Fire Stories* (1908).

'The Brown Hand': *Strand Magazine*, May 1899; Collected in *Round the Fire Stories* (1908).

'Playing with Fire': *Strand Magazine*, March 1900; Collected in *Round the Fire Stories* (1908).

'The Legend of the Hound of the Baskervilles' from *The Hound of the Baskervilles*: *Strand Magazine*, August 1901; *The Hound of the Baskervilles* (1902).

'The Leather Funnel': *McClure's Magazine*, November 1902; Collected in *Round the Fire Stories* (1908).

'The Silver Mirror': *Strand Magazine*, August 1908; Collected in *The Last Galley* (1911).

'The Terror of Blue John Gap': *Strand Magazine*, August 1910; Collected in *The Last Galley* (1911).

'The Blighting of Sharkey': *Pearson's Magazine*, April 1911; Collected in *The Last Galley* (1911).

'Through the Veil': original to *The Last Galley* (1911).

'How It Happened': *Strand Magazine*, September 1913; Collected in *Danger! and Other Stories* (1918).

'The Horror of the Heights': *Strand Magazine*, November 1913; Collected in *Danger! and Other Stories* (1918).

'The Bully of Brocas Court': *Strand Magazine*, November 1921; Collected in *Tales of the Ring and Camp* (1922).

'The Lift': *Strand Magazine*, June 1922; Collected in *Tales of Twilight and the Unseen* (1922).

THE CAPTAIN OF
THE 'POLE-STAR'

Weird and Imaginative Fiction

The first printing of the Ash-Tree Press edition of
The Captain of the 'Pole-Star'
was published on 22 May 2004
and is limited to Six Hundred copies
with additional copies produced for
legal deposit and contractual purposes.

Ash-Tree Press

Titles Published

1994

Lady Stanhope's Manuscript and
Other Supernatural Tales
(Card Covers)

1995

The Five Jars
by M. R. James

The Alabaster Hand
by A. N. L. Munby

Intruders: New Weird Tales
by A. M. Burrage

They Return at Evening
by H. R. Wakefield

Nine Ghosts
by R. H. Malden

1996

Sleep No More
by L. T. C. Rolt

Randalls Round
by Eleanor Scott

Conference With the Dead:
Tales of Supernatural Terror
by Terry Lamsley

Forgotten Ghosts
(Card Covers)

The Executor
and Other Ghost Stories
by David G. Rowlands

Old Man's Beard
by H. R. Wakefield

Ghosts in the House
by A. C. and R. H. Benson

The Stoneground Ghost Tales
by E. G. Swain

A Book of Ghosts
by S. Baring-Gould

The Occult Files of Francis Chard:
Some Ghost Stories
by A. M. Burrage

1997

In Ghostly Company
by Amyas Northcote

Under the Crust
by Terry Lamsley

Unholy Relics
by M. P. Dare

Imagine a Man in a Box
by H. R. Wakefield

The Rose of Death
and other Mysterious Delusions
by Julian Hawthorne

Midnight Never Comes
edited by
Barbara and Christopher Roden

The Haunted Chair
and Other Stories
by Richard Marsh

Someone in the Room:
Strange Tales Old and New
by A. M. Burrage

Annual Macabre 1997
edited by Jack Adrian

1998

Binscombe Tales:
Sinister Saxon Stories
by John Whitbourn

Out of the Dark: Volume 1
by Robert W. Chambers

The Night Comes On
by Steve Duffy

The Clock Strikes Twelve
and Other Stories
by H. R. Wakefield

Ash-Tree Press Occult Detectives
Aylmer Vance: Ghost-Seer
by Alice and Claude Askew

Twilight
and Other Supernatural Romances
by Marjorie Bowen

The Fellow Travellers
and Other Stories
by Sheila Hodgson

Nightmare Jack and Other Tales
by John Metcalfe

The Black Reaper
by Bernard Capes

The Terror by Night
by E. F. Benson

Lady Ferry
and Other Uncanny People
by Sarah Orne Jewett

Annual Macabre 1998
edited by Jack Adrian

Nights of the Round Table
by Margery Lawrence

1999

Six Ghost Stories
by T. G. Jackson

Ghost Gleams
by W. J. Wintle

The Night Wind Howls:
Complete Supernatural Stories
by Frederick Cowles

Binscombe Tales II:
Sinister Sutangli Stories
by John Whitbourn

Ash-Tree Press Occult Detectives
Norton Vyse—Psychic
by Rose Champion de Crespigny

Out of the Dark: Volume 2
by Robert W. Chambers

The Terraces of Night
by Margery Lawrence

Strayers from Sheol
by H. R. Wakefield

The Wind at Midnight
by Georgia Wood Pangborn

The Passenger
by E. F. Benson

The Phantom Coach:
Collected Ghost Stories
by Amelia B. Edwards

Annual Macabre 1999
edited by Jack Adrian

The Talisman
by Jonathan Aycliffe

Warning Whispers
by A. M. Burrage